L. P. Hartley (1895–1972) _____ David
Cecil as 'One of the most _____ one of
the most original'. His best _____ h was
made into a 1970 film. Other written works include: *The Betrayal*, *The
Brickfield*, *My Fellow Devils*, *A Perfect Woman* and *Eustace and Hilda*, for
which he was awarded the 1947 James Tait Black Memorial Prize. He was
awarded the CBE in 1956.

L. P. Hartley

The Boat

JOHN MURRAY

First published in Great Britain in 1949 by Putnam & Co. Ltd.

This paperback edition first published in 2013 by John Murray (Publishers)
An Hachette UK Company

1

A CIP catalogue record for this title is available from the British Library

ISBN 978-1-84854-811-4
E-book ISBN 978-1-84854-812-1

Typeset in Sabon MT by Hewer Text UK Ltd, Edinburgh
Printed and bound by Clays Ltd, St Ives plc

John Murray policy is to use papers that are natural, renewable and
recyclable products and made from wood grown in sustainable forests.
The logging and manufacturing processes are expected to conform
to the environmental regulations of the country of origin.

John Murray (Publishers)
338 Euston Road
London NW1 3BH

www.johnmurray.co.uk

To Miss Ethel Sands

Gaze on the wretch, recall to mind
His golden days left long behind.
                              Emily Brontë

CHAPTER I

'THIS is a quiet little hole,' said the cook. She was telephoning to a friend in the market town of Swirrelsford, eight miles away.

'I don't think I shall want to stay here long. And Effie doesn't want to either. Her feet play her up something terrible. All stone floors they are in our part, and the scullery, you never saw such a place, a real death-trap. And then there's that man. What's that you said, dear? Oh not him, he's all right in his way, a bit potty, if you ask me. No, it's *him*. . . . Oh, I thought you understood who, dear. I wouldn't demean myself by mentioning his name. The gardener, if you can call him one. You'd have to laugh if you saw what he brings in. Yesterday I took the basket straight in to Mr. Casson, just as it was, and showed him. 'That's for three people,' I said. I didn't need to say any more. So I just said, 'Will you please speak to him about it?' But he won't, not he, he hasn't the spirit of a wood-louse. And where does it all go to, that's what a good many of us would like to know, because it doesn't come in here. It's not very nice, is it, dear, having to deal with people like that? that you can't trust, no, not an inch. And what makes me mad is that Mr. Casson likes him, just because he sponges up to him. But of course he's lived abroad and doesn't understand what honesty is. Italians are not people according to our ideas, and anyhow they'll soon be fighting against us, the dirty tykes. Ice-creamers, some call them, but it's too polite for them. So under the circumstances I shall give in my notice. . . . Why don't you say something, dear, you leave me to do all the talking. . . .

'I don't know what you mean. Of course you could have got a word in. Anyhow you have now, haven't you? You've said quite a lot. Yes, of course he is a single man, I admit that, at least I suppose so, you can't be sure with anyone who's lived abroad, and he doesn't go poking his nose into what isn't his business. He wants to have guests though, but I put my foot down about that. "I can manage," I told him, as straight as I'm telling you, "if you don't have guests." "I get rather lonely sometimes," he said. "Yes," I said, "but think if you were in the trenches like our poor boys are. They've got good reason to be lonely, they have." People ought not to talk that way even if they are too old to be out there. He didn't say anything, what could he say? Besides the tables are turned now, they can't talk to us like they used to, they know they can't get anyone in our place. The boot's on the other foot now. That's why I shall give in my notice. You aren't saying very much, dear, you never used to be so silent. . . .

'Yes, I can, I know it is nice to be near you, dear, but I could get a place in Swirrelsford any day, and the buses only run from here three times a week. Yes, I should think he's fairly well off, it's not that, and I must think of Effie first, as I always do, and she always has liked the country. She says the air would be doing her good if it wasn't for her feet. But I don't know – the mists that come up out of this old river – why, sometimes you can't hardly see across the lawn. I shouldn't call it healthy. But Mr. Casson says he wants to go out in his boat. He must be mad. Think of boating in this weather. We ought to have central heating with Effie as delicate as she is.

'Yes, dear, I'll think over what you said, but I think I shall give in my notice all the same, because it never does to be put upon, and if I do, he will understand better how difficult things are here and what I have to put up with from that man. Goodbye, dear, cheerio, Abyssinia.'

She put down the ivory-coloured receiver, opened the shutters, switched off the light, and left the telephone room to glimmer pallidly in the winter dawn. In the hall she found Effie, sweeping the black and white square tiles.

'Oh, Beattie, what were you saying?' The housemaid was tall and slender, with pretty, fluffy, faded golden hair and a small round face flushed with tea and exertion. Beatrice was short, dark and compact, her powerful nose a curving ramp beneath her continuous black eyebrows.

'What made you tell her you were giving in your notice?'

Making a great effort, Beatrice turned on Effie a look that was almost hostile. 'I wish you wouldn't listen at the keyhole, dear.'

'I wasn't listening,' cried Effie, indignantly. 'You don't know how you raise your voice when you get excited. Anyone can hear you. I expect Mr. Casson could hear you quite well. Hark! He's running his bath.'

The two women listened to the sound as it came sliding down the curving stair.

'I don't care if he does hear,' said Beatrice. 'Do him good, that's what I say.' She paused to savour her defiance, and then went on in a different tone.

'But what's come over you, Effie? The other day you were as keen to go as I am.'

'Oh I dunno,' said Effie, 'I can't be forever chopping and changing. You go if you want to. I shan't, not for a while, anyhow.'

Beatrice looked at her in consternation.

'But we've been together all these years.'

'You don't need to tell me that,' said Effie airily. 'Maybe we should get on better on our own. A change is good for everyone, they say.'

The pause that followed was broken by the rasp of hob-nailed boots grating on the flagstones in the kitchen.

'There he is!' cried Beatrice. 'I declare the sound of him makes me want to gag. Come with me, Effie. I really dursn't face him alone.'

'Why, what's wrong with him?'

'What's wrong with him? And you of all people to ask me that!'

'I've got my sweeping to do and my table to lay,' complained Effie. 'He's no different from other men. He won't eat you.'

'Oh, Effie, and I done the telephone room for you and opened up the shutters.'

'Very well, then,' said Effie. 'But talk about people wanting their own way!'

Propping her brush against the white panelled wall, she followed Beatrice through a swing door down a short passage which ended in a side door, and had a door on the right which led into the kitchen.

'Good morning, ladies,' said the gardener, straightening himself from the stooping position which gardeners so readily assume. 'How are you, this fine morning?'

His bright brown eyes held them. He was a thickset man of about forty-five, whose breadth made him look shorter than he was. His brown moustache was inclined to be ragged, and even at this early hour his hands were caked with earth.

'Mind your muddy boots on my clean floor,' snapped Beatrice. 'I had to do it all over again after you yesterday.'

'There now, isn't that a shame?' said the gardener, shifting his glance from Beatrice to Effie. 'If I'd known, I'd have done it for you.'

'Like hell you would,' said Beatrice, but her tones lacked conviction, and the taunt fell flat.

' 'Tis Mrs. Burnett that do the scrubbing anyhow,' said the gardener. 'You've no call to grumble.'

'Mrs. Burnett didn't come yesterday,' said Beatrice, triumphantly establishing her ground of complaint. 'She sent a message to say her mother was took ill. There's some folks in this village whose relations are always falling ill, I'm thinking.'

The gardener smiled at Effie.

3

'What a nasty sarcastic tongue your friend's got,' he said. 'I wonder you don't get kind o' sour, listening to her day in, day out.'

'Well, she does get a bit on my nerves at times, but I don't mind, do I, Beattie? I dare say your wife says a few words to you on occasion.'

'Oh no, Mrs. Wimbush doesn't, not she,' said the gardener. 'She's got plenty to do without that. She's got five children to look after, not counting me. She wouldn't know what to do with herself if I was a well-off single gentleman like Mr. Casson. Some people has all the luck.'

'Meaning who?' demanded Beatrice.

'I shan't mention no names because you wouldn't like it if I did. And I don't mean Mr. Casson, either.'

He winked at Effie, who found it increasingly easy to keep her temper as the others were losing theirs.

'Now, you two,' she said pacifically. 'You'd argue the hind leg off a donkey. Don't pay any attention to him, Beattie, he only wants to tease.'

'I wish he'd clear out of my kitchen, then,' stormed Beatrice. 'The proper place for gardeners is in the garden.'

'All right,' said Wimbush. 'You can bring your own wood in next time. I'm not going to get it for you, you old so and so. . . .' The rest of his remark was drowned by the sudden whirr of an electric bell.

'That's him,' exclaimed Beatrice. 'Now he'll be wanting his breakfast. Men are all alike – they've no consideration.' She bustled into the larder, slamming the door. Wimbush picked up the empty skep and said to Effie:

'Don't you ever get fed up with that old bitch?'

Effie drew herself up. 'What a horrid word to use, Mr. Wimbush. I won't talk to you if you speak of my friend like that.' She looked at him again and at his big earth-caked hand, as brown and tough as the skep that dangled from it, and something in her melted. 'Well, I do a bit at times,' she said.

'Now *you're* different,' said the gardener. He squared his shoulders, and smoothed his hair with his free hand. 'You and me could get on quite well together.'

'Oh Mr. Wimbush,' tittered Effie. 'You oughtn't to say that.' The larder door opened, and he stumped out.

4

CHAPTER II

TIMOTHY CASSON sat down at his writing table. It was of oak, or imitation oak, stained nearly black, and very solid; large brass studs clamped the scratched and faded leather to the wood-work. It had the inertia, without the strength, of massiveness; it was a dead weight, which challenged his mind to lift it. He looked across the ink-stained surface to the snowy scene beyond. The light streamed up at him, filling the cornices behind his head with pale blue shadows. Gingerly he pushed open the shell-inlaid lid of the converted knife-box; it fell back with a startling rattle, as though guillotined. Lined with violet velvet, the deep slots did not surrender the quarry easily, but at last he fished up a sheet of paper, and began to write.

THE OLD RECTORY,
UPTON-ON-SWIRREL,
Nr. SWIRRELSFORD.
16*th January*, 1940.

MY DEAR MAGDA,

I am here at last. As a matter of fact I 'moved in' just before Christmas, but seem to have had no time to turn round. Not that I've much to do, but you know how curious and unreal one feels in a strange house. Nothing here is mine, of course; my things are all at Villa Lucertola, in the care of dear Amalia and Armando: you remember them – you thought them such a handsome couple. I know you don't like Italians much, but they weren't really Fascists, though latterly they had to pretend to be.

Well, I took this house furnished. I can't imagine what you'll say to the furniture; it's what you most dislike, heavy and dark brown, everything upholstered and self-important like a stage dowager of the 'nineties, with some shiny stream-lined pieces of modern date among them, hard and sharp and engine-turned, that look as though they would hurt if you touched them. The house itself is rather nice, or might be; it's been bedevilled, of course, but the garden-side isn't altogether un-Queen Anne and has such a lovely view. There's the substratum of a little terrace, and then a dipping lawn, and then the river; and beyond the river, on the opposite bank, a Stonehenge effect of fantastic pink Wagnerian rocks, leaning affectionately towards each other, like drunken dolmens, and the green of the moss on their sides and the yellow grass on their crests – I can't tell you how vivid it is against the pink. Not now, of course; now they're covered with snow, and the pink, which shows in patches, looks almost black. Snow falsifies every colour-value, doesn't it? but I must say the Welsh hills, which must be any number of miles away, do look rather wonderful, and with that remote, high, mystical light on them where their summits touch the sky.

The boat-house you would *love*. It's Gothic Revival, with stained-glass windows and a pointed roof, which just shows from where I'm sitting. And I needn't tell you there's a boat inside, my boat that I had brought here – indeed I took the house, really, to give a home to the boat. For reasons too boring to go into I haven't been able to use it yet. But I shall. What do you think I ought to row in? Shorts do not become my advancing years (forty-nine now, dear Magda) and flannel trousers are so dull. But now I must, if only to keep my figure from falling too far below your exacting requirements. Tell me when you write. You have an absolute sense of period – but I never quite know what period I belong to!

I haven't mentioned the war, have I? But then no one does. Most people think it's practically over. But you're in a better position to judge than I am, with your work at the Ministry of Appearances. I expect I ought to have tried to get a war-job, but then I am *so* unwarlike. And you have always said that one has but one duty – to look right for the circumstances. But I'm not sure I could look right in a war. Khaki's the only wear.

Timothy paused, thought, and sighed heavily. On the blotting-paper he tried to make a drawing of Magda's face. The parrot beak was a vile travesty of her nose, which was really only a little pronounced; and the wavy hair, that was always dressed so smartly and as though it had a special understanding with the brush, had turned to copper-wire.

By the way, did you get a small token from me at Christmas? A bottle of scent – I got it at Bertini's the last day I went shopping in Venice. The name would have amused you, but it was so embarrassing that I soaked the label off, so as not to shock the Customs. Italians love up-to-date English slang, but they don't always know when to use it. I can only say (and this is a compliment, so don't be offended) that if the object had really been what it was so quaintly called, to have given it to you would

6

have been like sending coals to Newcastle. All the same, little as you need it, I can't help hoping it reached you!

My spare rooms aren't quite what I could wish, but when they are more comfortable, you will come, won't you? Such heavenly country, and only five hours from London – a mere nothing.

Ever yours, TIMOTHY.

I like your cagey address. But you seem to have turned into an algebraic symbol!

He took an envelope and wrote—

Mrs. Magda Vivian,
Box 2xy, W.C.D.O.

Timothy got up and walked about, rubbing his hands, for the wood fire did not suffice to warm the room. But he regarded the fire with pride and affection and it warmed his spirit because he had cut the logs himself, with the help of the gardener and a two-handed saw. Coal was already getting scarce, but Timothy, like others in those early days, found an exhilaration in answering the call to austerity.

His circulation restored, he sat down again, and again angled for writing-paper in the finger-pinching velvet.

'Esther, my dear,' he wrote,

'This is just to wish you, rather late, a very Happy New Year, and to give you my news, such as it is.

'As you see, I took the Upton house after all – you called it a golden plan, and I hope it will turn out to be. In the end I decided in a hurry, and without showing the agreement to my solicitors, which was perhaps not very sensible—'

Timothy broke off. Esther had a wholesome horror of a grievance, and after all he had only himself to blame.

'Miss Chadwick, my landlady, is a very nice woman, and descended, I should think, from a long line of Deans. She has a patina of 1880 Isle of Wight high bourgeois culture, which I like. She wasn't in the least impressed when I told her I was "Lombard" of the *Broadside*; she only said, with acid sweetness, that my article made the rest of the paper seem so high-brow, and added "I'm afraid you won't find our farm labourers as picturesque as your peasants." To my relief, the *Broadside* is keeping me on, to write about the English countryside instead of the Italian, and my job is listed as a reserved occupation, which means I shan't be "directed into industry." "Pictures of Britain" they want me to call my sketches. At any rate I

7

ought to have a fresh eye, not having lived in England, except as a visitor, for eighteen years.

'The only drawback is, the people round here are much less forthcoming than my friends on the Brenta; so the one article I've written so far was a landscape without figures. Miss Chadwick said something about behaving in a neighbourly way, and I fully mean to, but she also said that village people are naturally reserved with strangers: so how am I to begin? At present I rely on the society of my servants, two middle-aged women of extreme respectability, who have always been in service together. I think I am going to like them very much. They are a little distant with me, but of course that is the way with English servants, and doesn't mean that they like one less. My gardener is an amusing fellow, a regular card; and I think they all have good times together in the kitchen (Servants' hall we have none. This is a small house, six bedrooms all told). I can hear their voices sounding most animated over their elevenses. I think we are a happy nucleus.

'But to return to my neighbours, or lack of neighbours. I feel you can advise me about them, having lived so much in the country. I wish I'd taken notes, all the times I've stayed with you at Langton Place! Only of course it's different for you: your family is the pivot on which the village has turned for generations. If you want to know anyone, you merely have to call on them. I can't do that, I have to wait to be called on, it seems. (In Italy, as you know, it's the other way round.) But I have one acquaintance in the district – a very important one, only I haven't seen her yet: Mrs. Lampard.

'She is important because she is the chief landowner round here, she rules the roost; and she is specially important to me because, apparently, I have to get her permission before I can use my boat. It's a question of the fishing-rights. The agents told me—'

Timothy thought, frowned, and scratched 'the agents told me' out. Esther would not want to hear the tale of their misdeeds.

'Miss Chadwick told me that the fishermen would certainly resent my rowing my boat on their private waters. I said I knew nothing about fly-fishing; but surely it doesn't begin till the mayfly rises? She said, "No, but the fish have to have a quiet time to breed." I went into this with my gardener, who after all belongs to the place and knows how fishes behave, and he said it was rubbish, because the fish withdraw from the main river and go into creeks and inlets to breed, so my boat couldn't disturb them. "Anyhow," he added, "Nature is nature, and if the fish wanted to breed neither your boat nor a battleship would stop they from breeding." I challenged Miss Chadwick with this, and she

8

said, with a slight air of superiority, that one would not go to gardeners to learn about the habits of fish. In fact she disabled his judgment. "And in any case," she said, "if you do put your boat on the river it will be regarded as an unfriendly act and make a bad impression. But of course if *Mrs. Lampard* says you can!—"

'So what luck that I know Mrs. Lampard. At least she was brought out to lunch with me at the Lucertola – twice, if I remember. And she asked me to call on her in London, but I never did. That was a good many years ago; she was rather formidable then, and I gather is more so now. But I wrote to her just after Christmas, reminding her of our meeting and asking if she had any objection to my using the boat; and her secretary replied, quite civilly, but rather formally, and not referring to our having met abroad, to say that Mrs. Lampard was not very well but she would let me know about the boat later. And there for the moment the matter rests. Don't worry! – I shan't make a grievance of it!

'It looks as if the war might fizzle out, doesn't it? But I expect you are frightfully busy, helping and organizing and smoothing things over. I haven't any evacuees yet, and I rather hope I shan't, for Beatrice and Effie, my very nice maids, don't like the idea of them. So at the moment I have three spare bedrooms, or shall have when I've collected a few more sheets and blankets. Miss Chadwick—'

Timothy erased 'Miss Chadwick'. He hadn't realised how the scores were mounting up against her. He went on – Langton is a long way off, but if you could spare a few days at the week-end or in the middle of the week, you know how welcome you would be, dear Esther, and you would raise me in the esteem of my staff (who have had rather 'good' places, they tell me). Just send a telegram.

Timothy signed his name and had already written on the envelope 'The Hon. Mrs. Morwen, Langton Place,' when he paused, shrugged his shoulders, sucked his lips in, puffed his cheeks out, opened and closed his hands. To weigh one imponderable against another, what a hopeless task! He took up his pen again.

'By the way, did you get a small gift from me at Christmas? Very likely not, so many things go astray, besides, the shop may have forgotten to put in my name. It was a thermos flask – a dull, *empty* present, but I'm told they may get scarce. Don't bother to write if you *have* got it – what *can* one say about a thermos flask? But send me a postcard if you haven't, and I'll stir up the shop.'

Two letters by eleven o'clock and such long ones; already he had something to show for the day. But not very good letters: too much about himself and not enough about his correspondents. Mme. de Sévigné would have made them feel, from the first word, that they were living in her mind, and that they were the object of these letters which, without them, and her need to get into touch with them, to glorify them and surround them with a pearly nimbus of affection, could never have been written. And she would have contrived to give them news of herself, all the same – only, herself mingled with them, drenched in their consciousness of her. And he had said almost nothing about the war.

What would they think of that? Though so different, they were alike in being far more war-minded than he was. Mme. de Sévigné frequently referred to the wars – 'The success of the French in every country surpasses belief, and I give thanks for this in my evening prayers.' But enough of her.

Posterity, at whose dim, unexpectant face Timothy sometimes peered, would learn nothing about Magda and Esther from these letters. It would not see Magda's tall slight figure with its awkward grace, or hear her throaty voice, a little huskier, perhaps, from the cock-tails and cigarettes; they would not realise how purposeful was her transcience as the air parted and closed behind her in flat and bar and restaurant and night-club. She hated to linger; she must move on or be overtaken by the boredom which was ever at her heels – her only constant companion. Of her two husbands there remained no trace, not even the name of the last one. She was about as permanent as a manicure or a massage, much less permanent than a permanent wave. And she had rather that effect on one; that was why people liked her (those who did like her). She was a wash-and-brush-up, a shampoo; to those whom the phrase applied, a beauty treatment; astringent, but freshening. One associated her with any fashionable resort, but not with any special place.

Whereas Esther was inconceivable apart from Langton, and the many-voiced creative stir of its shifting or indigenous population – the relations, the children, the guests, the dogs, and now (Timothy felt sure) the soldiers and the evacuees. Timothy stayed with her whenever he came to England. She did not always notice him when he was there, but she wanted him in her system; she was indignant if he delayed to come, and rather reproachful when he went away. No one ever stayed with Magda, except for bed and breakfast, even in the days when she had a husband and a home; for long together, the non-amorous proximity of another person bored her.

Writing to them had made him wish for their company. He was handicapped, as always in writing to these two old and dear friends, by the fact that Magda had an æsthetic, and Esther a conventional, view of life. Two broad and comprehensive fields of vision; but anything that fell outside Magda's bored her, and anything that seriously smacked of unconventionality puzzled and irritated Esther. They did not like each other very much, Timothy reflected; neither would be pleased to know that he had written to the other. To Magda, Esther seemed frumpish, muddle-headed, untidy, dull-edged if not dull; while Esther thought of Magda as too smart, too stream-lined, too soignée; trembling, no, poised on the edge of a world she did not care to know, not quite second-rate, but nearly; perhaps, in her hard bright glitter, a little selfish. . . . No, not selfish, for Esther, as a woman of the world, was chary of moral judgments. She would say that Magda was restless or unreliable or disappointing, or that she had thrown away her chances.

Thinking of moral judgments reminded Timothy that he still had a letter to write. But his mind, launched on its career of evocation, would not be turned aside. Suddenly it was filled with light, a light far warmer than the bluish pallor reflected from the ground beyond his window; the light of a July afternoon in the Piazza in Venice; and out of this radiance stepped Tyrone MacAdam, hatless, his wispy hair flickering over his oncoming baldness, like flames round an egg – unshaven, untidy, in fact almost dirty, swinging in his hand the paper bag in which he so often carried his lunch.

'I've come from Verona,' he announced. 'I was just in time to see the last performance of *Ballo in Maschera*. Quite good; but they did it better at Dresden in 1934, and at the San Carlo in 1936, and not much worse, if the soprano hadn't been so frightful, at Basle in 1931. You've seen it, of course?'

Timothy had to admit that he had not.

'Oh, you disgust me,' exclaimed Tyro, accepting the chair that Timothy pushed out, squeaking, on the pavement towards him. 'You well-off English people – yes, I will have some tea, thank you – you come out to Italy and what good do you get from it? You hang about in places like this where you simply see other people like yourselves, gorging and guzzling like yourselves, killing time and killing thought; then just when it's time to go home you have a look at St. Mark's and the Doge's Palace, and then you go back to England and say how rude the Fascists are, because they make you take your feet off the seats in the railway carriages, and how cruel to the Abyssinians, because they use against them the weapons of modern warfare which the English never use, oh never, against races less civilised than themselves. You could have learnt all that by staying at home and reading the paper. It makes me so angry when I see supposedly intelligent people like yourself doing that kind of thing.'

'But I don't, I don't,' protested Timothy, while Tyro with a grimy pocket handkerchief wiped his fingers and then his face. 'I don't like the Fascists, it's true, and Italy has been far less pleasant since they came into power – for the Italians, as well as us. But I'm not politically-minded in the Continental sense, and I don't want to be. I don't think any good comes of it.' Timothy glared at his friend, who was staring at the strollers and paying him very little attention.

'I beg your pardon, Timothy,' he said, with the charming smile and beautiful manners that every now and then flashed through his habitual air of crossness.

'I was saying I didn't want to be politically-minded.' The remark sounded less striking when repeated. 'I like the Italians very much, just as much as you do, only I don't want always to see them in a contrast, and as one side of an argument. I just want to get on with them, and enjoy being with them as I have done, most gratefully and happily, for eighteen years, and mean to go on doing.'

'You won't go on much longer,' said his companion, with gloomy relish, 'because there's going to be a war, and all brought on by people like you, with no moral sense.'

'I like that!' cried Timothy, 'I've done my best, in a small way, to foster good feeling between England and Italy. I've even had a row with the editor of the *Broadside* because I haven't more openly condemned the régime.'

'Oh, I know your "Lombard" stuff, exuding sunshine and sweetness, and the signore inglese, cosi buono, cosi ricco, distributing kind words and kinder soldi among the snivelling contadini – cosi grati, cosi ricon-oscenti. That's not what's wanted. What's wanted is to tell the English that, with their record, they have no right to take a high moral line against aggression. Such hypocrisy! It only brings morals into disre-pute. As an Irishman and a Scotsman, and for all I know, as a Welshman, I can tell you that when I hear the word aggression on an English lip it makes me sweat at my knee-caps.'

'But you always said you were an American.'

'By birth, yes. But don't speak to me of nationalities. I'm a citizen of the world, I hope. It makes me so angry when I hear people vaunting their beastly birthplaces, just as if there was some virtue in being born a Siamese or a Hottentot.'

'Oh come now,' said Timothy. 'Your morality is a form of war-mongering too. But couldn't we dine together? Where are you staying?'

'My usual address – care of Cook's.'

Timothy directed a baffled glance to where, on the left side of St. Mark's, the homely English name, writ large on the Venetian wall, had begun to assume, in this troubled and menacing summer of 1939, an air as comforting and reassuring as the word 'policeman' to the well-doer.

'Couldn't you stay at the Lucertola, and still be care of Cook's?'

'I suppose I could. Thank you, Timothy. "Be given to hospitality," the Apostle said, and you are. But don't imagine your hospitality will avert a European War. I suppose you think, from the way I spoke just now, that I'm in favour of Fascism?'

'It sounded a little—'

'Well, I'm not. I'm not in favour of any country, and not particularly keen about the human race. There's not an ounce of good in any of them, as you'll find out if you live long enough.'

'My dear Tyro,' wrote Timothy, and stopped, for he could not remember his friend's address. Care of Cook's would find him, no doubt; but it was discouraging when you had written someone a letter, as Tyro had to Timothy, a long one, to discover that not only had the recipient failed to keep it, but had not even troubled to make a note of the address.

Timothy had a large correspondence, some of it from Italians both in Italy and England, commenting on his articles. Scarcer than they used to be, the letters from Italy also took longer to arrive, and they were disfigured with large rectangular smudges as of lamp-black, around which could be described a few limbs of letters, tossing like disjected fly's legs on an inky sea. To think that his communication with Italy, once perfect and complete, should be reduced – when the correspondent had anything he really *wanted* to say – to meaningless pot-hooks!

Timothy had a habit of leaving small caches of letters wherever he sat or lingered; they sprang up like rubbish dumps in the hollows round a village. He regretted them, but could not stop them. Now he must visit each in turn, like a Government employee collecting salvage. How gay and welcoming the hall would be if only the fanlight over the door, and the larger lunette, above the somewhat exiguous window on the staircase, were not permanently blacked out with cardboard! Dark, dark, dark, total eclipse! No, not total, for the severely rationed, snow-sunlight filtered shyly through the banisters. Slender, twisted, closely set, they had an air of breeding, and Miss Chadwick had been right to beg him not to break them.

Up he went, and down a dark passage on whose indigo-tinted skylight the snow lay piled; and so to his bedroom with its blue rep carpet and the two deeply-recessed windows looking on the river. On the long pointed roof of the boathouse snow lay in patches; the little cluster of bamboos in which it nestled, shivered, he could almost hear the dry rustle, as the wind stirred their yellow stems and withered leaves.

But here, too, his search was vain, for the heap on the dressing-table only yielded long bluish letters of business cut, from which Timothy's mind shied away. Downstairs again, and into the telephone-room. This pile was much tidier than when he left it: Effie had done her work well – or was it Beatrice who 'did' the telephone-room? They each had their bounds beyond which they might not pass. He fingered the miscellaneous missives and at the bottom lay Tyro's.

A feeling of guilt mitigated Timothy's triumph, for the letter was much too private to leave lying about. Still, it gave him the address he wanted, and he wrote it down at once, – The Censor's Office, Liverpool. Then, he went on.

'I'm sorry you find your fellow-censors unsympathetic, but at any rate you have someone to browbeat, which is more than I have here. The village seems to be divided into two nations: not Disraeli's two, the rich and the poor, but the old stagers and the newcomers. The old stagers are retired soldiers and professional men; the newcomers are of all sorts, but chiefly refugees from the Midlands fleeing from the bombs to come. (I don't think there will be any, do you?) My gardener, who is my chief source of information, tells me the two factions don't mix at all: they are like oil and water, he said, and indeed he always says it, whenever these Montagues and Capulets are mentioned. Nor, I gather, do the villagers in his own walk of life mix much: he told me with pride that in the twenty years he had been here, no one had crossed his threshold for a cup of tea, nor had he crossed anyone else's. 'It's the only way,' he said, darkly, 'It's the only way.' To what? I wondered.

'I have never knowingly set eyes on one of the gentry; perhaps they only come out at night and by day are shut away behind their high garden walls and thick box hedges. (I picture them as old, but of course they may not be.) The invaders, on the other hand, wallow in visibility; they walk down the street four abreast, the women in trousers and the men in sporting checks, pushing perambulators and summoning the straggling toddlers in no uncertain voices. They pass the time of day, and would do more, I think, only I don't know how much I want to be involved with them – it isn't just snobbery, but I do have to protect my time a little – also I feel that of the two sets I would rather make friends with the old-timers – I have a special reason for wanting to be in their good graces – from which friendship with the others would apparently debar me. . . .

'You ask how long I've taken the house for. Well, thereby hangs a tale. I was considering the agreement and going to send it to my solicitor in London, when the house agents rang me up and said that unless I signed at once they would offer the house to someone else. I'm sure this was a bluff, and they couldn't have done it legally, with the negotiations so far advanced; but there's such a scarcity of houses that I didn't dare risk it. Now I have had a reproachful letter from my solicitors telling me I've taken the house for five years without the power to break the let (though my landlady can), that I can't sublet without her permission, that I shan't be able to store the fruit, only pick it up off the ground, or eat it as it becomes ripe (you can imagine me gobbling all day and dying of a surfeit), that my landlady may 'enter' at any time, 'having given sufficient warning.' And she does: only yesterday she entered and took away a pair of sheets saying that as a bachelor I could not possibly need them.

'But what I really mind about is the boat. The house-agents' prospectus said "Boating and Bathing on the River Swirrel." I came, I saw, I liked the house, and I loved the boat-house. The day I signed the Agreement I wrote to a boat-builder and ordered a boat. It is a lovely boat; it cost me eighty pounds, ninety, counting the carriage from Oxford. It arrived at the door on a nondescript vehicle capable of carrying a fire escape; it was unlaced, untied, and found to have suffered no damage. Two men in baize aprons bore it reverently through the stableyard and across the lawn. It was all I could do not to get into it. Step by step I kept pace with them, in an agony lest they should drop the lovely, fragile, chestnut-coloured vessel; we rounded the bamboos and reached the inlet, the artery to the boat-house. There they launched it with the softest imaginable splash; it hurried into the water as a duck does, and seemed so thankful to be in its element. Where the water touched it, the wood turned a darker chestnut, and the ripples beneath its bows reflected broken tawny lights. The baize aprons were not, of course, as excited as I was, but they felt the lustre of the occasion, their faces shone, and they whistled a little, as they gently backed the darling creature into the boat-house, where it lay, quietly heaving, and looking almost *sanctified* with blue and red and orange bars of light playing on it, rainbow-like, from those *heavenly* stained-glass windows.

'Well, it was rather late, and windy, and I seemed to have all time before me; and the next day it rained, and I contented myself with visiting the boat-house every hour or so, just to make *sure*. And the day after, in the morning, Miss Chadwick (who has moved into a smaller house within striking distance of this one) called, and said with an air of great empressement that she had been talking to some of my neighbours, and they all expressed consternation when they heard I had imported a boat. How had they heard? I asked. She replied that such an event could not be kept secret, and that somebody had said it was the greatest misfortune that had happened to Upton for thirty years. 'It is not for me to advise you,' she said, 'but the strongest feelings have been aroused, and if you persist in using your boat, the consequences may be grave.'

'Of course I complained to the agents, but I got very little satisfaction from them. They advised me to apply to Mrs. Lampard (the local grandee), or the Catchment Board, a rather mysterious body whose headquarters are in Bristol where, it is said, they dine most lavishly on profits made out of traffic on the river.

'I do apologise for this outburst, but one of the comforts of writing to you is that one need not conceal one's grievances of pretend that things are going better than they are. My feelings about the boat are utterly disproportionate, I know; what *does* it matter (and in a European war!) whether I go for a row or not? And what a comedy, to take the house for the boating, and then not to be able to boat! But of course I shall, as soon as I get in touch with Mrs. Lampard.'

Timothy broke off. He flinched from the next part, and Tyro perhaps more than the other two would resent being reminded.

But it would be pusillanimous not to mention the matter, and Tyro, if he ever remembered, would scold him less for speaking out than for failing to.

'By the way, did you get a little thing from me at Christmas? a fairly early copy of Swift's "Conduct of the Allies," not in the least valuable, but I thought you might like to have it with your other Swiftiana. Just send me one of those service cards – you know, "I have, have not, received your parcel." Of course a letter would be still more welcome, but I know how busy you must be.'

CHAPTER III

TIMOTHY had bought a small car to take him about the countryside in quest of subjects for his Pictures of Britain. The petrol restrictions made it impossible for him to go far afield at present, but he had applied for an extra allowance in connection with his job. Once or twice he went alone, then it occurred to him to ask Beatrice and Effie to go with him. He knew they liked to go out together, and when the weather got warmer he meant to spend the day out, so that they should be able to do the same. As it was, they often had to take turns, unless Mrs. Burnett could oblige in the kitchen, which she never could be sure of doing, she had so many relations in the district who needed her help, and other employers more short-handed than Timothy.

Effie, whom Timothy asked first, shook her head mournfully and said they were much too busy. There was neither gratitude nor disappointment in her voice, but an obvious pleasure in saying 'no,' and a suggestion, too, that Timothy might count himself lucky that he could take the afternoon off while other people had to work. Feeling the justice of this, Timothy retreated hastily from the kitchen, an action which was already easier for him than entering it, and slipped out through the side door into the stableyard, where the frozen snow crunched beneath his feet. One of the loose boxes had been converted by Miss Chadwick into a rough sort of garage which Timothy used for his car. In a neighbouring shed, open to the elements, stood another car, a ramshackle affair which had seen much hard service, and of which Timothy knew nothing except that it was not his. It was his habit to take things for granted, and had the shed been occupied by an elephant he would not have wondered how it got there. But today something – perhaps it was pique at Effie's refusal to accept his offer of a drive – kindled his curiosity about the unsightly vehicle, and he called out to Wimbush, who happened to be passing, and asked him whose it was.

Wimbush approached ponderously and laid his hand on the car's battered hood, as though he could more easily explain its presence if he was physically in touch with it.

'It belongs to Mr. Edgell, the Rector's son,' he said, 'Miss Chadwick let him leave it there, while he went to join up, like.' He became aware of Timothy's hostility to the car, and added, ' 'Tisn't an ornament, sir, is it?'

'Well, no,' said Timothy. 'And I think he might have asked me, don't you? After all, I may want to use this shed for a guest's car. I'm expecting some guests, before long.' Timothy was surprised to hear the resentment in his voice.

'He mightn't have known that Miss Chadwick have let the house,' remarked Wimbush. 'Happen I see him about, I'll tell him to take it away. He's got plenty of petrol in his tank; four gallons, I shouldn't be surprised.'

'Oh no,' exclaimed Timothy, too much taken aback to wonder how Wimbush knew there was so much petrol in the car. 'You mustn't do that. I only thought he might just have asked me. What sort of a fellow is he, Wimbush?'

'Regular harumscarum he is,' said Wimbush, 'a proper clergyman's son, they all say. Not that I've anything against him. We keep out of each other's road. That's always safest, I say.'

It was not the first time Timothy had heard Wimbush proclaim his policy of isolation.

'But I expect you know the Rector?' Timothy pursued.

An inscrutable look came into Wimbush's red brown eyes. 'Oh yes, we all know him.'

'Is he . . . is he?' Timothy began.

'Yes, he is,' said Wimbush, to whom Timothy's vague question had evidently meant something quite definite. 'He's all that and more, sir. But he's got his faults like the rest of us; he wouldn't be human if he hadn't. Mrs. Purbright, of course, she's different.'

'Different in what way?'

'Well, the money's hers, for one thing.'

But for the moment Timothy was more interested in the Rector's failings than in his wife's money.

'What sort of faults?' he asked.

'Well, one that isn't really a fault in a man, sir, not like it is in a woman, I mean he's got a terrible temper. When anything upsets him he goes off alarming, just like you or I might, except that he dursn't use bad language. Some of the chaps annoy him for the purpose, just to see him get his rag out. But his worst fault is that he hasn't got much to say to a working man, not like you have, sir, and Mrs. Purbright.'

Timothy did not like having to share this compliment with Mrs. Purbright. 'I'm afraid I chatter a great deal,' he excused himself, insincerely.

'Oh I wouldn't say that, sir,' said the gardener. 'Only having vegetated abroad in a manner of speaking, you haven't quite got the ways of the gentry. But you will. Not but what some of them's very nice people. There's Colonel Harbord, for instance. He nearly went down on his knees to me to go to him. He have a really big garden, more like a park, it is, that need two or three men. He's a great fisherman too. He's one of them that makes the river what it is. He and Commander Bellew, and Sir Watson Stafford at the big house up to Cumberledge, and several more I could name, only they wouldn't mean anything to you, being a stranger, begging your pardon, sir.'

'They're all tenants of Mrs. Lampard, I suppose,' said Timothy.

'Bless you yes, sir, as far as the eye can see. All except this house, that belong to Miss Chadwick, as it did to her brother the judge, before her, and she won't sell it, not for love nor money.'

'I'm glad of that,' said Timothy. 'And all the people who have come from outside to live here, are they Mrs. Lampard's tenants, too?'

Wimbush disengaged himself from the car, stood upright and shook his head. 'You couldn't rightly call them tenants,' he said earnestly. 'I don't know what name to give them, really I don't, that wouldn't sound rude. But legally speaking, yes, they be tenants of Mrs. Lampard, seeing as how the whole village belongs to her. And they pay good money for all those cottages that she had dolled up and fancified, you wouldn't believe.'

'I expect there are some nice people among them,' said Timothy, but he felt priggish defending them.

'Don't you be too sure, sir. All I know is they don't mix with the gentry, any more than oil mixes with water. I shouldn't want to have anything to do with them.'

Sounds came from behind them, the shutting of a door, the scraping of shoes on stone, discreet coughs and throat-clearings. Timothy turned his head. Standing on the doorstep were Beatrice and Effie, dressed for the afternoon; they were looking in his direction, and already had the reproachful air of people who have been kept waiting. They had changed their minds and were coming after all.

Scarcely had Timothy left the kitchen when the larder door opened and Beatrice appeared, belligerence on her brow.

'Oh, Effie, why did you say not to go with him?'

'Well, haven't you always said we're not to give way to him over every little thing?'

Beatrice had not expected this argument. She was silent, and Effie pressed her advantage.

'At this rate he'll be thinking he can take us anywhere he likes, at any time. It isn't very nice, is it? You don't know what he might do.'

Beatrice recovered herself. 'Not with me there. I can look after you if he starts anything.'

'It might not be me; it might be you.' Effie looked out of the window. She saw Wimbush talking to Timothy, who looked thin and slight beside him.

'Oh go on with you,' said Beatrice. 'I dunno what's come over you lately. You never seem to want to get out of this hole. If it was someone else, I might think you were in love.'

Effie turned away from the window and sat down in a basket chair. The image of Wimbush was so vivid in her mind, that obscurely she felt it must be reflected in her face. She said airily, 'What if I was?'

'You couldn't be,' said Beatrice scornfully. 'There's not a man in the place, except him.'

'It would have to be a him, wouldn't it?' Effie's tone was sarcastic, but the self-betrayal that love demands took the stiffening out of her voice.

Beatrice stared at her. 'If I thought it was *him*, I should kill you and myself, too.'

Like an animal that scents danger, Effie was at once on the alert. 'You and your hims! You're a regular hymn-book. But if you're going to get all worked up about it, I don't mind, I'll go. Anything to keep you quiet. But don't blame me if he takes it as an encouragement.'

'Good!' Timothy called out as soon as he saw them. He liked the idea of company, and was happy to think that the maids wanted to come. 'Wait a moment, and I'll have the car out.'

This needed a certain amount of manœuvring. Wimbush stood in front, rather in the attitude of 'he' in Blind Man's Buff, encouraging, advising, warning. Timothy was afraid he might run over him. At last the car was brought to where the maids stood. With an exaggerated flourish Wimbush held the door open for them. Beatrice swept past him without a look; Effie, whether by accident or design, stumbled, but deftly eluded his outstretched hand. Settling themselves delicately, they took the rug Timothy offered and pulled it round themselves. 'All right behind?' he asked. The car started with the jerk which Timothy had never been able to eradicate. Blowing on his hands, Wimbush watched them go.

* * *

Timothy returned in a contented state of mind, but sadly short of petrol. On the outward journey he had made a détour to show Beatrice and Effie the ruins of Merrivale Abbey, a Cistercian building romantically situated on the banks of another river. This would be killing two birds, for the abbey was certainly one of Britain's pictures, and many writers had tried their hands at describing it. Few had seen it under snow, however, and none had the advantage of having Beatrice and Effie with them. This was the Age of the Common Man. Timothy did not mean for a moment to suggest that Effie and Beatrice were common women; but he thought it would strengthen his hand if he could embody in his article the appeal the abbey made to untutored but beauty-loving minds. Later, he realised that their comments would have to be carefully edited; but Timothy had no scruples on that score. Merrivale Abbey, ruin though it was, was one of the things we were fighting for.

Musing thus, he caught sight of the dilapidated hood of the intruder: seen in the mingling moonlight and snowlight, it had a ghostly quality. His animosity towards it had completely melted: but an idea came to him: why should he not use some of the petrol, which Wimbush said was interned within it, for his own car? Two gallons would take him seventy miles, and reveal who could tell how many pictures of Britain, far beyond the reach of Wimbush's bicycle which he sometimes borrowed for these necessary excursions. A letter to the Rector, who had not yet called on him, would be a friendly gesture, and perhaps, too, a milestone on the road to Colonel Harbord, Captain Sturrock, Commander Bellew and the rest, even a slight advance in the direction of Mrs. Lampard. Already Timothy saw himself in the boat, gliding gently along the forbidden river, always with a watchful eye to the trout who were misconducting themselves (but quite laudably) in its depths. The scenery along the banks (unimaginable, for the road seldom approached the river, and, except at the village bridge, only crossed it at points two miles above and below Upton) would be worth at least one picture of Britain: but that was not the point; the point was the sum of psycho-physical sensations that Timothy would capture with the first free stroke of his free sculls on the free water: the release, the renewal.

He told the Rector how lucky he felt himself to have found a house in such a beautiful place as Upton; how much he looked forward to living there; that his non-appearance at church, which he greatly deplored, was only the result of the difficulties, in wartime, of getting settled into a house. He looked forward to making many friends, among them the Rector, his wife, and his son, whose car he was particularly glad to be able to accommodate in his garage. The car would not be in the way, not in the least, he hoped the Rector's son would feel free to leave it there as long as he liked. But he had just one request to make; as the Rector's son was not, and would not be using the car, might Timothy take for himself by a simple operation, known, he believed, as siphoning, some of the petrol that was in it? If he might, not only would the car be a delightful addition to his other furnishings, but a very useful one as well.

The letter was in time to catch the post.

The next morning announced a thaw. Water lay in blue-black hollows in the snow, the river had risen and changed its colour to a dirty yellow. The boat was a foot or more higher than when he last visited it, and the rainbow lights from the stained glass touched it in new places. Timothy could not help feeling he was in church, even to the point of tip-toeing about with subdued movements; and his sense of isolation from the outside world, of being alone with a presence that commanded awe, was absolute. Save for the whispering chuckle of the water there was no sound; save for the almost imperceptible rise and fall of the boat, no movement. Timothy's senses were stilled in a kind of ritual. He opened the door quietly and went out.

What had Beatrice and Effie really said? They had reacted to the ruins in a strictly professional spirit. The church itself left them untouched; their imaginations did not conceive the idea of worshipping there. But the monastic buildings, the use of which Timothy explained as well as he could with the help of small, leaden notices planted by the Board of Works, these they found both interesting and undesirable. Fancy cooking, sleeping, washing, feeding in these old places! No comfort, no convenience anywhere. All stone floors and nowhere to sit down. And the cold! The snow which thickly covered the ruins lent weight to this objection; Timothy could not convince his pupils, and could hardly convince himself, that the snow would have been out of doors, not in.

Triumphantly Timothy was able to assure them that the monks *had* grumbled. In contemporary records their complaints were still preserved. Not of the cold, strangely enough, but of the heat; of the sunlight striking on the water, which, they declared, hurt their eyes; of the soldiers in the border castle of Chepstow, who came over and pinched their livestock, and with menaces demanded food and shelter; of the better conditions prevailing at the abbeys of Tintern and Much Wenlock. At these evidences of imperfection, Beatrice and Effie pricked up their ears; it was clear that they liked the idea of Merrivale Abbey seething with discontent better than when they thought of it as a haunt of ancient peace. To the great natural beauty of its situation, lassooed in a loop of the river, with the pinkish cliffs on one side, and on the other, snow-sprinkled woods sloping upwards with an effect of infinite depth and distance towards the mountains of Wales, they seemed indifferent; but as they turned away Effie remarked that she wished they could see the place on the movies – it would look so pretty there.

They were getting into the car when Timothy looked back and saw what the monks complained of: a shaft of light striking the river with almost unbearable brightness. Half blinded, he called to the maids to come and look; but by the time they had got out, the dazzling ray was gone, and he was left wondering if he had seen it or imagined it.

'Damaris and Chloe,' Timothy wrote, 'rightly felt that the domestic arrangements of the abbey compared unfavourably with those we enjoy in England today. In England today we have both sorts of luxury; the thousand material comforts that surround us from bedtime to bedtime, *and* the incomparable beauty, so refreshing to the spirit, which the monks of Merrivale bequeathed to us – a beauty, one should add, perhaps more poignant because more elegiac than that of the monasteries of Italy, where Time, kept captive by the Catholic Church, is not allowed to show his majesty. Yet the bare ruined quire of Merrivale is not dead; Damaris and Chloe, typical figures of today, stepping delicately among the snow-covered ruins, exclaiming with delight at what they saw, were quick to appreciate the humanity and humour of the old chronicler, Walterus ex-Oxoniensis, with his tales of eye-strain from the sunlight on the river, and the exactions of the soldiery, foraging or, as we should say, scrounging, in the abbey ponds and pastures.

'A hint from Chloe that scenes like Merrivale would merit the attention of the film-producer seemed to me a happy one, and I hope it will be taken up. But we must remember if we see this lovely relic flashed upon the screen, that its home is not in a hot and possibly rather stuffy room in London or New York or Paris, with no other context than the backs of innumerable heads wreathed in tobacco-smoke, a spot-lit figure at an organ, and illuminated notices showing the audience where they can get out; its home is not in these cosmopolitan and possibly ephemeral surroundings, contrived to give recreation to tired workers of our industrial age, but in the depths of the English countryside, with centuries of English history flowing over it; and round it, audible to an ear attuned, the devout whisperings of the Age of Faith. These imponderables can only be appreciated *in situ*, as they were by Damaris and Chloe, those intelligent and decorative nymphs; they belong to no Odeon or Plaza or Rialto, but to one valley of one county of England, which has been free for nearly nine hundred years, and which we mean to keep so.

'I have been betrayed into attempted eloquence. Let me finish on a lighter note, the note of comedy with which our visit also finished, reminding us that the valley we were leaving was not only beautiful but merry – merry as Merry England. Turning to me with mischief in her eyes, Chloe said—'

What *could* Effie have said? Timothy tried to think; his readers expected a light touch from him, and he must not disappoint them. He tried an experimental smile, for the mind is sometimes pleased to take a hint from the body, and as it was broadening into an idiotic grin the door opened to admit as much of Effie as, on certain occasions, she was prepared to show. 'The Reverend to see you, sir,' she said.

'The Reverend?'

Effie compressed her lips to imply that it was not her fault if the visitor had an unusual name; also, that he was close behind her. And as she grudgingly opened the door wider he walked in. Timothy wiped the humour-engendering smile off his face, substituted another more suitable, and rose.

'How do you do, Mr. Purbright? This is a pleasure.'

'How do you do.'

The Rector's smile flickered and went. He was a tall, ascetic-looking man, whose swarthy complexion seemed to cast a permanent shadow on his face.

'You find me writing an article,' said Timothy, immediately feeling called on to justify himself. 'But I can't tell you how glad I am to be interrupted.'

'I am sorry if I have disturbed you,' said the Rector, ignoring the second part of Timothy's remark. 'But I got your letter, and I felt I must come round at once.'

'Do sit down. You mean my letter about the car?'

'Yes. I hope I am in time.'

'Of course,' said Timothy. 'There was no hurry at all. I'm glad you came, but I'm sorry you hurried.'

The Rector's face relaxed somewhat. 'It was to save you from committing a serious imprudence,' he said.

'Imprudence?' echoed Timothy.

'You did not know that the expedient you suggested, of – er – siphoning the petrol from my son's car into your own was forbidden by law?'

Timothy was taken aback. He did know that to transfer petrol from one car to another was illegal; but he had heard of many people doing it, and supposed that the law winked at it.

'You might have got us all three into serious trouble,' said the Rector impressively. 'I could not possibly be party to such a transaction. People have been sent to prison for less.'

Timothy's sense of guilt now became tinged with irritation. The Rector was sitting in front of him for all the world like a policeman. 'I could not have dreamed,' he said, a little stiffly, 'of taking the petrol without first asking your permission. That was why I wrote. Your son left his car in my shed without my leave or knowledge. I could charge him rent for it, I suppose. I should not, of course, do that; but it did not seem unreasonable, in the circumstances, to ask him for a *quid pro quo*.'

The Rector's dark face turned darker. 'I am sorry you take my friendly advice in that spirit, Mr. Casson,' he said. 'Edgell is now with the R.A.F. He kept his car here at the invitation of Miss Chadwick, as we have no room for it at the Rectory. In his haste to answer his country's call he forgot to take the car away. A good many of us are rather busy with war work, Mr. Casson. I think you will agree that an oversight, which I sincerely regret, is hardly to be balanced against a deliberate infringement of the law.' He rose. 'If you will allow me, I will take the car away with me now.'

Timothy felt that matters must not be left like this.

'Oh please, Mr. Purbright,' he said, rising in his turn and smiling into Mr. Purbright's unsmiling face, 'don't let us misunderstand each other. Of course take the car if you want to, but I shall be most happy to keep it here. Believe me, I had no wish to do anything that might embarrass you.'

A struggle appeared in the Rector's face, as though he was reminding himself of the duty of Christian forbearance. The movement of his moods seemed to demand a corresponding movement in his bloodstream. But presently his brow cleared and he said,

'That is kind of you. I accept your offer gratefully, and I thank you, too, on Edgell's behalf.' He drew a long breath, a Cease Fire over the battlefield, and looked round him, a trifle dazed. Timothy at once came to his side, and together they moved towards the window.

'A very nice place you have here,' said the Rector. 'In Judge Chadwick's time it was the scene of much simple hospitality. His sister,

Clara, could not keep up the gracious tradition. Straitened means, I fear. You have met her, of course?'

Timothy said he had.

'Bookish, very, a remarkably well-read woman, in fact. You will enjoy many a literary crack with her, I trust. Not a bad woman of business, either. You will find that most of your neighbours are not great readers. Fishing is their main occupation – perhaps I should not say that, but certainly their main recreation. There are some very good fellows among them, very. Colonel Harbord, a great gentleman; Captain Sturrock, one of the best. Commander Bellew, a little brusque ... naval, you know, but delightful when you know him. Watson Stafford – he likes us to forget the "Sir" – a self-made man – he would be the first to admit it – but wonderfully generous, wonderfully. And, of course, there is Mrs. Lampard.'

Timothy said he had met Mrs. Lampard, many years ago.

'You met Mrs. Lampard?' asked the Rector in surprise.

'Yes, in Italy,' said Timothy.

'Oh, in Italy,' said the Rector, as if to meet Mrs. Lampard in Italy was not at all the same thing.

'She came to luncheon with me once or twice,' said Timothy carelessly. 'She was very handsome then; what is she like now?'

'A princess,' said Mr. Purbright earnestly. 'A Tudor princess. If you ask me which Tudor princess, I could not tell you, my history is rather rusty, I'm afraid. But she could have held her own at the court of Henry VIII; she would have kept her head, ha-ha.' Timothy, too, appreciated the joke. 'It is some time since we were bidden to Welshgate, and the war takes toll even of such an establishment as hers, but the entertainment was regal.'

'Is she a good landlord?' Timothy asked, fully expecting an overwhelmingly affirmative answer, and was surprised to see a shadow cross the Rector's face.

'I have not always seen eye to eye with her,' he said. 'In that and ... and in other matters. But it is greatly thanks to her that our river has won and kept its nation-wide reputation as a fly-fisherman's paradise. Are you a fisherman, Mr. Casson?'

Something in the Rector's manner made Timothy feel that he already knew the answer to his question; but he was so pleased with himself for having turned away Mr. Purbright's wrath, and so anxious to enlist him as an ally in the battle for the boat that he threw caution to the winds, and explained exactly how matters stood.

'Do come out and see the boat,' he wound up. 'I have called it the

Argo, provisionally, you know – suggesting a quest. To have called it the Mayflower might have been provocative, don't you think, challenging comparison with the mayfly. You will see how little water it draws – six inches at the most – and though I am far from being a polished oarsman, I am careful not to put the sculls in deep. I cannot believe that the progress of my boat would disturb the daily routine of a minnow!'

Carried away by his fancy, Timothy failed to see what effect it was having on his visitor. Alas, alas, Mr. Purbright's face had clouded again, not so much with anger, it seemed to Timothy, as with embarrassment.

'Quite, quite,' he was saying. 'And I sympathise with your devotion to what is in ordinary circumstances a healthy and an unexceptionable pastime. But I am afraid that you will find—' He broke off, mis-liking what he was going to say. 'The fishing-rights here are very jealously preserved, and I do not think my parishioners would tolerate any infringement of them. One's duty to one's neighbour, Mr. Casson, one's duty to one's neighbour. This is a gentleman's river, not a public thoroughfare like the Thames with its rowing-boats and gramophones. If I were you I should not try to insist—' He lifted an appealing eyebrow to Timothy, whose face fell.

'You see, I came here,' said Timothy, 'largely for the sake of the rowing, and bought the boat. It's a very nice one. . . . I have written to Mrs. Lampard.'

'What did she say?' asked the Rector quickly.

Timothy said he was still awaiting her reply.

'I hope it may be favourable,' said the Rector doubtfully. 'That would certainly clarify the situation. A ruling from her, though of course she has others to consider besides herself . . . would carry much weight. You have friends in the locality, Mr. Casson?'

Timothy admitted that he had not.

'I ought to tell you,' said the Rector, 'that your . . . your attitude to the river may cause a slight barrier, a faint feeling of distrust. . . . I myself take great pleasure in walking.'

Timothy said he also liked walking.

'What about a dog?' said the Rector suddenly. 'A good dog, preferably of a sporting type, makes an excellent companion, and gives confidence, if you know what I mean: a man with a dog at his heel soon seems part of the place. A dumb animal, you know, quickly finds its way into people's hearts.'

'H'm,' said Timothy.

'Yes, they stop and – er – pat him, and after that it's a short step to breaking the ice with his owner. I'm sure there would be no objection to you having a dog, as long as you kept him away from the coverts.'

'I'm afraid I'm not very fond of dogs,' said Timothy as politely as he could.

'Not fond of dogs?' The Rector shot him a quick glance and sighed. 'Well, well, it was just an idea, in case you should be feeling lonely. By the way, you must come and see us: my wife will ring you up.'

Timothy said how delighted he would be.

'And thanks for your hospitality to Edgell's car. I'm afraid I was a little hasty, but the law is the law, isn't it, and I didn't want you to start off with the wrong foot, to use an expression of my son's. I hope I have not spoken too plainly, or what he would call "out of turn." We older people will have to learn a new vocabulary. And now I must get along and leave you to your writing.'

Master of the situation, he turned from the window. Timothy, following him, was moved to say:

'You'll have a drink before you go? A glass of sherry, or some gin and vermouth?'

The bottle and glasses were standing on a tray in full view, and it would have been useless to ignore them. Besides, Timothy much preferred to drink in company.

'No, thank you,' said the Rector, eyeing the bottles distrustfully. 'I only drink to celebrate an occasion. But I am distressed by the amount of drinking that goes on, or has begun to go on, here, in a little village like this. I am afraid that some of our Midland friends have set us a bad example.'

Starved of gossip, Timothy pricked up his ears.

'Rather well-to-do people, some of them, I gather, with little feeling for the country or understanding of country life, regular townees, if that's not a harsh word. The village doesn't like them very much, but they bring plenty of custom to the Fisherman's Arms, and do not always come out, or indeed go in, as sober as they should. You may have noticed some of the women's clothes, perhaps: flashy, not to say fast. And their relationships seem, well, irregular. A regrettable element. As my wife says, we must make the best of them, but I'm afraid it will be a poor best. I was one of those who deplored Mrs. Lampard's action in doing up those rather dilapidated but picturesque and serviceable cottages for the week-end use of prosperous tradesmen, leaving more than one excellent family of farm-labourers homeless. But à la guerre comme à la guerre, and we must all make sacrifices. Good-day, Mr. Casson.'

Timothy saw the Rector to the door and then, fortified by a glass of sherry, went back to his work.

'Turning to me with mischief in her eyes, Chloe said. . . .'

CHAPTER IV

'I CANNOT understand,' wrote Tyro, 'why you did not jog my memory sooner about "The Conduct of the Allies." It was really rather careless of you, dear Timothy – such a valuable book and far too good for me. You know how I detest possessions, but at the same time I should have felt really upset if a gift from you had gone irrecoverably astray, as it well might have, after such a long lapse of time. Yes, I got it, in the throes of moving to this dreadful place, and I hope I shan't sound ungracious if I say that the fear of losing it was not the least of my anxieties. I have always forbidden you to give me presents, which, if unwanted, are a nuisance, and if treasured (as I fear this may be) only make the idea of death more distasteful; all the same, I must take this opportunity of thanking you, even while I implore you not to do it again.

'You have done well to bury yourself in the country and hold yourself aloof from this disgraceful conflict (for such, I suppose, was your intention). If I had had the means I should have done the same. Ever since 1914 I have loathed the spectacle of humanity in collective action; they are homicides to a man, and what is nationalism, or patriotism, or whatever you choose to call it, but an excuse for legalising and sanctifying the homicidal impulse? The State is man's greatest enemy, as I have often told you, my dear Timothy; and the State disguised as "my country" is the most hateful form of the disease. What an experience it was, all through Munich, to see one's warlike friends straining at their leashes, feeling "smirched" (their favourite word) because the world was not plunged in tears and blood! And even now I see a daily disappointment in the faces round me because the war refuses to develop, and give them their vampire feast.

'Well, here I am, not liking it, of course, but earning my keep and glad in a way of the chance to have my convictions about the human race so amply confirmed. (You, in your little rural paradise, cannot have the faintest idea what "they" are really like.) Sunday is the great day, of course, in which all the most popular newspapers, thrusting the war into the smallest headlines that decency allows, regale their five million readers with all the instances of murder, robbery, rape, incest, burglary, and blackmail that they have been able to collect. You would think, wouldn't you, that in this crisis of humanity's existence, when all our lives are in jeopardy, when the world has had such a crop of atrocity stories to delight it as it has never known before, that the craving for this special form of spiritual vitamins would have been somehow satisfied?

'Well, re-reading your letter I see that you have not altogether escaped the universal passion for swindling, graft, double-crossing, etc. You won't be able to store your apples, you may have to keep your house on for five years, whether you like it or not, you live among factions who clearly hate each other's guts, and you are not allowed to row the boat which was your strange reason for wanting to live at Upton-on-Swirrel. Just as I hope the war will fizzle out, so I also hope that all these gloomy predictions will be falsified; that your apple-room will be stinking with apples; that you will sublet the Old Rectory for an enormous sum the moment you tire of it, that you will be the toast of the entire neighbourhood, and float up and down the Swirrel in your barge or whatever it is, like Cleopatra or King Arthur. But if things shouldn't turn out like that, and your enemies get the upper hand, please, *please*, dear Timothy, don't speak of the joke or the comedy of it all. Don't pretend that it's your fault, don't pretend that you're enjoying it, and *don't* say anything about poor suffering human nature. If you do, you will forfeit my friendship. The brutes know perfectly well what they are about, their sufferings are entirely their own fault, and if they decide to down you, they will not be put off by the smile on your face, or your wish to see them as an aspect of comedy.

'I do congratulate you on having found such satisfactory servants – I congratulate them, too. I remember, from the days when I had servants, what a difference they made to one's life. I never had any good ones, but I can see they would have made a difference, too. Mine lied and stole, cheated and generally misused me. And you know what I can be like: I was an angel to them. Oh how much better I have always behaved than 99 per cent. of the people round me! This is a thing, dear Timothy, one should never forget, or let anyone else forget, on pain of being party to the Great Conspiracy, made fashionable by Rousseau and Dostoievsky, though no doubt existing long before their time – which consists in promising to say you are no better than other people on condition that other people will say they are no better than you. The Immoral Contract, one might call it, for it makes socially acceptable only the lowest standard of value and behaviour. I must not profess a respect for human life because to do so would put Crippen out of countenance.

You must not say you pay your bills, because to do so would hurt the feelings of Whittaker Wright. I know hardly anyone who would not rather boast of a bad action than a good one, and glorify the Devil rather than God. Prig is a word invented by the Devil to discredit virtue; next to being called a bore, it is this charge that the educated modern man fears the most. But I glory in both, as you must have noticed, and hope I always shall.

'As to coming to stay with you – you know how I hate visits and the insincerity that always attends them – the meaningless conversations that politeness requires, drained of every thought or expression that could possibly give offence to a bundle of noodles whose one idea is how they can use their neighbours' collective stupidity, codified and called conventional morality, to cheat them. Oh, what I have suffered at those gatherings – the effort not to tell my fellow-guests their glaring faults, not to demonstrate to them that they have enough malice and meanness among them to be the motive-power of a world war! And all because I will not, I *will* not, Timothy, adopt a cynical attitude, perhaps the truest of simplifications, but the most boring and the most despairing. What can life be like to a cynic? Nightly I pray to be defended from cynicism. But with you I know that I can always speak my mind, and that you will not expect from me a greasy Collins, wallowing in falsehood and saying that what was really a purgatory has been the happiest time of my life. So that if the Office should ever relax its stranglehold (it has promised to, one week-end in six months, but what are promises worth?) – I will join you in your funkhole and together we will curse the human race and the misery it has brought on itself, and us. The Fall, the Fall, how often it has been repeated, and each time Eve discovers a new attraction in the apple, and Adam snatches at the much-chewed fruit.

'Well, thank you again for your delightful present – Swift, my favourite author, "The Conduct of the Allies" my favourite theme. I shall enjoy re-reading it, and then perhaps put it in the Bank for safety. You must never give me another present, but if you do, please make sure that it reaches me. You are a good friend, Timothy, but tidiness, promptness, efficiency and in a sense, consideration for other people were never among your virtues.

Love from your affectionate

TYRO.

P.S. – Don't imagine from this that I have any time for letter-writing – I haven't.'

* * *

It took Timothy some time to read this characteristic effusion, closely typewritten on large sheets of paper so much resembling toilet paper that one could scarcely tell the difference. He was familiar with Tyro's misanthropy, and knew that it was genuine in spite of the froth of exaggeration and overstatement that poured off it, like steam and bubbles from a boiling saucepan. As always, it exhilarated and comforted him. He, too, sometimes had doubts as to the general good faith of human beings, and was accustomed to still them by precisely those mental subterfuges that Tyro had denounced. Who am I to sit in judgment on other people? I am the worst of sinners, he would think; or, how funny it all is, what a joke, what a comedy. Tyro's tirades, by painting the picture so much blacker than, even in moods of despondency, it had ever appeared to Timothy, reconciled him to the human countenance as it rose, moonlike and enigmatic, above the garden wall of the Old Rectory. How much happier he was, and would always be, than the hunted fugitive of Tyro's fancy, scuttling to and fro like a beetle on a board, pursued by the malice, the indefeasible moral turpitude of his fellows, his only solace his conviction that he was right and 'they' were wrong! By reaction, Tyro's letter restored him to the world where morality was only one of many issues, and had not devoured the lot, like a swollen modern state, jealous of every independent being within its borders.

Relieved of the strain of the moral outlook, inoculated against pessimism, Timothy remembered, with an anticipatory thrill, the world about him, hibernating, winter-bound. What leaves, what buds, what blossoms, would it soon put forth?

The post had come betimes today: there were two more letters with his early morning tea. The long pale blue envelope with Magda's handwriting on it exuded a faint perfume, aromatic rather than sweet, the herald of her presence: she never came unannounced, or without considering the effect she was to make on all one's senses. 'One-Fifty-Five Park Lane,' ran the address, in cursive almost copper-plate lettering, white on the blue ground, like an aerial message printed on the sky. 'Timothy dear,' the scent began to enfold him,

'I hate not having written to thank you, it's so Falangist, somehow, to forget to thank people. In Russia they have a habit, Lurya Libidinsky tells me, of always sending with a present a picture postcard of one's favourite Commissar, addressed to the donor, and saying, "Nicolay Polaiechev (or whoever it may be) and I thank you for your gift." So no present ever goes unacknowledged. I find that charming, and it quite takes away the sting of the personal, the eternal anti-social arrogance of the I. So Litvinov and I gratefully thank you for that darling bottle of scent, and try to forget that it comes from Abyssinia-torturing Italy.

'I never liked Italy after Fascism came in, and never understood how you could live there. It was different on the Lido, of course; the de Hautevilles had their French friends, and one hardly spoke to an Italian. Those black shirts made them look so swarthy, and I never could believe they were properly washed. And the Roman salute is so unbecoming to a rather dumpy body and short legs, which most of them have.

'Valentine de Hauteville was a friend of yours, wasn't she? She said something about the Spanish War which offended me, and I never saw her again. By the way, are *you* quite sound, Timothy? Somebody told me something you had said, that there had been cruelty on both sides. That may be true, though I deny it: the point is, it's not the thing to say, and I shall try to think you didn't. As long as I live, there will only be one War for me – the Spanish War. People tell me I'm not sane on the subject, and I don't want to be, if sanity means listening to arguments on the other side.

'As to this war, well, we are in it, I suppose, but I don't feel happy about it. It's phoney, for one thing. And I'm not at all sure that it isn't capitalist and imperialist as well – the old business, a secret understanding with Germany aimed at Russia and the workers. Otherwise, why hasn't Russia come in with us? Of course, you couldn't expect her to, after being snubbed at Munich; if we had fought then, the war would be over now. But both Tanya and Manya Benediktov (comrades from the Curzon Street Cell – they wouldn't interest you, but they are people who know what's going on underneath) say that Russia really hates Germany and only made the Pact for self-protection and to secure her just rights in Poland, Finland, Estonia, Livonia, Lithuania, Courland, etc., etc. And Lurya and Furya say the same. Who cares about the Poles? They look alike, and are all the same height and say the same things in the same boring voices and I can never forgive the Finns for stabbing Russia in the back.

'But I'm afraid you're not really interested in politics. I met your friend, Tyrone MacAdam, the other day, looking particularly dirty and unkempt, and was shocked by something he said to me about human beings having only themselves to blame for wars, etc. So moralistic and seventeenth century. To talk like that about human beings is sheer blasphemy. Can't he understand that it's the system that's wrong, and that all that's wanted is to get rid of capitalism? – and capitalists, as they have in the U.S.S.R.? I called a taxi and drove off.

'So don't worry because you're not taking an active part in a war to preserve capitalism. I work at the M. of A. simply for something to do that isn't taking bread out of the workers' mouths, as I should do if I let myself be directed down a coal mine. I don't like the thought of your house, a Victorian rectory is my idea of hell, and you will have a lot of stuffy neighbours who will insist on calling on you. That sort of scenery isn't the kind I care for either, I'm afraid, it's too fussy; I long for featureless plains and a wide sky, and men with broad strong faces raising angry fists – anything else, including this war, is rather like play-acting to me. And are you sure your boat is not a form of escapism? That's what's worrying me. Escapism is deviation Number One in our code, the one thing a comrade cannot forgive another. Lurya says she never eats a mouthful of caviare without a sense of purpose – to advance the cause of communism, and Nastya would give up vodka tomorrow if it didn't make her feel in line.

'I don't like women, as you know, but I make an exception for those two; they know how to dress, which is more than some of the male comrades do. The women in the office are frightful; no style, no make-up, no conversation. God, how they bore me! I should die if I hadn't this little place to come to in the evenings, and the Cell where at least they talk sense.

'So a week-end with you would be pure bliss, as we used to say. I'm not sure I like the idea of servants in a private house; in a flat it's different, they're not so oppressed by the sense of private ownership. I expect you spoil yours, Timothy, it's the last flicker of bourgeois conscience, trying to put off the inevitable. Of course, they see through it, and despise you. A personal maid is different, of course. Even in Russia an officer is allowed a batman. One puts one's personal efficiency at the service of the Party, and anything that sharpens the spear-head of revolution is permissible and even laudable. I hope you won't mind if I bring Nastya, though I must warn you that the country makes her laugh, she finds it so reactionary. She laughs a good deal at English servants, too, she finds them so funny, but she has perfect manners, of course, all Russians have. She laughs at the oddest things which you might not think amusing. I didn't, at first, but now when she laughs, I laugh, too, it is such a release to abandon oneself wholeheartedly to a proletarian impulse. One's whole being acts, and with the current of humanity, not against it. Nastya's laughter isn't anti-social, as yours (and mine) so often is: she laughs because she has tuned in to humanity's wave-length.

'All the same, I am bored – bored with myself, bored with my colleagues in the M. of A., bored with the war. I go into a nursing home to-morrow for a week or two.

Best love,
MAGDA.'

Timothy looked up, puzzled and disturbed. Magda's political phase was a new departure. Before the Spanish War she had known nothing about politics, and cared nothing. Gardening, music, the ballet, bridge, poker, had successively absorbed her. It was true that she seldom entertained two interests at the same time, and when one was in the ascendant she was apt to belittle the others; but certain things were constant: her liability to boredom, her feeling for the arts, her passion for dress, her absorption in the lover of the moment, and her serious affection for a few friends, of whom Timothy was one. Magda never changes, they proudly and fondly said. But Magda had changed. The personality in the letter had hardened and shrunk. Magda had always been sceptical about the value of a sense of humour; resting on a pleased recognition of imperfection, humour did not accord with the standard of æsthetic perfection she aimed at. There was nothing funny in being badly dressed, or in playing the wrong card, or singing the wrong note, or in dancing or doing anything badly: such weaknesses were just mistakes, to be dismissed with a grimace and a shrug. She had a sense of humour, and one that was all the more effective because it was forced out of her. Now she had stifled it, and built round herself a barricade almost forbidding in its exclusiveness. The barrier had always been there, hedging her about, making her more precious: but Timothy had always felt he was on the right side of it. Now he was not so sure.

To enjoy things, that is what endears. Magda's scornful impatience with the things she did not like had lent a fiery zest to her enjoyment of those she did. Her intolerance had been a bond, a private key to the central fountain of her enjoyment; by excluding, it enriched. Now, it seemed to Timothy, she was living on her exclusiveness, which she called comprehensiveness, and trying to enjoy the very act of disliking, for the sake of the stimulus it gave her; all she could do for a friend, for Timothy, was to invite him to dislike something, indeed to command him, for it was clear she would tolerate no disagreement. Cosmetics and politics; those were now her gods. And this expensive perfume, which always seemed to double his income, was their incense. Timothy sniffed it luxuriously and sighed.

He hoped the third letter would be from Esther, announcing the arrival of the vacuum flask, and drawing him into the complex system of her multitudinous family life, but the handwriting was unknown to him. Round and guileless, covering half the envelope, it inspired confidence, and he opened the letter at once.

DEAR MR. CASSON,

My husband so much enjoyed his little talk with you, and I am very anxious to make your acquaintance. We think it so generous of you to say you would keep Edgell's car; he will be here himself, we hope, in a few days' time to thank you personally. He is a dear boy, but rather scatter-brained, I'm afraid. Meanwhile could you possibly drink a glass of sherry with us on Saturday of next week, and I will ask some friends from the neighbourhood whom I think you would like to meet, and who I am sure would like to meet you. There is just a chance that Edgell may be here! Hoping to have the pleasure of seeing you about six o'clock,

Yours sincerely,
VOLUMNIA PURBRIGHT.

The sun poured in, the motes danced, the world glittered through his window, rejoicing in the thaw. A radical change of outlook, a complete spiritual revolution, took place in Timothy. Now he would meet them all – Colonel Harbord, Captain Sturrock, Commander Bellew and the rest. 'My dear fellow,' they chorused, 'of course we have no objection to your rowing on the river. It will keep the trout in training, dodging your nice little skiff. And by the way, our gardens, too, go down to the river, so any time you're passing just step ashore and have a drink or a cup of tea with us. No, we mean it! We shall be extremely disappointed if you don't.'

His breakfast scarcely swallowed, Timothy sped to his writing-table, which seemed to have lost its air of yielding unwillingly to his thoughts, and wrote to Mrs. Purbright a thoroughly fulsome letter of acceptance. Saturday would be a particularly convenient day for him. It was the day in the week when, having finished one article, he had not begun to worry about the next. He was overjoyed at the thought of meeting Mrs. Purbright, of whom he had heard, if he might say so, the most enthusiastic accounts, as he had of her son, who seemed to be especially beloved in the village. And he welcomed, more warmly than he could say, the privilege of meeting his neighbours. Looking forward enormously to these pleasures, he was hers very sincerely.

CHAPTER V

THE visit was still some days ahead, for Mrs. Purbright had given him ample notice, when Timothy found to his dismay that certain things that used to be in the house were no longer there. They were all small things, and being very unobservant, except when professionally training his eye on a possible picture of Britain, he wouldn't have missed them, if he had not been in the habit of using them himself – the clothes-brush that hung in the hall, the presentation ink-pot on his writing-table, a silver match-box, and a snowstorm paperweight, with which he often beguiled the weary intervals between his thoughts. His discovery of these depredations was spread out over several hours of one evening, when he had come back from an expedition on Wimbush's bicycle, in search of copy; he felt morally sure that before he left, all the things had been present and correct. Anyone might have taken them, for Effie and Beatrice had also been out for the afternoon. Disregarding the warnings of instinct, he rang the bell, never a popular move, and asked Effie if she could throw any light on the disappearances.

Effie's vague, lackadaisical manner stiffened at once. 'I'm sure I don't know anything about it,' she said. 'I never touched the things.'

'Oh, but when you dusted them?'

Effie did not deign to reply, and Timothy realised to his horror that he had made two gaffes. He must try to put the inquiry on a more impersonal footing.

'Of course, I don't for a moment,' – he began, but before he had time to say more, Effie burst into tears. Sobbing noisily and swaying, she went out of the room, leaving the door open; the sounds of her distress echoed down the passage until the kitchen door slammed on them.

Silence settled on the house, and seemed to penetrate, an active and malignant presence, into its furthest corners. Timothy tried to write, but in vain. He could not construct another world; his own, or rather Effie's, was too much with him. He had committed an unforgivable sin; by his clumsiness, his stupid directness of approach, he had destroyed her peace of mind. Walking up and down, glad to be making some movement in the static, hostile room, he pondered what he should do.

Follow her into the kitchen and try to calm her? But what could he say? The things had disappeared, and cossetting Effie would not bring them back.

Footsteps sounded down the passage, a firm steady tread; they crossed the hall, and Beatrice, dark and square and lowering, stood in the doorway.

'If you please,' she said, 'Effie and I wish to give in our notice.'

Timothy's heart turned over, and a void, whose walls yearned painfully inwards, opened within him. He heard himself say:

'I'm very sorry to hear this, Beatrice. Won't you tell me why you want to go?'

'We would rather not say anything about it,' Beatrice said, her face getting still more set and square.

'Oh, but you must tell me,' said Timothy, who already knew only too well. 'Has it anything to do with the things that have been . . . lost?'

'We don't like being in a house where such things are said,' Beatrice remarked.

'I never said anything,' Timothy retorted, irritation lending him courage. 'I merely asked Effie a question. Surely there's no harm in that.'

'You say no harm,' said Beatrice with relish. 'You say no harm. Effie's in bed now with a sick headache.'

'Oh dear,' said Timothy, looking round for a way of escape that was not blocked by Beatrice. 'I am so sorry. Tell her not to get up until she feels better.'

'She won't do that, you needn't worry,' said Beatrice grimly. 'She won't get up to be insulted. Once is enough.'

'Oh, very well,' said Timothy. 'But I think you're being rather unreasonable, you know.'

'We don't know anything about that. We've got our good name to consider,' Beatrice answered. 'We've got our pride, too.' When Timothy made no rejoinder to this, she said, 'I shouldn't be surprised if it was him as took them.'

'Him?' asked Timothy. 'Who do you mean?'

'Why did you pick on us,' Beatrice countered, her gaze directed so unwaveringly at the square of carpet between Timothy's feet that he felt it must be boring a hole there, 'when there's him as well? He has the run of the house, same as us.'

Timothy felt a twinge of distaste. 'I suppose you mean Wimbush. Of course, I shall ask him, since neither you nor Effie seems disposed to tell me anything.' He turned away.

'That's right, trying to put the blame on us,' said Beatrice. 'We could tell you a thing or two about him, we could.'

Timothy found that the ostrich-like policy of not looking at Beatrice lessened the strain of talking to her.

'I'd rather not hear any more,' he said, sitting down at the writing-table, with his back to her. 'When do you wish to go?'

To his surprise Beatrice had no answer ready. For the first time she lifted her head, but her eyes did not meet his. 'I'm ready to go tomorrow,' she grumbled, 'but I've got Effie to think of. It's not very nice, is it, asking us straight out like that? I should have thought you would have shown more consideration.'

This small victory made Timothy feel magnanimous.

'Very well,' he said pacifically. 'Let's hear what Effie says.' Resolutely straightening his back against Beatrice, he reached for the writing paper; and a feeling of détente in the room, rather than any physical sign of her withdrawal, told him that she had gone.

'The Manor House at Yoreham Parva,' he wrote, 'is a particularly attractive specimen of the Jacobean style, straight on the north front, a hollow E on the southern, garden side. Between the two brick wings is a two-storeyed stone porch, most elaborately decorated. In front, a balustrade with statues, Italian or in the Italian style. The house was empty, the gardener told me; the family had left because they could not get the staff to run it. I asked him how many servants they kept, and he said, six, and eight in the old Squire's time. I remember villas on the Brenta much larger than the Manor House at Yoreham Parva, which were run by three or four servants, and my own, which was more modest but wonderfully un-labour-saving, was managed by a couple: they never complained that the work was too much.' Timothy frowned, shook his head, but let the sentence stand.

'Italian servants are more adaptable, I think, than English servants. They are not trained, of course, in the sense that ours are. They don't efface themselves, far from it; they consider that their employer's business is theirs too, and seldom hesitate to give him their advice. But, dear reader, you have already heard too much about Amalia and Armando. Both their virtues and their faults are clearer to me now that I see them in the light of my relationship – a very happy one, let me add – with my own servants here.'

Timothy paused, and reminded himself that he was painting a picture of Britain, not taking a photograph.

'Italian servants in their felt slippers, smiling their way through the day, working very long hours, apparently not wanting any time off, setting vocation above vacation, not always to be found when wanted but always wanted when found, would exasperate many a skilled English housewife; they slouch about like soldiers on fatigue, they never, as soldiers on parade are told to, look as if they owned the piece of ground they stood on. Humility shows in their mien, and humility and style are seldom found together.

'English servants have their pride. Much has been said against pride by pens abler than mine, but one cannot help respecting it even if its manifestations are sometimes disconcerting. To take a hypothetical case, suppose I say something which Belinda, quick to notice where one has overstepped the mark, takes amiss. Ruffled, wounded, she says at once, "I have my pride." Simple, magnificent, unanswerable.

'Would an Italian servant have said that? No. With them, *amor proprio* is a quality to grace the boards of the opera, but not to be used as a weapon (their only weapon, for what other have they?) to humble a despotic employer, to resist the power that corrupts. Mussolini took from the Italians their pride and vested it in himself; lowly in their own lives, they could strut in his. He could not have done that rape on Belinda; and as long as her type survives to withstand the petty tyrant of the drawing-room, Fascism will get no foothold here. Pride is a stubborn thing, and once roused does not quickly strike its flag: to awake it rashly is an unchristian act, for which one may pay dearly – as dearly as one pays for rousing the British lion. But Belinda is not implacable. *Si foret in terris*, Democritus could win her with a smile, and if I go to her and say, "Belinda—"

Timothy laid down his pen. What could he say to Beatrice? Writing about her, arguing her case, he had persuaded himself that she was in the right. Had she come in at that moment he might have found a playful formula that would have appeased her. But the only answer to his thoughts was the loud, startling peal of the dinner bell. He followed the welcome summons into the white-panelled room, with its glowing electric fire and blue and fawn curtains of figured cotton damask.

Beatrice was putting in his place a plate of soup. It steamed with friendliness, and perhaps rather to it than to her he exclaimed, 'Oh, Beatrice, how good that soup smells!' But she did not answer; nor did she when he again complimented her on the taste of his first mouthful of mutton. Her presence behind him was like something heavy and sour-smelling draped across his shoulders. He waited till she had gone, and then fetched himself a bottle of claret from the wine cupboard under the stairs. It was Bordeaux of no special mark, but of the 1929 vintage. Unwarmed, unbreathed, undecanted, it came to his side like a guest who has had no attention paid him, who has not even been greeted: but its subtle unfolding fragrance, its crimson glow in the glass, lit by a shaft of red, the soft shadow on the surface soon to be broken by his lips – kindled a mood of anticipation in him. He drank; and drinking asked something of the wine which it at once supplied: a sense of comradeship, of good manners, of age-old responsiveness to human needs. What he wanted, it had; and the second glass had it in even fuller measure than the first.

He did not notice Beatrice's third entry; did not hear the swish with which she took away his dirty plate or the clatter that heralded the clean one. Unconsciously he registered the fact that the dish which she clutched to her, so closely that, stretching, he almost had to pluck it from her bosom, was a cheese soufflé, and cheese is a friend to wine. A friend to wine! And what is wine to man? Almost more than a friend, so it seemed at that moment to Timothy, deprived of the sound of the human voice, sent to Coventry but reconciled to his banishment. The sense of otherness, which belongs to friendship, was present in the glass and awaited him in the bottle; in neither was there pride, or anger, or unkindness, merely a silent invitation to an exchange of critical appreciation, the capacity for which, in both of them, broadened and deepened with every sip.

The wine likes me, Timothy thought, the wine likes me; and the more I like it, the better it will like me. For a while his mind busied itself with the distinctions which claret, being an intellectual draught, demands. But soon its influence stole to other seats of sentience, as the sound of music confounds the lightning of the composer's thought in the soft thunder of its sensuous appeal; pleased and comforted, his whole being glowed with responsiveness and gratitude, and the only shadow on his happiness was the shadow declining in the bottle each time he held it to the light.

Far from waking with a sour stomach and a heavy head, he felt on excellent terms with the morning, and it was only when Effie came in with his tea that he remembered he had something hanging over him.

'I hope you're feeling better, Effie?'

She gave him a sad little smile. 'I was ever so upset by what you said.'

Oh dear, thought Timothy.

'But your headache has gone, I hope?'

'I shouldn't like to say.'

'Then I think it must be better.' With a lighter heart Timothy began to pour out his tea.

'Beatrice doesn't think we ought to stay, after you've suspected us.'

'But I haven't and I don't,' cried Timothy. He would have liked to add, 'But I soon shall,' but refrained, believing that fair words soak up ill-feeling as charcoal absorbs acid in the stomach.

'I don't know what to say, I'm sure,' said Effie with a twitch and a simper. 'It all depends on Beatrice.'

Leaving Timothy on tenterhooks, she withdrew, and presently rejoined Beatrice in the kitchen.

'Did he say he didn't mean it?' asked Beatrice.

'No. He was too proud. But he asked if my headache was better.'

'And you said no?'

'I wasn't going to tell a lie, so I just said I couldn't say.'

'It's no good giving way to him, Effie. We'd better go.'

'All right, you tell him then.'

At that moment Wimbush came into the kitchen, with Timothy's shoes, looking small and fragile, swinging from his earth-stained fist.

'Good morning, ladies. Pleased to find you up so early. If there's anything I can do for you, you have only to ask me.'

His glance slid past Beatrice and rested on Effie; there were reddish glints in his tawny eyes. Effie always found it hard to keep still when anyone spoke to her, and Wimbush's remark produced quite a crop of tremors. She sat down on the table and giggled weakly.

'Don't speak to her like that, she's upset,' said Beatrice severely. 'We had something unpleasant happen last night, and she was ever so poorly. We've given in our notice.'

'Oh, that's too bad,' cried Wimbush, 'and just as we was beginning to get on so nicely. You don't mind how you disappoint people, does she, Effie? And what was this unpleasantness, if I may ask?'

'Don't tell him, Effie,' said Beatrice sharply. 'It's no business of his. Why does he go poking his nose in? If Mr. Casson had spoken to him, it might have been a different tale. . . . Drink this, dear, it'll do you good.' She poured her friend out a cup of tea.

'Thank you,' said Wimbush, stretching out his hand and with extreme insouciance taking the cup from Effie. 'I don't mind if I do. I'm that thirsty.'

'Well, of all the cheek!' Beatrice stormed.

'Now, now, we don't want any more unpleasantness.'

'Who's being unpleasant, I should like to know?'

Beatrice darted forward as though she meant to snatch the cup away from Wimbush; but he had put the shoes down and was holding it in both hands, making it part of himself. As he lowered his broad face to the cup, Effie could see his eyebrows, sticking out, fierce and wiry, beyond the line of his temples; he blew on the tea to cool it and his moustache swayed, lifted by his breath. He looks like a lion, drinking, she thought.

'I don't know as I want to leave all that much, Beattie,' she said. 'It wasn't so much what he said, as the shock. He ought to have warned us first.'

'What did he say?' asked Wimbush, lifting his head from the cup.

Before Beatrice could intervene Effie told him all the story 'It was the shock more than anything,' she repeated.

'I know where those things have gone,' he said darkly. 'And 'tisn't you have taken them, either. Not a nice girl like you. Now Beattie might have.' His mocking look reduced Beatrice to speechless fury. 'But she didn't. You just tell Mr. Casson to come to me.'

'Oh, do tell us,' pleaded Effie. She had quite recovered now. The colour had returned to her cheeks, and to her movements a fragile grace, a strain of race and breeding that lit up the kitchen like a vase of flowers, and was not lost on Wimbush.

'Well, if you promise not to leave,' he said.

'We won't promise any such thing, will we, Effie?' put in Beatrice. 'We shall have him accusing us of murder, next.'

'Oh, Beattie, do give over,' said Effie wearily. 'She acts like she was my gaoler, doesn't she, Mr. Wimbush? She won't hardly let me call my soul my own.'

'Effie!' exclaimed Beatrice, in a heart-stricken voice.

'There, there,' said Wimbush. 'Don't quarrel, ladies, please, or I shan't know whose part to take, shall I, Effie? Now you kiss and be friends and I'll tell you who took those things. . . . But you've got to come nearer, because stone walls have ears.' His arms made a wide embracing gesture. Beatrice edged away, but Effie, with a little giggle, drew closer to the sketched circumference.

Meanwhile, upstairs, Timothy was reading Esther Morwen's letter.

'So many things came at once, as they do at Christmas, dear Timothy,' she wrote.

'My presents, and Henry's and William's and Daphne's and Susan's (they were all with us) and then the grandchildren's, six of them – you know what it's like on Christmas morning! Four other people had had

44

your lovely idea, and before you could say "knife" one of the grandchildren (Priscilla, I think it was, but you wouldn't know her now, she's grown so much) had pounced on those lovely, gleaming, enamelled flasks and set them in a row for ninepins! We managed to save them in time, but in the confusion all the cards had got hopelessly mixed up, and *yours* was never seen again! so I couldn't be *sure* you'd sent anything. But I thought you would let me know if you had, and I do so enjoy getting your letters.

'When you come here (and you *must*, I'm heartbroken that you haven't come already, but oh, how *can* I ask you to venture into this Bedlam – and we may have to take a dozen evacuees – just think of it) when you come here you must tell me which of the flasks is yours, and we'll have a special party for it, if it's still in being!

'I can't tell you how excited I am that you've come to live in England. It took a war to uproot you! I grieve for the Lucertola as if it had been my own; but no one could want to be away from England at a time like this. Munich was terrible – the suspense – and last summer nearly as bad, only we'd been inoculated.

'It's such a relief, now, to see one's way absolutely clear. Henry and William expect to go abroad at any time; Daphne's husband, Peter, is training cadets, and Susan's fiancé, Alan Ledward (I don't think you've met him) is moving heaven and earth to get the Foreign Office to release him – but so far they won't. He frets, poor boy, I am so sorry for him. How it brings back 1914! I was twenty-five then; David and I had been married for four years; Henry was three and William was a baby. Somehow I never thought I should be a war widow. Mercifully the pattern of one's life is hidden from one. I had a breakdown then, you may remember; I was so ashamed of myself that I couldn't take it as many other women did. But I never felt any bitterness, and I don't now. The thing is so much greater than oneself, and the certainty all round one – the country's heart beating so steadily – makes everything easy – well, not easy, but inevitable. David gave me so much – the children, the house, the village; we have all grown older and shared our experiences; there is a strength in that which makes sacrifice only a word for something we all do together, like turning to the east in church. I think of it as fulfilment, not sacrifice. Sacrifice means that someone has to be appeased, like Hitler; and I feel that I am not sacrificing but ennobling and even glorifying myself by resisting him.

'Why doesn't Italy come in on our side? I can't understand those dear people, whom I love almost as you do, being aloof and almost hostile to England. Surely Fascism is a kind of mask they have put on, a wax mask which will melt when the light of truth strikes it? I expect you feel puzzled – not divided in mind, for that you couldn't be – but distressed by this seeming breach in our friendship with Italy, such a horrible thing, like a rift in a family or a feud among one's servants. I don't see how another country can *really* disagree with England, for England is every country's other self. I won't say better self, or you might think me prejudiced! But the self they come back to when the fighting is over, just as children come to themselves after a good cry. There is a lost England in every country. That is why, to me, England is all-important and worth dying for; we *are* the sanity and spiritual health of the world.

'I wonder what you are doing? I'm ashamed to tell you I've lost your letter, but I know you said something about a boat. Was it for fishing? I know the Swirrel is a great fishing river; an uncle of mine used to have a rod there. Well, I wish you luck with the boat, whatever you want it for. Oh, and you spoke of neighbours, and asked me how to get into touch with them. I've always been in touch with mine – too much so, sometimes, but of course in war-time one can't be! – they'll call on you, I expect. But no, a single man who's taken a furnished house, I'm not sure they will. It would be different if you were married, or had bought the place. Fishing may be a link, or war-work: I expect you'll be doing some. And church, if you go to church; but perhaps you became a Roman when you were in Italy? The Rector would take you by the hand, I'm sure. Everyone meets nowadays, and are in and out of each other's houses. (My fear for you is much more that you won't find your neighbours very interesting. I should be cautious how you approach them, and leave yourself an avenue of escape!) Now it comes back to me: Julia Lampard. She's a sort of cousin of mine – her mother was a Cumberforth, and we came out together. She never liked me very much, and I never felt easy with her. She always lived among swells. She is a law unto herself and doesn't mind what people say. . . . I could write to her and ask her to look you up; but I don't think she's your sort. I don't suppose she opens a book. She's rather ruthless, and it's easy to get on the wrong side of her.

'How lucky you are to have such good servants. Cling to them, they'll soon be worth their weight in gold, if they're not already. It's much easier to dispense with neighbours than with servants, I can tell you!

'As to staying with you (you see I remember *all* your letter) nothing could give me greater pleasure. I *long* to see you. But how to get away, that's the question. I'm so tied with family and war-work here. Ask me

46

again when it's warmer and we can go out in your boat! But remember you are welcome here *any* time, if you can put up with our hugger-mugger way of living.

> My best thanks for the flask, and love
>> from
>>> ESTHER.'

Timothy re-read the letter gratefully. Of the three, it was the one that warmed him most. But wasn't there something lacking in all of them? Two things, really: the writer's self, and his. Or rather, they were dwarfed and overshadowed; in Tyro's letter by his conviction of the wickedness of the world; in Magda's by politics; in Esther's by patriotism. In one way or another, though with such different results, the war had taken possession of their minds, crowding out the he and she. The clear call of one personality to another was muffled by a drum-beat. To each, Timothy's Christmas present, his ambassador, his representative, had arrived as some kind of interruption to the tenor of a mind set on other things. One and all they had found it convenient to ignore or to forget. Perhaps a petty affirmation of the ego was out of place at a time like this? If the absence of acknowledgement implied a rebuke, as perhaps it did, he should not be above taking a lesson. He tried to remember his own letters; and their insistence on his trivial concerns, in a world at war, made him hot to think of.

Yes, but at any rate he had kept the banner of friendship flying; surely that was something; the book, the scent, the vacuum flask might have burdened a war-clogged postal service, might have laid an added strain on minds tired by war-work. But the values they symbolised – the right and duty of each human being to treat another as an end in himself, not as a flag or a coloured shirt or a sinner, these were what we were fighting for: freedom of access to another's heart. His letters might be laboured and diffuse; but at least they were carefully differentiated; not only the address on the envelope but every word had been written with a careful sense of the person it was meant for. No jealous estranging 'ism,' no hint that there was something in his life more important than they were, had been allowed to intervene between him and his correspondents. Or had it? Had it? As Timothy sipped his tea, his eyes strayed out of the window to where a peaked roof showed above a cluster of bamboos. The boat; he had forgotten the boat.

CHAPTER VI

TIMOTHY was sensitive to the content and quality of silences, but breakfast was a meal with so many voices – purring, sizzling, crackling – that it was almost a companion in itself. Until Effie appeared, he hadn't noticed her absence. Her face was portentous, an expression it was by nature so ill-equipped to bear that her slim, tall body seemed to buckle beneath a physical weight.

'Mr. Wimbush would like to see you, sir, when you're free,' she said, her voice faltering and tripping between the words.

What now? thought Timothy. Is Wimbush going to leave, too? He picked his way between the blobs of dirty snow, grey and porous, that lingered on the terrace, and made for the kitchen-garden, the long red-brick wall of which ran parallel with the right side of the house, and far beyond it. The gate, surmounted by stone balls, was approached by a path flagged with mill-stones; at one point this broadened out into a circular paved platform, in the middle of which was a sundial, flanked by four stone seats.

'Stone, Stone, Marcus Stone,' intoned Timothy, who found this part of the garden particularly nostalgic and lacking only a beautiful, pensive, sad-eyed lady in evening dress and a picture hat, with her hand resting on a deer-hound equally distinguished, wistful and expectant. They were looking along a terrace, much grander than this, and bordered by clipped yew hedges, for someone who did not come, perhaps for Timothy. *Magari*! The lady, possibly fearing pneumonia, faded into the pale, cold light of the January morning, but the dog remained, for a dog is an ice-breaker, and Timothy remembered the Rector's advice to provide himself with one, as a companion and as a gage – of what? General trustworthiness to the people of Upton. Knitting his brow he glanced at the sundial, which, true to its boast of only recording the sunny hours, ignored this one. Feeling his weight inadequate to the massy pavement he glided on. The wrought-iron gate swung outwards ponderously; its closing clang let him into another world. The satyr of the vegetable garden had his back to Timothy; he was digging and did not seem to hear him come; but he redoubled his efforts, and when Timothy drew near turned round with a look of surprise which at once broadened into welcome.

Timothy greeted him warmly, adding, 'You said you wanted to speak to me.'

Wimbush leaned on his spade. 'Yes, sir, what would that be about?' He seemed mystified.

'I was expecting you to tell me,' said Timothy.

Light appeared to dawn on Wimbush. ' 'Tis they girls, I expect, sir. They were having a little game with I.'

'Yes, Wimbush?'

'They seemed all in a dither and 'twas about nothing, so I said I'd tell you, sir. 'Twas only for the joke.'

Timothy always welcomed a joke and was specially glad to think of one in connection with last night's affair; but he did not want to hurry Wimbush.

'That Beatrice only has to hear a pin drop but she begins belly-aching.'

Timothy pursed his lips, out of loyalty to Beatrice.

'And, of course, between you and I, sir, 'twas Miss Chadwick who took those things. But don't be telling her I said so.'

'Of course not, Wimbush.' Miss Chadwick! Why hadn't he thought of her? It was not her first raid on the house. But before, she had always let him know she was coming and asked if he would mind – or rather, told him that he would not mind. Moreover she had always taken, or caused to be removed, substantial objects like beside lamps or coffee-tables. It had not occurred to him to connect her with the disappearance of trifles like match-boxes and paperweights. Timothy's relief was immense, for after all the things were hers, and the notion of theft which had hung about his mind like an unpleasant smell, could be dismissed. But the thought of what a fool he had been still rankled.

' 'Tisn't quite fair, is it, sir,' Wimbush was saying, 'seeing as how you've taken the house furnished, in a manner of speaking.'

'Well, perhaps not quite fair,' admitted Timothy.

'Miss Chadwick's a very good lady and I'm not saying anything against her,' Wimbush went on, 'but she knows the colour of a half-penny as well as anyone else.'

'I expect she has to be careful,' said Timothy tolerantly. Since she had rescued him from his domestic dilemma, Timothy refused to think unkindly of Miss Chadwick.

'She promised me a rise, she did,' said Wimbush, 'not long before you came, sir, and then she seemed to forget about it.'

'I'll remind her, Wimbush. I'm sure I pay you far too little.'

'There isn't many as would tackle this garden single-handed, and with gentlemen offering me more money all the time to go to them.'

'No indeed, Wimbush, it's very good of you to stay.' Timothy thought a moment and said, 'I hope she won't come when I'm not looking and take you away.'

Wimbush laughed delightedly, rocking to and fro and digging the handle of the spade into his midriff. 'That's a good one, sir, that is. She'd have a job to shift me. Do you know how much I go?'

'Go where?'

'On the scales.'

'Twelve stone?' ventured Timothy.

'Thirteen stone ten, sir, and that's not with all my clothes on either.'

'You don't say so!'

'Effie, she wouldn't believe it.'

'About the clothes?'

'Ha! Ha! sir, but a man's clothes do weigh a lot more than a woman's.'

Timothy wondered if the conversation was quite seemly. The silk-clad lady in the Marcus Stone picture rose before him, and mentally he tried to weigh her, with and without clothes. He felt that Wimbush must be reading his thoughts; but what if he was? It seemed a long time since Timothy had talked to anyone.

'Beatrice must be a good weight for her size.'

'That's right, sir. All that cooking make a woman heavy. The fat gets into them somehow.'

Timothy hesitated, then said with a rush, 'She gave me notice yesterday.'

Wimbush whistled and looked extremely shocked. Then he said, 'I shouldn't pay any attention to that, sir. They know when they're well off. Besides, Effie, she's a *good* girl.'

'You like her better than Beatrice?' Timothy was annoyed with himself for saying this: it was all wrong. Talking to servants was a bad habit he had picked up abroad. Most English people would think it unconventional and unattractive. But he must talk to someone, and who else had he to talk to?

'Well, of course, they're nothing to me, sir, neither way,' said Wimbush rather loftily. 'They come and they go. But of the two, *of the two*, Effie is the one I should like to meet Mrs. Wimbush. I can't say fairer than that.'

'No, indeed,' said Timothy, and made a mental note to call on Mrs. Wimbush without delay.

* * *

Before the reconciliation with Beatrice and Effie, to which he much looked forward, Timothy felt he must get in touch with Miss Chadwick and raise the question of the removals. It would be better to have confirmation from her own lips. This he could do on the telephone, and without betraying Wimbush's confidence; all that was needed was a little diplomacy. At the same time a certain display of moral indignation was justified. He took up the instrument.

'Yes, this is Miss Chadwick speaking. Who is that?'

'Timothy Casson, Miss Chadwick.'

'Would you mind speaking a little more distinctly, I'm afraid I didn't catch the name.'

'Timothy Casson.'

'Siegfried Sassoon?'

'No, Timothy Casson, Miss Chadwick, your tenant.'

'Oh, it's Mr. Casson. I'm afraid the line's not very good. Well?'

'Forgive me for worrying you, Miss Chadwick, but a rather tiresome thing has happened. One or two things are missing from the house, and I thought I ought to let you know.'

'Missing? What sort of things?'

Timothy told her. There was a moment's silence, then Miss Chadwick said, with a little laugh, 'Didn't it occur to you that I should have taken them?'

'Well, really, it didn't.'

'But what use would a thief have had for a rather worn clothes-brush?'

'I expect they brush their clothes,' said Timothy, nettled.

'Perhaps; but they would hardly risk imprisonment in order to look smart. Really, Mr. Casson, for a writer you did not show much imagination.'

'Well, as long as it was only you,' said Timothy, feebly rude.

'Don't think I don't appreciate your kindness in telling me. And if anything of value disappears, I hope you will at once inform the police.'

'But how shall I know?' Timothy began. 'And there's the inventory.' He lived in terror of this inculpating document.

'I think you can safely leave that to me, Mr. Casson. Was there anything else?'

'Yes,' said Timothy, nervously determined. 'I wanted to ask you if I might raise Wimbush's wages.'

'Why?'

'I thought that with prices going up—'

'Prices will go up if wages go up, Mr. Casson. It is an inevitable consequence.'

'I know, but sometimes one has to put sentiment before economics.'

'A dangerous doctrine but it shall be as you wish. Only, have you asked Colonel Harbord?'

'Colonel Harbord?'

'Yes, I think it would be more neighbourly to consult him. We live in a community, and cannot escape its obligations.'

'But I don't know Colonel Harbord.'

'Not know Colonel Harbord?'

'I mean, he hasn't called on me.'

There was a perceptible silence. Then, in an altered tone, Miss Chadwick said: 'In that case you had better act on your own initiative.'

Trying to recover his position, Timothy said carelessly, 'But I'm hoping to meet him next week at the Rector's. Perhaps I had better leave it until then.'

'I think it would be more tactful. You will find him very understanding, and anxious to help. I hope you are comfortable at the Old Rectory, Mr. Casson?'

'Very comfortable, thank you, Miss Chadwick.'

'It's a dear old house, a very dear place. I can't get used to living in a modern villa, and though I have many of my own things round me, they look awkward and self-conscious, as if they had been stolen from somewhere.'

Timothy laughed gaily.

'My servants would say they had been.'

'Had been? I'm afraid I don't quite follow.'

'They think the things were stolen.'

'Oh. But I couldn't very well steal my own property, could I?'

Timothy put down the receiver with mixed feelings. Relief was still uppermost, but he wished he had given a better account of himself with Miss Chadwick. Really, her referring him to Colonel Harbord deserved a snub. His mind, relieved of the paralysing pressure of the moment, invented several withering retorts. But, he comforted himself by thinking, one cannot be rude to a lady, especially a lady older, much older, than oneself. He might have told her so. But that would have been to put their relationship on a strained footing, the attitude of mistrust which haunted the nations of Europe and ended in universal war. And he might have to ask her a favour later on. It was much better to finish with a laugh, even if the laugh had been on him.

Beatrice and Effie, however, did not share his pacific outlook; they were extremely angry with Miss Chadwick. Primed with the news, bursting to tell them that the culprit was found out, he had bearded them both in the kitchen; but the revelation was an anti-climax; he saw at once that they knew already. Nothing more was said about the notices, so Timothy assumed that these had been tacitly withdrawn. But though the two women were indignant with Miss Chadwick, they were not pleased with him, and still less pleased when he told them, with triumph, of his diplomatic interview with her on the telephone, and the merry laugh with which it ended. They thought he had behaved in a very poor-spirited way.

'But what about us?' demanded Beatrice. 'She may not be a thief, I don't say she is, but she comes into the house like one, and what do you do? You accuse us. It isn't very nice, is it? We have our good name to think of, even if she hasn't.'

Beatrice seemed to be unable to understand that Timothy hadn't accused them, so he agreed it was not very nice.

'She's a nasty old so-and-so, that's what she is,' said Beatrice, and Effie, who had hardly spoken but contented herself with wincing and undulating and making inarticulate sounds to underline what her friend said, echoed with satisfaction, 'That's what she is, a nasty old so-and-so.'

Grimly pleased with having summed up Miss Chadwick in a phrase, they exchanged nods over tightly shut mouths, and seemed to be allowing their resentment to relax. But a moment later Beatrice said, 'And you won't like it either, sir, when you find she's taken something you really want, like that old boat.'

It would be very inconvenient, Timothy agreed, and he began to wonder whether a policy of appeasement was the best way of treating Miss Chadwick.

'And her a judge's sister, too.'

Yes, that did make it worse. She ought to know better, and he would consult his solicitor – quite informally, of course, and take the opportunity to mention his disappointment over the boat. It would be only prudent to find out what the legal position was.

'I sympathise with you, of course,' his lawyer wrote.

'But I'm afraid I can't give you much encouragement. It was a pity that you did not allow us to examine the terms of the lease properly before you signed it. Miss Chadwick undoubtedly has the right to come into the house – not without giving you notice, of course, but I doubt if you can legally object to that, especially as she seems to have notified the gardener, who is your servant. That she should take things away without asking your permission is, I admit, very irritating, but I question whether it is actionable. Your argument that you took the house with certain things in it is difficult to answer, but these matters are governed a good deal by custom and etiquette. A certain latitude is always allowed to ladies, whose ideas of business are subject to caprice in a way that ours are not.

'As to your inquiry about the boat, again we regret that we cannot offer much encouragement. A house-agent's prospectus is, as you probably know, not intended to be an exact description of the property; Messrs. Leeson & Renton's reply, that boating had been enjoyed by previous occupiers of your property (as witness the undoubted existence of the boat-house), and they had taken for granted that it could still be so enjoyed, absolves them from the suspicion of ill-faith. We do not think that this unfortunate circumstance could be construed as a breach of contract on their part, or that you could, in a court of law, establish the claim that you had taken the house on false pretences.

'We appreciate your disappointment (oh, do you? fumed Timothy, growing more and more ruffled) at having provided yourself with a boat which respect for local feeling prevents you from using. Again we must regret that details such as these were not examined more carefully before you signed the contract. As to the further point you raise, whether you would be within your rights to put your boat on the river and take your pastime regardless of the wishes of your neighbours, we are inclined to think that this must remain a question between you and your social conscience. Fishing rights are, of course, very strictly preserved, and the propulsion of a rowing boat or skiff over waters in which fishing is being enjoyed would probably constitute an act of trespass, unless it could be proved, as it probably could be, that boating was enjoyed on those waters before they were leased for fishing. Your situation seems to be, in the legal sense, without precedent. The case of Piscator and others *versus* the Blue Barge Haulage Company, in which the horse, drawing a train of barges, took fright and knocked into the water several anglers who were fishing from the towpath cannot be held to apply, and if applied would only weaken your case, since the anglers obtained heavy damages from the Company, while the Company's counter-claim for damages, based on the plea that one of the fishermen, by waving his hat and other intemperate gestures frightened the horse, which also fell into the water and was unable to resume its duties for some weeks, was dismissed with costs.

'We shall be happy to act for you if you wish us to, but we think you will be well advised to make the settlement of these questions a matter of private negotiation with the persons concerned.'

Beatrice and Effie were not more put out by Timothy's surrender to Miss Chadwick than was Timothy by the lamentable lack of fight displayed in Messrs. Givin and Givall's letter. Their frequent and hollow use of the word 'enjoyment,' where no enjoyment was, increased his chagrin. To console himself he wrote them another letter, slightly subacid in tone, inquiring whether, if Miss Chadwick took away *all* the furniture from the house, stripping it bare, he would still have no legal remedy against her; was there no limit, he asked, to the chivalry required of men in their business dealings with ladies? And would not the inventory, for the making of which he had paid half, be soon as worthless as the paper it was written on? And as to the boat, how could he enter into private negotiations when the person chiefly concerned, Mrs. Lampard, did not answer his letter, and the others resolutely remained outside the pale of his acquaintanceship?

No sooner had Timothy written this peevish outburst than his anger cooled, and he began to await the solicitors' reply with trepidation. Nor were his fears groundless. Messrs. Givin & Givall's answer was decidedly crisp. It would be time to act, they said, when Miss Chadwick *had* stripped the house bare. Meanwhile, if she took away, without Timothy's leave, any important piece of furniture such as a sideboard, bed, or article of essential domestic use, he was at once to inform them, and they would seek an injunction against her. With regard to the boat, they were sorry but they could add nothing to what they had already said. It might happen that under stress of war Timothy would find, as others did, that fishing was a sufficient outlet for his energies.

The prick of conscience often turns to rage. Why should it be patriotic or praiseworthy for *them*, Colonel Harbord, Captain Sturrock, Commander Bellew and the rest, to dangle their fishing rods in the water, sitting or standing with idiotic expressions in silly-looking hats from dawn to dusk, coming home only when light failed, to carouse over their whiskies and sodas, and tell each other fishermen's tales, which were notoriously untrue? How could this be thought more helpful to the war effort than a brisk row up or down the river, eyes glued to the bank in quest of pictures of Britain? And the return, refreshed and renewed, to, perhaps, a modest gin and vermouth to refresh his imagination while the picture came to life?

Comparing their relative usefulness, Timothy grew even more indignant that the fishermen should escape censure and he not. It was sheer snobbery on the part of his solicitors to imply that fishing was a more reputable war-time pursuit than boating. Boating was a proletarian pastime; fly-fishing was a privilege of the rich; that explained their attitude. Almost for the first time Timothy felt himself warmly proletarian, a champion of the have-nots against the high-ups.

Besides, Colonel Harbord, Captain Sturrock and Commander Bellew were professional members of the fighting services; they ought to neigh like war-horses instead of lining the river bank or paddling in it protected by the waders which they ought to have sent to the nearest lifeboat crew. They approved of war; they were overjoyed, no doubt, to see Europe in flames; they were no doubt disappointed that the conflagration seemed to have been checked. They held the view that death in war was a worthy sacrifice, and one that every gentleman should be proud to make; to them the battlefield was the seed-bed and forcing-house of virtue, a general purification from which those who survived came back better men to beget clear-eyed, straight-limbed sons who would also gladly perish in war when their turn came. They might even – who knows – subscribe to the appalling doctrine that it didn't matter killing people so long as you did not hate them; cut-throats with a cheerful smile and a kind word for their victims. But no; the eyes that narrowed with cruelty over the dying struggles of an exhausted fish, the faces that hardened above the hands that held the gaff (or whatever it was) were not likely to spare as much as a grimace for the death-agony of a Boche. They lived for their blood-lust, thought Timothy; nothing that satisfied that would come amiss. Every day, in one form or another they indulged it, either at the expense of the brute creation or of their fellow-men; and after the orgy, no doubt, when the instinct for cruelty which lurks in all of us had been appeased, they might even appear between six and seven over their whisky, or between nine-thirty and ten-thirty over their port, thoroughly amiable and good-natured; more amiable, more good-natured, perhaps, than those of us who have all our lives repressed such impulses, and must pay the penalty for those innocent and innocuous years in a fit of irritability or moroseness now and then.

For he, Timothy, wished ill to nobody and nothing; a Buddhist priest could not have more reverence for the sacredness of life! If he saw a German about to rape his sister—

56

The whirr of the telephone bell interrupted Timothy's orgy of self-justification. Indignant thoughts streaming off him like drops of water from a tired swimmer struggling in the surf, he dashed into the white-panelled room and snatched up the receiver as if it was a life-line.

'Yes?'

'Can I speak to Mr. Casson?' said a woman's voice – surely not Miss Chadwick's?

'Yes, this is him speaking.'

'Oh, Mr. Casson, this is Volumnia Purbright. I just wanted to remind you about Saturday. I was afraid it might have slipped your memory. I expect you have a great many engagements.'

'Oh *no*, Mrs. Purbright.'

'Well, I just wanted to say how much we are looking forward to seeing you. It's going to be, for us, quite an occasion. *Such* a lot of people. You're going to meet *all* your neighbours.'

'That *will* be a pleasure.'

'I'm sure they'll think so. And one more thing, which is really the reason why I rang you up. *Edgell* will be here!'

'How perfectly splendid.'

'I do so want you to meet him. He is such a dear boy. He has literary leanings.'

'I shall love to talk to him.'

'That's all right, then. You didn't mind me disturbing you?'

'You couldn't have done me a greater kindness.'

'Do you know, your voice reminds me of Edgell's? I feel we are friends already.'

'So do I, Mrs. Purbright.'

'Au revoir, then, Saturday.'

'Goodbye, Mrs. Purbright.'

Treading on air, Timothy returned to his writing table. How much more workmanlike it looked, stripped of the inkpot (a converted stag's foot, which he never used), the silver matchbox, which gave Effie extra work to clean, and the childish and distracting snow-storm! Miss Chadwick had done him a kindness by taking them away. What an admirable woman she was, clear-headed and prompt in action, the sort of person one could respect. And his neighbours were looking forward to seeing him, were they? Timothy blushed for the thoughts he had just been entertaining about them. They were not in the least what he had imagined. They were elderly country gentlemen, living quietly on inadequate pensions, not having much fun, not able to entertain each other very much, barely able perhaps to give each other a drink. Their deeds and decorations in the Army and the Navy had made a stir at the time, but the generation that remembered how Colonel Harbord won the D.S.O. was passing away: with a patient shrug the retired officers acquiesced in this partial oblivion, for they had never been pot-hunters; all they needed, in the way of fame, was the tacit recognition, each by the other, that he had served his country well; and for recreation, a little fishing – so easy to reconcile, by neighbours who were looking forward to meeting him, with the brief sorties of Timothy's boat – gliding down the shallows where the water hurried over sunlit pebbles, lingering on some green pool overhung by willows, interfering with nobody, disturbing nothing, leaving hardly more trace of its passage through the water than did the mayfly itself!

And besides the solitary joys, the party at the Rectory would initiate Timothy into exactly the kind of social life he liked – the society of rather staid, elderly people of set manners and habits, who kept engagements, and to whom he would appear almost young; whereas to those bright bare-legged beings, in trousers and pullovers, who haunted the Fisherman's Arms and with self-conscious bravado, three or four abreast, pushed their perambulators down the village street, and sometimes cast a friendly glance in his direction – to them he would be simply an old fogey, utterly out of date. Of course, he would not find them at the party; the Rector had made his attitude to them quite clear. The people he would meet would be precisely those whom he wanted to meet: the backbone of the district, the guardians of the river. And Mrs. Lampard, wondered Timothy, would she be there?

It was Thursday; only two days to wait. Tomorrow he would arrange an expedition with Beatrice and Effie to visit Keystone Castle, a Border stronghold which would be sure to interest them, for in no mediæval castle in England were the arrangements for the housing of the serfs, servers, villeins and other varlets better preserved. As a picture of Britain, it showed how far we had progressed, and as an object lesson to Damaris and Chloe it might be useful, too.

CHAPTER VII

'MY DEAR,' – wrote Timothy, and stopped. For the first time in his life he wanted to write a letter and did not know to whom. He shook his pen. A spreading blot showed that it was ready: readier than he. The imposing silhouette of Keystone Castle, the most recent subject of his pen, with hard-won phrases floating from it like balloon captions in an advertisement, threw its shadow across the Rectory drawing-room, and the clear tones of Beatrice and Effie, loudly condemning the Middle Ages, contended with the subdued murmur of voices courteously deferring to each other which had greeted Timothy on his arrival at the cocktail-party.

'But,' Damaris flashed at me, 'Why did they put up with it? That's what I want to know. Why didn't they give notice?' Because, I explained to the intelligent but historically uninstructed girl (for Damaris is no *femme de lettres*) under the Feudal System it was practically impossible to give notice; you were part of the pyramid which had its apex in the King, and could no more detach yourself from your position, high or low, than a brick can wriggle out of one wall and insert itself into another. 'Well, I call that most unfair!' 'Yes, and we've progressed a great deal since then, haven't we, Chloe?' Chloe, perhaps readier to agree than Damaris, thought we had. 'You are free to leave me at any moment' (I continued the lecture), 'but I can't leave my house, even if I wanted to.' 'You can't?' said Damaris incredulously. 'No, because I hold it on an unbreakable five years' lease. You might say I was still living under the Feudal System and Lady Gloria Fitzpatrick (in vulgar parlance Miss Chadwick) is my overlord. I am bound to her by a complex system of dues and services.'

At this point Damaris merged into Edgell Purbright.

'I say,' he exclaimed, 'five years is a long stretch! Won't you get a bit sick of us by that time?' Timothy didn't think he would. 'It's just the place I was looking for,' he said, glancing at the snowdrops, massed companies of them in finger-bowls, with here and there a frilly aconite, which nodded at him from the window-sills. 'It's just the place I've been trying to get away from,' Edgell Purbright said, 'but don't tell the parents.' Involuntarily Timothy looked up and saw all round

59

him, clustered on tables, piled on cabinets, balanced precariously on brackets, glimmering from behind glass, the most heterogeneous agglomeration of objects that he had ever beheld in any human habitation. Hanging from the ceiling, clinging to the walls, springing up in thickets from the floor, were spoils from the four corners of the world. Of all styles, shapes, sizes, colours and substances; of ebony, ivory, mother-of-pearl, silver, lacquer, china, tortoiseshell and lapis-lazuli, they solicited but did not clamour for attention. A League of Nations! But how much more decorative, how much more effectively creating unity out of diversity, than parallel assemblies at Geneva and the Hague! Mrs. Purbright's catholicity of taste had wrought a miracle. For what can be more selfish, more intolerant of each other's claims, than works of art? Here, towering in pyramids, or reaching outwards in espalier formations, they each contributed their own quota of beauty to a collective beauty that was not their own.

The drawing-room at the Rectory was a long room made out of two, with two fireplaces, in each of which a fire was burning. On the frontier between them stood a low table carrying the drinks, a plentiful supply, yet so arranged, Timothy noted with admiration, as not to seem ostentatious or excessive. Within reach of this table Edgell Purbright had taken his stand, and Timothy with him; and two or three more lingered on the borderline, casting glances every now and then at the two firesides, as if they were wondering which group to join. Timothy knew where he would like to be; with the group on his left, where the Rector was sitting, smoking contentedly and talking to a straight-backed middle-aged man, his face so closely shaved as to seem almost polished, in whose bleached blue eyes when they were at rest there was a hint of strain and sternness. A sailor, he seemed, perhaps Commander Bellew? Timothy distinguished other male figures, giving an impression of grey hair and grey clothes under the grey cigarette smoke; and among them, several ladies, equally neat and self-contained, equally unemphatic in bearing and gesture, looking like a masculine idea translated into a feminine language.

'You're looking the wrong way,' said Edgell Purbright, before Timothy had time to speculate further on the identities of the Rector's circle. 'Eyes right.'

Timothy braced himself to meet a blast of colour. But he was disappointed; the invaders were more soberly dressed than their opposite numbers across the barrier. There were no bare legs, no trousers, no pullovers of scarlet or pale blue; black predominated, black that clung close to slender bodies and spoke with an urban accent, rebuking tweeds. Timothy had the impression of a man or two, but these did not lessen, they rather increased the general effect of femininity. Tactfully, as she thought, but mistakenly as it turned out, Mrs. Purbright had put on her gayest things. Very tall, she had draped herself across a chair and a footstool so casually that she almost seemed to be putting her feet up; she was smoking a cigarette through a long black cigarette-holder tipped with silver, with which from time to time she made a wide gesticulation. The air of vague and comprehensive benevolence with which she had drawn Timothy into the room was more than ever in evidence, and there was something aristocratic and reassuring in her unself-consciousness.

'My mother's so excited by all these pearly-queens,' said Edgell. 'She thinks she'll get them to come to church. She wants to bring the smart set and the old contemptibles together. What a hope! But I like those jolly girls, some of them. There's one I don't know: that fair one with her back to you. She's rather pretty.'

Timothy saw whom he meant, but the back of her head told him little.

'But it's you my mother really wants to know,' Edgell confided, 'and shall I tell you why, or one reason why, though it isn't very flattering. She thinks you might have a steadying influence on me – though why you should bother! And anyhow I'm in the Air Force now. . . . Wait a moment, I must take this tray round. But let's each have another first.'

There was still some gin and vermouth in the cocktail shaker, but it had grown watery, and Edgell refreshed it generously from the bottles. 'I don't care for this sort of show, do you?' he went on. 'At least I like the drinks, but not the social part, it's all meaningless. Those girls are all right in the Fisherman's Arms – and I don't mean in Harbord's arms, or Sturrock's – they'll never be there! But this is all make-believe. Mother would have them, but Father didn't want them and he was right. If I was a writer like you are, and writing about present conditions in England, I should say that everything those people stood for' – he nodded in the direction of the fishermen – 'was finished. They don't belong any more. Now, if you'll excuse me, I'll go and give them something to drink.'

He moved away, taking the tray with him, and leaving Timothy to the companionship of his glass. At the same moment his host and hostess detached themselves from their respective groups and converged upon him. A silence fell on the company, and Timothy felt the impact of a cross-fire of speculative eyes.

Mr. and Mrs. Purbright reached him simultaneously. The Rector's forehead flushed at the contretemps, but his wife laughed.

'Well, Mr. Casson,' she said. 'We both had the same thought. We couldn't let Edgell monopolise you any longer. Now which of us would you rather go with?'

Timothy flashed an appealing glance at the Rector, on whom was hung, almost visibly, the key to the polite society of Upton, the key that might unlock the boat-house door. He said to Mrs. Purbright:

'You must answer for me.'

Focussed on the two alternatives, Mrs. Purbright's dark blue eyes squinted slightly. 'Then I shall claim him, though I expect he would much rather go with you, Edward.' The Rector's brow cleared. 'Ours is a mothers' meeting. Are you interested in babies, Mr. Casson?'

'Well, in an academic way.'

'I'm glad to hear that. I think everyone should be.' She drew Timothy with her. The Rector, with the air of one who unexpectedly finds an empty seat in a crowded train, returned to his place. Mrs. Purbright's voice grew more confidential. 'They're so important, babies, I mean. Such a trouble for one thing.' She sighed. 'But you're not married?'

'No.'

Mrs. Purbright stopped. 'What a pity. But why should I say that? I expect you're very happy.'

'Well—' began Timothy.

'You needn't bother to tell me. I expect you have a great many relations?'

'Oh no, almost none.'

Mrs. Purbright stubbed out a half-smoked ciagrette, and taking another from a silver box fitted it awkwardly into her long cigarette holder.

'No parents; for instance? You might have – you look so young, sometimes.'

'I've been an orphan almost longer than I can remember.'

'How sad for you, how very sad. But some people are happier without out ties. Or don't you think so? You mustn't bother to answer – people tell me I think aloud.'

Timothy detected the elusive current of her sympathy, a sort of Gulf Stream lapping against the shores of his mind.

'Men have other interests, of course,' she went on. 'I sometimes envy them. Fishing all day! You must have seen them on your rambles.'

'I don't think I have,' said Timothy. 'Isn't it perhaps a little early?'

'Of course, how stupid of me! I shall never learn. The mayfly! What I meant was, you have a boat, haven't you?'

Timothy said he had.

'A boat!' Her eyes grew dreamy. 'I can understand so well! The Standridges had a boat once. I wonder what became of it? The river was not so private then; more fun in a way, I suppose. You like sharing things, Mr. Casson?'

'I should be delighted to lend you the boat at any time,' said Timothy eagerly.

'How kind you are! But I didn't quite mean that. Our boating days are over. And I doubt if Edward. . . . You see, we represent what you would most dislike.'

'Oh!' exclaimed Timothy, aghast.

'Yes, but that needn't prevent us from being friends, need it? I feel we are, already. Only this question of the river. I do so sympathise with you; I should like to help you.'

'Help me?' echoed Timothy.

'How silly I sound, and perhaps rather patronising. No, not help. But I shall always be glad to tell you anything I can.'

'About the river?' Timothy was mystified.

'Well, yes. And about, – what shall I call them? The customs of the country. I expect everything was different in Italy – no fishing, or not the same kind. They live on pasta, mostly, don't they? But I could tell you something about the river, too. Let me see. There's a waterfall called the Devil's Staircase—' She broke off, for a third person had joined them, the woman, as her empty chair showed, whom Edgell Purbright had pointed out to Timothy. She was tall and strikingly fair. A cataract of pale fine hair, drawn smooth as silk on the top of her head, rippled to her shoulders and rebounded in a thick gold mist. Long lashes curled over blue eyes that held something of a baby's wondering regard, innocent, questioning and wistful. Where had Timothy seen her before? In a picture, but not a picture of today, she was much too unsophisticated; in a garden with stone balls and clipped yew hedges, standing on some steps: the lady with the dog!

'I'm afraid I must go, Mrs. Purbright,' she said. 'I've got to put the che-ild to bed.' Her voice had a faint lilt, an undertone of sing-song.

'Oh, how lucky you are,' sighed Mrs. Purbright. 'How old is he?'

'She's a girl, I'm afraid,' the lady answered, 'and she's just going to be five, I think. I'm never quite sure of their ages.'

'Oh, you have more than one, then?'

'Yes, there are three of them. Sally's the baby. She's only eighteen months.'

'And the middle one's a boy?'

'Oh no, I'm afraid not. She's a girl, too.'

Mrs. Purbright tried not to look disappointed, and said, 'But how nice. Three little girls.' She tried to put some enthusiasm into this remark, failed, and said encouragingly, 'But you'll be having a little boy one day.'

'Perhaps,' said the lady. She turned her beautiful sad face to Timothy and added, 'But I must get married first, mustn't I?'

Mrs. Purbright and Timothy stared at her. 'But I thought—' began Mrs. Purbright, puzzled.

'That the children were mine? Oh no, they're not. They're Frances Bingham's. I promised to put them to bed for her.' She laughed; her eyes lit up and her whole face sparkled, then suddenly resumed its melancholy cast.

Timothy and Mrs. Purbright joined in the laugh rather uncertainly, and Mrs. Purbright said:

'I am so dreadfully vague. Names float in front of me. You must excuse me. I was just going to introduce you to Mr. Casson as Mrs. . . . . Miss, I mean. . . . .' She stopped, confused. The lady smiled, but did not help her out. Mrs. Purbright plucked the strings of her mind for the chime, the tinkle of recognition that a recovered memory gives. She did not catch it, but she had heard several names new, or nearly new, to her that evening. Selecting one at random, she said:

'Angell, that must have been it.'

'Miss Angell,' said the lady with the ghost of a smile, which somehow missed Mrs. Purbright and fell on Timothy. 'Mrs. Purbright likes boys better, but all angels are females, aren't they, Mr. Casson?'

How clever of her to have got his name so pat. 'I've always thought so,' Timothy said.

'And unmarried.'

'Of course.'

The lady smiled. 'But I'm afraid you're mistaken. My name isn't Angell.'

'Oh dear!' said Mrs. Purbright. 'Angell seemed so right for you, somehow.'

De-angelised, the lady shrugged her shoulders slightly.

'Would you tell me your name again? It was stupid of me to forget.'

'Cross.'

'Cross! Miss Cross! Of course! But do you know I'm almost sorry, because the other name suited you so much better. I shall always think of you as Miss Angell. And now you must go. What a pity.'

Miss Cross's face grew sadder under Mrs. Purbright's gentle scrutiny.

'Or must you?' Mrs. Purbright went on. 'Stay a moment and talk to Mr. Casson.' 'Well, just a moment,' said Miss Cross.

With a curious feeling of confidence, Timothy led her to a chair and fetched another for himself. Mrs. Purbright returned to her circle, and the conversation, which had languished, renewed itself round her.

Miss Cross waited, with her hands in her lap.

'I really mustn't keep you,' Timothy ventured.

'Why not?'

'Oh,' said Timothy, 'the children. You must be feeling anxious about them.'

Miss Cross raised her eyes.

'To tell you the truth I was feeling terribly bored. You don't blame me, do you?'

'For feeling bored?'

'Oh no, not for that. You couldn't. But for saying I had the children to look after.'

'Hadn't you?'

'Oh no, it was just an excuse. I simply had to get away.'

'You mustn't let me keep you,' Timothy repeated.

'Well, just this once. You're the writer, aren't you? I've heard a lot about you.'

'Oh,' said Timothy. 'I didn't think anyone in the village had.'

'Indeed we have, we're all your fans. And we think it's terribly tough luck on you.'

'What is?'

'Oh, about your boat. We all think it's a frightful shame. We're all on your side.'

Timothy glanced round. The guardians of the river were smoking peacefully. They looked safe and comfortable. As soon as Miss Cross had gone he would get up and join them. But did he want her to go?

'We had quite an indignation meeting about it last night,' his champion went on. 'Frances said she wondered you didn't take a nice little tube or whatever it is of arsenic and poison the fish.'

Her voice, which was always clear, became positively bell-like at the last three words, and one of the fishermen looked round with a query in his eye. Timothy was horrified, but the next moment he couldn't help admiring Miss Cross for daring to speak her mind. 'We'd like to help you if we could,' she went on. 'We had all sorts of plans. But there was always one thing against them.'

'What was that?'

'You don't like us,' sighed Miss Cross. She spoke quietly, even sadly, but there was a click of finality in her tone. Timothy turned scarlet.

'Not like you?'

'I'm afraid not. You see, we're just intruders. We don't count. We have babies and do our own housework. We go to the pub and have a good time. You don't like that, do you?'

'I'm not a great pub-crawler,' admitted Timothy. 'I drink in solitude. But that's nothing to be proud of. And if you're an intruder, so am I.'

Miss Cross considered this.

'Well, in a way, I suppose, we are in the same boat. But what a tactless expression! It's just where we're not. Too bad.'

Her face filled with sympathy, and Timothy began to feel himself exceedingly ill-used.

'We ought to hold a council of war,' she said. 'Come any night to the Fisherman's Arms. You'll find masses of sympathisers.'

'But wouldn't that be rather public?'

'All the better. You can't do anything without publicity. You didn't become famous by writing your articles and putting them into a drawer.'

Timothy had never thought of himself as famous. He knew he had a certain reputation with the *Broadside's* less austere-minded patrons, but he didn't imagine that the general reader had ever heard of him.

'Of course we're very much afraid of you.' Miss Cross went on. 'Petrified, in fact. You walk down the street, not looking at anyone, and we hide behind our perambulators.'

'But I'm sure I should have seen you,' protested Timothy. 'Do you mean I walked past you without looking at you?'

She smiled her slow sad smile, and slightly shook her head.

'They all say the same. "Of course he doesn't want to know us, why should he? He's just holding himself aloof until he can get in with them." ' She nodded very perceptibly in the direction of the tweedy group who were talking to each other as members of the same family do, in monosyllables, with shrugs and upward pursings of the lips, showing no extra liveliness of voice or manner, thoroughly at home with themselves and with the Rector.

'They're a dull, up-stage lot, aren't they?' Miss Cross observed. 'About as much use as a sick-headache. I wouldn't mind seeing some of them strung up to lamp-posts.' Her face brightened, and she gave Timothy an enchanting smile. 'But I mustn't start crabbing your friends.'

'They aren't my friends.'

'No, but you'd like them to be. Unless you're waiting for an invitation from Mrs. Lampard.'

How on earth did she know? But in a small place rumour flies: Timothy remembered that in Venice his movements were known and reported to him, sometimes before he had made them, sometimes when he had never dreamed or would dream of making them. Looked at in the right way it was all rather funny. He laughed.

'Oh, I only wrote to her about the boat.' At once Miss Cross divined his change of mood.

'I know,' she said. 'What a damned shame. Look here, if you can bear to meet us, I'm sure we can think of something. A proper plan of campaign, I mean, not just a phoney war. Trust me, I'll arrange it for you. I'm just longing to have a go at them.' The lilt of her voice traced a pattern on the air; it stopped like a painter's pencil in midstroke, leaving her innocent, almost babyish face softened by a sweetness strangely at variance with her words. The power of her beauty stole over Timothy, bringing a delicious quickening of every sense; and at the same time the intimate moral comfort of having found at last an ally warmed those places in his heart in which love grows and courage springs; and his sense of humour, which, it must be confessed, had been nourished on the denial of many of his other faculties, took wing.

Only to see her, to be with her again! 'Of course I'll come,' he said. 'Any time you like. When? Where?'

Dreamily she looked at him, with tilted chin and lowered eyelids. The wistful lady with the dog faded away, to be replaced by the properties of another scene not altogether different, belonging to the same age but glowing with a more ardent poetry; a halo, a sundial, and a dove: Beata Beatrix. The room grew indistinct, but now there was another sound in it besides the hum of voices; the creak and drag of chairs rubbing on the carpet. Shapes rose and moved towards each other. One silhouette detached itself, and came to where they sat. It was Edgell Purbright.

'Sorry,' he said, 'but I've been deputed to break up your *tête-à-tête*. The governor wants Mr. Casson to meet his sporting pals and their worthy ladies – the backbone of the place,' he added, looking humorously at Miss Cross.

'Aren't you being rather rude?' she said, her face expressionless.

'I didn't say the beauty of the place,' retorted Edgell, quite unruffled. 'But you see, this is a getting-together party, and Dad feels that Mr. Casson ought to take the rough with the smooth.' He despatched a furtive, collusive grimace at the Rector's group, two or three of whom were now standing up and making discreet departure signals. 'Perhaps you would let me try to entertain you for a moment,' he said, lifting an eyebrow to Miss Cross.

Ignoring him, she turned to Timothy. 'I don't know how Mr. Casson feels, but I feel I've been insulted.'

Social training and the instinct not to make a scene struggled in Timothy with the desire to avenge Miss Cross. A thousand swords should have leapt from their scabbards; his did not. He stammered:

'Well, perhaps in the circumstances we might be allowed. . . .'

'Why, certainly,' said Edgell. 'It's up to you.' He gave them both a brief, unrecognising stare, and was turning on his heel when Miss Cross called out:

'Mr. Purbright.'

He faced them with a guarded smile. 'Yes?'

'You've got a button undone. . . . I thought you'd like to know.'

Edgell glanced down, and flushed. Revolving anxiously, his gaze swept the room. Where least danger threatened, he turned and fumbled.

'That'll teach him,' said Miss Cross. At the sound of her voice Edgell turned. He was wearing the King's uniform, the blue of the Royal Air Force, and he was not lacking in combative spirit.

'Improperly dressed on parade,' he said. 'What do I get for that?'

Immediately Miss Cross laughed. Dimples drew sickles in her cheeks, and a pang of jealousy stabbed Timothy.

'I'll let you go now,' she said to him, giving Edgell the full benefit of her pensive, demure regard.

Having received his congé, Timothy got awkwardly to his feet, but too late. Taking their cue from the others, the group round Mrs. Purbright had also risen, and the whole party was already on the move. The gentry began to file past Timothy – a clean hard line of jaw, a clipped grey moustache; a high-domed forehead over jutting, wiry eyebrows; and the ladies among them, high-cheek-boned, Roman-nosed, steady-eyed with plain gold, or pearl, or diamond earrings fitting tightly; figures firmly curved but not voluptuous; coats and skirts grey, rust-brown, purplish, that absorbed the light; restrained indoor movements braced for leave-taking. More than one, as they passed Timothy, cast a glance in his direction, discreet, incurious, yet measuring. And what did they see? In the pier-glass opposite, Timothy could see what they saw: Miss Cross in her dead-black close-fitting cloth suit, with its white collar, her beautiful legs, touching, caressing each other, showing the gleam of flesh through the mesh of her silk stockings; and above, the springing lily of her face, so young compared with theirs, and her blue eyes travelling slowly from one cavalier to the other. Of the two, it was Edgell who fitted into the picture, a smile of understanding lent experience to his boyish features; while Timothy, bewildered by competing hopes, grey-haired, middle-aged, felt uncertain where he belonged, but looked (the mirror had no doubt of it) the property of Miss Cross.

Without rising, without moving, she let the procession pass. Then when the goodbyes at the door had left a space round her, she got up, and looking at her own reflection rather than at Timothy or at Edgell, with all the confidence of her slender tallness she bore down on Mrs. Purbright.

'Why, it's you!' her hostess said. 'I was afraid you'd gone away.' Spying Timothy in Miss Cross's wake, she added, 'I'm so glad that Mr. Casson prevailed on you to stay.'

'It wasn't me,' said Timothy, inventing wildly. 'Miss Cross remembered there was someone in the house after all.'

'Ah!' exclaimed Mrs. Purbright, 'I felt sure there would be. I mean,' she hurried on, squinting benevolently at Miss Cross, 'Fate couldn't want to rob my party of so much prettiness!'

'I have enjoyed myself enormously,' Miss Cross answered, formally. 'Goodbye.'

'And we enjoyed ourselves looking at her, didn't we, Mr. Casson. . . . And you had the pleasure of a talk as well.'

'So did I,' put in Edgell. 'Miss Cross said a few words to me, too.' There was a touch of challenge in his tone.

'Then you were both of you *very lucky men.*'

Mrs. Purbright put a lot of emphasis on the last three words. 'You won't forget us, Miss Cross, will you? We're always here.'

Miss Cross assured her that she would not, and repeated her goodbye more decisively than before. Timothy added his, and was hurrying out after her, when Mrs. Purbright said:

'Don't run away. We've hardly seen anything of you.'

Timothy muttered something about wanting to stay but being afraid he ought to get back.

'Children to put to bed? No, of course not,' Mrs. Purbright answered herself. 'How silly of me. You're a bachelor. But we may all be having evacuees before long.'

Timothy's eye strayed to the door. 'I know, and my servants say they'll give notice if we do.'

'Oh dear, and servants are so precious nowadays. I shouldn't do anything to annoy them. Just say you are a man.'

'Wouldn't that be rather obvious, Mother?' asked Edgell. 'Wouldn't it be insisting on something that's self-evident?'

'I mean a man can't be expected to look after children. He really mustn't lose his servants.' Mrs. Purbright looked at Timothy with concern. 'I hope you have good servants?'

'Oh, they are treasures,' agreed Timothy, his eye trying to follow his mind through the door. The door opened to admit the Rector who had been saying goodbye to Miss Cross.

'Has she gone?' asked Mrs. Purbright, anxiously.

'Well, I shut the door on her,' the Rector said.

'Yes, I know,' said Mrs. Purbright. 'Only it doesn't follow . . . but you see what I mean, Mr. Casson, Edward and I have to do everything for ourselves – we do get some help, of course, neighbours are very kind – but such things as washing up and opening the front door.'

'Really, Mother, if you insist on keeping him against his will, you should regale him with more entertaining conversation,' said Edgell, offering Timothy a cigarette.

'I know, I know, and he must be used to talking to such clever people. *What* was I going to say?'

'I can't tell you,' said her husband. 'But I was going to say I was sorry we didn't get Casson into our little party.'

'Mr. Casson was otherwise engaged,' said Edgell, 'and I don't suppose he would have found their wit very scintillating.'

His father frowned. 'I may be old-fashioned, but I value many things more than wit. Besides, Sturrock can tell a very good anecdote, very good, nothing risky, of course, just honest fun. And Hector Bellew is a very widely-travelled man, well, naturally he is, he only just missed being an admiral. Harbord we *all* know; he's as straight as a die. Casson would have enjoyed talking to him.'

'Mr. Casson isn't interested in fishing,' said Edgell, maliciously, 'if that's what you talked about. He's an oarsman, aren't I right, Mr. Casson?'

'Well,' began Timothy, 'I have a boat. . . .'

'Yes.' The Rector cleared his throat. 'That was one reason why. . . . Naturally, everyone feels sympathetic. If we haven't been rowing ourselves, we have friends who were.'

'It came out in discussion. We have our . . . our . . . er . . . little infor-mal talks, Casson, our tobacco parliaments. That was why I was sorry you weren't able to . . . er . . . be with us just now, to find how sympa-thetic, how – what shall I say . . .? accommodating, the atmosphere was.'

Timothy said he, too, was sorry. But it wasn't altogether true, and his heart was outside the Rectory, looking up and down the lane.

'When people come together in a friendly spirit,' the Rector went on, 'something emerges, some way out of the difficulty that perhaps none of those present could have thought of for themselves. The situation is eased; there is a general tendency to waive rights. Harbord had one plan, to which Bellew – cautiously, mind you – was inclined to agree. Then Watson Stafford, bless him, proposed something quite different.'

'If it is a question of paying—' Timothy began.

The Rector held up his hand. 'Oh no, my dear fellow. Money doesn't come into it. In a sense of course it does; the fishings here are very costly; but it wouldn't influence such men as the friends who have just left us. Goodwill beats money every time. That is why I'm sorry – but it's no use crying over spilt milk. No, it's a matter of rights and prece-dents. If you were to use your boat—'

'I see,' said Timothy. 'Others might want to use theirs.'

'Exactly. And as Sturrock said, there would be pandemonium on the river, positive pandemonium.'

'Negative pandemonium wouldn't matter so much,' said Edgell, pertly.

The Rector frowned.

'Since you joined the Air Force, Edgell, you seem to have lost your sense of values. A most important principle is at stake. If you were to ask me what that principle is, I should be at a loss to define it, but it involves the whole relationship of the individual to society.'

'Haven't you left out Mrs. Lampard, Dad?'

'One thing at a time, my boy. I was coming to her. Of course we must wait for Mrs. Lampard to give us a lead.'

At the name Timothy sighed, and a silence fell on the room.

'Well, this isn't helping us to win the war,' said Edgell.

Timothy saw his chance.

'I really must be off. Such a bore, but I've an article to finish.'

He held out his hand to Mrs. Purbright, who disregarded it and said, 'Ah, now I remember! We were going to ask you to be kind enough—'

'No, no, Mother. He won't want to vet my literary efforts. We've got him into quite enough trouble as it is.'

'Trouble, my dear boy, trouble? I hope not.' Mrs. Purbright's mild gaze traversed the room like a gentle searchlight. Her son's eye followed hers.

'Too late, I'm afraid, the mischief's done.'

'I had wanted Mr. Casson to meet *everyone*, but sometimes it's more fun talking to two or three. Was that what you meant, Edgell? I hope he wasn't bored.'

'Oh no, Mrs. Purbright.'

'I know Edward doesn't, but I think all this new blood is rather a *good* thing, a transfusion that might help us. All those rejuvenating processes, they make one shrink, but ought they to? I mean, there's a great deal of beauty in blood—'

'Mother!'

'Well, there is. Think of a hospital nurse, very pretty, really lovely perhaps, with a hypodermic needle, and all the patients lying round, pale and listless – poor things, you know how hope droops in such places from the sameness of everything – why they'd welcome a dog's bark. Yet the patient has his own life, the comfortable routine of his sensations; even if they are all dulled and drained by illness he doesn't want them altered, he turns away, he dreads the prick—'

'Mother, you make us feel quite sick! Anyhow, some of those old boys have very thick skins. They'd turn a needle. And it didn't strike me they wanted rejuvenating. They seemed impervious to the charm of all your hospital nurses.'

Mrs. Purbright looked saddened and distressed.

'No, it didn't go quite as I should have liked. But I wasn't thinking of them so much—'

'Who were you thinking of?' said Edgell. 'Out with it.'

'Miss Cross seemed an unusual sort of young woman,' remarked the Rector.

'I noticed you took your time seeing her off.'

'Not at all. But she seemed a little uncertain of the way, so I paused to give her directions.'

'I'm surprised – I mean I'm surprised that she didn't know the way,' said Mrs. Purbright. 'But she's only been here a short time – she's staying at The Nook.'

'I should hardly have thought there was sufficient sleeping accommodation in that small house,' observed the Rector.

'You must tell her to mark her bedroom with a cross, Dad.'

'She wore such pretty clothes,' Mrs. Purbright put in, dreamily. 'One can't help feeling grateful to someone who looks as decorative as that. I quite fell in love with her.'

'I thought she was pretty, too,' said Timothy.

Now the Rector came forward with his testimony.

'Very striking, very striking. I nearly told her she was an ornament to the village. Pity she belongs to the . . . the other . . . camp.'

The three men seemed to warm to each other at the thought of Miss Cross. Their faces expanded, their gestures loosened and became freer, and Edgell was emboldened to say, 'She certainly does strengthen their side. I mean to see more of her.'

'Oh, but Edgell, darling,' his mother interposed, 'you're only here such a very short time. Your leave is up on Wednesday, isn't it? Think of the disappointment for her – that sounds like flattery, but in times like this, you know, we clutch at straws.'

'Who does? Who clutches? And am I the straw?'

'In my life I've had the most acute disappointments over the smallest things, haven't I, Edward?' Mrs. Purbright appealed to her husband. 'Out of all proportion – yes, and made scenes about them, I'm afraid. The young feel things so terribly. It's then that one needs to be clever about one's life; later, it doesn't matter so much, does it, Mr. Casson? But of course we should be delighted to see her – all of us, she would be wasted on one person.'

Edgell winked at Timothy.

'I don't think you'll get her here again in a hurry.'

'Oh why not, Edgell? You grieve me. Don't you think she enjoyed herself? We enjoyed looking at her so much.'

Edgell was silent, regretting what he had said. He did not take it back, however, for he knew that his mother's mind was hospitable to all ideas, and she would soon arrange this one in a position where it harmonised with the rest. Nor was he wrong.

'Of course we won't ask her, if you're against it,' she said. 'People should be themselves. It makes them much less interesting if the corners are rubbed off.'

'Miss Cross's corners were quite sharp, I can promise you,' said Edgell.

'Well, well,' said his mother, 'we've made a step in the right direction. Meeting people in a room is a very different matter from seeing them in church—'

'They don't go to church, I only wish they did,' said the Rector, and Timothy made a pious resolve, not for the first time.

'Perhaps they will now.' Mrs. Purbright lost herself in a day-dream in which sleek blond heads, bowed in prayer, were lit by coloured gleams from stained-glass windows. The organ swelled, the congregation rose to its feet, a splendid gathering such as Upton had not seen for years, filled the church. Not all the newcomers had brought prayer-books: the sidesman shuffled from pew to pew distributing them, receiving a shamefaced nod from the embarrassed worshippers, but still there were not enough to go round. Here came Edgell with a tray and glasses, wicked boy. Hands were decorously outstretched, and Mrs. Purbright's fantasy broke up. Edgell, who had an intuitive insight into her thoughts, said, 'You'll empty the church, you know, Mother.'

'My darling, how could you say such a thing? All they need is to feel they will be welcome.'

'Sturrock won't welcome them in his pew.'

'There are plenty of others. It's such a lovely church, Mr. Casson, isn't it? I never find it difficult to imagine Heaven when I'm there. I wish there was more praise, though. We have so much to be thankful for. Prayer and repentance are very good things, but there would be less need for them if praise came easier to us.'

All her three hearers looked uncomfortable, and the Rector's frown returned.

'The Church's liturgy was carefully designed,' he said, 'to meet the requirements of average believers. Thankfulness is enjoined upon us, as a Christian duty, but other obligations and observances come first. The thanksgiving of the heathen is mere sound and noise.'

Mrs. Purbright did not agree. 'Surely praise is a wider thing than that. God is praised in a beautiful face, for how should we know it was beautiful, unless it reminded us of Him? And when we are happy seeing it, that is in itself an act of praise.'

The three men still looked rather sheepish, but much less critical than before.

'It's rather unfair on Colonel Harbord,' remarked Edgell, 'that one can see his face without feeling at all thankful.'

'There are many kinds of beauty,' said Mrs. Purbright, speaking more confidently now that she had the ear of her audience. 'Colonel Harbord is a very fine man, Mr. Casson; you will appreciate him, I know. Think how sweet he was about Mrs. Eridge's pig, Edward; and he scarcely knew her, she had no claim on him at all.'

'Mr. Casson isn't a pig, Mother.'

'Of course not, Edgell dear. I only meant that the pig had been a great nuisance to the Colonel, breaking into the garden at Lawnflete and . . . and nesting among his beloved begonias. He was so understanding about it, not at all what he's sometimes thought to be.'

'Mother thinks he'll get to heaven on piggy-back, but I shouldn't try nesting among his begonias if I were you, Mr. Casson.'

'Naturally it's different with a dumb animal.'

'Pigs are not dumb, Mother.'

'No, my darling, I only meant that Colonel Harbord is quite capable of seeing someone else's point of view, even if at the moment it seems to conflict with his.'

'Yes, Harbord has shown up well on a number of occasions,' remarked the Rector. 'For instance, when his house was burgled and his loving-cup taken – that was before you came here, Casson – he appealed for a lighter sentence for the misguided culprits, hardly more than youths they were. And when the fire broke out in his garage, which looked like arson – a very serious matter, arson, Casson – he flatly refused to prosecute, flatly. And another time when those really horrible fellows, I hardly know what to call them' – the Rector's brow darkened, Timothy could see him struggling with the tide of anger – 'perhaps sweeps would not be too harsh a word, actually dynamited it, Casson, only a few yards from the lawn at Lawnflete, under his very fishing-rod, you might say, a cowardly act if ever there was one, for what chance have the fish, what possible chance? against high explosive, he would not let his man set the dogs on them, though Grappler and Boxer were only just down from the police college and were longing to go for them. In fact the Chairman of the Bench commended him for his restraint.'

The Rector turned on Timothy the glare that was meant for the sweeps; his whole being and presence seemed to dilate with indignation, and Timothy drew back a pace.

'I had no idea that such things went on here,' he said. 'I thought that this was such a quiet little place.'

'Of course it is, of course it is, my dear fellow.' A new gust of feeling from among the many circling round them fanned the embers of Mr. Purbright's wrath in Timothy's direction. 'Have I said anything to suggest that it is not?'

'Oh, no, nothing at all,' said Timothy hastily. 'Perhaps it's just that Colonel Harbord isn't a very popular man.'

'Not popular? What makes you think that?' demanded the Rector. 'I should say that with the possible exception of Bellew, and Watson Stafford (who, between ourselves, rather courts popularity) he's the most popular man in the parish.'

His raised eyebrows challenged Timothy to deny this. On an impulse Timothy said, 'Then you think that perhaps he won't object to my using the boat?'

The Rector's face changed instantly; his eyes narrowed and became grave and considering. Wrinkles of humorous craftiness spread out fanwise round them, and he said, 'That would be telling, wouldn't it, and we mustn't do anything undiplomatic, especially at this stage. Such a pity you didn't find it . . . er . . . possible to talk to our friends yourself. There were signs, there were distinct signs. Of course a great deal depends on the attitude of Mrs. Lampard, and we don't know what that is, yet. But don't give up hope.'

'No, don't give up hope,' pleaded Mrs. Purbright, and her large long face with its high, almost Italian colouring, suddenly looked extremely concerned. 'He must have his boat, mustn't he?' Her eyes, lit by a sibylline gleam of urgency, appealed first to her husband, then to her son.

'Mother thinks you want to praise God in that boat,' said Edgell lightly. A laugh started, in which, after a second's hesitation, the Rector joined. It seemed a sign for Timothy to to go. Cordial farewells accompanied him across the hall and to the doorstep. The sudden cold caught at his throat, and the night, pressing on his eyeballs, brought a sense of strain. Denuded all at once of warmth and friendship, he shivered, and broke into a run. But it was not, he soon discovered, really dark; the glow from a hidden moon lit his footsteps to the garden gate.

CHAPTER VIII

AT the junction with the main road Timothy paused. Something was moving in the shadow of the tall hedge opposite, something lustrous, owl-high against the hedge; it floated towards him, nodding like a lantern, and a woman's voice said 'I thought you were never coming.'

Timothy could now see the moisture of the night glistening on Miss Cross's hair. He apologised. 'I had no idea you were waiting for me,' he said.

'I wasn't sure of the way,' she answered mournfully, 'and believe it or not, I don't like walking down these country roads at night, all by myself. I expect you think me a fool.'

'Not at all,' said Timothy. 'I shall be only too glad to escort you. Do we go the same way?'

'There's only one way really, is there?' she said. Something in this remark struck Timothy as inconsistent, but she did not give him time to analyse it. 'I live just beyond the Green. . . . Will that be taking you too far?'

'Only a few steps,' Timothy said. 'My house is practically on the Green.'

'The house with the gravel-sweep?'

'How did you know?'

'I guessed. It's the kind of house you would have.'

'Oh, there are plenty of nicer houses, tucked away behind walls and trees.'

'You mean belonging to those old fossils we saw tonight. The ones we were talking about, who won't let you use your boat.'

'Oh, perhaps they will some day.' Timothy tried to sound philosophic.

'Not if you give way to them. They're like Hitler. I believe you're an appeaser at heart.'

'Well, one doesn't want to make trouble.'

'Not make trouble? Do you know you sound rather smug? If we'd been afraid of making trouble we shouldn't have stood up to Hitler.'

'I suppose not, but the cases aren't quite parallel.'

'Why not? You seem to be taking their side. You're afraid of offending them. You're a doormat. You don't really care whether they let you use the boat or not.'

'Oh yes, I do, desperately.'

'I don't believe you for a moment.' She studied Timothy as though she was looking for another weak spot. 'But why? Why are you so keen on it? Is it to keep yourself fit?'

'Yes, in a way,' said Timothy.

'But fit for what?'

Timothy hesitated. Not for the first time he asked himself why he was so set on having the boat. But no one had ever asked him before.

'The moment I get on to the water—' he began.

'Yes, what happens then?'

'Well, I feel different,' said Timothy lamely.

'How? And why should you want to feel different?'

'Well, doesn't one want to?'

'Perhaps. But go on.'

'It's a feeling of release, of going with the stream.'

'Even if you're going against it?'

'Yes, there's something in the motion, I suppose, gliding – no friction, no jolts. And then the reflections, which are so clear and still, and shadows under the boughs – the soft, black depth – I like that. But doesn't all this bore you?'

'No, why should it? I dare say I should feel the same thing myself. What I don't understand is why you aren't ready to fight for it.'

Timothy laughed. 'Well, I can't go to war without allies.'

'But you have allies. You have us. We're only waiting for the word. We're tired of being high-hatted by all these stuffed shirts. Who do they think they are?' Her vehemence died away, like a gust that blows itself out; and into the silence stole another sound, a low continuous susurration, hardly audible, as if Nature were turning restlessly or sighing in her sleep.

'Listen!' said Miss Cross sharply. 'Isn't that the river?'

They stopped and peered. The fields were enveloped in a milky mist, in which floated hedges, trees, and bushes – blurs and blobs of varying opaqueness. The retaining wall of the valley, a vast concave at the foot of which the river flowed, could just be seen, but not the river itself.

'Ugh!' Miss Cross shuddered. 'How could you? Do you think that's where the what-you-call-it, the Devil's Staircase is?'

'I never heard of it till tonight,' said Timothy.

'Well, let's make a plan. Do you ever go out in the evenings?'

Timothy said he had nowhere to go.

'Poor fellow, you must be lonely, aren't you?'

'Well, a bit.'

'We thought you must be, but we didn't know if you preferred solitude. Some of us aren't unintelligent, you know, and everyone's crazy to meet you.'

'I can't believe that.'

'Of course they are. You're much too modest. You under-rate yourself. Are you always like that?'

'I've plenty to be modest about,' said Timothy.

'Ha! Ha! But you're wrong. I was reading one of your articles coming down in the train. Jolly good.'

'Oh, did you enjoy it?'

'We all laughed our heads off. Tell me, who are Damaris and Chloe?'

'That's a secret.'

'I said I didn't believe you had any girl-friends.'

'I conceal them.'

'I'm sure you're right to. They don't sound very intelligent.'

'I'm educating them.'

'Are they two tarts?'

'Not at all, they are most respectable.'

'I don't believe they know how lucky they are. They sound rather dumb to me.'

'To tell you the truth, they are.'

'What a shame, when you take so much trouble with them. They don't know when they're well off. Do you get all that stuff out of a book, or do you know it already?'

'Half and half, you know.'

'Do they ever read what you write?'

'Oh dear, no. At least, I hope not.'

'You do make fun of them at times. Would you call yourself a satirist?'

'I have been called a whimsical sentimentalist,' said Timothy.

'That's most unjust. The man who said that must have been a fool.'

'It was a woman, actually.'

'I thought so. It must be heartbreaking, writing for such half-wits. Are you always getting fan letters?'

'As a matter of fact, I do get a few.'

'I bet you do. Any from this district?'

'I don't think anyone reads me here, but you – and Miss Chadwick, but she's not one of my fans.'

'She ought to have her brains tested. You're thrown away on this place.'

In spite of himself Timothy began to wonder if he wasn't. They walked in silence for a time, under the trees that soared into the clear sky above the mist. The moon was behind them, and Timothy suddenly saw their shadows on the road, advancing side by side with an air of intimacy that made the night seem much less lonely. The contrast between their silhouettes intrigued him. Hers took the shape of a tea-cosy or a bee-hive, whereas his resembled a tomb-stone with an urn on it. Turning to her, he saw her flowing hair, blanched by the moonlight, bright against the black stuff of her coat. As at a signal, she too half turned; and the moonlight, leaving her hair in shadow, rested on her beautiful pensive profile, as downcast and withdrawn as that of a young nun. The sight pierced him with an unimaginable sweetness; in that moment she meant to him everything that her face so eloquently expressed. As if aware of the change in his thought of her she suddenly said, 'Was I very rude just now?'

'Rude?' he repeated. 'When?'

She half turned away.

'I had to give that awful young man a lesson, hadn't I? But perhaps—'

'He certainly deserved it,' Timothy said warmly.

'Oh, I don't know. Only he seemed so sure of himself, just because he was in uniform. He'd been bothering you, hadn't he?'

'He was rather monopolising me.'

'I could see that, and somehow it made me angry. They all did, sitting around with closed faces, trying to look like generals at a conference planning the next move. They're no use to anyone—'

'I wouldn't quite say that.'

'Well, compared to you they're not. Even as soldiers they're hopelessly out-of-date. A man I know in the War Office told me that it's old dug-outs like them, rotting with antiquated notions, that may lose the war for us. They can't adapt themselves to the new conditions. Well, I expect I made a fool of myself.'

'Oh no.'

'Sure? If I did, it was a good deal on your account. I saw red for a moment.'

'That was very generous of you.'

'No, it was just . . . impatience with stupidity, I suppose, and because you seemed so different to them. More distinguished, though you don't give yourself airs. Anyhow, you didn't think me too awful?'

'Of course not.'

'Because, darling – you don't mind me calling you darling, do you?'

'I like it,' said Timothy.

'Because I should hate myself if you did.'

Timothy's heart began to beat hard. His footsteps dragged and faltered. Into his mind leapt a score of questions that could not be uttered. He did not know where to look, and whatever his eyes lighted on seemed transformed and unrecognisable. The shape and meanings of a new life began to steal across his consciousness; layer upon layer of feeling that had been pressed down and dried and buried began to stir and throb.

'You didn't mind my saying that?' she said.

For answer he slipped his hand into hers, which did not fail to return its pressure, and so they walked for a moment, hand in hand, until a radiance stronger than the moonlight, diffused mistily on the trees in front, showed them their silhouettes lovingly interlaced. Involuntarily Timothy pulled Miss Cross on to the grass verge and dropped her hand. But when the car, which was travelling at a snail's pace, had gone by, he took her hand again, as if by right, and held it until the Green, with its fringe of Lombardy poplars, opened out before them. Not a gleam of light came from any of the houses; and he would not ask her which was hers, counting each one they came to as a condemned man might count the minutes to his death. At last she stopped.

'I shall see you again?' he murmured.

'Why not?'

He looked at the house, a small one with a window on each side of the door, and three above.

'When?'

'You'll be coming to the Fisherman's Arms?'

'Yes. When, tomorrow?'

'Tomorrow would be perfect, darling.'

'It seems such a long time to wait. You couldn't come on to my house now, and have a drink?'

'I'm afraid not. Frances will be wondering what's happened to me.'

Something has happened to me, Timothy thought. 'Tomorrow there'll be so many people,' he said.

'But I want you to meet them. You'll like Frances, she's a splendid girl, absolutely super.'

'I'm sure she is. But it's you I want to see.'

'You seem to be very fond of me all of a sudden, darling.'

'Well . . . yes . . . I . . . May I call you by your Christian name?'

'I was hoping you would.'

81

'What is it?'

'Vera.'

'Vera – what a lovely name. It means true – but of course, you knew that.'

'Yes, somebody told me once.' She looked sad and thoughtful.

'It suits you, you know. You're not afraid to speak your mind.'

'Meaning I can be damned rude?'

'Oh no – just outspoken. I like it – one knows where one is with you. With some people one is never sure.'

'Why do you say "one" and not "I"?'

'Oh, just a way of talking, I suppose.' How bracing her sincerity is, Timothy thought.

'It sounds as if you were trying to hide behind someone. Say "I know where I am with you, Vera." '

'I know where I am with you, Vera.'

'That's much better. I don't like talking to "one," but I do like talking to you.'

'I wish we didn't have to stop.'

'I'm afraid we must. Talk's rationed tonight, worse luck.'

'There's just one thing you haven't said,' said Timothy suddenly.

'What's that, darling? I thought I'd said all there was to say. What have I forgotten?'

'My name.'

'Timothy.'

'How did you know?'

'Everyone knows.'

'Say it again.'

'I don't know that I will. I'm not sure it suits you.'

'Oh Vera, try to think it does.'

'All right, Timothy.'

He took her hand again with some vague idea of saying goodbye; but the hand had a message of its own which would not wait, and his lips obeyed it long before Timothy had time to say them nay. Kissing her he forgot her; when it was over and memory came back, she was still there for him to kiss again.

'Verochka!'

She gave him an awakening smile. 'I didn't know you spoke Russian.'

'I don't – the word just slipped off my tongue.'

They both laughed and slowly drew away from each other with fond, wondering looks, as if the happiness they had given each other still lingered, a visible winged spirit in the air between them.

'Tomorrow, then,' he said, taking her hand again, but formally, as if it was her hand this time, not his.

'Tomorrow, darling?' she repeated.

'Tomorrow at the Fisherman's Arms.'

A soft cloud of distress settled on her face, blurring its outlines.

'But Timothy, darling, I shan't be there!' she wailed.

'Not there?' cried Timothy, stupefied.

'No, darling, I'm going away at teeniest cock-crow, and I don't know when I shall be back!'

Such was the subject-matter of Timothy's projected letter. He wanted to ease his spirit of its burden, to lessen his pain by telling it, to put the episode of Vera's defection in a context of other happenings, other issues, where it might interest his mind instead of tormenting his emotions. Externalise, objectify, he told himself; and he had gone quite a long way before he laid down his pen, feeling that there was no one to whom he could send, no one who would have patience to read, such a pointless, unedifying story. Esther might appreciate his account of social life at Upton; but her sympathies could not help being with the other side, the anti-boat faction, for by birth she belonged to it; also, she would feel that the whole episode, with the issues that it raised, was odd and peculiar and tainted with shirking. Had Timothy been defending his fishing-rights from the encroachments of a newcomer with a boat, she would certainly have backed him up. And well as he knew her, he couldn't tell her even the first thing about the parting at the gate. Tyro would sympathise with him there; but Tyro was soured about women, as about so much else; at the best they were indifferent, at the worst they were hostile, to the Moral Law. Tyro would not look at the case on its merits, as something that had happened to Timothy; he would universalise it, and make of Timothy's afternoon out the text for a sermon on the depravity of mankind, and Timothy, as the protagonist, would not wholly escape censure. Magda was his best choice; Magda had not the smallest prejudice against men who kissed and told; she expected it of them and said she liked cads; he could tell her what had happened at Miss Cross's gate down to the last detail – not that there was much to tell; too little perhaps; he might have to embroider it to make it seem worthwhile. But the party at the Rectory would bore her even more in a letter than it would have in life; all this bourgeois bunkum would remind her that society should be classless and amorous. On the other hand she sympathised with his longing for the boat – not because she understood what it meant to him, but because she felt it was withheld from him by the power of Privilege. Vera, too, had sympathised with him. . . .

As the thought of her pierced his defences his wound bled afresh. Forty-eight hours had passed since they had said good-bye. He did not very well remember what had happened; he had made a kind of scene, he had reproached her and asked her what she meant by – by what? Leaving him? But he had only spent an hour in her company and for some of that time he had – was it possible? – almost disliked her. Letting him kiss her? But that was his idea, not hers. Breaking her promise to meet him at the Fisherman's Arms? But she had never said she would – 'darling, I never *told* you I was going to be there!'

And trying to recall their conversation he couldn't remember that she ever had. In his eagerness to see her again, he must have put the words into her mouth. Yet, as step by step, and over again, he retraced their walk, he could not banish the impression that she had somehow cheated him. Was it for a joke, just to see how he looked under the smart of disappointment? If so, it was quite a good joke; Timothy, a joke-monger himself, laughed at it wanly. Or perhaps it was a joke on the part of Destiny, a scherzo of some Ironic Spirit? In that case he need not think himself a fool, or her a – well, there were several Anglo-Saxon as well as Greek words for sirens who led trusting middle-aged men up the garden path.

But rationalise her behaviour as he would, the pain returned. He simply couldn't bear the thought of going to the place where she should have been but was not, and be among faces which should have included hers, but did not. Yet strangely enough on the morrow, when night fell, he had taken advantage of the darkness to hang about the entrance to the Fisherman's Arms. Every now and then the door opened furtively to let a customer out or in, revealing, behind the black-out curtain draped across the doorway, a gleam of light and an elbow lifted in good cheer, but nothing else. Also, both today and yesterday, he had yielded to an impulse to walk as far as The Nook (daylight confirmed that this was the name of the house where Vera had stayed). It was something between a cottage and a villa, without the picturesqueness of the one or the smartness of the other; but it might have been Hampton Court from the way he stared at it.

All this could not be put on paper, but some of it could be told, and perhaps most easily told to Magda. Pushing away the piled up sheets he took a new one.

'Dearest Magda,' he wrote.
'Upton is absolute heaven at this moment – the finest winter landscape you ever saw. And though you might not believe it, there are some

quite pretty faces among the villagers, and some really presentable clothes – but more of that later. Do try to come here next weekend. I've so much to tell you. . . .'

The door opened. So strong was his evocation of Magda, so convinced was he that his wish to see her would bring her, that he half expected to see her small, distinguished head framed in the opening. But it was Effie, coming to draw the curtains.

'Oh Effie,' he exclaimed, almost happily. 'I'm hoping to have a friend here next Saturday – Mrs. Magda Vivien.'

'The Society Woman?'

Effie was evidently a student of the picture papers.

'You might call her that, but it doesn't really describe her, she's interested in society with a small "s," you know, and in . . . in . . . improving conditions for everyone.'

Effie did not answer for a moment; she seemed to wilt, corkscrew fashion; a spiral of distaste ran up her.

'Beattie says she can't manage if you have guests.'

Timothy felt dashed, but only for a moment.

'Oh, I'm sure she doesn't mean that,' he assured the shrinking housemaid.

Effie gazed at him blankly and drew a sharp breath between her teeth.

'I don't know what we shall do, I'm sure I don't,' she muttered lugubriously as she turned away.

Timothy finished his letter in a less sanguine frame of mind, but he might have saved himself the trouble of writing and Effie and Beatrice their dread of an expected visitor; for Magda replied, in a very kind letter, that the Curzon Street Cell held its meetings on Sundays and for the present she was unable to get away.

CHAPTER IX

'GOOD MORNING, SIR,' said Wimbush.

'Good morning,' said Timothy, who for the first time that year had come out without his overcoat. 'It really is a good morning. Isn't that a primrose?'

'You're right,' said Wimbush. 'You're quite right, if I may say so, sir. But that little chap'll be sorry he poked his head out so soon before many days are over.'

'Oh, don't say that, Wimbush.'

'Well, I always say the first to come is the first to go. You've been with us now a matter of four months, sir.'

'It seems longer.'

'Well, sir, to a gentleman like you the time do drag, I expect. We working chaps has hardly time to count the days.'

'I know you're always busy, but so am I, in a way.'

'That's what I always say, sir, when folk speak of you as a gentleman of leisure. Gentleman, yes, you'd have to go a long way to find a better gentleman, but leisure, no. Why there's more than one in the house don't work half as hard as you do, mentioning no names.'

The field of conjecture was not wide. Timothy knew whom he meant. With an effort he refrained from encouraging Wimbush's wish to gossip, but the gardener did not need encouragement.

'I've known a good many cooks,' he said, 'and to tell you the truth, sir, I don't go much on them. I wouldn't dirty my hands by touching one.' He spread out his large grimy paws which no amount of handling cooks could have made dirtier. Looking severely at Timothy, he added, 'and when I say touch, sir, I must ask you not to misunderstand me. I speak in a moral spirit. They're a race that are no good to us gardeners. In my opinion, the world would be a better place if there wasn't a single cook left in it.'

'That's rather sweeping, Wimbush.'

' 'Tisn't, sir, not if you knew them women as I do. There's not an ounce of good in any of them. Take the one here, for instance, that they call Beattie.'

Timothy's look forbade him to take Beattie, but the gardener ignored it and went on.

'She's a sour-faced old so-and-so if ever there was one. I can't do nothing to please her, not I can, and I wouldn't try if I could. And she can't keep her tongue off other people's business. She'd pry on her own mother going to the privy, she would, sir – no mistake. Now Effie here, she's a *good* girl.'

'Oh, you like Effie?' exclaimed Timothy, relieved at the turn the conversation had taken.

'When I say "like," sir,' repeated the gardener, reprovingly, 'I wouldn't quite say I *like* her, that wouldn't be right, would it, and her's a single girl and me a married man. No, I don't say I like her, but I can put up with her, oh yes.'

'I'm glad of that,' said Timothy, always pleased to envisage harmony in his domestic arrangements.

'She's a girl that I wouldn't mind bringing into the presence of Mrs. Wimbush, except the ladies, sir, they never can get on.' He winked a tawny, leonine eye at Timothy.

'I have noticed that some of the nicest women seem, well, a little on their guard with each other,' said Timothy.

'Bless you, sir, they're all the same.' Wimbush smiled complacently, squared his shoulders and expanded his broad chest. ' 'Tis only human nature after all, and where should we be if they weren't jealous? I mean, the race has to carry on.'

Timothy agreed that this was so, and asked Wimbush about his family.

'The eldest boy, sir, he'll soon be old enough to go. He have tried twice at the recruiting office already, and they've turned him down for being under age. They said they'd do something to him if he tried again, pretending he was older than he was. He's the kind we want, but now he's gardener's boy at Captain Sturrock's. They think the world of him, there.'

'I'm sure they do,' said Timothy warmly, though he felt something stiffen in him at the name of Captain Sturrock. 'And you, Wimbush, I hope you're comfortable here?'

'As happy as a sandboy, sir, except for the other one in the kitchen. But then none of us last for ever.'

'No,' said Timothy dubiously, and he was going to say something in Beatrice's defence when a piercing blast on a whistle cut him short. Instantly Wimbush put on a business-like air, rubbed his hands down his trousers as though clearing them for action, drew a long purposeful breath, apologised to Timothy for taking up his time, and murmuring something about 'weeds won't wait' strode on to the flower-bed. Timothy called after him. 'But wasn't that the signal for your elevenses?'

Wimbush put his hand to his ear.

'Your lunch!' shouted Timothy.

Still looking invincibly hard of hearing, Wimbush returned from the flower-bed.

'Sir?'

'I think that whistle was a call to the cook-house door.'

Comprehension dawned on Wimbush and he laughed loudly. 'You know more about us than we do ourselves, sir. Well, I suppose I must go, mustn't I?'

He saluted Timothy and with a slight swagger moved off towards the house. Timothy hesitated a moment and stumbled down the grass slope, crossed the lawn which was beginning to look greener, and followed the cinder path to the clump of sere and ever-rustling bamboos that guarded the boat-house. The magic of the place, its numinous exhalation, came out to meet him, like a breath of sanctity from a shrine. The door had a key which he always carried with him; not that anyone was likely to steal the boat, but Timothy enjoyed the formal, ceremonial entry. There, in the dim religious light, the prostrate god was lying, its outriggers, extended like arms, reaching almost from one side of the narrow dock to the other. Steps went down to it, disappearing into the water. The river had risen, perhaps the springs were breaking, and today the boat floated higher than he had ever seen it. Transoms of blue and orange light from the oblong stained glass borders of the windows fell across it – across the teak, the mahogany, the many different kinds of wood of which, so the boat-builder had assured him, it was made. The water chuckled softly and the boat nodded, as if in agreement. It had the air of waiting for something. For what? For sacrifice, perhaps. Yes, yes, the beckoning fair one seemed to say; come with me, cast off, lower away, forget whatever it is that holds you back. The lure of the invitation grew stronger and Timothy could feel it tugging at his will. Involuntarily he glanced behind him; the slender, blue-bladed sculls were hanging on the wall, ready to his hand. He lifted one from the rests on which it lay; holding it at the point of balance, he scarcely felt its weight. A thrill went through him, almost a shiver; worlds were his to conquer, continents to explore. Light, the light of day, shone through the crack between the two doors that opened on the channel to the river.

Carefully he replaced the scull, trembling as if he had been exposed to some great temptation, and felt his spirit brace itself to bear its accustomed load, heavy, disappointed, but at peace. A sour-sweet reek of the river, which he had not noticed before, seemed to invade the boat-house; dark, fat gobs of slime coated the water-line, and the walls, now that he could see them better, were furred with mould and mildew, growing in tufts like hair on an old man's chest. This new manifestation of the god disturbed him, and without looking back he tiptoed softly from the boat-house.

Outside, the gentle air and the warm spring sunshine wooed him to prolong his stroll. Following the inward-curving line of the shrubbery which looked from the house like an ostrich feather lying across the lawn, his footsteps again took him towards the river. At the end of the shrubbery the river came into view, but still divided from him by another stretch of grass, a tiny water-meadow, now flooded. Timothy stopped at the edge of this miniature inundation. The turf beneath looked pale and pearly; here and there an island, perhaps an ant-hill, stuck out, crowned with tall grasses in a ragged cluster. The flood water was motionless; beyond it, where the submerged bank showed almost black the river hurried by, purposeful, glinting, crinkling with a thousand dissolving smiles. Here came a branch, quite a big one. Some unseen obstacle near the edge becalmed it. Released, it slid away sideways, to be caught in a mimic whirlpool and spun round and round. Then after a fidgety progress, all stops and starts, it was drawn with seeming reluctance towards the middle. Gradually it responded to the power of the current and shedding all resistance, with no pace of its own, only the impulse of the water round it, it glided swiftly past him to vanish round the bend. Timothy felt glad for it, as if it had achieved a liberation. After it had gone by his mind followed it, swinging down the potent centre of the stream.

He waited for another branch to come along so that he could watch its progress; but none came, and he lifted his eyes to the pinkish rocks opposite, now aglow in the sunlight, and to the mountains beyond them, on whose ridges no longer lay the creamy, mist-laden covering of snow, that, while it lasted, had effaced the skyline and brought heaven and earth together.

Beatrice was sitting at the kitchen table. Fragments of type-written paper, some flat, some curled like shavings, were spread out in front of her, as tantalising as the pieces of a jig-saw puzzle. As she was fitting them together (an easy task, for the letter had not been effectively torn up) she said:

'I shouldn't have done it, of course, only I saw the word "immoral" and then I knew I ought to. Look, here it is again, "immorality," and here again, "morality," but that's just the same, isn't it? People ought not to write such letters, nor they ought, there ought to be a law against it, and there is, too. And against receiving them as well, I daresay, for the receiver is just as bad as the other one in the eyes of the law. "Offence," they call it. I always thought Mr. Casson was up to no good, taking us for motor-drives and all that. And if I read this it may tell us what he *is* up to, and put us on our guard. I'm doing it for your sake, really, Effie. I can look after myself.'

Effie came back from putting a kettle on the kitchen range. 'I'm not saying no, Beattie, though I think you're wasting your time. If it's anyone it's that Miss Cross, but she's gone now and a good job, too. Why, dozens of people saw them in the lane together. And he had his arm right round her, too. I don't know how he could.'

'That's just what I'm saying. If he'll do it with one he'll do it with another, just you wait, my girl. Now there's a bit here. "Morality" (but it's the same thing really, you can't have one without the other) "like civilisation and like art and like everything worth-while, is middle class in origin, and will perish, is perishing, with the middle classes. The lower classes, some of them, have moral reactions, they know what to say when a man runs away with another man's wife; but they have no moral sense, I mean they wouldn't know when a man was justified in doing it and when he wasn't. The upper classes" – it breaks off there, I must find the next bit. It's a blessing he only writes on one side of the paper. But just think of it, Effie! What did I tell you? He says a man might be doing right to run off with another man's wife. Who's he thinking of, I'd like to know? Miss Cross, I shouldn't wonder.'

'Miss Cross isn't married, silly.'

'She may be, for all you know. And lower classes! I'd like to give him lower classes. Who does he think he is, anyway? Or Mr. Casson, either? A foreigner that nobody knows anything about. Oh here's the next bit. It isn't very interesting. He just says the upper classes are a law unto themselves.'

'I don't know why you want to read the letter at all. It's only two people writing to each other.'

'Don't you want to hear any more?'

'Only if it's a bit exciting.'

'Oh, but listen. "The woman you told me about sounds like a" – wait a moment – "bitch to me." '

'Bitch to me?'

'You heard what I said.'

Beatrice and Effie exchanged horrified glances.

'There you are, you see! He says bitch. That's the sort of man he is.'

'Which of them?'

'Well, both. Now I'm going on. "And I think you'd do much better to stick to your" – I can't pronounce these names – "Damn Arris and Coaly." '

'Who on earth are they? His girl-friends, I suppose. Oh Beattie, do dry up, the kettle's nearly on the boil.'

'Listen to this bit. "No doubt, if a seduction is what you want, either of these nymphs would only be too glad to oblige, in the convenient shelter of one of the abbeys or castles which you have been describing so eloquently in your recent articles." '

There was a pause, and a silence broken only by the singing of the kettle.

'Effie, he *does* mean us! We must give in our notice today.'

'I shouldn't pay any attention. I shouldn't lower myself. Whoever wrote that letter is potty. Who is it? I bet it's a woman.'

Beatrice searched among the pieces.

'I can't find a name anywhere. Oh, here's something. "It makes me so angry to think you are being prevented from using your boat by the . . . the embattled prejudice and ignorance of the countryside. It's that sort of thing that makes one despair of human nature. I've no objection to Colonels or even Majors as such: it's their selfishness I mind. Money doesn't matter, it's the morals of the people who have it. They know how they ought to behave, for they have the Law and the Prophets; but they won't listen, they do what they know to be wrong, as the house-agent did, when he told you you could use the boat, knowing full well you couldn't. This petty cheating is everywhere and it makes me sick." He seems to be preaching here, doesn't he, Effie? It must be a man.'

'If so, he sounds potty.'

Beatrice rummaged among the fragments.

'What a nuisance, I seem to be getting the same bit over and over again. Oh no, it isn't, it just begins the same. "It makes me so angry—"

'He's always angry, isn't he?' said Effie languidly. 'He ought to use something sticky to keep his hair on.' She tittered, and Beatrice joined in, but perfunctorily, for she wanted to keep the stage. ' "It makes me so angry the way the Government" – we don't want to hear about the

Government, do we? We hear too much about it on the wireless. Here's another bit. "The State is the great enemy. Not the Germans, not the Nazis, but the State in every country, especially in our own. The State is an immoral institution, designed to encourage and to perpetuate immorality. If an individual acted as the States does, he would be hanged before nightfall. The State is a criminal, and uses its sovereignty to make criminals of all its members." He didn't ought to say that, did he, it's treachery, he could be shot for saying that.'

'Oh, I don't suppose they'd bother with him,' said Effie indifferently. 'There, the kettle's beginning to bubble – we must blow the whistle.'

'What, for him? He can starve for all I care.'

Nonchalant but purposeful, Effie sidled up to a nail in the wall, from which hung various keys, and, attached to an exciting white lanyard, the associative effect of which was so strong that it seemed to turn the kitchen into a police station, an authentic, silver-bright police-man's whistle. Effie opened the door and blew a long, earsplitting blast. Beatrice took no notice except to raise her shoulders. Her hands were moving about the table with gathering speed, like a patience player's who sees the game at last coming out.

'I've got it,' she cried triumphantly, 'all the last four pages, though from the way he ends up, I don't think you could tell if he's a man.'

Four closely-typed sheets of foolscap lay before her, veined and marbled. They did not lie quite flat, so she ran the rolling pin over them before she began to read.

'Human nature has now reached a new low level and it will never be any better until it repents in a proper, old-fashioned way, in sackcloth and ashes. But it won't; in war the greatest devil is the greatest hero; the mob idolises suffering for its own sake, and doesn't care a rap where it may be leading. Before the last war my faith in humanity was just as strong as yours, and I used to proclaim it, which was more than you did; then it was shaken, now it is dead. We do know about the concentration camps; we don't know what the nations have got up their sleeves in the way of bombs and gas: but merely to have thought of using such things puts them, for me, outside the pale. If I'd committed a murder and been let off, you'd have said "Poor old Tyro, it was all a mistake, he didn't mean it," and have gone on asking me to tea. But if I'd done it again even you would have said "Poor Tyro, he's gone a bit too far this time. I'm afraid I must cross him off my visiting-list." That's how I feel about the H.R. after this second orgy of mass-murder. How can you regard a race of creatures as even remotely well-meaning, whose strongest impulse is to kill each other? Of all the thousands of created animals

92

there are only half a dozen, among whom we take pride of place, who kill their own species except from motives of sex. And the rest only kill from hunger or in self-defence – unless, like dogs, they have been corrupted by association with us. Yet we pretend to be shocked by Nature, and call it red in tooth and claw. What humbug!

'It's the humbug I mind more than anything. Apologists of the H.R. call it self-deception, a kinder term, but it convicts them of moral idiocy. If I told you I smoked in order to benefit the Imperial Tobacco Company you wouldn't believe me; nor should I believe you if you told me you dropped a bomb on a town full of women and children in order to improve their standard of values. And if there's one thing I hate, it's the kind of mysticism that pretends that one purges one's spirit by doing something one knows to be wrong, and that criminals are somehow especially pleasing to God because, having disobeyed His every law, they can plead no virtue of their own (which might look like spiritual pride) but must throw themselves utterly on his mercy. Salvation by degradation. Nothing in my hand I bring. We cannot plead our own merits, of course; but it is quite another thing to bring hands dripping with blood, as though God had no attribute except forgiveness, and would somehow be offended by the spectacle of virtue in human behaviour, since it would give Him less opportunity to exercise the quality of mercy.'

A shadow crossed the window, but Beatrice did not notice it, so absorbed was she by the effort of reading; and Effie, though she was only half listening to the words, was too much fascinated by the sound of Beatrice's voice, and the B.B.C. intonations which kept creeping into it, to see the shape go by the window, or hear the click of the lifted latch as Wimbush entered the kitchen.

'But we do take pride in our sufferings, and when we rejoice in our victories (if we get them) we shall equally be rejoicing in the sufferings of others, unless we can persuade ourselves that *our* victories entail no suffering to the vanquished, as we are quite capable of doing. We praise a man for dying for his country; we don't praise him for killing for it, though it would be more logical to do so, since a soldier's first duty is to take life, not lose it.

'And what hypocrisy, in this age of conscription, to talk of giving one's life for one's country. One might just as well talk of giving one's money to the Tax Collector. Both are taken from us by compulsion, in the name of the State; and the descendants of Hampden – who refused the King's demand for ship money because he did not happen to live by the sea, and resented the billeting of soldiers – meekly submit to exactions ten times greater than those for which Charles I lost his head. They thought themselves so clever for showing the sovereigns of Europe that a King's neck had a bend in it. Little did they dream, poor boobs, that they were exchanging one frail spinal column, which could so easily be severed, for the bull necks of millions of electors whose thick heads no amount of headsmen could cut off, more's the pity. We are all our own tyrants now.

'The modern world has legalised bloodshed and practised it on a scale never imagined before, all the while proclaiming from its pulpits and soap-boxes that God is Love. What blasphemy! And how lonely it makes one, to have a moral standard even a shade higher than one's fellows! I watch them sitting in the tram that takes me to work, their noses buried in the latest murder – yes, Timothy, even in this war in which millions may lose their lives, a murder is still front-page news – and I thank God I am not as they are, who have no thought, no existence beyond their blood-lust. Can you explain it, this itch to kill, to see the bright blood flowing, or not even to see it, to hear of it at second or third hand, to be able to gloat over it however remotely, and sniff its odour through the printer's ink?

'No, you can't, because you're not made that way, and if ever I quarrel with you, which Heaven forbid, it will be because you are a humanist, as I once was, and believe that man is his own moral criterion, and there is no appeal from what man does to a higher tribunal, a standard of transcendental morality. A little patience, a little forbearance, a little understanding, a little laughter, *gentle* laughter (forgive me Timothy) and all will be well. I seem to hear you say that, and it makes me angry. Patience has had her perfect work; forgiveness has been unto seventy-times seven; forbearance has died of constipation; laughter has split its sides; but all is *not* well, and the human race still yearns for homicide. Morality was made for man (you were once reported as saying) not man for morality. Forgive me, my dear friend, but that is dangerous nonsense. What is man without morals? A wolf, we say, insulting a noble animal. A devil? No, for devils have no experience of God. A human being without morals is a thing that wants a name, a curse too great for thought to conceive or words to utter. But what is morality without man? Rank upon rank, tier upon tier the blameless vegetation rises, a sampler of infinite majesty worked by a master-hand; and on every terrace the animals – when not engaged in little tiffs or personal encounters, involving no one but themselves – a display of heraldic valour lending quaintness to the scene – move or sleep in the nobility of their unspoilt natures, not desiring more blood than will last them from one meal to the next, or ensure them a faithful wife and healthy children. The sampler does not depict a Golden Age; far from it. Earth has scenes far lovelier than these terraces, animals far kinder than the round-eyed lions and whiskered leopards that frolic on them, nobler trees, brighter flowers. Why then does it seem a paradise? Because natural laws have limited malevolence; because blood-letting has its off-seasons, like any other activity: because Man is not there.

'But look! Strain your eyes! Surely behind that feather-tufted palm-tree lurks a sportsman with a rifle? In the heart of that hedgehog-pointing shrub is there not a soldier with his finger on the trigger of a Bren gun? Are there not men with knives and tomahawks lining the rushes where the stream goes by? Yes, and where they wash their excremental fingers, fouled by the viscera of the victims, the river runs with blood.

'Excuse this outburst, but my insteps ache when I see the harm the human race has done and is doing and will do, and all the while snivelling about its sufferings as if it had anyone to blame except itself. And even with you, dear Timothy, I could pick a quarrel for you refuse to see your neighbours as they are – a parcel of purse-proud provincial nonentities, who for some inexplicable reason have warned you off their precious river. You say you would like them if you could get to know them; believe me, you wouldn't, they would bore you to tears, and horrify you with their various forms of blood-lust. How one mouths and maunders, talking of the brutes; the one word that would annihilate them for ever escapes one, and one is left, a middle-aged cosmopolitan with a living to earn, snarling at their heels.

'I should not write to you like this unless I was absolutely devoted to you and so thankful you had not mixed yourself with this silly bloody business that Europe is plunging into. Keep yourself to yourself, my dear Timothy; as your excellent servants seem determined you shall. How wise they are to forbid you to have guests – though in spite of that I should try to come, for I adore giving trouble. I've studied the Bradshaw, but do you know by the time I've changed at Birkenhead and Chester and Birmingham and Gloucester, and got on to the one-class-only train to Swirrelsford and motored eight miles to Upton, I should only have ten minutes to embrace you and come back. Shall we ever meet again? I doubt it.

Love and warnings from

Yours affectionately,

Tyro.'

Breathless, Beatrice paused. She took the steel pince-nez off the bridge of her powerful nose and laid them on the table.

'Do you know what I think?' she said.

'I didn't know you did think.' At the sound of Wimbush's voice both the women turned round in a flash. Beatrice was the first to speak.

'Well, of all the nosy—!'

'Oh, I'm nosy, am I?' said Wimbush moving ponderously into the room and dwarfing everything in it. 'And what are you, if I may ask?'

But Beatrice was not to be intimidated.

'Can't I read a letter from my friend without an outdoor servant in his dirty boots glueing his ear to the keyhole?'

'You whistled for me, and I come in ordinary-like,' said Wimbush mildly, 'only you didn't hear, you was too busy reading Mr. Cassons's letter.'

'I like that,' stormed Beatrice. ' 'Twasn't his letter, was it, Effie?'

'Beattie has a friend who writes like that sometimes,' said Effie. 'We think he's potty.'

'Then why's it all tore up?' inquired Wimbush. 'And why does he call her Timothy? She's not a man, is she?'

Effie sniggered.

'That's because he's potty. Well, we got a laugh.' Her voice invited Wimbush to let the matter drop, and taking the hint, he said to Beatrice, 'You do have some funny people writing to you, I must say.'

Beatrice relaxed somewhat.

'Yes, I tore the letter up because I didn't think anyone should see it. He used a rude word.'

'Two for the matter of that,' remarked Wimbush.

'Oh, which was the other one?' exclaimed Effie, and when Wimbush didn't answer she said languidly, 'Of course I'm broadminded but I don't like bitch said to a dog.'

'No,' said Wimbush. 'Like that it sounds funny, and he shouldn't have said it to Beattie, either.'

Beatrice was indignant.

'He didn't say it to me. He said it of someone – well, Mr. Casson could tell you who.'

'What's Mr. Casson got to do with it?' asked Wimbush innocently.

'Nothing, really, only a man like that knows that kind of woman.'

'I expect your friend has only heard about them,' said Wimbush.

'I tell him to be careful what he writes,' said Beatrice, 'that's why I tear his letters up. He's an educated man of course, and that accounts for a great deal.'

'They're always the worst,' said Wimbush, winking at Effie. 'He sounds a bit of a Conchie to me.'

'I should say so!' exclaimed Beatrice. 'I was only passing the remark to Effie just before you come creeping in that people like that oughtn't to be allowed out.'

'I thought he was a friend of yours,' remarked Wimbush.

Beatrice tried to cover her mistake.

'Well, so he is, in a manner of speaking, but that don't mean I hold with what he says. Here, take your tea for goodness' sake. You'll be saying I let it get cold next.'

The cup looked white and frail in Wimbush's large brown fist, and his moustache dredged the red-brown liquid like a fishing net. To Effie, the tea, the eyes and the moustache all looked the same colour. Raising his head he said, 'Don't think I'm crabbing your literary friend, Beattie, but I don't feel that way about war. When I was a youngster in the last war you couldn't hold me back, and that went for most of the chaps round here. Nor you can't hold back my eldest youngster, either. 'Tis in the blood, you can't stop it. War isn't a matter of wanting to kill people, like he says.'

'He ought to be shot,' said Beattie. 'I was only saying so to Effie.'

'Of course I wouldn't say such a thing of your friend, Beattie,' said Wimbush rather pompously. 'And everyone must have their views. Mr. Casson now, he's a literary gentleman by all accounts, I wonder what he'd say to that letter.'

Beatrice struggled with herself and then said, 'Some of it's about him, as a matter of fact.'

'You don't say so! Well, personally I never hear nothing that wasn't meant for me, but perhaps he ought to be told.'

Beatrice's eyes opened in alarm.

'You wouldn't go and tell him? It might be illegal.'

'Of course not,' Wimbush soothed her. 'Don't get all upset. When him and I talk, we talk about other things.'

'What do you talk about, Mr. Wimbush?' asked Effie, pertly.

Wimbush turned right round to her, so that he seemed to address her with his whole broad person.

'Well, your ears might have burnt this morning.'

'You didn't talk about me?' cried Effie, giving a little scream.

'Oh no, we only said what a nice girl you were.'

Beatrice got up from the table where they had been sitting and began to move noisily about the room.

'What did you say?' asked Effie.

'Who's being nosy now? Do you think we mentioned the colour of your eyes?'

97

Effie pouted.

'He's not a bad old thing. But they don't like him in the village, do they? The milkman was only saying to me yesterday, "Your boss don't seem to have many friends here."'

'That's all he knows. A college-trained gentleman like Mr. Casson doesn't go to the local like you or me.'

'Oh Mr. Wimbush you are a tease. Fancy seeing me at the local. Why I shouldn't know what to do.'

'You'd be a nice girl anywhere.'

'I'm glad your wife can't hear you.'

The gardener stiffened slightly.

'Mrs. Wimbush wouldn't be interested, not within four square walls. She knows as well as I do,' he added cryptically. 'Besides, Beattie's about.'

'Yes, and wishes she wasn't,' said Beatrice gruffly from the grate. 'You should keep the other side of the door, that's your place. I suppose the garden minds itself while you sit talking here.'

'Do the potatoes boil any quicker because you're looking at them? They might, you look that hot and cross, doesn't she, Effie? She looks real red.'

'Oh that's nothing unusual,' said Effie, lightly. 'She often looks that way.' She meant to imply that Beatrice's moods were her own concern and not likely to be affected by anything that Wimbush might say; but Beatrice pushed past her without looking, and a moment later they heard the back door slam.

Wimbush moved his chair nearer to Effie's. Leaning forward he slid his arm along the table until his hand and lifted fore-finger were only a few inches from her.

'One place is as good as another, I say.'

Effie watched him fascinated, and his earthy, out-of-door smell, musty with tobacco and other less definable odours, enveloped her stiflingly, for she had a delicacy of perception amounting to hyperæsthesia.

'I don't know what you mean,' she said, but her body knew, and her breath came with difficulty. 'It couldn't be here.'

'Why not?' said Wimbush. His teeth showed under the boskage of his moustache and his eyes seemed to tilt still further inwards. 'You wouldn't say no, would you?'

His voice that had grated harshly now cajoled her, so that the fences she was putting up against him toppled over. No longer could she translate the emotions that held her into terms of yes and no; her spirit bent like a weed in the current.

Another bang announced the return of Beatrice.

'You wouldn't mind, Beattie, would you?' Wimbush asked of Beatrice's back.

'What wouldn't I mind?' She did not turn round.

'If I gave Effie here a kiss.'

'Yes, I should,' said Beatrice shortly.

'Not if it was just in fun, under the mistletoe? I'll kiss you, too, if you like.'

'Now get on, be off,' said Beatrice, angry, but keeping her head. 'Effie's got her work to do, and so have I.'

'Oh, I never heard you talk of work before,' said Wimbush pretending to be shocked. 'Besides, a kiss doesn't take that long. 'Tisn't like a mustard plaster.'

Effie looked from one to the other as if her fate was being decided. Her face followed every movement of her feelings, whereas Beatrice's changed but little. She knew Wimbush wanted to make her angry and she felt her anger rising; but love lent cunning and sublety beyond the reach of her normal mind. So she said as carelessly as she could, 'Oh, all right, but you must kiss me first.'

Wimbush hadn't expected her to say that; he was taken aback; the initiative left him, and he got awkwardly to his feet with his indecision written on his face. Beatrice stepped up to him as bold as brass, a moving bastion, swelling with defensive contours. His hesitation was momentary, but it was fatal. Just as the second of two smacking kisses fell on Beatrice's firm cheek the door opened and Mrs. Burnett, the charwoman, came in.

'Good gracious,' she said. 'Is this a love scene?'

A small, active-looking woman, with quick eyes and reddish-golden hair, she switched her gaze with bird-like jerks from face to face.

'We were having a sort of bet,' growled Wimbush, heavily.

'A bet – I like that,' cried Beatrice. 'He asked to kiss us both.' She saw the dull red precursor of a blush stealing painfully into Wimbush's unaccustomed cheek, and looked her triumph.

' 'Twas only a joke,' he mumbled. 'Mrs. Burnett knows me better than that.'

Mrs. Burnett, a native Uptonian, was inclined to side with Wimbush; but though he was well-liked in the village, his swagger had always been a subject of comment and criticism, and she couldn't resist the fun of seeing him mortified. There he stood, stalwart but helpless and crest-fallen, with his hands hanging down and his face, like the harvest moon, looking larger than its normal size; while around him surged waves of feminine scrutiny, three pairs of eyes, sharp, amused and critical, boring into the secret places of his male complacency.

'He ought to kiss Effie and me, too, shouldn't he?' remarked Mrs. Burnett.

'Don't say that, you'll make him shy,' Beatrice taunted him. 'He's forgotten how.'

Wimbush stood stock still, trying to think of a way of escaping from his predicament with dignity.

'We know which of us he loves now, don't we?' Mrs. Burnett's voice was light and ironical. 'He won't look at you and me, Effie, not while Beattie's there.'

'I can't think what's come over him,' crowed Beatrice. 'He was all agog a moment ago. Now he just hangs like an icicle.'

'Perhaps once was enough,' said Wimbush, 'and there's no more where that came from.' But he put no spirit into the retort.

'Come along, Mrs. Burnett,' said Beatrice. Her triumph had made her jovial; she looked and felt quite unlike herself. 'A good cup of tea's better than all his kisses. I've tried, and I know which I'd rather have, any day.'

She pursed her lips at him and raised her eyebrows and nodded once or twice to make her meaning clear. Wimbush had accepted his defeat, and was turning to go when suddenly Effie said, 'I'll kiss him.'

There was passion in her face, surprise and delight in his, and their kiss was a real kiss that made its quality felt in every corner of the room. If a gun had gone off the change of atmosphere couldn't have been more startling and complete. For a second afterwards Wimbush held Effie's hand, almost as though they were actors taking a curtain call. She looked oblivious of her surroundings, he triumphantly aware of his.

'Well, I never!' explained Mrs. Burnett. 'There's no telling what women will do, is there, Beatrice? Now I'm the next.'

But Beatrice did not answer her. The anger that had receded from the shores of her mind rolled back in an overwhelming tide. 'Get away!' she shouted. 'Clear out of my kitchen, all of you! Yes, and you, too!' she added, pointing at Effie as though unable to speak her name. 'You're the worst, leading him on!'

The moment she was alone she burst into tears.

CHAPTER X

THE wonderful summer of 1940 started in May; in the first week it was hot enough to bathe. Still anxious not to offend the deities of the river, Timothy made discreet inquiries of Wimbush as to whether bathing might be considered an infringement of the fishing-rights. He fancied that as far as the middle the river belonged to him; but a stroke or two might easily take him into forbidden waters, to find, perhaps, impending over him an irate Colonel in full fishing panoply who might even hook him with a well-directed cast. . . . For Timothy was still ignorant of the niceties of fly-fishing. Indeed, there was no one to teach him; as a social unit in Upton, he seemed to have lost rather than gained ground since the abortive party at the Rectory.

A second letter to Mrs. Lampard had met with the same fate as the first, and he felt like a spider in a wine-glass, unable to make headway on the hard slippery surface, but condemned to go on trying. It never occurred to him that in the end he might fail to get his way; he felt that gradually his will was dissolving the bulwarks raised against it, and some day when he was least expecting it the permit would turn up. It was like being elected to a club; you waited months, years maybe, and then one morning the forces of resistance crumbled and in you walked. All the more did it behove him, meanwhile, to behave in a circumspect manner, so that the rumour of his blameless, useful life, percolating through hall and cottage, would the more quickly bring him his reward.

Wimbush replied indignantly that of course Timothy could bathe; it would do the fish good to stir them up a bit, they got that fat and sluggish lying there among the weeds. Mention of Timothy's riverine scruples and uncertainties always made Wimbush angry; but Timothy could get no practical advice, still less any moral ruling out of him. He would declare with equal vehemence that Timothy was the master here and could do what he liked; or that the river was free for all; or that it was a damned shame that it was not; or that the fishermen would welcome any move that Timothy might make; or that they would do their utmost to hinder him, but what the hell did it matter? Obscurely he seemed to feel that his being in a temper somehow clarified the situation and made everything all right for Timothy, and Timothy found these gusts of temper on his behalf very comforting.

But his mind was not quite at rest, and one morning, after first making sure of a specially delicious bathe, he sauntered back over the fragrant, sun-dried sward, which held all the freshness of spring and all the heat of summer. The twilight that reigned in the heart of the house, vowed to half-mourning as a result of the permanent black-out of the hall window and the fanlight, had depressed Timothy during the winter months. But today it was grateful to his eyes, almost blinded by the glare on the terrace, and the cool, black and white pavement seemed made for such a day as this.

Feeling quite equal to a talk with Miss Chadwick, he dialled her number.

'Oh yes, Mr. Casson, is there anything I can do for you?'

'Well, there was just a question I wanted to ask you.'

'Not about the boat, I hope?'

'Oh no, I mean, not exactly. You haven't heard anything about it, by any chance?'

'No, and I'm afraid you'll find the mayfly rather a formidable competitor.'

Timothy sighed.

'You're still doing your best for me?'

'Naturally, but I don't get much encouragement. There is a slight feeling . . .' Miss Chadwick broke off.

'Yes?' prompted Timothy.

'I hardly know how to put it. . . . You have seen this morning's paper, of course?'

'I just glanced at it,' said Timothy guiltily.

'I'm afraid it merits more than a glance. Our friends here are very much alive to the danger, Mr. Casson.'

'Yes, indeed,' muttered Timothy.

'Well, forgive me for reminding you. . . . But you wanted to ask me something?'

Shame quickly turns to annoyance, and Timothy suddenly felt annoyed.

'Yes,' he said defiantly. 'In the prospectus of the house, you may remember, Miss Chadwick, among the inducements held out, were boating and bathing on the river Swirrel. I have refrained from using my boat, out of consideration for the feelings of my neighbours. Do you suppose I ought to refrain from bathing, too?'

After a pause, Miss Chadwick said, 'You sound as if you thought us unreasonable, Mr. Casson.'

'Not you, Miss Chadwick,' said Timothy reassuringly. He still found great difficulty in making a nakedly hostile remark to anyone. 'But as to the others . . . well . . .'

'Why do you ask me, if you have already made up your mind?'

'I haven't, that is why I wanted your opinion.'

'Wouldn't it be simpler to ask, for instance, Colonel Harbord?'

'You see, I don't know him.'

'I remember, you told me. What a pity that your boat has cut you off from so many interesting friendships. But perhaps, after all, he would think the question frivolous.'

'Are fishermen very serious-minded men, in your experience?'

'Surely you are aware of the difference between fishing and bathing?'

'Aren't they both water-sports?'

'Juliana Berners and Izaak Walton would not have thought so.'

Glad to be able to confront Miss Chadwick on the field of culture, Timothy said, 'Juliana Berners wrote about angling, not fly-fishing. She was a lady of the court and . . .'

'Precisely. The two pastimes belong to very different worlds.'

'Isn't that rather a snobbish distinction?'

'Good heavens, Mr. Casson, you're not a Communist, I hope? Somebody was asking me only yesterday. I said you were more probably a Fascist.'

'It was kind of you to defend me.'

'Not at all. They were puzzled, I think, by seeing you with your servants somewhere in the neighbourhood of Dangerfield aerodrome.'

'Oh yes, we were looking at the rather interesting barrows.'

'They must be intelligent girls. How lucky you are to have them. Servants are a bachelor's prerogative, nowadays. Weren't you a little near to the camp, perhaps?'

'Nobody challenged us.'

'All the same, I believe there were inquiries. War-time isn't like peacetime. You should keep to the beaten track.'

'At the cost of boring my readers?' asked Timothy pertly.

'I'm only telling you as a friend that archæological investigations in the neighbourhood of military areas are liable to be misunderstood. You don't want to get the girls into trouble, do you?'

'I beg your pardon, Miss Chadwick?'

'I mean, you don't want to get them talked about.'

'I still don't quite understand you.'

'Then I must leave it to your mature reflections. We live in a small community, you must remember that. Personally I never pay the smallest attention to gossip, and we all enjoy your articles so much.'

'Thank you, Miss Chadwick.' Timothy was immediately mollified.

'By the way,' said Miss Chadwick in a slightly different tone. 'I'm sorry to hear about your domestic difficulties.'

'Oh, what . . .?'

'Naturally you wouldn't want to discuss them. Wimbush is an excellent gardener, but of course he hasn't got an easy temper.'

'I get on very well with him,' said Timothy, mystified.

'Perhaps you spoil him a little. You raised his wages, I believe?'

'I told him not to tell anyone,' said Timothy.

'You've a lot to learn about village life, Mr. Casson. You couldn't expect her not to be jealous.'

'Oh, who?'

The latch clicked. Timothy turned round. Effie was standing in the doorway. Timothy signalled to her with his eyebrows, but she held her ground.

'The relationship between cook and gardener is traditionally difficult. It will all blow over, if you're patient.'

Miss Chadwick's enunciation was remarkably clear, and it seemed to Timothy that everything she said must be distinctly audible to Effie, who had closed the door behind her and was standing with drooping eyelids in a pose that suggested unbearable weariness combined with a stern sense of duty. He could think of nothing to say.

'I'm not sure it pays to try to make friends with one's servants,' Miss Chadwick went on. 'Their outlook is so very different from ours. Kindness is so often construed as weakness or worse, and familiarity is always a mistake. Hullo?'

'Yes, I'm here,' admitted Timothy.

'I was afraid we had been cut off. Your parlourmaid seems a very superior girl, but she looks rather delicate. Is there any family history of tuberculosis?'

'I never heard of any,' said Timothy.

'It might be worth while to make inquiries. Motoring, of course, doesn't suit everyone. It would be a thousand pities to let your kind intentions be the cause of injuring her health.'

Timothy glanced at Effie's drooping figure and remained tongue-tied.

'Hullo? Again I thought we were cut off. It's lucky your cook takes such good care of her, but even the warmest friendship can't take the place of medical advice. She wouldn't resent you taking her to a doctor, would she? Sometimes they cannot see what is best for them. Dr. Melhuish is a very good man.'

'I'll remember what you say, Miss Chadwick.'

'And I shouldn't worry about Wimbush. Those things blow over. But it must be awkward if they're not on speaking terms.'

'To tell you the truth, I didn't know they weren't.'

'How strange! I shall ask people not to talk about it, though, to be sure, quarrels between servants are no reflection on the master of the house. But I'm sorry, we were always such a happy household in my brother's day.'

Timothy made suitable noises, and having inveigled Miss Chadwick into saying goodbye, he put down the receiver and apologised to Effie.

'Did you want me for something important?'

'It's all right now, sir,' said Effie faintly, 'but he gave me quite a turn.'

'I am sorry, Effie, you do look rather pale.'

'Well, he walked right in, sir. I hadn't expected that. I don't expect to see them in the house. It isn't very nice.'

'No, I'm sure. Who is he?' asked Timothy getting up and involuntarily looking round for a weapon.

'He may have gone now, sir, you were so long talking to the telephone. He said he was in a hurry. And of course I didn't like what Miss Chadwick said. It frightened me. She didn't ought to have spoken like that, she gave me a turn. And her knowing so much about me and Beattie. It doesn't seem right.'

'No, well, we'll talk about that later. Now who is it who's waiting to see me?'

'I left him in the hall,' faltered Effie. 'But he may be anywhere now. I believe they can go anywhere they like. Nothing's private. Oh, I do hope it isn't one of us.'

Thoroughly alarmed, Timothy went from the brightness of the telephone-room into the cool twilight of the hall. A helmet, looking enormous in the gloom, stood on the table, and sitting beside it on a hard hall chair, as though keeping watch over it, was a policeman. The policeman rose to his feet, slowly, as if by standing he committed himself to a new line of behaviour, and said:

'Beg pardon, sir, but I called to see you about a small matter.'

Timothy hoped he didn't look as guilty as he felt. 'Oh yes,' he said. 'Can I help you in any way?'

'Well, it's like this, sir. In your premises you have, I understand, a shed.'

Timothy felt extremely reluctant to admit that this was so, but didn't think it wise to deny it.

'That being the case,' went on the policeman, who was tall and fair and young, 'are you of the opinion that the shed is one in which a car could be accommodated?'

Trying to see a catch in this, Timothy admitted that a small car might be.

'Such a car as Mr. Edgell Purbright's, for instance?' said the policeman with a slight twinkle in his eye.

Clearly the policeman was omniscient.

'Yes,' said Timothy, 'he used to it keep there.' Now for the summons, or arrest, or whatever it was.

'Well, sir,' said the policeman, with the air of a commander who having cleared the ground now advances to the attack, 'in view of what you have just stated, would you allow a car to stand in the aforesaid shed?'

Timothy was so overwhelmed with relief that he could have embraced the policeman.

'Of course, my dear fellow!' he exclaimed. 'I should be only too delighted.'

But the policeman was not to be put out of his stride.

'The car would be an eight horse-power saloon job, with carmine red body, and black wings. It is very nicely upholstered in a red leatherette. I may add that it is altogether a lovely-looking little outfit.'

'I congratulate you,' said Timothy. 'Is the car yours?'

'It has only done 6,000 miles,' the policeman went on.

'Think of that!'

'It cruises comfortably at forty-five.'

'What a marvellous car! Did you say it was yours?'

'It gets away as good as any high-powered American make.'

'I can hardly wait to see it,' said Timothy.

'And the price was only a hundred and fourteen pounds.'

'What!' exclaimed Timothy. 'I thought you were going to say a thousand.'

'A hundred and fourteen it was,' the policeman said, 'I suppose in consideration for my uniform.'

'So it does belong to you!' exclaimed Timothy.

For the first time the policeman looked slightly put out, as if Timothy had unfairly forestalled him. He had clearly timed this disclosure for a later stage in the conversation. But he said good-humouredly, 'Since you ask me, it does.'

'How splendid.'

They gazed at each other in delight, marvelling at the miracle of the constable's precious possession. The elation of his pride in it entered into Timothy, reviving his trust in the joy of living; it seemed for a moment as if nothing in the world could go wrong, when a man could be so happy in his motorcar.

Suddenly the policeman banished ecstasy from his brow, and looked more business-like. His air of severity returning to him, he said, 'I believe you stated that the shed had been already used for the purpose of accommodating a motorcar?'

'Well, you said so, as a matter of fact,' remarked Timothy.

The policeman looked serious, as if levity was out of place in a transaction of this sort.

'That being the case, might I inquire what sum the tenant paid by way of rent?'

'He didn't pay anything,' said Timothy.

A look of disapproval crossed the constable's face, indicating that this was not the way business should be done. But relief struggled with it, and dropping his official manner, he blurted out, 'I could manage five bob a week.'

Timothy was touched.

'Oh no,' he said. 'You're quite welcome to the shed, such as it is.'

The policeman stared at him a moment, and wiped his brow with the back of his hand, and Timothy realised what an effort the offer to pay must have cost him.

'The wife will be grateful to you, sir,' he grinned. 'She didn't want me to buy the car at all, she was dead against it.'

A stab of pleasure went through Timothy, a warm gust of gratitude at having been able to take so much care off the policeman's shoulders. But he repressed it, realising that he could claim small merit for a benefit which cost him no more to confer than the breath with which it was given.

'Now you'll be able to keep an eye on us,' he said.

'You don't suspect anything wrong, sir?'

'No, indeed. I was only joking.'

As the policeman was reaching for his helmet the front-door bell rang. Excusing himself, Timothy went to the door. But in his haste he turned so quickly that he slipped and with a crash measured his length on the flagstones.

'Are you hurt, sir?' asked the policeman, looking down at him impassively.

'Oh no,' said Timothy, preparing to get up.

The policeman raised a warning finger. 'Would you just make sure, sir? Only a routine precaution, I hope.'

Feeling rather foolish, Timothy made swimming motions on the floor.

'Quite all right.'

The policeman stooped down and helped him to his feet.

'It doesn't do to move them at once, sir,' he explained, 'in case there should be any bones broken.'

'Very thoughtful of you,' Timothy said, and waving away Effie, who had fluttered into the background, he opened the front door himself.

Mrs. Purbright was standing on the threshold. She looked white and frightened.

'Come in, come in,' he said.

But she had caught sight of someone inside, and recoiled. 'I see you are engaged. Another time would be better.'

'Oh no, please come in.'

'But the morning is such an inconvenient time.'

'Not at all, I am at my best then.'

'Very well,' said Mrs. Purbright reluctantly. 'Why, it's Nelson! How do you do?'

They shook hands, and Mrs. Purbright said, 'I am so glad to find you here. It's most unexpected and reassuring. Such a good friend for Mr. Casson to have – I mean, he needs looking after. Nelson is a good friend to us all,' she went on, 'a very present help in time of trouble.' The words recalled something to her, and her expression changed. 'There has been nothing unfortunate, I hope? There is so much misfortune in the world, against which even Nelson cannot protect us.'

'Nothing wrong at all, Ma'am,' Nelson answered her. 'We were only having a friendly talk, as you might say.'

'Oh, I am so relieved,' said Mrs. Purbright. 'Now that I know everything's all right, may I tell you what I thought I saw as I was standing on the doorstep? But perhaps you'd rather not know?'

'No, please tell us.'

'I thought I saw Mr. Casson lying on the floor among the rushes and you were there, too, Nelson, which was why I was so surprised, and yet not surprised, to see you.'

Timothy and the policeman exchanged glances, and Timothy told Mrs. Purbright of his mishap. She nodded, without appearing to share their wonderment, and said, 'I can't see very well – the black-out makes everything so dark. But are there any rushes on the floor? It was one of those nice mediæval customs.'

'There are some in the corner,' said Timothy. He glanced at the converted umbrella-stand from which protruded, moth-eaten and with the stuffing coming out of them, the long, brown velvet fingers of Miss Chadwick's bullrushes. 'Perhaps it was these you saw?' he suggested.

Absently Mrs. Purbright agreed that it might have been. 'But I interrupted your talk with Nelson,' she said, distressed. 'You can talk to me at any time.'

Timothy protested that he and Nelson had finished all they had to say.

'Oh but conversation is so important!' cried Mrs. Purbright, shaking her head and looking extremely worried. 'I'm sure you would agree with me, Mr. Casson, and Nelson must have to talk to so many people who are in trouble of some kind – who are angry, or ill, or frightened, or miserable, or who . . . who . . . have done something wrong?' She looked at Nelson in an agony of interrogation.

'I suppose I do see the seamy side, Ma'am,' said the policeman, not without complacency. 'But the worst thing about my job is all the silly questions I get asked.'

He reddened, suddenly realising that Mrs. Purbright had asked him a question, but she didn't seem to notice, and swept on.

'Yes, it must be most boring for you. But how nice to be able to tell people where to go and what to do, and never make a mistake! I envy him, don't you, Mr. Casson?'

Timothy admitted that he envied Nelson.

'You wouldn't, sir, not if you knew what I've got to do now,' said the policeman. 'But I won't tell you, not in front of Mrs. Purbright, she's that tender-hearted.' For the second time he reached for his helmet, and having opened the door so as not to do discourtesy to the house, he stood on the doorstep to put it on. 'Good morning, ma'am, good morning, sir, I'm very much obliged to you,' he said, as he saluted them goodbye.

'Such a nice man,' sighed Mrs. Purbright, protestingly allowing Timothy to lead her into the drawing-room. 'I won't ask you what he came about, I'd rather not know.' Timothy took this for an invitation, and was beginning to tell her, but she held up her hand. 'No, I'd much rather you kept it to yourself. There's too much common knowledge – it's such a pity. Now I expect you know quite well what brings me here.' When Timothy declared he did not, she seemed astounded.

'You wouldn't have received me so graciously if you had,' she remarked. 'I am a bird of ill-omen.' She gave him her sad, penetrating stare and asked his permission to smoke. She refused his cigarettes, and fitted a thin yellow Russian one into her long black cigarette holder. 'Of course it all depends,' she said, 'on how long you're staying here.'

Timothy explained about the unbreakable five years' lease. 'But I don't want to go away,' he wound up.

Mrs. Purbright said she was glad to hear him say so. 'And of course we don't want you to go – it would be a calamity – yes, a calamity – for the district. All the same,' she stuck to her guns, 'you might want to go away, for a time.'

Timothy reminded her of the lease.

'Oh, the lease!' said Mrs. Purbright vaguely. 'I expect you could soon find a way out of that. Solicitors can, you know, and Clara Chadwick is not a woman to stand in the way of her own advantage.' Timothy raised his eyebrows; what could Mrs. Purbright be driving at? But she was already explaining. 'All I mean is, you mustn't let yourself feel shut in here. There are other places, Mr. Casson, other valleys as beautiful as this.'

'You sound as if you wanted me to go,' said Timothy reproachfully.

'Do I?' said Mrs. Purbright. 'How one's words betray one! I should miss you sadly, we all should. Such a distinction for this little place. It would be a disaster for us. But as I said, there are other houses, other rivers – Windrush, Evenlode, such lovely names. Swirrel sounds so shallow and scratchy.'

'But where should I go?' asked Timothy.

'Don't speak of going, don't think of it! But you have friends in this country, of course, a man of your literary standing must have many friends. I can imagine how much they must long to see you. And relations too, or did you tell me you hadn't? Excuse me, I hate to seem prying. At my age – not at yours, of course – one needs a context. This is mine – these woods, these hills, this horizon, how near it seems!' – she waved her cigarette holder towards the window where the line of hill-top like a screen shut out the sky – 'these friends, these neighbours – you saw some of them at the Rectory, these Nelsons, these – could I count Miss Cross? – and my own dear family – such good, good people! And yet, Mr. Casson, I know you won't misunderstand me if I say that sometimes I should be glad to get away from it all.' She paused. 'In Italy, I expect, you felt quite free?'

One confidence deserves another, and Timothy, rather haltingly, for the facts do not always give the flavour and meaning of one's own life, even to the most sympathetic listener, told her how he had been the child of his father's old age and of his mother's late maturity, how they had died while he was still a boy, leaving him to the care of a guardian, a man of great integrity, devoted to his parents' memory; how to this Victorian business-man he had been not only an absolute obligation, but also an object of affection, almost of love, and shielded from the harsher, and above all from the practical contacts of the world. It was he who in the first instance had taken Timothy to Italy for long holidays in the legendary time before the first World War, and introduced him, insensibly, to the life of æsthetic appreciation which he had led ever since.

Culture had been a kind of religion to his guardian, and business closely linked with morals; ostentation was abhorrent to him, they travelled in comfort but never in luxury, and in all he did he was influenced, if not guided, by the criterion of what a man in his circumstances could afford. He had never married, and though he rarely mentioned the subject to Timothy he gave him the idea that attention to business, the continual improvement of one's mind, regular habits, the kind of social life that consisted in a dinner party for six or eight people, with excellent wine, beginning soon after eight and ending soon after eleven, the exact and punctual discharge of every duty, and a self-discipline that need never amount to stoicism – that these constituted a routine sufficient for life.

What lay beyond he treated with impenetrable reserve; 'I don't think he denied its existence,' said Timothy, 'he once or twice quoted Pascal to me – "je mourrai seul" ' (Mrs. Purbright nodded) 'and implied that certain experiences must be faced alone and without help from anyone else. And certainly in his own last illness, which was long and painful, and in which he needed the help of a male nurse for all the smallest bodily necessities, he never complained except playfully or allowed one to feel that one was visiting a sick man. He was most particular about that, and disliked any extra attention, or even inflexion of one's voice, that showed that one was sorry for him. Towards the end he showed a little asperity – a sort of weakening of control, I suppose – it was one of the indulgences he had denied himself before. He saw less and less of his friends – he said he preferred people should remember him as he used to be – and in the end only me and the nurse and the doctor.'

Mrs. Purbright took the cigarette holder from her mouth, and sat quite still.

'One felt his absorption in what lay before him the moment one entered the room,' said Timothy. 'The world outside seemed muffled and far away, and time had no quality except its tick, as it has when you are waiting for a clock to strike. I admired him very much and loved him then, but it was too late to tell him so, and would have sounded false, for we had never made each other professions of affection. One's mind recognises the approach of death, and I did not need warning when the time came for me not to leave him. I had been sitting by his bed, holding his hand and not speaking, to spare him the effort of reply, when suddenly he said, in quite a strong voice, "I have waited until now," and a few minutes later he died.'

Tears came into Timothy's eyes, and blurred his utterance. Usually the scene brought him little emotion, he had thought of it so often; but when he tried to put it into words, and all the circumstances came back, his grief renewed itself. He had almost forgotten Mrs. Purbright and was startled to hear her voice.

'What a privilege, and how thankful you must be!'

As Timothy turned to her, a wild light sprang into her eyes, a sway-ing violet flame that lit up her whole face. He felt hurt and disap-pointed, and said, shortly, 'It was the saddest day of my life.'

Her expression of exaltation did not change, however.

'But think of what it meant to him!'

'To him? He's dead,' said Timothy.

'No, no!' cried Mrs. Purbright. She laid her long blue-veined hand, with its single sapphire, on his arm. 'You must never say that! Never think it! But you don't; you speak against your feeling. The grief is for you; it is a precious possession, Mr. Casson; cherish it, guard it always! It is not too much for you – believe me, it is not! But for him the waiting is over; be thankful for that, as he was, and do not let your sorrow cast a shadow across his fields of light! Be sorry for your loss, yes, for that is irreparable, but not for him. Who knows, where he is gone, he may still need your faith, your joy joined to his, to recognise himself in the company of the blessed, to assure him that it is he, he, your guardian, the companion of your happy days, to whom this bliss belongs!'

She paused and looked at Timothy as though for confirmation. He felt her words beating against the bastions of his mind, hardened by years of another way of thinking; they could not force an entrance, yet the garrison pricked up its ears and manned the walls.

As though aware that she was leading where he could not follow, Mrs. Purbright changed her voice and thanked Timothy formally for what he had told her.

'Do your thoughts often go back to that afternoon?' she added.

'Oh yes.' Timothy did not remember telling her that his guardian had died in the afternoon. 'I went into the room but I sometimes wonder if I ever came out.'

'Oh no,' said Mrs. Purbright, anxiously, 'no. You mustn't say that. The windows are open and we are all in the world. No, I see your guardian well, a noble portrait by Vandyck, a head above a ruff, grave, sensitive, serene. I expect he influenced you greatly. What there was to look at then, he saw; and the best of it. But now, what a different prospect! His face condemns what we see; but still, we must look at it, though it is harder for us, who have seen through his eyes.'

'I always took the line of least resistance,' sighed Timothy. 'What he left me enabled me to do that. He wouldn't have liked me to skim the cream without doing the milking, but there! I'm like many belated Victorians, I suppose.'

Again a ferment of flame in Mrs. Purbright's eyes, a startling intensification of her regard, a protest, a challenge. It died out, and she merely said, 'Humanism might have been one's religion in those days.'

'But not now?' said Timothy.

Mrs. Purbright shook her head.

'We can inherit the gifts of Christianity but not hand them on: I mean, the third generation must renew its faith.'

Timothy wondered to which generation, in Mrs. Purbright's view, he belonged. Her next remark did not really enlighten him.

'You are a regular attendant at church, Mr. Casson,' she said. 'In a Roman Catholic country my husband would take that for granted. Here, he naturally is pleased.'

Timothy felt extremely uncomfortable. His reasons for having become a church-goer were not the right ones, certainly not the best ones.

'I like the feeling of being in church,' he said, apologetically, 'the bowed heads, the subdued movements, the ritual, that varies so little and so much. And the sense of worship round me is comforting to me, even if I don't share it. I expect a barn-door fowl is grateful for its wings even if they scarcely lift it from the ground.'

Mrs. Purbright listened to him attentively, but no elation, no upflung spark of sympathy, ignited in her eye.

'So glad,' she murmured almost mechanically. 'So very, very delighted. Who in the congregation, I wonder, could say as much? Who would wish to say more? Can you think of anyone?'

She darted the question at him with extraordinary intensity, as if a great deal hung upon his answer.

Timothy smiled.

'Well, you see, I hardly know any of them, even to speak to, much less to exchange religious views with.'

'But it is a beginning, isn't it, to be with them, enjoy the bowed heads, the ritual, the spiritual comfort – isn't it a short step, then, to a friendly understanding, not perhaps on the spiritual plane' – a wave of her hand seemed to dismiss the spiritual plane – 'but to a feeling of neighbourliness – I mean the kind of relationship in which all you have done for us, Mr. Casson, might be acknowledged by something, however little, that we could do for you?'

'But I have done nothing!' exclaimed Timothy. 'I only wish I could.'

Mrs. Purbright looked at him.

'Shall I take you at your word?'

'Please.'

She smoothed out her blue dress under the black fur, took another cigarette, changed her position as if she were changing her mood and seemed to assume another personality.

'On my way here I called on Colonel Harbord.'

'Ah!' said Timothy. It sounded like a snarl. Try as he would he could not keep the hostility out of his voice.

'He is, of course, an old friend of mine,' said Mrs. Purbright. 'We do not touch, we do not meet, our gestures are lost upon each other. I come into his house as a bird might, through the window, and as he is fond of animals he does all he can not to scare me, and keeps the window open so that I can fly out again.'

'I shall shut the window,' said Timothy. He rose to suit the action to the word. It was not a mere politeness, for at the mention of Colonel Harbord's name he had become aware of a keen draught. Mrs. Purbright called him back.

'No, please let us breathe this exquisite spring air,' she said. 'I was very open with Colonel Harbord, I rated him severely. Do you know why?'

Timothy kept a childish, obstinate silence.

'I see you do know. And what do you think he said?'

'I can't imagine.' The spurt of rudeness in his voice startled Timothy, and he added, 'I mean, I wouldn't be likely to know.'

'He was so funny, so serious about it all.'

'Well, I am serious, too. I don't know if I'm funny,' retorted Timothy.

Mrs. Purbright became grave at once.

'No, for you it is a necessity. I told him so.'

Obstinacy would not let Timothy inquire what reply Colonel Harbord had made, but he could not help saying, 'I suppose he told you it all depended on Mrs. Lampard.'

'She was such a dazzling creature when we first met her,' said Mrs. Purbright. 'She wasn't married then, she had only just come out, and was startling everyone with her unconventionality. That was in London; we heard about it before we saw her; she came to stay at Welshgate Hall – she was a distant relation of old Mrs. Lampard. The old lady used to give large parties, and we were asked to one. Do you dislike arrogance, do you think it wrong? Her manner offended many people, but I thought it was just high spirits. Where will you find great art without arrogance? A masterpiece is there to be admired, and she was a masterpiece, not of art but of nature. It was her art to be natural. Do we think the worse of a child or a cat or a swan, because they sometimes rebuff us? Don't we feel the more elated, when it pleases them to be pleased? And she could be so melting, so irresistible when she was in the mood. It was not that she was kind and good. She could have wheedled the keys out of a gaoler, or the rifle out of a sentry if she had had the mind.'

'I remember when she came to lunch with me,' said Timothy, 'that she made it seem an altogether unusual event.'

'When was that?' Mrs. Purbright asked.

'It was in September, 1927. Funny that I should remember,' said Timothy carelessly.

'Wouldn't it be funnier if you had forgotten? I mean, at that time, not now, perhaps. Now she is quite different, I'm told, not that we ever see her. She shouldn't have married Randall Lampard. Oh no, it was a great mistake.'

'Wasn't he a good match?' asked Timothy.

'Oh yes, too good, too rich, too handsome. But he was twice her age and besides, he was married already.'

'I never knew that!' exclaimed Timothy, a little put out at being found wanting in worldly knowledge.

'She wasn't happy with him, who could have been, but they were just struggling along, and poor thing, she was so hoping for a child who might have brought them together. He complained of her childlessness, but who knows whether he really wanted her to have one? This is what Nelson calls the seamy side – life is incomplete without it, I suppose – but when Julia began to lay siege to him she didn't realise – she was barely nineteen – what it would mean to an older woman. She may have thought – let us give her the benefit of the doubt – that he was being sacrificed to a loveless marriage. But it wasn't easy for Julia, because he was far too spoilt to fall in love with her. Other men did, oh but a great many. We heard all about them when she came to live in the district.'

'Oh, did she?' said Timothy.

'Yes, the Palliters of Deepdene were her cousins. She spent weeks, months with them. Edward and I used to go there often – there were plenty of young men – I sometimes think that youth was an Edwardian phenomenon – and she flirted with them like a charming young tigress. It was delicious to watch her.'

'Did they find it delicious?' asked Timothy.

'Oh surely! Why else did they go? Can you have a queen without a court? And do the courtiers mind? Wouldn't they lose their occupation if she didn't smile at them? One mustn't judge those days by these. In those days there was so much happiness to fall back on – cushions, mattresses of happiness; and if you weren't happy you could always feel that other people were. Life was padded against accident. Now, if one scratches one's fingers, the whole world bleeds.'

'How do you mean?' asked Timothy.

'I mean we've sold our capital of happiness, our reserves are gone, we must build them afresh. Isn't that what you are doing in your articles, showing the delight and beauty that still waits in England, through your own eyes, through your servants' eyes, catching us all in your golden net?'

Timothy reddened.

'You pick it up from the earth, you reach for it from the air – not with your will, I think, but may I say with the communicating effort of your nature, that stretches out to beauty and love.'

'Yes,' said Timothy, who had collected himself. 'But you forget the third element, water. I also look for a spiritual harvest there.'

Mrs. Purbright's face fell.

'No,' she said. 'I don't forget. I was coming to that. But where was I?'

'You were talking about Mrs. Lampard's young men.'

'How odd it sounds, put like that. Well, finally she got engaged to one of them. People say now she never meant it seriously – that it was part of her plan – but I don't like to think so. I think the plan came later, when she saw that Randall Lampard really minded the engagement.'

'Did she break it off?'

'Not at once,' said Mrs. Purbright slowly. 'Not for quite a long time. They used to ride over to Welshgate Hall together, she and the young man, and drop in casually. I don't want to seem censorious, but I think it was then that she made a mistake. You see, she wanted him so much.'

'But is it wrong to want something?' asked Timothy.

'Oh no, *no*! How else would the world get on? But don't you sometimes feel a current flowing that draws your own will with it, like the wind that bends the ears in a cornfield? You know the shimmer that passes and gladdens one's heart, because something in one answers to the movement and would be distressed if even a single head leaned the other way? If she felt it she didn't heed it. I used to meet her on the road to Welshgate, sometimes alone, generally with her fiancé; she looked magnificent on a horse, as she still does. Sometimes she would greet me as her oldest friend; sometimes with a kind of amused smile as if I had interrupted a private joke she was having at my expense. Her lips came together and her eyes sought his, bright with complicity. But as time passed I saw him more seldom, and in the end she rode alone. He's married now. I wonder if he ever thinks of those rides.

'The neighbourhood thought she was behaving badly; I believe that her friends and relations pleaded with her and entreated her to go away from Upton, but she stayed on and on. She never became a laughing-stock, oh no. There was something first-rate about her, unchallenge-able, that couldn't be made to look silly. Her pride stood up to the strain. Singly she was a match for them all, and even in corners people only whispered, as if the shadow of a hawk was on them. But she got a strained, intent look, as if she was watching something on a distant hill; you could tell that nothing existed for her except her object. All the elasticity was gone. I used to pity her on those solitary rides. And then one day I met her coming the other way, and Randall Lampard was with her. She looked triumphant, but not happy or at rest. But why am I telling you all this?'

'No, please,' said Timothy, 'go on. I've so often wondered about her.'

'I haven't much more to tell because, well, you know what our position is, and after the divorce and everything our relations with Welshgate became merely formal – to my sorrow, for it was then she needed sympathy. And then the war came with its invisible cloak altering everything, changing values; old Mrs. Lampard died, and the Hall became a hospital; and soon after that he got a job in Paris, something to do with the Peace Settlement, and she joined him there, and gossip says they each went their own way. Well, that was the way she had always gone, and he too, though for a moment he went hers. When I saw him, just before he died, he was a distinguished-looking elderly gentleman with sleek hair, almost green.'

'Death was very obliging to her,' said Timothy.

'Yes. It mowed a swath in front of her, for it took his first wife too – not that she made any resistance, poor thing. Some people are in league with death, it enters into their calculations, they count on it. They would take any risk. That was what Edward meant when he said she was like a Renaissance princess. But she was different when she first came to Upton, a young girl in love. The waiting and planning changed her nature.'

'You don't see any parallel between her career and mine?' asked Timothy.

Mrs. Purbright opened her eyes wide.

'Oh, Mr. Casson, how could you suggest such a thing? No, no. There never were two people less alike. I can't remember how we came to talk about her. Yes, I do. I am so anxious you should use your boat, and before you come to want it too much.'

Timothy laughed.

'How kind you are. But is there no way of getting round Mrs. Lampard? Has she no soft spot anywhere?'

Mrs. Purbright thought deeply.

'Like Jephthah, she has a daughter.'

'Oh, she has a daughter?'

'Yes, indeed, Désirée. She was born in Paris, six or seven years after they were married.'

'She was a disappointment, I expect,' said Timothy. He felt as though the subject of Mrs. Lampard had turned his mind to vinegar.

'Oh, no,' said Mrs. Purbright. 'She loves her with a jealous affection. A boy was what *he* wanted. Désirée has been most carefully brought up, and sheltered in a way that seems old-fashioned nowadays. I've met her once or twice. She seems a sweet girl, rather shy, hardly with a will of her own. She's just twenty but she never goes out alone, there's always a groom or someone with her. Yes, Mrs. Lampard is a very strict and careful mother and the parties at Welshgate are exceedingly conventional, so I am told. Mrs. Lampard has cold-shouldered her past life, and doesn't recognise it; she is very particular and correct and not very kind to other people's failings. Yet how can one not admire her, for having the pluck to live it all down? And not for her own sake – I don't suppose she cares a scrap for the world's opinion – but for her daughter's. Have I made you like her better? I hope I have.'

To his great surprise Timothy was suddenly aware of a warmer feeling for Mrs. Lampard.

'Do you think if I rescued the daughter from some dangerous situation – of course it would have to be in full view of Mrs. Lampard – she might—'

'I am sure she *would*,' said Mrs. Purbright, her eyes kindling at the prospect. 'We must think of a way. A little plot! What fun it would be.' Her eyes narrowed. 'So much can be done through the affections.' She gave him a quizzical look. 'Do I know you well enough to appeal to yours?'

'They are always at your service,' exclaimed Timothy. His conversation with Mrs. Purbright, twenty minutes of almost complete emotional accord, had entirely won him to her side, and he felt ready to do anything for her.

'But as I said,' she reminded him, 'it depends on how long you're going to stay in Upton. You may not want to stay, when you know my errand.' Her glance was questioning, almost hopeful. 'Colonel Harbord looked rather blank, and Mrs. Harbord almost flabbergasted, when I asked them.'

'You're still trying to drive me away!' cried Timothy.

'Oh no, *no*! If you only knew how anxious we are to keep you! But listen. I am the billeting officer,' she said tragically, 'and I've come to ask you to take some evacuees.'

'Oh!' The ejaculation was forced out of Timothy. He felt physically and emotionally winded, and it took him an appreciable time to re-arrange his face.

'There!' said Mrs. Purbright sadly. 'I should have told you at first, and not tried to win your confidence with unkind gossip about people I hardly know. For the sake of the pleasure of your society I took a mean advantage. Do you ever feel the burden of your sins, Mr. Casson? Not that you have any, I'm sure.'

Timothy was bewildered by her change of mood and subject. 'Well, just lately I've been thinking more about other people's.'

'Exactly! and how right! And now you will be thinking about mine. What a hypocrite she is, you must be saying to yourself, to ramble on about the dangers of purposefulness (I mean in the case of Mrs. Lampard, of course) when all the time she had one idea, to make me do something which will ruin my life.'

Mrs. Purbright's raised hand dropped into her lap, and her expression became utterly woe-begone.

Timothy had now recovered himself.

'Of course I should be only too pleased—' he began.

'Yes, yes, I know you would. But if I just tell them you don't know how long you may be staying, the whole question can be dropped.'

Timothy had a momentary vision of the taxi at the door, and what was that behind it, a kind of trailer carrying the boat? Goodbye, Upton! He was off. The evocation glowed with the relief that lightens the last moments of almost any departure but he put it from him, and said:

'It's my servants, you know. They say they won't stay if I have evacuees. They say all the bother would fall on them.'

Mrs. Purbright knit her brows.

'And it's true. Poor Mr. Casson! Do you ever feel a longing for hotel life – no orders to give, no one to propitiate, everthing at regular hours – writing letters in one's bedroom, or one of those nice quiet writing-rooms they often have – no responsibility, no pressure of life, even the black-out arranged for you! I know of such a delightful little inn on the river below Swirrelsford, with everything you can wish for, even boats – I often think I shall retire to it! But you say they are quite adamant?'

'My cook is,' sighed Timothy, 'and Effie generally agrees with her.'

'If they left,' said Mrs. Purbright, 'what would you do?'

'Leave, too, I suppose,' Timothy said. 'They tell me, and all my friends tell me, that I should never get any more.'

Mrs. Purbright stroked her chin with a masculine gesture. 'You know, I believe you *are* the only resident in Upton with a proper staff of servants. Isn't it a tribute? Nearly all the rest of us depend on a daily woman. We're quite envious of you. Oh to be a bachelor! But most households have a wife or a sister or an aunt, some female drudge, to keep them fed and tidy. You would be sadly at a loss.'

'Yes,' said Timothy. 'I really *should* have to leave.'

For a second Mrs. Purbright's face didn't alter. She seemed to be accepting Timothy's announcement with resignation, even with relief. Then animation spread through her, in almost visible waves, like the return of feeling to a limb that has gone to sleep.

'Let me talk to them, let me talk to them!' she cried, springing to her feet. 'I'll see if I can't persuade them!'

Timothy escorted her to the kitchen door, and returned to his writing table, where a letter from Magda lay unopened.

'I'm still terribly bored,' she complained, 'and if I was a man I should be a conscientious objector. They are the only people I respect. And as you know, many of the Comrades are Conchies. I was talking to one who had been wounded three times in the Spanish war and tortured by the Fascists, and he said nothing would induce him to fight in this. A good-looking man with a perfect figure and as fit as you could wish, but that's what he said. "It's not *our* war." Naturally, if he had refused to fight on religious grounds, I should have despised him utterly.

'I am sick of my job here and if I thought it contributed to what they call the "War Effort" but what ought to be called the enslavement of the workers, I should throw it up at once. London is so completely dreary now, the food uneatable, the drink poison, and the people shabby beyond belief. And dirty. Next to being a Fascist that's the thing I mind most. Cleanliness is next to Communism and as a rule they are both found together – not always, for some of the Comrades look a bit dingy. I confess that in them I find grime rather endearing and anyhow it's not their "fault" (to use an old-fashioned expression), it's the fault of the conditions most of them have had to live in. In Curzon Street we have the Collective Courtesy Room scrubbed with disinfectant daily and it's more bearable than the scent most people use.

'Rural areas are notoriously out of step, and your situation vis-à-vis the fishing snobs sounds the kind of thing we ought to inquire into. I've sent a memorandum about it to headquarters and if you like I'll have someone sent down to Upton to make a report, and incidentally strengthen the resistance to the snob-centres that you say already exist in the neighbourhood. You needn't be afraid it would get you into a jam (I know you hate that); whoever went would work strictly on their own. The Government doesn't exactly encourage our activities but it's still a free country, thank God. I would come myself if I wasn't so tied up here.

'Do you know, in spite of your anti-politics pose, I detect a welcome strain of class-consciousness in your last letter? You are beginning to see who the real enemy is, after all, and will have to come down off your fence. *A propos*, I was dining for my sins at Lucullus's the other night, and who should I see but Julia Lampard and her daughter – they were dining together and seemed quite wrapped up in each other. I don't approve of Julia, of course, she's a hopeless reactionary – and that dreadful habit of crumbling her bread! But I've always liked her freedom from bourgeois prejudice, though I've never admired her looks – those bloodhound eyes, that bee-stung lip – and now she has the suspicion of a Lely-esque dewlap. The daughter is rather pretty in a dark-eyed, pale-skinned way, but has no style: I suppose Julia thinks she is too young for that, though she must be nearly twenty. She hardly looked up when two young men stopped at their table to speak to Julia. My friend wouldn't have interested Julia, he is a night-club addict who doesn't improve with drink and I was thoroughly bored with him before the evening was over. Men of that sort are so deadly un-serious, or serious about the wrong things: racing is nearly as much an opium of the people as religion. I doubt if he has ever heard of Marx. As you've never been in love you can't realise what a much better tonic hate is – but you will, you will, I recognise the symptoms. You couldn't be doing the cause a greater service than by living as you do, quietly ignoring the warmongers and raising ill-feelings against the boss-class. Soon you'll find what fullness and purpose it gives to life to know that there are several million people who are asking to be shot; and you are one of them, dear Timothy: yes, I'm afraid you are.

Comradely salutes, we don't deal much in love

MAGDA.'

The letter worried Timothy. Had Magda really sent a report on his affairs to her Communist friends? Would some nondescript person carrying a parcel with a bomb in it suddenly materialise on the Green at Upton? One never knew what people would do, what breaches of confidence they might commit, once they got inoculated with one of those political viruses. And had his letter to Magda really shown the kind of feeling she professed to detect? Surely it was no more than a humorous exaggeration of his chronic grievance, meant to amuse her? Talking to Mrs. Purbright he had almost forgotten the grievance, and to be reminded of it, and congratulated on it, as if it was a virtue, and told to cherish it, was disturbing to him in his present mood.

The door opened and Mrs. Purbright came in. She plunged uncertainly towards him, and he could not tell from her eyes, which in moments of absorption looked as sightless as a Greek statue's, how she had fared in her mission.

'No, no,' she said when he offered her a chair. 'You mustn't let me sit down. I've taken up too much of your time already – the woman from Porlock, and on such distasteful business. But how nice they are, your servants. They seem so fond of each other. And of you, too. They said they couldn't do enough for you.'

Timothy showed his pleasure at this news.

'But not for the evacuees?'

An expression Timothy couldn't decipher crossed Mrs. Purbright's face.

'It seems so presumptuous to say it, and really I don't know how you'll take it – but yes, I succeeded, I prevailed.'

'Well done.'

Mrs. Purbright didn't seem to share his elation.

'Time will show. I'm afraid it will be an awful bore for you – another tie, pleasant for us but cruelly binding for you. To think I should be the one to clip your wings!'

'Oh, but this is my chosen perch.'

Mrs. Purbright spread out her hands.

'They will undertake sole charge. You need not see, hear, or think about the little exiles. And perhaps they won't come, in which case!' – she made a wide gesture, embracing the heavens. 'And believe me, your generous action will be widely appreciated, very widely.' Timothy recognised an inflection from her husband's voice. 'I shall see that it is. No, don't thank me,' for Timothy had begun to stammer words of gratitude, he hardly knew for what – 'regard me as your evil genius. I, I am to blame for anything that happens. All, *all* your just resentment must fall on me. *Good*bye.'

'Why did you say we'd have the children, Beattie?' Effie demanded as the kitchen door closed on Mrs. Purbright. 'You've always said we couldn't, you know that quite well.'

'Oh, I don't know,' said Beatrice, wearily. 'It was her, I guess. She made me properly mad.'

'I don't know what's come over you lately,' complained Effie. 'You don't seem to mind how much they put upon us. We could have said "no" to her just as easily as we could to him. Who does she think she is, anyhow? And she didn't want us to take the children. Quite the opposite. "They will disturb Mr. Casson's work, and add to yours. I strongly advise you to refuse," ' quoted Effie, giving a plausible imitation of Mrs. Purbright's manner.

'That's what riled me,' Beatrice said. 'If she'd asked us to say yes, I should have said no, of course. He must have put her up to it, telling her we wouldn't. What business is it of hers, anyhow? And her saying he ought to go to a warmer place because he'd lived abroad. I soon put a stop to all that.'

Effie assented rather dubiously to Beatrice's reasoning. 'Of course it wouldn't be fair to us if he went away. Now that you mention it, she did seem as if she wanted to get rid of him. And all that money he puts in the collection! Ten shillings every Sunday, they say. It seems a shame.'

'Who told you that?' asked Beatrice sharply.

'A little bird,' said Effie airily.

'Not so little,' said Beatrice darkly. 'I wonder why you demean yourself. Silence while he's in the kitchen, that's my rule. And you won't have so much time to chatter when the evacuees come.'

'Well, you wanted 'em and you can look after 'em.'

Beatrice's eyes softened and her pose of no surrender to aggression relaxed.

'I don't mind,' she said. 'It'll be like being young again. And it'll take my mind off other things.'

'What other things?' asked Effie, innocently.

Beatrice jerked her chin up.

'You should know.'

CHAPTER XI

THE tremendous, bewildering international events of May followed, but they reached Timothy only as a murmur, hardly more menacing to him personally than the far-off rumble of guns, which sometimes made the windows rattle but which, once he got used to them, confirmed his idea of the war as something that was taking place outside his experience. He was doubly insulated, by the hills of Upton, and the woods, just turning green, that thickly clothed and cloaked them, and still more by the solitary life he led, enclosed in his cocoon of self-generating and infertile thoughts. The war to him was something that was happening in a history book which it would one day be his duty to learn: he could not recognise himself in the situation it created, nor could he profitably compare notes with other minds, for Effie and Beatrice were as little able to grasp world events as he was. Their reactions were confined to general denunciations of Hitler, while Wimbush, when questioned about this war, generally answered by describing his experiences in the last one. There remained Mrs. Purbright, whose company Timothy cultivated more and more; her house was always open to him. But she never asked anyone to meet him, and her feelings about the war were, he gradually learned, only an intensified version of her general view of the human lot. For her, suffering was a mystery pregnant with beauty and redemptive value, and the greater the suffering the greater were the opportunities for spiritual gain. At least he imagined that to be her view, but her mind was elusive and tangential and most unwilling to let its principles be known; any attempt on Timothy's part to anticipate its workings she eluded and would often impatiently disown her opinions of yesterday if he quoted them against, or even for her.

Her husband's mind, on the other hand, was as plain sailing as a channel marked out by buoys; with him the only risk was a sudden gust of temper which might spring up over anything, not only when he disagreed but if he thought a question unsuitable for discussion. These visitations of Satan were well-known to the Rector, who tried to guard against and put them down, but the struggle was embarrassing both to him and to his interlocutor. Timothy never started a controversial topic with him if he could help it; though any subject was likely to become controversial. Still, the Rectory was a haven for Timothy; he felt at home the moment he turned in at the gate – and all the more so that other gates, snugly set in walls and split-wood fences, were barred against him.

The evacuees duly arrived, two little boys aged five and seven, and were warmly welcomed not only by Timothy but by Beatrice and Effie. They were shy and tongue-tied and almost paralysed in Timothy's presence, but as soon as his back was turned they broke into violent movement, kicking up their heels like colts and shouting at each other in strong Midland accents that caused some amusement to Beatrice and Effie. Questions arose about where they were to go and what parts of the house should be out of bounds to them; Timothy took them for a sight-seeing tour from room to room; they gazed wide-eyed but without seeming to take in what they saw, or kept each other's spirits up with nudges and whispered confidences when he was looking the other way. At the beginning he determined to see them every day after tea, before they went to bed, and talk to them or read to them; but he found their attention difficult to win, so strong was the undercurrent of private understanding between them which he could not enter. They came in with flattened hair and strained, set faces, almost like sleep-walkers; they hurried off in a flurry of whispers, shoves, and all the signs of a joyful reunion. Soon he discontinued these interviews which were obviously as much of an ordeal to the children as to him, though he sometimes went to see them in bed, when the approach of sleep was diminishing their high spirits and their small, rosy faces, side by side on the soft pillows, looked angelic.

Timothy's part of the house held few attractions for them, but not so the garden, and it wasn't long before Beatrice came and announced, in an expressionless voice and with a studied moderation of manner, that unless Wimbush acted differently to the children, she couldn't stay.

'What has he done?' asked Timothy with a sinking heart.

'It's not what's he done, sir, it's what he says he'll do.'

'Oh,' said Timothy, relieved. 'What does he say he'll do?'

'I'm not one to tell tales,' said Beatrice, compressing her lips. 'But he says he'll skin them.'

'Oh, I don't suppose he means any harm. Did he say so to you?'

Beatrice looked immeasurably affronted.

'Mr. Wimbush knows better than to speak to me, sir, and if he did I shouldn't lower myself to listen. No, he said it to the boys.'

'I'm sure it was just his fun.'

'They didn't think so and nor will their Mum and Dad when they hear.'

'Is there any reason why they should hear?' asked Timothy.

'It wouldn't be fair to keep a thing like that from them, sir, and there's the Society for the Prevention of Children, too.'

Timothy stared at Beatrice, hoping to find some sign of relenting in her attitude. But every line was square.

'Has he ever, well . . . knocked them about?'

'He wouldn't dare to lay a finger on them while I'm here, sir. But when I'm gone—' and to Timothy's astonishment Beatrice began to sob. He tried to comfort her.

'Well, you mustn't go.'

Beatrice continued to sob.

'I couldn't stay, not with him threatening them the way he does. You must speak to him, sir, I can't.'

She left the room, blubbering but somehow invested with the dignity of grief. Through the french window Timothy espied the stalwart form of Wimbush, vigorously weeding a flower-bed. Timothy went out to him.

'Morning, sir,' said Wimbush, 'it do take all my time to get the better of they weeds.'

Timothy complimented him on his success and asked him if the boys gave him any trouble.

'Trouble? Not they, sir. I like 'em. Regular little imps of Satan they are.'

'Sure they don't get in your way?'

'Oh no, sir. Of course I has to keep my eye on them, otherwise they'd be all over the place. Regular boys they are, as full of mischief as a cartload of monkeys. But 'twouldn't be proper if they weren't.'

'You mustn't let them be a nuisance to you,' said Timothy.

Wimbush laughed.

'Trust me, sir. Only yesterday I says to Billy, "If I catch you on that flower-bed again I'll skin you."'

'Wasn't he frightened?'

'Bless you, no, sir,' he laughed.

'Of course we have to remember that they've never been away from their parents before, so I expect they feel a bit strange.'

'I know, sir, that's why I talk to them like their father would. Makes them feel at home, like. They're fine boys, they are, sir, up to any mischief. I used to be like that myself.'

A manifold disturbance, a tornado of sight and sound, made itself felt in the distance, and soon Gerald and Billy were scampering towards them across the grass. At the sight of Timothy they halted abruptly, seemed to confer, and then advanced sedately, looking about them in an interested manner. A few yards away they stopped, put their hands in their pockets, stuck out their elbows, turned their eyes downwards, and leaned their small bodies heavily, first on one heel and then on the other, apparently to see which could make the deepest dent in the turf.

'Say good morning to Mr. Casson,' said Wimbush. 'They seem to have lost their tongues.'

'Hullo,' said Gerald to no one in particular, and Billy, after a moment's hesitation, contributed another 'hullo.'

'Say "sir." '

'Sir,' said Gerald doubtfully. Billy remained silent, and looked at Timothy from under downcast eyelids.

'He's regular obstinate, the little one,' said Wimbush admiringly. 'If he don't want to speak you can't make him. But they'll talk like one o'clock the moment you've gone away, sir.'

'Well, perhaps I'd better go,' said Timothy. Then, remembering Beatrice's accusation, he asked, 'Are you quite happy?'

Billy gave Gerald a nudge with his elbow, and Gerald, studying his feet, replied tonelessly, 'Yessir.'

'No complaints?'

They did not seem to understand this, and Wimbush interpreted. 'Mr. Casson means do you miss your Mummy?'

At this, the little one's underlip began to quiver, and Gerald took his arm and, pointing to the horizon, said, 'Mum's only just over there.'

'Mummy's coming to see you next week,' said Timothy. 'She's going to spend the day here.'

'And is Dad coming, too?' asked Gerald.

'Yes, they're both coming by a train.'

'Mr. Casson will tell them what bad boys you are,' said Wimbush in an affectionate tone, and as if this was the kind of report the parents would wish to hear.

'We aren't, are we?' asked Gerald.

'No, you're very good. What will you tell them about us?'

The boys moved uneasily from one foot to another, with half-smiles, unwilling to answer.

'What will you say about Mr. Wimbush?'

'He's champion,' said Gerald. 'He's given me a catapult. Will they take it away?' he added anxiously.

'Oh, I don't suppose so.'

'But it's Beattie that dresses us,' the older boy went on. 'She's ever so nice. But she doesn't like Mr. Wimbush. She doesn't want us to play with him.'

Timothy saw the storm gathering between Wimbush's leonine brows, and said hastily, 'Oh, but he likes to play with you.'

'Yes, you do, don't you, Mr. Wimbush?' asked Gerald in a small pale voice.

Wimbush said nothing but pulled up some groundsel with as much energy as if he was eradicating Beatrice.

'He calls us his mates,' said Gerald proudly. 'He says we're good little beggars. He don't lay into us, never.'

'I'm glad to hear that,' said Timothy.

Pleased with his success, Gerald let his glance stray over the house and garden.

'Does it all belong to you?' he asked.

'No, it really belongs to a lady called Miss Chadwick. I'm only the tenant.'

'Oh,' Gerald seemed disappointed. 'Don't none of it belong to Beattie?'

'The kitchen belongs to her in a way, of course, but Miss Chadwick is the real owner.'

'Could she turn you out?'

'Only if I did something wrong.'

A shadow of apprehension crossed Gerald's face.

'You wouldn't, would you?'

'I hope not,' said Timothy. 'Do you like it here?'

'Yes,' said Gerald, 'but our house is a home.'

'Well, isn't this?' said Timothy.

'No, it's too big for a home. It's more like an 'ospital. I've been in 'ospital once. So has Billy. We thought this was an 'ospital when we first come. We thought you were the doctor. Then Beattie said, "Oh no, he isn't, he's only Mr. Casson." '

Timothy laughed, and the gardener, who had worked off his ill-humour, laughed too.

'Well,' said Timothy, resolved on a last bit of detective work. 'Now I'm going to leave you to Mr. Wimbush.'

He saw the relief, the sunrise of anticipatory joy on their faces as he turned to go; and through the french window he could see how quickly they regained their self-assurance in Wimbush's company. An exuberance of gesture took hold of them; they waved their arms about and stamped their feet as if they had broken loose from invisible cords.

Without giving his resolution time to cool, Timothy went straight to Beatrice and told her that he had seen Wimbush and the boys together, and that they all seemed to be on good terms. Wimbush's language might be a little rough, but Timothy was sure he meant no harm. Beatrice listened to him in a sceptical silence that was more baffling than argument, and when he had finished merely said she didn't suppose that Wimbush would set about the children as long as Timothy was looking on; all she could say was, she would never trust the gardener with any child of hers – her tone suggesting that whereas Timothy was culpably childless, she was not. At this point Effie came in, and Timothy appealed to her.

'You don't think Wimbush would be unkind to the children, do you, Effie?'

Effie glanced at Beatrice, moistened her lips, moved her head uneasily as if testing a stiff neck, and said:

'I don't know why you should ask me, sir. I hardly ever speak to Mr. Wimbush. He doesn't come into my work at all, it wouldn't be natural if he did. Mrs. Burnett, she might know. I really couldn't tell you if Mr. Wimbush is safe with children, could I, Beattie?'

Beatrice did not answer, and Effie seemed to be so flustered that Timothy let the matter drop. He made a mental note, however, to ask Mrs. Burnett and was reminded of it the next morning when, on emerging from his bedroom, he found her on her hands and knees blocking the doorway. Complimenting them all on their kindness to the children, he observed that he was glad that Wimbush had taken such a fancy to them.

'Well, sir,' said Mrs. Burnett smiling radiantly, 'he have five of his own, so two more don't make much difference. They need a man, sir, boys do, as knows the meaning of discipline, otherwise they'd grow up nohow, which isn't to say you couldn't do it yourself, sir, only it has to be someone they can respect.'

Timothy agreed. 'Is Wimbush a strict disciplinarian?' he asked, casually.

'Well, sir, his children all have clean faces and nice habits, and that don't come from just leaving Nature to take her course.'

Timothy wished he hadn't consulted Mrs. Burnett.

'I fancy that you and I were brought up more strictly than the children of today,' he said. 'The latest theory is to let them do as they like.'

'You're right, sir,' said Mrs. Burnett warmly, 'and a great pity it is. But you needn't be afraid that Wimbush holds with them notions. He's old-fashioned. You can trust him to do what's right by the boys, same as their own father would. If you like, sir, I'll say a word to him in private. 'Tisn't fair that a gentleman like you should have the worry of walloping 'em.'

'Oh no, no,' cried Timothy, dismayed by the turn the conversation had taken. 'Please don't say anything of the sort.' Mrs. Burnett promised not to, and with that he had to be content.

The parents' visit was a strain, but Timothy thought that on the whole it went off well. The father worked in a baker's shop; the mother stayed at home. Timothy was right in believing they would come in their best clothes, and glad that he had put on his. They arrived in the early afternoon, and he took them round the garden, which, as is the way of gardens, seemed to be between seasons, the spring flowers being over, and the summer flowers not yet out. Mr. Kimball was a sweet-pea fancier, and knew more about them than Timothy knew of all of the rest of the world's flora put together. Like most experts, he had an attitude towards his subject which no amateur could hope to enter into; the beauty of the flowers he took for granted; what interested him was their size, shape, colour, the difficulties attendant on rearing them, their habits of growth and above all their prize-winning capacities. But even this last was devoid of excitement for him; the thrill of the prize was subordinated to and almost lost in the various technical points necessary to secure it. The winning of the award was not so much a crowning glory as the logical outcome of having fulfilled all the conditions, and he expatiated at equal length on Mariposa which had taken several first prizes and on Wolverhampton Wonder which, owing to an exaggeration of certain qualities, attractive to the public but fatal to the true harmony and balance of the bloom, was never more than Highly Commended. Timothy listened, bored as one must be with an accumulation of details outside the grasp of one's mind, but respectful, because he recognised in Mr. Kimball's dispassionate approach to his hobby the signs of an austere idealism which was lacking in his own art. From time to time Mrs. Kimball supplied the personal touch that her husband had left out – 'Mr. Kimball stayed up until three o'clock the night he thought Bradford Belle had caught cold,' and so on, but he clearly deplored these womanly intrusions, and quickly elbowed them out of the conversation.

When they came to the children, it was her turn; and Timothy soon saw that both parents had a different attitude to them from the judicial temper Mr. Kimball kept for his sweet peas. All the family had tea in the drawing-room with Timothy. Effie, bringing it in, contrived to suggest by her deportment that their presence there was highly irregular; carrying the tray, she steered her way between them as though they were recently imported pieces of furniture designed to trip her up; and Gerald's wistful question, 'Why is she going away? Isn't she going to stay and have tea with us?' she woundingly ignored.

Timothy heard many tales about the children punctuated with 'Didn't you, Gerald?' and 'Speak up, Billy, he isn't usually so shy,' and shared their embarrassment. If only they could all put off their company manners and change into their old clothes! But no; this was a prestige occasion, and the more earnestly that Timothy hunted for a common ground of experience – the trials of travelling in war-time, the shortage of foodstuffs – an unlucky gambit for it turned out that the Kimballs had brought masses of food with them, which, out of delicacy, they had not, so to speak, declared – the more self-conscious, the more sharply aware of personal, family, and class rivalry they all became. It was soon revealed to Timothy that the Kimballs, in casting their children upon the world, were doing the world a favour, which they expected the world to acknowledge; and to the Kimballs that Timothy was a harassed, over-worked bachelor, with a beautiful house and an extensive and well-kept garden which he was, from motives of public spirit, putting at the disposal of a class of people who would never otherwise have enjoyed such privileges.

Hollower grew the voices, more careful the accents, more constrained the gestures; politeness caught them in its vice and was cramping their every thought when Billy, who for half an hour had been denied every outlet which his nature craved, suddenly dropped his tea-cup. Catching a chair leg it broke in pieces. Splayed brown fingers of tea ran across the carpet, and Billy raised a tremulous wail in which, after a second's study of the faces round him, Gerald joined. To Timothy it seemed the happiest sound he had heard since he came to Upton. At once the knot of tension broke; Mrs. Kimball, between scoldings, soothings and apologies, gave expert advice as to how to deal with tea-stains; everyone rushed about, dishcloths were fetched, mopping operations started, fragments of tea-cup collected, smiles broke out on every face, and Billy, from being the villain became the hero of the hour. Only a small disaster is necessary, reflected Timothy, to deliver us from ourselves.

After a tour of the house, which they extravagantly admired, Mr. and Mrs. Kimball returned to the kitchen, and later Timothy drove them to the railway station. The prospect of reaching home at two in the morning did not daunt them; they declared they had never spent such a happy day.

After this the boys lost their shyness of Timothy, and when they spied him in the garden, they would hurl themselves upon him or ambush him from behind trees, armed with wooden models of sawn-off shot guns; a tremendous barking as of machine-gun fire betrayed their presence, and then the two gunmen would rush out and tell Timothy he was dead. If he lay down on the ground and shut his eyes they were transported with joy, and danced a war-dance over him. They did not take such liberties with Wimbush, though it was he who had provided them with their weapons, remarking to Timothy, 'They can't begin too young, they can't begin too young.'

Of one person on Timothy's premises they never lost their awe, and that was Nelson. Timothy saw but little of Nelson; he had his own times for coming and going and often his new, sleek, shiny car, so reminiscent of him, never left the shed for days together. But occasionally he was to be seen stalking about the stable yard, exuding majesty, or standing with Wimbush, who was a friend of his, in wordless conversation, for neither of them seemed to speak, though each of them looked as though something the other had said had exhausted the subject, whatever it was, and left them both with their worst fears realised. Even Timothy could never quite repress sensations of guilt when Nelson hove into view, and the little boys, so Timothy learnt, were so alarmed by their first encounter with him that Billy was unable to eat his dinner.

Timothy, too, had reason for despondency. The war news was as bad as it could be, and he himself had received a private blow which increased his feeling of uncertainty and insecurity. The *Broadside* had written to say that in view of the paper shortage they could no longer find space for his weekly 'Pictures of Britain' feature; they hoped that he would occasionally contribute an article, but that was all they could promise him.

For nearly fifteen years Timothy had been writing regularly for the *Broadside*. Its columns conveyed prestige, and his association with the paper had become so much a part of his life and mental habits that he could not imagine himself without it. They did not pay very much, it is true, but with taxation at its present level and several of his investments suffering a wartime shrinkage, the weekly five guineas had become an object. Besides the job was a 'reserved occupation' and carried with it quite a generous petrol allowance in excess of the basic ration; without it he might be directed down a coal mine, or, even if allowed to stay above ground, find himself more than ever cut off from the outside world.

Events move quickly in war-time; his next article, the Editor regretfully informed him, must be his last.

What should be his final subject? Perhaps it was as well that his job was coming to an end, for he had already exhausted all the 'sights' – houses, castles, abbeys, churches, beauty-spots and the reflections on England's greatness that they inspired – in a radius of thirty miles of Upton. There still remained one, the most obvious of them all. Yet for reasons much less obvious he had not included it in his survey; he had always put off going there.

Welshgate Hall was fifteen miles away. It was never open to the public, but from certain points of vantage, he had been told, a good view of it could be obtained. Timothy's mind began to consider its pictorial possibilities. 'Welshgate Hall, a hideous example of the worst period of English architecture, "una vera porcheria," as the Italians say, is the property of a Mrs. Lampard, a woman who would scarcely stop short of murder to attain her ends. Having broken up her husband's first marriage, and sent the unhappy widow post-haste to the grave, she had the effrontery to return to his house and adopt airs and what for want of a better word I must call graces, which would have sat ill on a woman of such proved probity as Queen Victoria herself. A petty tyrant of the countryside, she used her wealth and influence to uproot the flower of freedom wherever it raised its head – especially in the monstrous conservatories – fungus-growths, glassy sheets of toadstool which disfigure the already sick-making brickwork of Welshgate Hall.'

Timothy pondered. Yes, it would be a revenge, a rich revenge. It would teach her to ignore a distinguished writer who had once entertained her lavishly at the Villa Lucertola.

It was Beatrice and Effie's afternoon out; they were going to the cinema in Swirrelsford. He would have liked to take them with him but did not want to ask them to change their plans. Lately they had seemed reluctant to accompany him, and Damaris and Chloe had dropped out of his pictures. Never mind; he could invent their comments, as he had often done before. 'Is this Welshgate Hall? Why, it looks like a workhouse!' Hitherto his pictures of Britain had been discreetly laudatory. Would the editor object if the last essay in the series was less favourable? Well, he would have to print it, Timothy's swan-song, and must shrug his shoulders if its tone was a little tart. 'What hast thou done for me, England, my England?' he thought, his eye catching the bamboo clump where the boat-house lurked. 'I have written thee up in twenty-six articles, and what is my reward? The sack. My life since I left Italy has been a continual struggle,' he thought resentfully. 'Everyone conspires to thwart me; only Mrs. Purbright understands me.'

Gerald and Billy were playing on the lawn. What a business it had been to find someone to look after them for the afternoon! Usually, when Beatrice and Effie went out, he stayed in to keep an eye on the children, and give them their tea; that was no great hardship for everything was left ready for him; he only had to boil the kettle. But today he simply must go out, it was his only chance of seeing Welshgate Hall, for the article must be in by Monday. Wimbush had kindly ransacked the village for volunteers; Timothy had offered a handsome reward; but no one would give up her Saturday afternoon. Eventually Mrs. Burnett's niece had promised to come. She had promised to come at two o'clock: it was now nearly half-past and there was still no sign of her. He dared not wait any longer.

He walked across the lawn to give a last word of caution to the two little boys. Shouting their battle-cries, they raced towards him. For a moment Timothy pretended to be dead. Gerald sat on his chest and Billy on his feet; their small fists pommelled him, their excited voices uttered the most fearful threats. Scrambling to his feet and shaking off the grass, for the lawn had been newly mown, he told them that a nice lady would soon be coming to play with them, and then put them through their catechism.

'Where are you not to go?'

'Not on the road,' said Gerald promptly, and Billy echoed, jumping about, 'not on the road, not on the road.'

'And where else?'

'Not near the river.'

'And where else?'

'Not inside the boat-house.' This was a routine answer, for the boat-house was kept locked. Gerald paused and said, in his lilting, plangent voice, 'Why won't you let us go inside the boat-house, Mr. Casson?'

Timothy hesitated. There were several reasons for forbidding the boys the boat-house, but the chief one was that he did not much want to go there himself. Since the evacuees arrived he had not bestowed upon his treasure so much as a single glance.

'I'll take you some time,' he temporised.

'Now! Now!' they chorused, clinging to him, but he shook his head.

The memory of their clutching fingers and teasing, pleading faces lingered with him as with surreptitious glances at the map – for maps were suspect in the hands of private persons – he nosed his way along the lanes in what he believed to be the direction of Welshgate Hill. The signposts had been uprooted; the hedges were high; the fifteen miles seemed more like fifty. Suddenly there was an ominous hiss, a spiteful exhalation as though Destiny were discharging her ill-humour at him. The car listed and limped and mutely declared itself to be no longer his servant.

Timothy was an inexpert mechanic, and by the time he had changed the wheel it hardly seemed worth while going on. But he would have to rejoin the main road. Where was it? He drove on and presently came to a high arch framing a gateway with a lodge on each side of it. The wrought iron gates stood open, and just inside a man was sitting at a table.

Timothy went up to him, but before he could ask the way the man said, 'Did you wish to see the Hall, sir? I'm afraid it's just on closing time.'

Timothy noticed a roll of tickets and a pie-dish half full of silver coins.

'Why, what place is this?' he asked.

The man looked at him in surprise.

'It's Welshgate Hall, sir. It's open today for the Queen's Nurses. Pity you didn't come earlier. It's never been shown to the public before.'

'Could I just drive up to the door?' Timothy asked, trying to conceal his disappointment.

'If you think it's worth two bob, sir,' the man grinned. 'Only you must be out again by five o'clock. The orders were strict. You won't let me down, will you?'

Timothy promised not to.

Welshgate Hall was a Palladian house with a portico, reminding Timothy of the Villa Malcontenta, near Venice, but much larger. Three rows of windows with nine windows to each row stretched across the front. It lacked the elusive beauty of Malcontenta; Palladio's inspired mathematics had here been reduced to a formula; but it was an imposing structure. Beneath the great portico was a door-way tall as the entrance to a baroque church; and this door-way was reached by a double flight of steps curving up from either side, rather small for the size of the façade but intimate and friendly against the impersonal expanse of stone. It intrigued his eye and invited him to mount; but was it worth while, to go in for five minutes?

While he debated, the figure of a girl came towards him from the opposite side of the drive. She was making for the staircase, but when she saw him she hesitated and then came up to him.

'Did you want to see over the house?' she said.

She was slender and pale-skinned, with dark grey eyes that were full of light.

Timothy told her of his misadventures, to which she listened as sympathetically as though no one had ever had a puncture before. 'And now I'm afraid it's too late,' he wound up, and the stable clock, striking five with a high, unfamiliar note, gave point to his words.

'Oh no,' she said, 'you must see the house now that you've come all this way – from Upton, I think you said? And we've had so few people, we hoped for many more, it's because of the petrol rationing, I expect. Aren't you tired? Wouldn't you like some tea? I was just going to have mine.'

Now Timothy realised that she must be the daughter of the house. He hesitated. Confronted with the idea of meeting Mrs. Lampard, he had an impulse to flee.

'Mother had to go away for the week-end,' she said, 'and I'm all alone, but if it wouldn't bore you, I'm sure she would like you to stay to tea.'

She spoke more formally, as though shouldering the dignity and responsibility of a hostess. I must seem very old to her, Timothy thought; that's why she feels she can ask me; her mother would never let her entertain a younger man alone.

'It will be a great pleasure,' he said.

'And afterwards I'll take you round the house. There's not much to see, really. Some fairly good pictures and some French furniture, if you like that. I do, because you see, I was born in France and I love it. I think I mind about France more than anything else in the war, so far. I say I have French blood in my veins, but Mother swears we haven't. Are you fond of France, Mr.—?'

'Casson.'

She turned to him, startled, and her hand, which was touching the knob of the front door, dropped to her side.

'Then you must be *the* Mr. Casson.'

'I shouldn't think so,' said Timothy, smiling.

'Oh, this is so exciting! What a pity Mother isn't here. We've heard such a lot about you, but I never thought you would be so nice.'

'I've heard about you, too,' said Timothy, 'and I must say I did expect to find you nice.'

'I'm afraid I sounded rude,' she said penitently, but still without opening the door. 'It was such a shock to find myself with the hero of a cause célèbre!'

'You won't want to have me to tea, now,' said Timothy.

'Of course, of course, all the more!'

She pushed the door open and led him into a square, lofty hall. 'I'm simply dying to talk to you. We shall have so much to say.' She hesitated. 'Look, that's supposed to be a Vandyck,' and she pointed to a full length portrait of a man in a ruff glowing richly against the grisaille. 'But I'll tell you about him afterwards. Now let's have tea.' He followed her down a saloon lined with pictures to its cornice. The three chandeliers were all turned on, for the glass roof which should have lighted the gallery had been blacked out. Ahead, the light of day struggled through a doorway. This led to a small room, hung with crimson damask. A silver kettle gleamed among the tea-things.

'You know,' she confided to him as they sat down, 'I've always been on your side.'

'How?' asked Timothy.

'Well, it sounds funny, doesn't it? but I mean about the boat.'

'Oh, the boat,' said Timothy.

At the sound of that short word constraint fell upon them, only slightly eased by the ceremonious handing of plates.

'Perhaps you'd rather not talk about it?' Miss Lampard said, anxiously. 'Would you rather just talk about the house, or—'

'Ourselves?' suggested Timothy.

She smiled delightfully at him and then looked serious again.

'Oh, but this is such an opportunity!' She watched Timothy's face, where suspicion and resentment still smouldered. 'And I've always admired your writing so much – not that my opinion is worth anything.'

When Timothy told her his job was coming to an end, she looked quite miserable.

'Oh, and what will you do now? It's more than ever important—' she broke off, knitting her white brows. 'You see, it's all been such a muddle! Twenty years ago, before I was born, nobody would have said a word – but now the fishing has become quite sacred, and of course it's to Mother's interest it should be – she gets such colossal rents! But perhaps you're a Socialist?' she added. 'I know that many writers are.'

Timothy disclaimed being a Socialist, but Miss Lampard looked thoughtful.

'Sometimes I think one ought to be. Well, every kind of suggestion has been made – like certain days of the week, and certain times of the year, being set aside for you to row on – and well, perhaps I oughtn't to say this – your being asked to rent a certain stretch of the river as though it were a fishing – and then, though they all say it's a shame you shouldn't row, they disagree among themselves and then seem to think it's *you* who have turned the proposals down, as if you were a kind of enemy who had come amongst us. It's so unfair! "But he'll never consent to that," they say, or "it's no good asking him *that*, he'll be sure to refuse!" I said to Mother, "But he's never been consulted!" Mother's a darling, you know, and I'd kill anyone who said anything else, but she belongs to her generation, she doesn't – how shall I put it? think that a rule should have exceptions and she doesn't like modern ways – she was so carefully brought up herself – but she isn't a bit *hard*, I should hate you to think she was.'

'I gather the decision doesn't really lie with her,' said Timothy.

'No, but of course she could influence them – they're all her tenants, except you. They'd do what she wanted, no one can help it. She has a way with her, you know. But I shall tell her,' her daughter went on firmly, 'I shall tell her you came and how nice you were, and then she'll do something about it, I'm sure she will. I shall tell her you're not in the least like what people think.'

'What do they think?' asked Timothy.

'Oh, they've got it all wrong. You don't mind me being frank, do you, they think you're an eccentric kind of person, half a foreigner, and perhaps a sort of revolutionary, you know – who wants to upset established customs – and turn the valley into – well, a sort of Lido, I suppose, destroying its character, and so on. At least I think that's what they think. I hardly ever see them. Mother has so many tenants.'

'I suppose she has,' said Timothy.

'Yes, and you wouldn't believe what a nuisance they can be at times, wanting so many repairs done and never satisfied. That's why I am so excited to meet you, because you really are *someone*, and not just a tenant. Are you going to write about our house?'

'Well, I might.'

'How thrilling. And will you put me in?'

'Perhaps in a very veiled way. Should you mind?'

'I should adore it. And Mother will be pleased, because she's very proud of the house, though she pretends not to be. Between ourselves, that was why she went away. She couldn't bear the idea of people she'd never seen tramping round and perhaps stealing the writing-paper – you know, to look as if they'd stayed here. But you won't put that in your article, will you? How will you begin? "At the door I was met by a withered crone?" '

'I shall stick strictly to the truth.'

'Well, have you had everything you want? Another cake? another cup of tea? Then let's begin.' She rose. 'This is called the Ambassador's room. . . .'

Timothy did not get away unscathed. The gate-keeper upbraided him for having outstayed his time. 'She's a regular madam,' he said, alluding to his employer; 'she'll have me on the mat for this all right.' But a tip seemed to appease him, and Timothy drove back through the slanting sunshine aware of a more real peace than he had known for months. Fostered by the feeling that each in thought had been unfair to the other, the new acquaintance had ripened into friendship. To Timothy she seemed a delightful child, touchingly vulnerable and innocent, and he believed he had made a good impression on her, for she hung on his lips and laughed at his feeblest sallies. He had been flattered, and for a long time no one had flattered him except Mrs. Purbright, with whose appreciation, generous as it was, there sometimes mingled a note of warning, like the sound of a bell-buoy on a calm day. Most of the young men she knew spoke slightingly of France, which hurt her; she pined to return to it and would have gone but for the cruel turn the war had taken. And Timothy found himself confiding in her in a way that wouldn't have seemed possible a few hours earlier. It was as if the accumulated small grievances of his life at Upton, instead of barring his spirit's egress, now urged it to freedom. They promised to meet each other again; he was to come to Welshgate Hall, and she, with her mother's sanction, to the Old Rectory. As to the question of the boat, that could be regarded as already settled.

The high tenor note of the stable clock had sounded seven times before he left. Already he was revolving in his mind phrases for his last article. It should have an elation, a confidence that none of the others had had; an ecstasy of farewell. Ave atque vale! The spirit of England in a Palladian setting; our gift for borrowing and transforming what was best in the art of other countries; a great house where the name of France was held in equal honour with our own. Timothy had never had a special feeling for France before; its people, he thought, were ill-tempered, its art over-spiced with cleverness; geographically it was an unavoidable stepping-stone to Italy. Now he remembered its great services to civilisation; its ceaseless intellectual energy; its sense of style, more tenacious even than its sense of beauty; its magnificent refusal to be over-governed, its wholesome instinct to choose corruption, in which there is always life, in preference to tyranny, which spells death. Yes, Welshgate Hall was a monument to France as well as to England, and in its serene survival, its evident indestructibility, was a symbol ready to his hand. Hitherto he had always avoided the topical as exotic to his mind, which flourished in the climate of the past; now he would explore the present in all its most hopeful implications, guided by the genius loci of Welshgate Hall – a nymph with a French name, but was she really flesh and blood, or a spirit, a gracious ghost from the time of Louis Quinze wafted across the water with those commodes and bergères and escritoires, whose gilded gleam gave back the evening gold, poured molten in through the tall windows?

Here shortly would be entertained, so his guide told him – if guide she was – those members of the Free French Forces who had risked all to throw in their lot with freedom, and the furniture would glow again to hear its own tongue spoken, and feel its long exile ended, by theirs, which had begun – no, not begun, for here, at Welshgate in England, they would be at home.

Savouring the enchantment of the hour he drove slowly, for there was no hurry to get back.

Turning into the stable yard, he saw Wimbush and Nelson, deep in wordless confabulation. He was in no way surprised to see them, and having put the car away he called out 'Good evening' and was making for the side-door when the two men came towards him.

'Excuse me, sir,' said Nelson, in a tone more ominous than he had ever used to Timothy before, 'but I take it you haven't heard the news.'

'What news?' asked Timothy, his heart sinking.

Nelson and Wimbush exchanged glances.

'It's to do with the boys, sir, Gerald and Billy Kimball,' said the policeman, eyeing Timothy closely.

'What about them? Please tell me, Nelson.'

'Well, sir, they've disappeared. At least, they can't be found.'

Timothy stood still, twisting his hands.

'But I left them playing on the lawn.'

'What time would that be, sir?' asked Nelson, producing his notebook.

Timothy told him.

The policeman nodded as if the hour confirmed his worst fears.

'Was there anyone with them when you left?'

Feeling and looking like a criminal, Timothy explained that Mrs. Burnett's niece had promised to come and keep an eye on them. 'I left the side-door on the latch so that she could get in,' he added.

Nelson looked up from his notebook, and said, 'Would it surprise you to hear that Miss Cornett, Mrs. Burnett's niece, failed to arrive?'

'But she promised faithfully to come,' said Timothy.

'On inquiring at her house,' said the policeman, 'she stated that she had forgotten the whole matter and gone out for a walk.'

'With young Tom Sutton,' put in Wimbush.

'He confirmed her statement,' Nelson said. 'The last person to see the boys was yourself, sir.'

'Then who—?' began Timothy.

'The alarm was given by Beatrice, Miss Kinghorn, I should say, who informed me at my cottage shortly after returning from a visit to the cinema at Swirrelsford about 6.30 p.m. She said she could find the boys nowhere, and asked me to assist in the search, with which I at once complied.'

'And you couldn't find them?' said Timothy stupidly.

'I obtained the help of Mr. Wimbush, and together we made a thorough search of the house, premises and pleasure-grounds, but we could find no trace of them.' Nelson paused. 'We examined the river bank, but there were no signs of footmarks, discarded clothing or anything to indicate a tragedy.'

Timothy said with an effort. 'Did you look inside the boat-house?'

'We went there first, sir. But it was locked.'

'Those old boys always had a rare fancy for the boat-house,' Wimbush put in. ' 'Twas because you told 'em not to, like as not, sir. Boys will be boys.'

In the context this well-worn phrase seemed to Timothy unbearably pathetic, and his voice shook as he said, 'Had anyone seen them in the street?'

'I made inquiries in the vicinity, but failed to receive a satisfactory answer. Children were seen, but the passers-by could not identify the boys in question.'

There was a long pause. The two men seemed to expect Timothy to contribute something to the situation, but his mind would not work on it.

'Is there anything more we can do?' he asked.

'I telegraphed to the next of kin, in this case the parents,' said Nelson. 'I used your telephone, sir.'

'Quite right,' said Timothy. 'How did you know the address?'

'Miss Kinghorn was able to supply it, sir.'

Wimbush sniffed.

'I'm afraid the girls will be terribly upset,' Timothy said.

'Effie did rather give way,' said Wimbush, 'which is not to be surprised at, being so tender-hearted, but the other one really created more, which I own I didn't expect.'

'I advised weak tea with plenty of sugar,' said Nelson, 'for shock.'

'I'll go in and see them,' said Timothy.

Beatrice and Effie were sitting in the kitchen red-eyed and speechless, Beatrice still catching her breath. They had nothing to add to Nelson's story, though they were loud in condemnation of Mrs. Burnett's niece, of whom, it seemed, they had expected nothing better. They were inclined to blame Timothy for not waiting longer, but not as much as he blamed himself. The three of them mingled self-reproaches with half-hearted surmises as to what might have happened; they even argued a little, and then fell silent. What they all feared, they dared not say.

Timothy wandered out of the kitchen into the house, which wore a silent, stricken air: he did not realise how much the little boys, though they were not encouraged to come 'his way,' had peopled it. He went from room to room, looking perfunctorily into cupboards and under beds; he went into their room, but retreated hastily, so painfully did the sight of their small belongings affect him – their pocket-knives and pistols, the coloured stones they had collected, the twist of paper which still had some sweets packed into the corner. Remembering their passion for ambush and concealment, he climbed on to the roof, where they had been strictly told not to go, wanly hoping that the rat-tat of a machine-gun would greet him from behind some chimneystack. But all was silence and emptiness and thick, level sunshine. From this height the boat-house, its pointed roof rising steeply from among the sheltering bamboos, looked like a little chapel; the drunken rocks across the river were a deep rose; the untroubled beauty of the evening hour was like something aimed at his heart.

Closing the trap-door behind him, he returned to the little boys' bedroom, feeling that some effluence of their presence might linger there, and more than ever ashamed that it was such a poor room; for he had set aside the two best rooms for the week-end visitors who never came. Not seeing very clearly he turned on the light. How untidy the room was; Beatrice, whose especial charge the little boys were, had always kept it neat. He pulled open a drawer in the drab-painted chest of drawers. It was empty. Another gave the same result. He was puzzled, and a suspicion, as yet a feeling rather than a thought, began to form in his mind. A moment later his mind grasped it.

The boys had not disappeared, they had been taken away.

As if that were a worse fate, he found himself trembling. Kidnapped! The word had horrible associations. It had gone screaming through the nineteen-thirties, warning mankind that the age of clemency was over. To confirm his fears he walked across to the bed. The coverlet had been disarranged. He felt underneath it for their nightshirts. They were not there, so he put his hand under the pillow; and as he did so something fluttered from the back of the pillow on to the floor, away from him. It was a piece of paper, he found when he got round to it, scribbled on in pencil. Holding it to the light he read:

We have taken the boys away.

You will hear from us later.

Mr. and Mrs. KIMBALL.

So intense was Timothy's relief that he felt as though the boys had been given back to him from the dead. Nay, more, as if they had been created on the spot, miraculously, to give joy to their ageing parents and to him. But Beatrice and Effie received the news in a different spirit. Joy lasted long enough to dry their tears; then they became indignant: a little with Nelson, who had told them to touch nothing in the room, thereby preventing them from making the discovery; a little with him, for forestalling them; but most of all with the parents who had given them such a fright. 'People like that didn't ought to have children.' Soon Timothy began to share their indignation, for really the Kimballs had behaved in a most outrageous manner; whatever they might plead in their letter, nothing could excuse them.

Pleased to have succeeded where the arm of the law had failed, Timothy went out into the stable yard where Nelson, to fill in time, was making a round of the loose-boxes. Nelson listened with an impassive face, as if surprise was an emotion unbecoming to his calling. 'It's not the first time,' he said darkly. 'It often happens, and mark my words it will happen again. They don't like them out of their sight – 'tis only natural.'

'Yes,' said Timothy, 'but the boys seemed so happy.'

'That's what you think,' said Nelson, looking down at Timothy with a kindly smile. 'I'm not saying they weren't, I'm far from saying they weren't. This is a good home, sir, and let me tell you I've seen a good many. But who can tell what goes on in a kid's head, sir? Why, they might have thought you was a kind of Bluebeard, for instance.'

Wimbush, who had been listening, said warmly, 'Mr. Casson laid hisself out to please they little devils. 'Tisn't every gentleman, let alone a gentleman who does head work, as would lie down on the ground and let 'em mess him about, same as Mr. Casson used to.'

'Doesn't do to be too familiar with people of that sort,' said the policeman. 'They don't appreciate it, and only take advantage.'

'That's right,' said Wimbush. 'When they come from Birmingham you don't know where they come from.'

Nelson agreed that the Midlands were incalculable, and turned to Timothy.

'All's well that ends well, as they say, sir. Though we've had a lot of trouble for nothing, and on a Saturday afternoon, too. But there, a policeman's time's everybody's time. I shan't say nothing about your little mistake, sir.'

'Oh, what mistake was that, Nelson?' Timothy reviewed a lifetime of mistakes.

'Well, touching the things in the boys' room, sir, might be called obstructing a constable in the execution of his duty. But you didn't mean any harm, and it's all turned out for the best.'

'I daresay Mr. Casson won't be sorry to see the last of them,' said Wimbush. 'They treated him that rough. And I shan't have 'em trampling down my flower-beds. But there's one as will miss them, and that's the other one in the kitchen.'

'You mean Beatrice?'

Wimbush nodded, as if he could not bring himself to utter Beatrice's name. 'She'll cry her eyes out,' he added, not without satisfaction.

'These unmarried women have feelings that you and I don't know about,' said Nelson. 'I could tell you a thing or two.'

Wimbush turned out to be right. Beatrice's eyes on the morrow were still red and swollen, and to her habitual taciturnity was added a bitter sense of loss and grievance. To Timothy the house seemed strangely silent and under-populated, but he scarcely had time to miss the children, so busy was he writing his article in praise of Welshgate Hall. The war had more meaning for him in proportion as he could visualise it as a union instead of a conflict; and in this farewell essay there was a double reconciliation, for each glowing sentence took him nearer, he felt, to an understanding, an entente cordiale, with Mrs. Lampard, and was musical with the plash of oars. For surely, surely after this she would not deny him the boat?

He laid the praise on thick, awarding it equally to France and England, co-inheritors of the civilisation enshrined in this stately and splendid monument, which was so well worth dying for. And if it was worth dying for, so, by implication, was its owner, thanks to whose care and taste it still maintained undimmed its ancient glory; thanks to whose generosity the public could see it as it used to be, with the bloom of private ownership still on it, an organism, a living entity, not a State-owned museum from which the soul had fled. The soul which might be symbolised – here Timothy paused, for he was enveloping Désirée in a plethora of symbols – by the guide or sprite (was she really there in the sunlight, or did he only see her in chambers where the curtains were half-drawn?) who seemed to accompany him from saloon to staircase and from whose lips the French language – evoked by so much that they saw and touched and talked about – floated as easily as her own.

Carrying his last article to the post box, Timothy felt triumphant rather than sad, for in his mind, at his writing table, he had brought together so many opposites that it was like a fulfilment of his personality. The world might not be at peace with itself, but he was at peace with the world.

Monday morning brought no letter from Mr. and Mrs. Kimball, but it did bring Mrs. Burnett, and Timothy, although still in the mood of finding everything for the best, felt he must ask her for an explanation of her niece's conduct.

Usually brimming with good humour, Mrs. Burnett seemed to think the query rather tactless and parried it more than once, by the simple expedient of scrubbing without answering, before she faced it.

'Well, sir, of course it was her day off, like everyone else's.'

'I know that, Mrs. Burnett, and it was very good of her to say she would give up her afternoon. Only I wish she would either have come, or let us know that she couldn't.'

'Yes, sir, it's a good deal to expect of a girl to give up her afternoon out, and my niece is a good worker, there's no denying that.'

'I'm sure she is, only she said she'd come, and we got rather a fright.'

'Well, sir, no one has ever said anything against the girl, and I'm sure my sister would be very upset if she thought anything had been said. It isn't very nice, especially when you've gone out of your way to do a favour, as she had.'

'I appreciate that, Mrs. Burnett. If only she could just have let us know!'

'But she couldn't have stopped them taking them away, could she? After all they were the children's parents. She might have got mixed up with something nasty, and then what would my sister have said?'

'I know, but that isn't quite the point. She said she would come, and—'

'Well, sir, we're only young once, and there was a kind of feeling, all round our way, that it wasn't fair to ask a girl as has a steady young man to give up her afternoon to doing what's really a nursemaid's duty. There was quite a strong feeling, sir, and it's got stronger since what's happened.' Mrs. Burnett's voice changed and deepened. It registered affront: tears stole into it, and a hint of menace. 'I think the girl's had a lucky escape, sir, and there's many that thinks with me. Mrs. Pilling, at the local last night, she came out quite strong. But of course if you're not satisfied, sir,' here Mrs. Burnett's voice almost broke – 'well, I should like to give in me notice, that's all.'

Timothy was aghast.

'Oh please don't do that, Mrs. Burnett.'

'Well, sir, I'll think it over this time, but there's no one can't say I don't do a good day's work, and if my niece is to be insulted I shall know where to go.'

'We won't say anything more about it,' said Timothy soothingly.

'You may not, sir, but things of this sort don't lie down so easily when anyone's been unjustly accused, and there's no fire without smoke. There's some as might want to give the house a wide berth after what's happened.'

'Well, it wasn't our fault,' said Timothy defensively.

'I'm not saying it was, sir,' said Mrs. Burnett, and resumed her scrubbing.

With quickened step and smarting spirit Timothy retreated from the house. Try as he would, he hadn't been able to persuade Mrs. Burnett that her niece should have kept her word. The niece hadn't a leg to stand on, yet somehow her aunt had managed to carry the war into his country. The war! Better forget it, for this was his first day of freedom, the day he had looked forward to and dreaded for so many years, when his weekly task was over, his time unmortgaged, his mind unfettered, free to roam where it listed. He leaned on the white gate and looked across to the Green with its girdle of Lombardy poplars. Where do we go from here? Which way freedom? The Swirrelsford bus, always at hand when one wasn't waiting for it, stopped on the far side of the road. Some people got out; others got in; the driver seemed to look inquiringly at Timothy. On an impulse Timothy signalled to him, jumped on the bus, and found himself sitting next to the birdlike, highly finished profile of Miss Chadwick. Raising her lorgnon, she said:

'Mr. Casson! Whither away?'

'Nowhere in particular!' he answered gaily.

'What, nowhere in particular! Not looking for a picture of Britain?'

'I've found it here!' he smiled at her. 'But—' and he explained his position.

'You mean that the *Broadside* has fired you?'

Timothy laughed.

'But this is serious. What shall we know of England, who only Casson knew? And what will you do now? Join the L.D.V.?'

'I hadn't thought,' said Timothy lamely.

'We must rope you in for something. Do you know your First Aid?'

Timothy attempted a joke.

'Well, I always try to help myself.'

'Ha, ha, your best *Broadside* manner. But I'm afraid it's helping others that matters. You should get in touch with Mrs. Harbord.'

'I'm afraid I don't know her.'

'Not know Mrs. Harbord?'

'No.'

Miss Chadwick thought a moment.

'There is the factory down the road. They welcome part-time workers.'

'With me, it would have to be all or nothing,' said Timothy.

'What about fire-watching?'

'In the summer?' said Timothy innocently. 'I'm afraid I've let my fire out.'

Miss Chadwick shook her head, then lowering her voice, she said, 'What a mysterious business about your evacuees, Mr. Casson. So many rumours are going round. What really happened?'

Timothy told her all he knew.

'But there must be something behind it,' insisted Miss Chadwick. 'If only to allay suspicion you ought to find out. Mrs. Purbright is a friend of yours, we know, a great friend; but unless this is cleared up, she will hardly dare to repeat the experiment.'

'I'm not sure I want her to,' said Timothy rashly.

'It isn't for myself I mind,' Miss Chadwick went on, 'but my dear brother would have so hated the idea of anything . . . well, unfortunate, happening in his old home. He was a scholar, of course, I expect that makes a difference. He shrank from any kind of publicity.'

The bus was slowing down, and Timothy saw his chance. 'This is where I get off,' he said, waving Miss Chadwick goodbye. What is freedom, unless it enables us to break away from disagreeable situations? All the same, conscious of having made a fool of himself, he walked home in a chastened and sober spirit.

CHAPTER XII

SHALL I read her the letter, Timothy wondered, shall I just tell her its drift, or shall I falsify it?

He read the letter again.

'DEAR MR. CASSON,

'We ask you to excuse the liberty we took in taking the children away, but after Miss Kinghorn had written to us the way she had we couldn't rest. She said not to tell you as it would do not good, so I shall only say that someone in your pay has threatened to use the children something terrible unless they stopped doing something that being children they couldn't help doing. It seems funny, doesn't it, after she said that about not telling you but she also said that it wasn't any good her saying anything but if we complained to you you might send the person away. But we shouldn't like to ask you to do that knowing the shortage of labour at the present time, also people can't help not wanting kids about, they can be a regular nuisance at times and some people are real set against them, though kids can't help being kids.

'Our purpose in coming over was really to talk it over with you in case some way out could be found, because it isn't your fault, sir, you're one of the best and we don't blame you at all. But when I come the train was late and we found the boys playing on the lawn like you told them to with no one to look after them in case anything should have happened to them which it might being only children and the river so close, and we had to decide in a hurry with only a few minutes left to tell the taxi to turn back and catch the train. Mr. Kimball can only get away on a Saturday that was partly why we were rushed, that and their being no Sunday trains. So we thought what would be the best thing and which would give least trouble in the long run would be for us to take the children away there and then, leaving a note on the pillow as the most likely place. We had no thought of giving you anxiety and worry such as you must have had judging by your telegram and letter when you kindly sent the boys things back. I am very sorry for that both of us and would wish to take the opportunity to thank you for all your kindness to the boys whilst under your care. They often speak of you and Miss Kinghorn with real love and ask when they are going back again, and mention the other person who they was evidently more afraid of than you being stricter. They never say he laid a finger on them though he sometimes spoke rough but you can't tell with boys can you, they're as silent as owls if anything's wrong they won't tell on their oppressors, it's instinct I suppose like the public-school spirit.

'But we are very sorry that it happened because otherwise the boys couldn't have had a better home nor a kinder friend than you and Miss Kinghorn, she was like a mother to them. And we apologise and are truly sorry for any inconvenience caused by our hasty action trusting you will understand and meet as friends after this dreadful war is over.

'Wishing you always the best,

'Yours respectfully,

'MR. & MRS. KIMBALL.

'P.S. You will be pleased to know the boys are in good health and increased weight. They send their love and kisses to Miss Kinghorn.'

The kisses, in great numbers, followed.

Timothy put the letter in his pocket and with no clear plan of action went towards the kitchen.

Bowed over the rolling pin, Beatrice looked very forbidding.

'I've just had a letter from Mr. and Mrs. Kimball, Beatrice,' he said, as casually as he could.

No answer.

'It's a very nice letter,' he persisted, 'and there are a lot of messages for you.'

'I'm not interested, I'm afraid,' said Beatrice, but he saw the lines of her face stiffen and her eyes grow more intent.

He fluttered the letter in her direction, but she kept her eyes averted, and he returned it to his pocket. An idea came to him.

'The whole thing seems to have been a mistake,' he said. 'Mrs. Kimball seems to have had a dream or something – you know what mothers are.' He paused; Beatrice could not possibly know but she might feel flattered to be raised for a moment to the status of mother-hood. 'If any of us had been here at the time we could have put every-thing right. It wasn't our fault that there was no one here,' he went on, throwing Mrs. Burnett's niece to the wolves.

'That girl deserves to be strangled,' said Beatrice, breaking silence in a voice cold with hatred.

'Oh, we mustn't be hard on her, she's only young. The whole thing was so unlucky.' Feeling that Beatrice had thawed a little he told her something of the circumstances of the Kimballs' visit, and then going to the window, on the pretence of getting a better light, he read out the parents' tributes to her. By a stroke of luck the kisses had a whole page to themselves, so he was able to show her them.

'What's the good of telling me all this?' said Beatrice in an unsteady voice. 'It's too late now.'

Now was the moment for Timothy to spring his surprise on her. 'I don't think so,' he said. 'I think with a little persuasion they'd let the children come back.'

He saw Beatrice struggle with herself and a tear fall on the much flattened pastry.

'I don't know as I want 'em now,' she said. 'Children should be in a happy house. This isn't a happy house.'

'Not happy? Why not?'

'Because there's people about as don't want it to be.'

'Oh, I'm sure you're wrong, Beatrice.'

'I'm not,' she answered stubbornly. 'You don't know because you live all to yourself among books and papers as has no feeling in 'em, and folks with airified voices who pretend that nothing matters.' (Beatrice must have had in mind some former employer; no one with an airified voice had been to the Old Rectory in Timothy's time – he wished they had.) 'I don't know what Mrs. Kimball dreamed,' she went on recklessly, turning the slab of pastry over, and rolling it on the other side, 'but if she dreamed there was someone here who didn't wish the children any good, she wasn't far wrong.'

'I'm sure you're mistaken, Beatrice,' said Timothy with all the firmness he could muster. 'You're just imagining things. Now do let me write to Mrs. Kimball and say we all hope she will let Gerald and Billy come back.'

For a moment he thought she was going to yield. Then she threw up her chin and said, 'You must do as you think best, sir. But if the children come back *I* shan't stay. They're well out of it, if you ask me.'

Timothy saw her shoulders twitch and heard her sniff before he left the kitchen.

The hum of the mowing-machine tempted him out of doors. Wimbush was at the far end of the lawn. In front of him, perpetually renewed, a green wave sprang up and broke in a foam of daisy-heads upon the grass. The gardener's forehead was furrowed and his eyes were bent upon the ground. At sight of Timothy his face lit up with smiles.

'Warm work!' he said, brushing his brow with a brown hairy forearm. 'This'll bring out the willow-pattern on you.'

'I know,' said Timothy. 'We must get that motor-mower.'

'I don't want no motor-mowers,' declared Wimbush. 'Motor-mowers are for young chaps who don't know what work is. Commander Bellew he have one, and so do Colonel Harbord, he's gone all haywire about grass, they call him Colonel Lovelorn. I don't say there's another man would do this single-handed; but then, as I say, what's a man for?'

Timothy could not answer this.

'I was only saying to Nelson the other day, "You haven't half got a cushy job, standing about at street corners holding your hand up." He didn't like it, sir.'

'I suppose not,' said Timothy, doubtfully.

'He didn't. But bless you, sir, he's a good fellow, Nelson is, only he talks too much.'

'*Does* he?' exclaimed Timothy, who had never thought of Nelson as a chatterbox.

'Yes, he do, sir, begging your pardon. I said to him straight, "If there's any wrong 'uns knocking about round Upton, they'll get away while you're shooting your mouth, as the Yankees say." He didn't like it, sir.'

'Well, you were a bit severe, Wimbush.'

'Oh no, sir, he takes it in good part. Why, only yesterday he was talking about that sing-song that the L.D.V. and the police together are getting up.'

Wimbush gave Timothy a significant glance and Timothy blushed.

'I expect I ought to be in the L.D.V., Wimbush. You are, aren't you?'

'They made me corporal first go-off and from the onset. But it's different for a gentleman working on his head.'

Even Wimbush had to find excuses for Timothy.

'Of course they want every able-bodied man they can get, sir,' Wimbush went on, 'specially with the news so bad.' His face brightened.

'What news?'

'The Germans have crossed the Seine, and Italy has declared war on France.'

'You don't say so!' cried Timothy, aghast.

'It's true, sir, I heard it on the wireless. You look all upset, sir, but it'll do a lot of good, that news will. It's what the country's been waiting for. I wish I was younger.'

'Did you enjoy soldiering in the last war, Wimbush?'

'I wouldn't have missed it, sir, for all the tea in China.'

Timothy did not answer. Wimbush's comment seemed to make nonsense of many of his pet theories.

'I'm not speaking only for myself,' Wimbush went on, as though Timothy had accused him of boasting. 'We all felt the same. I was only saying to Nelson, "you should be in the Forces, a young chap like you, not in the Force." '

'Did he like that?'

'It wouldn't do for a policeman to be taking offence at every chance remark,' said Wimbush. 'Besides, he was approaching me about you, sir.'

'About me?' Timothy felt as if he was already half-way to prison.

'To see if you would be interested in the draw, sir.'

'What draw, Wimbush?'

'It's for the smoking concert. He didn't know if you'd be interested, not being in the L.D.V. or the police. So he asked me to approach you.'

Wimbush's pause invited Timothy to make the next move; 'How can I show my interest?'

'Well, sir,' said Wimbush, 'there's more ways than one. Some gentlemen buys a ticket; some gives a prize – Captain Sturrock have promised a bottle of Scotch – and some—' here Wimbush spread his hands out, as if to suggest that the generosity of an ingenious patron might take infinite forms. Seeing Timothy still look puzzled, he added patiently, 'It all helps to win the war, sir.'

'Could I contribute something?' asked Timothy, wondering if this was right.

Wimbush looked surprised and slightly shocked.

'We wouldn't either of us dream of asking you, sir. I hope you didn't think that?'

'Of course not,' cried Timothy. 'I should be delighted to. Would money do?'

'Nelson wouldn't say "no" to money,' remarked Wimbush cautiously.

Making a rapid calculation, Timothy decided to treble the amount of Captain Sturrock's gift.

'Oh, that's too much, sir, that's more than Mrs. Lampard's given.' Wimbush allowed Timothy half a second to change his mind, and went on, 'Nelson, he will be pleased. 'Tisn't everyone wants to give money to the police,' he added slyly. 'Some people might call it corruption. As I was saying to Nelson, "Now we know where you got the money to buy that smart car of yours." '

'Did he like that?' asked Timothy.

'Well, he turned a bit red. But as I said to him, " 'Tisn't as if you were a working man earning your daily bread. You're paid out of the rates by such as me and Mr. Casson, and we have a right to know where the money goes," I said. He couldn't deny it.'

'Well, I hope the party will be a great success,' said Timothy. He pulled out his pocket-book. 'Can I trust you to give Nelson this?'

For a moment Wimbush looked grave; then he burst out laughing.

'Ha, ha, sir, you can see a joke as well as anyone.'

I wonder if he liked that, thought Timothy, walking away.

'I hope you aren't joining the hue and cry against the Italians,' wrote Tyro. 'All this talk about the "stab in the back" simply sickens me. Has any nation ever hesitated to stab another in the back? Did Napoleon wait for Prussia's convenience at Jena? Or Austria's at Wagram? Did Wellington ask Napoleon to choose the ground at Waterloo? And I must say, Timothy, that your country has surpassed itself in tactlessness in its mismanagement of Italy. All that good will (perhaps the only real good will between two countries) thrown away, just because you couldn't bear to see Italy becoming a power in the Mediterranean. And talking of broken promises, as if you yourselves had not broken the Treaty of London, which brought Italy into the last war. And preaching to them about the wickedness of invading Abyssinia, as if you had not yourselves done the same thing scores of times. Do you know you now control nearly 4,000,000 square miles of Africa, more than a third of the area of the whole continent; and Abyssinia, which you once invaded yourselves but I suppose did not think worth annexing, is only about a fifteenth of that?

'Did no one remember the Boer War, did no one think of the Transvaal, of the many wars against the Ashanti tribesmen, of the ultimatum to Cetewayo? – and yet one's English friends blandly assumed that not only was it in their interest, it was their duty, to stop what they called Italian aggression. If Henry VIII had appointed himself a judge in the Divorce Court, it would have been reasonable, it would have been positively edifying, compared with the spectacle of the English Satan rebuking the Italian sin. I have no territorial ambitions, remarked the thief, his pockets so bulging with loot that he could hardly stagger – loot which he calls the White Man's Burden. We have reformed. We do not intend to give back any of the swag, of course; but we mean to see that no other nation shall offend. So hands off Abyssinia! What you can't see, among much else, is that you give justice a bad name by taking up its cause, it suffers under your patronage, just as it did when Jeffreys held the Bloody Assize. Well, well, if you win the war (which seems very unlikely at this moment) we shall see the Walrus and the Carpenter, draped in Union Jacks, gobbling up the Italian oysters on the shores of the Red Sea and the Mediterranean, tears pouring down their cheeks.

'Don't let yourself be stampeded into any kind of war effort, will you? This war-fever is a nasty thing, and has made many of my friends utterly impossible: in these past months I've written and received more rude letters than I should have thought possible – and the pleasure I get in writing finis to a friendship! I believe you are the only friend I have left, but you won't be, if I hear of you giving way to the universal madness. If I thought that would happen, I should throw up my job and come to Upton by the next train: failing such a catastrophe I must view your blessed inactivity from this respectful distance.'

Magda also wrote.

'DEAREST TIMOTHY,

'This must be a sad day for you, and I hasten to send my sympathy. I know Italy was like a second country to you, you had lived there so long and were so fond of it. I never cared for Italy, even before the Fascist régime – I hated to think of people being happy in such squalor and the dreadful ignorance of the peasantry always appalled me. You will find it wherever the Roman Catholic Church hoodwinks the people with tales of rewards and penalties in another world. And I disliked their obsequiousness and their tooth-paste smiles and persistent chattering and vibrato voices and petty dishonesty. Of course I don't mind dishonesty as such – honesty is what makes the Swiss so dull, that and their looks. Life without crime would be even drearier than it is. Think of Oslo, where you can drop a five pound note in the street and find it again next year, or the island of St. Kilda, where crime is unknown. What do the inhabitants find to do, I ask you? I like dishonesty in the Spaniards, it has so much panache, and the big French frauds always make amusing reading; and Russian dishonesty is too sweet – it's so naive and childlike, you can see them coming a mile off, and of course now it's organised it's becoming a valuable asset to the Party. But Italian dishonesty before Fascism – God, how old it makes me feel – was so hopelessly small town – it just meant stealing your luggage, or a diamond pin in a hotel bedroom – just for gain – no fantasy or political sense behind it.

'What they've done now isn't very pretty, is it? It isn't that I mind treachery but I do care so intensely about France. I won't ask if you defend them, for I don't want to quarrel with you, dear Timothy – I prefer to quarrel with people who call you a reactionary, for I know that *au fond* you think as I do, and must be feeling as sick as I did when

156

Russia made the pact with Germany. But that was to throw dust in the eyes of the Capitalist countries, and how well it succeeded!

'I don't feel half as deeply as I should about these things. Some of the comrades here just live for hatred of everything Fascist. It's like a flame that burns up all that one used to mean by life – personal relations, art, food, sex – though they have to make time for that, or where should we get new Communists? And they are never bored, never. I haven't attained to that yet. I still can't bring myself to hate everyone on the other side of the barricade, otherwise I wouldn't be writing to you, my beloved Timothy: believe me, I do feel for you, even if I ought not to. And you have the right attitude to the war, although for the wrong reasons, and are helping to sabotage it in your quiet way. As I told you, certain quarters I'm in touch with are quite interested in your little trouble about the boat. You have allies you know nothing about! But I expect you've come to terms with the local Fascistry and are taking them for rides up and down the river, flying the Swastika.'

Timothy mused. On the banks of the Brenta the corn would soon be golden and ripe for cutting. But there wasn't much corn by the river, he reflected. There, everything was green; the dark green of the vines and the acacias, the silver green of the willows and the poplars; the yellow-streaked green of the maize. How flat the landscape was, and yet how shut in and secret, with its arbours and trellises of vines, a honeycomb of intercommunicating cells, with feathery summits, and here and there a pollard tree shorn and tufted like a poodle, lifted above them. In these green compartments mysterious shadows lurked, and the dust-pink cottages encrusted with ancient stucco – like lichen, like barnacled sea-shells on the sea-shore – were up to their eaves in the green tide. Barefooted children, and keen-eyed dogs with pointed muzzles loitered round the doors, and the ground was moist and sticky from the wash-tubs. Now came the father of the family with his stiff gait, his face stern from combating the wiles of men and the malice of the climate: not angry yet, but quite ready to be; and his wife as hardbitten as himself but watchful for his moods. They meet and exchange a mono-syllable or two, unsmiling, before he lumbers into the house.

The whole scene is stripped for action; reduced to the essential requirements of wringing a bare living from the soil, there is no adventitious prettiness, no loving tidiness in the ground about the house, where an English farm-labourer's cottage is always tidy; the vineyards and maize clumps are tended more carefully than the garden. Indeed, there is no garden, in our sense of the word, only a few ragged flowers growing haphazard, among which the chickens peck and cluck, and a flimsy arbour of vines, to make a shelter from the sun. Yet this place is full of beauty and peace; it seems to lie at the centre of the heart's experience, to be as fruit-laden as a Georgic, as poetic as an eclogue: civilisation at its simplest and most enduring.

Timothy's mind travelled on down the rough white weedy track where the tramlines ran, to the station, also vine-girt, with its high, stencilled rooms, into which, even in memory, he was thankful to withdraw from the noonday glare. Other passengers had already arrived, dressed in their Sunday black, regardless of the heat, for this was a festa, and they were all bound for Venice. Several of them saluted Timothy, for they knew him well, the signore inglese of the villa Lucertola; they hailed him with delight, they told him how well he was looking, they were extravagantly pleased to see him. Relations of the friends came shyly forward and were introduced; the exchange of compliments grew almost fevered; the air hummed with protestations of good will. Not all the friends, not all the relations, were in happy circumstances; some were ill, some were suffering cruel financial hardships; some had lost their nearest and dearest. There were sighs, head-shakings, even tears, and cries of 'poveretto!' But the smiles returned as the tram came in, clanking, grinding and squeaking; two or three got out, everyone got in; there was no room for them, the tram was full already, but they piled in somehow, and those who couldn't, clung like flies to whatever foot- and hand-hold the tram afforded. Jolting and squeaking it moved off, taking the points so recklessly that the passengers were thrown against each other. A young man offered his seat to Timothy and would take no refusal.

The hilarity increased with the bumping and swaying; the sun-drenched greenery rushed by, and now they were running along the river bank, beside the long sleepy barges, with their staring bulbous eyes. On, on, until the vegetation ended and the lagoon appeared, deep blue except for little crests of foam, whipped up by the sirocco; and the air danced with freshness. A moment more and they were rattling into Fusina, with the Venice that Shelley and Byron must have seen, lying ahead, an argosy of ivory and coral, anchored to the floor of the lagoon. The obese little steamer was turning round, churning up the water; from its tall funnel, black evil-smelling smoke was whirled towards them on the fragrant wind. Often as Timothy had done the journey the tingle of excitement that this moment brought was always new. The tram pulled up, on the edge of the sea; the passengers jumped off, dropped off, walked off, were helped off; they scurried past the ticket collector and down the corridor that led to the boat. Timothy lingered, partly to savour the moment, partly to find his ticket; he was just giving it up when he felt a touch on his arm. Two men in black shirts were barring his way; the ticket collector had fallen back a pace, his hands hanging at his sides.

'We are here to arrest you,' said the taller of the two men. 'You must come with us.' 'But why?' asked Timothy. 'War has been declared,' said his captor, 'and you are now an enemy. Do not resist.' They hustled him into a closed car that was standing near, and drove rapidly away in the direction of Padua.

The dream, and the feeling of distress it left, did not disperse easily; here in England, in the bright summer morning, the indescribable defilement of captivity hung about him and he could almost smell the hostile presences in the room. But gradually his mind persuaded his more instinctive and mistrustful faculties that he was free; free to get up when he wanted, free to drink his cooling tea, free to read the letter that lay still unopened on the blanket. The address made him start. It was the Police Station, Swirrelsford; but the rest of the missive was reassuring. The Superintendent of Police thanked Timothy for his generous donation to the expenses of the concert, and in the name of the police and of the L.D.V. expressed the hope that he would be able to honour the occasion with his presence.

CHAPTER XIII

THE room filled up slowly. Anxious to make a better impression at this, his second public appearance in Upton, than he had done at the Rector's cocktail party, Timothy arrived betimes, and was escorted to what could only be called the High Table. Arranged for dramatic perform- ances, the village hall had a stage at one end, and on this a table had been placed. Below the salt two long tables on trestles ran down the body of the hall; Timothy could imagine himself back at Oxford. His place at the end of the table which he was to share with another guest was a point of vantage; he looked down his own table, and by turning his head could see what was happening at the others. He wondered who his neighbours were going to be.

The room was decorated with the flags of the Allied Nations; the Stars and Stripes were there; large coloured portraits of the King and Queen hung at the back of the stage, and along the walls were pictures of generals and maps of the war, interspersed with peace-time prints of a much earlier date: 'Bubbles,' and others in which figured rollick- ing and bibulous monks, large and kindly dogs, cottages under snow or with roses round the door, lovers delightedly meeting or sadly saying farewell. Accordion-pleated paper swags of red, white and blue swung from one wall to the other and from the ceiling hung frilly balls and bells of the same colours; the whole effect was so gay and pretty that Timothy began to feel his spirits rise. Singly or in small knots the guests drifted in, peered along the tables and took their places with much whispering and laughing. Wimbush and Nelson were sitting together; Timothy waved to them and received a discreet salutation in reply. At his table the guests were slower in making their appearance; perhaps, thought Timothy, they expected to be bored and meant to make their purgatory as brief as possible. Presently the Rector arrived, resplendent in purple and accompanied by a clerical friend; they were given places of honour near the centre. Mr. Purbright having sat down got up again and came round to Timothy. 'Glad to see you here,' he said. 'Come to the Rectory afterwards if you feel like it, there'll be several of us there.' Timothy got up to speak to him, and when he sat down again he found that his left-hand neighbour had arrived, a genial-looking red-faced man of fifty, of great breadth and girth.

'Daykin, my name is,' he announced, 'Sergeant-Inspector Daykin to the members of the Force.'

'My name is Casson,' said Timothy.

'You needn't tell me that,' remarked the Inspector with a smile.

'What, do you know me?' said Timothy.

'It's our business to know everyone,' said the Inspector, 'but it isn't always we have the pleasure of talking to gentlemen we know quite well by sight and reputation.'

'I hope you know nothing against mine,' said Timothy with a nervous laugh.

'Nothing at all, Mr. Casson, on the contrary. People sometimes feel funny when they meet a policeman, I know, but he's really there to help them. Ah, here's the Captain.'

A tall, spare man with iron-grey hair was sitting down at Timothy's other side. He was just going to say something, when, with a loud scraping of feet, the whole party rose, and silence falling on them the Rector said grace.

'Just in time,' said Timothy's new neighbour when they were all seated. 'I thought I was going to be late on parade. Let's see,' he said looking round, 'Daykin's an old friend, good evening, Inspector.' He glanced interrogatively at Timothy, 'I suppose I ought to tell you my name, such as it is. Sturrock.'

'Cas—' began Timothy, but before he had got his name out Captain Sturrock exclaimed, 'Of course! Didn't we meet once at the Rectory?'

'Well,' said Timothy, 'we didn't exactly meet.'

'I remember! You were engaged with a fair lady, a dazzling blonde. We all envied you and wondered who she was.'

'Miss Vera Cross,' said Timothy a little stiffly.

'That's the name! Quite pretty, wasn't she? But we didn't get a look in – you had the whole field to yourself. She didn't pay any attention to us old fogeys.'

His smile robbed the words of any offence, and Timothy, getting rather red, remarked casually, 'Oh, I think she was one of those people who are here today and gone tomorrow.'

'I haven't set eyes on her since,' said Captain Sturrock. 'But then we don't see much of the floating population – all the young matrons in trousers.' He paused reflectively. 'You staying here some time, I hope?'

Timothy gave a brief outline of his plans, or lack of plans.

Someone was standing behind them with a bottle.

'Thanks, I will have some sherry,' Captain Sturrock said. 'Those poor chaps down below aren't getting any, but no matter, they'll soon be well away on beer. I'm glad to have this opportunity of talking to you,' he added, altering his tone, 'because, well, we're all neighbours and this is a jolly little place, isn't it?'

Timothy said he liked Upton very much.

'Yes, we're a very happy family,' said Captain Sturrock, his glance embracing with approval the other members of the High Table, of whom Timothy had counted fourteen, radiating outwards from the distinguished looking red-tabbed soldier in the middle, 'and of course we want to help each other and not get in each other's way. I should very much like to have a talk with you, Casson, not about anything in particular, but a general pow-wow.'

Timothy said that nothing would please him better.

Captain Sturrock thought for a moment. 'I'll get the missus to write you, that would be best, wouldn't it? As you're a single man she can't call on you, it wouldn't be proper. I don't understand these mysteries myself. Yes, please,' he said over his shoulder, 'I will have some claret, aren't they doing us well?'

Sipping his wine and watching through the alcoholic fumes the sunburnt faces at the table below him growing flushed behind their tankards, Timothy began to feel much mellower.

'There's one thing I can say now,' said Captain Sturrock, 'because we've all talked about it and we're all agreed, I mean it seems a damned pity you shouldn't be able to use the river.'

Timothy had heard something like this before, but all the same, he pricked up his ears.

'Of course it needs a certain amount of adjustment,' Captain Sturrock went on, 'but it shouldn't be beyond the wit of man to arrange.'

'A lot depends on Mrs. Lampard, doesn't it?' said Timothy cautiously.

Captain Sturrock raised his eyebrows. 'On her? I don't see what it's got to do with the old girl as long as she gets her rent paid. You would be willing to come in on that, wouldn't you?'

'Of course,' said Timothy. So the Rector had been wrong in thinking that money would not talk.

'Well, that would be one item on the agenda. By the way,' Captain Sturrock lowered his voice, 'are we leaving the Inspector in the cold?'

Inspector Daykin was staring, with the feigned interest of the un-talked to, at the paper streamers and pendent balls and bells.

Timothy nodded to Captain Sturrock, and said to the Inspector, 'Pretty, aren't they?'

'They are quite tasteful,' replied the Inspector, 'but what I'm thinking is, if this room gets much hotter we shall see all that paper stuff floating up to the roof.'

Timothy was suddenly aware of the heat, and looking closer noticed a swaying movement among the decorations as if they were captive balloons straining at the guide-ropes. The heavily blacked-out windows and the unshaded electric light bulbs added to the impression of heat.

'I'll open the door a chink,' said the Inspector. 'It won't show because of the curtain across the porch.'

He rose with surprising agility for so big a man and brought back with him a puff of air which soon settled down into a hard-working draught. Draining his tankard and looking round in a marked manner for replenishment, which immediately came, he said, 'Well, what do you think of Upton, Mr. Casson?'

'I think it's charming,' said Timothy flatly.

'You would say that this was a quiet little place, wouldn't you?'

Timothy said he would.

'You'd say that the people just fed the chickens and milked the cows and ploughed the fields and scattered, and then had a glass or two at the local and then went home to bed?'

Timothy said he supposed that their lives followed some such course.

'And you'd think that the police have nothing to do but sit on their beam ends and count the hymn-books in church?'

'Well—' began Timothy.

'You'd be wrong,' said the Inspector. 'You'd be absolutely wrong.'

There was tremendous, crushing finality in his tone, and his face closed like a trap. Timothy looked at him inquiringly. Jerking his head back he said, impassively, 'There's people in this village who look as mild and meek as you, Mr. Casson, who would give the London police a run for their money. They would indeed.'

'Really?'

'Yes, and there's some in this hall—' his prominent eye-balls swept the festive tables – 'who are lucky to be in this hall, and not somewhere else.'

'Good heavens!' exclaimed Timothy, in spite of himself agreeably thrilled. 'You don't say so.'

'And some who might be sitting next to their own fathers without knowing it.'

Timothy couldn't help looking as if he had hoped for something more sensational.

The Inspector fixed him with a gimlet eye.

'And one who's his own father's grandson, in a manner of speaking.'

Timothy registered amazement.

'Think it out, Mr. Casson,' said the Inspector, leaning back. 'Think it out.'

Timothy couldn't, and begged to be enlightened.

The Inspector told the story with many circumlocutions and short-cuts. It was a tale of ignorance and passion and of pathos which gained rather than lost by the Inspector's terre-à-terre recital. His attitude was severely professional; the feelings of the parties seemed to mean nothing to him except in so far as they furnished clues, and he disapproved of their carelessness much more than of their wrong-doing. In this respect the woman's conduct had been especially culpable. 'She asked for it,' he said. 'If she hadn't cried when they mentioned his name to her, she wouldn't ever have been found out.'

Timothy was much affected by the story, and could only say, 'I suppose that sort of thing only happens among the very poor.'

'Well, with the poor you can watch 'em,' the Inspector said. 'Some of 'em don't rightly know it's wrong, so they don't take the same care that you or I would. When they slip up it's generally from the love-motive. Now with these foreign elements that have just come to the villages you don't know where you are.'

He drained his tankard and paused a moment while it was being refilled.

'It's bicycles they're after,' he said, 'and illicit petrol, and all sorts of tricks they've picked up in the towns. Hot-beds of crime, some of those big cities are. And of course we get all sorts here. We can't keep 'em out. The gentry don't like 'em, nor do we. Why, some of those girls is positively provocative. You don't go much to the Fisherman's Arms, Mr. Casson?'

Timothy said he didn't.

'It was a good house once,' the Inspector said. 'I don't live here, Swirrelsford's my home, but if I dropped in of an evening I'd find, well, perhaps half a dozen of the gentlemen who are sitting at this table with us. Now you won't find one. Just pullovers which are hardly decent and trousers which in my opinion are worse than bare legs. It's putting ideas into people's heads, isn't it, Captain?'

He leaned across Timothy towards Captain Sturrock.

'What is, Inspector?'

'The way some of these foreigners act at the local. They might be ladies who earn their daily bread by night. And talk about careless talk!'

'We're old-fashioned, Inspector,' said Captain Sturrock. 'But what can we do? We can't run them out of the village.'

'Treat 'em as the French people do the Jerries, by all accounts,' said the Inspector. 'Look at 'em as if they weren't there.'

'Some of them are rather pretty,' said Captain Sturrock slyly.

'That sort of prettiness comes off with a little soap and water.'

'What do you think, Casson? But perhaps it isn't a fair question.'

'It's a blonde question,' said Timothy.

The Inspector turned away, not seeing the joke. Captain Sturrock smiled and said, 'Now that I've got your ear' – he sneezed violently, 'Good God, that draught! Must I catch my death of cold to prevent Daykin having a stroke? What I was going to say was, I do hope you'll come round, old boy, and have a chat and tell us what you think of the proposal.'

'I should love to.'

'That's agreed then. You'll find us all plain people – no blondes, I'm afraid.'

Timothy said he did not prefer blondes.

Captain Sturrock laughed. 'And not highbrows either. You'll have to make allowances for us. But my Missus is keen about Italy, though she doesn't like Musso.'

'Nor do I.'

'We've got a picture of the Grand Canal and another of St. Marks, so you'll feel quite at home.'

'I'm sure I shall.'

A chair scraped, and a hush fell on the tables.

'Gentlemen, the King!'

Looking back on the evening, a painful exercise of memory, Timothy wondered where he went wrong, at what point his sense of his own welfare, his instinct for co-operating with his best interests – the instinct that prevents one from biting one's cheek or from being run down by a passing motorcar – abandoned and betrayed him. For it would have been so easy, it seemed afterwards, not to get into the state of mind in which he made the mistake, to preserve the coolness and judgment which would have made the lapse impossible. And, what was so mortifying to reflect, if he had acted as his nature prompted, held aloof, keeping himself mentally and emotionally free from the spirit of the evening, not let himself be caught up by the afflatus of good fellowship, all would have gone well. And if he had not drunk so much, that might have helped. But everything had conspired against him – his will, his inclination, and above all his mood of the moment.

Not only was he determined that the villagers, above and below the salt, should think of him as one of themselves, but he was persuaded, thanks to his success with Captain Sturrock, that they already did. Not only was the boat within his grasp – the sculls already in his hands and his feet in the stretcher – but he had already begun to enjoy in anticipation the whole complex of emotions that went with that event, the elation of victory and the swearing of eternal love and friendship with the vanquished. Into his mind floated pictures of picnics in some secluded creek with Captain and Mrs. Sturrock, with Mr. and Mrs. Purbright, with Tyro, with Magda, with Esther Morwen, bright with conversation and vivacity and the exchange of compliments; drowsy afternoons alone, half dreaming half awake, exposed body and mind to the healing influences of this almost unparalleled summer, whose sunshine never burnt or stifled, in whose bland zephyrs there was never a treacherous under-breath of chill.

True, Captain Sturrock had complained of the draught and from time to time he sneezed violently and indignantly, but had too much public spirit to get up and shut the door; while Timothy, too well warmed in spirit to notice, was happy watching the tobacco smoke, whirled hither and thither in blue-grey eddies as the current caught it. So thick was the smoke as practically to veil the naked hanging lights and to make indistinct the faces and figures of the performers as, one after another, they left their places on the benches and stood by the piano at the far end of the hall. One or two of the artists were professionals or near professionals who had come from London or the Midlands bringing the latest songs. Uptonians by birth, they had names known far beyond the village, and their presence lent the occasion a lustre, a metropolitan air, to which Timothy was not insensible. With their songs and recitations, duologues and tap-dancing, they bore the brunt of the attack; but soon there was a call for local talent. Favourite performers were summoned by name, and greeted with affectionate or ironical and encouraging cheers; fumbling and stumbling they extricated themselves from the benches, and stood, sheepish and awkward, with large red hands and redder faces, under the battery of eyes and ears.

After the sophisticated patter of the professionals, crammed with topical allusions, and their croonings about love, which were generally meaningless or bitter, the Victorian ballads favoured by most of the Uptonians had a strangely wistful ring. They were songs Timothy's mother had sung to him, and he experienced a thrill of emotion to hear them sung again, in country accents by rough male voices who made up by fervour what they lacked in skill. The accompanist, an old hand at his job, waited for them or hurried after them or changed the key of the song when they were getting into difficulties.

The Minstrel Boy went to the war again, and Johnny came marching home; the last rose of summer shed its petals on the grass; the luckless maid lingered on the Banks of Allan Water. Many of the singers began shakily, but they waxed bolder as they went on, and if they were nervous of the audience they were never afraid of the sentiment of the song; throwing themselves into it as if it was something they had felt for a long time and could now at last express. All this moved Timothy and loosened his emotional control, so that he found himself with smarting eyelids and a lump in his throat.

Then the professionals came back and the concert began to change its character. Almost imperceptibly the jokes became broader and the tone of the entertainment moved from the drawing-room to the smoking-room. Had the line of demarcation been more marked, had a bell rung or a whistle sounded, Timothy might have taken warning, and so might the Rector who, after smiling benignly at the first few daring jokes, began to look uneasy as their impropriety became more and more difficult to ignore. He shifted in his chair and looked to right and left, obviously longing to make a bolt. But it was too late; to leave the concert now would be to register disapproval, and this the Rector was determined not to do. His companion in the cloth, a pale man with a dog-collar much too big for him, looked less uncomfortable, for after all the moral tone of Upton was no concern of his.

Timothy hoped that the outbreak of indecency would die down as suddenly as it started, but no; it had captured the imagination of the house, and like the rumbling of a distant storm came nearer and nearer, until, like a clap of thunder, came a joke which combined suggestiveness with profanity. The laugh that followed shook the room; the Rector's face turned dark red, and his hand made a sudden sharp gesture of anger and impatience. Timothy saw this with dismay; unfortunately several of the company saw it, too, and their faces lit up with grins. 'He didn't like that one,' said the Inspector in a whisper that seemed to carry across the room; 'I'll make him sit up when my turn comes.'

He did not have long to wait. By now the professionals had again stood down, and the amateurs were once more called upon. Some merely told a risqué story, which was often drowned in roars of laughter, for laughter now possessed the hall; others sang soldiers' marching songs very slow in coming to the point, of which they could only remember the spicier fragments. Each got its laugh, and after each scores of eyes were turned towards the Rector, to see how he had taken it. Timothy stole a glance at him. His face was mottled, his eyes were fixed upon the table, and his friend and guest now shared his embarrassment as painfully as did Timothy. The wild idea came to Timothy that he, too, might be called upon to sing a bawdy song, on pain of being denounced, and perhaps thrown out as a kill-joy and a prig. Even the Rector might have to give his quota. . . . The fantasy was working on him like an onset of hysteria, when suddenly he heard a scraping at his side and the Inspector staggered to his feet, and announced in a loud, thick voice: 'I've only come down for the day.' A burst of laughter and a round of applause greeted him, and Timothy's corner became the target of all eyes: it was almost as if he were singing himself.

Nevertheless, for a moment he relaxed, for he vaguely remembered the song, and as far as his memory went there was no harm in it. But soon he realised that the Inspector knew another, more colourful version, which began almost at the point where its more decorous original left off; verse followed verse in which ever more preposterous and improper proposals were put before the man who had only come down for the day. They were not very funny but they were very scandalous, and Timothy's much tried self-control gave way before them. When the crowning salvo of laughter and clapping came, it found him in a paroxysm of hysterical fou-rire, which went on, with a noise like that of mingled whooping-cough and sobs, long after the acclamations had died down.

The next performer, already on his feet, waited politely for Timothy to recover from his mirth. But the Rector did not wait. Bestowing on Timothy a look of hatred which Timothy, his forehead bowed almost to the table, happened just to catch, he laid his hand on his friend's arm and shepherded him out of the room.

There was a dead silence, and the singer who was standing up looked about him uncertainly for guidance, and getting none, sat down again.

168

Little gusts of conversation started up here and there; the voices were subdued as if the speakers did not wish to be heard; but one of them called out to the discouraged singer to begin his song. It was only mildly indelicate, or seemed so, now that the Rector had gone; it was sung half-heartedly and the applause that greeted it was half-hearted, too. Much shuffling and stirring followed, there were questioning looks and nudges and sotto voce exhortations of 'Come on, now!' but nobody volunteered to sing.

The red-tabbed general stepped into the breach with a short speech in which he said how enjoyable and successful the evening had been; he thanked the organisers for an excellent dinner and the performers for their part in the entertainment; he congratulated the L.D.V. and the police on the valuable work they were doing, and exhorted them not to relax their efforts as sterner times lay ahead. His voice and manner and the authority with which he spoke did something to restore the morale of the assembly, faces cleared, the rout became a retreat, and so with 'Auld Lang Syne' and 'God Save the King' the party came to an end.

Timothy, who felt as if he would never dare or even know how to laugh again, muttered to Captain Sturrock, 'I'm afraid I made an awful fool of myself.'

'Oh no, you didn't, old boy, it might have happened to any of us. You coming along to the Rectory?'

'I think I'd better not,' Timothy said.

'All right then, be seeing you in a day or two.'

It seemed like four in the morning, but actually it was only ten o'clock when Timothy regained his room. He sat down at once and wrote a letter of abject apology to Mr. Purbright. The letter proved to be the most difficult he had ever written. The more he explained, the more there seemed to be to explain. He had never been intimate with Mr. Purbright; their friendship had been founded not on mutual sympathy but on respect and good will, and it was precisely these that Timothy had violated. The best he could do was to make himself out an hysterical nincompoop with a strain of perversity which always made him laugh in the wrong place.

In the morning he hardly dared to face Wimbush, but a morbid instinct to hear the worst got the better of him. His reception, however, was agreeably different from what he had expected.

'Well, sir, and how did you enjoy our little entertainment last night?'

Timothy took a deep breath.

'I enjoyed it very much.'

A twinkle came into the gardener's eye.

'We saw you did, sir.'

'Yes, I'm afraid I made rather an ass of myself.'

Wimbush's surprise seemed quite genuine.

'Indeed you didn't, sir. The chaps were only too pleased you enjoyed their bit of fun. They think all the better of you for it. Why, it was the joke of the evening when you couldn't stop laughing. The Rector now, he hasn't done himself any good by going out with his nose in the air.'

Ashamed of the tide of relief that was rolling over him like water on a desert, Timothy said, tolerantly:

'I expect it was a little difficult for him.'

'Why, sir, he ought to be able to take a joke, even if it is a bit broad. 'Twasn't as if he'd been in church. The chaps didn't like it, sir. There's quite a few say they won't go to church in future, as a kind of protest, like.'

'Oh that would be a pity,' said Timothy, aghast at the idea of having decimated Mr. Purbright's congregation. 'But they never went very much, did they?'

'That was quite different, sir, if you'll excuse me. They wouldn't go now if they could. The fact is, they feel they've been insulted, sir. When a gentleman like you can take a joke, why shouldn't a clergyman like Mr. Purbright?'

On the whole the interview had been reassuring, and Nelson felt much the same about the "incident" as Wimbush had. The Rector had sunk in the community's esteem, while Timothy had risen.

All the same, he awaited Mr. Purbright's answer with misgivings, nor did they prove unfounded. It was a formal note of acknowledgment, bringing a rather frosty breath of Christian charity, but no suggestion that bygones should be bygones, or that a resumption of Timothy's visits to the Rectory would be welcome. There was a postscript, however. 'I cannot help feeling glad,' the Rector added, 'that Volumnia was away when this discouraging and regrettable little episode occurred. I was not myself when I reached home, and had to ask the friends who came on later if they would excuse me. My wife's Christianity is of a more elastic type than (I am afraid) mine is, she sees evidences of spiritual-mindedness where I cannot; but she will be inexpressibly grieved to hear – as hear she must, for we have no secrets from each other – that my twenty-five years' ministry in this parish has borne so little, and such bitter fruit.'

Mrs. Purbright! In his multitudinous concern for the consequences of the incident, Timothy had almost forgotten her. She was a woman of strong feeling, he knew. Would he lose her friendship, with her husband's? He did not like to ring up the Rectory, but Wimbush discovered, by methods of his own, that Mrs. Purbright was still away and it was not known when she would be back.

CHAPTER XIV

WIMBUSH was right: Timothy's breakdown at the dinner did seem in some way to have endeared him to the inhabitants of Upton, and as he walked along its street, hands of men he did not even know by sight were raised in salute. Almost any form of popularity was sweet to him, and as he had been starved of it so long, he found himself welcoming these rather equivocal signs of favour. Moreover, any day now he would be receiving a summons to The Old Stables, as Captain Sturrock's house was called. Wimbush was right, too, that the Rector had lost ground by his discourteous and priggish gesture. One or two of the passers-by who saluted Timothy stopped and made sly little digs at Mr. Purbright, and the attendance at church (for Timothy still went to church) seemed to have fallen off. Wimbush made a joke about this: 'I heard that the whole village was there, both of 'em,' and Timothy couldn't help being amused and half pleased that a party seemed to be forming against the Rector.

Returning one day from his afternoon walk, which now had no object except air and exercise, he found a letter from Esther Morwen, from whom he hadn't heard for several weeks. She apologised for her silence: 'It's so boring,' she wrote, 'to say I lost your address again, but I did. I meant to write the day Italy came into the war – I knew how you would mind it, that dear country which has been a home to generations of Englishmen. No country has understood them so well as we have; we helped them to their freedom at the time of the Risorgimento, didn't we? and Browning said that Italy would be found graved on his heart. They have been rather ungrateful, haven't they? when we have done so much for them, and it would be easy to feel they have betrayed us, but somehow I can't; it is just a momentary blindness, not seeing eye to eye with us, and as soon as we win, and get rid of Mussolini and those horrible Fascists, who are so anti-English, and put in the kind of statesmen who understand our point of view, all the old good feeling will come back. Victory will be like the sum of our good intentions made manifest; it won't be for the imposing of our will – that would be tyrannical and un-English; but the wholesale recognition, by them, of the sacrifices we have made really *for* them, to bring them back to the kind of standards we have always stood for.

'You wrote so sympathetically and understandingly about Denis; poor boy, he was only twenty and had a brilliant career before him, he was in some ways the most gifted of them all. Daphne was inconsolable at first; but she begins to realise that all he meant to her, and us, and to the world, isn't *lost* – I couldn't believe a thing so horrible even if it were true – it lives on among the good things that grow out of the battlefield as naturally as fruit and crops and flowers do.

'I thought your letter was a little wistful. Village life is a habit you can't easily acquire if you're not born to it – you may so easily magnify differences and quarrels which are really only ripples on the surface – signs that the sap is rising. It's all so *sound*, really, the instinct that makes English people of that kind apparently so critical and hard on each other; it means they are keeping each other up to the mark, it's the opposite of decadence, and some of it is *so* enjoyable! I wouldn't miss the little upsets we sometimes have here for the world. In the end they bring out everyone's essential niceness, which is somehow inseparable from the instinct to make a scene. I don't always try to pour oil; it makes them think you superior, and even inhuman, if you never take their squabbles seriously or take sides. But I'm afraid I'm a born partisan; I never could agree that one becomes less oneself by fighting for something that one loves – to me, that is the most the self can aspire to, the height of self-hood, I might say.

'It's a pity you laughed – but you'll find the Rector will be the first to forgive you, they have so much experience of every type of human nature, and so much worse things to fight against than a laugh! And even if the villagers think it was a bit off-colour, they'll just put it down to your foreign ways!

'I'm so glad you think you may get leave to use your boat, though I never quite understood why it means so much to you, especially in these times when everyone, more or less, has his shoulder to the wheel. Fishing, of course, is a definite contribution to the War Effort; it helps the food supply, and besides is something that people like ourselves have always done; whereas a boat only leaves behind ripples that die away when they reach the bank. But you always have been a law unto yourself – it's one of the things I love about you—'

Timothy heard a sound and looked up. Effie was standing at the door.

'Miss Lampard, sir.'

'Who?' Timothy had heard, but couldn't believe his ears. Effie repeated the name.

'Ask her to come in,' said Timothy.

She came in slowly, with an air of not noticing what she saw. Her eyes were bright and her face was flushed, and she was breathing quickly. She looked nervous – frightened almost – but resolute. Even so, her presence lit up the room.

'Do sit down,' said Timothy.

She looked around her vaguely, and then sat down on the edge of the worn green armchair.

'I mustn't stay,' she said, 'but I felt I had to come.'

'Tea will be here in a moment,' said Timothy. 'You'll stay for that?'

'How kind of you. Well, just a cup. I left my horse in the stable yard,' she added. 'Your gardener kindly tied him up for me. I hope it didn't matter?'

'Of course not. You rode over, then?'

'I couldn't help it. We're nearly out of petrol. The car would have been safer.'

'Safer?'

'I didn't want to be seen.'

Timothy looked at her inquiringly.

'Mother doesn't know I've come here,' she said with an effort. 'She . . . she'd be angry if she knew.'

'I'm sorry,' said Timothy.

'But I couldn't *not* come,' she said, as though repeating something she had often said to herself, 'when you had been so kind.'

Timothy assured her that the kindness had been all on her side.

She disagreed. 'You were so nice about the French. Some people are horrid about them. And you wrote such a lovely article about our house – at least I thought so.'

'Your mother didn't?'

Désirée did not speak for a moment, and the light faded from her face.

'No, she didn't like it at all. She thought it was – well, rather vulgar. And she didn't like me showing you over the house.'

'I'm sorry,' repeated Timothy.

'I'm not.' She spoke with sudden animation, defiantly. Then her face fell. 'I made you so many promises,' she said, sadly.

'Well, you have carried out the most important of them.'

'By coming here? How nice of you. But I'm afraid I shan't be able to ask you back.'

'I didn't expect you would,' said Timothy. But he had expected it.

'Mother says that since your article heaps of people – strangers – have written to ask if they may see the house, and some have called and asked to be shown over.'

'I'm sorry,' said Timothy again. How could he have foreseen that this would happen?

'She hates publicity more than anything. It was the first time the house had been open to the public, and she says it will be the last. She almost refused to let a party of Free French soldiers see over it the other day, although she knew one of them quite well. He was such a charming boy. They all were, but he specially.'

Something in her tone made Timothy say, 'Have you seen them again?'

She hesitated. 'I wanted to – one or two of them. The one that Mother knew, as a matter of fact. His father was a friend of hers – he's dead now – and François is the Duc de Charleroi, not that it makes any difference. But she doesn't want me to see him again.'

'And that does make a difference?'

She flushed a little. 'Yes.'

Timothy pondered. How delightful she was; what possibilities of happiness went with her, what a glow of life. And he owed Mrs. Lampard nothing, unless it was a poke in the eye with a burnt stick.

'Couldn't you meet him here?' he said.

She started; the colour came and went in her face; she clenched her hand and looked away from Timothy.

'How could we arrange it?'

'I could write and ask him. It would be quite natural to offer hospitality to the Free French. People are asked to.'

She frowned and shook her head once or twice, as though denying herself something. Timothy got up and offered her a cigarette. She looked at the clock and said, 'No, I mustn't,' and then changed her mind. He lit the cigarette for her, and she smoked it with quick puffs, like a child.

'It would be risky,' she said. 'Mother would be so angry if she found out, and you don't know what she's like when she's angry.'

'She's angry with me already, I'm afraid.'

'She does seem to be. But what have you done? That lovely article – she said it was like a house-agent's blurb, and people would think she wanted to sell the place.'

'She doesn't, does she?'

Désirée laughed. 'Oh no. And then, there's another promise I have broken.'

'What, another?'

'About the boat. She doesn't want you to have it. She's seen a lawyer who says the tenants of the fishing could sue her for breach of contract if you got in their way.'

'Oh, but she could persuade them. A word from her—'

'But she won't say it. I've asked her twice: you can't ask her anything three times.'

'But if the tenants themselves don't object—'

'That would be different, perhaps. But she wouldn't like it, even then.'

'Miss Lampard,' said Timothy, leaning forward and speaking in a voice that shook, so wrought upon was he by the thought of Mrs. Lampard's intransigence, 'if you want to meet the Duc de Charleroi here, you have only to tell me.'

The trouble and the joy returned to her face, chasing each other like shadows. 'Oh how kind you are,' she said, jumping up. 'How grateful I am I met you. Whatever happens, I shall always be grateful to you.'

'Don't go yet,' pleaded Timothy: 'Here's tea.'

Effie's arrival changed the subject of conversation. Gone was her habitual languor; her manner was gracious, her movements deft and sure. The room lost its bachelor bleakness and became intimate and domestic.

Timothy asked his guest to pour out the tea.

'What will you say if I spill it?'

'I'm sure you won't.'

He watched her hands moving among the tea-things.

'What pretty cups,' she said.

'They've never looked pretty before,' said Timothy. 'Are they French?'

She coloured charmingly and her face soon lost its look of strain. Unwatched, the hands of the clock crept round the dial. Suddenly, as though angry at being ignored, the clock struck six.

'Oh dear,' she said, 'Now I must go.'

Timothy didn't try to detain her.

'This is a nice house, isn't it?' she said, as they went to the door. 'It must be about the same date as ours, the mouldings, I mean.' Timothy looked up at the cornice which repeated, in a whisper, certain grandiloquent utterances of plaster and stucco at Welshgate Hall. 'And the hall would be so pretty,' she said as they crossed it, 'if it weren't for the black-out. It's just the same with us, do you remember? the picture gallery's quite spoilt by all the horrible felt stuff on the roof.'

Timothy was charmed by the naturalness with which she compared her house to his.

He held her horse while she mounted, and walked beside her down the drive. She talked to the horse in peremptory and to him in dulcet tones; with the buoyancy of youth she seemed to have thrown off her fear of a scolding. But when the bend of the road brought the poplared green into view she leaned towards Timothy and said, 'Perhaps I'd better say goodbye to you here.'

Timothy was loth to let her go.

'Tell me if there's anything I can do for you,' he said. 'If any questions are asked, you must say your horse had a puncture.'

'That's a good idea.'

'And you'll let me know about the Free French.'

The baffled, anxious look returned, and she said, 'Oh, I *wish* I knew what to do.'

'Nothing venture, nothing have.'

'I know, I know. But mother and I are such great friends. I love her and admire her more than anyone else in the world. I can't bear to do something she doesn't like.'

'She can't keep you on leading-strings for ever,' said Timothy.

'You don't think it's wicked of me to go against her in this case?'

'No, I think you should stand up to her.'

Désirée frowned.

'She's never been like this before. We've never had the smallest disagreement. She isn't like herself – I think she must have got something on her mind.'

'Perhaps she's rather possessive – mothers sometimes are. I can quite understand her not wanting to lose you.'

'But that would mean she was selfish, and she isn't a bit.'

'Perhaps she doesn't like the idea of your marrying a Frenchman.'

'She isn't very nice about the French,' Désirée admitted. 'And she used to like them so much. Oh, if only I could *talk* to her!'

'Is she difficult to talk to?'

'Impossible, if it's something she doesn't want to talk about.'

'But this is so important.'

'I can see you think she's selfish,' said Désirée, troubled.

'No, but I expect she's forgotten what she felt like at your age.'

Désirée looked at him with a gleam of suspicion in her eyes. 'Why, have you heard anything?'

'Only that she was very much in love with your father.'

Désirée seemed relieved.

'Yes, she was. Perhaps I'm like her. But she said such cruel things. She said she'd rather see me dead than married to him.'

'How could she be so cruel?'

'And that I was throwing myself at his head, though I've only seen him twice.'

'Is she often as unkind as that?'

'Never, oh no, never, and I don't want you to get a wrong impression of her.'

'I think you're marvellously loyal,' said Timothy. 'I only wish I could find someone to stand up for me so nobly.'

'Oh but I do!' Désirée cried. 'I always fight your battles.'

'Against whom?' said Timothy.

She saw herself caught out, and blushed.

'Oh, no one, no one in particular. Perhaps I was thinking of the boat, it does seem so unfair. And your article, whatever anybody says, I love it, and I've pasted it into my scrapbook, and ordered six copies to send to friends. There! I must be off. Goodbye, Mr. Casson, and thank you for that perfect tea.'

Horse and rider passed through the gate and disappeared, but Timothy found himself listening to the clatter of hooves long after she was lost to view. Turning back to the house he caught sight of his shadow stretching out in front of him, long and thin. A trick of distortion gave it a sinister twist, as of someone creeping about with no good purpose, Iago perhaps.

Days of perplexity ushered in July, leaving Timothy, whose temperament was usually equable, a prey to contradictory moods. By some obscure mental process, which he himself did not understand, he had come to regard permission to use his boat as a sign that he had been accepted by the community of Upton; until that happened, he was still a foreigner, an out-lander as the natives called it. In some moods he regarded the permit as a victory, the imposing of his will on theirs; the one had prevailed over the many; like Julius Cæsar he had come and seen and conquered Upton. At other times he regarded it as a favour they had conferred on him, a privilege that recognised his outstanding merit, but something that he could be grateful for, and Timothy, when not flown with pride, was quite content to be grateful.

On the plane of practical politics he had convinced himself that if Mrs. Lampard's tenants agreed to let him row, she would have to withdraw her objection, though this did not diminish his wrath against her, rather the reverse. He longed for a letter from Désirée, authorising him to arrange a clandestine meeting between her and the Duc de Charleroi; the rôle of go-between appealed to him mightily, and he told himself he did not mind what the upshot was so long as Mrs. Lampard was check-mated. But the days passed, and no letter came.

Nor, to his growing disquiet, did the promised invitation come from Captain Sturrock. This was much more serious. Had he forgotten? Had the Rector, whose influence was considerable, in the parish, persuaded him that Timothy was an undesirable element, to be looked on askance, and cold-shouldered, like the floating population of Midlanders whom they both disliked so much?

Timothy brooded over this, and the more deeply because he had now very little else to do. The moment when he gave up his job, or rather when his job gave him up, had been like a deep draught of free-dom which his thirsty spirit drank like wine. And for some time after-wards, when in thought he evoked it and put it to his lips, the elixir still worked. But soon it lost its potency. Freedom turned into leisure, and leisure into ennui; the mornings became deserts of inactivity, to be got over somehow; and the period between tea and dinner, for Timothy the most fertile season of the day, was almost frighteningly empty. And when the day came round that should have brought his monthly cheque, he felt that freedom stank.

He tried to kill time by filling in the many gaps in his reading. Miss Chadwick's bookshelves were well stocked, and he started on a course of Thackeray. But reading was a receptive occupation, a centripetal process paring the self down to its core; it was no real substitute for the creative activity of writing, during which the self expands and blos-soms, breathes new air and sees new sights, albeit only for an hour or two. Reading was listening, listening to a dead mind; writing was communication, words sent out to the living, and Timothy longed to communicate. Soon his body caught the infection of his mind's rest-lessness, and made its voice heard. Physical activity was not the same as creative activity, but it was a better substitute than reading. Why not join the L.D.V.?

Timothy had debated taking this step ever since the smoking concert had brought into his solitary life, however unfortunately and briefly, the warmth of fellowship. The salutes of the members in the village street, the sight of Wimbush in his uniform, kept his intention alive. He decided that he would broach the matter at Captain Sturrock's tea-table. It would be another symbol of his achieved solidarity with the village, it would be a subject of conversation, of congratulation, and they would like him the better for it. But the invitation had not come, and Timothy, who had unconsciously begun to regulate his actions, and even his thoughts, according to some fancied relationship, hostile or friendly, with the entity of Upton, said to himself, 'No invitation, no L.D.V.'

Leaning over the parapet of the bridge at Swirrelsford, where he had gone one afternoon to see a cinema, and decided not to, among other loiterers as aimless as himself, he suddenly saw, on the bend of the river, almost out of sight, a boat-house, a landing stage, and a flotilla of rowing boats. Why had he never seen them before?

Timothy had to stand for a long time in a queue, but at last the boat-man, a quiet, sad little man, hooked up a boat for him; it was chipped and dirty and much the worse for wear, it had a fixed seat, the sculls did not meet in the middle and one was longer than the other; even in the open air it seemed to smell of unwashed urchins; but it was a boat; and although stepping into it did not mean that he had received the freedom of Upton, did not mean that he had been taken to its heart or it to his, in fact meant hardly any of the things that embarking in his own boat at Upton (try not to think of that!) had come to mean, it meant something; the pushing off from the shore, the making for the middle of the stream, that gliding motion, the short cramped strokes and then the long swing – it meant something that satisfied Timothy's needs in a way that nothing else could.

The Swirrel at Swirrelsford was a different river from the dimpled sparkling stream that laved the garden of the Old Rectory. It carried on its surface flotsam that the eye turned away from it; it received noisome tributaries, frothing obscenely from electric-light plant and gasworks; it was discoloured and polluted, the town had demoralised it.

Moreover, at the point where Timothy embarked, the Swirrel was as congested as a side-canal in Venice or as the Serpentine on a Bank Holiday. His fellow pleasure-seekers did not proceed up and down the river in an orderly manner; soldiers and airmen mostly, sometimes escorting girls, they pulled wildly from one bank to another colliding with each other to the sound of splintering wood, screams, giggles, and loud, mirthless guffaws. Timothy's sense of oarsmanship was outraged by the way they rowed – often sitting two abreast, each holding an oar and not troubling to keep time with the other. He had to row looking over his shoulder to avoid the impending bumps. 'Look ahead, sir,' he shouted, but they only laughed the more, for to them collisions, he discovered, were a great part of the fun. Frowning and irritable he fended them off with his hands; but they were unconscious of offence

– they smiled amiably, or laughed raucously, and he quickly realised that their attitude to the pastime was totally different from his.

He remembered that when he rowed his sandolo on the Brenta or through the crowded canals of Venice the boatmen there would smile at each other, but for a different reason. They, who rowed for a living, could not understand how anyone could do it for fun. Timothy, when he realised this, did not mind their being amused at his expense, and he soon felt the same about these soldiers and airmen who, obliged by military discipline to spend a great part of the day performing, with set, expressionless faces and bodies clenched into an unnatural rigidity, correctly and well, exercises which were doubtless boring to most of them, looked forward to their outings on the river as an opportunity to relax, to assume whatever attitude came easiest, and to handle their boats as incorrectly and badly as they liked; for to do a thing badly is an affirmation of independence, whereas to do it well is to confess oneself a slave to other people's standards.

So Timothy's irritation passed away; but all the same he was glad to be rid of the jostling. As he pressed his way upstream, the shouts and laughter died, the water grew clear and sparkling; the river regained its country state. On one side the bank was low enough to see over; channels with sluices pierced it, the relics of an ancient system of irrigation, long since disused. Willows and water-meadows, pearl-grey in the heat, carried the eye to a low range of hills. On the other side a railway embankment rose steeply, blocking out the view. Suddenly there was a rattle and a roar, and a train came along, in a flurry of steam and busy speed. The fireman was leaning out of the cab with his eyes fixed on the distance. Timothy waved to him, and the man, with a broad grin, waved back. Presently another train passed, going the other way, and again Timothy gave, and received, a salute.

Afterwards Timothy came to count on these greetings from the unknown railwaymen. The embankment and the river only marched together for a few hundred yards, so it was essential to be punctual at the rendezvous. He found himself making great efforts to achieve this. If he failed, it appreciably lessened the pleasure of the afternoon; if he succeeded, he was correspondingly elated. The men always played up, though they had their moods and expressed them in gestures of varying enthusiasm. Sometimes the fireman only would take the salute, sometimes the driver joined him; sometimes a languid hand would be raised, sometimes two arms would shoot up as though on wire. Sometimes the men would call out messages, obviously of a facetious nature, which he tried in vain to catch.

Whatever it meant for the railwaymen, for Timothy the ritual exchange of signals represented whatever of general goodwill he still had to give. The return journey into the clashing boats, the laughter and the gramophone records, was something of an anti-climax. To reach the boat-house Timothy had to pass under the town bridge, and as often as not there was a pop-eyed urchin hanging over it, with working cheeks and protruding tongue, waiting to spit on his head. This was a different way of communicating with a stranger. Usually the missile went wide, but sometimes it hit, and stuck, and Timothy would look up angrily and see the mischievous little face broaden with satisfaction before its owner took to his heels and scurried away out of reach of its victim's impotent wrath.

Fortified by tea in the town Timothy rode his bicycle back to Upton (for the infrequent buses did not serve him) a good eight miles over hilly country through the lengthening shadows; it was an effort, riding both ways, and though it soothed him physically, it sometimes left him tired and cross, reminding him he was past the fifty mark, and ought to slow down. A glance at the hall-table did not show the wished-for letter with the Upton postmark, and the long evening, scotched but by no means killed, lay coiled in front of him.

On one such evening, not in the best of tempers, he was riding into the stable-yard to put his bicycle away when he saw a man he did not know leading half a dozen greyhounds on a leash. The fellow seemed to know his way about; he gave Timothy a glance over his shoulder and proceeded without further ado to open the door of the last of the four loose-boxes and lead the dogs in. After several minutes he came out, shutting the door behind him, and was crossing the stable-yard to go out into the village street when Timothy stopped him.

'What are you doing with those dogs?' he said.

The man, who was wearing leggings and an old coat of whipcord, rather long for him, and had a sharp-featured face, like a jockey's, seemed surprised at the question.

'I'm putting them up for the night,' he said.

'But these stables are mine,' said Timothy. 'Who authorised you to put the dogs in them?'

The man looked sullen.

'They're Captain Sturrock's hounds,' he said, 'the same as he always has for the coursing meeting.'

'But I don't understand,' said Timothy angrily. 'Did he say you could put them here?'

'I don't know anything about that,' said the man. 'My orders were to put them in the stables at the Old Rectory, same as usual.'

'Who gave you these orders?'

'Captain Sturrock, of course.'

'Where do you come from?' demanded Timothy with growing indignation.

'What's that to do with you? I'm paid by Captain Sturrock to look after his hounds when they come here for the meeting.'

'And supposing I order you to take them back to Captain Sturrock?'

'The Captain might have something to say to that,' said the man nastily.

'Do you threaten me?' asked Timothy fiercely.

'I don't threaten you,' said the man looking Timothy squarely in the eye, 'but I pity you if I set about you.'

'Come on then,' shouted Timothy.

In the scuffle which followed he managed to land a fairly hard blow on his opponent's cheek. The man staggered and put his hand to his face. Timothy was following up his advantage when he heard the sound of wheels. A car stopped at his elbow and Nelson jumped out.

Timothy and the dog-man were leaning towards each other, breathing hard, their coats bunched up at the shoulders, their wrists bare. Seeing the police-constable the man stepped back, and without looking round, shambled off quickly through the open doors of the stable-yard. Nelson seemed to be on the point of following him, but Timothy shook his head. Opportune as the policeman's arrival had been, he felt wretchedly ashamed at having been caught in a common brawl. Nelson asked if he could do anything for him, but again Timothy shook his head. He sat down on a chopping block and put back his tie, which had come out, and pulled down his sleeves and smoothed his hair. Nelson, who had averted his eyes from Timothy's toilette, when it was over turned round and said admiringly:

'On passing through the gates I saw you give him a lovely wallop, sir. He won't forget that in a hurry.'

Timothy felt comforted and even appeased, and began to tell Nelson how the quarrel had arisen. But the recital brought all his anger back, and Nelson's comments which, though complimentary in general, were critical of particular points, did nothing to allay it. He begged the policeman not to tell anyone what had happened, and Nelson promised not to.

Timothy was almost sick from anger and excitement. His heart beat so violently that he could scarcely stand. He went into the house and sat down in an easy chair with his hands along its arms, seeing nothing, aware only of the spring of anger that was welling up in him, staining his vision with the colour of blood. After a time he got up and went to his writing-table. His hands still trembled and his mind was too confused with feeling even to express its anger; but at last the letter was finished.

'To CAPTAIN STURROCK,
'SIR,

'I notice that you are very careful of the rights of private property where your own interests are concerned. I wish you were as considerate for other people's. I should have found it easier to excuse your impertinence in sending your dogs to be lodged in my stables without asking my permission if the man who brought them had not also been intolerably rude. If you think this is conduct befitting an officer and a gentleman, I don't, and suspect that though you may once have been the one, you can never have been the other. But even if you had had the common decency to ask me, I should not have allowed my premises to be used for the purposes of a brutal, degrading and unmanly pastime for which I have a particular abhorrence. Unless the animals are removed before ten o'clock tonight, I shall turn them into the street.

'Yours faithfully,
'T. CASSON.'

The letter became more literary as Timothy worked on it, and before the final draft was achieved, some of his anger had evaporated. But now his thoughts and his will came to the rescue of his failing rage; he remembered the months of frustration inflicted upon him by Captain Sturrock and others of his kidney, their bland refusal to have anything to do with him, and he hardened his heart. What rankled more than anything was Captain Sturrock's promise, already more than three weeks old, to ask him to his house. Timothy had built so much upon that invitation; until this very evening he had not quite ceased to hope; now he realised that these people's promises were so much pie-crust, dodges to gain time, face-saving devices under cover of which they could indulge their selfishness undisturbed.

He took the letter and went out, with knees that still had the tremor of temper in them, into the red-gold, slanting sunshine. The Old Stables was only five minutes' walk. Timothy observed, with the detached curiosity one feels when looking at a place one will never see again, the trim lawn, the clipped bushes, the sarcen stones lining the path, the military order and tidiness of the garden. The house was old red brick, long and low; it still bore traces of its former function, but the process of conversion had robbed it of character, and there were one or two disgusting whimsies, an over-rustic porch which did not suit it, and hanging from the porch, a nasty arty little square lantern, which probably represented Captain Sturrock's idea of the old-world.

Triangular mounds of rusty cannon balls flanked the doorway, as though to remind the visitor that Captain Sturrock's notions of warfare dated from the Commonwealth. He heard the letter drop into the letterbox, and walked slowly away, taking care not to look into the over-large, over-white, round-topped ugly windows.

Timothy had little appetite for his dinner, and contrary to his custom, and much to Effie's concern, left half his food on his plate.

'Beatrice will be disappointed, sir. And that nice chicken, too. They're ever so difficult to find.'

'And expensive to pay for,' snapped Timothy, still ruffled. 'But I'm afraid I can't oblige her, Effie; I'm off my food tonight.'

'It's nothing you've had to eat, I'm sure,' said Effie. 'There's something catching going about the village: I hope it isn't that.'

'Oh, I shall be all right tomorrow,' said Timothy.

'Beatrice will be ever so upset, when she's taken so much trouble,' Effie warned him again.

'I'm sorry, Effie,' said Timothy, more gently, 'I couldn't eat another mouthful.'

'You haven't had any bad news, sir? There's so much bad news going about.'

Timothy assured her he had not; but he noticed that her movements took on a kind of ritual solemnity, and she looked at him with respect, almost with awe, as someone on whom the distinction of calamity had fallen.

He was applying himself, without much success, to 'Esmond' when Effie reappeared, still with her air of assisting at a tragedy.

'Captain Sturrock's at the door, sir, and says he would like to speak to you.'

Timothy did not raise his eyes from the book. 'Tell him I'm not well, please, Effie, and cannot see him.'

Presently Effie returned, and said, or rather chanted, 'Captain Sturrock presents his compliments, sir, and says he is sorry you are ill, and may he take the dogs away now?'

'By all means,' said Timothy.

In a minute or two Effie was back again. 'Captain Sturrock wants to know where the dogs are.'

Timothy told her. 'You show him where they are, Effie.'

'I will sir,' said Effie with alacrity. 'He seems ever such a nice gentleman.'

'Does he?' said Timothy indifferently.

Timothy spent a miserable night. The adrenalin, or whatever it was his temper had let loose, seemed to course round and round; then it collected into a hard ball in the middle of his stomach and no amount of bicarbonate of soda would disperse it. By three o'clock all that was left of his ill-humour was a disagreeably thudding heart, unconquerable flatulence and a longing for sleep. His rage had petered out in indigestion. Will it turn into a gastric ulcer? he wondered, having recently read somewhere that this complaint had doubled since the war began. But although his body accused him of misusing it, his mind protested that he was in the right. 'I must get used to being angry,' he told himself, 'it's only a habit like any other.' At cock-crow, calmed by this resolve, he began to doze, and dreamed that he was a hare being chased by greyhounds. 'Stand up to them!' cried a voice, and he stopped in his tracks and looked round fiercely. All he saw was Captain Sturrock, who held out his hand, but Timothy would not take it.

The hand proved to be Effie's, carrying his early morning tea.

'I hope you feel better, sir?' she said solicitously.

Timothy said he was much better. 'I hope *you're* all right,' something in the tone of her inquiry made him add.

'Well, sir, both Beatrice and I are naturally upset, you couldn't expect us not to be after what happened.'

'Oh, did anything happen?' asked Timothy, surprised.

'No, sir, but it might have, you being taken queer the way you was. And Captain Sturrock, he seemed quite upset, too. Beatrice said to me, "Has Mr. Casson had a death?" We felt sure you'd had bad news, sir.'

'I'm afraid it was more bad temper than bad news,' said Timothy, and felt the better for this small confession.

'Oh, but you're never bad-tempered, sir,' said Effie. 'Why, a gentleman was only saying to me the other day, "Mr. Casson has only one fault, he's too good-tempered." '

'What a nice thing to say,' cried Timothy, sitting up and reaching for the tea-pot. 'Who was it, Effie?'

'Well, sir, if you won't repeat it, it was Mr. Wimbush.'

Timothy couldn't understand why he felt a little disappointed. Was he hoping she would say Captain Sturrock?

The envelope was the one he had long been looking for; the one with the Upton postmark and the address written in an unknown hand. 'DEAR CASSON,' he read,

'I don't know what you will think, not having heard from me for all this time, but perhaps you have forgotten that on the evening of the L.D.V. beano you promised to come and see us. I was looking forward to that and the Missus was going to write to you, but as ill-luck would have it that damned draught (do you remember it?) caught me in a tender spot, and I'm ashamed to say it, it sounds so silly in the middle of summer, but the thing turned into bronchitis and I was laid up for weeks – sign of anno domini, I'm afraid – and I only got up a day or two ago, feeling as weak as a rat. But I daresay somebody told you, or not seeing me in Church you concluded I was on the sick-list.

'However, all's well that ends well. I've cheated the undertaker this time and my wife and I will be most happy if you will come to tea with us on Thursday, if you are free, and we'll have a general pow-wow, not about anything in particular, of course, just a sort of survey of the lie of the land. We're asking Harbord, and Bellew, and one or two more of the old familiar faces, and very much hope to rope you in.

'Now I'm going to ask you a great favour. I don't know if your interests lie that way, but it's our annual Coursing Meeting the day after tomorrow and as usual I've entered some hounds. Such a pretty sport, coursing, don't you think, if only this beastly electric hare doesn't kill it. In the past, Judge Chadwick always let me keep my hounds in the stable at the Old Rectory for the two days of the meeting, and his sister did, too, while she was there. So it's become a sort of tradition. Quite a lot of hounds come down for the meeting, and there's nowhere else in the village for mine to go. So I would take it as a great kindness, old boy, if you would give them the hospitality of one of your loose-boxes. There's a chap looking after them, so they won't be any bother to you. If they yap in the night just shout out of the window and tell them to go to hell. I'm sure they won't, but I feel the whole thing is rather an imposition and if you decide you would rather not take it on I shall quite understand, but look forward to seeing you on Thursday.

'Yours sincerely,
'JAMES STURROCK.

'P.S. – Since writing, I've heard the hounds are on the way, so this may be rather rushing you, but hope you won't take it amiss.'

Long ago Timothy's guardian had advised him always to examine a coincidence, because as often as not you'll find it isn't a coincidence at all, but a link in the chain of cause and effect. Was it the more comforting, he wondered, to regard the mistiming of Captain Sturrock's letter as a blind hit of chance, or as one of a series of seeming mischances, ordered and inevitable as the rungs of a ladder, which the logic of his nature required for its development? In either case he was the loser; but if character was destiny, and if he attracted to himself fiascos as a magnet attracts iron filings, the outlook was dismal.

Was it his destiny to be friendless? In England friendship had been hard to come by, but in Italy, on the Brenta, the golden afternoon had been loud with the voices of his friends. They had just arrived from England; they were astonished and delighted with what they saw; even Mrs. Lampard could not withhold her praise. On the green ramparts of Asolo, in the romantic clefts of the Euganean Hills, in the enchanted alleys of the garden of Valsanzibio the many toned voice of friendship chanted in thanksgiving. To whom? To Timothy? No, of course not. But to something (was it too much to claim?) that came into being where he was, that flowered spontaneously in his climate. He had been a conductor of happiness, a channel of good fellowship. Was that too much to claim? Say rather that his friends, his guests, his servants, his acquaintances round the Villa Lucertola, brought all that radiance with them. Still, he reflected it, he was the mirror in which they saw their joy. And now the visit's over; adieu, glorious days of sunshine (but not more glorious than this in Upton), and the car to take them to the station is waiting on the opposite bank of the river. They see it but they are loth to go, they linger on the steps of the modest portico, they look around them, finding new forms of appreciation, new modes of expressing their thanks to Timothy the magician (but that is claiming too much!) who has conjured all this up for them. They surround him with gratitude and affection, so that there is not a part of him that the raw air touches, not a fibre of his mind that is not satisfied. But now they must go; the servants are waiting with the luggage, Armando in his blue-striped coat, Amalia in her unmourning but habitual black; like sentries they stand on the water-steps, unarmed sentries, sentries wreathed in smiles, sharing (how often have they been told of it!) the glory, the honour, the unparalleled delightfulness of the visit. And below them, ready to ferry the returning guests across, shabby but gay, old but serviceable, nestling in the rushes, lies the boat.

The boat!

Effie was right when she said that Captain Sturrock was a nice gentleman. The letter showed he was. Timothy glanced at it again. It was like a present of glass or china that should have been a pleasure to receive, but owing to faulty packing has arrived broken, beyond repair, and is now an embarrassment both to giver and receiver. Perhaps Timothy could never have made a friend of Captain Sturrock; their differences were too great. He was ready to withdraw brutal, degrading and unmanly, as epithets for coursing, but he could not agree that it was a pretty sight – two large dogs chasing one small hare. And in any case he had said too much. One can apologise for an injury, but not for an insult; in other days Captain Sturrock might have called him out. Timothy had acted in haste and must take the consequences, that was the only dignified course. What they would be he had no idea; but he had again made a fool of himself, and this time he would not get off so lightly.

In refusing the Captain's invitation to tea he said he very much regretted the hasty expressions he had used in his previous letter. The fact was he had lost his temper with the man who was looking after the dogs. He was very sorry about the Captain's bronchitis, and trusted he would have no return of it. He added that he hoped the Captain would be successful at the meeting; but this he deleted, feeling that the situation had gone beyond the reach of an olive branch.

CHAPTER XV

As he was taking his bicycle out of the garage ready for his afternoon ride, Wimbush came up to him. There was a twinkle in the gardener's eye, but his manner was unusually respectful.

'Well, sir, I heard you had a little disagreement last night with a gentleman who spoke out of turn, as the saying is. I must congratulate you.'

Timothy's heart sank.

'I asked Nelson not to say anything about it,' he muttered.

'I'm not saying that Nelson did, sir,' said Wimbush warmly. 'Nelson has his faults, but being a policeman he knows how to keep his mouth shut. No, it was the fellow hisself who was seen at the local, and he had two black eyes as big as hen's eggs.' The gardener chuckled.

'Oh, but Wimbush, he couldn't have had, I hardly touched him.'

'Well, sir, there was several as saw him, and said his nose was bleeding, too. You gave him a proper pasting, sir, you spoilt his beauty all right.'

Timothy sighed despairingly. What would the village think of him now?

'Everybody's talking about it, sir, there was two or three stopped me on my way home to dinner. They said we didn't think Mr. Casson had it in him, being a church-goer and almost a Christian, you might say.'

'I'm very sorry about the whole business,' said Timothy wretchedly.

The gardener's tawny leonine eyes opened in astonishment; red flecks were dancing in them, and he looked as if he might be going to roar.

'You shouldn't say that, sir, begging your pardon. Why it might easily have been the other way round, him being a tough customer, by all accounts, and you only a gentleman. You'll excuse me saying it, sir, but if it had been known the fight was coming off the odds would have been nine to two against you.'

Timothy wondered how these figures had been arrived at, but felt too ashamed to inquire. 'It was all a mistake,' he said, 'and such a bad example, too.'

Wimbush looked very serious.

'You're wrong there, sir, you're quite wrong. Why, all the chaps think the world of you. You're the kind of man the village wants to wake it up, and give it a lead, like. Gentlemen like Colonel Harbord are all very well in their way, I'm not saying anything to the contrary, but you'd hardly know they were soldiers, they go about so quiet. They may be all right for map-reading but they wouldn't be no good in a rough house. They'd let the other fellow have the last word, if you take my meaning.'

'That's what I ought to have done,' said Timothy.

'No, sir, you mustn't say that. You taught the chap a lesson he'll remember all his life. 'Tisn't as if he belong to Upton. He's just a chap from nowhere in particular – Birmingham, like as not, he speaks that broad – and what does he do? He forces an entry and uses insulting language and behaviour – those were Nelson's very words.'

'Oh, but I thought you said Nelson—'

'I did say so, sir. Those are the words Nelson would have used if he hadn't been careful not to say anything. He could do no less. He said he'd have charged the man but you wouldn't let him. He said he was sorry about that because it would have brought him credit. When the high-ups in the police find a village constable like Nelson not reporting anybody they think he must be slacking because it stands to sense there must be crime everywhere, in Upton as well as other places.'

Timothy said he was sorry Nelson had missed his chance.

'Bless you, sir,' said Wimbush, 'he don't hold it against you. He said to me, "There may be better garages in Upton than Mr. Casson's, I'm not saying there aren't – there's Colonel Harbord's that has hot pipes and an examination pit, but I wouldn't put my car in any of 'em, not if Mr. Casson himself asked me to."'

Timothy felt much touched and warmed at heart to be so firmly supported by the arm of the law.

'Well, I'm glad you think I did right, Wimbush.'

' 'Tisn't only I, sir, the whole village be saying the same thing.'

The village street was drowsy at this hour. The depth of summer, the depth of the afternoon, lay upon it, a two-fold weight, heavy as an enchanted sleep. No process was at work towards growth or decay: all was fruition; Nature at its prime. The light could do no more; it had given to visibility all the word could mean, all that Giorgione saw; the air was like a luminous fluid whose unseen pressure retarded movement, whether of people, smoke or trees. All things had lost their own quality and partook of the quality of summer. The ducks languidly dabbling their bills in the pond, the cat crossing the road, its tail as vertical and motionless as the plumes of smoke from the chimneys, the flowers and still more the weeds, which rioted on the patches of untended ground between the houses, and sometimes in the gardens themselves, had reached their peak hour of luxuriance. A halt had been called in the eternal effort of the year.

Only Timothy, it seemed, felt the need for further striving, for moving his position, for altering his state of mind, for going one better. Not that he was the only human being astir in Upton. One or two farm labourers lumbered towards him, perhaps on their way from one field to another. Their gait, the slowest that was consonant with progress, scarcely disturbed the idle rhythm of the afternoon, for they, too, had yielded to the spell of summer. But when they saw him they nodded with a quick lateral jerk of the head that was intimate and full of complicity, and not, Timothy thought, devoid of admiration. Even so might Joe Louis be saluted, swaggering down the streets of Harlem after another lightning knock-out. He saw to it that their tributes did not go unacknowledged.

And here was someone else, a lady walking down the middle of the road, but walking was hardly the word, for she moved like a child, at almost every pace between running and standing still, between swinging majestically and tripping delicately. Plunging and dipping, she came onwards like a pinnace. Timothy recognised her from afar, but had she recognised, would she recognise, him? An inner glow, he knew, absorbed her vision; of the outer world she saw only what she chose to see, her long thick eyelashes made a sort of filter in which visibility was effortlessly sifted; had a giraffe passed her she might not have noticed it and yet the creature could not feel affronted; it was only that today was not her day for noticing giraffes. But Timothy felt his situation so delicate, after all that had happened, that the chance of being invisible to her was a risk he dare not take. Dismounting in a flurry of arrested movement, he barred her way.

'Why, it's Mr. Casson!' she said. 'How strange to see you here! But how silly of me, I should have said, how delightful – but it is always strange to meet someone who has just been in your thoughts.'

'Was I in yours, Mrs. Purbright?' asked Timothy, in spite of his misgivings feeling at once that heightened state of awareness that her presence always brought him.

'Did I say you, Mr. Casson? How stupid of me. Of course, you are a constant guest, my preferred visitor. But no, it was someone who vaguely reminded me of you, not you at all, a sort of doppelgänger. We were talking en tête-à-tête.'

'And I interrupted you!' said Timothy.

'But how opportunely! I would rather converse with you than with your shade. An image gets out of date; how can I tell if you are the same as when I saw you last?'

'Do I look different?' asked Timothy.

'Do you know, I think you do. Don't ask me how. One notices changes, being away so long.'

'A month, was it?'

'Very nearly, and what strides summer has taken! This garden' – she waved to it – 'was full of roses when I went away. Where are they now? And these nettles, how tall they have grown! And all this dark, heavy greenery, shrouding everything! It's like August. The year has grown much older since I went away.'

Timothy considered this.

'I do get the feeling of a turning-point,' he said.

'You do? How interesting, because I was only saying the same thing just now, when I had you, so to speak, in the dentist's chair.'

'Was I a good patient?' asked Timothy.

'Oh, very good! You never complained, not even when my clumsy fingers touched a nerve.'

Timothy leaned on his bicycle, for he thought this might be a long business.

'Tell me some of the things you said.'

'Oh no, Mr. Casson, I couldn't dream of it. Our conversation was entirely private, and to speak of it, even to you, would be a breach of confidence. I see I'm keeping you from your ride, and exercise is so necessary for you. Good-day.'

She was moving off, out of his life to join the circle of shadows that surrounded him. He called her back.

'Oh please, Mrs. Purbright, just give me the gist of your conversation.'

She turned back, irresolutely. 'Oh, it was nothing at all. So interfering and so one-sided. I'll only tell you if you promise me to think of my interlocutor not as yourself, nor even as my idea of you, which may be quite mistaken, but as an independent entity, an abstraction, a victim of my meddlesomeness. Shall we call him X?'

'By all means,' said Timothy. His personality seemed to ebb away from him: he was anonymous at last.

'But we mustn't go on standing in the middle of the road,' said Mrs. Purbright urgently. 'Do you know I sometimes tremble for your safety?'

'Or for the safety of X?' said Timothy, wheeling his bicycle to the side of the road.

'For the purposes of my respectful regard and concern,' said Mrs. Purbright, 'you are as one. Shall we stand under the shadow of this tree? Aren't you afraid of sunstroke, going without a hat?'

'I always did in Italy,' said Timothy.

'But X told me that in Italy, dear Italy, the dangers are not the same as they are here.'

'I wonder what he meant,' said Timothy.

'I was afraid to ask him.'

'Afraid?' said Timothy.

'Yes, he has such an excellent sense of humour, and when he laughs there's no stopping him.'

Timothy detected a gleam under Mrs. Purbright's long lashes.

'How inconvenient for him!' he said.

'Yes, but only for him. He gets embarrassed, but everyone else rather enjoys the joke.'

'Everyone?'

'Oddly enough X raised that point. He thought his laughter might have given offence. I told him, on the contrary. There was no one, literally no one, who did not, either at the time or upon reflection, feel the better for his outburst.'

'How X must have enjoyed his tête-à-tête,' said Timothy. 'I wish my dentist was as comforting.'

'Yes, but wait. I got out my little probe, and told X he had been unkind to avoid places where his society had always been welcome.'

'I can think of a good many things X might have said to that.'

'He did say them.'

'Did he say he wished you hadn't been away from Upton at the time?'

'Yes, but I dismissed that as flattery. I said it was ridiculous for a man like him to feel that in a small place such as the one we had been discussing he needed an interpreter or a protector. Be yourself, I said; people will appreciate you far more for what you are than for what you want them to think you.'

'That was a touch of the drill. Did he flinch or cry "oh!"?'

'He was extremely patient at first, but he began to argue.'

'How very unlike me this man X is.'

'Oh, completely. I said so, didn't I? A hypothetical case. But I suppose I had touched a tender spot, for he got rather angry.'

'Angry? With you?'

'Yes, and not only with me, with everyone. For a moment I hardly recognised him. I felt quite frightened, as though a stranger was talking to me.'

'X is proverbially a bit of a problem.'

'I suppose so. But he had always seemed such a good-natured man.'

'Remember you told him to be himself,' said Timothy.

'Yes, but this was being someone else. And he didn't stop at words, he actually came to blows.'

'With you?'

'No, not with me, though I felt the impact of his anger quite distinctly. He wouldn't have hurt a woman, I am sure. No, with some person of no account who was passing through the village. They actually had a fight.'

'His name must be mud,' said Timothy.

'Quite the opposite, quite the opposite. He is the hero of the hour. I told him so. Everyone, I said, who has any kind of grudge against society, or against his neighbour, or against himself, who has hard words or hard feelings to dispose of, gets twice as angry when he thinks of X.'

'This X must be a popular fellow,' said Timothy.

'He is, Mr. Casson, he is. With his own party, of course he is. With the Exites, or should I say the exiles, since many of them are living far from their own homes, his name is a rallying point, almost a battle-cry.'

'X forever! The unknown quantity, the dark horse!'

Mrs. Purbright smiled.

'But there is another faction, who are much less vocal, but just as convinced, the anti-Exites.'

'Can there be such people, Mrs. Purbright?'

'X asked me precisely that question. I told him, as we walked along, that there was hardly a house in which there was someone who was not for him or against him, and some were divided against themselves.'

'Is the Rectory divided?' asked Timothy.

'The Church is above politics, Mr. Casson. It only seeks a remedy.'

Timothy was silent for a moment or two, then he said, 'How was X reacting to all this?'

'Oh!' said Mrs. Purbright, 'what a difficult question. If only I knew! It is so different talking to a private person and parleying with a general at the head of his army! Falstaff cannot take the same liberties with King Henry that he did with Prince Hal.'

'You found X so much changed, then?'

'Rather I would say, so certain of being in the right.'

'I don't think X sounds a very nice man,' said Timothy.

'Oh, but he is! Only one would not wish to feel altogether in the right.'

'No?' said Timothy doubtfully.

'No.' Mrs. Purbright's voice was firm.

'Had you any advice to offer to this dangerous man?' said Timothy at last.

'Oh, Mr. Casson, how should I dare? I painted him a picture of the village as it soon might be, split into two camps; I pointed out the discomforts and risks of such a cleavage, at a time when we ought to be united as never before; I showed him the stiff lips and averted eyes, the decline of mutual helpfulness, the increase of mutual suspicion; I recalled from the past small acts of spite that had made feuds between families, long, septic quarrels which even now impair the harmony of village life; Cassandra-like I prophesied words, blows and bloodshed; I mentioned the added burdens on my husband whom Nature has not fashioned for a peacemaker, though he does his best to be; I referred, but only in passing' – Mrs. Purbright waved her hand – 'to my own small share in the life of the community, suspected by each party of sympathising with the other, going from house to house shunned like an infected person; seeing the little gatherings I have to preside over dwindle, being criticised for everything I do.' She paused and looked away from Timothy. 'And I even ventured to tell X what effect all this . . . this cancer of ill-will might have on him.'

'Ah,' said Timothy, clutching his bicycle. 'And what effect did you foresee?'

'Oh, Mr. Casson, how can one enter into the mind of another person, especially a person who is sure of being in the right, and can command a large, devoted following? How put oneself in his place? I spoke in the most general way of the risk to a sensitive, imaginative nature, much alone, as X unfortunately is – of dwelling too much on one thought, and that a resentful one; of the avenues of experience that this might be expected to stop up, of the over-development of the will at the expense of the other faculties, of the danger to health and even to sanity. I didn't say much, how could I? I spoke of the plots and counter-plots, the conversations all ending in one conversation, the thoughts all ending in one thought. I tried to indicate what his new way of life would be like – seeing how far he could go, stopping just in time, looking for adherents in unlikely places, sowing discontent. I warned him of betrayals, and of fidelities that would be worse than betrayals. I told him of the lies he would have to tell, the deceits he would have to practise. Speaking like a doctor, I gave his moral nature six months to live. But there was hardly anything I could say, for you see, his mind was made up.'

'You seem to have said a good deal,' observed Timothy.

'Oh no, I barely touched the fringes of the subject. I could have gone much further but—' here her voice was drowned by the roar of a low-flying aeroplane. Timothy waited for the din to subside.

'But what?' he said.

'Well, you see,' said Mrs. Purbright, 'I had a proposal to make.'

'Can't you tell me?'

'Oh no, I think I'd better not. Let our little fantasy end here in this dear old village, so different from the place I have been describing, and let us bury X, for soon he will have to be buried.'

She spoke with so much vehemence that Timothy started.

'Tell me your proposal, Mrs. Purbright. What do you want me to do?'

Mrs. Purbright stared at him.

'You, Mr. Casson? But we were talking about X.'

Timothy felt himself trembling and saw that perspiration had broken out on Mrs. Purbright's forehead. She made a gesture of utter weariness.

'What is the use? X rejected my proposal, Mr. Casson.'

'But I might accept it.'

She shook her head.

'I have talked far too much. And yet I have not talked to you, though for weeks I have been looking forward to it. How silly of me. You must go now. I mustn't keep you. But just tell me this: how have you been getting on?'

'Well, so-so. A few little ups and downs, you know.'

'Village life is so dull,' said Mrs. Purbright. 'Nothing ever happens. Sometimes I feel I should like to shake it up, and send everyone flying, as Alice did the pack of cards.'

'As X would have done,' Timothy reminded her.

'We mustn't go back to X.'

Timothy sighed. 'You are so tantalising. You offer me something, and then you snatch it away.'

'Only to save you the trouble of handing it back to me. Besides, you probably know what it is.'

'I haven't the remotest idea.'

'X said that.'

'That man again! I hoped I was cleverer than he is.'

'You are much cleverer,' said Mrs. Purbright. 'Only you see his position gives him great power.'

'He is so unlike me,' said Timothy, 'that I don't see how you ever fitted us into the same thought. Power for good, or power for evil?'

'For both. I told him so. It was the basis of my appeal. You hold us all, I said, in the hollow of your hand. Only you can save us.'

'And didn't he respond? The man must be a kind of Heathcliff.'

'He thought I was exaggerating. I assured him I wasn't. But how could I convince him? By saying the river would run with blood? By saying he would see half the people he knew strung up to lamp-posts? By saying that the village would be laid waste, and left a prey to the crows and ravens? Dare I use such arguments to a man of X's elegant and sophisticated mind, and with such a keen sense of the ridiculous? I did, and I said that all this could be averted if he would make one sacrifice. I reminded him of the value of the spectacular in turning people from a fixed idea; I said that his act, like a column of fire shooting up to heaven, would change the character of everybody's thoughts. They would be lost in amazement; their minds would go up, with the leaping flames; they would join hands and dance round the great pyre singing hymns of thanksgiving and praise.'

'To X?'

'To him and to all the heavenly powers.'

'And he refused the boon?'

'Yes, he said the sacrifice would be too great. But I forgot to mention one thing.'

'What was that?'

Mrs. Purbright looked fixedly at Timothy, and dropped her voice. 'Have you ever considered if the river was suitable for rowing, Mr. Casson?'

Timothy, his mind jolted and jarred, could only repeat, 'Suitable?'

'Well, safe. When I besought X to burn his boat, I forgot to put that question to him.'

In the glow of his great renunciation, Timothy rode on towards Swirrelsford. Thinking over his conversation with Mrs. Purbright, he realised that he had reached his decision long before she had told him what the sacrifice was to be. He had not guessed what was in her mind, but when she told him, it seemed inevitable, so perfectly had she adapted the means to the end. Somehow she had managed to cut the thousand filaments that bound him to the boat, and now it seemed just as necessary to part with it as before it had seemed essential to keep it.

The two gestures were complementary; both had come to involve his strongest feelings, both were intensifications of his inmost self, both were symbols of victory. But whereas one meant the contraction of his entire being, the discarding of all desires except the single impulse to have his own way, the other was an enlargement of himself, a holocaust on to which he could gloriously fling every impulse, great or small, that he had ever entertained, every accretion of experience, every variation of personality, that had visited him since the dawn of self-consciousness.

With every revolution of the wheels he felt his obligation to Mrs. Purbright increase. She had performed a miracle, and at no small cost to herself; she was quite done up with all the nervous energy she had put out. He, too, had been exhausted by the conflict with her will, so exhausted that he wondered if he should go home and postpone his expedition until tomorrow. But the mood of sacrifice was on him and he did not want to break it; besides, with the wish to free himself of the boat, had come the knowledge of how he must set about it, and that entailed going to Swirrelsford.

He almost wished Mrs. Purbright had not brought up the point of the unsuitability of the river. It was a good debating point, no doubt; but it tinged his act of self-sacrifice with the leaden hues of self-inter-est. Just as two excuses are less effective than one, so two reasons for doing the right thing are likely to damage each other. Moreover, he was certain she exaggerated. All through, indeed, she had exaggerated. Timothy was not conceited enough to suppose that his determination to retain the boat would set the village by the ears and divide it against itself. That was picturesque overstatement, which might contain a grain of truth. But to say the river was dangerous was a plain mis-statement, a characteristically feminine appeal to his fears. Timothy had never seen the Devil's Staircase, on which she based her warning; not many people had seen it, for it was situated in closely preserved waters a mile or so below the village. But Wimbush had seen it and he said that far from being a kind of Niagara it was in normal times the merest trickle between boulders, resembling, Timothy gathered, the Swallow Falls in a dry summer. It might easily be impassable to a boat, simply for lack of water deep enough to float it. True, below the falls was the so-called bottomless pool, beloved of fishermen; but Wimbush was of opinion that any full-sized man, such as he or Mr. Casson, would be able to stand up in it, and in any case it could only be reached from below; the rocks of the Devil's Staircase would be an effective barrier to any boat coming from above. Thirty or forty years ago, before the river was so

strictly preserved, picture postcards were sold in the village shop showing a most imposing cataract, the rocks scarcely visible in bursts of
spray and rushing, mud-green water; but Wimbush had never seen it in
such angry mood; and was it probable something would happen, which
had never happened yet in his experience?

Thus the legend of the falls had been debunked; and the only grievance Timothy had against Mrs. Purbright was that, to strengthen her
plea for the abolition of the boat, she had tried to scare him with it.

At first he had been so dominated by her picture of the destruction
of the boat that he had assumed that that was the only way to dispose
of it. It would be lifted from its shrine among the stained-glass windows,
dragged across the lawn and through the stable-yard, like a witch, like
a heretic, like a malefactor, on to the village green; and there faggots
would be piled under it, anointed with all the pitch and tar and paraffin
that the village could produce. Thus it would remain for a day or two,
awaiting combustion, the cynosure of all eyes; little boys would press
around it, with matchboxes in their pockets, longing to have a chance
to set light to it before its time. In the end it might have to be roped off.
Then, when its presence had been fully advertised, and its meaning
made known to everyone, Timothy would issue invitations, beginning
with Colonel Harbord, Commander Bellew, Captain Sturrock, Sir
Watson Stafford and the rest, to a dinner party; and when they had all
eaten and drunk as much as they could, or more, they would repair to
the Green, shortly before midnight, where they would find the whole
village, massed in a hollow square, motionless and silent. There would
be a brief ceremony of dedication; Timothy would make a speech
protesting his affection for the village, which would be greeted by a
deep-throated rumble of congratulation and approval. Following this,
a whispered conversation between Timothy and his guests in which the
honour of setting fire to the boat would be disclaimed by them and by
a general vote conferred on him; and he with a brand or torch soaked
in kerosene, flaming smokily and smelling strong and resinous, would
advance to the pyre.

At once, scarcely giving him time to leap back, the flames would
start up, smoke-crowned, with a crackle and a hiss; the sentinel poplars
would be flood-lit to their summits; a murmur would go through the
ranks of the spectators, rising to a roar that would drown the roar of
the flames; everyone would stand and cheer and slap each other on the
back; and Timothy and his guests, flinging off their tail-coats and
white waistcoats and possibly more, since the heat would be almost
unbearable, would dance like dervishes round the pyre. From time to

time, wild-eyed and with her hair in disorder, Mrs. Purbright, the prophetess, would dart forward with an inarticulate cry and fling upon the conflagration sweet-smelling oils, filling the air with the scent of jessamine and honeysuckle.

A boat is a frail thing, hardly thicker than matchboard, though composed of so many and such costly woods. Now it is alight all along the delicately-lined gunwale; now the seat at the back has caught; the smouldering cushions have burst into flame; and see, the very sculls are burning; a tongue of fire is licking round their blades. Timothy dashes forward and picks one out and holds it, flaming, high above his head. A new wave of cheering bursts out, stamping feet mark a rhythm; they are all singing 'For he's a jolly good fellow.' The Green is now as bright as day; radiance streams up into the firmament; the bonfire has conquered the darkness in the heavenly places, as well as in the human heart.

But what is this distant, but insistent throbbing, with its missed beat and syncopated rhythm, that, half-heard at first, now begins to throb in their ears like the pulse of blood? No need to ask; the first stick of bombs has already burst, miles away, but in a minute, guided by the bonfire, the raiders will be right overhead. 'Take cover! Take cover!' In a trice the Green is deserted; the noise of scurrying feet dies away, the terrible, inexorable iambics overheard grow louder. All the spectators have vanished into the night. Timothy is the last to leave the scene; he watches it from his gate. The boat is now quite consumed, yet its form is perfectly preserved, a long, glowing skeleton along which the wind plays in waves of whiter heat. Suddenly its spine breaks and it dissolves into ashes, already blackening, and at the same moment a prodigious crash announces that the Germans have discovered Upton.

No, the idea of the bonfire must be abandoned, if for no other reason than that it would contravene the black-out regulations. But in any case, thought Timothy, now restored to reality, why destroy the boat? He couldn't help smiling at himself to think how literally he had taken Mrs. Purbright's metaphor. The boat was valuable, it could still be a source of pleasure, it might even be a source of profit. Everything had increased in price since the war began; why not a boat? It might already be worth twice as much as he had given for it. Timothy had lost his job; some of his investments were not paying as they should; a hundred and sixty pounds would be most useful. To part with the boat as if it were an investment that had gone up in value was no doubt a less spectacular way of getting rid of it than a public cremation; but was it not more rational? And less vulgar, less ostentatious? The village would appreciate his gesture none the less because he had not, financially, been the loser by it. Indeed, if he burnt it they might think he was batty, or that he had decided to do away with it in a fit of pique, because he wasn't allowed to use it. They would shake their heads and tap their foreheads. Whereas if he sold it they would realise that he was a practical man like themselves, making the best of a bad job. 'Jolly sensible of Casson; now that he's got rid of his boat, we can all get together.'

And think of the children who would enjoy rowing in it, and trailing their fingers in the water! And the soldiers and airmen, poor fellows, who were at a loose end in the afternoons; how many of them it would save from less salutary and healthful pastimes! Up and down the river it would go, carrying loving couples, helping to increase the waning stock of the world's happiness; it would lose its status as an amateur, of course, it would ply for hire; it would be a public conveyance. But wasn't that better than rotting slowly away, in a twilight stained with blue and orange gleams, and smelling of decaying weed, where no one, not even its owner (for it was weeks since Timothy had unlocked the door) ever saw it? And sometimes, if he was lucky, he might find it next on the list, awaiting its old master, and he could hire it and pretend it was his. He would still be a benefactor, to himself, to the public, and to the Swirrelsford boatman, who had often complained to him of the difficulty of replenishing his fleet.

Compared with the other, it would be an ignominious exit for a guest that had made so proud an entry – that, even when caged and bound and denied its freedom, had carried the cargo of so many hopes, that had been launched a thousand times in his imagination, although in reality it had never left the shore. When my ship comes in! – but his had never gone out; it had stayed indoors, and so had he. Where were the friends he should have made, the houses that should have been open to him, the harvest of shared experiences that he had meant to lay up for himself at Upton, as he had garnered them on the Brenta? Experiences he had had, of course, but they were all negative, all in opposition, all strengthening the will at the expense of the inclinations. Somebody must be humbled in order that Timothy might stand upright. It was a dreary record, and he was glad to be writing finis to it, and turning over a new page free of grumbles and grievances, a blank page.

He hurried on, for his conversations with Wimbush and Mrs. Purbright had made him late and today he had a special reason, which he had forgotten until now, for not falling behind his schedule. It was a ridiculous reason which to think of made him hotter than he already was; but as the suburbs of Swirrelsford drew near, the black and white houses, the gardens gay with marigold and geranium, he redoubled his efforts. He wanted to keep his rendez-vous with the two trains. Unbelievable as it was, considering the scanty nature of the acquaintance, but he had had a tiff with them. Not with the trains themselves, though now he viewed them with much less favour than before – they were obviously branchline trains incapable of doing more than forty miles an hour – but with their moving spirits. How had it happened, when, except for inarticulate shouts and cheers, he had never exchanged a word with them? Well, twice, on two successive days, the men had failed to return his greeting. They must have known he was there, for he was always there; but inexplicably, when they converged, the men on the railway line and he on the water, they had been woundingly occupied with something else. Once the fireman had been feeding his engine, which he could quite well have done at another time; once he was staring through the look-out hole, with an expression of great intentness, at a line which, even Timothy could see, was perfectly clear. And in the other engine the same indifference reigned; they had purposely looked away from him. They wouldn't play, they thought the joke childish, they had cut him out of their lives. The old buffer in the boat must be put in his place.

There was only one thing to do, and Timothy did it. He made up his mind long beforehand. As it happened, next time the trains came by, the drivers waved with all their old abandon. But Timothy rowed on, his eyes fixed on the boat. A second time they tried again, rather languidly, as Timothy could see under his raised eyebrows, but it was a definite salute. Again Timothy hardened his heart, and after that rebuff, they waved no more. The warning rattle of the trains, which had once filled him with agreeable expectation, was now the signal to guard his self-esteem against the memory of a slight; tension, a clenched mind, a furrowed brow, reigned in the boat, and in the cabs of the two engines who knows? perhaps the same emotions, perhaps (still more mortifyingly) entire forgetfulness. Timothy could feel the hostility mounting in him. He never reached the point of hoping the train would crash, but he did catch himself wishing that these extremely unpleasant, ill-mannered artisans might be late once too often, and be degraded to driving a goods train.

In his new mood, freed of his incubus, and the self-regarding, self-esteeming emotions it engendered, Timothy felt that he must not lose a minute in repairing the breach with his old friends. If necessary he would stand up in the boat, at the risk of upsetting it; and if pride still restrained them from answering, he would repeat the gesture every day for a fortnight. It should be his first act in the new manner, his first act to show that he asked nothing of humanity except its love.

So absorbed was he in his vision of the coming reconciliation that he did not notice, as he crossed the bridge and began to lead his bicycle down the tow-path, the altered aspect of the river. Indeed, it was not unusual, when he arrived, to see no boats about; it had happened before, and the boatman had always kept one for him. He knew where it would be, but it was not there now. He put his bicycle into a shed which the boatman had placed at his disposal, and stepped on to the long broad shallow barge moored to the shore, that served the boatman as a landing-stage. There was no one about. He knocked on the door of the cabin, and the man came out. His features were always drooping and despondent, but today he looked so woe-begone, so utterly insulated and enclosed by grief, that Timothy forgot his customary greeting, forgot the mutual inquiries and comments on the affairs of the day that were the recognised preliminaries to business, and baldly said:

'Can I have a boat?'

'Afraid not,' the man replied.

'Oh,' said Timothy. He looked round. There were no boats on the river, none at the landing stage; it was a boatless world.

'It's no good your looking,' the man said heavily. 'I've had to take them in.'

'Oh why?' said Timothy.

'They were all being knocked to pieces, that's why,' said the boatman. 'People nowadays don't know how to use a boat. They use 'em same as you would those motorcars that crash into each other at a fair. Only the cars are built to stand up to it and my boats aren't. Why, already this summer I've lost five boats simply through rough handling, and three pairs of oars. I can't replace them and I wouldn't if I could. It's murder, sheer murder.' He looked at Timothy as accusingly as if he had been a ring-leader of the boat-killers. 'And that's not the only reason,' he added darkly. 'There's another thing they do.'

'What's that?'

'They take a boat, for an hour, and when the time's up I look round for the boat to let to another customer. But it isn't there. I wait, two hours, three hours, still the boat doesn't come in.' He paused and looked hard at Timothy. 'Mr. Casson, that boat never comes in. And why? Because they've left it by the bank somewhere, perhaps two or three miles away – upstream and downstream there's a five-mile stretch of river, as *you* know – left it and walked home across the fields.'

'Why do they do that?' asked Timothy.

'Why, can't you see? To get off paying, of course, or because they're too tired to row back, or because they've damaged it so much they daren't.'

'What a shame,' said Timothy.

'A shame? It's worse than a shame,' cried the boatman, his indignation beginning to choke his utterance. 'It's a crime. People like that deserve to be shot. Why, last Sunday there were eight boats that didn't come in, and I had to spend five hours on Monday morning collecting 'em. A full ten miles I rowed, counting both ways, and once with five boats in tow, and one of them was shipping water so badly I had to keep stopping to bale it out. And I'm not so young as I was.'

He really did look years older, Timothy reflected.

' 'Tis all these Army and Air Force chaps,' the boatman went on. 'They wouldn't do it if they was living in their own homes. But as soon as they get into a uniform, and have a number instead of a name – same as nobody can't trace 'em – they think they can do anything they like. And the good ones learn it from the bad ones.'

'I expect it's partly thoughtlessness,' said Timothy.

'Thoughtlessness!' echoed the boatman, scornfully. 'Thoughtlessness! They do a good bit of thinking if you ask me. If they didn't think, they'd bring the boat back in good order, same as you used to, sir, and same as most people did before the town was overrun by these chaps from nowhere. They think with the wrong side of their brains, that's their trouble. So I've done a bit of thinking, too, and I've decided to go out of business till the war's over. I've got to. My stock wouldn't last out another season, not at this rate.'

The man's depression seemed to put him beyond the reach of sympathy, and the river looked so inviting with the sun shining on it that Timothy felt almost as disconsolate as he did. He began to offer condolences, but at each word the man shook his head impatiently, like a retriever shaking himself after a swim.

'I suppose you don't want to buy a boat?' Timothy wound up. There was no need to explain, for he had already discussed every point of his skiff with the boatman many times.

'That I don't!' cried the man warmly and almost pleased, it seemed, after all he had suffered, to be able to inflict a small disappointment on someone else. 'What should I want with another boat, I ask you? I wouldn't take your boat as a gift, a good boat like that, not even if things were different. Why, it wouldn't last a day, the way they handle boats on this river. And you won't find anyone else as will want to buy it,' he went on with gloomy satisfaction. ' 'Tis the same everywhere, by all accounts, sheer murder to a boat to put it on the river, and will be till people come to their senses and know what's due to a boat. You hang on to your boat, sir, and perhaps you'll be able to use it when we've beaten Hitler.'

Suddenly Timothy had an idea.

'Couldn't you let me keep my boat here, at your landing-stage, so that I can come over from Upton and use it?'

'I've nothing against it,' said the man. 'But there'll be nobody here to keep watch, and by the time those old boys' – he waved his hand to indicate some youngsters who were standing on the towpath with their eyes turned inquiringly on the boat-house – 'have found it there won't be enough left of your boat to boil a tea-kettle.'

What a different conflagration from the one he had envisaged! Still murmuring sympathy Timothy proffered a parting present to the boat-man. Mollified by the tip, the man accompanied him a little way along the towpath. 'It's my belief,' he said, 'that people nowadays just live to do all the harm they can.'

Timothy rode back over the hills to Upton in a strange, neutral mood; his sense of anti-climax so strong as to be almost a negation of living. Nothing that he saw held any meaning for him, he could not associate himself with the landscape or the way he was going; even his fatigue seemed to belong to another person. Not a tremor of desire stirred in him; volition was stilled; he functioned as mechanically as the bicycle. He seemed to have no future beyond the crest of the next rise, no past more distant than the last one. Where do I go from here? he asked himself. The hum of the turning wheels was his only answer.

Dropping down into Upton, he felt its familiar atmosphere begin to enfold him with something of the feeling of home. Unconscious of the revolutions, the street fights, the changes of government that had taken place in his heart and mind since he set out, the village awaited him – the only field for his activities that now remained. The coronal of poplars pierced the sky like gigantic exclamation marks. As he drew nearer to his house, the comfort of the known had a steadying effect. He passed one or two of the villagers whom he knew by sight, and their nods and smiles of recognition cheered him. Now he was overtaking two ladies. One had bare legs, the other, who was pushing a pram, wore trousers. The foreigners, the out-landers, were still only on the fringe of Timothy's acquaintance; with some he was just on bowing terms, and he was wondering how definite a salute he should accord to these, when the disengaged lady on the left, the fair one, whose hair had been catching the sun, but whose legs were surprisingly white, heard the sound of his bicycle and turned. She smiled and moved directly into his path, so that Timothy perforce had to dismount.

'Why it's you!' exclaimed Miss Cross.

Clumsily Timothy tried to manœuvre his machine so as to be free to shake hands with her. She watched his operations with amusement, but when, after barking his ankles on the pedals, he had reduced the refractory bicycle to obedience, and was stretching out his hand, she made a tiny motion of withdrawal and absently raised her hand to smooth her hair.

Timothy's arm dropped to his side.

'I never expected to find you here,' she said.

'Why not?' asked Timothy.

'I thought the fishmongers would have frightened you away.'

'Oh no, I'm still here.'

'And boating?'

Timothy smiled. 'No. I've missed the boat.'

'I knew it,' exclaimed Miss Cross. 'I knew you wouldn't do anything if I went away. I suppose you've taken to fishing?'

'No.'

'Are you doing war-work?'

'No.'

'Are you writing your articles?'

'No.'

'Good God, what do you do?'

'Nothing.'

'Nothing? Hold me, Frances, I think I'm going to faint. An able-bodied man, and he does nothing. Don't you even go to the local?'

'No.'

'I see it was high time I came back,' said Miss Cross. 'Will you promise me to be there this evening without fail?'

'Yes, if you will,' Timothy said.

'Nine o'clock, then. You know Frances, don't you? Well, then, shake hands with her.'

Timothy and Frances shook hands with the reserved and slightly guilty air of people who should have performed this ceremony long ago, but for one reason or another have not thought it worth while.

'I want you two to be buddies,' said Miss Cross. 'She's a girl in a thousand, much nicer than I am.'

She may be nicer, Timothy thought, but she isn't half as pretty.

'I haven't got an engagement for this evening, have I?' Miss Cross suddenly asked her friend.

Timothy braced himself to bear a disappointment.

'I don't think so, but you don't tell me all your dates,' Frances said.

Miss Cross turned to Timothy.

'What should you do if I didn't turn up?'

'I should be heart-broken.'

'Very well then, I will. But only on one condition.'

'What is that?'

'I'll give you three guesses.'

For a long time Timothy's life had been so barren of alternatives, which are the prerogative of the free-minded, that he had quite lost the habit of looking for them. He seemed fated to do one thing, and that the wrong thing. No doubt Miss Cross's life was fertile in acts of choice. He tried to think of three possible solutions to her problem.

'That you pay for the drinks?' he ventured, archly.

'Not a very gentlemanly remark. I took it for granted you would,' she answered, almost without a smile.

Timothy thought again.

'That I put on a black tie?'

'What a good idea. I hadn't thought of that. But you must, though . . . I won't come if you don't. But it's not the real condition.'

Moth-like, Timothy's mind fluttered round the most perilous and delicate suggestions. He looked at Frances, in case he should see in her expression some hint of how far he might go. But she was looking as inscrutable as only a woman knows how to.

'That I behave myself properly,' he said at length.

'I'll see to that,' she said. 'Now shall I tell you what the condition is?'

'Please.'

'You won't like it.'

'I'm always doing things I don't like.'

'You won't like doing this.'

'What is it?'

'You must promise to take me with you in the boat.'

Timothy stared at her in silence. The setting sun spilt orange over the red-faced houses, it gleamed on their windows like fire; but from his mind the radiance faded, and the chill of twilight stole through all its corridors.

'Perhaps . . . sometime . . .' he mumbled.

'No, not sometime, tomorrow.'

'Will you really not come unless I promise?'

'No.'

'Then,' said Timothy slowly, 'I'm afraid we shan't meet.' Not from rudeness, but from a kind of hopeless preoccupation with the unending pattern of his disappointment, he mounted his bicycle and rode off without a word. Miss Cross began to laugh, and her laughter followed him down the street. The passers-by looked round.

'Timothy!'

It was so long since he had heard his Christian name that he hardly recognised it and she had to call him twice.

'Timothy!'

He turned round slowly and rode back. The two women were standing where he had left them, and Miss Cross had silenced her laughter with a bewitching smile.

'Darling, you looked so funny riding off like that. Were you angry with me?'

'Of course not,' muttered Timothy.

'Darling, I believe you were. Do you know, the back of your neck is quite red? You are an old silly. Of course I'll come, and you can go and drown yourself in your boat for all I care.'

Her smile turned the words into a blessing, but Timothy scarcely noticed what she said, so bewildered was he by the unlooked for reversal of his fortunes and the call to rejoice instead of weep. On the way back he could not help grinning inanely at everyone he met, and even a sharp nod from Captain Sturrock, who was turning into the drive of The Old Stables, did not damp his spirits. 'Now I know which side I'm on,' he thought, but there was no hostility in his mind, only the sweet sense of unquestioning loyalty to another person. Back in his house he banged about, as if the enlargement of his personality demanded an outlet in increased noise. He sang in his bath and afterwards, in an ecstasy of opening and shutting drawers, he began to hunt for the dress clothes he had not worn since he left Italy, nearly nine months ago. Bang, bang, here was his black tie, discreet symbol of a festive occasion; but would he still remember how to tie it? Here was his waistcoat; would it fit? Here were his trousers, but oh horrors! What was this rash that had broken out on their sleek sides, these disfiguring streaks and perforations in the soft, even nap? He took the garments to the window. . . . Yes, the moth had got into them; while civilisation tottered and crashed, the hateful insect had seized its opportunity. As Litvinov had said, peace was indivisible; and the rent in the fabric of Europe had its humble counterpart in Timothy's dress-suit.

Full of misgiving Timothy slipped the trousers on, challenged the looking-glass and tried to give himself the admiring smile that even the least vain keep for such occasions. He recollected he was going to a bar. At a bar, one stood. If he did not bend, or stretch, or sit, or lie, if he turned away from rather than towards a fellow-reveller, if he lurked in a shady corner instead of coming out into the open, if he could remember to take short steps instead of long ones, if he could keep himself from sliding or stumbling or falling, if he could remain rigidly still and inflexibly upright, he would still present, to an uncritical eye (not Magda Vivien's!) the appearance of a pre-war gentleman going out to keep an engagement with a pre-war lady.

He chattered all the way through dinner, and though it was to Chloe rather than to Effie that he talked, he found her concerns of absorbing interest. She could not fail to be impressed by his animation, and afterwards in the kitchen, when they heard the front door slam 'fit to shake the house,' she remarked to Beatrice:

'I don't know what's happened to Mr. Casson. He's become quite cheerful all of a sudden. And all dressed up, too! He must have had a birthday.'

CHAPTER XVI

IT was some time before Timothy would acknowledge, even to himself, the strength of his attachment to Miss Cross. He tried to persuade himself that the eccentricities of his behaviour had nothing to do with her. If he went out into the village street in the middle of the morning, and lit a cigarette, and walked up and down studying the cottage gardens, it was because he wanted to do this, not because, a few days ago at much the same hour, he had run into Vera there, and fondly imagined that her movements were guided by a time-table.

Timothy's day was punctuated by such sorties, all of which he believed spontaneous, but all of which were really inspired by the desire to meet Miss Cross. His procedure was always the same: the cigarette, the uninterested air, the starting and stopping, the sudden absorption in the sky. This last occupation was plausible enough, for Upton was a hive of low-flying aircraft. They swooped down, cutting short conversation, obliterating thought. Besides, August was well advanced, and the village had seen the silver gleam of many a daylight bomber, and at night had heard the heavy grunt and watched the reddened sky-line. To those he met when off on these patrols (how rarely they turned out to be Miss Cross!) he was often over-effusive, holding them in conversation as if it was they whom he had really come to see; and if they happened to be friends of hers (Timothy now numbered most of the 'foreigners' among his acquaintance) he tried extra hard to make himself agreeable, feeling that by being civil to them he was somehow recommending himself to her. He never mentioned her to them, but if they mentioned her to him it almost counted as a meeting, so sweetly did her name sound on their lips. Indeed, he treasured every little word they said about her, for it helped to build up an image with which his thoughts could afterwards make free.

But he seldom, at this time, dropped in at the Fisherman's Arms, which was the most likely place to meet her; partly from shyness of the faces turning at his entry, partly because it was, well – one thing to saunter down the street, looking here and there, and another to sidle into the pub, with his purpose shining in his eyes. When he met her there it was generally by appointment. Timothy felt there was much virtue in an appointment; it betokened regularity and order and was something of which his guardian would have approved.

Actually his mind was in chaos, its furniture turned upside down, its lighting lurid and fitful, its atmosphere tingling as though with an electrical discharge. It was no place to live in – that was one reason why he was so often out of doors.

To his surprise he did not find her difficult to talk to, for he spoke to draw her out, to explore her mind, to hear what she would say; it didn't much matter what she said, the important thing was that she said it, and to him. He did not always like what she said at the moment when she said it; but a second later he had invented a score of reasons for finding it commendable. Her flattery was sometimes crude, her conversation bristled with booby-traps; her callousness sometimes startled him; but all these could be turned to favour and to prettiness by one simple trick of mental alchemy; she was nearer to nature than he was. By living a sheltered life among books and pictures, by adopting the detached, judicial attitude of a sight-seer, he had interposed a wall of æsthetic judgment between him and experience. This barrier she was breaking down, for she was the raw material of art, the essential thing from which artists drew their inspiration; talking to her, he was refreshed at the original fount. He had been told that his work was too literary, that it was bleached by irony and drained of nature; well, the colour would now be restored, the nature put back; for she was a child of nature and unconsciously illustrated its workings.

Thus he silenced the questionings of his critical faculty, if ever it seemed suspicious of her. But it seldom did, for the emotions control the mind much more easily than the mind controls the emotions, and Timothy was only too glad to feel the current of his being running one way. Gradually, as it seemed to him, but rapidly by the reckoning of days and nights, the milestones on his way to her were passed. It had seemed dashing to meet her at the Fisherman's Arms; soon it became the usual, though never taken-for-granted climax of his day; it had seemed daring to enter The Nook, and wait on the boldly-striped divan side by side with dolls with dangling limbs and decadent faces, while Vera and Frances put the children to bed. Not without set-backs these goals were won; for sometimes Vera would fail him at the pub, and he would sit, with one eye on the door, draining his tankard and trying to hide his disappointment from the watchful eyes around him. And sometimes when he escorted her to her home, expectation tightening at every step, she would leave him on the very threshold, saying she had things to do: 'So sorry, darling, I must throw you out,' when she hadn't even let him in.

He could count on his love for her, though not on her. But his love throve on these set-backs which, as he seldom really believed in her excuses, he would put down to some deficiency in himself, some clumsiness of approach, some tactical error; he must be as various, he told himself, as she was capricious; he must discover, at the eleventh hour, the right word to say, the right look to give, to make her want him. He tried to snapshot himself at the moment of admittance so that he could be the same another time, and repeat his success. 'But it's Frances I really want to see, not you,' or something in that vein, had proved an Open Sesame more than once.

But she would not even promise to visit him at the Old Rectory. 'No, I couldn't, what would they take me for?' she said. Timothy, when he first heard this felt the thrill of pride in her refusal to cheapen herself that any man might feel. But when he got home to the empty chair in which so confidently he had seen her sitting, he was overwhelmed with disappointment. Vacancy invaded him, darkening his mind like a barren twilight; nothing that had gone before, none of the painful progress he had made, seemed to count beside this last rebuff; and when he met her in their accustomed haunts the magic and the thrill had gone, simply because they were not his house. His longing to see her was as strong as ever but the actual encounters brought him little delight and an uneasy sense of frustration; she was like an object of virtue that the collector longs to possess, and comes back time after time to look at, tormented because the owner will not part with it and must not be asked again.

One evening, however, when he had resigned himself to the static nature of their friendship she suddenly said, 'Why have I never seen the inside of your house?'

Timothy could not answer; his heart beat in his throat and he looked at her inquiringly.

'When will you come?' he muttered.

She laughed and said, 'Darling, you always want to make an engagement. Do you never do anything without putting it down in your diary first?'

'It's to have it to look forward to,' said Timothy.

'Well, what day is it today?'

Timothy tried to remember; he had been losing count of the days. 'August the seventeenth, I think.'

'Well, shall we say December the seventeenth? That will give you plenty of time to look forward.'

Timothy's face fell. 'Oh, that's too far ahead.'

'October the seventeenth?'

Timothy answered more lightly than he felt, 'But I might be dead then.'

She smiled. 'Well, so might I. You don't seem to think of me.'

'I think of you all the time,' said Timothy.

'I don't feel flattered,' she said moodily. 'You'd rather think of me than be with me. What about September the seventeenth? Have you the book handy?'

Timothy brought out his diary and opened it. Day followed day, week followed week, great empty tracts of time, to be got over somehow. September now seemed much further off than December had, a moment since.

'Come on, put it down,' she said, covering the day with a scarlet finger-nail. 'V. at the O.R. or whatever code you use.'

Her voice was impatient, but Timothy still hesitated; writing down a date seemed final to him; by claiming her for the seventeenth of September he forfeited all hope of getting her before.

'What's the matter?' she said. 'I don't believe you want me at all. It was just a ruse to put me off, this diary business.'

Timothy could not speak; he took the book from her and slowly turned the pages. 'Look how blank they are,' he said. 'Not a single engagement.'

Bending her head until it almost touched his shoulder she watched the procession of dateless days. 'What's this day?' she asked, suddenly, her finger pouncing.

'That? Oh, that's today, August the seventeenth.'

'Well, what's wrong with August the seventeenth?'

'But it's today,' repeated Timothy. 'You don't mean—?'

'Of course I do. I only said the other, because it gave you more time to look forward.'

Timothy stared. Why had he been so foolish? Yet even then, in the full flood of his relief and joy, he couldn't quite abandon himself to the current; his mind searched wildly for some cable to tether him to the world he knew. They were standing in the village street, en route for The Nook.

'But won't Frances be expecting us?' he said. 'Won't she wonder what's happened?' The words sounded silly as soon as he had uttered them and he looked at Vera apprehensively; she had a sharp tongue and she had often told him that she had no patience with his sheep-dog moods. But unexpectedly she was all honey.

'Don't worry, darling,' she told him; 'I warned her that I might be a bit late.'

So she was sitting in his chair after all; her face broke the curve of its back just where he thought it would, and her pale hair against the olive-green upholstery held shadows in its depths that were almost green too. On the octagonal mother-of-pearl table lay her handbag, just as he had pictured it; Miss Chadwick's drawing-room was taking the impress of its new visitor. But how unwillingly! He felt he had to fight with many shadows for her right to be there, and some of them were in himself; some could only be appeased by presents, extensions of himself that, in her possession, were like passports to the house's favour. Against these gifts she fought, she was no gold-digger, she said; but presently another handbag lay on the nacreous table, and then another. And at last, after infinite persuasions, and a day of bitter estrangement, a jewel, a tiny diamond clasp, sparkled on her shoulder.

Thus the house came to know her – the hall, the drawing-room, and the dining-room; and in the dead season when she wasn't there, which was after all the greater part of every day, Timothy could imagine she was, for he knew how those places looked when lighted by her presence. They were transformed by it as much as he was; they belonged to his conception of her, just as she answered more readily to the call of his imagination when she carried with her something he had given her; something that had a place on her dressing-table or in her chest of-drawers, that greeted her familiarly in the morning and parted from her last thing at night. He could find it in him to be jealous of these objects which were so much more intimate with her than he was, which could return the pressure of her hand for hours together, whereas he must be content with minutes; which could spend the whole day on her shoulder, while he—

But as he went upstairs and stepped outside the circle of her ambience, the vision of her faded; she was a ghost that haunted the ground floor, and was bound by the conventions of a common caller, her dearness overlaid and distanced by the ceremony with which he must approach it. In rooms where she had not been, how could he call her his? – and she would not, *would* not even pretend an interest in what lay above the level ground of their companionship. This companionship had become for Timothy as humdrum and lacking in allure as had his former meetings with her at the inn and in The Nook; his imagination no longer kindled at the thought of them, they were like hard-won peaks which the mountaineer no longer notices, so far are they below him.

'But what do you want to show me, darling?' she once asked. 'Is it your toothbrush and your face towel? – because I can imagine those. Or is it some monster that you keep hidden in a cupboard? You've seen me tidy my hair and make my face up; are you jealous of the smallest, tiniest little things I do to myself?'

Timothy protested that he wasn't. 'But I shall like my room better if you've been in it,' he said.

'But, darling, it's not a show place,' she reminded him, 'and besides, what would the servants say?'

What indeed? At one time Timothy would have minded very much what they said, but since the return of Miss Cross his relationship with the staff of the Old Rectory had become almost dreamlike. Beatrice and Effie were hardly more than names; they slipped in and out of his consciousness without leaving a trace of their passage. He talked to them, perhaps more easily and naturally than before; but he no longer tried to mix his personality with theirs or find a highest common factor for their intercourse. Even with Wimbush his exchanges were perfunctory; he could not remember afterwards what either of them had said. His household had receded with the rest of the world from the centre of reality and were dimly visible on the confines of his mind.

Besides, the world itself was unrecognisable. Bombs were raining down on London. Even the direction of men's eyesight was changed. It was turned upwards; like miniature search-lights their tired eyes swept the zenith. 'Take shelter! Take shelter!' was the cry. All but the bravest people felt in jeopardy; like rabbits they had at the backs of their minds a place where they believed they would be safest. At the Old Rectory it was under the stairs; here he and Effie and Beatrice would foregather and drink tea and while away the weary minutes between 'alert' and 'all clear' with desultory, meaningless conversation that was like the very language of boredom, for it expressed nothing except their desire to hide their fears. We are all ostriches with our heads in the sand, thought Timothy, building shelters round our bodies and our minds to keep out the reality of danger, living in caves like troglodytes. Everyone is busy taking cover; they look up or down, no one looks round or over; each and all we are enclosed and perfect in our separateness. Who will mind, who will even notice, in the middle of a world war, if I take Vera Cross upstairs and show her the appointments?

So he argued, but Vera only smiled at him and never gave so much as a glance to the climbing staircase, though sometimes, when he was seeing her off, he would mount the first step, lay his hand on the banister and from this eminence, with head half turned and swinging foot, detain her in what he fondly imagined was bedtime conversation.

In vain. Muffled, muted and ingrowing his life went on, describing a descending spiral of ever-lessening diameter, shedding the accretions of experience and thought and culture with which the soul seeks to protect itself against the inexorable egotism of the flesh, until his whole being was emaciated and his shrunken consciousness had lost all substance and only existed in the spark that fed it. Nor had he any outlook or mental landscape other than the series of receding mirrors that showed him his desire.

But above all this his being hovered, lonely in its new element, like a kite that floats above the hand that holds it to the earth; and if his thoughts were impoverished his sense of the mere act of living had never been so keen. Never had the sensations of hunger and thirst, energy and weariness, heat and cold, and his awareness of their contrasts, been so sharp and pure as now. His sensations seemed far more real than his discarded thoughts and moreover he could share them with Vera, they brought him nearer to her. If he felt tired, so perhaps did she, and if she said she did, he had the thrill of approximation to her, a kindling sense of union, as though the same skin clothed them both. He would ring her up to tell her what he was feeling, and if she felt the same it brought a closer sense of contact than any identity of views. What matter if such intercourse sometimes involved a little cheating, a few misrepresentations before harmony was reached?

'I had a slight headache this afternoon.'

'So had I.'

'I'm so sorry. When did yours come on?'

'About half-past three.'

'How extraordinary. So did mine.' Actually Timothy's headache had arrived somewhat later in the day, but at any rate the two visitations must have overlapped, and by doing so brought the lovers together in a way that no clean bill of health, no radiant expanse of featureless well-being, could ever do.

United by a headache! But they were not united; they were separated by the height of a staircase.

One chilly evening, for the year had now expended its seemingly exhaustless store of warmth, she drew the silver fox fur round her and said, 'You were quite right, darling, I was angry at the time but what a comfort it is. And you ought to have one, too, wandering about the cold passages in this rambling old house.'

'Why,' said Timothy, 'what makes you think they're cold?'

'But, darling, they *must* be! My commonsense tells me so. It was arctic in the hall; what must it be like upstairs?'

'Ah, that's a secret!' said Timothy.

'Don't think I want to pry or to be tiresomely maternal, but I should like to know what you wear when you go from your bedroom down the freezing passage into your bath-tub piled with ice-bergs?'

'What do I wear? Why, my dressing-gown, of course.'

'Darling, I supposed you did, but what sort of dressing-gown?'

'Oh, a brown hairy one.'

'But doesn't it tickle dreadfully? Do you wear it next to your *skin*?'

'Well, sometimes I have my pyjamas underneath.'

'What are they made of? I have to ask, you see you never tell me *anything*.'

'Artificial silk. I could show you—'

'No, no, just tell me. I only want to be sure that you are warm. And what do you wear on your feet?'

'Oh, just some ordinary bedroom slippers.'

'Ordinary? What colour are they? You see, you make me drag things out of you.'

'Oh, just blue.'

'Blue, how dull. Wouldn't you like me to give you some really nice ones?'

'I should, but you mustn't bother.'

'Bother? What an awful word to use. How would you like it if I told you not to bother?'

'I suppose I might feel hurt,' admitted Timothy.

'Darling, I should think so. You speak to me as if I was a lost umbrella. I should have to know the size, of course.'

Timothy told her.

'But that's such an extraordinary size. No shop would stock it. Have you very peculiar feet?'

Rather self-consciously, Timothy made his foot revolve on the pivot of his instep. Vera watched him with admiration.

'Think of being able to do that! You must be double-jointed.'

'Oh, I don't think so.'

'Take your slipper off and let me look.'

Timothy obeyed.

'Darling, I don't like your socks. They are the kind a clergyman might wear. I believe they were a present from Mrs. Purbright.'

'Mrs. Purbright doesn't give me presents.'

'She ought to, if she's as rich as people say. Isn't that a tiny little hole?'

'I'm afraid it is.'

'Is your skin really that colour?'

Timothy blushed. 'I suppose so.'

'Darling, it's so much paler than your face. Please take your sock off, I must just see.'

Timothy's embarrassment increased but a feeling of excitement mingled with it. He took the sock off. Inside out, it at once gave the room an air of squalor, and he slipped it in his pocket.

Vera gazed in ecstasy at his bare foot.

'But you have such wonderfully *clean* feet! Put it here a moment.'

She dug a little nest for it on her lap.

'But I shall fall over!' said Timothy, getting up and coming towards her.

'Not if you hold on to the chair. There. I love your little toe, it's too sweet.'

'Oh, but it's such a long way away from me.'

'Can you kiss it? Try.'

Timothy leaned forward until his thinning hair mingled with hers. 'I'd much rather you did,' he murmured.

'Darling, you do expect a lot.'

But all the same she bent down and brushed his toe with her lips. 'It's like sending a telegram. Have you got the message yet?' she asked anxiously, turning her eyes up to his.

'I'm just beginning to.'

She smiled and put his foot down gently on the floor.

'Look, we mustn't waste time. Get a bit of paper and a pencil and I'll draw your foot so that there shan't be any mistake about the size.'

Timothy brought her a sheet of foolscap.

'Shall you draw the kiss?'

'I might put a tiny little cross, but it won't take up any room. They'll think it's a corn. Now press your foot down flat.'

Timothy wriggled as the pencil began to press against the tender ticklish hollow of his instep.

'Darling, stand *still*! I might be a blacksmith shoeing you, the way you flinch!'

At last it was over. Vera surveyed the drawing critically.

'They'll never believe it, but it's true,' she said. Folding up the paper, she put it into her bag.

Timothy, deflated, began to put on his sock, shivering slightly as he did so. Vera laughed.

'Darling, you must be pretending. You can't really be cold! It was only your foot. Think if you'd been posing for me in the nude!'

Timothy thought of it and said hastily, 'What colour will the slippers be?'

Vera knit her brows. It was a gesture most unusual with her, indeed he did not remember ever to have seen her forehead furrowed.

'It depends on what they've got to go with. Your dressing-gown's brown, you say.'

'Yes.'

'And your pyjamas?'

'Well, I've several pairs, as a matter of fact.'

'How extravagant you are. Which do you like best?'

'Well, there are some flame-coloured ones—' Timothy felt a fool.

'How dashing!' Vera pondered. 'Flame-colour and brown *could* go together. May I see your slumber-wear, or is it too personal?'

Timothy stood up.

'I'll go and fetch it,' he said.

'Oh, but isn't that a bother?'

'You mustn't use that word,' Timothy warned her. 'They're only just upstairs.'

'Is that far?'

'Only a few steps.'

Vera looked up at him.

'Perhaps I ought to go with you. Clothes look so different in the hand.'

Suddenly everything in the room seemed brighter and more distinct to Timothy, as though the electric light had gained in power. But he couldn't bear to risk another rebuff.

'I can quite well bring them down,' he said, evenly.

Vera gave him her sad smile. 'But, darling, I think I'll come up. I could tell so much better if you just tried them on.'

Timothy's bliss was of brief duration, for four days later Miss Cross left Upton. She could not tell him with certainty where she would be, or when she would be back; but she gave him an address in Curzon Street from which letters would be forwarded.

She begged him not to come to London; London was being bombed and she hoped to get away from it. Let them make the most of their time together.

This they did; even with the shadow of separation hanging over him, they were the happiest days Timothy had ever known, for they were days in which he was lost to every consideration except his love. The third evening in the new era came, and they parted, for Vera was leaving at dawn, she said, and she did not encourage him to see her off. 'Do you know, I'm shy of being seen with you,' she told him. Timothy was still enveloped in the sweet sense of her yielding; she had withheld nothing from him, and so uplifted was his heart with gratitude that the bitterness of impending loss could scarcely force an entrance. She was the symbol of his joy, and his joy would represent her, he felt, even when she was not there. But all the same the concourse of feelings was, for a man of his age and untried temper, almost too tumultuous to be borne; dimly he descried himself struggling in gigantic, rainbow-tinted seas, with no knowledge of how to act, or experience of how to feel; disciplined and rule-ridden as his nature was, he parted from her speechless and in tears.

What then was his astonishment to hear her voice on the telephone the next morning saying that she had had to put off her departure for twenty-four hours; she had things to do which would occupy her until the evening but she would be free to dine with him.

Timothy passed the day in a fever of expectation. He was to see her again! The reprieve had brought him an entirely new crop of sensations, a jubilation so intense that it could not be contained in minutes but seemed to range backwards and forwards over his whole life-time, past, present and to come. He even felt he must have done something to deserve so signal a blessing, and searched his recent behaviour for some act of surpassing merit, without however finding one.

The day dragged on. In the village street people crept about like flies, like beetles; all the energy seemed to have gone out of the world. He went for a long walk and tried by tiring himself to anæsthetise his sense of time. But it would not work, for Time will only hurry for those who accept the small change that it offers; for them it moves, and not for those who demand from it a capital sum.

Timothy had rehearsed their meeting a hundred times before she came, but he was unprepared for the film of sadness, slight but unmistakable, which blurred her presence and touched with languor and a pensive lack of zest every little thing she did. His joy at seeing her made him for a time immune to her mood of melancholy; he felt that it would pass if he ignored it. But when, after dinner, the cloud was still there he plucked up courage to ask if anything was wrong.

At first she put him off: there was nothing the matter; she was only a little sad at leaving him. Couldn't he understand that? How selfish I have been, thought Timothy: what was a victory to me, a lustreless, middle-aged bachelor, may well seem a defeat to her, the young and lovely Vera. I have the spur of satisfied vanity to help me over the first few hours of this separation; but what has she? Only the inevitable reaction from generosity, the unexhilarating sense of having yielded to pity and importunity. I can strut and preen myself, while she! He felt very humble, and disgusted with himself that in her presence he could not realise what her absence would mean. But it could not be just his inadequacy as a lover that had wrought this change in her.

'I am sure you have something on your mind,' he said. 'Please tell me – I shall be so unhappy if you don't.'

'I'm afraid you will be unhappy if I do,' she answered; and then it came out how, that very evening, Frances had been sitting in the Fisherman's Arms – 'I wasn't there' – and had overheard two of those men, the fishing snobs, saying something about her, Vera, and Timothy. 'I won't tell you what it was, darling, because words stick and I don't want you to be haunted by it – but it was *so* disagreeable. Promise me you won't ask Frances.'

Timothy promised, adding, 'I didn't think *they* came now.'

'Darling, don't you believe me? And promise me one other thing, you won't want to, but it's only this, that whatever happens, you won't make friends with any of them, will you? I could never come here again if you did – you'd understand why, if you knew what they'd said.'

Timothy felt so sick with hatred of the fishermen that he could hardly speak; but at last he got the promise out.

'Oh, darling, you look so funny when you're angry. You look as if you might murder them.'

'Well, I should like to,' said Timothy.

'Please don't do that, but if you get a chance of putting a little gaff in their gills, you will, won't you? So many people would be pleased, as well as me.'

Fervently Timothy promised that he would.

Even as he spoke he saw the shadow lifting from her brow and her movements regain their life and confidence.

'It'll be another secret for us to share,' she said. 'And now for the last one. Can you guess what it is?'

Timothy looked completely mystified.

'Why do you suppose I stayed an extra day?'

Timothy said he thought it was on business.

'It was, your business.' And opening the capacious shopping-bag Timothy had given her, she took out the flame-coloured slippers. When they had been duly admired and exclaimed over, 'Shall I put them on now?' asked Timothy, eagerly kicking off his pumps, for he was wearing his dress suit.

All at once her melancholy returned.

'No, darling, not tonight. Wear them when I'm gone.'

Timothy could not believe it. It was as though someone else had spoken.

'Oh, but I wanted you to . . . to see me in them.'

'Another time, darling, when I come back.'

Timothy was silent. He could not look at her.

'Is it . . . because of them?' he asked, at length.

'I don't know, darling, but I think it is. You see, they were so *very* rude about us.'

CHAPTER XVII

THE second desolating morning dawned, but this time it brought no reprieve. It did, however, bring the comfort of a bulging envelope from Tyro, and at this reminder of his discarded life Timothy stared, curious yet fearful to know what, after his long absence from it, the world would have to say to him. But Tyro was not the world; he was perhaps Timothy's most intimate friend; and whatever might be Timothy's mood of the moment his mind told him that Tyro was an anchor.

'MY DEAR TIMOTHY,' he read,

'So the Battle of Britain is on at last! I won't bore you with bomb-stories or tell you how near the nearest came to hitting me – you will have found plenty of people to tell you *that* – it is extraordinary how every man woman and child feels that they are the object of the enemy's special malevolence, and the world has somehow been delivered from destruction because *they* have escaped. I should have less patience with them if I did not feel the same myself – if I did not feel, when the swish that paralyses and the dull thud that bruises one's mind, is over, that here I still am, and while I am here there is still someone to face the music and carry the war on against Hitler.

'In your last letter you said, "I am beginning to agree with you that the human race is probably innately quarrelsome" – and you told me something about the dissensions in your household, which you evidently regard as a microcosm. Well, dear Timothy, without offering any opinion as to that – for I have no household – I really think you were a little mistaken and perhaps lacking in the spirit of true friendship, to back me up in such a preposterous sentiment. I have always spoken frankly to you and I rely on you to do the same with me. If I did say something of the kind – and I'm sure I did, or you wouldn't say so – it was because, being a foreigner and belonging, in a manner of speaking, to three nationalities all of which have had grievances against England in the past – the remote past – I didn't realise clearly the part England is playing in this struggle for liberty; and I thought – I must have thought since you say so – that there were faults on all sides. And of course there are; none of us is perfect; but that does not prevent one side being largely right, and the other largely wrong. Justice is above such small considerations. After a motor accident it is not the man of comparatively blameless life, but the man who has driven his car with care who wins his case. In my search for a simplification which would fit the circumstances I may have said we were all to blame; and having suffered in my ancestors from England's expansionist policy (a policy which I see now has brought untold blessings to the world) I may have been blind to her magnificent record in the present struggle – I believe I was.

'But you, Timothy, have no such excuse. You are an Englishman, as I only wish I was; and I frankly cannot understand those passages in your letter which wear a war-weary, almost a defeatist air. Even if England has been guilty in the past of acts of aggression, as you seem to suggest, and even if human beings are innately quarrelsome (which I take leave to doubt), it does not affect the incidence of right and wrong, in the present issue. Would you say that because all men are sinners that therefore the church, which is composed of sinners, is, vis-a-vis say, the Camorra or the Ku Klux Klan, an immoral institution? Right and wrong cannot be measured by sums of addition, intended to calculate the private virtues of individuals throughout the world; it is the general perfume that rises from their thoughts and acts; and if you take a sniff at the Nazi cauldron and then at the English alembic surely you can be in no doubt as to which should be preserved?

'And in saying this I leave out all their known, documented record, unparalleled in history for cruelty, treachery, and breach of faith – yes, and of combining these into the credo of a religion that will forever debase and dehumanise mankind.

'But all these are just platitudes, mere statements of fact, scratchings of pen on paper in a smelly, stuffy room (all the same, an ante-chamber of liberty!) with the fag-end of my mind, scraped bare by sleepless nights. You'll find them more convincingly expressed in any newspaper. But what grieves me is that you shouldn't feel the strength and majesty of the moment, the chance it gives one (though I hate to bring myself into it) of living beyond oneself and of meeting other human beings on the plane of selflessness. You write of your irritations and sore places, you complain of your household, you say your neighbours are unfair to you; but what do you expect, if you insist on standing aside and letting others do the work? I was amused by your account of the Home Guard dinner and laughed heartily over your attempt to dispose of your boat – though evidently you didn't. You took it all so seriously I wondered what had happened to your famous sense of humour. The war does odd things to people; nearly everyone I know is immeasurably the better for it, and by better I do not mean only in the narrow moralistic sense, but more fully alive to social obligations, better adjusted, better integrated, completer men and women.

'At least that is my experience, and I think it would be yours if you could spend a few days in this office. Why not try it?'

Timothy was so infuriated by this letter that momentarily it took away the ache and smart of Vera's leaving him. He lost no time in composing a reply. Searching Tyro's surviving letters for sentiments the reverse of those he now professed, he put examples of the two in parallel columns, with a lavish commentary of footnotes and exclamation marks. Like most mild-tempered men who have had little practice in disagreement he expressed himself much more violently than the experienced controversialist who keeps his weapons graded; it was not Tyro's views he attacked, but Tyro. An uneasy conscience no doubt lent venom to his pen, he felt the justice of some of Tyro's strictures; but for a long time now he had been losing the habit of entertaining thoughts and emotions of the middle register: they must be extreme, extreme as his feeling for Vera, else they were no fun to hold. So he heaped on Tyro all the ridicule he could muster, without respect for their past or concern for their future friendship: indeed, he felt himself trying to kill it; wherever the body still seemed warm and living, he planted another dart, another poisoned scratch; until with a faint sigh, just audible in the quiet room, his affection for his old friend gave up the ghost.

'Good morning, ladies,' said Wimbush, coming into the kitchen. His face brightened. 'Good morning, lady, I should say, seeing that the other one seems to have hopped it.'

'She knew you were coming, that's why,' said Effie archly.

Wimbush sat down heavily in a chair and spread out his knees. 'She isn't the only one that's hopped it, either,' he remarked.

'You're right,' said Effie, tightening her lips.

'Now you women are all alike,' said Wimbush, 'but I thought better of you, Effie, I really did.'

'It's all very well for you,' said Effie. 'You didn't have to wait on her. That's what I mind. If we hadn't felt sorry for him we should have given in our notice.'

'Sorry?' said Wimbush. 'I don't know as you had any call to feel sorry. Quite the opposite, I should say.'

'It isn't very nice in a house, is it?' said Effie, changing her ground.

'It's nicer in than out,' said Wimbush, accepting in a lordly manner the cup of tea that Effie offered him. 'It's nicer in than out,' he repeated. 'What's a house for?'

'Oh, Mr. Wimbush,' tittered Effie, 'I shouldn't know.'

'Now speaking for myself,' said Wimbush weightily, 'speaking for myself, I'm not sorry she's gone. Mr. Casson hasn't had a word for me all these last weeks. Perfectly civil-like, oh yes. But he might have been talking to a block of wood.'

'Well, what was he talking to?' asked Effie, pertly.

Wimbush ignored this sally and blew on his tea.

'If you ask me, he didn't know whether he was coming or going. It's bad when it takes them at Mr. Casson's age. Not that I mean any disrespect.'

'Men can do what they like, I suppose,' remarked Effie languidly. 'It's her I blame, making up to him. And then all those presents. She might have been the Queen of Sheba. But Beattie thinks she's a German spy.'

'What makes your friend think that?'

'Because she's so blonde, the type that Hitler falls for. And she's always asking questions.'

'What about?'

'Oh, about the river. She reckons it's a shame that Mr. Casson can't row on it. But Beattie thinks she wants to signal to a German submarine.'

Wimbush sniffed. 'That's not the sort of signal she makes, believe me.'

Effie looked serious.

'Beattie says we're not to know anything about it. She might be a manicurist, she says.'

'I thought she said she was a German spy.'

'Well, she could be both, couldn't she?'

'And supposing she *was* a manicurist?'

'Well, she'd have to trim his toe-nails and so on. She couldn't do that in front of everybody. It's beauty-parlourwork. They're often alone with gentlemen for hours together.'

'I see,' said Wimbush portentously. 'I see. So that's what we're to say.' He sighed heavily, put down his empty cup, and rested both hands on his thighs, with the elbows sticking outwards.

'Do you know what they say in the village, Effie?'

'No. Don't tell me if it's anything upsetting.'

'They say he won't stay on in Upton now she's gone.'

'He stayed before she came.'

'Yes, but that was for the boating. Now that they've turned his boating down, and she's gone, he won't stay. He was only saying to me yesterday, "Wimbush," he said, "I'm about through with Upton".'

'He hasn't got anything to do, that's his trouble,' said Effie.

'Yes, he rambles about like a ship in distress.'

'He starts to write a letter – Dear so-and-so, and then tears it up. Beattie counted six.'

'I didn't know she could count so far,' said Wimbush. 'He ought to have someone to live with him – a companion, like they advertise for in the papers – someone who could talk a foreign language, perhaps.'

'Why should he want to talk a foreign language?' asked Effie.

'Just to give him a break. 'Twould take it off a bit.'

'Take what off?'

'Well, what he feels when he thinks about her. He's sure to fret, 'tis only human nature.'

'He ought to be ashamed by rights,' said Effie, but without conviction.

'You are a hard-hearted girl,' said Wimbush. 'Wouldn't you fret, if I went away?'

' 'Twouldn't be the same thing at all,' said Effie primly.

Into the silence that followed, Beatrice entered.

'What are you two being so talkative about?' she asked, not ill-pleased at finding Wimbush and Effie with nothing to say to each other.

'Oh, we were just talking about Mr. Casson,' Effie said.

'There's plenty of others doing that, you may be bound,' said Beatrice, 'without you adding your bit.'

Wimbush rose to his feet.

'She's so sharp, isn't she, your friend, Effie? We were only trying to be helpful.'

'Well, that's something new,' said Beatrice.

'Mr. Wimbush thinks Mr. Casson ought to have a companion,' Effie said.

'Companion's a nice way of putting it.'

'Now please be serious, Beattie. Mr. Wimbush says someone who talks a foreign language.'

'And doesn't talk much, either,' put in Wimbush. 'Just a steady flow, you might say, same as I do.'

'He'd have to be fond of walking,' said Effie.

'And be – you know – there when he was wanted, like, and not when he wasn't, and run errands, and perhaps do a bit of digging in the garden.'

'He might do some housework, too,' said Effie.

'You couldn't ask a man to do that,' said Wimbush. 'But he could lock up at night and keep away undesirable persons when Mr. Casson was out. The chap I'm thinking of would be a steady fellow of about fifty, who's seen a bit of life and knows his way about, and maybe has a wife and family at home as he wouldn't miss too much, domesticated-like, but with a bit of spirit too—'

Carried away by his evocation of the sort of companion who would suit Timothy's needs Wimbush stretched out his arms in both directions, his eyes opened wide, his breath came fast, and his whole person and personality seemed to dilate.

'Sounds as if he was trying to describe himself, doesn't he, Effie?' remarked Beatrice drily. 'Perhaps he's after the job. He does speak broad – I can't always understand him – but you couldn't call it a foreign language.'

Wimbush's arms fell back to his sides and he spluttered wrathfully: 'Anyhow 'twouldn't be anyone like you he'd want, you big old parrot-face, that can't talk in your own language fit to be heard, let alone a foreign one.'

They glared at each other, and Effie, with a trembling spiral movement like the resultant of their two forces, said, 'Oh, please, Mr. Wimbush, don't upset her. She hasn't been herself all the time that manicurist has been here, playing about with Mr. Casson's toes; she felt the disgrace of it more than you ever could, being a man.'

At the sound of her weak, pleading voice Wimbush's features relaxed somewhat, and the reference to his masculine immunity from shame evidently pleased him. But he felt that it would mean a personal defeat, a serious loss of face, if he ceased to be angry, and he said, less truculently than before:

'What makes me so mad is her pretending she wants to do something for Mr. Casson to make him look his own height more, and less of a rat-tail, and then when I come forward with an idea taken from quite another person, as Effie knows, she starts crabbing and says I'm thinking of myself, as if I ever did. But she doesn't suggest anything herself, you notice.'

'I could,' said Beatrice, 'if you stopped recording yourself for a moment and let me get a word in.'

Wimbush threw his head back.

'Well, what's the big idea?'

'You think I should tell you?'

'There you go again.'

'It's someone who could do all you could, and speak a foreign language, too.'

A silence followed this announcement, and the trio held their positions without moving, like a group waiting to be photographed.

'I suppose it's one of the friends who write you those funny letters you find in the waste-paper basket,' Wimbush sneered.

'No, he talks quite plain, even you could understand. And he could do a bit of digging, too.'

Wimbush shrugged his shoulders. His turning heel grated on the flagstones. 'All right,' he said over his shoulder. 'As long as it's not you, I don't care who it is.'

'Oh, do tell him, Beattie,' said Effie wearily. 'He'll have to know sometime.'

Beatrice hesitated, and Effie beckoned to Wimbush. He came forward rather with the air of someone who has been asked to confirm the suspicion of a gas-escape.

'If I do, it's only because of Mr. Casson,' he said.

'And I'm only telling you because of Mr. Casson,' said Beatrice.

The three conspirators bent their heads together.

CHAPTER XVIII

ABOUT this time a rumour began to get about that Désirée Lampard was engaged to be married. Timothy heard it originally from Effie, and it was Effie, too, who contradicted it, saying that Mrs. Lampard was said to be much opposed to the match, as the young man was a Frenchman, 'one of these Free French'. She was even reported to have forbidden it; and various surmises were afloat as to what her daughter had done, or would do, in the face of her mother's refusal. These ranged from committing suicide to entering a convent. Eyewitnesses at Welshgate Hall reported stormy scenes. It was said that the couple were secretly engaged, then that they had secretly been married; Mrs. Lampard had summoned her solicitor at dead of night, and made a will disinheriting her daughter if she insisted on marrying the Duck, as he was always called.

The neighbourhood, Timothy gathered, didn't specially look forward to a French consort at Welshgate; it would be contrary to tradition and besides, the French had let us down. But they sympathised with Désirée not only because she was crossed in love but because they liked her. Mrs. Lampard was not popular but she commanded awe; anything she said or did was news; she possessed the force of personality that creates a legend. Her rudeness was notorious and as it was expressed with an incisiveness that amounted almost to wit, her remarks were often quoted. Even the many who had been worsted by her were not ashamed of relating their discomfiture, while the few who had had an answer ready could never tell about it often enough. A new addition to the existing store of Lampardiana was sure of a welcome – either in the Upton district, or indeed, in London. The neighbourhood could not help feeling proud of owning, and being owned by, a woman of so much character. And what made the present situation so specially piquant, such a particularly alluring tit-bit of gossip, was that Mrs. Lampard, though she cared for nobody else, was known to be devoted to Désirée. In other encounters she came out scatheless because her emotions were not involved. In this case they were; if the daughter suffered, the mother suffered, too. Mrs. Lampard had at last met her match, and in what an unexpected quarter.

At first Timothy took less interest in the matter than he would have a few months ago. He had been a little hurt that Désirée had not written or made him another sign; for a short time he believed he had found a friend in her. He wished her well, the memory of her youth and freshness haunted his mind, but was obscured by all the happenings of the summer, the wearing psycho-emotive crises provoked by his efforts to come to terms with Upton, but most of all by his entanglement with Vera which had produced a crop of new emotions with which his nature was at once too young and too old to cope successfully. He was an idealist who could not easily act without first convincing himself that some good purpose was being served, some end beyond the gratification of his immediate desires; and the contemplation of his behaviour stripped of any relish of salvation made him uneasy. While Vera was with him she swept out of his mind all considerations that did not arise out of his love for her; and for the first few days after she was gone his being throbbed and ached with all its swollen and lacerated tissues, so that he could not think of anything else. Writing to her was a solace, but her answers were slow in coming and brief when they came; they whetted his hunger for her but did not satisfy his mind or help him to the discovery of a tolerable routine of existence without her.

It had not been very satisfying before she came, but at any rate the people who made his world had seemed life-size, sometimes, from the trouble they gave him in dealing with them, larger. Now they had shrunk; Effie, Beatrice and Wimbush hardly seemed to achieve the stature of human beings, so inadequate were their responses to the kind of emotion he had got used to feeling. It was Gulliver's progress in reverse. From consorting with Brobdignagians he now found himself among Lilliputians. So might a general feel who, after commanding in a campaign, was condemned to play with toy soldiers. Between him and Vera's friends, whom he saw from time to time, there was the barrier of a common embarrassment; they did not know how much to talk to him about her, and he was shy of speaking of her to them. As her entourage, whose mannerisms and turns of phrase recalled her to him, rather painfully, they had shone with reflected light. But without her they were colourless reminders of her absence, all except Frances, that perfect duenna, who, though always loyal to her friend, sometimes answered his inquiries about her with a sudden reserve and soberness of manner that vaguely troubled him.

As to the old residents, whose acquaintance had once seemed so desirable, they might have slipped from his consciousness altogether had not Vera's parting message revived his ancient grudge. The duty of revenge had been laid on him, as it had on Hamlet, and all the more urgently because he now had her to avenge, as well as himself. Like Hamlet he did not want to; as far as he knew what he wanted, it was to make his life a frame – and not even an elaborate frame, a mere passe-partout oblong – for her picture. But her letters contained reminders that he must take action against the fishing-snobs; and as, despite the proverb, the power of love perforce grows fainter in the absence of its object, and other emotions assert themselves, other objectives for desire to aim at, and as he often needed other material for his letters to her besides professions of love which would interest her and bring their minds in touch, he did, like the prisoner of the Château d'If, half in fun and half in earnest, begin to devise plans for the downfall of the retired gentlemen of Upton. But as their paths never crossed, he did not know how to begin.

One figure alone kept something of its old stature and challenged him from the past – Mrs. Purbright. All through the Vera episode he had kept in touch with her. True, a good deal of the life had gone out of their relationship since the fiasco of his attempt to sell the boat. The memory of that hot still afternoon, charged with crisis, had left them both feeling rather shy. The episode had taken hold of his imagination with the force of a symbol. Destiny had delivered such an unmistakable snub that he no longer conceived it possible to dispose of the boat; if he did, it would return to him, he felt, like some doom-laden amulet in a fairy story. So he walled it up in the recesses of his mind, and neither he nor Mrs. Purbright ever referred to it, except as a kind of joke. And there was another subject which was taboo: Miss Cross. Timothy felt exceedingly self-conscious if her name cropped up, though neither Mrs. Purbright nor the Rector gave him any cause to.

Yet in spite of these multilations of his old intimacy, he was glad to frequent their house, for he found there, not embalmed but still oper-ative, the standards which, he fondly imagined, he had brought with him to Upton. He had discarded, or was discarding them; he was now, he told himself, a realist content to see himself as the elderly hero of a French farce, whom senile passion for a woman half his age had rendered wholly ridiculous and a little pitiable; this was his rôle and he must accept it. The emotions he entertained for Vera did neither of them any credit, they were nothing to be thankful for, you could not praise God with them, nor did they increase the world's store of beauty and gladness; they were the reverse of romantic, the kindest reception they could hope for from a world which on the whole was kind to lovers, was a shrug. Never mind; they happened to people, and they had happened to him. He could not ask for sympathy from Mrs. Purbright for those kisses rewarded, if not bought, with handbags and furs and diamonds, ingenious though she was in turning a railway sleeper into a spring-board.

Perhaps he would confide in her some day; and meanwhile it was comforting to sit among her encompassing treasures, redundantly proclaiming the breadth, length and height of her aspirations – an earthworm content with the ground, and listen to her hopes and fears for the drama at Welshgate Hall. Her sympathies of course were with the lovers but she felt for Mrs. Lampard, too.

'How easy it is, Mr. Casson, to be unfair to the feelings of older people, especially when they seem to conflict with the . . . the requirements of romance! Mrs. Lampard's daughter is everything to her; could one expect her to give her up without a struggle? Why did she not re-marry, why is there no step-father at Welshgate Hall? Her daughter knows the answer to that question. It was not, it still is not, for lack of opportunity; Mrs. Lampard has had many offers, I believe; and do the feelings grow less strong with age?'

She appealed to the room as much as to him, but Timothy answered on behalf of the feelings of the elderly.

'Of course they do not!' Mrs. Purbright went on. 'With the young, love is a spontaneous flowering of the emotions, one takes it for granted. June roses are delightful, no doubt, but are they as precious as the roses of December? Do they cost the tree as much effort, do they bespeak the same tenacity of Nature? Which is the more worthy of our regard?'

'The roses of December sometimes look a bit bedraggled,' said Timothy. 'Probably they wish they had come out earlier.'

'But we don't,' said Mrs. Purbright, 'and they bloom for us, as well as for themselves.'

'Do you really think so?' said Timothy.

'I am not in the secret of their intentions,' said Mrs. Purbright. 'I can only answer for their effect on me.'

Timothy was silent for a moment; then he said, 'But Mrs. Lampard preferred her daughter to a second husband.'

'Oh, I am only surmising, but to a woman of her passionate nature the temptation must have been great.'

'Perhaps she has had a lover,' suggested Timothy. But, if he had hoped to startle Mrs. Purbright he was disappointed.

'Perhaps,' she repeated, absently. 'It may sound unconventional in a clergyman's wife, but I should not want to criticise her. Autumn hath violets as well as spring, and age its sweetness hath, as well as youth. But perhaps I botanise too much?'

'No, no,' said Timothy. 'I love the language of flowers.'

'Your tone challenges me to defend us older people,' said Mrs. Purbright. 'Against what charge? For caring too much? Is that a vice? Is it because you see something inelegant in later love? I sympathise with Mrs. Lampard's attachment to her daughter, for I shall not find it easy to let Edgell go.'

'But you would not stand in his way?' said Timothy.

'It depends, it depends. In certain circumstances I believe I should stop at nothing.'

Timothy walked slowly home. Was it imagination, or did the fires that blazed upon the crests or smouldered in the deep hollows of the autumn woods carry the message Mrs. Purbright meant them to? If there was such beauty in corruption and decay, then perhaps he might claim for his love that it was not just a warning beacon, a brothel gas-fire set upon a hill? The thought soothed him, and for the first time for many weeks the forms and colours of the landscape made a harmony. Why do I want to see myself as an agent of the good? he wondered. How much happier I should be if it wasn't for this absurd presumption! And dragging Nature into it, too, as if I had never heard of the pathetic fallacy! Low overhead an aeroplane zoomed and roared; the frightened birds fled squawking from the threat of its black shadow. Timothy's mood wavered; and here was Colonel Harbord's gateway, the pretentious portal to Lawnflete. An arc of iron spanned it, with a lamp on top. How easy to fix a booby-trap there, attached to a tempting string that the incoming colonel could hardly fail to twitch! 'Darling Vera, he looked so funny with the tar streaming down his old red face! It's only a beginning, of course! I've got something much juicier in preparation for the others!' How childish it seemed; and yet how pleased she would be; and how could he better please himself than by pleasing her?

He wandered on, a prey to conflicting thoughts.

The afternoon post brought a letter.

'DEAR MR. CASSON,

'What must you be thinking of me – that is, if you think of me at all, but I expect you've quite forgotten Welshgate Hall, and the girl who called on you so unceremoniously one afternoon, in June, I think – but it seems years ago. I hope you remember, because *I* can never forget your kindness to me that day. And I should have written long ago to thank you, if it hadn't been for all the things that have happened since – terrible, unbearable to look back on.

'It's all come right, and we're engaged and the announcement will be in the papers shortly – but I wanted you to know before almost anyone, because, you see, it's through you it happened. I owe all my happiness to you. This is quite serious because, if it hadn't been for your advice, I could *never* have persuaded Mummy to give us her consent. I suppose I could have married him without, but it would have killed me to. Does this sound silly? It wouldn't, if you knew what we have always been to each other.

'You told me, do you remember, to stand up to her. You suggested she was selfish. I resented that at the time, but as I rode home I realised you were right. And I did stand up to her. She said the most terrible things to me – you would have thought she could not love me, but I know now that it was love that made her say them. Can you imagine loving anyone like that? I can't. In the end I didn't answer; think of it, for a whole week I didn't speak to her! Meal after meal went by and we didn't even look at each other! I don't know how I kept it up – I never could have, but somehow I trusted what you said. Then I got quite ill like someone in a book, and he was so miserable about it he begged me to give him up. He has behaved like an angel all through – Mummy admits that now, she has quite come round to him, or I shouldn't be writing to you like this. But for weeks she didn't – she tried to make me go into a home, somewhere in Scotland. But I wouldn't. I got quite dazed and light-headed and sometimes forgot where I was, like a very old person does. I suppose I had a kind of breakdown, and Mummy nearly had one, too, she looked so ill and strained and miserable.

'Does it all sound rather funny, two women behaving like that to each other? It wasn't, I assure you.

'Then at last, she began to grow different, she began to talk to me in an ordinary way and to mention his name, which she never would before – it was one of the things that hurt me most. And then she said he could come to the house, and do you know, the very first time he came, she welcomed him as if he had been her son.

'Well, now, I've told you everything, at the risk of boring you, but gratitude will out, I simply had to, for you have made two people blissfully happy.

'But oh dear, oh dear, the gratitude is all on my side for I've done none of the things I promised you I'd do. I'm sure they haven't let you row your boat, I should have heard if they had. And you've never been to see us at Welshgate again! My only excuse is, that you wouldn't have enjoyed it if you had. But you must promise to come as soon as François and I are married. Oh the happiness it gives me, just to write those words! And you really shall have your boat! Mummy wouldn't refuse me anything now.

'It's to be a country wedding because of the war and there won't be many people, but you will come, won't you? The date isn't fixed yet, but it will say on your card. It has to be at a Roman Catholic Church, which Mummy rather hates; indeed her chief reason for not wanting me to marry François was that he is an R.C.

'Once again let me say thank you, dear Mr. Casson, and for François, too: I've told him what an angel you are, and he is immensely looking forward to meeting you. Only think, if you had never come sightseeing to Welshgate, this could never have happened and I should have been condemned to being an old maid, for I would never, never, *never* have married anyone else!

Always yours most gratefully,
DÉSIRÉE LAMPARD.'

It would be scarcely too much to say that this letter caused a revolution in Timothy's state of mind. He trembled with happiness. He did not trouble to ask himself the reason – whether it was the satisfaction to his power-complex, having at last got the better of Mrs. Lampard, or whether it was the snobbish satisfaction contained in the prospect of an ampler social life, or whether it was the revival of his old desire for the boat. Certainly his first act, after he had written to congratulate Désirée, and tell her how much he looked forward to the wedding, was to go down to the boat-house. He had not visited it for months, although, from some kind of superstition, he kept the key always in his pocket. The lock turned stiffly and he had to push the door open; damp and leaves and cobwebs and disuse combined to keep him out; it was like breaking into the palace of the Sleeping Beauty. The goddess slept in her soft narrow bed, transoms of coloured light falling on her. She did not seem to have changed; but raising her reverently by the rowlock he detected on her polished flank a narrow ridge of green, and from the rudder wisps of water-weed were trailing like green hair. She has grown older, he thought sadly; even here in her shrine she has not escaped decay. To rot away unused! – he put the thought from him and substituted another, brighter one; the glorious morning when he and Wimbush would take her out, and cleanse and deck her for her maiden voyage. And with that promise he left her.

Meanwhile there was the wedding-present to get. Of late Timothy had spent a lot of time and money buying presents. Of the first he had plenty to spare, never so much; of the second increasingly little. His stockbrokers had been pleased, their judicially-worded letters, solemnly comparing this holding with that, almost convinced him that it was wiser to sell his investments than to keep them; but his solicitors, to whom he had to write for his share-certificates, warned him against the inroads he was making on his capital. But what was the loss of a few pounds a year compared with the rapturous pleasure of the purchase, the sudden access of power as the goods crossed the counter, and the sight of the recipient's face, alight with eagerness and curiosity as she took the parcel from his hands?

Timothy's present, for which he travelled much farther afield than Swirrelsford, was as beautiful and nearly as expensive as he could have wished. It was a Chinese sang-de-bœuf bowl, wonderfully lustrous and faintly iridescent. The potter seemed to have poured on the colour with a careless hand, leaving, at the base, patches and streaks uncovered; it took time for Timothy to realise how much these seemingly artless lacunæ enhanced the colour's value, and how the beholder's eye would never weary of the incompleteness.

At first he refrained from taking his present from its wrappings, fearing that he could never tie it up again. But he was tormented by the desire to look at it and soon found reasons why he should: one was that he had forgotten to put his card inside. Another and (he persuaded himself) a better one was that he ought to show it to Beatrice and Effie, for whose education in the arts he still felt responsible. By this time the engagement had been announced in the papers and it would be a natural and at the same time dramatic way of letting his staff know that he had been invited to the wedding.

Beatrice and Effie did not fail him; they expressed the warmest admiration for the object, Effie's only misgiving being that she would not like the job of dusting it. Timothy told her she needn't; as long as the bowl was in his care he would dust it himself. It could stand in the corner cupboard, out of harm's way, but resplendently visible whenever he chose to look at it.

Thus fortified, he settled down to possess his soul in patience and await the appointed day, meanwhile losing himself in wedding fantasies of top-hats, grey waistcoats, morning-coats and spats, all of which he possessed but had hardly expected to wear again. Sunshine and crowded staircases and high gold and white rooms thronged with excited, smiling faces – how it all came back; with sadness and nostalgia, but also with joy and hope, and with the vision of himself as a golden intermediary, a celestial Pandarus, floating along the gilded cornices, showering down benedictions, publicly recognised and acclaimed. Foiled for so long, Timothy's unconscious fantasy of himself as a general benefactor was at last fulfilled.

He could not get it quite straight – could not quite square the apotheosized, hymeneal Timothy with Vera's secret lover. To her also he had been a benefactor (it might be claimed) but in a hole-and-corner fashion, and far from disinterestedly. That episode was a stain on the white radiance of his present feelings, his longing to identify himself with the happiness of Désirée and François, and when he wrote to Vera he was sharply aware of the discrepancy, for his pen misliked the subject, and would only touch on it belittlingly – 'a marriage has been arranged, and will shortly take place, between our old friend Mrs. Lampard's daughter, Désirée, and a young, titled Frenchman whom the natives call the Duck. The old lady doesn't seem to like the idea. You will be amused to hear that I'm going to the wedding.' No, it would not do; better not mention it at all. The art of having a mistress, and combining devotion to her with the other, more easily avowable interests of one's life was essentially French. It was an art that Timothy was not too old to learn; but how vexatious these conflicts between loyalties could be, – rending the bosom, sapping the integrity of one's thoughts, splitting the atom of one's personality!

But Vera was far away – indeed he did not quite know where she was, for her notes seldom told him her immediate whereabouts – and Désirée and François were close at hand. For the time being he would abandon himself to the idyll of their marriage, whose architect he could claim himself to be.

The days passed in a trance of pleasant anticipation, and Timothy used them to overhaul his feelings for the village in general; he must think more kindly of all its inhabitants, for soon he would have to meet them at the great occasion. He still did not know the date, and was greatly surprised, one morning, when Effie told him.

'The 24th! Why, that's in a week's time! How did you happen to hear, Effie?'

'Mrs. Burnett told me, sir. She obliges for Mrs. Harbord when she can spare the time, and she saw the invitation card on the mantelpiece, in full view it was, so she couldn't help seeing it. Besides, Mrs. Harbord told her.'

'How interesting, Effie! I expect I shall be getting mine soon.'

A tiny fear clutched at Timothy's heart that could only be exorcised by action. The 24th! It was high time to send his present. He could not do that, of course, until he had received his invitation; but he could at any rate tie up the parcel, and this he did, taking all the morning over it and using enough straw and shavings to ensure safe transit for a dinner-service. 'With my warmest good wishes', 'With heartiest good wishes', 'With all good wishes', at last he chose from among them, and having crossed out the Mr. in front of Timothy, to show he was a family friend, he slipped the card into the gleaming and capacious belly of the bowl. Packed to resist a train smash, it stood in the hall, waiting.

Timothy, too, waited. Curiously enough, after the surprise of Effie's disclosure he regained his confidence, and watched the posts come in with absolute assurance that the next would produce the wished-for envelope. Of course the invitations could not all be sent out in one day, or even in two. Meanwhile he had to hear from Effie and Beatrice and Mrs. Burnett a great many details about the approaching ceremony; the dresses that Mrs. Lampard's tenants in Upton were going to wear if the weather was wet or fine, cold or warm, bright or cloudy; how they were arranging transport, who was to be given a lift in who's car, to save petrol; guesses as to where the honeymoon would be spent; speculations as to what Mrs. Lampard would do now that she no longer had her daughter to keep her company. The wedding came to be regarded as an unofficial Bank Holiday; other dates were reckoned in relation to it: 'That'll be before, or after, the wedding.'

Though not all Mrs. Lampard's tenants were invited to the ceremony, all or nearly all were to be entertained at Welshgate Hall; and of these the less affluent had subscribed to a joint wedding present. As the day drew nearer a feeling of relaxation made itself felt, edged with expectation; the village began to slow down, look about, and metaphorically lick its lips. Like an audience at the play it leaned back and confidently waited for the curtain to go up, and Timothy tried to lean back, too, and look as though the spectacle was meant for him.

But his faith was being shaken, and on the Tuesday morning, two days before the wedding, when the invitation had still not come, it had sunk to a low ebb. He had given the servants to understand that he was going; he had had his morning clothes cleaned and pressed. Now Beatrice and Effie were asking for the day off, so that they, too, could stand in the crowd at Swirrelsford, leaving Wimbush, who was not interested in weddings, to look after the house. Pulling himself together, Timothy told them that he might not be present at the ceremony but that they could certainly go, and he would get his lunch somewhere else.

It cost him so much to say this, and meet their raised eye-brows and tactful silence that he almost decided to leave Upton for a couple of days and come back when it was all over. But he shrank from such a public show of pique; he would stay, even if he was the only man left in the village, emptied of folk that pious afternoon. Besides, there were several posts still to come. Aware of his disappointment, Beatrice and Effie ceased to refer to the wedding, indeed they ostentatiously avoided it.

On the Wednesday morning Timothy's spirits had sunk to a new low level. After much cogitation, and making sure that Beatrice and Effie were out of earshot, he rang up Welshgate Hall. Could he speak to Miss Lampard? Evidently his name conveyed nothing to the butler who politely asked, was it very important because Miss Lampard was extremely busy? Timothy said it was rather important.

After a long pause Désirée came to the telephone. Her voice did not sound like her. It was extremely embarrassed, and she laughed a great deal. She thanked him effusively for his good wishes and his letter; she agreed with him that she hardly knew whether she was on her head or her heels; but she said nothing about seeing him at the wedding or afterwards.

In the afternoon Timothy decided to take a long walk; he felt more comfortable in motion. He walked over the hills, unconscious of fatigue, spurred on by bitter thoughts. So Mrs. Lampard could refuse her daughter something, after all; she could refuse to ask Timothy Casson to her wedding.

He felt he hated her. She was a poisonous woman. All the frustration of his life in Upton, his foolish and exaggerated behaviour, his failure to be of any use to himself or anyone else – all, all could be laid at Mrs. Lampard's door.

Thinking such thoughts, linking together a score of barely related circumstances to make one long indictment, feeling that if he met Mrs. Lampard he would strike her, he descended the hill into the next valley. Suddenly he noticed that all along the grass verge, as far as his eye could see, an endless serpent trailing down the hill, was a line of books. Some were propped together, backs up as in a bookcase; some lay on their sides; some were open, their pages fluttering in the breeze; some lay face downwards, their leaves bent and crumpled, as though a care-less reader had wanted to keep his place. Then Timothy remembered that the little town below him had been organising a salvage drive;

241

leaflets had been sent round begging people to contribute their unwanted books. He himself had received one, but had been too wedding-drunk to act on it.

There they lay, a small selection of civilisation's most precious and characteristic output, naked to the elements, uncared for, finished, waiting for the knacker's cart to come and convert them into bombs.

Walking slowly Timothy bent over the volumes, like a general reviewing an awkward squad. Dust from the road had gathered on their pages; raindrops had spotted them; many had been torn and dirty and defaced before they were thrown out for cannon-fodder. They were not looking their best; but even so Timothy had to admit that, intrinsically, few of them were worth the trouble of taking home.

Still, he felt an impulse towards rescue work and would fain save one of them from salvage. How many old books of reference, what numbers of bound magazines! The Victorian Age would not feel flattered if it knew how many of its popular favourites lay abandoned by the roadside, elderly, unfashionable children of the humane century, exposed to perish on the heights above Upton.

He picked up a book, and presently discarded it for one he liked better, and so on down the pathetic, dingy line, until his faculty of choice began to sicken. Perhaps he was stealing, for these books were not ownerless, they were the property of the State, and the State was treating them as all modern states treat their children, as Moloch treated the children of Carthage. The State would resent, might even prosecute him for giving shelter to an embusqué volume.

Someone was coming up the hill, a Government agent, perhaps. Timothy bent down hastily. Here was a find, Pascal's Pensées, bound in calf. Who could have had the heart to throw this book away? He opened it at the book-plate. Travelling downwards his eyes took in first a helmet, then a warrior's arm, clenched in a rigid right-angle and terminating in a mailed fist clutching a battle-axe. Below was the motto, 'What I have, I hold', and last, the owner's name, in thin, copper-plate writing, 'Julia Lampard'.

Anyhow she hadn't held the Pascal. Timothy checked a childish impulse to throw the book down, and continued his inspection. All these French books, upon examination, proved to be Mrs. Lampard's. They did not all bear the same book-plate. In Tallemant des Réaux's memoirs there was a lady of the period with her finger to her lips, and below, the motto 'A moins soyez discret'. Not very discreet, perhaps, to jettison these nice French books at the very moment her daughter was going to marry a Frenchman; there must be hundreds of them, several book-cases full, devoted to destruction. Still, probably no reader's eye but his would ever look at them again. He wandered on, still preferring the Pascal to any book that caught his eye. At this point the calf-bound volumes ended, and the novels in paper jackets began. These in their turn gave way to almanacs and telephone directories and finally to railway guides, in faded orange covers. He picked one up; a nostalgic whim seized him to find out at what hour, in 1924, the Simplon-Orient Express left the Gare de Lyon for Venice. As he picked the book up its leaves fluttered open and a slip of paper fell out, writing-paper with a coronet at the top. It was a short letter, very short.

June 1st, 1924.

Madame,

You can say what you like, but I assure you that the little Désirée is as much mine as yours.

Charleroi.

So this was the secret of Mrs. Lampard's opposition to her daughter's marriage: François was Désirée's half-brother.

As Timothy was staring at the letter the man coming from below drew level with him. He did not seem to be a Government agent; at any rate he grinned at Timothy and said:

'Found something?'

Timothy waited until the man had got some way ahead, and then slowly followed him up the hill. At the crest he paused. Below him in the brittle October sunshine lay Upton-on-Swirrel, much as it must appear to the pilot of a German bomber, carrying his lethal load. Should he drop it, or shouldn't he? No doubt it was his duty to, for his country was at war with ours; perhaps, too, he had private reasons for wanting to harm us, a mother or sweetheart to avenge, an old score to pay off. But he couldn't help hesitating, for the village looked so innocent and defenceless.

Tossed like a cork between thought and feeling, starting and stopping, straying from one side of the pathway to the other, with as little sense of direction as if he had been a landmine, Timothy drifted down on Upton.

He did what at the time he believed to be right; he put the Duc de Charleroi's letter in an envelope and posted it to Mrs. Lampard. But afterwards, in the misery of self-reproach, he used to wonder whether he would have done so if, on his return, he had found an invitation for Désirée's wedding waiting for him. Would he have? Would he have?

Because, until the last, he was in two minds about sending it; so undecided, indeed, that he went out and stood beside the pillar-box and waited until the postman came; waited until the man had actually cleared the box before he could bring himself to put the letter in his hand. He had written the address with his typewriter; the Upton postmark would be the only clue to whence it came.

About noon the next day Effie came to Timothy and told him with a grave face and heightened manner that word was going round Upton that the wedding had been cancelled. Timothy by that time was beyond thinking or feeling any more about it. It had been for Mrs. Lampard to decide. But wherever he went in the quiet house he seemed to hear the sound of sobbing.

CHAPTER XIX

BEATRICE was indignant at the cancellation of the wedding; she spoke as if the whole thing were a put-up job, a hoax, aimed at all Upton and at her particularly. Mrs. Lampard, she suggested darkly, knew all along it wasn't going to come off. It wasn't fair on people, she insisted, to behave like that. Everyone had been left looking silly (this reflection gave her a certain grim satisfaction) except Mr. Casson; she congratulated him, in effect, on not having been led by the nose. 'At the time we thought it was a shame you weren't asked, sir, but now we know better.' Effie, on the other hand, adopted a pensive demeanour that clung to her for several days. 'Poor things,' she said, 'they will be so disappointed. I don't know about him, being French, perhaps he wouldn't mind, but she was so *lovely*.' Putting Désirée into the past tense, she seemed to put herself there, too; and perhaps to identify herself a little with the stricken girl. 'They all say it was Mrs. Lampard that did it, she's so proud, she didn't think he was good enough for her daughter.' Then Effie brightened a little. 'Perhaps it's all for the best – she'll marry some nice Englishman now.'

Timothy hoped that Effie might be right, but he was still haunted by Désirée's distress and the thought that his had been the hand that snatched away her happiness. Yet what else could he have done? Her mother had been prepared to take the risk; might he not have done the same, if he had been on better terms with her? How much of pure revenge had lain behind his action? Plenty, he knew, when it first occurred to him: none, he hoped, when he handed the envelope to the postman. Yet the first thing he had done, when he got home, was to see if the invitation had arrived. If it had, might he not have joined Mrs. Lampard in her gamble with society?

He tried to find out what had happened at Welshgate but an iron curtain had descended, and though rumours were rife, no one in Upton seemed to know for certain whether the mother and daughter were still there. Mrs. Lampard's gift for evading publicity did not fail her now.

After the traditional nine days, during which it was in everybody's mouth, the Welshgate Wonder ceased to be talked about. The war absorbed it. But on Timothy it left a scar that did not heal. One after another the shoots that his nature tried to put forth had been snapped off; the sap bled at the breaks and then fell back. He was a shrub that could make no growth. And a corresponding inertia had overtaken his mind, which grew more and more suspicious of any activity presented to it. None of his faculties would act in concert. Even the name of Vera was not the battle-cry it had been. Her letters spoke the language of love; but too perfunctorily to carry across the distance, and her diatribes against the fishermen sometimes seemed unreal to him. He wanted to act with, not against somebody. He had no background of companion-ship with her to make her a food as well as a stimulant, and his longing for her was a wasting asset to his emotions, and resented, as a cuckoo, by older-established loyalties and habits of mind.

Yet how drab and spiritless, even in absence, she could make her rivals seem! Indeed, how all his affections, using the word in its widest sense, warred against each other! If only he had Mrs. Purbright's gift of making them co-operate, and pool their several lustres, instead of always taking the shine and meaning out of each other! For instance, Timothy should have been touched by Tyro's answer to his rude, queru-lous and wounding letter. Tyro professed himself astonished that Timothy should have received his recantation in such a hostile spirit.

'My dear fellow, what a Junius was lost in you! I could hardly have believed my eyes. Is this my Timothy? I asked myself. Honestly, I am only now beginning to recover from your bludgeonings. You are as right, of course, in one way as you are mistaken (dare I say so?) in many ways. I ought to have apologised for changing my opinions. No, not apologised, for no apology is needed when one leaves the wrong path for the right: but like a motorist I should have held my hand out. I shall not insult your intelligence, Timothy, by suggesting that you regard consistency of opinion as a virtue; an opinion is only valuable in so far as it is true. If the word apostasy has an unpleasant ring, it is because men have apostatised from fear, under duress. I would change my opinions twenty times a day if by doing so I felt I was bringing myself, and others, to a nearer apprehension of the truth. I shall not change them now, because I believe them to be right. It is not that I have been influenced by propaganda, as you seem to think. My work in this office, trivial as it is, gives me an insight into the feelings of ordinary men and women which could be got no other way; and my 'conversion' (as you scornfully term it) to a more sanguine view of human nature has not been a self-generated movement of my mind, induced by a consider-ation of abstractions, though many better men than you or I, Timothy, have arrived at their opinions by that route. No, it has been brought about insensibly, by listening to the multitude of voices, many of them illiterate and inarticulate, which 'speak one message of one sense to me'; and I could no more be mistaken than, when listening to the buzz and murmur of a crowd, one could fail to tell whether it was angry or goodhumoured. An inherited instinct, Timothy, an inherited instinct.

'But I do apologise for expressing my views in such a way that you, my oldest friend, seem to have taken offence. It never occurred to me that you would misunderstand my natural vehemence, or I would have taken steps to curb it. In future, my letters to you will be in a flatter tone. . . . I have plenty of examples round me: how flat these letters are, that I have to search for innocent or deliberate indiscretions! Yet, in a way, I like them the better for it, for have we not lived too much among clever people, for whom the form of a thought is more valuable than the content? You seem to have convicted me of self-contradiction: all you have really done is to make me realise, more clearly than I did myself, that whereas once I held one opinion, now I hold another. Before, I was impatient with humanity because of its indifference to moral issues; now I see that as soon as those issues are put before it in an unmistakable form, a large part will rally to the cause of Right. What would right be, if it could not be expressed in terms of human behaviour? An abstraction. And what value would that abstraction have, if it could not be apprehended even when confronted by its opposite?

'As you never, I think, shared my misanthropy and pessimism, I imagined you would welcome my change of attitude, for though it has no importance for the world, it has for me; things make sense to me in a way they never did before. I am much happier than I used to be. And I know you are fond enough of me to let this count, even if, as your letter suggests, you no longer wish us to be friends.'

Timothy replied at once, taking back almost everything he had said in his previous letter. In an effort to justify himself, he said that the proto-Tyro had been a more effective missionary than perhaps he realised: some of the mud with which he had daubed the visage of mankind had stuck. Now under the influence of the deutero-Tyro, he would try to wipe it off. He assured Tyro that their friendship was unimpaired, and that he felt no animosity towards him. This last was nearly true; but as the letter dragged itself along, loaded with generalisations and efforts to meet Tyro on his own new ground, he felt that he was attitudinising, and that the letter had no more to do with Tyro than an essay has with the master it is shown up to, and meant no more to Timothy than an exercise in schoolboy dialectics. He had to think of something to say, and this was the result. It was an irreproachably polite and reasonable but lifeless study in agreement, and Tyro might mark it β—. 'Casson is a trier, but his work lacks individuality and conviction'.

One morning, when she called him, Effie asked Timothy if he had heard anything about the dog. 'Dog?' said Timothy. Oh, he hadn't heard then, because Mr. Wimbush had said something about one. 'Not in my hearing,' said Timothy. 'Has a dog been killing the chickens?'

'Oh no, not that sort of dog, it was just a dog that Wimbush happened to have mentioned.'

'Is he fond of animals?' asked Timothy. Effie seemed quite taken aback and wilted visibly. She disclaimed all knowledge of the gardener's tastes.

Timothy dismissed the matter from his mind, but later in the day, when he was interviewing Beatrice about the food, she remarked, 'No one can say I'm wasteful, but I often have to throw things away that would make a good meal for a dog.'

'Dog, what dog?'

'Oh, no special dog, but any good sized dog that wasn't too particular what it ate.'

'Have you seen a dog about?' asked Timothy.

'Oh no, sir,' said Beatrice, almost huffily. 'There's nothing here that you don't see, sir. I take good care of that. But there are dogs and dogs.'

'Quite true,' said Timothy. 'But I don't know much about them, I'm afraid.'

'We live and learn, sir. There's no harm in a dog if it's kept in its place.'

'No indeed,' said Timothy warmly. 'But I'm afraid I'm not a doggy person. They're so noisy, and besides, they smell.'

Beatrice's mouth closed like a trap, the angles of her face stuck out and she said no more.

A dog! In spite of Beatrice's disclaimers Timothy could not rid his mind of the idea that there was a dog somewhere, and putting on his overcoat, for the days were growing chilly, he went into the stable-yard and peered into the loose-boxes, where a dog might easily lurk. Not a yap, not a bark, not a growl. Then Timothy remembered that the subject had originated with Wimbush, and set off to find him.

'Good morning, sir, were you taking a look round the premises?'

'Well, just to make sure everything was in order.'

'Them outbuildings, sir, they are a proper hidey-hole for tramps.'

'Have you ever found one there, Wimbush?'

'They wouldn't come with me around, sir, but of course I can't be here all the time.'

'Naturally not.'

'Of course,' said Wimbush reflectively, 'there's nothing like a dog to keep off tramps.'

That dog again!

'But we've got Nelson,' said Timothy. 'He's as good as a watchdog any day.'

'Ha, ha, sir, but a dog's so companionable. Nelson's only a policeman.'

'But you often talk to him.'

'Well, sir, just to pass the time. And Nelson can't bark,' added Wimbush almost wistfully.

'But what a good thing!' said Timothy. 'Do you want him to?'

Wimbush looked as crestfallen as his naturally sanguine cast of features would permit.

'Well, sir, Nelson's talk is all plain-sailing – if you see what I mean. A child could understand what Nelson says.'

'He uses rather long words, sometimes.'

'Oh yes, sir, he learned them in the police college. But you'd find them all in the English dictionary, if you took the trouble to look. A dog, now, he speaks what you might almost call a foreign language.'

Timothy agreed that this was so.

'A foreign language,' Wimbush repeated. ' 'Twould be a kind of change, sir, hearing a foreign language.'

Timothy considered. His thoughts flew off to Italy, as Wimbush meant they should. The mellifluous *lingua Toscana*, especially when pronounced by the *bocca Romana*, did not invite comparison with any dog's bark he had ever heard; but those harsh-sounding monosyllables that the Venetians shouted at each other from traghetto and fondamenta – the '*stai*!' and '*premi*!' of the gondolier rounding a corner – well, bark was just the word. He had said 'barked' himself, more than once, in alluding to them. His face must have grown dreamy with reminiscence, for Wimbush added, hopefully:

'And there's other noises a dog can make besides barking, sir. It can growl and howl.' He paused, and taking a plunge, added, 'just like those Eyties do.'

By what different routes, reflected Timothy, have our thoughts converged.

'I'm not saying they're the *same* language,' said Wimbush, 'but what I mean to say, I realise you must get tired of hearing all of us speaking the King's English.'

Wimbush spoke with a proud humility which Timothy found touching. He said he was always pleased to hear Wimbush talk, and not having grasped the gardener's drift was turning to go, when Wimbush said:

'Beg pardon, sir, but Nelson have heard of a dog.'

Puzzled, Timothy stopped. 'Has he? How interesting.'

'What I mean to say, if you were to approach Nelson—'

'Approach Nelson, Wimbush?'

'Yes, sir,' said Wimbush doggedly (there is no other word). 'He have heard of a fine dog, but he'd rather tell you about him himself, sir.'

'I shall be pleased to hear about the dog, of course,' said Timothy, rather grandly. 'Is it a kind of police dog?'

'Oh no, sir, it's a very affectionate animal, Nelson says.'

'Is he going to take it about with him in his car?'

Wimbush looked shocked at the idea. ' 'Twould be against regulations, for a policeman to have a lap-dog. Not that he is a lap-dog,' Wimbush went on, rather indignantly, as if someone else had made the suggestion. ' 'Tis a proper man's dog by all accounts. But talk of the devil, here *is* Nelson. He'll explain to you better nor I can.'

As though at a pre-arranged signal Nelson was seen advancing with measured tread across the lawn. He saluted Timothy. After they had exchanged greetings there was a noticeable and pregnant pause.

'I have broken the ground with Mr. Casson,' said Wimbush at last to Nelson, 'and he sees no objection to your idea of a dog.'

Timothy was like the victim of a conspiracy who feels the toils closing round him but cannot tell exactly what they are. 'Well,' he began, 'not to the idea of a dog, perhaps, but as to a dog itself, I—'

'It's like this, sir,' said Nelson. 'I'll make it all perfectly plain. The dog would be a good dog.' He paused, heavily.

Timothy said he was sure it would be. Remembering Nelson's technique in broaching the subject of his car, he also felt sure the dog was his. Probably he wanted Timothy to let him keep it in the stable.

'The dog in question is a golden retriever,' said Nelson. 'It's age would be about four months, as far as can be at present ascertained.'

'Oh, quite a big dog,' said Timothy fatuously.

'But not too big, sir,' said Nelson firmly. 'It's just the right size for a dog. Not too trumpery, like a peke, or too massive, like a Great Dane. As a policeman, I speak with some experience of dogs.'

Timothy nodded.

'A dog should be fierce in defending its master's life and property against unauthorised persons, but not so aggressive as to keep away visitors.'

Timothy agreed.

'That being the case, sir, you could not want a better dog than the one I have in mind.'

'He sounds a treasure.'

'He is well feathered down the legs, he has large, speaking eyes and a magnificent rudder.'

'I congratulate you, Nelson. Did you want to keep him here?'

'Well, sir, a dog couldn't want a better home.'

'Nor a better master!'

Nelson looked rather embarrassed. He took off his helmet and with it a good deal of his authority.

'As to that, sir, I was coming to that. The dog would not, in a manner of speaking, be mine.'

'Oh, I see. Whose would it be?'

Nelson looked down with a kind of indulgent severity at Timothy, as at someone who has unwittingly transgressed a bye-law. 'Well, sir – if it was agreeable to you, the dog would be yours.'

Timothy glanced at Nelson, whose face, under the helmet which he had now replaced, was utterly impassive. Wimbush had turned away and with almost unbearable delicacy of feeling was staring at a celery trench.

'It's most kind of you,' said Timothy at last, 'but I'm not sure that I want a dog.'

Both Nelson and Wimbush contrived to give the impression that Timothy had uttered a blasphemy but that they were too much men of the world to be shocked by it. Wimbush was the first to speak.

'We thought he'd be a companion for you,' he said.

Timothy did not know how to reply. He was not fond of dogs and did not understand them. At the same time he was touched by the men's thought for him, and reflected that sometimes other people knew what was best for one.

'Most people like a dog,' went on Wimbush. He spoke in a neutral, take-it-or-leave-it voice, as though Timothy's unconventionality was his own affair, and must be respected. 'A dog's not like a human being. More reliable. More affectionate, too.'

'Yes,' put in Nelson. 'There's many a motorist as wouldn't scruple, if you understand me, to run over a human being, pulls up short when they see a dog in the road.'

Timothy reflected upon this.

'And of course a dog like the one I've been speaking of is a great help socially. I mean,' Nelson took himself up, 'he would be among chaps of our sort. People who would never think of speaking to you if they saw you by yourself, would speak to you fast enough if you had a dog with you.'

A memory stirred in Timothy's mind. Had not the Rector said something to the same effect – that a dog inspired confidence and that people quickly made friends with him, and so with his owner? In spite of all the rebuffs, Timothy had not quite relinquished the hope that one day, one day, he might be a welcome guest on the lawn at Lawnflete.

Nelson realised that he was weakening. 'You wouldn't have to be ashamed of him, quite the contrary,' he said eagerly. 'His rudder alone! Why he's got strength enough in that rudder to break a man's arm, I shouldn't wonder.' He looked for confirmation to Wimbush, who nodded gravely several times.

'And he's a grand water dog, you need never be afraid of upsetting when you went out in your boat. He'd bring you to shore whether you liked it or not.'

Timothy sniffed.

'Of course I'm not pressing you to have him.' Nelson suddenly adopted an air of judicial detachment. 'I want you to feel quite free. Only in my view it's an opportunity too good to miss, especially as the animal would be, in a kind of way, a present.'

'A present!' exclaimed Timothy, dog-like pricking up his ears.

'Well, sir, in view of your kindness in giving me the use of your garage my friend would be prepared to make a substantial reduction in the price. To you, sir, it would be fifteen guineas, not a penny more.'

'Fifteen guineas doesn't seem much for such a big dog,' said Timothy, wanly.

Simultaneously Wimbush and the policeman came a step nearer and closed in on Timothy. The effect was of a gigantic convergence, an irresistible pincer-movement.

'You'd never regret it, sir,' said Nelson, his breath beginning to come rather fast. 'It's the chance of a lifetime. Buster'll be a godsend to you. He'll never leave you, night or day.'

Timothy succumbed.

The next morning Nelson appeared in the stable yard, leading Buster. But that is putting the cart before the horse, for it was Buster who was leading Nelson; nor, in all the course of their relationship did Timothy ever know the order reversed. His face set in horizontal lines of outraged majesty, Nelson leaned back, making an obtuse angle with his straining charge such as the handle makes with the Plough in the celestial constellation.

'You see how he pulls, sir,' gasped Nelson. 'He's only a youngster yet, he'll soon tone down.'

Meanwhile Buster had reached Timothy. Getting on to his hind legs he put his front paws on Timothy's chest, and his long, pink, sickle-shaped tongue wavered towards Timothy's face. His eyes wore an expression of humorous craftiness.

'Geddown!' shouted Nelson, jerking at the lead and upsetting Buster's balance so that he nearly fell over backwards. Panting and triumphant the dog gazed hungrily at Timothy as though longing to repeat the assault. 'He doesn't do that to everyone,' Nelson apologised. 'If you weren't the owner here, sir, he'd know in a minute. He wouldn't let you touch him. He mightn't bite at first but he would if you meddled with him.' 'Hey, Buster!' he cried, moving towards the dog with a threatening attitude. 'Go for him, boy! Seize him! Lay hold of him!' Buster watched the policeman closely, as he danced ponderously round him, anxious to do the right thing but not knowing what it was. Meanwhile Beatrice and Effie, having heard the noise, had come out and were standing by the back door; and Wimbush, also wondering what the hubbub was about, had strolled in from the garden and was watching Nelson's provocative caperings with amusement.

'Go on, boy!' Nelson cried. 'Fetch him out! Worry him!' It seemed he could only be referring to Timothy, who drew back a step and looked round nervously. Buster put his head down, arched his back, and barked excitedly. It was not a proper bark, but an adolescent imitation, with no hostility in it; he wagged his flail-like tail, and his eyes looked round anxiously for approval.

'Good boy, good boy,' said Nelson, satisfied with this exhibition of ferocity. 'You see, sir,' he said, turning to Timothy, 'he's got the makings of a first-rate house-dog. Only you mustn't be too soft with him, or else he'll take advantage. Now just hold his lead and walk him about a bit, to get the feel of him, as I might say.'

Timothy's fingers closed on the leather thong and Buster at once started off, ventre-a-terre, swaying on his big soft paws, tugging at the leash and snorting every now and then as the pressure on his collar threatened to throttle him. He seemed to know at once where he wanted to go and to think it did not matter what happened to his body, provided his head got there. In this case his destination proved to be the chestnut tree in the middle of the stable-yard. Having reached it he stopped, with an air of absorption so intense it seemed as though he would never move again. Then he slowly made a circuit of the trunk, examining it with a strictly professional and slightly sceptical air which sat oddly on his youthful features. Satisfied with his inspection he started off again, this time in the direction of the house. Timothy's arm felt as if it must be pulled out of its socket, and his expression became as intent and agonised as the dog's. Looking up gingerly he saw the four spectators, who were now all standing together, smiling broadly and giving an impression of complete harmony, all defensiveness put aside, all differences sunk.

Nelson strode up and, with negligent condescension, patted the straining Buster who, diverted from his purpose by this overture, sat down, mouth ajar, wagged his tail, panted self-consciously and put on the absurd and conciliating grin of an elderly stage-favourite taking a curtain-call. Everyone, Timothy included, beamed back at him.

'The gentleman that owns him calls him Felix,' announced Nelson, 'because his dam was a Felixstowe bitch.' Timothy winced at this plain-speaking, but Nelson didn't notice and went on, 'But Felix isn't a proper name for a dog, so I call him Buster. 'Tis more manly-like.'

'Oh,' said Timothy. 'But I much prefer his old name. I shall call him Felix.'

Nelson looked pained.

'But you won't spoil him, will you, sir?' he pleaded earnestly, as if Timothy's preference for the sissy name was evidence of such intention. ' 'Tis wonderful the way that dog has taken to you. I thought he'd be more stand-offish. But you mustn't think the worse of him for being so friendly. As I stated just now he's only a puppy. He'll soon grow out of that.'

Felix, however, did not grow out of it, and remained to the last unable to distinguish between friend and foe, since he regarded everyone as a friend. Unable and perhaps unwilling. He did not want to be a watch-dog. He hated being alone, and sometimes if Beatrice (for she early became his favourite) was out of the house he would yelp in a strangled and heart-broken manner; but if anyone came to the door he was only too glad, and however suspicious the intruder looked, gave him a warm but noiseless welcome.

At first he was made to sleep in the stable, but whether from fright or loneliness he howled so dismally that Beatrice, grumbling, brought him in and let him sleep in her room. He was a milksop in some ways, in spite of his great strength, and Timothy was content he should remain so.

Felix's advent had a curiously pacifying effect on the Old Rectory. Alone of its inmates he never suffered from nervous exasperation. He was totally free from resentfulness. He never harboured malice. If you patted him while he was eating a bone he would growl, but that was only, Timothy decided, because he thought he ought to. He was far from obedient, and would ignore any word of command uttered at a distance of more than thirty yards, pretending not to hear it. He was never quite reliable with chickens, and having passed them by a dozen times with an expression of lofty disdain would, on the thirteenth, launch a treacherous attack, and send them flying amid a flurry of squawks. It was no use beating him, for any blow that would have hurt him would have been beyond the strength of an ordinary mortal to inflict; and such a blow if delivered, would have deserved the attention of the Society for the Prevention of Cruelty to Animals. Appeals to his better nature were more effective, for though like love he was too young to know what conscience is, he did not like being called a bad dog, and would reduce his native exuberance to a mere glimmer, like a motorist diminishing his headlights. But it was hard to tell how far he was really penitent, for his habitual expression, when not animated by the promise of a walk or food or other distraction, was one of deep and suffering sadness. Or he would wearily lift his great head from his paws with a look of mingled nobility and boredom that wrung the beholder's heart.

But his patience was inexhaustible, and the moment that one invited his co-operation it was forthcoming in unstinted measure. He responded to the smallest attention. A single pat would set the ponderous machinery of his affection working. He would slowly rise, and after a few preliminary rubs and nudges to establish contact and turn on the current he would, in pantomime, devour the image of the beloved object. He had in an almost literal sense an appetite for affection; whatever it was he wanted from one – those effluences that his quivering tongue detected – seemed to go straight down his throat. He would also take into his mouth whatever parts of one's clothing he fancied, and fondly bite one's wrists; but these gestures were only the emblems of his love, the concrete symbols of his intense emotional craving. Intense and insatiable; for Beatrice was quite right when she said, 'He can't have too much of that.' He also obviously experienced great pleasure in throwing his weight about; he liked to be supported; he would lean against the tottering object of his devotion and heavily relax. Most people, surfeited by his caresses, soon got angry with him. Then Felix's sense of humour would assert itself. Wearing a smile high up on his face that showed he knew quite well what a bore he was being, he would redouble his efforts, artfully planting his large rump, whence his strength sprang, with lighthouse-like solidity between his victim and the door.

Such was Felix; a golden nature, as golden and soft as his own coat. As Wimbush (who took a less professional view of the functions of dogs than Nelson did) frequently remarked, 'He hasn't got an ounce of vice in him anywhere.' Timothy was soon wrapped up in him. At first the responsibility of owning Felix weighed on him. He was afraid that the dog would fall ill, and then what would he do? Happily Beatrice and Effie, no less than Nelson and Wimbush, though their prescriptions did not always agree, knew exactly what to do if Felix should fall ill. Indeed, they seemed to hope he would, so ready were they with suggestions as to how his condition might be remedied. Actually Felix never did fall ill; his health was as inexhaustible as his benevolence, and Timothy, from regarding him as practically an invalid, soon came to think of him as immortal.

Outside and in the village Felix did not immediately have the social success that Timothy expected and that the Rector and Nelson had confidently foretold. One of the qualities in Felix that Timothy always deplored was a lack of diffidence amounting to brazenness. Welcoming himself, he expected always to be welcome. He rushed up to everyone he met, and immediately enveloped them in the boisterous expressions of his good will. Especially was he attracted by children, hesitant bicyclists, and ladies with shopping-bags. Such was the vehemence of his onslaught that occasionally his objectives would topple over even before he reached them. This delighted Felix, for, prostrate and helpless, a human being was much less able to resist his advances; but the victims, crying, picking themselves up, or dusting themselves as the case might be, were far from pleased, and Timothy was involved in innumerable apologies. He could see that they had every right to grumble, at the same time he thought them very unreasonable to be afraid of Felix, who advertised his good intentions with every movement of his body. Soon, whenever Felix appeared, there was a marked tendency on the part of the weaker members of the community to scatter and seek shelter; perambulators were stopped and flushed matrons, gathering their toddlers round them like angry hens, prepared to stem Felix's advance. Felix would return from these encounters with a jaunty and self-important air which soon turned to bewilderment when Timothy, loudly but half-heartedly, began to scold and threaten him.

So instead of the triumphal progress down the village street that Timothy had pictured, the congratulations on his new acquisition, the pattings and strokings, their joint effect was that of two bullies, gauleiters almost, from whom everyone fled in terror. Timothy was exceedingly disappointed, for he believed that all English people were fond of dogs. Reluctantly he put Felix on a lead, after which things went better, and quite a few of the congratulations he had hoped for began to come in. Timothy was by now a passionate partisan of Felix and inclined to regulate his feelings for his neighbours by the way they treated him. Love me, love my dog. Highest in the scale came those who had welcomed Felix in his unfettered state. But had he examined himself he would have had to admit that Felix now meant more to him than any of them.

So the autumn passed into winter, and returning spring found Timothy still a dog-lover. To love Felix was a simple matter, he made no conditions, he had no moods, and on his broad golden brow, sometimes furrowed with puppy-wrinkles, it was easy to imagine Cupid enthroned – not Cupid twanging his bow, not the naughty boy who engineers heart-breaks, but Cupid asleep, with a liquid gleam of dark bright eye showing in the cleft of his deep soft eye-lids. Every now and then he would stretch and sigh, to make himself still more comfortable, and his expression would register an even deeper contentment; it seemed as though waking he consciously enjoyed the bliss of sleep. His big clumsy paws were stretched towards the blaze, whose warmth he received full on his fringed chest and stomach; he gave an effect of relaxation and defencelessness that was most touching. Watching him Timothy almost held his breath, so wanton did it seem to disturb his quietude.

Beyond a casual reference in a letter to Vera, which she had not taken up, Timothy had told no one outside the village of his new playmate. He did not want to share Felix even in thought. Esther was fond of dogs; her house was littered with them. Nondescript animals for the most part, they were indispensable to the routine of life at Langton Place. They were valued, they were looked after, they were taken for walks, they were sometimes made the subject of conversation. But they were not regarded as an end in themselves, they were not idolised; on the contrary, it was their function to contribute to the full realisation of that ideal of country life which, perhaps unknown to herself, coloured Esther's thoughts; she kept dogs because country life required it. What country life consisted in, she would have been at a loss to define, but she knew what its constituents were and their relative importance. Not to have kept dogs would have been eccentric; but not, perhaps, so eccentric as to keep one dog and lavish upon it, in secret, all the emotional output of one's nature. To keep dogs was a sign of balanced behaviour and united you with people of like tastes; it was equally a gesture of conforming and an affirmation of standards that must be conformed to. By having dogs Esther did not cut herself off from other people, she proclaimed her solidarity with them.

Timothy would have liked Felix to be a bond with the people of Upton, but it had turned out differently, and instead of being a link with he had become a substitute for human affection.

But Felix did not mind that, indeed he liked it, and Timothy's great wish was to please him.

So he did not write a doggy letter to Esther, nor, though he often thought he would, to Magda. A trivial thing prevented him. Magda, too, had had many dogs in her time, and Timothy in his unregenerate, non-dog days, had sometimes criticised them. They were small, shrinking, shivering, repulsive creatures, griffons or griffonesque; objects of luxury, wearing coats, and often to be mistaken for a scarf or a muff or something she had left lying about. When they barked it was an impotent, dry sound, like some very old person coughing. Magda called them angelic and divine and said she doted on them; but their point was that they looked peculiar, and decorative in a smart, outré way. She might be fond of them but there was no room in them to be fond of her; the great warm heart of dogdom did not beat in them; and if Timothy went into raptures over Felix's too obvious qualities, his silky coat, his speaking eyes, his noble head, his propeller-like tail, and above all his inordinate craving to be liked by everybody – Magda would only yawn and declare that he was altogether too roly-poly and honest-to-God for her. She might even call him sentimental. And Timothy was too sensitive about Felix to run the risk of hearing him disparaged, even from a distance.

Nor did he confide in Tyro. One of his earliest bonds with Tyro had been their dislike of dogs; to admit that he now liked them would be an apostasy at least as estranging as Tyro's conversion to humanism. Timothy could not bring himself to do it; besides, he did not want to. Since their recent controversy he had felt quite unable to tune in to Tyro's new wave-length.

So, a topic too secret, if not too sacred to be mentioned, the slumbering Felix had come between Timothy and his friends. To stroke Felix was easier, far easier, than to write a letter; and to receive his caresses a more satisfying and a much more immediate reward than the replies which, when at last they came, so often contained something critical, or

Soon these desertions became a regular occurrence, and not only in the evenings. Whenever Felix had given Timothy more than a few minutes of his company he grew restless and asked to be let out. The lure of the kitchen, of Beatrice and the 'something' she had ready, was proving too strong for him. One day Timothy tackled her about it.

'Felix has quite fallen in love with you, Beatrice,' he said.

Beatrice's face stiffened and she looked away from him.

'It isn't only that, sir,' she said, elliptically, 'though I suppose a dog has his feelings like the rest of us. It's Effie.'

'Oh, Effie?'

'Yes, sir. Effie says she can't stand it any longer.'

Timothy's heart sank.

'Oh, what can't she stand, Beatrice?'

'Him leaving all his hairs on the drawing-room carpet, sir. It's a day's work getting them up.'

Felix certainly did shed his coat more freely than most dogs, and it was Effie who had to clean up after him, not Timothy. But all the same—!

'Doesn't he leave them in the kitchen, too?' he said, trying to make the question sound unprovocative.

'The kitchen has a stone floor, sir, that's why it plays up our feet. But it doesn't collect the hair like a carpet does.'

'I suppose not.'

'Effie can't stand it, sir, and it makes her cough, too. Some of those hairs get right down her throat and into her chest and curl themselves into knots. It isn't healthy. A big dog like that doesn't want to be in the room.'

'He used to want to be,' said Timothy, deliberately misunderstanding her.

Beatrice gave him a quelling look.

'A person's health is more important, sir, than a dumb animal.'

CHAPTER XX

IT was only when Felix's visits had ceased altogether that Timothy remembered his present to Désirée Lampard. After the fiasco he had not wanted to unpack it; he had put the hat-box away, out of sight. Suddenly a vision of the bowl slid into his emptying mind, glowing with a soft lustre. Unpacking it was such an excitement that he scarcely felt a twinge when, deep in the heart of the bowl, covered with shavings, he found the visiting-card which still carried his best wishes.

Standing in the middle of a low round table, to ensure the utmost visibility, its unageing glory lit the room. It was a proud object and Timothy did not presume to be familiar with it. Indeed, it did not repay familiarity of any kind. Not that it was exactly stand-offish. But it represented the transcendent; it was perfection's ambassador; it demanded homage, not love, and homage is a tribute that must not be paid too often, for it is subject to a law of diminishing return. The uplifting effect of humility ceases to operate if it becomes a habit; even the Emperor of China, the Son of Heaven himself, only required a limited number of kow-tows. And like a royalty it must not be seen too often; for prestige is a sensitive plant that shrivels with thoughtless or intemperate usage.

> 'So am I as the rich whose blessèd key
> Can bring him to his sweet uplockèd treasure,
> The which he will not every hour survey,
> For blunting the fine point of seldom pleasure.'

Having been warned, Timothy took care not to look at his bowl until he had wanted to at least half a dozen times.

But though the treasure repelled familiarity, it did not refuse intimacy. Even a queen may have lovers; and Timothy sometimes, and with due formality and inward preparation, allowed himself to approach the bowl and finger its exquisite surface, cold and hard as marble, but of a smoothness so remarkable that it seemed to give new meaning to the word.

How different was this contact from the feel of Felix's warm yielding coat, how much rarer and more refined (if one thought of comparing them) the pleasure that it gave! Those unconsidered pats and smacks and strokings, the expressions of a casual and unregulated regard, given without respect and received without dignity – how could they compete, as examples of civilised behaviour, as gestures worthy of the spirit, with the finger-tip caress, the bated breath, the absolute stillness and concentration of mood demanded by communion with the sang-de-bœuf bowl! How compare the grandeur implicit in this noble and most fragile object (dating, who knows? from the Ming dynasty), the centuries stored up in it, the garnered worship, the æsthetic tradition distilled from the beauty-loving aspirations of millions – with the commonplace allure of good, kind, clumsy Felix, a dog without pedigree or distinction, a transitory bundle of flesh, not always very agreeable to the nose, who would be forgotten dust in a dozen years?

And idiotic as it was, Timothy could not help feeling aggrieved with Felix for his defection, his preference for the kitchen and the company of Beatrice, to the drawing-room, and the surely more manifold delights of Timothy's society. No doubt it was only cupboard love on Felix's part, but it was disappointing and undignified, conduct more befitting a human being than a dog.

So that when Timothy came across Felix in the stable-yard or in the garden, or saw him holding court in the kitchen, his new kingdom, he seldom stopped to speak to him and sometimes did not even look at him, a calculated slight which Beatrice, though not Felix, was quick to notice.

A favourite has no friends. Someone else had observed that Timothy had cooled towards the golden retriever. Felix was not a good gardener. He believed himself to be welcome everywhere and could not understand why Wimbush should object when he gambolled on the flower-beds, leaving footprints which, so Wimbush said, were so large they might have been made by an elephant. That Wimbush had been the prime mover in bringing Felix to the Old Rectory failed to soften his resentment, and the fact that he had become Beatrice's plaything greatly aggravated it. Not, it must be admitted, that he was unfair to the dog. He continued to say that Felix had not an ounce of vice in him. But whereas before, at the time when Timothy followed Felix about with doting looks, he contented himself with admonishing Felix for his misdeeds, he now gave him an occasional cuff and once or twice took a stick to him.

He did not do this without first consulting Timothy.

'Should you mind if I give him a wallop now and again, sir? It doesn't matter so much now, but come the summer, you won't get a bloom from those delphiniums. They'll be flat, same as if they'd been bombed.'

'Well, so long as you don't really hurt him,' said Timothy. He blushed for himself, but Wimbush laughed.

'You can't hurt him, sir, his skin's much too thick.'

Felix took the beatings in good part for, as Wimbush said, it was next to impossible to hurt him and in any case the gardener did not want to. He merely wanted to warn him off the flower-beds and in this he was beginning to be successful, for Felix was far from stupid and the desire to please went to the root of his character.

It happened, however, that Beatrice witnessed one of these chastisements and her ever-smouldering animosity against the gardener flamed up anew. She at once sought out Timothy and complained to him.

'Wimbush'll be killing Felix, one of these days.'

But Timothy remembered Beatrice's former charge against the gardener and could not take this one seriously.

'Oh, I'm sure you're exaggerating, Beatrice. Besides, dogs have to be trained, just as children have. It's not fair to Wimbush to have him running wild over the garden. He *is* rather disobedient, you know.'

He saw the storm gathering on Beatrice's brow as she said, 'You wouldn't have said that this time last week. You were all over him then.'

Timothy reddened and said crossly, 'I wish you wouldn't speak to me like that, Beatrice. He's only a dog after all.'

Beatrice trembled and her colour came and went.

'He's more like a Christian than some people I could name,' she said. Timothy knew she was referring to Wimbush, but it sounded as if she meant him, and the rudeness of her manner stung him.

'I've a good mind to get rid of the dog,' he said brutally. 'He's not worth the trouble and expense. How would you like that?'

'I'd give in my—' began Beatrice. But the operative word was never uttered. She burst into tears and went out sobbing.

Timothy found himself staring at the bull's blood bowl. What a blessing that it could not make scenes and answer him back and thoroughly upset him; that it did not appeal to any human feeling at all except the highest – the love of beauty. Could one live on that? he wondered. Could one make oneself independent of human contacts, stop one's ears against the sirens' song, as did the sailors in the Odyssey? Left to themselves, unheeded and unheeding, the emotions would atrophy and petrify, leaving the consciousness as hard and gem-like as the bowl was; and one would go through the motions of living, an automaton, saving one's spiritual energy for one's reactions as a connoisseur, just as some people keep theirs for business or sport or football pools. The age was an age of specialists; one must be selective, the devotee of a single activity, and not slop over on to life, like a bucketful of water thrown over a backyard; and limit one's responses to one's fellows to the 'Fares please' and occasional 'thank-you's' of a bus-conductor. How grateful people were, at bottom, to the conductor's impersonality, to his functional, unemotional visitations, which did not exclude the cracking of a joke, and which required of them nothing but a token action, a routine payment of what was due – and due to the company, a vast anonymous body, not to him.

Fairness, justice, those were the valuable qualities; and they could only be attained and administered by the absolute suppression of the personal, by a companion state of mind to that in which one appreciates a work of art.

He had been less than just to Beatrice, perhaps; certainly to Felix. It was not sentimental to think of justice in connection with a dog; even beasts must be with justice slain – not that there was any question of killing Felix, but of course his flower-bed antics had to be put a stop to – rather a shame in a way, for he always looked particularly pleased with himself and certain of approval when he was sending the earth flying. Such a good game! Such a good dog! Digging for victory! And the truth was, he wouldn't have been so diligent in digging if Timothy hadn't, just lately, discontinued his habit of taking him for walks. Felix was really a terrible nuisance on a walk. Apart from his penchant for bowling over babies, and when leashed, tugging at the lead until one's arm was stiff, he could not be relied on to behave properly on the open hillsides. He would suddenly vanish to reappear in the distance as a golden feather, moving at high speed against wall or hedge or sky-line. Timothy's voice would get hoarse with shouting; while Felix pretended that it was just another of those peewits, which he loved to chase. . . . And then there was the threat, vague but omnipresent, of the 'coverts,' where he had no business at all to be. How could one keep up a clear, harmonious flow of thought when every minute one had to be telling Felix not to do something?

No, it was no fun taking him for a walk, and Timothy was relieved when Felix's treachery and ingratitude gave him an excuse for dropping them. But obviously he must have exercise, whether he was a good dog or not, it was only fair, besides he would otherwise fall ill. Lead in hand, Timothy went to look for him. The maids had finished their luncheon but Beatrice's eyes were still red.

Felix, who was also finishing his dinner, jumped up delightedly and his tail smacked against the table-legs.

'I'm going to give him another chance, Beatrice,' Timothy said, forbearingly. It had never really entered his head to part with Felix, but he had many grudges against Beatrice to pay off, and Felix was obviously a weak place in her armour. He was rewarded by seeing in her eyes a gleam of fear, which she immediately suppressed.

'If only he would leave the flower-beds alone,' Timothy went on, still talking to her. 'We may have to put you on a chain, Felix, if you will do that.'

Felix acknowledged this remark by jumping up and trying to lick Timothy's face. It always pleased him to be spoken to, and Timothy did not sound angry. But Beatrice's brow darkened.

'The man doesn't keep the borders all that neat,' she said. 'He calls himself a gardener, but that rose-bed under the kitchen window's a disgrace. I never saw such a crop of dandelions in all my life.' Timothy tried to placate her.

'You're right,' he said. 'It is a bit untidy. I must remind him about it. Well, come on, Felix.'

On the hillside, away from Beatrice, away from flower-beds, away from the explosive atmosphere of the Old Rectory, Timothy's affection for the dog came back. For the moment Felix seemed to have turned over a new leaf. He put away childish things and adopted a strictly professional air. Perhaps he imagined himself at a shooting party; beaters and other dogs surrounded him. He was being ordered this way and that by stern-faced men with guns. There was not a moment to lose; his reputation as a retriever was at stake. Backwards and forwards he galloped, with his lilting, rocking-horse action, examining with the rapt attention of a botanist this or that grassy phenomenon. Until he had satisfied himself that the secret was solved, nothing would move him from the spot. Then suddenly, as though stung by a wasp, he would leap aside with a supple flourish of his outflung body, and be off.

Timothy had taken Felix to a distant field which he believed to be free of cattle, sheep, pheasants, anything that Felix might be blamed for chasing. Hitherto, they had always had it to themselves, but to-day someone was walking on the sky-line, a woman clearly, though by the freedom of her stride she might have been a man. Timothy's first reaction was to call Felix; but he was already outside the radius of obedience, racing towards his quarry. Would she turn and flee? Timothy set off at a rapid walk, breaking at times into a run, and rehearsing to himself the well-worn phrases in which abject apology struggled with suppressed irritation that anyone could be so silly as to be afraid of

Felix. With a sinking heart he saw Felix execute a few vertical bounds, but the lady held her ground without flinching, and when Timothy came up Felix was trotting round her, plucking playfully at her elbows, as his manner was, but not attempting to knock her down.

'That's a nice dog you've got,' she said, before Timothy could speak.

Where had he heard that voice before? But before trying to place her he must say his piece.

'I'm so sorry he came up to you like that. I've tried to break him of the habit but he will do it. He's only young you know, and does it out of friendliness and high spirits. He wouldn't hurt anybody, but they're not to know that. Felix, you bad dog.'

Felix withdrew a pace or two, panted like a steam-engine and tried to look ashamed.

'Don't worry yourself,' the lady said. 'I'm not afraid of dogs and I know the breed. They're all the same.'

Liking her at once for liking Felix, Timothy still felt he could not let this implied criticism of him pass unchallenged, for Timothy was a one-dog man, though Felix was far from being a one-man dog.

'Oh, but he has a lot of personality. He isn't really like other dogs. For instance, he . . .' In vain Timothy searched his mind for ways in which Felix was 'different'. 'He scarcely ever barks,' he concluded, lamely.

'Retrievers don't bark much, in my experience,' said the lady, and a shutter of indifference came down over her face. She was wearing dark glasses, so large and opaque that they hid her eyes. Where had Timothy seen it before, that rather long oval, the full mouth and the proud, short nose? Her complexion was yellowish: it was the only thing about her that looked unhealthy. He wondered if she was older than he was.

'I was looking for someone,' she said abruptly. 'A tall girl, about my height, and rather like me. We were to have met here. You haven't seen her?'

Timothy told her he had seen no one.

'It's odd,' she said. 'I expected her yesterday, too. I've been expecting her for some time. This is a place we used often to come to, for picnics. She knows it quite well, she couldn't have missed her way.' A look of worry came into her face, which she banished immediately.

'Excuse me,' Timothy interrupted her, 'I must just call Felix.' Felix, who had taken advantage of their conversation to retreat to a strategic distance, came galloping up with an air of invincible innocence.

'Good dog,' said Timothy, and turned to the lady. 'I'm so sorry. If I did happen to see her, shall I tell her that someone is looking for her?'

'Yes, her mother,' said the lady. After a moment's pause she added, 'No, don't say that. It might be a shock to her. Just say I am waiting for her at the usual place.'

Timothy was puzzled. 'She will know who it is?' The worried look came back.

'Of course she will. She must. When all's said and done, we still have the same name. *You* know who I am, don't you?'

In that moment Timothy did know, but he couldn't keep the tremor out of his voice as he said, 'Yes, Mrs. Lampard.'

'I rather hoped you didn't. This place is teeming with spies, Germans some of them, I shouldn't wonder. There's a man living in Upton – he's been a perfect plague to me. Nothing has gone right since he came. She knew him. She wanted me to ask him to her wedding. When I refused, she cried. But he was no good to her. Half our troubles came from him.'

Timothy said nothing.

'If you see her,' Mrs. Lampard went on, 'ask her to come back to me. I've asked her, of course, but she might pay more attention to a stranger. She's joined the A.T.S. or the Wrens or one of those things. So unnecessary! She says she's happy, but how can she be happy away from me? With a shiny nose and thick stockings, too? Don't say I'm her mother; say I'm someone with a message from him. She'll know who it is.'

'I will, Mrs. Lampard.'

She went on in a sharper tone.

'And for God's sake don't tell her what a bore I've become, or it might put her off. They used to say we were like Mme. de Sévigné and her daughter. I always felt sorry for Françoise de Grignan with her doting mother. But the French are so emotional. I've only written Désirée two letters since she left me. Do you know why?'

Timothy said he didn't.

'Because they open them. That's how it all started – with someone reading a letter. I wish I knew who it was, or how they got hold of it.'

Timothy was silent.

'They won't come to any good, whoever they are.' She stopped and raised her hand. 'Look, isn't that someone coming?' But Felix had already seen the distant figure and was streaking towards it.

'Felix! Felix!'

Obedient this time, Felix came trotting back. 'She wouldn't mind!' exclaimed Mrs. Lampard. 'She likes dogs, too. Look, can you see who it is? I'm sure it must be her.' She became extremely agitated. 'Perhaps you'd better go now.'

Timothy strained his eyes.

'I'm sure it's her,' Mrs. Lampard repeated. 'I couldn't be mistaken. It's her walk, exactly. Why don't you go away? I asked you to.'

Confused and miserable, Timothy said, 'I will go away, Mrs. Lampard. But I don't think it's her, I don't think it's your daughter.'

'Why not? Why not? What makes you say so? Do you know my daughter?'

Timothy mumbled something about having seen her once.

'You've seen her? Why didn't you tell me? You're keeping something from me. You're . . .' She looked at him searchingly. 'You're trespassing, do you know that? Tell me your name.'

Timothy hesitated. The strange woman was quite near to them now; he could see the grey stuff of her clothes and her kind but resolute expression. Felix trotted up to her sedately with his tail in the air.

'Look, Mrs. Lampard, here's someone who wants to speak to you,' said Timothy.

Petulantly she turned away from him.

'They always know where to find me,' she grumbled with an angry sigh. 'I shall have to look for another place. Only then *she* won't know where I am. I don't want to speak to her in front of strangers – I hate the whole pack of them.'

The nurse raised her eyebrows slightly to Timothy and said, 'Come along now, Mrs. Lampard. It's time for you to go in.'

Mrs. Lampard said to Timothy, 'You see I live under orders now.' She shrugged her shoulders, gave a little laugh, and said, 'But I'm afraid you don't know each other. How remiss of me. Nurse Pynsent, this is Mr. . . . . Mr. . . . .' She waited for Timothy to supply the name. An amused light came into her eyes. 'Isn't it odd, Nurse, but he doesn't want us to know his name. I wonder why. But I know it – I can tell you!'

She looked mockingly at Timothy and said, 'Shall I break the news?'

He stared at her, his blood turning to ice.

'It's Casson, Mr. Timothy Casson.'

She chuckled, a low delicious gurgle of amusement, and added, with a smile that wrinkled downwards from the corners of her mouth, 'Aren't I right, Mr. Casson?'

'No,' said Timothy firmly. 'I'm afraid you're mistaken, Mrs. Lampard. My name is Peabody, Adolphus Peabody.'

His dignified, affronted stare outfaced her incredulity. 'Peabody,' she repeated dreamily. 'What a curious name. It suits you, I think. But I'm sorry you're not Mr. Casson; there was a great deal I wanted to say to him.'

Suddenly her manner seemed to detach itself from the whole scene, the entire proceedings.

'Goodbye, Mr. Peabody. Remember what I said.' Barely acknowledging his bow she moved away towards the hill-top, with the nurse following her, a pace or two behind.

'Do you know who that was?' said Timothy to Felix, when the lady of the manor and her escort had passed out of earshot. 'It was Mrs. Randall Lampard, and she's quite, quite mad.'

But Felix was not interested. Indeed the whole interview, which held him on an invisible leash and made excessive demands on his conscience, had been extremely tedious to him. He celebrated his freedom with longer and more daring escapades amid the gorse and bracken, not disdaining, in his appetite for pleasure, to snap at the brimstone butterflies tempted out by the late Spring sunshine. Following his technique of gradual withdrawal he reappeared from time to time, but at longer intervals and a greater distance. Finally he disappeared altogether. Timothy did not worry about him, for the shadow of the hawk, that might have punished his venturesomeness, had passed away from the lonely hillside. Mrs. Lampard had other things to occupy her than the preservation of her game.

Musing upon her career, and his own association with it, Timothy had ample opportunity for tasting the sweets of revenge. But his stomach was not robust enough for them; his imagination kept following her back to Welshgate Hall where, amid shrouded furniture and diminished daylight, she lived a life that was also shrouded and diminished. Try as he would to absolve himself from all responsibility for her fate, he could not help feeling that it added a darker shadow to his own; and he was glad to see the roofs and chimney-pots of Upton, embedded in their fresh spring greenery, with the sentinel poplars keeping guard, the river gleaming in the meadows before the thick woods claimed it, and the garden and stable-yard of the Old Rectory – an asylum in the best sense of the word.

CHAPTER XXI

BUT he could not dismiss Mrs. Lampard from his mind, she haunted his pillow, and on the morrow he sought out Wimbush, feeling sure that the gardener could supply some gossip.

Wimbush did not lift his head as Timothy came along the path that he was hoeing. There was nothing surprising in that, for he always became more deeply absorbed in his work at Timothy's approach. But this morning the start and the broad smile of welcome were missing, and he let Timothy pass by without looking up.

Feeling like someone whose bluff has been called, Timothy turned back.

'Good morning, Wimbush, not a bad morning, but how different from last May.'

'Different in more ways than one,' Wimbush grunted, still without lifting his head.

Puzzled by his uncordial tone Timothy tried to count their blessings.

'I don't think the situation is any worse, the world situation, I mean,' he finished up.

Usually Wimbush was very ready to give his opinion on world affairs, so his answer, when at last it came, was all the more discouraging.

'What happens in the world outside doesn't affect us much in Upton, I reckon.'

Momentarily and for the sake of argument Timothy descended from his ivory tower.

'Oh, but Wimbush, it does. Quite a lot of Upton people have relations living in London and other towns, as well as at the war. Think of the relief to them, being able to sleep soundly at night.'

But again the result was disappointing.

'Bombs never did worry me,' said Wimbush, 'nor bombardments either. There's been a lot too much fuss made about these blitzes, as they call them in the papers. 'Tis just a word for a few bombs dropping.'

'Oh, but Wimbush,' persisted Timothy, 'when you think of the autumn of last year, and the danger we were in then, of invasion and so on, and then the winter, with so many women and children being killed – you must agree that things are better now.'

'Perhaps they are, perhaps they're not,' said Wimbush. 'In my opinion 'twas the Home Guard, and not all those Beaufighters and such, that kept the Jerries from these shores.' The indifference in his voice was edged with reproof, and Timothy was troubled.

'Still, we have much to be thankful for,' he struggled on. To find a want of sympathetic accord, amounting almost to opposition, in Wimbush was a new experience. 'England, this country, seems to be saved for the time being. And what terrible misfortunes some people have!' He lowered his voice. 'I met Mrs. Lampard yesterday, Wimbush.'

'Oh?'

The 'oh' was as clearly against him as a railway-signal, but Timothy decided to ignore it. Still in a voice artificially hushed he went on. 'You know what's happened to her?'

Wimbush shrugged his shoulders and attacked a dandelion, whose head came off, leaving a stump with a milky scar. 'They do say she's gone potty.'

'Yes, isn't it terrible? Do you know how it happened?'

'All along of that daughter of hers not marrying that Duck, they say,' said Wimbush. 'Good lord, if people go mad for a little thing like that, they can't have much to worry about.'

His reasoning was not clear to Timothy but his lack of sympathy with Mrs. Lampard was; and there was the added suggestion, painful because of the animosity behind it, that Timothy himself might go mad, and welcome, if having nothing to worry about was a sufficient cause.

Timothy could not bring himself to let the subject drop, however. 'I'm sorry for the daughter, too,' he said.

'I shouldn't waste my sorrow on such as her,' Wimbush advised him. ' 'Tisn't as if he had been killed, which might happen to any of us, and nobody be the worse.'

Again the vindictive tone. Timothy had never known Wimbush in such a difficult mood. Shifting his ground he said, with a feeble attempt at jocularity, 'Well, anyhow everything in the garden's lovely. I never saw it looking better than it is.' He glanced about him in exaggerated appreciation.

'That's not what you said yesterday,' said Wimbush grimly.

Timothy was completely at a loss. 'Yesterday? I didn't see you yesterday.'

'No, sir, but you saw someone else and they told me.'

'Who?'

'The other one in the kitchen.'

For the first time Wimbush looked up and Timothy realised how angry he was. 'Beatrice?'

Wimbush nodded without speaking.

Timothy tried to remember, but his encounter with Mrs. Lampard had wiped his memory clean of what happened just before. 'What did I say?'

'You said the rose-bed under the kitchen window was a disgrace.' Wimbush spat the words out as if it hurt him to utter them.

'Oh no I didn't, Wimbush. I said. . . . I said. . . . I may have said it was a bit untidy.'

'Why didn't you say it to me, sir?'

'I . . . I meant to, Wimbush. I hope you haven't taken it in bad part?'

Wimbush straightened himself, and his anger altered the shape of his face.

'I'm just about fed up, sir. I'm giving in my notice now and you won't see me again after a week come Saturday.'

'Oh, Wimbush, you mustn't say that. I . . . I didn't really mean it. It . . . it just slipped out. Untidy doesn't mean anything. We're all of us untidy,' Timothy pleaded.

'Disgrace does, sir, and that was the word used.' Wimbush was trembling. 'If you'll excuse me, sir, we won't say anything more about it. I didn't expect it from you, sir, I really didn't.' He went back to his hoeing.

Shaken and miserable, Timothy wandered back to the house. How had he given Beatrice this opportunity for mischief-making? He remembered how; thinking it was the best way of placating her, he had criticised Wimbush; and she had struck where she knew it would hurt Wimbush most, in his pride. To have been the means of wounding Wimbush, with whom he had never had an instant's disagreement, made him feel quite sick – his best friend in the place, next to Mrs. Purbright.

Should he consult her? No, he had already given her too many exhibitions, exhibitionisms, of spiritual nudity; she must be as shy as he was of these immodest displays. Better, braver, to beard Beatrice and give her a terrific talking-to. But he was in a weak position; all she had done was to repeat as his something she had said herself, and something to which he had, substantially, agreed. Disgrace, that fatal word. She was too old for him to try to reform, and besides, psychologists could find a dozen excuses, reasons almost, for her acting as she had.

He passed her in the passage with a scowl and sank down in a chair, thinking of his existence at Upton without Wimbush's support, thinking of their long and happy relationship, terminated by a word, in an explosion of rudeness and unkindness; and thinking, too, it must be admitted, of the black picture Wimbush would paint of him in the village, who had always been his staunchest advocate.

A gleam like a sunset broke through his musings, parting the clouds. The red bowl at any rate had no quarrel with him; its pride was not of the kind that would take umbrage. The expression of the potter's passion for his art, it dwelt in a region of crystallised achievement, of emotional stability sealed against change. It fortified his spirit, and he found comfort in the thought that when his eyes had turned to dust it would still be there, an abiding testimony to the joy men once found in their work, if never in their dealings with each other.

By the next morning Timothy had persuaded himself that Wimbush would have recovered his temper and be ready to withdraw his notice, if not to apologise. But he was mistaken. The gardener's manner was much less surly, but it was even more unyielding. Scores of times, he said, he had been on the point of giving in his notice, all owing to that woman; he had only stayed on for Mr. Casson's sake. If only Mr. Casson had spoken to him instead of to her! From Mr. Casson he would have accepted any reproof; the wife would bear witness that he was ready to cut off his hand for Mr. Casson. Effie, she was a good girl, he had no complaint against her, but the other one! He shook his head and went on digging.

It occurred to Timothy to try and enlist Effie's support.

'See if you can make him change his mind, Effie. He likes you, he said so.'

Effie's look of unhappiness changed to apprehension.

'Oh, I couldn't possibly do that, sir. He might think I wanted him to stay.'

'Well, don't you?'

To his surprise Effie burst into tears and ran from the room.

Twice in the next few days Timothy again tried to prevail on Wimbush to reconsider his decision, but without avail, though the gardener's manner had now regained some of its old cordiality. Saturday came and Timothy, with a heavy heart, counted out the curious, un-round sum which represented Wimbush's wages minus his share of the stamp money, and added a parting present.

It was nearly one o'clock but Wimbush was working away as usual, and there was no sign that these few minutes were the last that he would spend in Timothy's employ.

'Well, Wimbush, the ghost walks again.' This was Wimbush's own playful metaphor for the ceremony of pay-day.

Wimbush took the money into his mud-stained fist and transferred it to his pocket.

'And there's this as well.' Timothy held out the notes.

'What's that for, sir?'

'Just for remembrance and to show there's no ill feeling.' Wimbush looked away.

'I couldn't take it, sir, I couldn't really. It would stick in my throat.' He gave a gulp.

'Please take it, Wimbush. Don't think it comes from me, if you'd rather not. Pretend it's a bonus, or something you picked up in the street.' Wimbush's face softened, but he still hesitated.

'It doesn't seem fair, sir, not with me leaving you against your will, as you might say.'

'Don't leave me, then.'

Wimbush shook his head.

'I couldn't stay now, sir, not after what's passed. I should never hear the last of it. I should be a laughing-stock. I couldn't hold my head up in the village if I let her down-trample me like that. I shouldn't have any heart in my work, either, if I knew she was going to reap the benefit.'

'You take her too seriously, Wimbush,' said Timothy, feeling that he had nothing to lose now by plain-speaking. 'She's only a sour, sad woman with a bitter tongue. You shouldn't pay any attention to her. I don't,' he added, untruthfully.

' 'Tis all very well for you to say that, sir,' said Wimbush. 'You can speak to her distant-like through the veil of authority. But how would you like it if she came up to you in a nasty way and said I had said something about you discreditable which I hadn't really said, she said it, but I had said something, which would make it all the worse?'

'I expect I should be annoyed,' Timothy admitted.

'I'm sure you would, sir. And you haven't got your position to think of, like I have.'

'No, Wimbush.'

'But of course I never should have said anything discreditable of you, sir, you understand that, it was only to drive my meaning home the plainest way.'

'Yes, I appreciate that, Wimbush.'

'Because I couldn't have wanted a better master, sir, whatever you may think of me.'

Timothy was silent.

'This is a good job and I'm not saying it isn't. I'm not one of those who fly off the handle at a word and I shouldn't now, sir, if you'd said whatever you did say to me instead of her.'

They were back at the starting-place again.

'I'm very sorry about that, Wimbush, I've told you so.'

'Yes, sir, and there's many as wouldn't say as much, which is what I tell them when they ask me how I've stuck it so long here where a she-cat couldn't hardly breathe.' Wimbush was working himself up again. His tawny eyes flashed and his frame dilated. The air around them seemed to hold its breath and far away in the distance the church clock struck one.

'Time's up,' said Timothy, forcing a smile.

Wimbush sighed and the lines of tension relaxed and his large frame seemed to sag.

'We'll be seeing each other, sir.'

'Yes, of course. Where will you be working now, Wimbush?'

'Mrs. Lampard's agent have been looking for a water-bailiff, and of course he offered it to me as the most likely man.'

'I congratulate you,' said Timothy. 'It sounds a good job. Perhaps we shall meet on the river.'

Wimbush laughed and slapped his thigh. 'That's a good one, sir. We can always trust you for a laugh, in or out of season. There'll be a lot of things won't seem so funny, when you're not there.'

'It does take two to make a joke,' said Timothy.

Wimbush laughed again. Then his face grew serious.

'The new chap, sir, he may not see the funny side like I do.'

Timothy shrugged his shoulders.

' 'Tisn't everyone as would, not with her around.' The gardener's manner changed. 'Some of this gear, sir, belong to me. There's a spade, and the scythe, and these clippers—'

'You must take everything that is yours, Wimbush, of course.'

'I only mention it, because Miss Chadwick mightn't remember. There's the padlock on the chicken-house, too, but I'll leave that.'

'Thank you very much.'

'That's all I can think of now, but if there should be anything else you won't mind if I come and take them with your permission?'

'Of course not.'

'Oh, and there's the Dutch hoe and the oil-can. When you've been a long time in one place 'tis surprising how things mount up.'

'How long is it?'

'Eight years come Michaelmas. And how much longer do you think of staying, sir?'

'Well, I've got the house for another three and a half years.'

Wimbush whistled.

' 'Tis a tidy time.' Noticing Timothy's depressed look he added, 'But I expect it'll go quick.'

'It would have gone more pleasantly in your company,' Timothy said.

'I'm far from denying that, sir,' said Wimbush warmly. 'And it goes for me, too. If anyone had told me a fortnight ago that I should be leaving here, why, I'd have knocked the words down his throat.'

Timothy could not think of a reply and his eyes strayed down to the notes he was still holding in his hand. Wimbush's glance followed his.

'You'd much better take them,' Timothy said. 'I should, in your place.'

'I'm sure you would, sir,' said Wimbush, with emphasis, 'I'm sure you would. That's what makes me hesitate. 'Tisn't the way I ordained to go, not by any means, not as a man who puts his pride behind his back. But since you wish it, sir, I will.'

He pocketed the gratuity and, looking round the garden, searched his mind for a suitable comment.

'If you should ever want me, sir,' he said at last, 'you know where to find me. I can't say fairer than that. I hope you won't because it might mean you were in a jam, but you couldn't come to anyone better, you know that.' Timothy thanked him.

'I'm not saying I shan't miss you, sir,' Wimbush went on, as usual making his thoughts fit his words, rather than the other way round. 'A better gentleman it's never been my privilege to serve, alive or dead.'

Timothy's eyes grew moist.

'Nobody shan't ever say anything else in my hearing,' Wimbush declared. 'And if I had my way I should be here now, not somewhere else. Goodbye, sir.' He grasped Timothy's outstretched hand, held it a moment, and walked off without looking back.

Breaking the news to Miss Chadwick was not the least of the evils connected with Wimbush's departure. She was in one of her moods of not hearing, and Timothy had to repeat the distasteful tidings several times.

'Believing Wimbush? I've always found him perfectly truthful, as far as people of his kind ever are.'

'No, I said leaving, Miss Chadwick. In fact he's left.'

'I'm afraid I can't hear what you say. You'll have to speak a little more slowly and a good deal more distinctly. You mean politically to the Left? Most of the working classes are, in these days, more's the pity, and you yourself—'

'No, he's left my employment, gone away, hooked it, if you will pardon the expression.'

'I'm afraid it's new to me. Hook? I must ask you to translate.'

'I mean he's taken his departure.'

There was a pause, and then Miss Chadwick said in an altered tone:

'Now I understand. Why didn't you say so before? This is serious. Wimbush is a most valuable servant. How did it happen?'

After many false starts and circumlocutions, Timothy succeeded in telling her.

'What an unfortunate affair,' said Miss Chadwick, when he had finished. Her enunciation was perfect; every syllable rang.

'You told him to come and see me, I hope?'

'I'm afraid I forgot to.'

'Naturally I should like to hear the story from his own lips. My dear brother was exceedingly attached to him, and so was I.'

'And so was I,' said Timothy.

'But not enough to keep him, it seems. Hullo?'

'I told you how it happened,' said Timothy.

'Of course we all know your cook is a difficult woman. Still, it's no use crying over spilt milk. Let's hope the breach is only temporary, like so many war measures.'

'You think he'll come back?'

'When the present emergency is over I'm sure he will. He has no quarrel with the Old Rectory. . . . Yes?'

'The war doesn't look like being over,' said Timothy.

'No. Perhaps we ought not to discuss such subjects on the telephone. I hope you are comfortable in other ways, Mr. Casson? I'm afraid you live a rather lonely life?'

'Oh, I have plenty of interests, you know.'

'The Old Rectory used to be such a centre of social life. Friends poured in. There was a continual va-et-vient. I had hoped you would carry on the tradition, but now, from outside at least, the house has rather a forsaken air. And Wimbush leaving, too. . . . I had so much confidence in him. I doubt if you will be able to replace him, there is such a shortage of good gardeners. And of course the garden must be kept up. I'm afraid the prospect isn't very rosy for you.'

'Perhaps it would be better if I went away,' said Timothy. As Miss Chadwick did not answer, he repeated what he had said.

'Thank you, Mr. Casson, but I heard you the first time. No, that is quite out of the question. The lease has still more than three years to run, and besides you are an ideal tenant.'

'I was afraid you thought I was letting the place down.'

'Oh no, you are a perfect caretaker. From my point of view, you understand, it is better that the house should not have people tramping through it: there is less wear and tear. I couldn't consider any sub-letting, and the lease makes no provision for it. No, I am perfectly satisfied. It was you whom I felt sorry for.'

'Oh, I shall jog along.'

'But you will try to find another gardener, won't you? A garden so soon gets out of hand, especially at this time of year.'

Timothy promised to try.

'And if you don't succeed,' Miss Chadwick wound up, 'you had better take up gardening yourself. It's very good exercise, much better than boating.'

Miss Chadwick's misgivings proved unfounded, for hardly had Timothy laid down the receiver which, when she was talking through it, had the air of a lethal weapon, than he was summoned by a dismal-looking Effie to interview a prospective gardener. He was a sad-eyed sallow little man who seemed unable to rise above the worry of the moment; and his favourite phrase, which he used several times in the course of the interview was, 'It makes it so bad for everybody.' From the war down to the cigarette shortage, everything he touched on seemed to have this effect. But he had unexceptionable credentials from his previous employer, and his only reason for wanting to leave Sir Watson Stafford was that the girl there interfered with his tools. He said it made it so bad for everybody. Exactly how she interfered he did not specify, but Timothy promised it would not happen here, and engaged him on the spot – so thankful was he to have found a gardener at all.

Afterwards he regretted his precipitancy, for later in the evening two other men offered themselves for the post, both of whom were more likely-looking candidates than the defeatist Simpson, and both of whom expressed regret at being too late. In spite of his disappointment Timothy couldn't help feeling pleased that people were forthcoming to take service at the Old Rectory, and that it was not, as Miss Chadwick had managed to suggest, a place with a hoodoo on it.

Writing to Vera he told her of Wimbush's departure. He did not think it would interest her, but he was obliged to eke out endearments with such news as he had. And he thought that one aspect of the episode would please her.

'The new gardener is leaving Sir Watson Stafford to come to me, so at least one of the fishing-snobs will have reason to curse the name of Casson.'

CHAPTER XXII

FELIX was in disgrace again. It was the old story; he would make a playground of the flower-beds. Simpson's comment 'it makes it so bad for everybody' was not strictly true, for Felix enjoyed it. But it would have to be made bad for him too, for, as Timothy told Beatrice, if gardeners started leaving the Old Rectory in a procession the place would get a bad name. That he was emboldened to speak thus openly to Beatrice surprised even Timothy; but since Wimbush had gone her manner to her employer had become cordial, almost ingratiating. And she was loud in praise of Simpson: he could do no wrong. Had he offered to do Felix grievous bodily harm she would no doubt have hated him, for he only enjoyed her esteem, whereas Felix possessed her heart. But he didn't; he was terrified of the retriever, and Beatrice could easily forgive him for that.

And this was not Felix's only offence. Latterly, perhaps as a result of Wimbush's harsh treatment, he had taken to running away. An R.A.F. camp, about seven miles from Upton, seemed to have an irresistible attraction for him, and three times they had rung up Timothy to fetch him back. The first time Timothy went in his car, but he had no petrol for the other journeys and had to ride his bicycle. Bicycling with Felix was a tricky business, for Felix as usual wanted to help; moreover he had to be kept on a lead, which was known to be cruel. But it was the only way of getting him to follow, and Timothy did not mind if he was a little out of breath, for it would teach him not to run away from a good home and a nice kind master, whose one wish was to make everybody comfortable. If Felix took to pretending that the Old Rectory was not a happy house it would really be too much. Beatrice must have infected him with her discontent; he was her creature, almost indistinguishable from her; and when he lagged behind, mutely demanding yet another breather (for Timothy often got off to let him have a rest), Timothy would harden his heart and twitch the lead, half thinking it was Beatrice he had in tow, Beatrice whose loud panting was as music to his ears.

To revenge himself for the loss of Wimbush, Timothy again denounced Felix to her and had the satisfaction of seeing all his darts go home. The dog was a menace; he doubted if anyone would take an animal with Felix's black record, which Timothy could not, in honesty, conceal from an intending purchaser. It cost a great deal to feed him, more perhaps than it cost to feed a human being. Many slum children had to live on less than Felix got. No one would want him if it meant going short themselves. Much as he hoped it would not happen, he might have to consider putting Felix down.

So Felix's continuance hung on a hair. It was arranged that he should be tied up in the kitchen, and only taken out under strict personal supervision. Tiresome as he was, Timothy hated to curtail his liberty, for he was now the only member of the household who used his life for enjoyment. The rest of them, and the rest included Timothy, had let circumstances get the upper hand. They could react, but not act. Now Felix would join their sad society, for he would be in reaction against his chain.

But Timothy was wrong. Felix's powers of enjoyment were too great to be bounded by a chain; indeed he seemed to like it and regard it as an adjunct of his importance. At first, when his bonds were made of cord, it gave him keen delight to break them. A single bound sufficed; and how clever he felt, and looked, trotting away with a frayed piece of clothes-line hanging from his collar! Thicker and thicker grew the ropes but they all met with the same fate; and Beatrice secretly shared Felix's pride in their destruction. Had she dared she would have boasted openly of his prowess. Several chains went the same way before a cable could be found stout enough to hold him. Now he was securely tethered but he did not seem to mind; he gnawed at the cable with an expression of great contentment or made it rattle excitingly on the flags of the kitchen floor. No other dog could boast of so magnificent an ornament. . . .

But Effie, it appeared, did not share her friend's affection for Felix. She seldom spoke to him or noticed him. She had never been a great talker, but now she talked much less, and when Timothy entered the kitchen he felt he was disturbing a silence that had endured for days. Once she asked him if he had been seeing Mr. Wimbush. Timothy told her yes; he had run across him in the village and they had had quite a chat. He seemed to like his new job pretty well but didn't think he would stick to it permanently; gardening was his real calling. Effie hesitated and then said, 'Do you think he'll come back to us?'

'I wish he would,' said Timothy, 'but you know, he can't get on with Beatrice.' He thought it was better to say it, but the light faded from

Effie's face and she looked so fragile that he felt concerned for her. 'You don't get out enough,' he said. 'You ought to go for a walk sometimes instead of always to the cinema with Beatrice.'

Again she hesitated. 'We don't go out together now,' she said. 'We haven't been seeing eye to eye just lately.' Timothy said nothing, and Effie went on as if she couldn't help it. 'When you saw Mr. Wimbush, sir, did he happen by any chance to mention me?'

Timothy couldn't remember but he at once said 'Yes, he asked after you very particularly.'

The colour crept back into Effie's cheeks. 'Which day would that be, sir?' she asked. Timothy told her. 'And about what time? And where-abouts did you say it was?' Again she spoke as if under compulsion.

'Just in front of the post-office, I think.'

Her eyes grew distant as though she was fixing them on the scene and she said as casually as she could, 'I don't suppose he's in any special place now – I mean he has the whole river to look after.'

'Yes,' said Timothy, 'he has the run of it, I suppose.'

Effie thought a moment and said, 'It must be very pretty down there, below the bridge.'

'I've always heard so,' said Timothy. 'But it's private property. You should ask Wimbush to take you.'

Effie started and her colour came and went. 'Oh, I couldn't do that, sir, not unless it just happened.'

'Well,' said Timothy smiling. 'Perhaps it will.' He left her, uncertain whether he had cheered her up or not.

Meanwhile, his interests were antiquarian – at least, they took him to antique shops. The Chinese bowl looked lonely: he must find kindred objects to keep it company. Not so expensive, of course; he could never again be guilty of such an extravagance, especially for himself. Besides, he was jealous of the bowl's supremacy; his purchases must be little things, designed to show it off, acolytes kneeling at a shrine. In the choice of these it would have been natural to consult Mrs. Purbright who had a fine taste in such matters; but he was still shy of her and besides he wanted this buying to be a pure act of desire, free from any taint of compromise with another's wishes; and if the price was more than he could afford (and he knew he ought to save money, not spend it) so much the better, he could enjoy the delicious loosening of control, like a high dive, the tingling split second of recklessness that preceded the purchase.

Often he could not wait for the parcel to come through the usual channels but carried it home in his bicycle-basket, bumping dangerously, but more undeniably and effectively his, in this first frenzy of ownership, than it would ever be again.

And so, gradually, the low round table began to be covered with a muster of small objects, foothills to the mountain in their midst; however many he collected there always seemed to be room for one more, and if the pride of possession wore off and he no longer thought of the things as extensions of himself, they soon began to speak for themselves and assert their own individualities, though always with due respect and homage to the divinity that towered above them. For the bowl itself Timothy began to entertain feelings of reverence almost mystical, and he deliberately encouraged himself in this idolatry, believing that by cultivating it he could put himself beyond any temporal vexation of spirit.

Returning one evening from an expedition to Swirrelsford, where most of his pot-hunting was done, Timothy left his parcel in the hall and went up to have a bath, a lustration which had become an accepted prelude to the evening ritual of bowl-worship. Much of his weariness and preoccupation with less important things went down the drain-pipe, and a mood of happy expectancy was born. Bounded by the white enamel of the bath, and the white shiny tiles above them, his thoughts became as hard and glazed and lustrous as the porcelain downstairs. The white soap, the white skin, the white bath towel were further reminders that white is the colour of eternity – the eternity which china, of all the works of man, comes nearest to attaining. Timothy did not go so far as to put on a surplice, but he steeped himself in the white idea until he regained the hall and the package which, when undone, revealed a little vase about six inches high, not white indeed, but as nearly white as the Chinese potter cared to aim at. Holding it lovingly, and mutely instructing it in the life of praise and adoration that lay before it he opened the drawing-room door. But he got no further than the threshold, for scattered on the carpet, like the fallen petals of a peony, lay all that was left of the bull's-blood bowl.

Afterwards, and it was a crowning irony, Timothy discovered that none of the smaller objects on the table had been touched. But for the moment all he could do was to stand and stare, and then to revolve slowly round the remains, keeping as far away from them as he could, like someone suddenly confronted with the corpse of his beloved.

'It doesn't matter, it doesn't matter, it doesn't *matter*,' he kept repeating, until the slogan became meaningless, but gradually the repetition of it calmed him, and he began to wonder what he would say to Effie who, he supposed, was responsible for the bowl's destruction. Resolutely he rehearsed phrases of forgiveness. 'It's quite all right, Effie, anyone might have done it, it's bad luck of course, but china will get broken,' and 'Don't cry, Effie, you couldn't help it, you didn't do it on purpose.' After a while the words began to awaken in his mind echoes of their true meaning and the sense of forgiveness, so much sweeter to the forgiver than the forgiven, began to steal over him. He found himself going much further. 'Really, Effie, you have done me a service by breaking the bowl, I was becoming too much attached to it,' and 'Be careful, Effie, when you're sweeping up the pieces. You might easily cut yourself.' When he was satisfied that he had got into a state of mind becoming to a person who has lost an object valuable from the monetary, but quite worthless from the cosmic standpoint, he rang the bell.

Effie came in with a look of surprised inquiry, shut the door, advanced into the room, and stopped dead, staring horror-struck at the litter on the carpet.

'Whoever done that?' she said at last, in a voice hardly above a whisper.

Timothy hadn't bargained for this. All his mental exercises had been thrown away. He felt entirely at a loss.

'You don't know how it happened?' he said, choosing his words carefully.

'I'm sure I don't, sir. If I break anything I always tell. I don't know why you should pick on me.'

In spite of himself Timothy felt irritated.

'I wasn't picking on you, I only asked you if you knew how it happened.'

Slightly mollified, Effie answered with a sniff.

'I don't know at all, sir. Anything might have done it. It might have been the wind.'

'I don't think it could have been the wind. Besides, the window's shut.'

'Or it might have just rolled off,' said Effie, at last coming nearer, and eyeing the remains with fear and distaste, as if they were a bomb that might go off. 'You'd be surprised the way things roll.'

Timothy admitted that things rolled, but did not think that the bowl could have. In his opinion it had been dropped from a height, it was broken into so many pieces.

By now they had lost their superstitious horror of the corpse, and were standing right over it. The broken edges of the porcelain, which had not felt the air for several hundred years, looked startlingly white against the red.

'I didn't do it,' said Effie. 'That's all I know about it. And it's tempting Providence to leave such valuable things lying about. Why, it might have been stolen. It isn't fair – it's asking for trouble. It's as though you wanted someone to break it.'

Timothy assured her he did not. 'I'm not angry, Effie,' he said with an effort. 'I just want to know how it happened. I don't suppose Beatrice has said anything?'

Effie, who had been teetering sideways, drew herself up.

'I wouldn't say anything behind Beatrice's back,' she said. 'She wouldn't tell me in any case, she's been funny lately. You must ask her yourself, sir, but she won't stay to be cross-questioned like I have. She has too much pride. A human being isn't like a bit of china that can't be upset no matter what you do to it.' And with this ill-chosen simile Effie withdrew, in all the dignity of wounded feelings.

Little as Timothy relished the prospect of his interview with Beatrice, it never occurred to him either that she had not broken the bowl or that she would deny having done so. But she did most emphatically deny it; she never, she said, went into the drawing-room unless expressly summoned; the drawing-room was Effie's department, and what should she be doing there? She was bitterly insulted; she said she had never worked in a house where such things happened and such accusations were made; she had only seen the bowl two or three times and hardly knew what it looked like. They were both perfectly innocent, but since Mr. Casson chose to believe that they were both guilty they would join together to replace the bowl even if it took the last penny of their savings.

Timothy's exercise in forgiveness was wasted, for there was no one to forgive.

To his surprise neither of the women even offered to give notice. Indeed, they never addressed a word to him and only answered, if they answered at all, in monosyllables. And, he soon discovered, they spoke to each other as little as they spoke to him. In the kitchen, when he was compelled to visit it, absolute silence reigned. The silence lay about the house in layers, thicker in some places than in others. Here and there it was so dense one seemed to be swimming in it, breasting the waves; elsewhere it merely gave an impression of greater emptiness and space, and a ghostly feeling of recent habitation, as though someone who had been in the room had just gone out, and left it waiting and expectant.

And where was Mrs. Burnett? Timothy was not very observant, and sometimes days passed without his noticing her presence, for she only came in the mornings, and when he did see her she was only a bent back and a scrubbing-brush. Now he felt he would like to exchange a word with her, for she was always ready for a talk. But where was she? He searched the house from top to bottom, but there was no charwoman, only Effie on her knees apparently doing the charwoman's work.

'Effie,' he said, and his voice echoed in the silence like a stone striking against the walls of a well, 'what has happened to Mrs. Burnett?'

Effie's eyebrows registered surprise at Timothy's daring to transgress the silence code. Then she staggered to her feet and closed her eyes.

'It's my back,' she complained, in a voice hardly above a whisper.

'I'm so sorry. But why are you doing Mrs. Burnett's work, Effie?' Timothy persisted.

Effie turned a blank face, as though the name of Mrs. Burnett conveyed nothing to her.

'She's not here, sir. She's not been here for several days. Ever since the vase was broken,' she added, rather as though the breaking of the vase had been Timothy's culminating offence.

So that was it. Mrs. Burnett was one of the casualties of the vase. Perhaps she thought that Timothy had accused her of breaking it. Perhaps she had broken it. Why hadn't he thought of asking her? Suddenly he remembered why.

'But the vase was broken in the afternoon – it was all right when I went out after lunch, and Mrs. Burnett only comes in the mornings.'

Effie's outraged glance suggested that he had said something monstrously unfair. 'She said she did not wish to stay.' Effie clearly wanted him to think that Mrs. Burnett had shared in the general disgust over the vase episode; but Timothy was not convinced. Perhaps Effie was concealing something.

'She seemed quite happy before,' he ventured, though it was incongruous to think of happiness in connection with the Old Rectory.

'Mrs. Burnett was not all what she seemed, sir. She was not at all sincere.'

'Oh?'

'She took no pride in her work and had a very jealous disposition.'

'Had she?'

'Yes, sir, those things had nothing to do with her, they weren't part of her work.'

'What things?'

'I couldn't mention them to you, sir, I was so upset. She interfered, that's all.'

287

'Perhaps Beatrice could tell me,' said Timothy rashly. Effie's thin lips tightened. 'It's no good asking Beatrice, sir. Beatrice knows nothing where I am concerned. It's better to bury them in the past.'

'I'm afraid I don't understand what you're talking about.'

'No, sir, and for decency, if for no other reason.'

Effie had adopted Beatrice's most discouraging manner, but Timothy's curiosity was aroused.

'I didn't know she was that kind of woman,' he suggested. Effie shrugged and spiralled.

'She wouldn't have looked at the things, sir, if she had been a modest woman, much less passed a remark. And in any case it wasn't her business.'

'What wasn't?'

'I have charge of your things, sir, and I hope I look after them all right.'

'Indeed you do, Effie. Who says you don't?' Effie's lips began to tremble.

'She did, sir. She made an insinuation about my work.'

'You should have come to me.'

'I couldn't, sir, in a matter of that kind. It wasn't for a gentleman to hear.'

Timothy was more than ever intrigued. Perhaps, if he could prevent Effie from bursting into tears, he might yet find out what Mrs. Burnett had done.

'I'm quite old, you know, Effie,' he said. 'I don't suppose I should be shocked.'

'It was the impertinence, sir, and the surprise. I couldn't help flaring up.'

'Can you remember what she said?'

'Remember, sir, am I likely to forget? She shouldn't have been in the room at all by rights, she ought to have finished it.'

'Yes, but what did she say?'

'She said she'd only come to fetch her dustpan and brush, which she always leaves about, as you must have noticed, sir, but I knew better.'

'Well, there was nothing really rude in that.'

'No, sir, it was what she said afterwards.' Again Effie's face began to crinkle.

'And she couldn't really see them properly, only just the— Oh, I *can't* say it!'

'Please do. You'll feel better if you tell me.'

Effie spoke as solemnly as if she was taking an oath.

'She said they ought to go to the wash.'

'What ought to?'

Effie's manner became extremely agitated.

'I wouldn't tell you, sir, if you didn't force me to. It was your pyjamas.' She put her hand to her forehead.

'But did they?'

All at once Effie recovered her poise and her dignity. 'No, sir, if they had, I should have sent them. It was not for her to pry, and I told her so.'

'You were quite right, it wasn't. What did she say?'

'She answered me back, sir. She's a violent-tempered woman, Mrs. Burnett, she's like Beatrice for that. But I gave her as good as she got, and as calm as I am now. I said, "Leave those pyjamas to me, please." '

'And what did she reply?'

'I'd rather not say, sir. These village woman have no delicacy in such matters. They live all together like animals, so they have no respect. She couldn't see any difference between your pyjamas and her husband's.'

'Did she say so?'

'No, but she presumed it. She said she knew more about pyjamas than I did.'

'Good heavens!'

'But I didn't mind her dirty tongue. It was the interference, the interference with my work. And criticising me, too, when I was defending your interests. I should have known without looking whether they wanted sending to the wash. Of course, she was jealous, plain jealous. I just said, "They're not your pyjamas. . . ." '

'Quite right.'

' "And I'll thank you not to poke your nose into them." '

'Well, I suppose she hadn't quite done that.'

'No, sir, but to all intents and purposes she had. So she said, "Good-day, you won't be seeing me any more," and flounced out, not even taking her dust-pan and brush.' Effie's nose wrinkled at the remembrance; indignation had dried her tears. 'So that's why I'm doing her work, sir, though I never said I would, and it's too much for me, or for any woman. Beatrice should be doing it by rights.'

Dropping on to her knees Effie resumed her scrubbing, with a desperate, spasmodic vigour, as if she were trying to scrub away from the Old Rectory every trace of Mrs. Burnett. But with the closing of the door the harsh sound ceased, and silence enfolded the house. This was Effie's swan-song.

*   *   *

After two or three more days of being deprived of the sound of the human voice Timothy grew restive. The house was so oppressive that he spent as much time as possible out of doors, listening to the cheerful if inarticulate sounds of summer. He even went out after dinner and sometimes ventured into the Fisherman's Arms, though he was shy of doing that, in case he should meet the people who had coupled his name so disagreeably with Vera's. Her infrequent letters seldom failed to remind him of that insult; like the utterances of Hamlet's father, they were hollow with injunctions to vengeance. Her friends could tell him nothing more of her than he already knew, and they were a little reserved with him, which was not to be wondered at, for he only frequented them when she was there. Though beer did not suit him he would try to feel he was enjoying it; seen in the long glass clasping his tankard, he looked comfortable, even if he was not. The rustics were always welcoming, but he could never exchange more than a few sentences with them of the most general character, into which nothing more personal than the feeling of good will entered. He began to wonder if he was losing the power of speech. Then, with a timid and self-conscious 'Goodnight all,' he would creep back, under cover of the late summer twilight, to the dark house and the detesting maids, and in silence and indigestion betake himself to bed.

Soon he was driven to try to make a confidant of Simpson.

'Do they ever speak to you, Simpson?' he asked.

'Well, in a manner of speaking, they do,' said Simpson guardedly. 'That is Beatrice, she still speaks, though not like she used to, and the other's voice was always so faint, it don't make much difference if she speaks or not. It makes it so bad for everybody. I don't know what I should do if I hadn't got the wireless.'

The wireless! Timothy had never taken advantage of the opportunities of communication that the wireless offered. Now he turned it on by the hour, as loud as it would go, and the house was resonant with synthetic sound. Often he forgot to turn it off, and coming home after an absence of perhaps some hours, he would hear a resolute voice booming from the drawing-room and imagine for a moment that somebody had called. When he got in, the room seemed all the emptier for not being silent.

But listening is not the same thing as talking, nor has it the same power of relieving loneliness. Under cover of the radio's blare Timothy caught himself talking to himself, a symptom that alarmed him, especially as what he said in these soliloquies was nearly always of a self-justificatory nature and sometimes expressed in the third person.

'Timothy Casson' (he heard) 'had always wanted to get on well with the inhabitants of Upton; he had made continual demonstrations of good will, as witness the following instances.' (The instances followed, at great length.) 'It was they, they, who refused his advances and cold-shouldered him; and for the inevitable ensuing tragedy they alone were to blame.' Tragedy? Had he got persecution-mania? Surely not, he, he, the popular, hospitable, much-loved padrone of the Villa Lucertola?

On the banks of the Brenta the maize was ripening again, the grapes were swelling, and three visitors from England were expected that very evening. What excitement reigned, what tireless happy industry! Rooms were turned out, mattresses put out into the rain to air. 'But surely, Amalia, they will get wet! They will be dangerous! The signori will catch a terrible, infective cold! Please bring them in, and put them round the stove!'

'But, signore, the air always does good! A little rain does not matter at all! In England, yes, where the air is thick with fog and smoke; but in Italy we have l'aria pura, limpida, and the mattresses are all the better for it!'

More housewifely preparations; bath-mats, soap, towels, firewood for the bath, for the water has to be heated in a cylinder, by hot air, a long, perilous process, pregnant with opportunities for explosion.

'The signori will take a bath the very moment they arrive?'

'Well, perhaps not the *very* moment, Amalia; they may want to have a rest first, they will be tired after a night in the train.'

'But, signore, the signori inglesi always want a bath before anything else; you have often told us so; there is nothing the English hate so much as being dirty!'

'Well, perhaps you're right; as soon as they come I'll tell them the bath is ready for them.' 'Va bene, signore,' and having won her point, she bustles off.

Darling Amalia, but sometimes, it must be confessed, she is a little stubborn. She is so used to ruling the household, as all good Italian housewives are, that she has got into the habit of ruling Timothy, too.

But much still remains to be done. The food has all been arranged for; that is Amalia's province, and Timothy is only too glad to have it taken off his hands. But the drinks, they are his concern, the choice of white or red, of a fiasco of Orvieto or Chianti (decried by Armando as made-up, fortified wines), or the wine of the district, much purer and more wholesome (according to Armando) but an acquired taste, sour and rough to a palate unaccustomed to it. And here is the vermouth and the gin, the gin at which Armando holds up his hands in horror:

'troppo forte!' – much too strong for the uncorrupted constitutions of wine-loving Italians. What a lot of alcoholic support these foreigners seem to need! And now for the liqueurs. Aurum, yes, strega yes, good Italian products, gentle to the mouth and balm to the stomach. But the heroic travellers may also require brandy to revive them. Here is the bottle all right, but where is the brandy? Sunk to the very bottom, a couple of tablespoonsful at most. Timothy is sure the bottle was three parts full when he last looked at it. He summons Armando. 'But what can have happened to it, Armando?' Armando shakes his head and looks blank. 'I don't know, sir. None of us have touched it. Amalia does not drink cognac, nor do I. It is much too strong for us; we do not even know the taste of it. Perhaps you left the cork out and it evaporated.' Timothy looks doubtful. 'Perhaps the rats found it, and drank it by dipping their tails in the bottle and then licking them. They are intelligent beasts and known to be fond of cognac.' Timothy laughs. 'But they couldn't put the cork back again, could they?' Armando looks grave and shrugs his shoulders. 'I hope the signore does not suspect . . .?' 'Of course not, Armando. I'm sure there is some natural explanation. Perhaps in future I had better keep the bottle in my medicine-cupboard, in case any of us should feel ill. Brandy is really a medicine.' Armando is all smiles again. 'As the signore wishes. Shall I go and buy another bottle from the trattoria?' 'I think you had better, there is just time.'

'You have been listening to the broadcast of a conversation between Mr. Timothy Casson, late of the Villa Lucertola, near Venice, and his servants, Amalia and Armando. Mr. Casson lived much in Italy during the Fascist régime, and was inclined to believe that at any rate the humbler part of the Italian population surpassed our own working-classes in such qualities as commonsense, honesty and tractability. This little dialogue, which is authentic and comes from a well-stored memory, shows that Mr. Casson realises that he has done our people an injustice, and is anxious to make amends. You will have to look a long time before you find any virtues in a Fascist. Isn't that true, Mr. Casson?' 'Yes, I think it is.' 'And you would agree that we must fight to the last drop of our blood to extirpate this evil from our midst, as much for their sakes as for ours?' 'I should.' 'And you would agree that the only good Fascist is a dead Fascist?' 'Yes.' 'Thank you, Mr. Casson.'

A tremendous volley of applause greeted Timothy's recantation. It died away to a murmur and suddenly swelled to an even greater volume than before, as though Timothy was showing himself to the audience. Again and again it rose and died away. The house vibrated with it;

Timothy could almost see tormented particles of ether slapping against each other. He rolled off the bed (for things do roll sometimes) on which he had been having his siesta and went downstairs to turn the wireless off. Instantly the cohorts of silence, which had been waiting outside, on the roof, under the eaves, pressing against the doors and windows, entered and took possession. Unpleasant as the clapping had been, the ensuing vacancy was worse, and Timothy hurried out of the house into the sunshine.

In the stable-yard he found Nelson with his car. He often dropped in to have a look at it when his duties brought him that way. Sometimes he tinkered with it, sometimes he stared at it with a bemused expression, much as Timothy used to stare at his bowl. Timothy hadn't seen the policeman since before the Wimbush episode, and was rather chary of encountering him, so many question-marks hovered gnat-like between them. And Nelson's assumptions of ignorance were so tactful that it was difficult to know where to begin; for everything that Timothy said seemed to cause him intense astonishment – Not really! You don't say so! – totally at variance with his habitual demeanour of imperturbable, unsurprisable omniscience.

'And so Wimbush has gone,' Timothy concluded lamely. 'I'm very sorry.'

'In view of what you have just stated, sir,' said Nelson, 'Wimbush would seem to have acted hasty. In the story as it was told to me, told to me,' he repeated with emphasis, 'he seems to have been subjected to acts of provocation extending over a period of many months.'

Timothy agreed that this was so.

'Sooner or later,' he added rancorously, 'everyone seems to quarrel with Beatrice. It's Effie now.'

Nelson expressed so much sympathy and concern that Timothy told him the whole story of the broken bowl, and the present unsatisfactory state of affairs. 'I really don't know what to do,' he wound up. 'I can't understand why they don't both leave.'

'You can't, sir?' said Nelson, with his loftiest air of patronage. 'I can.' Timothy begged for enlightenment.

'Well, first of all it's a good place, sir, and they wouldn't get a better. And secondly Beatrice wouldn't leave, she's that fond of Felix.'

'I see,' said Timothy. 'But Effie? Effie isn't fond of Felix, and as far I can judge she isn't any longer very fond of Beatrice.'

'There are others she might be attached to,' said Nelson, in a voice so portentous and mysterious that Timothy exclaimed, 'You don't mean me?'

'It wouldn't be outside Nature if she was,' replied Nelson. 'But I didn't mean you, sir. She doesn't cast her eyes as high as that, she looks nearer to the ground.'

Involuntarily Timothy, too, looked down, as though hoping to find in the cobbles of the stable-yard a clue to why Effie wanted to stay. Nelson enjoyed his bewilderment.

'Of course if the other party was free it might be a different story.'

Still Timothy couldn't guess and Nelson said, 'We policemen don't gossip, otherwise I should tell you it was Wimbush.' He paused to relish Timothy's astonishment. 'Why, it's an open secret. She won't leave, sir, not as long as Wimbush is about. You can set your mind at rest.'

'But that's just what I can't do,' said Timothy, 'when they won't speak to each other, or to me.'

Nelson straightened himself.

'Was the bowl an object of value, may I ask?'

'Well, I gave over seventy pounds for it.'

The policeman whistled.

'It must have been a very special make of bowl. You could purchase a small car for that.'

'It was. Ming, possibly.'

Timothy hoped that Nelson would ask him what Ming was, but the policeman seldom asked a question unless it was going to cost the questioned some effort to reply.

'And you think it may have been broken in malice?'

Timothy explained that he didn't see how otherwise it could have been smashed into so many pieces. The table was only a foot or so above the floor, and the carpet was thick. It must have been thrown down violently, or hit with something hard.

'Has anyone anything against you, sir?' asked Nelson.

Timothy thought a long, long while. The whole history of his sojourn in Upton began to unroll itself. Yes, plenty of people had something against him. But that way madness lies.

'Not that I know of, Nelson.'

'You insured the article, of course?' With the feelings of guilt that Nelson's demeanour always engendered, Timothy confessed that he had not.

'That was a mistake, if I may say so, sir. Did you tell them that the article was not insured?'

'Who?'

'The suspected persons.'

'No, I didn't,' said Timothy. 'They weren't interested in my loss, only in the injury to their own pride.'

He spoke bitterly, but Nelson ignored this intrusion of the personal and said thoughtfully:

'Then they're not to know. If an Insurance Company have grounds for suspecting that an object or article of value has been damaged in malice, they may send down a representative to make inquiries, which being so, a charge may be made. Did you preserve the fragments of this ornamental bowl, sir?'

Timothy said he had.

'In that case finger-prints could be taken.' He looked hard at Timothy's hand. 'Would it surprise you to learn, sir, that many people, especially those of the class in question, object to having their finger-prints taken?'

'I shouldn't like it myself,' Timothy admitted.

'Exactly, sir, and you are an educated gentleman and almost, in the matter referred to, an innocent, if I may say so. Those of whom the allegations have been made will be much more upset, especially if interrogated in the first instance by a man in uniform.'

A faint shiver of distaste went through Timothy.

'What did you think of doing, Nelson?'

'Well, sir, officially it would be improper for me to do anything. But having regard to the suspicions entertained and the identical behaviour of the persons concerned, I should not stand on etiquette, but entering the kitchen as I am entitled to do with your permission and finding the women there, not having been notified of my visit, or in any way fore-warned, I should put before them in the plainest terms the consequences likely to ensue from the attitude they are at present adopting.' Nelson paused, thankful and proud to see daylight through the tunnel of the sentence. 'The impact of a policeman,' he went on, 'is something you wouldn't understand on the uneducated, especially when allegations have been made. To speak frankly they get the wind up and let out what under normal circumstances they would keep in.'

Timothy pondered.

'It's most obliging of you, Nelson. When did you think of doing this?'

Nelson's face lit up.

'I'm free now, sir, and the women referred to are sitting at the kitchen table over their elevenses, though not speaking.'

Timothy glanced through the window. Yes, there they were, the unsuspecting suspects, drinking their tea and nursing their estrangement. They looked worn and old. He disliked the idea of Nelson's shock tactics; he felt doubtful of their legality; he had an uneasy feeling that a year ago he would have unhesitatingly declined the policeman's offer. But much had happened since then; unsettled scores had mounted up, and justice was justice. To discover the culprit would not restore the bowl or the world which had been shattered with it; but it would restore, in a small degree, the balance of fair dealing which, Timothy thought, was tipping more and more against him.

'All right, Nelson,' he said, almost ungraciously. 'You go if you want to.' He felt much the same as he had when telling Wimbush he might punish Felix.

'Very good, sir,' said Nelson, saluting smartly. Tall, blue and young, helmeted and ominous as Achilles, he strode in the bright sunlight towards the kitchen door.

'And so, my dear Magda,' wrote Timothy, 'my experiment in the life of the pure æsthetic emotion came to a sad end. I don't feel I can take it up again, for, though I know this is a weakness, one cannot altogether dissociate in something the element that pleases one from the thing itself. They are inseparable, I think. I could give you a list of the many qualities in you which delight me; but they are only real to me because of you. If – absit omen – you died, and I tried to find them in other people, or, against all probability, in one other person, they wouldn't mean the same to me, because they wouldn't be you. How silly of me to labour this! – what I mean is, I was attached to the bowl itself, not only for its beauty, nor because it was mine. How I wish that the virtues and graces could be appreciated apart from the vehicles that hold them! Then, contemplating them, meditating upon them, one could never be lonely. But I am lonely, and I long for the act of hospitality which has been denied me for so long. And there is no one I should like to share it with so much as you. Do come, dear Magda, I am sure you could get away just for a week-end. I won't hold out any inducements, for there aren't any, only my need of you. Here, I get involved in so many barren entanglements and have such violent revulsions of feeling, all about nothing. . . .'

More and more obsessed by what was passing in the kitchen, he put down his pen and went out through the french window into the garden. The sunshine proved to be a shy, capricious blessing, and shorter-lived than one's faith in it. Still, it lit up the grass and warmed the flesh, if not the spirit. The place was too familiar now for him to take much notice of it; the magic of novelty had worn off, and he no longer felt that the flowers bloomed more brightly because his eye rested on them. It was Miss Chadwick's garden, not his. He was under contract to keep it up for her, not for himself. Even the boat-house, at which he glanced in passing, sheltered a stale secret. Was it his fault that his visual sense had sickened, and that none of his senses served him as they had last year? Was it his fault that he no longer responded to these things and that his inner life, all that was left of it, nourished itself on enmity and pain? Surely there was some way out, some altar which could still receive his offerings? All his life he had beguiled himself with the mirage of a coming fulfilment; he had no idea what it would be, any more than a plant can foretell its flower, but he believed implicitly in the movement towards fruition. And now it had stopped; the sap no longer rose; the flowers had withered and on the branches hung fruit that was not good to eat. . . .

Nelson was striding across the lawn towards him, pride in his step and triumph in his eye.

'It's all right, sir,' his young voice sang. 'One of them's owned up.'

'Oh which, Nelson?'

'Beatrice, she done it. Only it was an accident. She was holding the ornament up to the light, she said, to see the markings better, and it slipped through her fingers. She's a tough one, that old girl. I didn't half have a job with her. They're all right now, they're both crying their eyes out. You won't have any more trouble with them, sir, they'll eat out of your hand.'

CHAPTER XXIII

TIMOTHY'S reaction was one of unmixed relief. He could almost see the smoke-cloud of suspicion in which they had all three been living pouring out through the windows and rolling away over the roof of the Old Rectory, obligingly making off with many other, older grievances which had been lurking in its holes and corners. A general spring-clean. Even in the garden, the air seemed fresher, easier to breathe. Ripe for reconciliation, armed anew with forgiveness, he walked towards the house.

It now seemed an easy task to finish his letter to Magda. Even their points of difference seemed convenient pegs on which to hang his thoughts. He made prodigious efforts to meet her views. He said that he was gradually realising the virtues that resided in the proletariat, and coming to a better understanding of their point of view. It might not be such a bad thing after all, he said, if we were governed by them, for their feelings were still direct and natural, not vitiated by theories of behaviour. If an instinct of self-preservation made them try to cover up their faults, it was after all only an instinct of decency, like covering one's body. But they had too much conscience not to suffer from the repression, suffer really far more than he did, who could interpose between himself and his remorse all kinds of alleviating sublimations and rationalisations, the infertile offspring begotten upon the intellect by the unconscious mind. And when they repented, they repented whole-heartedly, they cried their eyes out, whereas his remained dry.

Confiding all this to Magda, he was aware that he was investing her with a personality very unlike her own, but did that matter? He must tell someone, and if his letter meant nothing else to her, it would show her how much he wanted her to come.

Having sealed the envelope he waited, vaguely expecting that Beatrice would come in bringing the tearful explanations he was only too anxious to meet half-way. But when an hour had passed and she did not come he decided to go in search of her. It was nearly lunch-time.

The maids were sitting in the kitchen, both crying, and no preparations were being made for lunch. Felix had his head on Beatrice's lap. When Timothy entered he jumped up, dragging his chain across the flagstones, and made his usual show of welcome. Beatrice and Effie hardly raised their eyes. Timothy did not know what to say but at last he blurted out something about being so glad that the mystery of the bowl had been cleared up. He was perfectly satisfied, he said, and the matter could now be closed.

Neither of them answered but both got up and began to move about the kitchen, Felix following Beatrice with devoted eyes, as far as the chain would let him. Embarrassed, Timothy began to stroke Felix who at once sat on his feet and leaned against him, butting him gently with his head. 'Felix seems in very good spirits,' said Timothy idiotically, trying to stem the tide of the dog's affection, which had just reached biting stage. 'Now, Felix, be careful of my wrist-watch.' Effie went out of the room and Timothy said awkwardly, still trying to curb Felix's transports, 'He does do credit to you, Beatrice. I think he's grown in the last four weeks.' Beatrice did not look round, but her sobs started afresh. 'Please don't think any more about the bowl,' said Timothy. 'It's perfectly all right and I quite understand your not wanting to tell me before. Look at Felix,' he went on fatuously. 'He doesn't worry about breakages, do you, Felix?' Felix, who always liked to be spoken to, grinned widely and deeply. His ears went back a quarter of an inch, making his expression foolish beyond words. 'He is a good dog, isn't he?' Timothy said, for Felix liked to be called good, and did not, as most Christians would, resent it as a deadly insult. 'He *has* found a friend in you, Beatrice. I don't know what he'd do without you.' But Beatrice wouldn't be drawn, and hopeless of breaking her Trappist silence, Timothy left the kitchen.

He found Effie laying the table.

'I'm afraid Beatrice is taking this very hard, Effie,' he said in a low voice.

'It's not to be surprised at, sir, when you set the policeman on us,' Effie answered. Her voice trembled but it was a voice, and Timothy felt relieved.

'Well, that was Nelson's idea, I didn't particularly want him to. But it's better to have the whole thing cleared up, don't you agree? Though I never thought it was you, Effie, you know that.'

'He upset us both so terribly,' said Effie. 'He showed no consideration at all, we might have been in the dock. It was horrible the way he went at us. You wouldn't believe it, not in such a young man.'

'I suppose they get used to talking in that way to people,' said Timothy.

'I knew it was something when he came in,' said Effie, a certain relish creeping into her voice. 'He had me crying at once, oh it was awful the way his eyes bored into you, just like gimblets. Oh, I wonder he could.'

'Still, all's well that ends well,' Timothy soothed her.

'It was wonderful the way Beatrice held out,' said Effie. 'She gave him word for word. I dursn't have, in her place. You could see he was a man, without his helmet. That's what made it worse. He's so big he seemed to take up all the kitchen. Oh, I was glad it wasn't me. Of course, he never laid hands on us.'

'I should think not.'

'They do sometimes . . . you read of cases. And his voice was awful when he said, "Do you want your finger-prints taken?" That was when Beatrice gave way.'

'If only she'd told us at *first*, Effie.'

'That's what I said to her, sir. And I shan't ever forgive her. She let me suffer in silence. If it hadn't been for him! But it was dreadful the way he went at us, two helpless women, for Felix is no good. He didn't try to bite him or anything. I still hardly know what I'm doing. I said to Beatrice, "Wasn't it lucky I wasn't out, you might have had to face him alone." ' Effie began to weep again.

'Please don't cry, Effie.'

'Oh no, sir, I wouldn't have missed it, of course, him being so angry and all that, I didn't think such a young man could be, and his buttons flashing. I should have confessed if Beatrice hadn't, I couldn't have helped myself.'

'I'm afraid Beatrice doesn't seem very happy,' said Timothy.

'Well, sir, what could you expect? It was one against two.'

Three or four uneasy days passed. Timothy hoped that things would settle down, but they didn't; Beatrice remained offended, sulky and mute, and Effie also retired behind a cloud of silence. Then the letter arrived. The scrap of lined paper bore no address or date, but the post-mark on the envelope was Swirrelsford.

SIR,

I think you ought to know it wasn't Beatrice Kinghorn that broke your piece of property nor Effie either but someone else who won't tell, not even if you call a policeman.

FROM SOMEONE WHO WISHES FAIR PLAY FOR ALL.

Timothy was puzzled by the letter itself and still more by the question of how to treat it. He was heartily tired of the subject of the bowl and would have gladly let it drop, but the re-opening of the mystery fretted him and he thought that both the women were still labouring under a sense of wrong. Like a relapse in an illness from which one believes one has recovered, it found him with impaired resistance, and all the more susceptible to disappointment. Try as he might to free himself, he seemed fated to flounder more deeply in the quick-sands of other people's feelings. Far better have no feelings at all, he told himself, than waste his time trying to make adjustments with the unadjustable. Kant's maxim that every human being should be treated as an end in himself was a counsel of perfection, for any human being, so treated, would see to it that his requirements were unending.

Usually one has quite a definite idea, though it may be mistaken, of what will happen if one pursues a certain policy. Mentally Timothy confronted Beatrice with the letter, but his prophetic soul gave him no inkling of what her reaction would be. He tried it on Effie, with the same lack of result. Then, in imagination he summoned them both to him, and flashed the letter at them simultaneously. But still nothing happened; the situation would not develop, the needle of intuition never quivered, it seemed to have lost its propensity for the North.

Finally he invoked the puissant shade of Nelson, helmet in hand, buttons gleaming, and this time the needle did move; it rotated wildly through all the points of the compass. Timothy took this as a warning not to consult Nelson.

There remained Mrs. Purbright. Timothy had not overcome his shyness with her; he felt for her as one might feel for a doctor, or a priest, to whom one has taken some fancied ailment, or some scruple of conscience, and profiting by the consultant's sympathy and readiness to come half way, has so overcharged the episode with meaning that it can only afterwards be referred to with a smile and a shrug; but meanwhile, as on the sands at low water, there remain the marks of the high tide, of which each is secretly envious yet ashamed.

This time, he told himself, the conversation should not leave the ground.

He found Mrs. Purbright, as he had hoped he would, alone. She was flushed and agitated and vaguer than usual. Several times her mind started out in quest of parallels and parables but forgot what it was looking for and returned empty. She seemed to be holding him off with small talk. Timothy was not prepared for this and rather resented it; it was he, not she, who was to keep the conversation earth-bound. At last he said, 'You remember my bowl, Mrs. Purbright?'

'Your bowl, Mr. Casson? I'm sure I do, but remind me.'

Describing it gave Timothy a double pang, one for its loss and another for the thought that beauty should be so quickly forgotten.

'Of course, I remember it perfectly.'

But Timothy wasn't sure she did.

'Well, it's been broken.' A second's pause followed this announcement. Then Mrs. Purbright said:

'Oh, how terrible for you. What a calamity. What a cruel loss. I do sympathise.' Her glance strayed round the room; it was well bowled, over-bowled – one might make a joke about that. Every table seemed to bear a bowl, some were upturned and carried on their bases other bowls, hour-glass wise. Confronted by so many bowls it seemed frivolous to complain of the loss of one.

'Of course, the loss was nothing,' Timothy said, mendaciously. 'It's what happened afterwards that I wanted to tell you about. May I?'

'Please do,' Mrs. Purbright murmured. 'Perhaps I could help. I've had so much experience of mending china.'

Having finished his recital Timothy produced the anonymous letter. Long-sighted, Mrs. Purbright held it away from her. It looked dirty and germ-laden in her blue-veined, blue-ringed hand. She will want a wash afterwards, thought Timothy. Mrs. Purbright gave him back the letter with a sigh.

'How pathetic, how unhelpful,' she said.

'Can you think of anyone who might have written it?' asked Timothy.

Mrs. Purbright suggested it might have been a friend of Beatrice's.

'Yes, I suppose so,' said Timothy. 'But it doesn't get us any further, does it, and what an awkward position it puts me in! How they love to shift the blame on someone else! What does the writer of that letter expect me to think? It means that I shall now suspect three people instead of two, though who the third is I've no idea. What would you do if you were me?'

'Oh, Mr. Casson' – Mrs. Purbright's face took on a hunted, almost agonised look. 'Don't appeal to me. Who am I to give advice? I tried to advise you once before, do you remember, in a certain matter?'

Timothy nodded.

'You took it most kindly, with exemplary Christian patience, but what a mistake it was! I mean, to suppose that I knew what was best for you! What presumption!'

'I didn't think so,' said Timothy, astonished. 'The pity was that circumstances made your advice unworkable.'

'They always would,' declared Mrs. Purbright. 'The only thing is to act according to your own sense of the matter.'

'My sense of the matter was to consult you.'

Mrs. Purbright groaned.

'I deserve it, I deserve it. But, Mr. Casson, let the lesson in humility be mine for once. Don't tempt me to be meddlesome. Do you know, I sometimes think you bring out the worst in people?'

'Do I?' exclaimed Timothy.

'Yes, somehow with you it is difficult not to give way to one's beset-ting sins. I believe you expect it of us.'

'I'm quite sure I don't,' said Timothy, bewildered by this novel view of his requirements.

'Where would you be,' said Mrs. Purbright suddenly, 'how would you feel about yourself, if nearly everyone in Upton hadn't done some-thing to hurt and mortify you?'

'I must have notice of that question,' Timothy said. He thought for a moment, trying to see where the trap lurked, for he was sure there was one. 'I should be in an altogether more comfortable state of mind,' he said lamely.

'Would you?' said Mrs. Purbright, with a hint of scepticism in her voice. 'Supposing it was you who had prevented Mr. Timothy Casson from rowing on the river? Supposing it was you who had broken his cher-ished bowl? Supposing it was you who had sulked and refused to speak to him, supposing it was you who had written him an anonymous letter?'

'I should be properly ashamed, I hope,' said Timothy, waxing indig-nant at the picture of this monster to whom Mrs. Purbright was liken-ing him.

'Exactly,' said Mrs. Purbright. 'With all our faults and tiresomeness you must allow us this – we haven't made you feel ashamed.'

So that was the trap and he had fallen into it. Timothy pondered over the implications of Mrs. Purbright's inquisition. A figure emerged very well pleased with himself, timid and resentful; swollen with vanity at the idea of other people's failings, feeding his self-righteousness on his awareness of their sins, indeed, like an agent-provocateur, prompt-ing and drawing out those sins, so that he might seem the more virtu-ous by comparison.

'I don't see why you say "we", Mrs. Purbright,' he said, peevishly. 'You haven't hurt or mortified me. Why do you include yourself with those who have – if they have?'

She did not answer at once, and he saw that he had puzzled her.

'Oh, Mr. Casson,' she said at length. 'But are we not all at fault?' A suggestion of her husband's pulpit utterance crept into her voice. 'What right have I to say that I am not the worst of sinners?'

'You have every right,' Timothy said crossly. 'And I don't think it's fair that you should enrol yourself with my . . . my enemies, if you like, so as to make it harder for me to attack them.'

'Attack them?' said Mrs. Purbright, wonderingly. 'Enemies? I didn't say enemies, I said sinners. Indeed, I hope we are not enemies. Or do you think they are the same thing?'

Another trap. Perhaps he did think that enemies and sinners were the same thing. But he was determined to dislodge Mrs. Purbright from her stronghold of sinnerdom, even if the conversation had to leave the ground and be fought out in the air.

'It is possible to excel, isn't it?' he demanded.

'Certainly,' agreed Mrs. Purbright, surprised.

'And if you were, say, Paderewski or Tilden, it would be generally acknowledged that you played the piano, or lawn tennis, better than most people?'

'Very true.'

'And if you played them better than other people you would, being an intelligent person, know that you did?'

'I believe that the great executants are notoriously vain,' said Mrs. Purbright.

'Yes, but vanity apart, would not their pre-eminence be a fact, that could not be gainsaid?'

'Even great reputations in the arts are at the mercy of fashion.'

'Yes, but not the greatest. The greatest are above criticism; they do not abide our question. And are not the virtuosi, the champions, the aces, sustained and confirmed in their supremacy, by a conviction, every time they exercise their art, that they are better at it than other people?'

'They may be,' said Mrs. Purbright. 'I don't know. I could never play lawn tennis, or the piano. I was always a duffer.'

Timothy swept this aside.

'And you would not blame them for knowing they were better?'

'No.'

'Or for saying so, if asked, since it would be an affectation, as well as a lie, to deny an obvious truth?'

'No,' said Mrs. Purbright. 'That is what you want me to say, isn't it?' She looked anxiously at Timothy and her breath came quickly.

'Mrs. Purbright,' said Timothy, with all the impressiveness he could muster, 'when you walk down the village street and see three people I will call X, Y and Z, three people who do the village no credit, and are known not to, when you see them and recall all the trouble they have

304

given, the ruined homes, the heartbreaks, the suicides – the' (Timothy curbed his imagination) 'the . . . the sorrow and tragedy they have caused, and when you remember as you must, Mrs. Purbright, you *must*, let me jog your memory – the acts of benevolence, small and great, the unending solicitude for the welfare of other people, even late-comers to the village, who have no claim on you, when you remember the words of gratitude you have listened to, the letters of thanks you have received, when you hear the inarticulate buzz of praise and appreciation which starts up at the mention of your name—' Timothy took a breath – 'do you not think yourself better than those three?'

Mrs. Purbright looked away.

'I should say, there but for the grace of God . . .'

'No!' cried Timothy passionately, and he thumped the arm of the sofa. 'You must never say that – it is a betrayal of the cause of goodness, a gross, vote-catching piece of humbug! What would you think if Paderewski, when the applause was over, came to the front of the platform and said, "Ladies and gentlemen, you clap, but any school-girl could have played that piece as well as I did. Do not mortify and humiliate yourselves, my dear friends, by thinking I play better than you do. I am the worst of players." He fixed his eyes sternly on Mrs. Purbright. 'Would you be impressed by such a declaration? Would you not say that, apart from being a liar, he was pandering to the worst instincts of his audience, their envy of his talent, their fear of feeling small in the presence of his greatness, their desire to be confirmed in their mediocrity?'

'But you said they were applauding him!' cried Mrs. Purbright.

'Only because it is the fashion, and not to applaud would seem superior, as though one possessed more critical judgment than one's neighbour. And anyhow it was just a paltry hand-clapping. But do you know what happened when he had made his speech belittling his talent? The whole audience rose to its feet and cheered and stormed the platform and carried him shoulder-high into the nearest bar, singing, "For he's a jolly good fellow" – because you see, they knew that the tyranny of standards was over and the right to do everything badly had at last been recognised.'

Mrs. Purbright smiled; she thought that Timothy's mood had spent itself in this vision of high jinks at the Albert Hall, but instead he went on with mounting excitement,

'Mrs. Purbright, you are our Paderewski of the moral art. You are the virtuoso of our spiritual life. You excel in goodness.' He stared at her fiercely. 'Admit that you do.'

She was silent.

'Has it come to this, that I must not even *accuse* you of goodness? That you still deny the imputation, even if I acquit you of all responsibility, and lay the blame on the workings of Divine Grace and the intervention of the Saints?'

Still she said nothing.

'Say after me, "I, Volumnia Purbright, am a good woman, much better – and by better I mean better at being good – than ninety-nine per cent. of the inhabitants of Upton, not excepting Timothy Casson. It grieves me to say this because I know it will give offence to many; but in the interests of truth, I must." '

Mrs. Purbright shook her head.

'Then I'll say it for you, and defy you to disagree.'

In an oratorical tone, and addressing the serried ranks of objects round him, he repeated the declaration as nearly as he could, but when he turned to Mrs. Purbright to claim her answer he saw that she was in tears.

Timothy was appalled. The cloud-capped fabric of his fantasy crumbled, reality rushed in, the reality of a woman and a dear friend bludgeoned into tears by an unfeeling interlocutor.

Much more embarrassed than she, he stammered out his apologies. He had to speak, for she could not. 'You bring out the worst in me!' he reproached her, sadly. 'It's because I never seem to talk to anyone now – I'm out of practice,' he maundered on, 'and the machinery gets hot from not being used. I didn't mean to talk like that. It was the way an old friend of mine used to talk, and I must have caught it from him. I didn't really mean what I said. How did it all begin? I know, I asked you about my servants, and you said you couldn't advise me because we were all sinners. You were quite right, of course.'

Mrs. Purbright was beginning to recover herself. 'In my infancy,' she began, dropped that thread and started again. 'Soon after Edward and I were married. . . .' But that cock wouldn't fight either. 'Just before you came to Upton. . . .' Still the annals of her past life yielded no precedent to mitigate the impact of the present; she had to face it as it was.

'I wasn't really upset,' she said, 'only it is so long since anyone thought it worth while to talk to me like that. I'm glad you did, for it has cleared my mind, and now I can give you some advice, if you still want it.'

Timothy nodded.

'You must get rid of them,' she said, 'misery-makers, enemies of happiness.'

Timothy hadn't expected this.

'Oh, but I couldn't. They haven't really done anything, besides, I should never get any others.'

'All the same, I should get rid of them.'

'I'm quite fond of them in a way.'

'You must steel yourself.'

'But they've done a lot of work for me.'

'You must harden your heart.'

'But they *won't go*!'

'Then you must be the angel with the flaming sword.'

Upton a paradise! Timothy remembered with nostalgia the days when it had seemed so.

'But if they went,' he said, 'I should have to go, too.'

Mrs. Purbright clasped her hands together, and almost wrung them. Inarticulate sounds came from her throat. At last she said, 'Even so, I should send them away.'

When Timothy did not answer she added in a different tone, 'But all the same I hope you won't.'

Ignoring her last remark, Timothy said, 'You think it would be better if I left Upton?'

Mrs. Purbright hesitated.

'Oh no, no, Mr. Casson. We have all *immeasurably* benefited by your presence here. We should all be desolated if you left. But I do wish you could have a companion – not one of us, you have tried us, haven't you? You have given us a *good* trial – but something like your beloved bowl, but not so fragile, or so precious, or so perfect, something that could be a handmaid, not a magnet to your thoughts. Perhaps I have something here.' Her glance swept the room; she rose abruptly and went to a small table on which stood a vase almost as large as itself. Taking the object in her arms she set it down on the floor in front of them.

'Do you like cloisonné?' she said. 'I don't, very much. But I've always been fond of this. Chinese art is usually static, isn't it? arrested – nothing seems to move. Perhaps that's why we both like it. Even the landscape is windless! But here there is an effect of movement, don't you think?'

Timothy rested his eyes on the lustreless, grey-green enamel of the vase, upon which, each enclosed in a margin of dull gold, floated flower-forms of every shade between pink and mauve and brown, with butterflies to match; and as he looked it did seem as though the whole mass was in motion, turning slowly round, like a revolving globe; and the petals, so firmly embedded, did seem to have a certain liberty of movement in relation to each other, and to widen or decrease the gap between them. So indeterminate and recessive were its lines that, for all its bulk, the vase seemed to have been conjured out of air – a materialisation of garden tints at twilight.

'Please take it,' Mrs. Purbright said, 'if you can fancy something that makes no claims for itself and is so used to being ignored. I have always found it companionable, and it isn't touchy, it wants to go to you – see how pleased it is to be changing hands.'

Suiting the action to the word, she put the vase into Timothy's lap.

'Oh, but I couldn't accept such a wonderful present!' Timothy exclaimed, his fingers tightening on the vase.

'It's not a present,' Mrs. Purbright said. 'I should like to give you a present some day. This is only the apology that I have owed you for so long. Whenever you look at it it will say, "Mrs. Purbright regrets." '

'If I ever catch it making such a remark,' said Timothy, 'I shall take a hammer to it.'

He was still fondling the vase as if he was afraid that Mrs. Purbright might change her mind, and still loading her with thanks when the Rector came in.

'Why, Casson, you're quite a stranger!' he said. 'What have you got there, a baby?'

'It's something Mrs. Purbright has given me,' Timothy said, and added hastily, 'much nicer than a baby. But I don't think I ought to accept it.'

'I shall be eternally indebted to you,' the Rector said, 'if you will take away some of my wife's junk. By the way, has she told you the great news?'

Timothy looked up in surprise.

'Hasn't she told you that Edgell is coming home on a month's leave?'

'We had so much else to talk about,' Mrs. Purbright interposed, 'but it was always at the back of my mind and made me a bad listener, I'm afraid. It isn't altogether a matter for rejoicing, Mr. Casson, because he has been ill, poor boy.'

'But you are always bidding us rejoice,' observed the Rector. 'Casson will bear me out.'

'Yes, but it is so much less easy for the young, in these days, and when they have got used to wider horizons. Edgell is quite a man now, Mr. Casson.'

'Well, that is something to be thankful for,' said the Rector, playfully.

'Yes indeed, but if only he would devote himself to his literary work! He has a real gift for it. Perhaps you would help him, Mr. Casson?'

'If I'm still here,' said Timothy.

'What, is Casson thinking of leaving us?' the Rector asked.

'Oh no!' cried Mrs. Purbright, and Timothy thought he caught in her eye the flicker of an appeal. 'Only he has had domestic difficulties.'

'He's lucky to have them,' said the Rector grimly. 'We should welcome that sort of difficulty, shouldn't we, Volumnia? At any rate there'll be one thing less for you to dust.'

Timothy looked guiltily at the great vase lying on his knees.

'Can you really bear to part with it, Mrs. Purbright?'

'It is asking to be yours, Mr. Casson.'

Timothy got up, rather in the attitude of some classical figure who is going to draw water at a well. Stooping down he picked up the lid, with its band of dull gold, and slipped it in his pocket. Mrs. Purbright also rose and fetched from another part of the room a small statuette, which she put on the table where the vase had been.

'It looks better there,' she said.

The room enfolded Timothy in its many-surfaced glow. Suddenly he felt impelled to testify.

'How I envy Edgell,' he said, 'coming home to be with you! I should ask for nothing better, nor, I am sure, will he.'

Timothy walked home thoughtfully through the evening light, hugging his vase. Its firm metal body comfortably returned the pressure of his. 'I'll show it to them both,' he thought, 'and tell them I've forgotten about the bowl.'

But the presentation did not go off as he had hoped; Beatrice and Effie would hardly look at his new treasure, deputising modestly for the old one. His spirits sank and Mrs. Purbright's drawing-room seemed very far away. Misery-makers, enemies of happiness, she had called them. Should he act on her advice and sack them? For a moment she had persuaded him to take his future into his own hands, to assume the direction of what was happening to him, instead of fighting a perpetual rearguard action against circumstance. Then, with her second thoughts, her concern for Edgell, she had blurred the bright image of resolution, resurgent in his mind, leaving him as doubtful as before.

'Isn't it pretty?' he repeated, hoping that by reiteration he could get them to admit it was. He flipped the enamel with his finger and it gave out a hollow ring, unmistakably metallic. 'And you couldn't break it, no matter how hard you tried.'

The 'you' was indefinite and not meant to be taken personally. But perhaps the whole sentence was unfortunate. Beatrice and Effie, exchanging furious glances with each other and with him, as at a signal turned away, and, heads erect, walked slowly to the door. Formerly Timothy had had a keen sense of the difference between them; they had seemed as unlike each other as two human beings could be. Now the same spirit seemed to inhabit them both and make them indistinguishable. It was a spirit of mindless hostility which, so long as he had been able to regard it in the abstract as an offence against charity and good manners, he had been able to find excuses for and even to think funny. But now he felt their naked enmity directed at him, with no cushion of humour or patience in between, and he responded as fully as they could have wished.

'Stop!' he shouted. The two women paused on the threshold and looked round, disdain contending with apprehension in their eyes.

'Come here!' he ordered, too angry now to care what happened. Beatrice and Effie came towards him, their faces (which annoyed him all the more) wearing an identical expression of hauteur masking fear. 'You don't seem very happy,' he accused them, and suddenly he remembered having used this tone before; at school, when he was Head of the House, and had occasion to rebuke refractory lower boys. 'You seem pretty pleased with yourselves,' he went on inconsequently, 'I don't know what it's all about.' He glowered at them, determined to wipe the struggling sneer from off their faces. 'You come to this house and you think yourselves God Almighty, but you aren't.' His heart rejoiced at the phrase, coming so pat to his tongue after over thirty years of mealy-mouthedness. 'You seem to think you've come here for a picnic, but I'm going to show you you're mistaken. I've had about as much of you as I can stand. Have you anything to say for yourselves?' Beatrice and Effie stared at him blankly; apparently they had nothing to say and Timothy's next move should have been to tell them to bend over. Rejecting it brought him to a nearer sense of the reality of the situation. 'You have a good home and comfortable quarters and I've done everything I could for you,' he declared, keeping his utterance as magisterial as possible. 'But you're a couple of selfish, disagreeable women, bent on making trouble, and the sooner you go out of this house the better I shall be pleased. You can take a month's notice from to-day.'

Timothy, who had been standing, sat down in a chair and drew a book towards him. 'You can go now,' he said. As he watched their retreating backs, one short and broad, the other tall and willowy, another phrase from his schooldays came into his mind. 'And shut the door after you,' he thundered.

Timothy spent the evening in alternating states of elation, apprehension and remorse. Several times he was on the point of begging the maids' pardon and entreating them to stay. If he did not do it then, it was because he could do it just as easily the next day.

But the next day brought a letter to say that Vera was arriving in Upton that afternoon, and Timothy's domestic problems slipped into the background.

CHAPTER XXIV

HE met her the same evening in the Fisherman's Arms, and the moment he saw her gold-dusted head shining halo-like in the blue tobacco-smoke, the preoccupations of the last nine months seemed infinitely remote and indistinct. How could he have concerned himself with such trifles? Though they had already lost their shape and meaning he could feel the scars they had left, like rocks on the sea-shore, disappearing under the tide of happiness. This was what he had been living for all the time that his energies had been squandering themselves, petering out in a delta of spite and grievance. He did not thus formulate to himself the details of his deliverance; he just had time to register the fact of freedom before he felt her hand in his.

She did not leave it there, however, for always they had practised a certain propriety in public and Timothy had been far too excited to notice who might or might not be in the bar. He had wished that their first meeting could be private; it was she who had suggested the Fisherman's Arms – rather to his surprise as well as to his disappointment, for she had so often reminded him of the remark that had been dropped there about them.

But he admired her courage, and actually their meeting had for him an added zest from being, however slightly, a gesture of defiance. They were not going to pipe down for anybody! Upton should know! There was a sweetness in the thought that she trusted him and was even proud of him as her ally; but it was not for that he wanted her, but for the sense of completion and fulfilment that she gave him, and the liberty to love her.

All this could not be expressed, but it could be damped down like a furnace and the under-glow felt, while they exchanged the breathless platitudes of reunion under the barmaid's practised, understanding, and not unsympathetic eye. And the feeling of the room was not against them as Timothy, once he had eased his heart by a loving word to Vera, soon discovered. Looking round shyly and a little dazed, like a swimmer who comes to the surface after a high dive, he met reserved but friendly recognitions, the friendliness for them, the reserve for their relationship, whose delicacy appealed at once to the sophistication that

312

lurks in the most untutored minds. 'Go on!' their glances, so economical of expression, seemed to say; 'behave as you must, we understand, we shall not be shocked unless you try to shock us.' Grave, measuring glances, critical of his performance, but ready to approve if he did well. So, turning round to her, he did not feel uneasy at exposing his back to their expert scrutiny.

'My darling,' he said to Vera, when they were outside, 'did we have to run that gauntlet?'

She turned her sad face to him, in which the rapture of the whole world lay.

'But, darling, it's such fun for them, and surely you want them on our side?'

'Yes,' said Timothy, doubtfully. 'But we are our side, aren't we? I don't want anyone else.'

Vera looked up and down the village street, collecting the wide-eyed homage of the passers-by.

'You are an old silly,' she said. 'You never know when you may want people.'

'I know when I don't want them,' said Timothy.

'I don't believe you do. Have you forgotten what that old hell-hound said about us?'

'Well, you never told me what he actually said.'

'I wanted to spare your feelings, that was why. But one thing I can tell you, it wasn't very pleasant. I hoped you'd have done something about it.'

'But what could I do? Call them out? And you never told me who they were.'

'Darling, you have such mediæval ideas. They aren't exactly popular, you know. Not half as popular as you are.'

'Me, popular?' exclaimed Timothy. 'Why, no one ever speaks to me.'

'That, darling, is because you're just a tiny bit of a snob, if you'll forgive me saying so, and don't speak to them. A few of the high-ups cold-shoulder you, and you know why, don't you?'

The unmentionable, alas, is not the same as the unthinkable. Timothy knew what Vera was alluding to; but superstitiously he refused to give it words.

'Oh, you mean something I have that they don't want me to use?'

Vera laughed.

'Darling, you make it sound so indecent. And it isn't indecent, it's perfectly proper. What could be more innocent than a—'

'Yes, I know,' said Timothy, hurriedly heading her off the forbidden word. 'But I've more or less got used to the idea of doing without it.'

Vera regarded him coldly.

'I wonder why I bothered to come back. I suppose you've also got used to the idea of doing without me?'

'Oh Vera, how can you say that? I've simply been living for your return.'

'Well, you may have to do without me.'

'Why?'

'To keep people from chattering about us.'

'But does it matter if they do? I don't mind my name being coupled with yours, if you don't. People *will* talk; it doesn't really mean anything. I tried to think of ways of retaliating, but in the end I felt the best plan was to ignore it.'

'I see,' said Vera lightly. 'Well, I suppose you know what suits your temperament.' Again she looked the village up and down. It was a high summer; but the summer of 1941 was but a faded transcript of its pre-decessor. The sunshine was paler, the vegetation less luxuriant; it was as though Nature had exhausted herself, like an artist whose best work is over. One could not lose oneself in the rapture of the season's mood, for like one's own, and like the world's, it was discouraged.

'You'll come back with me now?' said Timothy at last.

'Darling, I'm afraid I mustn't. You forget I have to be a nursemaid. Frances's hands are so full. I can't leave her to cope with everything.'

'But she has to when you're away.'

Vera looked at him in sad surprise.

'Dearest, you must forgive me but I never heard a more selfish speech. Don't you ever think of anyone but yourself?'

Timothy reddened.

'Well, come to dinner or come in afterwards.'

Vera shook her head.

'Not to-night. You see I *am* her guest, and I think she feels it a little that you didn't ask her when I was away.'

'I . . . I meant to,' said Timothy. 'I like Frances very much, of course. But it's you I'm really fond of, Vera darling.'

Vera looked at him.

'Are you? I wonder. You don't act as if you were.'

Timothy decided to ignore the implications of this.

'Oh, but I shall!' he cried, as confidently as he could. 'You won't want to be with Frances *all* the time.'

She shrugged her slender shoulders. 'I'll be seeing you.'

* * *

314

Timothy had to be content with that. He walked home soberly, his eyes on the ground, trying to see, in the dust that lay in thin drifts on the road, the quartz-like sparkle of a hope. He had to own that he was disappointed with Vera's reception of him; his feelings were still chilly from it. But his thoughts, scouting round, remembered a score of occasions when she had stood him off, only to take him back with added sweetness; this was but a temporary rebuff, a woman's ruse for making herself dearer. And well it had succeeded! Timothy's spirits were already buoyant with the hope of seeing her again.

As he entered the house the telephone bell was ringing.

'Hullo! This is Edgell Purbright here.'

'I'm delighted to know you're back,' said Timothy, as warmly as he could.

'Look here, I'm rather ashamed, but Mother said I was to ring you up.'

'I couldn't be more pleased.'

'You have to say that. Are you sure I'm not being a frightful bore?'

'Of course not.'

'You know what mothers are. They're simply remorseless in defence of their young.'

'Who's she defending you from?'

'I don't know.'

'I'm devoted to your mother,' Timothy declared. 'I'd do anything for her. What does she want me to do?'

'She wants me to see you at any cost – at any cost to you, I mean.'

'But that would be a great pleasure,' Timothy said. 'When can we meet?'

'I'm afraid I'm always at your service.'

Timothy thought rapidly. Tomorrow, Vera might be here. The day after tomorrow Vera might be here. The day after that she would almost certainly be here, all day; as indeed she might be on the preceding days. There was not a moment that was not bespoken by her; the whole future was hers.

'It's most tiresome, but I have one or two unforeseen engagements,' Timothy invented hurriedly. 'Could you come on Friday, about six-ish?' Friday was three days ahead.

'Splendid,' said Edgell's full, resonant voice, not at all the voice of an invalid. 'And you won't mind if I come armed with my literary works? Mother insists on that. She really is quite shameless.'

Timothy begged him to bring them first, 'or – or – just drop them into the letter-box if you're passing,' he added. 'Then I shall be in a position to make a report.'

Edgell promised to do this and their conversation bowed itself away in expressions of goodwill. Indeed, as the evening wore on Timothy began to regret that he had not asked Edgell to come round sooner, so heavily did the time drag and so fidgety did he become.

The next morning brought a letter from Magda. It was written from the nursing home in Grosvenor Square which she frequented when she felt in need of a rest. There was nothing unusual in that; what was novel was the superscription, heavily embossed in letters of scarlet: DEATH TO THE FASCIST DOGS AND TRAITORS.

'DEAREST TIMOTHY,' he read,

'Hitler's cowardly attack on the Soviets has moved us all deeply and left us in no doubt where we stand. What has all along been an imperialist, capitalist war has turned in a night into a war for the preservation of the proletariat, and *nothing else matters*. Whoever loses the war, they will win. Whatever other result the war may have, it now can only advance the cause of Communism. We in Curzon Street are straining every nerve; there was a new light in Nastya's eye this morning, when she told me that she lived only for one thing – to kill Fascists, to kill more Fascists, and to kill still more Fascists. And all the time the dear girl was saying this she was laughing with that deep-chested Russian laughter which no European, corrupted by centuries of bourgeois culture, can hope to understand. Two other girls whom I don't think I've told you about, Moucha and Groucha, joined in and laughed till the tears ran down their cheeks. I'm glad to say I was able to laugh, too. Niggling, individual emotions impede our march, but collective thankfulness is a tonic. I had to go away and make up my face. The Russian stalwarts didn't bother to do that, and much as I dislike tear-stained faces and what I can only describe as that nasty natural look, I didn't mind it in them, for they are always on active service, and only Nazi generals paint their faces on the battlefield.

'But I'm ashamed to say the whole thing was too much for me, so I rang up the Daimler Hire and here I am.

'Of course I shouldn't be writing to you if I didn't know that you would now be heart and soul in the war. You were right to hang back before, but there's only one reaction now. You are absolutely sound, Timothy, aren't you? I won't know anyone who isn't. You were always a little comfort-loving and I know how uncomfortable a turnover in one's convictions is – or I shouldn't be here, propped up on pillows, with these rather pretty but maddeningly silly nurses fussing round me, just when I want to be doing *something*, no matter what.

'But because we're all in it now doesn't mean we have ceased to keep an eye on the Fascists in our midst, and from what you tell me, and what I hear, there is quite a colony of them at Upton. All those retired soldiers and people who seem so patriotic, but are really fighting to enslave the workers. You haven't done anything about them, Timothy, in spite of all the provocation they've given you, and all the backing you've had. You really must, and to help you to make up your mind I'm going to accept the charming invitation you gave me so long ago and pay you a visit. As soon as I leave this place which will be in a fortnight at the latest, I'll come down to spend the rest of my leave with you, if you can bear it (the Ministry has given me three weeks off). I shall try to combine business with pleasure, and I shan't be a burden on your household because I shall have Nastya with me (I think I had your permission to bring her). She is a tower of strength and though she disapproves of servants and thinks them funny she gets on with them perfectly on the lines of class solidarity.

'So what fun it will be, to see places and people I've heard so much about, and have a drink at the Fisherman's Arms, and above all to be with you, dearest Timothy, in your absurd bourgeois stronghold. Don't think I shall be bored by meeting the locals. I want to see them all from Mrs. Purbright downwards, so please parade them for me. And if there's a chance of getting over to Welshgate to see Julia Lampard I shall go – poor old girl, she never cared much for me, but now she's batty she might like to see me. I always get on well with lunatics.

'How wonderful to be able to say au revoir!

MAGDA.

'P.S. You once asked me if I thought you grumbled too much. If you want my honest opinion, I think perhaps you do. All you really have to complain of is that things are no longer quite the same for people of your sort.'

Timothy's first reaction to this letter was one of alarm and despondency. He had longed for Magda to come; but that she should choose this very moment, just when Vera was here! Vera could never tell him how long she was staying; it would be cruel to lose her for a whole week. And Magda would be sure to find out about her (if she did not know already, she seemed so well posted in the gossip of Upton). She would not, of course, frown upon Timothy's liaison, indeed, she would give it her blessing, but how awkward the arrangements would be, demanding a kind of savoir-faire that he had never had. He was such an amateur, and Magda had no patience with amateurs, less than none with amatory amateurs of middle-age. To her trained eye, his conduct would seem woefully lacking in finesse; he might even muddle the whole thing, leaving Vera and himself looking shamefaced and ridiculous.

All the more was it important to regain Vera's favour without delay, so that they might snatch some happiness together before Magda came.

He looked at Magda's letter again. What a lot she knew about him and his doings, almost as if she had been making a study of Upton! It was unlike her to show curiosity; even in the days before her political phase she had always treated his other friendships as something quite outside her province. If he told her about them, she was frank in her comments, just as she was outspoken with him about her own concerns; but she never demanded confidences, she never probed, never for a moment suggested that she knew more than he had told her. But perhaps it was only his bad conscience that made him suspect her of doing so now – and in any case he ought to feel grateful to her, for Mrs. Purbright excepted, who else had bothered to speculate about him? To the others, friends, neighbours, acquaintances, servants, he was just a figure in their private fantasies, and usually an unwelcome and embarrassing one. Even to Vera he seemed hardly more than a convenient receptacle for her mood of the moment – moods which happened to be dearer to him than anything else.

So Magda must come, and she must be given a royal welcome, and Beatrice and Effie should now be told the news.

A year or more ago, when he had broached the matter to them, they had been far from enthusiastic. 'I can manage as long as you don't have guests,' Beatrice had said. But now, since he had given them notice, their demeanour had completely changed; they were friendly, civil, obliging, and nothing seemed a trouble. It was as though with the coming of the clash that they had so long been working for all their ill-humour had been purged. The certainty, the finality had cured them. Everything had been said that could be said; the air had been cleared, the axe had fallen, and they had returned to their best selves. An alternative, and more unflattering explanation was that they were thankful to be leaving Upton, the Old Rectory, and him; and no doubt they were. But had that been the only reason for the change they would have been less pleasant to Timothy; now, it seemed, they could not do enough for him.

Meanwhile, what was he to do when they went away? If he left Upton, where would he go? And what would happen about the unexpired lease of the Old Rectory? Miss Chadwick would not make it easy for him, she had told him so. He could not afford the rent of two houses; after the loss of his job, his extravagances, and the considerable wartime shrinkage in his income, he could scarcely afford to pay for one.

If he meant to stay he ought to write at once to an agency for domestic servants. Mrs. Purbright would advise him as to the best course. But she had made it clear that she wanted him to go (or had she?) and Timothy, too, had been resigned to going, had almost embraced the idea, only a few days ago.

He did not have to ask himself why he had changed his mind. The answer was at The Nook, but it was also in the air around him, it declared itself in all his movements, and in the face the mirror showed him. Upton had regained its magic.

The wisdom of experience is seldom proof against the emotion of the moment. Now that Beatrice and Effie were so amiable, why not tell them he had reconsidered his opinion, and ask them as a favour to stay on? In their present mood of delighted acquiescence in his every whim, it seemed as though they could not refuse. Something warned Timothy that such a policy would not work, that human behaviour had its laws which could not be mocked; but all the same he kept the project in reserve, and while he had it to fall back on, he could shelve the other.

As he expected, Beatrice and Effie received the news of Magda's visit with every sign of joy; their feelings, indeed, seemed to be far less mixed than his. It would do him good to have company; they would like his friends to know how well he was being looked after; they would be interested to see this Mrs. Vivian, the 'society' woman, whose photograph used to be in the papers, before the papers 'got so full of the war and that sort of thing.' This very morning Effie would put hot-water-bottles in the spare room bed; or would it be wiser to bring the mattress down and air it in front of the fire? Well, perhaps it would, Timothy said. But wouldn't it be a great bother? Oh, no bother at all; together they could do it easily. The kitchen fire would be best; Timothy wouldn't want a fire in the drawing-room this hot weather, and the mattress would look awkward and be in his way. But wouldn't it look awkward, and be in their way, in the kitchen? Not in the least, they could easily get round it.

Timothy wondered why he had ever found Beatrice and Effie difficult to get on with. Perhaps they were really longing to stay, and were just waiting for an advance from him. . . .

Edgell's typescripts duly arrived, a not too formidable parcel. The typescripts were somewhat faint, as though they had passed through many hands, but they were perfectly easy to read. For the most part they consisted of short stories, generally rather facetious in tone, their scenes laid in bars and night-clubs, street corners and dark entries, and the characters, who were often crooks or near-crooks, spoke a language flavoured with tough-guy Americanese. Through them flitted amorous and dazzling ladies, too beautiful to ignore, too ambiguous to trust. Seemingly as hard as nails, and with no flies on them, they rushed bald-headed into dangerous situations, and were always making appointments to meet equivocal males in deserted houses at nightfall. Many were the concussions they sustained from blunt instruments wielded in the dark; many were the knock-out drops they obligingly swallowed in their coffee; many were the rescues. Often the stories ended in a surprising twist, for the author did not always disclose, sometimes he never disclosed, whether the fair victims were angels or fallen angels, spies or counterspies. The stories had their dates attached; the later and maturer ones had an Air Force setting, bristling with Air Force slang. Timothy was impressed by this and by the fact that he could have written none of them himself. He liked what he remembered of Edgell, and was only too glad to give the benefit of the doubt to Mrs. Purbright's son.

But what a baffling mixture of sophistication and naiveté, of fidelity to the literary canons that Edgell had adopted, and of ignorance, or neglect, of all experience outside them! These bewitching blondes, for instance, always getting themselves and other people into trouble: did they really exist outside the pages of a novel? Were they not instances of the age-old fallacy that plain women were good, and pretty women bad? Had Edgell ever encountered one in real life? Had he, Timothy?

Well, there was Vera, of course (though Edgell, to be sure, had scarcely met her) and it was amusing to think how easily, to someone who didn't know her, she might seem to fit into the category of adventuresses who haunted Edgell's imagination. She was just as pretty as they were, indeed, much prettier, for she had her own face, darling Vera's face, with a hundred lights and shadows on it, not visible at a first glance, but visible to a lover's eye, utterly distinct from anything implied in that dreary, reach-me-down appellation, platinum blonde. And she was mysterious as woman is, as life is, not with the mystery of a siren in a shocker, factitiously imposed on her by a callow author in search of literary effects. True, she came out of the dark, she had no 'background' to 'place' her, for those who are interested in social cartography; but, are we not all the same, ships that pass in the night? Come to that, she knew very little about Timothy's background; neither had thought it worth while to impart to the other details of their past lives, and he had no reason to suppose that hers was shadier than his. People did not come together in their backgrounds but in their foregrounds, in the pool of bright light, as bright as Vera's hair, that the present moment shed around them. To inquire how they got there, by what streets and alleys, with what preoccupations, with the marks of what contacts, was as irrelevant and unfruitful as to try to trace the provenance of the half-crown in one's pocket. Really, how absurd Edgell was to connect these sleek, stream-lined creatures, simply because they were pretty, with all sorts of nefarious doings, sinister Chinamen, leaders of thugdom, and so on! No, he would never make a writer, because he saw life not as it was, but in terms of shocker-values; and the best way of convincing himself of that was to seek out Vera immediately, before she had time to leave the Fisherman's Arms, and persuade her to come back with him.

How innocent she looked among the warming pans and pewter tankards! If anyone in the bar was sinister, and needed his antecedents and intentions checking, it was Timothy; and Vera seemed to realise this, for she kept him at small-talk's length, fluttering on the surface of her mind like a moth trying to get in at a window – very different from the villain-heroines of Edgell's tales, who spoke in monosyllables, and then only to be rude. When he said he must go she didn't offer to accompany him; and when he proposed she should dine with him, on that night, or the next night or the next – a trap into which any of Edgell's young ladies would immediately have fallen – she only looked rather wistful and said that Timothy must not let her take up all his time.

Timothy ought to have welcomed these signs of incorruptibility, these proofs that Nature was far from imitating Art, and that to be blonde was not to be a baggage. But he did not. Regardless of the publicity of the bar, he took her hand and pressed it; he looked into her eyes; he let his feeling pass into his voice. All to no purpose: she was immovable on her stool.

The next day dragged by on leaden feet and the night followed, hardly distinguishable from it. So dark was Timothy's mind that the outward darkness brought no solace, it merely intensified the gloom in which he stood or sat or lay, repeating over and over again to himself the incredible news that Vera no longer cared for him.

He felt it was most important that he should face this fact. Reality was sacred; at whatever cost to his nerves and feelings, reality must be recognised. She had grown tired of him, he bored her; that was the truth.

There was nothing surprising in it and yet he could not believe it, for there had been no rupture, hardly the shadow of a difference since the time when she accepted – not very willingly perhaps (but what girl of nice feelings would have accepted them willingly?) – his presents, and his love.

The thing did not make sense, for even if she had been as chaste as ice (and she had never pretended to be chaste, why on earth should she, thought Timothy, impatiently shaking his head at the world's wagging forefinger) she need not suddenly have withdrawn from him every token of favour, and treated him almost as a stranger, so that all the feelings that sprang to life at sight of her, flooding his emotional constitution with an ichor that can only safely be absorbed by happiness, had become a poison to his mind and body.

He could not and would not think unkindly of her, for to do so only aggravated his misery, by robbing him of hope; besides, (his more reflective and philosophic self reminded him), what right had he to expect her to be constant to him, a middle-aged man leading a dull life, with nothing to offer her except a few gew-gaws? – while in return he demanded from her all the things that are most irksome to part with, unless given from a full heart? His position was one of the oldest and tritest known to the stage, the elderly protector abandoned by his young mistress; even the kindest and most tolerant of spectators would shrug his shoulders and feel that here was little to excite compassion – so little, indeed, that there was not one human being in the world to whom Timothy would have cared to confess his plight. You will get over it, he kept telling himself; suddenly you will see the whole thing in proportion – Timothy had great faith in proportion – and as something that is happening to someone else: perhaps even as funny. 'What a comedy!' – he had been teased, he remembered, for overworking this phrase.

But such exercises in externalisation only plunged him deeper into himself and forged new chains to bind him to his identity; for love is jealous of the other emotions, and the slightest exertion of the imagination, on a subject however unrelated, fans its flames. The torpor which is love's most dangerous enemy eluded Timothy, and the more he explored his dungeon the narrower did it seem.

That Vera should be in Upton and he not see her, except at meaningless encounters at a pub! And that she should acquiesce in this as though she did not care, as though she had not felt the depth of his affection, as though she wanted to take herself out of his life, as though he meant nothing to her, as though she disliked him—

* * *

322

One day, any day, musing thus, he heard the doorbell ring, a summons from the outer world which awoke no response in him. But the next moment Effie was in the room, and following her a young man in Air Force uniform whom, for a moment, Timothy did not recognize.

'You don't remember me,' the visitor said, looking down at Timothy with a self-deprecating grin. 'I'm Edgell Purbright. You did say Friday, didn't you?'

Recollection rushed over Timothy.

'Of course, of course, my dear fellow!' he exclaimed, getting up and pumping Edgell's hand. 'I can't tell you how glad I am to see you!' He felt his manner must seem strangely distracted, for Edgell couldn't know what a relief his presence was. 'Come, let's have a drink. I've had one already, two or three in fact.' He looked guiltily at the young officer, whose uniform gave him, to Timothy, the status of a much older man.

'I congratulate you, sir,' said Edgell, 'and I only wish I could say the same. Unfortunately, owing to a little disagreement between me and my tummy, I'm limited to one.'

'Oh, what bad luck!' exclaimed Timothy, gazing at Edgell with as much sympathy as if the young man had lost all his relations. 'I'd quite forgotten you were ill. What is it, if you don't mind telling me?'

'I'm ashamed to tell you,' said Edgell, taking his glass and bowing over it to Timothy, 'because it's what every lead-swinger has. A propensity to irritation, or what you will, in the duodenum. It's an odd thing – our M.O.'s are as brave as lions on our behalf, and they don't mind how many of us get killed in other ways, but you've only got to breathe the word duodenal and you're back in civilian life before you have time to kiss them goodbye.'

'Fancy!' said Timothy. 'But—' he looked at Edgell with concern – 'don't you feel ill?'

'Well,' said Edgell, 'every now and then the old pain comes back and gives me a touch of what for, especially if I have to stand for long together, like you do in church. I shall never be able to follow Dad's profession – that's definitely barred, it's much too strenuous. No pulpit work for me. I've got to be sedentary for the present. I dare say I shall find an opening as a lounge lizard. I could be quite good at horizontal sports, like love.'

He spoke lightly, but Timothy saw slanting shadows between his nose and the corners of his mouth which had not been there before. His face was paler and had lost its roundness, it had the look of maturity that suffering so quickly gives. He was broader and thinner than Timothy remembered him, and much better-looking.

'That's partly why Mother was so anxious you should vet my literary efforts,' Edgell went on. 'She thinks I might be deputed to write an official history of the Air Force, or something of that sort. I told her you wouldn't want to be bothered, and it was a shame to trouble you, but she simply wouldn't listen. Mother's a clever woman, you know, under all that sort of flowery stuff. But I'm her Achilles heel. Perhaps I'm every sort of heel. She's not quite sane where I'm concerned.'

'Your mother has been infinitely kind to me,' said Timothy, 'but even if she wasn't I should have been delighted to read your stuff.'

He paused, and Edgell said quickly, in another voice, 'You don't think it's too utterly shaming?'

'Indeed I don't,' said Timothy, but he could not quite keep his eyes on Edgell's face. 'It's not the sort of thing I could ever write myself,' he went on, choosing his words. 'I wish I could.' He thought he saw the shadows deepen on Edgell's cheek, and added, 'I'm sure there'd be a future for that kind of thing, and your Air Force studies are excellent – so first-hand.'

'You like them better than my rescue work among the blondes?' grinned Edgell.

'Well,' said Timothy. The thought of Vera, kept at bay for five minutes, pierced him and he could hardly go on. 'I thought them more carefully observed, truer to life, you know.'

'Man and boy, I have had some experience of blondes,' said Edgell, reflectively. 'In a way they do run truer to type than brown-haired girls, I find. Or perhaps it's just that I run truer to type when I'm with them. I don't seem able to keep them out of my stories. Do you remember meeting one at Mother's sherry party?'

'Mm,' said Timothy.

'Pretty girl, didn't you think so? She was the sort I mean.'

But before Timothy had time to answer he heard the whirr of the telephone bell. Glad of the excuse to turn his back on Edgell he hurried into the little white-panelled room.

'Yes?'

'Hullo, darling,' said a voice much more familiar to him than his own. 'I thought I'd just like to know how you were.'

'I'm getting on,' Timothy said, flatly.

'Darling, do you mean you're growing older? I couldn't bear that. I wouldn't have rung you up if I'd known you were going to tell me such dreadful news.'

'Well, why did you ring me up?' said Timothy.

'Has anything happened, my sweet? You sound so cross. I meant to ask you if I might come and dine with you, but I won't if you don't want me.'

'Please come,' said Timothy. 'Do come, Vera, please.'

'When shall I come?'

'Come now, right away.'

'Oh, I couldn't do that. I couldn't come as I am, if I'm going to spend the evening with you.'

'Of course you are.'

'It'll take me an hour or more. Will you still want me?'

'I shall have forgotten you by then.' Timothy paused. 'I've got a man here, but he'll be going any time now.'

'What sort of a man?'

'Oh just a man, nobody special.'

'Should I like him?'

'No, I don't think he'd interest you. He's quite a nice fellow, but a bit of an invalid,' said Timothy carelessly.

'I don't like the sound of him. Do send him away, my pet. Tell him his wife's been run over.'

'He hasn't got one, but I'll get rid of him somehow. You'll hurry, won't you?' said Timothy.

'I shall run all the way.'

He gave the receiver a resounding kiss.

Timothy returned to the drawing-room to find Edgell fingering the stem of his wineglass. Timothy offered to fill it up for him.

'No, I mustn't. But won't you have another? You look so well you can afford to.'

'Do I look well?' asked Timothy.

'Since you came back from telephoning you look a new man, if I may say so, sir. I hope it was good news.'

'Well, it means I've got an engagement,' said Timothy, 'which is rather a bore, but not at once. Now, about your stories—'

He put his finger to his lip, but no thoughts would come. Those that were not centred on Vera were banished by his sudden translation into bliss.

'Yes?' said Edgell, bending forward with his elbows on his knees. He turned his eyes, his mother's violet eyes, intently on Timothy.

'I was going to say . . .' Timothy groped, 'that work of that kind . . . should find a ready sale in magazines.'

To his disappointment, Edgell did not seem elated by the idea of magazines.

'I'd thought of trying them on some of the reviews,' he admitted, leaning back in his chair.

'Quite right,' said Timothy, eagerly. 'Try them by all means. They are just what high-brow editors want. I mean,' he hurried on, 'they have plenty of action and snap and ... and, of course, the feminine interest.'

Like a rocking-horse, Edgell leaned forward again. 'You think I handle the women all right?' he said, with an earnestness and deference that made Timothy feel all the more inadequate.

'You do! You do!' he cried. 'Those mystery minxes – they should – they should – go down well. Photogenic, too.'

Edgell raised an eyebrow.

'You were thinking of the films?'

'Well, yes. One never knows what will appeal to them. I mean,' said Timothy wildly, 'animals do.'

'Animals?' repeated Edgell, puzzled.

'Yes, yes,' said Timothy. 'Don't think I'm speaking recklessly, but next to women, animals are about the greatest draw to the reading public. Children adore them so. If only you could cash in on them!' He looked desperately at Edgell. 'Are you fond of animals, er ... er ... Squadron-Leader?'

'Only Flight-Lieutenant, I'm afraid,' said Edgell, politely. 'But please call me Edgell.' He leaned back again, and said a little sulkily but not without dignity, 'Yes, I'm quite fond of animals. I can't say I'm mad about them.'

'Because,' cried Timothy, ignoring his guest's lukewarmness towards the brute creation, 'I have the most delightful *dog* here.' Timothy said 'dog' as one might say 'unicorn' or 'phœnix.' 'Would you like to see him?'

'I should like to see him very much,' said Edgell, civilly, but with more than a hint of patience in his tone.

'Then if you'll excuse me I'll go and fetch him,' said Timothy.

Outside in the hall Timothy closed his eyes and drew several long breaths. The law of hospitality was one of the most sacred in the world. It was especially venerated by the Fiji Islanders. How could he behave so badly to this charming young man, who was moreover Mrs. Purbright's son, her heel of Achilles? Yet something had to be done to still the tumult in his mind.

Arrived in the kitchen he suddenly remembered he must tell the maids that Vera was coming to dinner. The news, announced with misgiving, was received with acclaim, and Effie said in her most refined voice, 'It will be quite nice to see Miss Cross again. She is quite a stranger.'

How generous of her, thought Timothy, how kind. His face glowed with gratitude. He thanked her, and said to Beatrice, 'Could I borrow Felix for a moment?'

At the mention of his name, Felix got up and ambled towards Timothy, his chain grating on the flag-stones.

'Do you want to take him into the room?' asked Beatrice. Did his eyes deceive him or had she turned a little pale? Certainly her voice was her old voice, at its most discouraging.

'Well, that was my idea.'

Beatrice hesitated. How jealous she is, thought Timothy; she can't bear him out of her sight.

'I should keep him on the chain, then,' she said, gruffly. 'He goes regular mad now, if he's let off.'

'Oh I'm sure he'll be good,' said Timothy. 'Down, Felix, down. Mind your hairs on my best suit. No, no, don't lick me. Now stand still just for one moment.'

At last the panting, straining Felix was unchained.

'I should keep hold of his collar, sir,' said Beatrice, anxiously. 'You never know what he'll be up to, and it isn't his fault, a dog can't help being a dog.'

Their progress down the passage and across the hall was like that of half a man and half a dozen dogs.

'Here he is!' cried Timothy, opening the door.

Startled by the tornado of noise and movement, Edgell looked up from his book. Felix made straight for him, propelled, it seemed, by the action of his tail; and the next thing Timothy heard was a dull thud followed by a tremendous, clanging crash. Headless on the floor lay the cloisonné vase; its lid rolled wobbling to Timothy's feet, and fell over.

'Oh dear!' cried Timothy. 'Your mother's vase! Felix, you bad, bad dog!'

Felix, his tail still waving, vouchsafed a backward look of light apology before launching his friendliness upon Edgell.

Timothy picked up the vase. Except for an almost imperceptible dent, which might have been there before, it was uninjured. He turned to Edgell, who had somehow subdued Felix's demonstrativeness to a display of manageable affection. He apologised for the dog and added, 'Such an extraordinary thing. It might almost make the subject for a short story. I'll tell it you if you like – though there are no blondes in it except this one.' He patted Felix's golden head – but cautiously, for a heartier caress would be sure to move the retriever to reprisals. 'I had a china bowl once, a rather nice one . . .'

Edgell was a flattering listener. Timothy did not tell him how the bowl came to be his, but laid great stress on Mrs. Purbright's kindness in furnishing a substitute. 'But you see how baffling it was,' he wound up. 'Felix was in disgrace at the time and I suppose Beatrice thought I should get rid of him if I knew he'd done it.'

Felix, who was now lying on the hearthrug with his legs stretched out and his creamy undershirt becomingly displayed, raised his head with a look of suffering nobility.

'It's a story with a happy ending,' said Edgell, 'for I take it that everyone's forgiven and there won't be any retrospective victim-isation?'

'Oh no,' said Timothy. 'It all seems so long ago now, and so trivial. I don't know why we all got so worked up.'

'But the blonde was the culprit, after all,' said Edgell, gently stirring Felix with his foot. 'You see I'm right, sir. They aren't to be trusted.'

'Oh, do you think so?' said Timothy, but he said no more, for in the doorway stood Effie, announcing with some pride, 'Miss Cross.'

CHAPTER XXV

ALL three got up, and Timothy, with a restraining finger on Felix's collar, said, 'Do you know Mr. Edgell Purbright, Vera?'

Ignoring Timothy, she walked across him and took Edgell's hand. She was wearing a black silk dress with touches of pale blue here and there.

'Know him, of course I know him. You weren't expecting me so soon, were you?' she said. 'I came early on purpose. . . . You might look pleased to see me, Timothy! You meant to keep him from me, didn't you?' Her glance brushed his, then gathering power, fixed its search-light beam on Edgell's face.

'Do you know what your friend said on the telephone?' she asked.

'I'm afraid I didn't eavesdrop,' Edgell said. 'I'm not in our Intelligence Department.'

'You don't look as if you were,' said Vera. 'Shall I tell him, Timothy?'

'I'm afraid I can't remember what I said.' Timothy was miserably embarrassed.

'Can't you, darling? I can. You said you had a man here, nobody special, and he wouldn't interest me.'

'I'm sure Mr. Casson was quite right,' said Edgell.

'I only meant you wouldn't be interested in what we were talking about,' Timothy said.

'You didn't say so, darling. You said I shouldn't be interested in him because he was an invalid.'

Timothy glanced despairingly at Edgell, and the latter said good-humouredly to Vera, 'I expect you only like tough guys like Mr. Casson.'

'I liked you the first time I saw you,' said Vera, lightly underlining 'first.' 'I wish Timothy hadn't told me you were an invalid.'

'Why?' said Edgell. 'Does it matter to you?'

'You're pretty rude, aren't you?' said Vera. Her voice grew softer as her face hardened. 'If Timothy had any guts he'd chuck you out. But perhaps you're both invalids. . . . I don't think I want to stay, Timothy; I'll go now. I'll leave the gentlemen together.' She turned and began to walk towards the door.

'Oh, but I'm going, too,' said Edgell, giving Timothy a quick look. 'Don't let me break up your party. You can't be sorrier than I am that I'm an invalid.'

Halfway across the room Vera stopped and looked back at Edgell.

'Are you an invalid, I wonder?'

'Well, don't I look it?'

'Perhaps you do,' said Vera. 'But Timothy was right: I'm not really interested.'

Timothy hovered uneasily between his guests.

'Then no harm's done,' said Edgell. 'I didn't think you were.'

While she hesitated, he strolled casually up to her, and experimentally held out his hand. 'Please let me grasp the nettle,' he said.

He was between her and the door, and by making the initiative of departure his, had robbed hers of its effectiveness.

Rather as if he had been offering her a dead mouse, she took his hand.

'Well, so long as it's goodbye,' she said, not looking at him.

'That's for you to say.'

She shrugged her shoulders and stood still, like an island in a river, while Timothy wound round her to join Edgell at the door.

He wanted to apologise to Edgell but Vera had made that difficult, and he could not think of anything that would not sound disloyal. Crossing the hall he said, 'You will come again, won't you, and have another talk? I'm so sorry we were interrupted.'

Edgell gave him a sardonic grin. 'Oh, that was quite all right. She doesn't seem to like me, does she?'

Timothy couldn't help feeling sorry for someone whom Vera didn't like.

'Oh it's just her way, you know. You mustn't take her too seriously.'

'I'll take care not to. And thanks a lot for the pep-talk, sir. I'll come back for another.'

Edgell walked out into the evening sunshine, a smart, soldierly figure. 'Give my love to your mother,' Timothy called after him, and Edgell answered, 'I forgot, she asked me to give you hers.'

When he returned to the drawing-room Vera was still standing where he left her.

'I suppose you have been pulling me to pieces,' she said.

'Oh no, Vera darling. I think he's fallen for you.'

'Good God, I hope not. What is the matter with him, really? Is it something unmentionable?'

Timothy told her.

330

'Oh, just indigestion. I think that's so unattractive, darling. I'm glad you don't have it. I expect he gets the wind up.'

Timothy laughed.

'No, I believe he's rather a good pilot.' He felt he could afford to be generous to Edgell. 'He's not a very good writer, I'm afraid.'

'Oh, does he write? What does he write about?'

'Well, chiefly about blondes.'

They both laughed, and Vera said, 'Darling give me a drink, if you haven't given it all to your boy-friend.'

They dined by candle-light and daylight. It was extravagant but intimate, and Timothy found a curious pleasure in watching the outside world recede and lose its meaning, while their world, the world between the candles, glowed and brightened, until there was nothing left in it but them.

Crushed by days of disappointment, almost lost sight of in the scene with Edgell, his love for her returned, the stronger for the interruption, and gilded and enriched by the months of separation. Disappointment, besides being one of the most unendurable of the emotions, is also one of the most remediable; healed, it leaves a scar tougher than untried skin. Timothy could not have enjoyed the hour so much if it had not been preceded by a long era of failure – failure to realise his wishes, failure to consent in their frustration. All these, in retrospect, were seen to be leading uphill and not down, towards a smiling prospect of illimitable extent, not to the narrow confines of a dungeon. The highest thing one could aim at was a perfect human relationship, and what was perfection worth if achieved without struggle, how could it be apprehended except in terms of previous set-backs? Far from destroying hope, these set-backs had only strengthened it, endowing it with a myriad shoots on which the flowers of rapture hung.

That Vera was an awkward customer Timothy did not deny, but in wooing her he had wooed the world in all its variousness, had embraced its capacity to wound as well as its power to bless, and in winning her, making her his, he had been victorious not only over the world, but over his own suspiciousness of the world, his tendency to seek out only those elements and people who consorted with his temperament, and whom by a forgivable but faulty logic he rated higher, morally higher, than the rest. Loving Vera was like loving nature. Human life and human beings were far too complex to be herded into such modish categories as nice and nasty, still less such time-honoured ones as good and bad; by doing so, by sitting in judgment, a man cut himself off from his fellows, and all he achieved, by his censoriousness, was to

331

define (for those who cared to know) what were the limitations of his own sympathies. More mortifying still, he betrayed (to anyone who was interested) his good opinion of himself, for those he chose to honour possessed qualities like his own, and his praise of them, his complacency in calling them friends, was an indirect encomium of himself.

People could not be judged, they could not even be understood, they could only be approached in love, as he was doing now; and by doing so he freed himself from the chains of self, which were never stronger than when attached to that kind of platform on which a man, by criticising those around him, really advertises his own faults.

What he felt with Vera now was the nearest thing to spiritual ecstasy that he, Timothy, could reach, nor was it, needless to say, dulled and muffled by the whisperings of argument like those just given. Indeed, his happiness partly consisted in not having to ask his mind for reasons. But all the same it rested on a foundation of some such unformulated thoughts, on the faith that security had been achieved not only in the emotional but the rational sphere. A man is grateful for the comfort of his bed, and does not speculate whether the mattress is of down or wool or horsehair; but at the back of his mind he knows that without one or other of these ingredients he would not be enjoying the well-being that he has.

When the curtains had been drawn and the blackout fixtures regulated, the room seemed snugger than ever and harder to leave. Leave it they must, for the evening was still young, and no stage in the ritual must outlast its proper length; yet Timothy was loth to go, to break the barrier of timelessness that joy builds round itself out of the most transient materials, to forsake the candles, the silver and the wine: the shining surfaces, the deep soft colours, that had become the visible embodiment of his bliss.

Yet leave it they must for it was but the threshold to a further state of happiness. Without the sequel, the inevitable sequel, their sitting thus together, not speaking much, and looking at each other without passion across the candle-light, would have had the sadness of finality and farewell that lurks in every rounded moment of experience.

Yes, they must go, though going would mean a change of thought and feeling more radical than a political revolution, would re-shuffle the pieces of the kaleidoscope until the pattern was obliterated, would jeopardise everything that the spirit's quietness, in the candle-light, had attained to, would mean strains and stresses that the waking mind could give no account of, and forbore to think of, so remote were they from the dignified and consistent image of itself that, on its daily occasions, it tried to show the world.

He opened the door for Vera to go through, and called down the passage, 'We've left the dining-room.' As he took her hand to lead her across the hall he heard Effie's answer, 'Very good, sir.'

'Very good, sir!' The well-worn phrase seemed to take on a new meaning.

'You know, Vera,' said Timothy, leaning back and trying to blow a smoke-ring, 'you know—' He stopped.

'What do I know, darling?' She spoke lazily and softly, but he heard quite well, for her head was resting on his shoulder. As he didn't speak, she added, 'If I know, perhaps it's hardly worth while telling me.'

'Oh yes, it is,' said Timothy, pressing her hand, as though to convey his meaning through it. 'At least it would be, if I could put it into words – the difference I feel now that you've come back to me. It must be extraordinary to be able to do so much for someone without trying to.'

'How do you know that I don't try, my sweet?'

Timothy considered this. 'You don't seem to, any more than a flower tries to be a flower.'

'Darling, I expect it puts every ounce of its energy into it. Think of being a peony. That must be a whole-time job.'

Timothy laughed.

'You're right. I ought to have thought of something else. Still a peony only tries to be itself.'

'And don't I?'

'You're not a bit like a peony, Vera darling.'

'Aren't I? Why not? A peony's such a heavenly flower.'

'I know. But it's not a bit like you. It's too red, for one thing.'

'Red's not a bad colour.'

'No, but it's not your colour.'

'It might be. I am rather red, as a matter of fact.'

'Are you?' said Timothy, indulgent and amused. 'Are you a Jacobin in disguise? You don't look a bit red, my darling!'

'Well, I am, and I'm not your only friend who is.'

Timothy tried to look at her, but she was too near for him to get a general view.

'Who else is there besides you?' He asked the question idly, with only the faintest prick of curiosity, and as though it referred to someone in a book; for at the moment no one existed for him except her.

'A woman I met in London, darling. She told me she knew you quite well.'

Timothy hitched himself up on the sofa.

'Who?'

'A Mrs. Vivian. But I expect she was just boasting. I don't suppose she ever set eyes on you.'

'Magda!' exclaimed Timothy. 'But of course! How strange you should have met her! You're quite right – she is rather red.' But it was the personal that claimed him, and he dismissed Magda's political complexion from his mind. 'She's a very old friend of mine,' he went on, sinking back into affectionate thoughts of Magda. 'I've known her all my life. What did she say about me?'

'All sorts of nice things, but she said you were a good man gone wrong.'

'Dear Magda! What did you say to that?'

'I said we should have to try to put you right.'

'My darling, you don't have to try. I told you so a moment ago.'

'She said she might be coming down here.'

'But she is, next week, as soon as she comes out of the nursing home.'

How delightful this was! What astonishing good fortune! They knew and apparently liked each other, and there would be no need for shyness or awkwardness or explanations; they were both women of the world and all would be plain sailing.

Timothy told Vera how glad he was.

'But, darling,' she said, 'how will you fit us both into your colour-scheme? Two reds don't make a white, you know.'

Timothy didn't understand. 'Do you think of me as white?'

'You would be to a Russian, my pet.'

Timothy laughed. 'Yes, but they would tolerate me now, because we're all on the same side.' He hesitated; even in a metaphor he disliked the word. 'I'll try to be red, too, to keep you in countenance.'

'Darling, is that a promise?'

'Of course it is.'

Vera looked round her vaguely, then, with growing purposefulness, her eyes strayed to the clock.

'Good heavens, it's nearly eleven. Darling, I must be going now.' She made a movement to reach her bag. It had an unmistakable air of leave-taking, and Timothy's heart turned over.

'Oh but Vera!—' She turned to him in surprise. 'Oh Vera, you can't go yet!' How well he remembered her wondering look.

'Not go?' she repeated. 'But I must. Frances is expecting me.'

'Oh but, Vera darling, it's our first evening together for . . . for I don't know how long. I've been so looking forward to it.'

'But, my treasure, you've had it, as they say. We've had a lovely time.'

In his agitation Timothy got up and looked down at her imploringly. 'But Vera, it's only just beginning – I mean we've seen so little of each other.' The words seemed inadequate, they had an ambiguous, vulgar ring that travestied his emotion. He reddened, and said hastily, 'Please stay, Vera darling, like . . . like you used to.'

'Like I used to?' she said, staring up at him with a blank face.

He took her limp hand in his and wrung it. 'Yes, please, Vera, like you did those . . . those other evenings, don't you remember?' As she still showed no sign of understanding what he meant, he went on, more and more wretched and embarrassed. 'You didn't leave at eleven then . . . no, nor at twelve, either.'

She dropped her eyes from his face, withdrew her hand from his, and said, 'I'm afraid I don't understand what you're talking about.'

'Oh but you must remember, my darling,' cried Timothy, agonised and frightened. 'Please, please think back!' He tried to find reminders more explicit, shied away from them, and sighed. 'We were everything to each other, then,' he went on despairingly, feeling as though she had gone deaf or turned into another person. 'You can't, you can't have forgotten!' He tried to possess himself of her hand again, but she drew it back. 'You can't have forgotten!' he repeated. 'Why, I haven't thought of anything else!'

But no gleam of recognition came into her face, and she only said, 'I'm afraid you are mistaken, darling. You've been imagining things. There was never anything of . . . of that sort between us.'

Desperately Timothy tried a last appeal. 'But the dressing-gown and the bedroom slippers—'

'Yes,' said Vera, 'I remember giving them you.' He stared at her with a fixed look of entreaty. 'But you've never been my lover,' she added softly.

With a blind gesture Timothy turned and sat down in the chair furthest away from her, and put his head in his hands.

So he remained for a time, feeling much and thinking little, and the next thing he was aware of was her voice, saying, 'Good-night, Timothy,' and he looked up and saw her in her slender tallness with her bag under her arm and her hand coming slowly towards him in fare-well. He got up awkwardly and uncertainly, but he could not look at her and did not take her hand.

'Good-night, Timothy,' she repeated.

He tried to frame the well-worn words but they would not come. In spite of everything he could not believe that she was leaving him, and all he could think of to say was, 'Why must you treat me so unkindly?'

She looked down at him in a puzzled way and said, 'Unkindly, darling? But I haven't treated you unkindly. We've had a lovely evening, at least I have, and I thought you enjoyed it, too.'

'I did enjoy it,' muttered Timothy. 'But—' he sighed – 'if you don't understand I can't explain to you.'

'Darling, I do know what you mean,' she said. 'But,' she went on almost pleadingly, 'you've got it all quite wrong, believe me. People often get those ideas into their heads: you're not the first. I expect you . . . you wanted to, and then you thought we had.'

Again, stealing through his misery but quite distinct from it came the frightened feeling, but this time it was not only her word that he doubted, but his own as well. Her word was as good as his. Could he have been mistaken? He made a little hopeless gesture with his hands and murmured, 'I can't say any more.'

She looked at him sadly and pitifully. 'But I can, darling,' she said. 'I hate to see you suffer when you've been so good to me. Only, what you thought of . . . what you spoke about . . . just now . . isn't easy for me. It isn't prudishness or coldness . . . but a sort of reserve, I suppose. But I'd do anything for you, you know I would.'

Timothy raised his eyes and seemed to see her again, not quite as before but less strange than she had been. But he could still feel no link between his mood and this new development in hers.

'It isn't that I'm not fond of you,' she went on, moving away from him towards the sofa and looking down at it, 'but it means something rather special to me. I suppose I'm rather . . . complex in these matters. Perhaps we all are.'

Automatically Timothy followed her towards the sofa.

'That's why I'm so sure,' she told him 'that it hasn't been as you thought. I should have to be . . . bound to the person in rather a special way.' She paused; the note of hesitancy in her voice invited a question.

'Yes?' said Timothy.

'May I sit down?' she asked. Timothy nodded but did not join her on the sofa. She put her bag on the arm, but she did not let go of it, her fingers kept playing with the strap, opening and closing.

'It's a kind of hero-worship, I suppose,' she said, almost dreamily. 'Not that you're not a hero, Timothy dear. . . . But few men are, in the

336

way I mean. I could love you without it, and I do, but not be *in* love with you.' Again her voice invited a question.

'Tell me,' said Timothy expressionlessly.

'It sounds so silly – but won't you sit down, I don't like to see you standing in your own house.'

Timothy sat down at the far end of the sofa.

'I expect I ought to have been born in another age,' she admitted, 'when men came home from the wars – they still do, of course, but with tin stomachs and duodenal ulcers – there's nothing very romantic in that!' She raised her eyebrows and gave Timothy half a smile. Neither his face nor his voice responded, but something in him warmed at her remark, though it was out of reach of his tongue.

'I'm afraid I'm too old to fight,' he said, shortly.

'Of course you are, darling, and I should hate to see you in uniform, it makes all men look alike.'

'What could I do, then,' said Timothy, 'that would make me seem heroic to you?'

She looked at him sadly. 'Darling, don't be sarcastic with me. After all, some people would think it was I who—' She paused and her glance slid down her dress to her black silk shoes. 'Actually it would take a very small thing to make you a hero in my eyes.'

'What?' asked Timothy bluntly.

'Darling, you know as well as I do, and you feel the same as I do really.'

'You mean—'

'Yes,' said Vera, 'but I want to hear you say it. Please say it, Timothy.'

Timothy got up from the sofa and began pacing the hearth-rug as though Vera was not there.

'Please say it, Timothy,' she repeated. 'It's childish of you not to.'

With furrowed brow and stricken face Timothy maintained his sentry-go.

'But what has it to do with us, Vera?' he burst out at length. 'You and me? What possible satisfaction can it be to you if I do something which I know is silly? What's the good of it? We shan't be any the better for it, either of us.'

'Oh yes we shall, darling,' Vera said, 'because we shall have done something for each other.'

Timothy thought this over. 'But it's so childish,' he said, resuming his march and speaking less to her than to himself. 'You say I'm childish because I don't want . . . er . . . to mention it, but you're more childish, it seems to me, to want me to, as if we were living in a fairy story! If it was something that would do you good, I wouldn't hesitate.'

'But it *will* do me good,' Vera said. 'After all, I'm the best judge of that. And, don't forget, it will do you good, too.'

Timothy gave an exasperated sigh. 'You wouldn't want me to if you knew how I felt,' he said. 'I have an instinct against it – call it a complex, a fixation, a superstitition, anything you like. It's haunted me ever since I came here. Every time I put out a thought in . . . in that direction, something goes wrong. It was all a mistake, I wasn't meant to use it. It's brought me a lot of trouble, and other people, too. And it would bring you into trouble, if you got mixed up with it.'

'But, darling. I'll take the risk,' said Vera. 'I'll go with you willingly.'

This brought Timothy up short. He stared down at her incredulously.

'You'll go with me?'

'Of course I will.'

'You mean,' he breathed almost in a whisper, 'that you'll go with me in the boat?' His eyes hung on her lips.

'Ah!' she exclaimed triumphantly, 'you've said it! The spell's broken! Yes, in the boat, any time you like. Now, if you like.'

She rose impulsively and came to his side and took his hand in hers.

'Think what it will be like in the moonlight, on the dark water, gliding between the trees! It isn't late, we shall have heaps of time. Do come, Timothy!'

They were behind the curtains that shielded the french window, invisible except to the moon and to each other. 'Kiss me!' said Vera, and Timothy kissed her; when he attempted a more ardent embrace she did not resist. He was lost in the rapture of being reunited to her, and it was her hand that, straying from its endearments, found the knob and gently let them out. On the lawn a fresh breeze met them, stirring the soft tendrils of her hair, those silken skirmishers, that seemed transparent when the moon shone through them. At a distance the black shadows on the lawn looked almost like holes, and Timothy, to whose arm Vera was clinging, instinctively guided her away from them, until at a closer view he saw that they, too, were moving with the gentle restlessness of the night. Down the grassy slope they stumbled, laughing and holding each other up; they crossed the moon-blanched lawn and took the path behind the shrubbery, which was too dense for moon or breeze to penetrate. And so they came to where the bamboos rustled, and sketched their spiky shadows on the walls and windows and peaked roof of the boat-house.

They key turned rustily and the door moved inwards grudgingly, as though someone was holding it against them. He left it open, for inside the darkness was so thick that at first they could see nothing but the dusky oblongs of the windows and the glimmer of the water at their feet.

'I ought to have brought a torch,' muttered Timothy.

'Try my lighter, darling.'

By the lighter's tiny flame they could only see each other, poised on an abyss from which came gentle whisperings and creakings. But when it dwindled and went out they began to see more clearly: a pale light as of dawn stole through the stained-glass windows; objects began to take on shape and meaning; something, not a mere random assemblage of surfaces, lay beneath them, something that seemed to have sense and will and intuition, and was offering itself to them: the boat.

'I can't see the sculls yet,' whispered Timothy.

He spoke in a whisper partly because all the sounds he heard were whispered sounds, but chiefly because it was a place in which he had never raised his voice since the day the boat was first entombed. He felt as he might have felt in a church at midnight, as a body-snatcher in a graveyard might have felt. . . .

'Darling, you're trembling,' Vera said. Her voice was incredulous and amused, but did not penetrate to the seat of his fear. 'You'll soon get warm rowing.'

'I haven't been in here for over a year,' he muttered, more to himself than to her. 'I don't seem able to get used to it. . . . Should you mind if . . . if we didn't, Vera?'

'Darling, it isn't I who'll mind, it's you.'

The tender edges of his consciousness struck against the steel thread in her voice.

'Do you still feel the same about . . . about everything?'

'How I wish I didn't, my treasure.'

Timothy could see the sculls now, they were hanging, one above the other, on supports on the opposite wall: two long, pale yellow shafts, for the blue blades were still invisible. Cautiously he edged his way to them, clinging to the sides of the boat-house, for the floor was damp and slippery, and nowhere more than eighteen inches wide. If he turned his head he could see Vera's hand and arm stretched down the door-post, silver in the moonlight; the rest of her was in shadow, and she seemed very far away, almost in another life, while the project to which she had committed him came nearer and nearer, presenting itself as something of tremendous complexity and peril, utterly beyond his strength. A few minutes ago it had seemed a simple undertaking; now the taboos which had grown up round the thought of it crowded into his mind, each with its warning message. But he struggled on; he had rounded two corners and his hand was on the handle of the scull when he heard the cry. Like an owl's cry yet unmistakably human, it made a furrow through the night.

'Hullo-o!'

He listened; the cry was repeated and seemed to come from nearer to.

'Don't pay any attention,' Vera's voice was urgent. 'Whoever it is, he'll soon go away.'

But Timothy was already making the return journey over the treacherous flagstones, much more quickly than he went.

'Don't go, don't go!' Her fluttering arms, stretching towards him in the darkness, barred his way.

'I must see who it is. Wait for me. I'll come back.'

'You won't.'

Timothy pushed past her and ran down the dark path on to the moonlight-flooded lawn. Above him on the terrace a man was standing, turning his head this way and that. 'Hullo!' he shouted, then saw Timothy and stood still.

Breathing quickly, Timothy came up to him.

'I'm so sorry, Casson,' said a pleasant voice, with a stiffening of authority in it that disclaimed apology. 'But I thought you ought to know that you forgot to draw your curtains, and there's a beam of light coming out that you can see from the road. I'm the Air Raid Warden.' (He omitted to say that he was also Colonel Harbord.) 'I knocked and rang, but I couldn't make anyone hear, so I came into the garden on the chance you might be about. I hope you didn't mind.' He kept his voice perfectly civil, clear of reproof.

Timothy thanked him and they walked quickly back towards the accusing beam, in which as they drew near it, the blades of grass on the shorn turf stuck out in vivid articulation, as white as if they had been frosted.

'Won't you come this way?' said Timothy. 'It'll be quicker for you.'

Colonel Harbord hesitated a moment, then, with a formal, 'That's very kind of you,' he followed Timothy through the french window. The latch clicked; the curtains, almost with the abandon of stage curtains, clashed together behind them. Blinking in the brightly lighted room they saw the hearth-rug in folds where Timothy's feet had puckered it; demoralised cushions crushed out of all shape; and, on the arm of the sofa, dominating all, palpably in possession, Vera's pale blue bag.

The room was less embarrassing when Timothy returned to it, after saying a crisp goodnight to Colonel Harbord. Indeed, it was almost seductive; and when he had put the hearth-rug straight, and plumped the cushions out, and put Vera's bag in a less challenging position, and exchanged a confidence with the cloisonné vase, he did not want to leave it. He did not want to leave it for the murky interior of the boat-house where swayed and slept on the stagnant water a direful deity, and where leaned against the lintel the priest-ess of the cult, all silvery white down one side and black through the rest of her body.

He knew he ought to go, but still he lingered, blunting his intention with delaying thoughts. Would Colonel Harbord have stayed for a drink, if Timothy had asked him? His demeanour had not been al-together unconciliatory. He seemed a friendly sort of man, a little stiff, perhaps. But what if Vera had come in, in the middle? Timothy tried to picture the scene, but his imagination could not carry it through to any but a disastrous conclusion.

He sighed and thought of Vera in the boat-house. How long the time must seem to her. He must go, of course, but before he went he would collect a few things for the expedition; some cushions and a rug for her, her fur wrap which was in the hall, his electric torch which might be in his bedroom. They needed lots of things, really. All this would take time.

How silent the house was, as he prowled round it! What a quality of expectancy and secrecy the lights had, screened from all participation with the night! So, too, was he cut off, a moving shadow among shad-ows that were fixed, invisible from without and hardly visible from within.

It was a long job but at last he was ready. He had collected every-thing they would and some things that they would not want, but it was better to be on the safe side. Bowed and lopsided he let himself out through the side door, not wishing to disturb the drawing-room curtains. In the moonlight his misshapen shadow looked like Father Christmas.

But when he reached the boat-house, it was empty.

She can't have gone far away, he thought, and searched the bushes round about, and peered among the rushes and ventured to use his torch in the darker places, and called her softly by name. But she did not answer, and he returned to the boat-house, half expecting to find her leaning against the lintel; but there was no one.

Slowly he started back again, and what was his astonishment to see, as he rounded the dark bastion of the shrubbery, the beam of light from the drawing-room lying like a sword across the lawn.

He hastened towards it, curbing in himself any impulse to reproach her, for it was he who was at fault for leaving her so long; and the words of apology were already on his lips when he entered the room. But he checked them, for there was no one there, no one and nothing; even her bag had gone. But yes, there was something, a pencilled note lying on the back of the sofa. His heart sank as he approached it. Without any conscious act of reading, the message printed itself on his mind.

'DEAR TIMOTHY,

'I have given you up. You won't expect me to explain why.

'VERA.'

Timothy waited a few minutes in increasing agitation and then telephoned. Vera might be home by now. He heard the bell ringing, but no one came to answer it.

He went to bed but his thoughts gave him no rest. 'I have given you up' might simply mean that she was tired of waiting for him; he tried to cling to that, but it was like a rock in a rising tide and he was soon dislodged. In the huge, encircling seas not a raft, not a spar appeared; not a gleam from the shore he had started from, not an intimation of land ahead. He was cut off from the past and the future, and the present had nothing for him but this ceaseless tossing. Already he felt a nausea akin to seasickness.

He sat up and turned on the light, and with the disengaged fragment of his mind asked himself some questions. Why had he got into this state? What was it all about? He was there, the same Timothy as yesterday, safe in his comfortable bed. True he did not feel very well, but that was just a functional disturbance of his nervous system and would soon pass. No dire disease threatened him. He had lost some money, he would have to be careful and economical, his solicitor had more than once told him so; but he was in no danger of bankruptcy or any kind of public exposure, and if he was, he had friends who would come to his rescue – one of them was shortly coming to stay with him. A girl had given him up – thrown him over might be a more accurate way of putting it; but did not that happen to scores of people? – people in their first youth for whom such a set-back might well seem the destruction of a lifetime's hopes?

Why then did he feel so wretched, so . . . why be afraid of a word? so suicidal?

Suppose he was with the army in some distant land, surrounded by foes waiting to kill him, how paradisal, by contrast, would his present state appear! Or suppose he was in the Air Force, as Edgell was, with the machine out of control and the ground rushing up to meet him! How enviable, then, to be Timothy Casson, sheltered from the malice of the elements, with nothing worse to complain of than a mild disappointment, a slight concussion of the feelings, so impalpable that no seismograph on earth could measure it! Was he not really very lucky, compared with ninety-nine people out of a hundred?

For a moment Timothy did almost feel lucky, and his mental pain withdrew as far as the end of the bed. But soon he felt it coming towards him, in thin layers of blackness, to envelop him in its clinging embrace.

Suppose he was in a German concentration camp, and this light that was shining in his eyes was ten times, a hundred times brighter. Then his dressing gown hanging on the door would be the Questioner, and the bed-posts torturers. The fire-irons would be their instruments and in the empty grate a fire could be quickly lighted. The clothes lying about the floor and sagging over chair-backs would be his clothes, for in an interrogation of this sort the victim would be told to strip. So Timothy was not lying warm in bed but shivering on the cold floor and the Questioner, bringing the thousand-volt lamp nearer to his sleepless eyelids, said, 'Now, for the last time, will you tell me what they make in the factory on the hills above Upton?' Timothy moistened his lips and tried to say, 'I can't tell you because I don't know,' but the words wouldn't come. 'You don't know?' said the Questioner, bringing the lamp so close to Timothy that the heat from it scorched his face; 'then we shall have to jog your memory.' At once the bed-posts began to close in on him, slender-looking trunks but with the strength of steel in them, and they dragged him over to the fireplace where the fire-irons and other sharper-looking instruments were glowing behind the bars. Then the Questioner, whose face was only in his voice, said, 'Have you ever known what it is to be in pain?' and Timothy, who could now remember only one thing from his past life, answered, 'Yes, the night that Vera Cross gave me up.' 'And is that all the pain you have ever felt?' asked the Questioner; 'all the pain you have felt in fifty-one years?' Timothy tried to remember, but his mind went blank. 'What we are going to do to you now,' the Questioner said softly, 'will hurt you so much that you will

343

look back on the night you spoke of as the happiest in all your life.' He paused, and then barked out, 'Put him on the floor, and start with the soles of his feet.' The shadows of the torturers, driven forward by the light behind, advanced and converged on him. . . .

Still possessed by the dream, Timothy opened his eyes, wondering where he was. As his terror began to loosen its hold he realised that he had fallen asleep with the light on. Sleepily he turned it off and after a moment saw the pallor of daylight on the ceiling above the curtains. His mind too deeply drugged by deliverance to be accessible to further pain, he turned over and slept.

CHAPTER XXVI

SEVERAL times during the day Timothy rang Vera up but she was always out. He whiled away an hour and more at the Fisherman's Arms, involuntarily turning his head when anyone came in, but his patience went unrewarded. As aforetime, at the beginning of their acquaintance, he hung about the village street at the times when she used to take the children for a walk. But not a glimpse of her did he get. And it was the same the next day and the next. In giving him up she had given up all her old habits. She had become invisible; and if it had not been for Frances's matter-of-fact announcements that she was out, he might have concluded that she had gone away from Upton.

He got through the days somehow because hope dawned anew each morning, waxed brighter as the day wore on, and only set when he laid his head on the pillow. Then his sufferings began in earnest. For several nights he had recourse successfully to scenes of horror; every inhuman act that the newspapers had recorded and that imagination could devise was re-enacted in Timothy's bedroom. It became a torture-chamber. And when he banished the bogies, and called back reality to his comfort, he would fall asleep.

But whoever tampers with reality does so at his peril. Timothy's reactions to his fancied horrors grew weaker, presently they ceased, and a night came when, instead of acting as a counter-irritant they joined forces with the foe, and Timothy lay in a kind of waking nightmare in which the terrors of Belsen and Buchenwald were reinforced by the nameless misery of his own plight. He could not divide them; he could not turn from one to the other, for they were on both sides of his pillow.

Nor did the phantoms he had summoned up abandon him during the day. They lurked in corners, only awaiting blackout time to come out and claim him. He was conscious of their presence all day long. They even followed him into the open air and accompanied him on the long walks with which he sought to tire himself. Still trying to find an antidote, for happiness does not give in without a struggle, he now compelled his mind to dwell on Magda's visit. What fun they would have! How Magda's cosmopolitan outlook and bright, shadowless mind would chase away these rustic spectres! How silly and trivial all his preoccupations would seem! The village would be reduced to its true scale, that is to say, it would be invisible. He wouldn't mind if she were a little cruel about it, he would even welcome jokes at Upton's expense. How they would laugh at it! In anticipation, and to keep his sense of humour lively, Timothy let out a trial guffaw; the meadows rang with it and a man who was walking along a hedgerow some distance away looked round in surprise. Embarrassed, Timothy met his glance. It was Wimbush.

His ex-gardener came towards him, a broad smile on his face. They shook hands.

'Why, sir, it's pleasant to hear you laugh so hearty-like,' said Wimbush. 'To tell you the truth, and meaning no disrespect, I thought it was a jay.'

'I'm afraid I was laughing at my own thoughts,' said Timothy, already finding humour up-hill work.

'And what better should a man have to laugh at?' said Wimbush, stoutly defending Timothy against the reproach of eccentricity. 'My mother used to say, "You must learn to laugh at nothing, for often there's nothing to laugh at." Ha! ha! And that's true, isn't it, sir?'

'It is indeed,' said Timothy, whose thoughts immediately took a soberer hue.

' 'Tisn't everyone as sees what it means, not at the first onset.'

They talked for a time of matters that concerned each other; of Wimbush's new job, of Timothy's new gardener; each allowed himself the luxury, and the other the compliment, of regret.

'If it hadn't been for that other one in the kitchen!' sighed Wimbush, and they both shook their heads.

'But I hear as they're both leaving now,' Wimbush went on, putting a great deal of delicacy into the statement. 'Would that be true, sir?'

Timothy said it was.

'Now Effie, she'll be a real loss,' said Wimbush. 'And I don't care who hears me say it. Another year or two, and we should have got sort of used to her, as we have to you, sir. It's these people that come and go so you can't keep track of them, they're the drawback.'

'Um,' said Timothy. They were walking along side by side and the sense of their old familiarity had returned.

'Mr. Edgell, of course, he's a bit of a harumscarum,' Wimbush said. 'But being in the Army do tone a man down, even if it's only the Air Force.'

Timothy said something in praise of Edgell.

'You're quite right, sir, only with that stomach of his he ought to lay off the ladies.'

Timothy glanced at Wimbush in surprise.

'You haven't heard, sir?'

Timothy protested ignorance, but Wimbush did not reply immediately.

' 'Twas what I meant by a drawback, sir,' he said obliquely, 'when you can't keep a proper check on 'em. Of course if I hadn't had the privilege of serving you for a long time, sir, and hadn't left of my own accord, I shouldn't be saying this.'

'But you haven't said anything!' cried Timothy.

'It wouldn't be my place, sir, you not knowing. But there's many here who wish you well, sir, as are quite glad it should be him instead of you.'

Timothy stood still and Wimbush stood still, too.

'Do you mean—?' Timothy began.

'I don't mean nothing, sir,' said Wimbush, holding his ground, 'only what I said. And I only said that because I thought you knew, and as man to man, though only a servant.'

Timothy guessed what Wimbush meant, but could not rest until he had turned suspicion into certainty. Making a great effort he said, 'How do you know this?'

'Why, sir, I've seen them together down by the river, and 'tis common talk.'

'You mean Miss Cross, of course?'

Wimbush nodded. 'We thought you'd ceased to take an interest, sir,' he said, noticing Timothy's expression. 'And we do feel it's all for the best.'

'Felix! Felix!' cried Timothy.

Down in the gully below them a little stream meandered, deep in summer rushes; and along this the retriever was galloping, every now and then stopping so abruptly that he almost threw himself into the air. Even from here one could feel his anxiety lest any detail of his business should escape him through inattention; it was a deeply personal matter, no one could see to it but himself. Down went his head and his tail waved to and fro, the varying rapidity of its movement answering to the intensity of his thoughts.

'Felix! Felix!' Timothy called again. 'Oh, that wretched dog! He won't do as he's told. He's just like he was when you were with me.'

But in saying this he did Felix an injustice, for the dog with a head-long sweep abandoned his cherished investigations and came racing up to where they stood.

Wimbush patted him and Felix, his eyes welling with delight, began to set in motion the cumbrous machinery of his affection.

'Down, Felix! Down!'

'I don't mind him, sir,' said Wimbush. ' 'Twas a pity he would muck up the flower-beds, but perhaps I was overhasty with him. How's the new man getting on?'

'All right, I think, but to tell you the truth I don't see much of him.'

Wimbush shook his head, as though this was only to be expected, and Timothy asked him how he liked his new job.

' 'Tis all right, sir, but I get fed up with trapesing along that old river and nobody to talk to.' They had said all this before.

'You never see Mrs. Lampard, I suppose?'

'Bless you no, sir, she's locked up, as a good many other people in this parish ought to be, if right was right.'

As he spoke, a shadow seemed to darken the hillside, quenching the uncertain sunlight of the summer and deepening the pain in Timothy's mind.

'Anyhow I'm very glad we met, Wimbush,' he said, trying to feel his way towards a gap in the surrounding blackness.

'And me too, sir,' said Wimbush. 'And I hope we shall soon meet again when we haven't neither of us so much on hand.' With this tactful reference to the fact that he was busy Wimbush was moving away; then he recollected something. ' 'Twas better not to leave you to find out, sir. Me telling you, that knows your style of thinking, as well as if it was my own, you won't fret half so much.'

'Thank you, Wimbush.'

Timothy put Felix on a lead and found, for the first time, that the retriever's persistent tugging and sudden starts after an invisible quarry were a relief rather than an irritation. They employed his mind as well as his body, and there was something forthright in Felix's nature that demanded an immediate response. One knew where one was with him. Not altogether, of course. An air of exemplary meekness was often the prelude to an act of signal disobedience. And sometimes he dissembled his love under an affectation of indifference, in order to take the victim by surprise. But he never concealed his indifference under a cloak of love.

It was most painful to Timothy to be angry with Vera; for his own peace of mind he instinctively invented excuses for her. If he could persuade himself that the breach was his fault it made him almost happy. But he never could, for long together. He did not really believe that she had given him up because of the boat. The boat was a pretext.

But he was handicapped in his efforts to get to the root of the matter by his unwillingness to think about the boat at all. The part of his mind where it lay, like a parasite encased in wax, was almost impenetrable to the probings of reason.

Edgell had stolen Vera from him; that was the true explanation. Young, handsome and attractive, he had come as a sneak-guest to Timothy's house and cast a spell on Vera. He had betrayed the laws of hospitality to do him this great wrong. Vera really loved him, Timothy; she had come prepared to tell him so. Then this pale and interesting stranger, romantic-looking in his Air Force uniform, had laid lightning siege to her heart. All the evening she had struggled against it but it had been too much for her and, snatching at the boat as an excuse, she had given Timothy up. What more natural? What had he to offer, what baits for love, compared with this martial invalid who, he remembered now, had an easy way with women and a fatal knowledge of the hearts of blondes?

At the time, he had to admit, he had felt sorry for Edgell, who seemed to be disconcerted by Vera's challenging manner. In reality it was an instinctive defence against a method of attack which Edgell had practised too often and too successfully. Now she was in thrall to a man who would do nothing for her, who would not think of marrying her, but would make her the victim of a hopeless attachment and the subject, perhaps, of a flashy and commonplace short story.

So Timothy reasoned and bade his mind stoke up the fires of his anger against Edgell, the cad, the heart-breaker, the abuser of hospitality. He told himself that but for Edgell he and Vera would now be enjoying the felicity of last August. Oh that he had never asked him to the house! Or if Edgell had come at some other time, at any time but that! How cruel of Fate to have ordained this fatal conjunction, setting the wolf where he the lamb might get! Miserably Timothy re-lived in memory all the circumstances that led up to the meeting, reminding himself of all the steps he might have taken to prevent it. Now he would never get Vera back; in her passions she was reckless and wholehearted, as he had cause to know. She was love's plaything, as she had been his.

But had she been? She said she hadn't.

He stirred in his chair. How changed the room was from the old days when he had felt almost a fondness for its shabby, unpretentious comfort. Now it watched him coldly, with an alien regard; even Mrs. Purbright's vase, so companionable to moods of the middle register, between joy and sorrow, had nothing now to say to him. No one had anything to say to him. . . .

The telephone bell rang.

'Hullo, who is it?'

'Oh, Mr. Casson. . . .'

For a moment he did not recognise the voice. 'Yes?' – rather impatiently.

'It's Volumnia Purbright.' Edged with anxiety though it was, her voice took its welcome for granted.

'Yes, Mrs. Purbright?' He could not feel his old affection for her, he could not.

'You don't sound very well. I hope you are?'

'Quite well, thank you.'

'I'm so glad. I had a feeling you might not be.'

'I have been a little bit under the weather.'

'I'm so sorry. Is there any chance of seeing you?'

'Well, just at the moment. . . .'

'Of course, I understand. And what I had to say I can say just as well now. But I'm afraid it will be tiresome – I apologise in advance.'

'I'm sure it won't be.'

'Mr. Casson, it's about Edgell. . . . Hullo?'

'Oh yes,' said Timothy tonelessly.

'I'm not quite happy about him. You see, there's so little for him to do here, everyone in the neighbourhood seems to be away, and we are such a dull old couple.'

'Oh no, Mrs. Purbright,' said Timothy, mechanically. 'You mustn't say that.'

'Yes, I'm afraid we are. You have been so good to him, and he likes you so much – he's quite devoted to you, you know.'

'Is he?' Timothy scarcely tried to disguise his scepticism.

'Yes, he is. He's a little in awe of you, of course.'

'Of course,' said Timothy, playfully ironic.

'Well, with the respect of an unfledged for an established writer. How badly I put it, and you have travelled so far beyond the need of hero-worship.'

'Yes, I am getting rather old.'

'Oh *no*, Mr. Casson.' Timothy could now hear the nervous intonations in her voice quite well. 'How I wish I could see you – this wretched instrument, I'm such a duffer at it. We all owe you so much, and I hate to go on imposing on you, but if you did have a minute to spare, and could give Edgell another little talk about writing, he . . . he would value it so much.'

'I'm afraid those things can't be taught,' said Timothy.

'Of course not, of course not. But in conversation so many hints are thrown out, so many sparks fly – and something is communicated. Even on the telephone.' Mrs. Purbright gave a nervous little laugh. 'Who should know it better than I?' she went on, uncertainly. 'I have often felt it was a shame – it has saddened me to think, Mr. Casson – that you should have been here so long – well, not very long really – and only we. . . . But I've said all this before. . . .' Timothy's silence produced another nervous laugh, almost a giggle. 'But you are what I hope I may call a friend of the family, and if you did feel you could give Edgell – I won't say encouragement, but—'

'Mrs. Purbright,' said Timothy brutally, 'it's no good. Your Edgell has many qualifications, I'm sure; but you can take it from me, he'll never make a writer.'

His laughter, as hysterical as on the evening of the smoking concert, filled the little room with descending arpeggios of mockery. Its effect must have carried to the other end of the telephone, too. Timothy heard an exclamation like a cry, the cry of someone who has been physically wounded; and then a buzzing that showed the line was clear.

Hateful to himself he went back to his chair, where the familiar pattern of what he saw brought back the familiar pattern of his thoughts. But another strand, darker if not more painful, was interwoven with them. How could he have spoken so cruelly to Mrs. Purbright? And taken so much pleasure in doing it, as if she was to blame for his loss of Vera? Alas, the answer was only too obvious, but its very obviousness made the lapse the more unpardonable. And he, too, would suffer for it – for he had lost, at one blow, Mrs. Purbright's friendship and the sense of self-respect which, badly holed as it was, had served him as a kind of raft – enabling him, with some hope of rescue, to run up distress signals to catch the attention of the passer-by. Now he did not deserve rescuing.

His impulse was to ring Mrs. Purbright up. If he could not take back what he had said, at least he could apologise for saying it, and try to restore the circulation between them, nipped by his sudden roughness. After all, Edgell had not meant to do him any harm. Had he, Timothy, when he first pressed his suit on Vera, considered whether he might not be robbing another man? He thought of the Rectory where he had always been treated as a favoured guest, though heaven knew how Mrs. Purbright had explained her partiality for him to her other friends. Now at the best his name would be greeted with a shrug from Edgell, a tight-lipped word of Christian forbearance from the Rector, and from Mrs. Purbright who knows? – perhaps a tear.

He dragged himself from his chair and slowly made his way across the hall to the telephone. Just as he was putting out his hand to take it, the bell rang. He started, and a quiver of fright ran through him, as though his senses had begun to play him tricks. He took up the receiver and a voice said, 'Upton 698? I have a telegram for you.'

The telegram was from Magda and said that she would be coming the day after tomorrow. She would be bringing Nastya with her. She gave him the time of the train's arrival at Swirrelsford, and sent him her dearest love.

Mrs. Purbright and her wrongs forgotten, Timothy hastened into the kitchen and there, with Felix pinioning his feet, he made elaborate arrangements for the reception and entertainment of this most cherished guest. Everything must be of the best, the food, the attendance, the welcome.

Beatrice and Effie showed themselves so co-operative that Timothy was again on the point of asking them to stay on. But he still felt doubtful of the wisdom of doing that, and anyhow, the question could be settled, along with how many others, by Magda when she came.

The stimulus of making plans, of moulding the future to his use, of stamping his image on events, soon passed, and when night came it found him hardly less depressed than before. He realised that Mrs. Purbright had been a life-line between him and what he valued, what really nourished his inner life; cut off from her, by his own unkindness, he was as helpless, faced by the task of clothing his spiritual nakedness, as a tailor without a tape measure. He did not know what he wanted; he could think of no boon to ask of the future that the future would not refuse to grant. So his mind occupied itself ceaselessly with the past, with going over all his old mistakes, correcting them and imagining the kind of life he would have had if he had acted differently. The sense of having used up the material of his life, of having borrowed on his expectations of happiness and squandered the loan, was torturing.

Yet Magda's telegram had brought him a moment's joy, and though he could no longer feel it, any more than one can feel the sunshine when the sun has gone, he could cling to it as a fact, a proof that his low spirits were not incurable; and as the hours dragged by, the promise of Magda's coming began to flash, like a lighthouse with a recurrent gleam, until, on the morning of the day, he felt, not indeed his own self, but as the sufferer from a chill feels when he is brought a hot-water-bottle. He spent the morning in a fury of activity; the house was to be embowered with flowers, Magda's room, Nastya's room should over-flow with them. From the cupboard appeared many of Miss Chadwick's vases that had never seen the light before; the borders were pillaged and all Simpson's protests set aside. Flower-conscious as never before, Timothy went to and fro laden with blossoms. The scissors snipped, stalks and leaves lined the basin and littered the floor; and though in all this activity Timothy had the feeling that he was trying to outstrip something that was close at his heels, the colour and the fragrance found their way to his senses, if not quite to his heart. He deliberately encouraged in himself the feeling of excitement, trying to believe it was the same as happiness; he quickened his movements and ran from place to place, just as someone might who was deliriously happy; and he could see by the light reflected on their faces that he had deceived Beatrice and Effie, even if he had not succeeded in deceiving himself.

There was the afternoon still to get through, and Timothy employed it by making a shopping-list. Many of the items, he knew, would be unprocurable in these days of austerity; but perhaps he could find some bath-salts, a pat of soap with a French name on it, some yellow roses, in which the garden was entirely lacking – and when he saw the shops themselves, other ideas would spring into his head.

He set off in his car early, to be in time before the shops shut. By now his impatience was really genuine; change of environment, and the wonderful pick-me-up of extravagance, had effectually banished his black mood. The shops themselves were far from encouraging, but in his passion for purchase he did not scruple to buy things that had only the faintest bearing on Magda's visit. Its mere scarcity made an object desirable and soon the back seat of the car was heaped with shoe cream, a bicycle lamp, anchovies in brine, cherries in brandy, weighty fancy cakes of brilliant hue, olive oil, an egg-whisk, a hair-sieve, elastic, hair-slides, cigarettes, matches, saucepans, and many other things that might be useful or enjoyable, if one had a crisis, equivalent to ship-wreck, in one's daily life. Each acquisition conferred a sense of power, and by teatime Timothy, the master of all these treasures, was also master of himself.

The train came in, forty minutes late. It was natural that Magda should not appear at once; she would have so many packages to collect, or to have collected for her. Timothy stood at the gate, watching the passengers go through. The soldiers on leave had tired faces, deeply sunburnt, and empty sometimes to the point of vacancy. Bowed beneath their equipment they walked with a clatter of hobnailed boots, laugh-ing and barging into each other. Anonymous, indifferent faces, these, not like the faces he was used to seeing, which reflected his moods almost as if they had been mirrors. Each of them was the centre of a complete solar system, impenetrable to Timothy and his problems. He found the thought soothing.

Now the stream was growing thinner; soon it was the merest trickle, leaving the platform bare. A whistle blew, the train drew out. A few of the station staff pottered about, relaxed and careless; but Magda was not among them.

She had missed the train.

Not unduly disheartened, Timothy settled down in an hotel in Swirrelsford to await the next. It was due in about three hours' time, a porter told him.

He telephoned to Effie, announcing his change of plan. Sitting in the lounge, he again felt the attraction of being unknown and adrift in an alien but not hostile world. To this was added, as he dined, an anticipation of the joy of seeing Magda keener even than before; it was as though he was going to find her again, after having lost her. She had become his favourite woman, his beloved, his only friend. In this sanguine mood he returned to the station. Ten o'clock brought the sunset, but did not bring the train. Not until the shadows had made their final pounce was he aware of a dull thudding in the east which deepened into a roar and then subsided into a rattle as the shuttered train, like a mortuary on wheels, clanked furtively past him. Narrow cones of dirty light in which the smoke still swirled were all he had to see by; he would have to recognise her by her silhouette, the slight stoop which was so far from being deferential. Once he thought he saw her and started forward, but it was not her, and he had to stifle the greeting that was rising to his lips.

The slow drive back, with lights so dim they hardly reached the hedgerows, was a new exercise in disappointment. No doubt an explanation awaited him – Magda's movements were often capricious – but an explanation is no substitute for an arrival, and it was an arrival that Effie was expecting when she flung the door open, letting out a glare of hospitable light, that had to be immediately quenched. Timothy saw the house as it would have looked, transformed by Magda's presence; then he had to tell Effie, and remind himself, that she had not come. 'But I expect you knew,' he added, blinking in the bright light shed by a chandelier that was not in ordinary use; 'there will have been a telegram or something.' Effie, shrunk to half her former size, and with all the lustre gone out of her, shook her head. 'Nothing at all, sir, and we've made it look so nice.' Timothy's assurance that it would look just as nice next day did not seem to console her, nor did it convince Timothy, for preparations timed to celebrate an occasion do not keep beyond it, and the house looked absurdly overdressed, lacking the reason for which it had been embellished.

Under the assault of artificial light, some of it coming from unshaded bulbs, the flowers, too, looked artificial, and their gaiety seemed strained and unspontaneous, as of flowers in a sick-room meant to banish the impression of illness. Even as a contribution to Magda's exotic effect they would perhaps have been exaggerated; as an end in themselves they were a failure, lowering the spirits they were meant to raise, and bringing out the shabbiness they were meant to hide. The rooms, as Timothy wandered through them, put him in mind of an old woman, made up and bedizened for a party that has not come off, there was even something macabre about them, a hint of the cenotaph. He did not like to think of the flowers watching all night in the unoccupied rooms, and had a mind to huddle them in the hall and on the landings, as they do in nursing homes, as they did, perhaps, in Magda's. It cost him an effort to go into her room and see amid the floral tributes the white sheet turned down. His own room had not escaped the universal beautification; Effie's solicitude had put flowers there, too; and when he turned on his bedside lamp, for Magda came between him and his sleep, he saw them looking at him with painted smiles and wished them away.

Morning brought a letter from Magda. He tore it open, asking Effie to wait to hear the contents, thinking, in his excitement, that it would explain her non-arrival. It was, in fact, written three days ago, so slow were posts in reaching Upton; but it was written after her telegram, to confirm it, she said, and was full of affection and anticipation. The blood-red slogan 'Death to the Fascist dogs and traitors,' twice underlined, was the only direct reference to politics. She felt extremely well, she said, and must really give up the nursing-home habit. But it was the only place in London where you were properly looked after, and being in Grosvenor Square was convenient for her friends in Curzon Street. They had been most attentive, poor darlings, and she was glad that the rules of the home allowed her to offer them a drink. 'I hope we shall have lots of river-life,' she wound up; 'I have brought all the necessaries, including a boater and a veil. Nastya thinks I'm mad. "You'll never put those on," she said. Little she knows – but of course not all the comrades understand that one can be presentable without and serious within.'

The letter recalled Magda so vividly to Timothy that it was almost as though she was already in the house. Even the reference to boating did not worry him; he could easily explain to her his changed attitude to that recreation. Going downstairs he felt that the flowers were once more perfectly in place.

Later in the morning he went into the kitchen to ask if the newspapers had arrived. Generally they came about midday; it was now nearly lunchtime. To his surprise he saw that they had, for Beatrice was sitting in a chair looking at *The Times* and Effie was reading it over her shoulder. So absorbed were they that they did not notice Timothy come in; only when Felix's tail began to thud upon the floor did they look up, and then it was only to look down again.

'Oh, I see the papers have come,' said Timothy, for the sake of something to say. 'But keep them by all means; I'm in no hurry for them.'

They both looked up at him blankly, and Effie turned without speaking and walked into the larder.

It was so like something they might have done in their old, undismissed, unregenerate days that Timothy was not surprised. After all their efforts and preparations they had good reason to feel chagrined.

At last Beatrice looked up. Her face was portentous.

'There's something in the paper, sir,' she said, 'but I don't want to be the one to tell you.'

Timothy's heart turned over.

'If you don't mind, I'd better hear,' he said.

Tears began to choke Beatrice's utterance. She rose and handed him the paper. 'Please, sir, look for yourself,' she said. 'I can't say it.'

Timothy's eye went straight to the entry.

VIVIAN . . . Suddenly, in a London nursing home . . . Mrs. Magda Vivian . . . No flowers, no mourning.

Timothy remembered that in all his letters to Magda he had never once asked after her health. He had assumed that her frequent visits to the nurisng home were simply another instance of luxurious living; that she went because she was bored, and idle, and could afford to. Indeed, by some muddled process of thinking, he had come to regard these disappearances as a proof of her perfect health. Most of her friends had done the same; and she was perhaps too proud and too reserved to undeceive them. They were not altogether to blame. Magda hated talking about health, her own or anybody else's; she did not think it was a subject for conversation. But how thoughtless of him never to have given the facts their weight; how callous never to have inquired!

He sat among the flowers, the flowers that she had forbidden, and felt that he had failed her, as he had failed everybody else. No one was the happier or the better for him. He tried to keep his thoughts away from himself; it was unseemly, in the presence of her death, to think of anything but her. A night of memories and sighs . . . Yes, he had given her that, but it was a tribute to the living Magda, who was coming to relieve his loneliness, not to the dead one, who could do nothing for him. Try as he would to accord her the selfless contemplation, the prayerful meditation proper to the dead, he could not help feeling how much more desolate his own position was, now that she had gone. . . .

He picked up her letter and re-read it many times. But it only spoke to him of a lost companionship, a friendship that he was too old and tired to look for elsewhere.

So he sat with the letter in his hands, and the minutes sped by and Effie, noiseless and almost voiceless, told him lunch was ready. He got up, and on an impulse, for the telephone room was on the way to the dining room, took up the receiver and dialled a number.

'Oh Frances, it's Timothy here. Is Vera anywhere about?'

'I don't think so, Timothy, but I'll go and see.'

A long pause, and then Vera's voice.

'Hullo, Timothy. How are you?'

'Well, a little upset as a matter of fact. But I can't tell you on the telephone. Any chance of seeing you?'

'Of course, why not? I'm always here.'

'What about dinner tonight?'

'Perfect.' There was a short pause, then Vera said, 'Are you going to strike a blow for freedom?'

'Yes,' said Timothy.

CHAPTER XXVII

'. . . AND so, dear Tyro, if you don't mind, I'll tell you all about it, and how it has come to mean so much to me, almost more than life itself. That won't sound so exaggerated to you as it would to some people, because you have always recognised the force of ideals, and know that they are the only things that really matter. I haven't always thought so, but now I *do*, which is partly why I'm writing you this long rigmarole – my apologia, you might call it, only that sounds so pretentious.'

Timothy paused to extract another sheet of paper from the finger-pinching velvet slot of the converted knife-box.

'I don't know whether you will sympathise with me, I'm afraid you won't, because, actively engaged in the war as you are, it will all seem so trivial. And it is trivial in a way, but the issues aren't. Anyhow, you're almost the only person left that I can write to, now that Magda is gone; unless I also write to Esther Morwen, just to have a second witness – though I'm afraid she will disapprove of what I'm going to do even more than you will. She'll think I've become a Communist! – which I haven't, in the least, though a friend of mine, who's in this with me, is a bit red.

'We haven't written to each other lately. I've been in an unsatisfactory state of mind and I knew I couldn't keep it out of my letters. It would be boring for you to hear about my troubles – sometime, when we meet, I'll tell you, if you can bear to listen, but the thing is, I've tracked them to their source. I know now why my life here has been a failure; it's all because I never had the courage to put my boat on the river. I was afraid of all sorts of things, public opinion, hurting people's feelings, being unpopular, breaking the law (though I've just consulted some solicitors who say the law is really on my side); and I was snobbish, too; I wanted to make friends with the "gentry" and I knew I never could, if I insisted on using my boat. Even the rumour that I meant to use it was enough to turn them against me. So I had no friends here except the Rector's wife, and she was always urging me to give way about the boat, and submit to "their" dictatorship – for that is what it amounts to. Now I've quarrelled with her, about quite another matter, and I'm sorry in a way, but perhaps it's just as well for she wouldn't approve of what I'm going to do. I did make another friend – the one who's helping me now – but she doesn't belong to the place, she's a foreigner, as I am.

'But all these eighteen months (and how long they seem, like a lifetime) the boat has been in my mind like an ulcer, poisoning it; and the more I tried not to think about it, the more harm it did me – we all know now what comes of harbouring an obsession – it made everything go bad on me.

'And not only on me, that's another point I realise now. The happiness of several other people has suffered, much worse than mine has. I came to live here with the best intentions, but I seem to have done nothing but harm. And why? Because I would not take action, though if I had it would have been to my own good and everybody else's.

'Think, there is this lovely river, one of the most beautiful in England, and the only people who ever get a sight of it, except at the bridge and one or two other places, are a parcel of stuffy, retired men who are no earthly use to anyone; not only do they cumber the land and the water, but they keep better people off it. You know how easily young people get into mischief; according to the statistics, more than ever did before; the figures of juvenile crime go up alarmingly. And why? Because, poor things, they have nowhere to go to amuse themselves except the pub and the cinema and the dance hall; they all pile into the Swirrelsford bus and spend their afternoons and evenings sweating indoors in a fœtid atmosphere, when they might be on the river, in the open air, communing with Nature, benefiting their health, and enjoying each other's society in any way they like (I'm not a puritan) in romantic and poetical surroundings, the influence of which will remain with them through life, quickening their response to the beautiful – which is also (I'm sure you will agree with me about this, so I won't stop to argue it) to *some* extent, the good.'

Timothy paused and remembered the damaged boats at Swirrelsford, and the boatman's opinion of his customers. But he dismissed these inconvenient facts from his mind, for when one is clearly in the right, it is both logical and laudable to ignore the arguments on the other side.

'But it's the younger children I think about the most, the kiddies who do so love the water. You remember the "Water Babies"? – I suppose it's old-fashioned now, but it's haunted me all my life with intimations of water-happiness, chucklings and gurglings – a perpetual murmur of invitation. It draws me by something in my blood – water on the brain, perhaps! – my spirit quickens the moment I see the river. And I know it's the same with the children here – you see them in these summer days splashing about in the shallow water by the bridge – "schoolboys play-ing in the stream" – you remember that lovely poem of Peele's? – and looking so blissfully happy – happy in themselves and with each other. If they could only stay like that – if the bright water could continue to be a condition of the spirit in which they could always play – they would never want wars or commit the horrors we are always reading about. In my mind's eye I can see a flotilla of nice tubby little boats moored by the bridge, and two or three good-natured boatmen ready to take out the youngsters – I wouldn't mind doing it myself, I can think of many worse occupations – and the happiness they would give, not only here, but to the children up and down the valley. They would come from far and near.

'But of course that's quite out of the question, a mere Utopian dream, so long as these sour-faced, half-witted colonels and people insist on appropriating the river and what is ironically called "preserv-ing" it for their elderly and far from innocent pastimes, with all their expensive paraphernalia of murder bought in Pall Mall and St. James's Street – never speaking, never thinking, just watching the water for a chance to kill, like a cat at a mouse-hole. And instead of children's laughter, a tense, waiting silence, broken only by the gasp of a dying fish, and the grim "That's got him!" of the fishermen.

'I know I ought to hate them but I can't quite bring myself to, because of course they don't realise all the harm their selfishness is doing – not only by depriving the humbler Uptonians of their rights to air and health and happiness, but far and wide, beyond this valley, by their example, rousing resentment, stimulating envy. People's lives ought to be made safe against envy, it isn't fair to expose them to it. The causes of envy should be rooted out and destroyed, like the causes of any other infection – not "liquidated," that's a horrid word – but some-how painlessly removed.'

Timothy paused and took another sheet. He felt that he was express-ing his ideas too baldly.

'All this is merely metaphorical, of course. I shouldn't like you to think I was animated by *hostility* to anyone, not even to the fishing-snobs, as someone has wittily called them. And I'm aware that if they had taken to me in the first place, I might not be writing of them as I am now. But that would have been weakness, the seduction of the corrupt system under which we live, and which perpetuates and sancti-fies all this unfairness. What I'm going to do now will be good for "them" as well, it will bring them to their senses and make them see that they *can't* go on as they are doing – they simply must be stopped.

360

They can't *want* to be enemies of humanity – any more than the Nazis, I suppose, *want* to be; but we had to stop them.'

Timothy thought awhile. He was uncertain about this part of his apologia, he did not quite know how it would sound; but since his reconciliation with Vera it had been running in his mind.

'It may sound exaggerated and fanciful, but it seems to me that what happened when I came here was a kind of Munich. I ought to have "declared war" *at once*, on the fishermen, put my boat on the river and taken the consequences. Then we should have known how we stood. It would have been from everyone's point of view the best course. Instead, I went in for appeasement. Like Mr. Chamberlain, whom I once admired, I let myself be put off by promises – sackfuls, my dear Tyro, *sackfuls* of broken promises – and all the time, of course, I was weakening myself by inaction, while they, aware of my criminal hesitancy, were strengthening themselves, drawing the chains of tyranny tighter, and making propaganda against me throughout the district – especially with Mrs. Lampard, poor woman – I don't think you know about her, but I realise now that it was they, not I, who really sent her mad. *If* they had given way – well, nothing of what has happened would have happened. And by acting resolutely *then*, before the situation had had time to develop and harden against me, and before people who were wavering had joined the other side – I could have *made* them give way – I am sure of it. I had so many cards in my hands which since have all been taken from me. Then they would have seen with whom they had to deal, the air would have been cleared, they would have respected me and we should have been friends.

'I've had an instance of the same thing in my own household. I think I told you how difficult my servants were; the more I tried to please them the more discontented they grew. They wouldn't let me have anyone to stay (which didn't matter much, as nobody could come), they quarrelled and made scenes so that at times I hardly dared go into the kitchen, they took offence at the slightest thing, they always thought they were being put upon, they made my life a burden. Until one day in a temper I gave them notice, and since then they have been angels, they can't do enough for me, and we are the best of friends. I suppose it's because their craving for a crisis has been satisfied; as long as I cheated them of that, making myself seem superior, which is unforgivable, they were unhappy, and so was I.

'If only I had taken the same line with the fishmongers! But it isn't too late for a show-down, and in three days' time, perhaps before you get this letter, I shall have staged it. Roughly, my plan is this. The friend

361

I spoke of (who more than anyone else has helped me to make up my mind) and I will start out in the boat, quite ordinarily and as though nothing has happened, and paddle down quietly to the village bridge. We shall be there by six o'clock. On the bridge will be gathered together all our supporters wearing their best clothes and possibly fancy dress and carrying the flags of the Allies, including of course the Hammer and Sickle. I'm a little against having the Red Flag, because as you know I'm not a communist and don't want to be thought one. We are having posters printed, and bills done by hand, A Free River for A Free People, and so on, some of which will be stuck to the parapet and some carried sandwich-fashion. Quite a few men have promised to come (my friend has gone from house to house and has a way with her as a canvasser) but the bulk of our supporters will be women and children, and young people for whom the closing of the river is naturally a special grievance. We hope the muster will be at least fifty strong. I can't tell you what fun it's been, collecting adherents. I had a feeling I must be unpopular in the village, but it turns out I am not; of course, since we started all this a week ago, I have increased my subscriptions and so forth, as people do in such circumstances. I don't see anything wrong in it, do you? It's such fun arguing with the waverers. My friend and I have lists, of course, with the names of all the villagers under the headings "For," "Against," and "Doubtful." It's easier to tell who is "against" than "for" because the "antis" show it in their face and manner, whereas I'm never sure whether those who welcome us with smiles are really well-wishers. Among the "doubtfuls" are the village policeman and my old gardener, Wimbush. I rather expected that the policeman would be on "their" side, being the guardian of the law; on the other hand I have a slight hold over him, because he garages his car with me and I've hinted I might not be able to let him keep it there any longer! Also, I've done one or two little things for him in the past; and he has told me he will be at the bridge at the appointed hour, to "keep an eye" on the gathering, in case anyone tries to break it up, which (between ourselves) I rather hope they will. More than that I couldn't get out of him; he retired, as he so readily does, behind the majesty of his profession, and I was quite satisfied.

'But I own I am a little disappointed with Wimbush, because we were by way of being pals, and there was a time when he used to urge me to put the boat on the river and damn the consequences. Now that he is employed by Mrs. Lampard, or rather her agent, and gets his living from the estate, he has changed his tune. He says he wouldn't object (so kind of him!) if I did it by myself but he doesn't hold with my trying to collect sympathisers and setting people against each other. As if one could get anything done without putting people's backs up (haven't I tried?): the whole point is that *I wouldn't do it for myself*, I'm doing it for everybody and to strike a blow for freedom. I tried to explain this to him but he kept shaking his head in a mulish way and saying "I don't like it." So we parted on that note and last time I saw him he didn't "move to" me (as they say here) which hurt me, I confess.

'On the other hand, it didn't hurt me a bit when Captain Sturrock (a leader of the enemy) passed me in the street and looked through me, instead of giving his usual curt nod. I was delighted, and like the Baker in the Hunting of the Snark I returned his stare with an impudent wag of the head. It is such a relief to be able to indicate one's hostility in an unmistakable manner – not of course that I am hostile to *them*, only to what they stand for.

'We hold informal councils of war in the village pub, under the sphinx-like gaze of the landlord, whom I've not yet dared to sound as to his leanings. But my friend has, and she thinks he's on our side. The pub is a good place because, ever since the "foreigners" arrived in the village, the "gentry" haven't seen fit to come. (By the bye, I've quite changed my mind about the "foreigners," they are excellent people, easy and informal, they give themselves no airs and are with us to a man – or perhaps I should say to a woman, as most of the husbands are away.) Here we discuss the plan of campaign and do a little quiet lobbying among the regulars, who are mostly farm hands and rather tough nuts, you can't quite tell what is in their minds they have such limited capacities for expression. But I rather think that several rounds of free drinks will have helped to bring them to our way of thinking.

'We were going to have had a Grand General Meeting in the village hall, with refreshments and so on, but have decided to give that up because the hall (isn't it typical?) is the property of the Church, and to hire it (for the night) you have to ask the Rector's permission and pay him a considerable fee. It isn't that I object to paying, of course (to tell you the truth, I've been spending money like water and am glad to part with every penny) but I don't think the Rector would let us have the place – of course he's hand in glove with "them." And for another reason I'm diffident about asking him. As I said, his wife used to be a friend of mine and I should be putting her as well as myself in a delicate position. I know that personal matters shouldn't come into a thing of this kind, and I also know that though a "good," well-intentioned woman, she has all along been my evil angel, trying to persuade me to submit to "their" dictatorship. My friend would like me to have it out with her, but I still don't think one should hurt people unnecessarily, so that I content myself, when she rings me up – which she has done several times lately – by telling my housemaid to say I'm out. As a matter of fact I never now answer the telephone myself, because I've had two or three calls from strangers who have been quite offensive – and though I'm glad of that afterwards, because it shows we are making headway, it embarrasses me at the time.'

Timothy sighed.

'Well, I've told you something about our preparations. I think we can claim to have divided the village into two camps, and ours is the larger. To make the division clearer my friend, who is really very clever with her fingers, has designed a "favour" for our people to wear on "the day" – a little paper boat, with "For Freedom" on it – such a charming little device. We shall all wear it in our button-holes.

'I've heard rumours of "clashes," but nothing has been substantiated yet. I don't really want actual *violence*. My friend does, but I think it might prejudice our cause. One or two rather seedy-looking customers have come along – not to me, as a matter of fact – and made certain proposals, but I have been very much against them, at any rate for the present. I never liked the idea of maiming horses and burning houses when they did it in Ireland, though I remember you saying it was the only way they could convince the English government that they meant business, so perhaps we shall come to it in time. But I wish it didn't have to be animals, which are much nicer than men, or houses, which are more beautiful, as well as harder to replace. I know I oughtn't to say this – it just slipped out – the fault isn't in men, who are, per se, the only standard of value we have: it's in the system which enslaves them and of which the rape of the river here is a humble but crying example.

'Well, I haven't apologised for boring you; it would be hypocritical, because I've done it deliberately. I got as far as the bridge, didn't I? The rest, as they say, is soon told. At the bridge there will be cheering and congratulations and I shall make a short speech, perhaps from the boat, perhaps on the bridge, and I shall hoist the Union Jack on the stern; and then (they tell me) they're going to sing "For He's a Jolly Good Fellow," which will embarrass me, and if they must do it I think I shall ask them to sing, "For We are Jolly Good Fellows," instead; it will be more comradely and make me look less of a pocket Führer. When the jollifications are over my friend (who's been very kind to me) and I will continue our voyage. As far as I'm concerned it will be a voyage of discovery, and I'm most excited about it. All I know of the course of the river is from hearsay and the Ordnance Survey map, which at last I've been able to get hold of. I don't suppose you'll want to think of me on the day, but in case you do, and I own I should rather like you to, here is a rough sketch of the "course." '

Timoth dived and fetched out another sheet. He pushed aside those he had already written and frowned over the blank page. Two efforts were unsuccessful; the third produced better results.

'You see it's quite a short distance – about half a mile – from my house to the bridge, and will be pretty plain sailing, I fancy. After that, the river appears to make an enormous loop, where the valley suddenly widens; it doubles on its tracks, going first east then west, and it's just after the loop that it runs over the so-called Devil's Staircase, which isn't marked on the map, nor is the "bottomless pool"(!) at its foot – but I think they are more or less where I've indicated them. When I get to the D.S. I shall turn back. I mean to explore it later but this is only a trial trip, a propaganda march, so to speak. There and back it will be about five miles, which is as much as I can manage, with so little training. I dare say my hands will be pretty sore, as it is, but they will be honourable scars! – won in defence of our rights and liberties.

'I don't think I have any more to say. If you ever get as far as this I dare say you'll smile at the idea of me as a village Hampden with dauntless breast withstanding the petty tyrants of these fields.

'Since I began to write I've somehow persuaded myself that your sympathies will be with me, for the sake of our old friendship; and that even if you don't quite like what I'm doing, you will appreciate the reasons why I do it. And I know you will be glad to hear that I am happy – happy at last and as never before. When this is over I shall write you a proper letter, if I can, I mean a letter from *me* to *you* – a communication, not a manifesto! – hardly mentioning the boat!

Till then, dear Tyro, believe me
Ever yours most affectionately,
TIMOTHY.

'P.S. I went up to London – for the first time since the war – to Magda's funeral. How changed it is! Those occasions are very sad, aren't they? I was thankful to get back here, where one has a task with the living, not with the dead. I've actually made my *will*, which I had always put off doing; however I found it a less depressing business than I feared. To make it was a recognition of reality – and now that I am living in reality at last, I realise what a tonic to the spirits it is. For some reason I felt there was a hurry, and I took the liberty of appointing you my executor. It was cheek, I know, and if you don't want to "act," please tell me. Also I've divided my "estate," such as it is, between you and two other friends – Esther Morwen is one. You won't think the worse of me for telling you, will you? Somehow I'd rather you learnt it from me than from a stranger. I don't approve of people being allowed to hand on their money, of course; but while the law is what it is one can only act within the framework of the law, and anyhow I have too little left to damage a principle!'

As Timothy was re-reading his letter, Effie came in. Her air was businesslike and important: she might have been the secretary of a political leader.

'Excuse me, sir, but Mrs. Purbright has rung up again. Shall I tell her you're out?'

'Yes, please, Effie.'

The letter disposed of, Timothy took another sheet. There were very few left: he would have to remember to order some more writing-paper. But would it be worth while?

'My dearest Esther,' he began, but he could get no further; the letter he wanted to write to Esther refused to be written. Should he take Tyro's from its envelope, and copy out the salient passages? After all, he only wanted to tell her certain facts; what did the personal count for, in a matter of this kind? But his literary conscience, surviving his recent transformation into an agitator, refused to take this easy way; with Esther he must adopt a different form of approach.

But would she ever read his letter? Would it get lost between the toast-rack and the tea-pot? Would one of the grandchildren get hold of it, and screw it into spills? Would the servants find it on the floor, and hurry it off to the salvage-can before she had time to read it?

A thought came to him.

'I am sorry to say that my two excellent maids are leaving me. It seems a pity, because we are getting on better than we ever did before; but I feel I ought to stick to my word. They are, in fact, due to leave me in a few days, and owing to the pressure of events, which I'll tell you about, I've taken no steps to replace them. I can still hardly realise that next week I shall be servant-less! Do you, dear Esther, know of anyone who might come? I know that you often take on, and train, girls from the district who have been unlucky in various ways; if you are in touch with any who haven't, from some reason of unsuitability, been called up, I *should* be so grateful if you would put them in touch with me. I don't a bit mind what their sins of omission, or commission, may have been! In any case it's society's fault, not theirs. I'm not particular, and they will find me perfectly sympathetic – *and* a bachelor! – which I believe is a recommendation. Do see what you can do. At the same time, I don't want to paint my domestic position as desperate. I haven't decided on anything yet, but I may not be staying here much longer. It rather depends on what happens during the next few days. I've had a slight difference of opinion with some of the local nabobs – excellent people in their way. You remember the boat—?'

After this, the letter went more easily. And as Timothy had found in writing to Tyro, the fact that his correspondent might be unsympathetic or even hostile to the letter's contents, hampered him much less than it would once have done. They must take it from him, they must take it from him. All the same it was a relief, though a relief of which he was secretly ashamed, to come to the bonne bouche at the end. How should he word it? Timothy was tired of saying the same thing in different ways; after all, it was most unlikely that the two recipients would ever compare notes. Making a resolution, as often before, to preserve the stamp, he tore open Tyro's envelope and started copying. 'For some reason I felt there was a hurry, and I took the liberty of appointing you my executor. . . . Also I've divided my estate, such as it is, between you and two other friends – Tyro MacAdam is one . . . and anyhow I have too little left to damage a principle!'

CHAPTER XXVIII

'IT's still raining,' said the Rector, going to the window of the dining-room, where luncheon for three was laid. 'It looks like being a wet day for the boating-party, Volumnia.'

His wife came and joined him at the window. A tumid greyness, flecked with white, was scudding across the sky.

'Perhaps Casson will call the whole thing off,' the Rector continued. 'He won't want to risk a damp squib.'

'We must pray for that.' Mrs. Purbright spoke with great intensity and her long interlaced fingers writhed in each other's clasp. Her face and her attitude were as strained as if she had been out in the rough weather, not watching it from behind glass.

'You mustn't take the thing too seriously, my dear,' said the Rector, taking his wife's arm and leading her away from the window. 'It's one of those little upsets that brew up suddenly like this squall, but they're forgotten as soon as they're over.'

'I wish I could think so,' said Mrs. Purbright.

'Have you tried to get through to him again?' asked the Rector.

'Yes, half an hour ago. He was out, the maid said.'

'You can say what you like in defence of the fellow,' Mr. Purbright exploded, with the relief of someone who has kept his feelings too long under control, 'but I call it exceedingly ill-mannered and ungrateful, after all you've done for him, fighting his battles, and so on.'

Mrs. Purbright shook her head.

'Oh no, Edward, I don't feel that at all. It's our fault at least as much as his. He's been driven into a corner. And I was so stupid to bother him about Edgell's stories, when I knew how upset he was. I have reproached myself a thousand times. It was the tone of his voice that took me by surprise.'

The Rector shrugged his shoulders.

'It doesn't seem to me a great deal to have asked him,' he said. 'It's all in the course of his work. Where is Edgell, by the way?'

'He's lunching in Swirrelsford.'

'Oh.' The Rector's face stiffened slightly and he looked away from his wife. 'Does he still talk of attending this silly function at the bridge?'

'I believe so,' said Mrs. Purbright, vaguely. 'Oh yes, Edward, I think he does. You see, he got on quite well with Mr. Casson. They were becoming friends. I was so sorry ... Naturally, he feels a kind of loyalty.'

'I wish he wouldn't.' The Rector's face darkened. 'It will look so peculiar. You and I know that he's an – an acquaintance of Casson's, but others may easily misunderstand. It was a misfortune that his leave happened at this particular time, when there are no young people in the village of our own sort. You were always charitable about the newcomers, Volumnia, but I never liked the idea of them. I'm afraid I was right.'

Mrs. Purbright's face grew troubled. She dropped into a chair and stared at the empty grate.

'Oh, Edward,' she said. 'Life is so complex. Think of all the strands of beauty in it. Does one want to tear them out, even if one could? Edgell is such a dear boy, I should not want to clip his wings.'

'He's got his wings all right,' said the Rector, in surprise. 'Oh, I see what you mean,' he added. 'Well, I'm afraid I don't agree with you, Volumnia. Laxity is a prevailing fault of our age, and we don't want to see Edgell drawn into it.'

'Yet even if what . . . what you heard was true,' said Mrs. Purbright, 'I could not regard it as an unmixed misfortune. We must remember the advice given to Peter, not to call anyone common or unclean. And you wouldn't in other circumstances, Edward, you know you wouldn't. What is our function in this village? Surely not to pass by on the other side? I wish you could feel, as I do, that beauty and goodness can no more be separated from other qualities than the flame can be separated from the coal it springs from.' She looked at her husband with an earnest frown.

'That's all right,' he conceded, grudgingly, 'quite all right in certain circumstances, Volumnia. But not, I think, in these.' His glance, avoiding hers, rested on the dinner table. 'But if Edgell is in Swirrelsford, who is our third?'

'Colonel Harbord; I asked him,' said Mrs. Purbright.

'Harbord? Good,' said the Rector. 'But why didn't you tell me? And—' suddenly he took in his wife's appearance which, husband-like, he had hitherto taken for granted, and words failed him. He saw the pearls, the rings, the bracelets, and the brooches, the lavender silk dress with its lilac fringes – all the concrete reminders, which she so seldom wore, that the money had been Mrs. Purbright's. She wore them so seldom that they did not seem to belong to her, yet they made their effect; in the dim light she glimmered like a stained-glass window.

'Good gracious!' said the Rector. 'Have you put on all that for Harbord?'

With a lifted hand she silenced his inquiry. 'I think I hear him in the hall.'

After luncheon, when Mrs. Purbright had gone to make the coffee, and the two men were together in the drawing-room, the Rector said, 'I'm afraid my wife is rather upset by this silly little demonstration at the bridge – the River Revolution, as they term it. Casson is by way of being a friend of hers. You know how charitable she is to everyone. I didn't altogether dislike the fellow, either. Of course he made a fool of himself at the smoking concert, but Volumnia accepted his excuses and persuaded me to. But I'm afraid my first impression was correct.'

Colonel Harbord shrugged his shoulders and asked leave to light his pipe.

'I've always been rather sorry for the chap myself,' he said. 'He led off with the wrong foot and his timing has been faulty ever since. More than once he was within an ace of getting what he wanted – wasn't he, Rector? – we were all ready to meet him half way, if he'd only known, but he always bungled it. Of course he ought to have gone somewhere else. A fishing river is no good to row a boat on. Apart from getting in our way, which would have been a nuisance, he'd have got stuck on the bottom half the time. I expect he will today, if he goes out.'

Involuntarily they turned their heads to the window. It was still blowing hard, but the rain had lessened.

'It's that girl he goes about with, more than him, in my opinion,' the colonel continued. 'She seems to be a regular firebrand. Good-looking little baggage, though.' He turned to Mr. Purbright with the minimum of inquiry in his eye.

The Rector stirred in his chair.

'Between ourselves, she's become rather a friend of Edgell's. I don't know how much Volumnia knows about it. He hasn't brought her here, of course.'

'Good lord, I should hope not,' said Colonel Harbord. 'In my day one didn't— She must be a girl of parts, keeping two beaux on one string, as they say. But I don't cotton to her, and I rather hope that Casson will tip her in the river.'

The Rector frowned. 'I do not wish her any harm,' he said, 'though I do not go as far as my wife, who seems almost to like the girl. She doesn't quite realise, dear Volumnia, what an awkward position it puts us in, Edgell apparently giving his . . . his blessing to this ridiculous outbreak. It's only a boy's freak, of course, but I'm glad to have this opportunity of apologising for him.'

Colonel Harbord smiled. 'I can assure you, my dear Rector, that we shan't hold it against him. It's just the sort of thing you and I might have done at his age.' The Rector shook his head.

'Well, I might,' Colonel Harbord amended. 'Just for the fun of the thing, you know. But it's different in Casson's case. He's old and ugly enough to know better. And as for his accomplice! Do you imagine they've made much headway in the village? They didn't canvass you, by any chance?'

'Indeed not,' said the Rector. 'Casson hasn't shown his face here for a month or more. It's hard to tell what progress they've made. As politicians know, countrymen are apt to be secretive when it's a question of revealing which side they're on.'

'They don't open up to you?' said Colonel Harbord.

'My inquiries have only elicited the vaguest replies,' the Rector said, 'perhaps because I cannot help showing that I regard the whole business as a serious piece of folly.'

'So you don't think we'll get murdered in our beds, or strung up to lamp-posts with our fishing tackle. "Hanged from a fishing rod" sounds rather good.'

The Rector shook his head. 'The villagers know which side their bread is buttered,' he remarked. 'From what I hear, Casson has been spending money lavishly, very lavishly. But I doubt if he really has a long purse, I very much doubt it. And country people are not easily impressed by display; no Englishman is, for that matter.'

'With the help of the rain, you think the revolution may just fizzle out?'

The Rector paused to light his pipe. 'Before the war, I should certainly have said yes. But today there is a new spirit, and a regrettable one, not only among the rowdier elements. Love of sensation, Harbord, love of sensation turns men into hooligans. Casson has the gift of the gab and he talks like a gentleman, even if he doesn't act like one.'

'I've only once had the pleasure of speaking to him,' said Colonel Harbord, 'and I don't think he was acting like a gentleman then – more like a man, perhaps. Ah, here's Mrs. Purbright.' He got up and shut the door after Mrs. Purbright, who, burdened by her tray, was walking with quick steps and a heightened colour.

She apologised for taking so long over their coffee. 'But I have to confess,' she said, 'that I telephoned, and that kept me.'

'You telephoned?' repeated the Rector, with a note of anger in his voice. 'And with the usual result, I suppose?'

'No, I didn't telephone to Mr. Casson,' Mrs. Purbright said. 'I telephoned to the post-office at Swirrelsbourn.'

'Why?' asked the Rector.

'To find out the state of the river there.'

Mrs. Purbright was breathing quickly.

'And they told you—?'

Mrs. Purbright poured out Colonel Harbord's coffee. 'Oh, I forgot – you like it black.'

'It doesn't matter a bit.'

'No, no. It'll do for me. I very much prefer it with milk. And here is yours, Edward. Please take all the sugar you like, Colonel; we have plenty.'

'But you haven't told us about the river,' the Rector reminded her.

'The river? Oh yes. They said it was rising fast.'

'Well, that's good news,' said Colonel Harbord. 'The water-party will be off.'

'Oh, do you think so?' said Mrs. Purbright. 'I wish I could. I feel so uneasy about the whole affair. I wish we could do something to stop it.'

'The Rector and I are for letting it alone,' said Colonel Harbord. 'You're playing into their hands by taking notice of them. Notice is just what they want.'

'You are quite right, Colonel,' said Mrs. Purbright. 'They want notice, and we should give it to them.'

She spoke with all the emphasis she could command, and stared hard at the two men, whose faces closed in wariness. The Rector cleared his throat.

'Really, Volumnia, I don't understand you. Opposition from us would be the greatest mistake. It would only inflame them further, besides making us look ridiculous. The only course is to ignore them.'

'You know, I think he's right,' said Colonel Harbord. 'I'm all for a fight myself, and so is he. But I do think, in this case, that discretion is the better part of valour. We all know you have the courage of a lion, and Casson hasn't, by all accounts. If you,' he went on, 'tackled him and told him not to make an ass of himself, you might bring him to his senses, mightn't she, Rector? By Jove, I wouldn't like to do something, if Mrs. Purbright told me not to. But even if she sent him away with his tail between his legs, there are still the others to reckon with, all the hoodlums of the place, not to mention his precious fellow-agitator, a nasty bit of work if ever there was one. They'd just cock snooks at you, Mrs. Purbright, they would, really. Far better take no notice.'

Mrs. Purbright listened with bowed head. At last she said, 'It wasn't that kind of notice I was thinking of.'

There was a moment's silence, then the Rector said, 'May we know what is in your mind, Volumnia?'

'Oh Edward, what can I say? How can I advise Colonel Harbord and you, who have so much more experience of practical affairs than I have? I am astonished at my impertinence. It was ju-jitsu I was thinking of.'

'Ju-jitsu, Volumnia?'

'Yes, isn't that a kind of wrestling in which the wrestlers don't try to resist each other, on the contrary, each gives way to the other, and the victory goes to the one who best knows how to yield?'

Colonel Harbord laughed. 'I believe it is something like that, Mrs. Purbright. Each man tries to make the other use his strength against himself. But in the end the victory goes to the one who twists the other's toes or squeezes his windpipe. . . .'

Mrs. Purbright closed her eyes. 'Surely it need not come to that. . . . Supposing you were Mr. Casson. . . .'

'Which of us, Mrs. Purbright?'

'Well, either of you – it is a great deal to suppose,' she went on hurriedly, 'but suppose you were in his boat, rowing down the river—'

'You aren't suggesting that Harbord or I should offer to be his passenger, Volumnia?'

'Oh, dear no, just put yourself in his place, with your heart full of, well . . . bitter feelings and then the bridge comes into view, and what do you see?'

'I should see, I suppose, a number of misguided fellows, sweeps, I might almost call them, the most undesirable elements we have, waving and cheering and uttering threats against Church and State and my good friend Harbord, and a few idle women who ought to be looking after their homes, and neglected, badly brought up children of a type with which we are becoming only too familiar—'

'Yes, and when you saw them, what would you feel?'

'Volumnia, you put a strain on my patience, obliging me to consider myself in a rôle, and I must say a personality, extremely distasteful to me. But when I saw them – er – egging me on, I should no doubt feel confirmed in my folly and do my best to encourage them in theirs.'

'Yes,' agreed Mrs. Purbright eagerly, 'you would. I mean—' for a look of disgust had settled on the Rector's face – 'in Mr. Casson's place you would. But suppose you saw some other sort of people on the bridge—'

'But, my dear Volumnia, there would be no other sort of people.'

'Let me beg you to use your imagination a little further,' pleaded Mrs. Purbright. 'Suppose you saw, leaning over the bridge and cheering with the others some quite different sort of people—'

'Do you mean ordinary aliens, or coloured people such as Indians or negroes?'

'No, no,' cried Mrs. Purbright. 'Though how nice that would be.' Lost in a confused vision of turbans and sarongs, she almost smiled, and it cost her an effort to dismiss the exotic throng. 'I mean,' she said unenthusiastically, 'people like ourselves.'

'People like *ourselves*?' repeated the Rector. 'But what would people like ourselves be doing there?'

'I told you,' said Mrs. Purbright, and her excitement brought the flush back to her cheeks, 'cheering with the others. He would recognise them, of course. They would not be his partisans, far from it, they would belong to the other camp, they would disagree with his principles and what he stood for.'

'The fellow hasn't any principles,' interjected the Rector.

'Perhaps not, but my point is that he would see, among his supporters, whom you, Colonel, correctly described as the . . . the less fortunate members of the community, people like ourselves, not sympathising with his intentions, indeed deploring them, but sympathising with him as a man, a fellow-creature, and in spite of everything, wishing him well.' Mrs. Purbright paused, like a speaker trying to gauge the feeling of the audience. 'What would his feelings be, as he draws near to the bridge, and sees, among the others, those faces that he had so little expected to see, not looking at him angrily or coldly, but with encouragement and understanding?'

The Rector shook his head, as though his wife had ventured into a region of speculation too remote for him to follow. But Colonel Harbord said, 'It would give him a turn, I see that. It would make him think again. It might even,' he smiled slyly at Mrs. Purbright, 'spoil the party for him.'

'Exactly!' exclaimed Mrs. Purbright. 'It would . . . it would disarm him. Colonel Harbord, it would spike his guns!'

Colonel Harbord gave the Rector a sidelong look. 'A sort of fifth column, eh? It might be a good plan,' he said doubtfully, 'but who's going to do it? Where'll you find the volunteers?'

Mrs. Purbright rose to her feet and stood over them. She was trembling, and the dawn of triumph, brightening in her face, transfigured it.

'Edward,' she said, 'Colonel Harbord, come with me to the bridge!'

She might have been a priestess with a taper in her hand, raised to the sacred vessel.

The silence was broken by the Rector.

'Volumnia,' he said, 'have you gone mad?'

But her mood was still too exalted to be cast down either by his words or the tone in which he uttered them. 'No, I've not!' she cried, like a child denying a groundless accusation from another child, and as if a simple assertion would prove her sanity. 'I'm not mad at all,' she went on, still in the same childish way. 'You agree with me, don't you, Colonel Harbord, that it's the only way to . . . to save the situation?'

Colonel Harbord's bright blue eyes looked at her uncertainly and then sought the Rector's. 'I must take my orders from my commanding officer,' he said.

The triumph faded from Mrs. Purbright's face; the taper was extinguished by the daylight. She swayed slightly and said, 'Oh, please, please, it's such a small thing to do. What is it, what does it amount to? Only a few steps to the bridge, only a few minutes on the bridge! Five at the most. What *can* you lose by it?'

Colonel Harbord's face was a mask; like a soldier on parade, when a general passes by, he betrayed nothing of what he felt. But the Rector's expression was startling, so little was there in it of his usual look, so utterly was it dominated by the feeling of the moment. Trying to keep his voice under control, he said, 'You don't understand these things, Volumnia. You look at them too . . . too emotionally. What you propose is totally unpractical. It would only make matters worse, much worse than they are, and might even earn me a rebuke from my Bishop. The only practical thing to do is to do nothing, as Harbord and I agreed, a moment ago.'

Mrs. Purbright threw her head back and drew a long breath.

'Edward . . . Edward, I implore you. I had not meant to mention it, because we have often discussed it and agreed that it should be treated with suspicion. It isn't second sight, of course, but for days I've had a most uneasy feeling about this . . . this boating expedition – it hurts me when I think of it, it hurts me!' She laid her hand on her breast, whence it fell to her side in a multi-coloured flash of jewels. 'Don't think of *them* – put *them* out of your mind altogether, and do it for my sake.'

The Rector turned away. 'It's no good, Volumnia, I can't. Do be reasonable,' he went on, more gently, 'how could a man in my position, or Colonel Harbord's, lend himself to this silly mummery? It isn't real, it's playing at life. As far as it has any meaning at all, we should be thought to be encouraging them, giving our support to the enemies of society . . . and . . . and of religion. And it would look as if we were frightened. Please, Volumnia, believe that in this case a man with practical experience knows best. I'm sorry not to . . . to oblige you, but I cannot go against my conscience.'

Mrs. Purbright stood, a figure of desolation, looking at neither of them.

'Mrs. Purbright,' said Colonel Harbord, 'I would do anything for you, but I feel in this instance I must abide by what the Rector says. And I'm sure your fears are groundless. Even a general in the field has to reckon with the weather. They won't turn out today.' Rising to his feet he gave her his most reassuring smile, but it was nothing to the smile the sun gave them, blazing through the window, gilding Mrs. Purbright's spoils with broken rings of brightness. Against the dark retreating clouds the trees looked as if they had been washed in gold; and the freshness of the air stole into the room. 'I must get home between the showers,' said the Colonel, holding out his hand. 'Mark my words, there'll be another downpour in a minute.' And thanking them for their hospitality he took his leave, memorising as much as he could of their conversation, to tell his wife.

Mrs. Purbright did not give up easily. All the afternoon she went to and fro in Upton, trying to prevail on the more substantial residents to go with her to the bridge. Naturally, she did not call on Colonel Harbord. Each of them received her kindly but the answer never varied. To attend the meeting would be taken as a sign of weakness; the best way to deal with the insurgents was to ignore them. Tired and dejected she returned to tea, hoping to find Edgell, but he had not come back. Tea was a miserable meal, neither she nor her husband speaking of what was uppermost in their minds. She did not tell him of her intention to go to the bridge herself; she could not face another altercation with him. Nor, at heart, did she feel it was any use her going. Alone, she would carry no weight; Timothy's party would welcome her, no doubt, but they would attribute her presence to her friendship with him, and to her well-known eccentricity; it would be a solitary gesture, meaning nothing, and it would anger her husband. Still, from loyalty to Timothy, and her sense of what was fit, she must make it. The Rector retired into his study, pointedly refraining from asking her how she meant to spend the rest of the afternoon.

Mrs. Purbright went to prepare herself for the party, but never had she done so with a poorer heart.

On her way to the rendezvous she saw in the distance the Swirrelsford bus stopping at the corner of the Green, opposite to Timothy's house. She did not notice it particularly. Only two passengers got out. One walked away from her in the direction of the village, the other came towards her, walking slowly and stiffly like an old man. She had to look again before she gathered who it was.

'Edgell!' she cried, hastening towards him. 'My dear boy!'

He looked up in surprise, almost with a start, but did not quicken his step.

'Hullo, Mother!' he greeted her. 'Where are you off to?'

'To the bridge!' she said, trying to make it sound the happiest destination. 'And you're coming with me, aren't you?'

'To the bridge?' echoed Edgell, stopping still and looking down at her. How pale he is, she thought. 'Did I hear you right?'

'Yes,' said Mrs. Purbright. 'I thought I would, and you told me you were going.'

'I was,' said Edgell, 'but to tell you the truth I feel a bit off colour, and I'm going home to have a lie-down.'

Mrs. Purbright tried to conceal her concern.

'Oh, my poor boy. I thought you looked a little tired.' He looked worse than that, but she did not want to scare him and he hated to be fussed over. She tried to think against the claims competing in her mind. 'Shall I come back with you and get you a hot water-bottle?'

'Well, it would be nice,' said Edgell. 'I do feel a bit rotten.' He had never said as much as that before, and Mrs. Purbright was alarmed.

'Would you like to take my arm?'

He smiled down at her from his commanding height. 'No, I can totter along. By the way,' he said, as they retraced their steps, 'does Dad know that you were going to Casson's show?'

His mother had forgotten about Timothy. Now the thought of breaking her unspoken pledge to him made her tremble.

'As soon as I've made you comfortable I could go back,' she said. 'I should only be away for a few minutes. It's just . . . just to put in an appearance.'

'I shouldn't bother to go, Mother.'

'My darling, I think I must,' said Mrs. Purbright. 'I don't want to fail him.'

'He's all right, you know, but he's a bit mad,' said Edgell.

'Oh no, Edgell, what makes you think so?'

'Well, from what I hear.'

Mrs. Purbright pondered. She was used to hearing people say that Timothy was mad: Edgell was not the first. But it hurt her, coming from him.

'I thought you liked him.'

'I did for a bit, and I didn't mind him taking a dim view of my literary efforts, but he needn't have put it quite so crudely. Spared the old feelings, you know. But perhaps he thinks I don't have any, being only a brutal and licentious airman.'

In spite of Mrs. Purbright's resolve never to pry into her son's affairs, her curiosity got the better of her. Where have you been all the day, Edgell my son?

'Oh, my darling,' she said, 'what makes you think he did?'

'Somebody must have told me, I suppose. But it's your fault really, you naughty woman. It was you who forced my effusions on the wretched man, though I begged you not to. They're not his class, of course. Though from what I hear he's not finding much of a market for his own stuff just at present.'

'I don't know, it's so long since I saw him. I'm sure he didn't mean to be unkind. But I think perhaps it was unkind of whoever told you. Things sound so different out of their context.'

'Oh no, I'd much rather hear the truth. I'm that sort of chap. To-morrow I shall diligently collect all the typescripts and make a terrific bonfire.'

Mrs. Purbright didn't quite believe him but she was deeply grieved at having been the cause of mortifying him. The unwitting cause: but someone had deliberately made mischief, and a nerve of resentment long buried in Mrs. Purbright's mind began to throb.

'You aren't angry with me, my darling, are you?' she said, speaking as lightly as she could. 'I couldn't bear it if you were.'

'Oh, no, Mother.' A stab of pain went through him, making him grimace. 'You have the vice of meaning well.'

The Rector was out, so a brief note in the hall informed them, and would not be in till supper-time. Mrs. Purbright boiled the kettle, made tea and filled the hot water-bottle. By the time she brought them up, Edgell was already in bed. She wanted to comfort him as if he had been a little boy; but the grown-upness of his head on the pillow, and the half unwilling respect which his manhood evoked in her, checked the endearments on her lips.

'You'll have to rest more,' she said, trying to keep fondness and anxiety out of her voice. 'No more visits to Swirrelsford.'

She saw she had made a mistake, for his eyes darkened with masculine secretiveness.

'It's all going according to plan. The doctor told me I should have these attacks. . . . Now, you buzz off, or you'll miss the bridge-party.'

'I dare say I have missed it. Sure you wouldn't like me to stay?'

'Good lord, no. I shall be quite all right as soon as I've made myself sick. Only I can't do that as long as you're here.'

'I wish you wouldn't, Edgell dear. I'm sure it can't be good for you. I distrust these drastic remedies.'

Weakness brought a flash of querulousness into his voice as he said, 'Oh, don't bother me, I'm always better after I've been sick. There's nothing like it for taking the old pain away.'

Distraught, almost agonised, wondering where her duty lay, she looked round the room helplessly, trying to see something that might give her an excuse to linger. Edgell closed his eyes.

'Enjoy the bridge-party,' he said, 'and come back soon. And if you see Casson, tell him I'm going to write a short story about him.'

CHAPTER XXIX

WALKING and running, dipping and rearing, Mrs. Purbright hastened down the village street. Her garden-party appearance was in odd contrast with her gait; the rustling silks, the gleaming jewels belonged to another scene and another kind of progress. And to another state of mind. She scarcely recognised herself, so much had happened that was at variance with everything she hoped for. She did not acknowledge the raised hats and the bows, the smiles that met and followed her. She was dismayed by the tide of anger that was rising in her, a dry, hot feeling that she had not known for years. Her mind was full of darkness and confused sounds. Muttering aloud, to the amusement of the passers-by, she argued for and against herself. 'Nonsense, nonsense,' she repeated to the summer evening, splashing through the puddles which the rain had left; 'you've got it all wrong.' Suddenly she pulled up short: a stream, almost a river, was running across the road in front of her.

On both sides of the obstacle were people who wanted to get across; the air rang with laughter and shouts. Mrs. Purbright saw that some of them were wearing in their buttonholes a kind of crescent, which, on examination, proved to be the paper silhouette of a boat. Now she noticed the feeling of excitement around her, excitement which increased when some of the boys and men took off their shoes and socks, turned up their trousers to the knee, and waded through the flood. A stalwart labourer offered to carry Mrs. Purbright across, but she declined. Just at that moment a car came up, and the driver made signals to her. She asked him to drop her at the bridge and he did so.

On the crown of the bridge, solitary as Horatius, stood Nelson. He was pulling something off the parapet; paper it seemed to be, for it came away from the stone in crumbling strips. At sight of Mrs. Purbright he straightened himself and saluted.

'Why, Mrs. Purbright,' he said, 'you're too late.'

'Too late, am I too late, Nelson? Oh dear.'

'You missed a fine show, Madam. Mr. Casson, he rowed a treat.'

'Oh, but Nelson, I feel so anxious.'

'Anxious, Mrs. Purbright, Madam? You haven't any call to feel anxious. I was here, so no trouble could take place. The crowd was quite orderly except for one or two hot-heads.'

'Oh, I didn't mean that,' said Mrs. Purbright, moving towards the parapet from off which, as she now saw, Nelson had been peeling the illegible and sodden posters that Timothy's supporters had affixed. 'No, this is what worries me.'

She peered down at the water, only a few feet below her. At the bridge the current was always strong; to-day the water had gathered itself into a smooth brown tongue, luminous at the edges, which flowed with so much force that where it rebounded from the pillars of the bridge it left a hollow. The gardens of the houses bordering the river were standing in water almost to the top of the black palings that divided them; crazily scraping against one of these fences was a hen-house; wooden gear of all sorts was floating slowly up and down, or twirling in miniature whirlpools.

The constable's face glowed.

'You don't see this every day, do you, Madam?'

Mrs. Purbright turned unhappy eyes to the other side of the bridge where the river, broadening out as it swept away from the village, showed a sliding, mud-coloured surface, flecked with gouts of yellow froth.

'I feel anxious for Mr. Casson,' she said.

'Mr. Casson, Madam? You needn't worry about him. Why, he gave such a display of oarsmanship as Upton hasn't seen in all its history.'

'I'm glad you enjoyed it, Nelson.'

'Enjoyed it, Mrs. Purbright, why it was an object lesson. I used to belong to a rowing club in Swirreslford so I know something about it. To begin with, you mustn't row with the arms, that's quite wrong.'

'Was he alone in the boat, Nelson?'

But Nelson was too much absorbed in what he was saying to notice her interruption.

'And it isn't the biceps either that matter, Madam. Them biceps is no use to you at all.'

'Did the crowd . . . did they cheer him, were they sympathetic?'

'It's your legs that matter, Mrs. Purbright,' Nelson went on, his eyes shining with enthusiasm. 'You wouldn't think so, would you, being a lady, but it's your legs that give you the power. Mr. Casson, he used his legs a treat.'

Mrs. Purbright was hardly paying more attention to him than he to her.

'It's just occurred to me, Nelson . . .' she began.

'Your legs and your back, Mrs. Purbright, Madam. It's there the drive comes from. And those hands, Madam, don't let those hands hug those thighs! Get them away!'

'If I went down Lovers' Lane should I be in time to stop him, do you think?'

Nelson was saying:

'And then there's feathering. Just look at my wrists, Mrs. Purbright, and follow my movements if you can.' He stretched his arms out, clenched his fists, bared his wrists, and moved his hands up and down with a sharp jerk. 'Try it, Madam, try it, you'd soon learn.'

Half hypnotised by his vehemence Mrs. Purbright found herself imitating Nelson's gestures.

'That's it, and now a long swing from the buttocks. Excuse me, Madam.' The spring of his eloquence broken, Nelson turned scarlet.

'I was thinking, Nelson,' panted Mrs. Purbright, 'that if I went down Lovers' Lane – you know it cuts off that big loop of the river – I might still be in time to warn him and make him turn back.'

'Turn back? Oh no, Mrs. Purbright, that would be a pity. The people wouldn't be here to watch him come back. He said in an hour's time, and the chaps are laying bets on it.' Nelson's voice was pathetic and reproachful. 'This is the best day Upton's had since I've been here,' he declared, 'and Mr. Casson's the hero of the hour, the hero of the hour. He's come into his own, at last, Mrs. Purbright, where you always wanted him to be. I wasn't in favour of it at all to start with,' he admitted. 'I thought he was just another of these so-called Communists. But he isn't, he's a first-rate oarsman, that's what he is, and Upton's going to be a paradise for oarsmen, like he stated, Madam, when he made his speech from the old water-steps down there. 'Tisn't what a man says, 'tis what he states that matters, and we shall have boats going up and down this river like they do in the grand canals of Venice.'

The policeman's face lit up at the vision.

'Thank you, thank you, Nelson,' breathed Mrs. Purbright. 'I am glad and grateful that you appreciate Mr. Casson so much.'

Leaving Nelson in possession she hurried away from the bridge, fumbling in her bag as she went. She could not find what she sought, and her back grew more bowed and her face more anxious.

Lovers' Lane, the short cut to the river, was only a few minutes' walk. Once it had been a public footpath; but when Sir Watson Stafford bought the property the right of way had fallen into disuse and he had, with very little protest from anyone, closed the path and sealed the entrance, which had been through a hole in the wall, with a door which he kept locked. But to several of his friends he gave duplicate keys so that they might enjoy the pleasure of the place: and Mrs. Purbright was one.

Just as she was abandoning in despair the search for the key she looked up and saw that she had reached the door, and it was open. As she passed through, the exultation which Nelson had managed to communicate to her lost its hold, the dreadful strength of the river came back like a physical sensation, weakening her limbs and filling her with foreboding.

When Vera Cross left Edgell at the bus she was, for once, in an un-decided state of mind. She had promised Timothy to join him at the Old Rectory for tea, after which they were to embark for the bridge. It was after half past five, too late for her to have tea with him but not too late to join him in the boat. At lunch in Swirrelsford she and Edgell had watched the rain and decided that Timothy would never make the attempt. The demonstration would have to be postponed. So she put it out of her mind, and thought of other, pleasanter things, for which Edgell gave her full opportunity, until in the late afternoon the sun burst through and reminded her that the expedition might take place, after all. As soon as she could draw Edgell's attention to mundane matters she put the question to him. He, not unnaturally, begged her to give the whole thing up, and stay and dine with him in Swirrelsford; and for a time she seemed to fall in with this. But she had already made up her mind to return, and the sight of her lover's disappointment only confirmed her resolve. Lovemaking was only incidental to her mission in Upton, it was not one of the results she had to show. In the end it was not so difficult to persuade Edgell to come back; he was already begin-ning to feel the strain of the day's delight, and wondering, though he would rather have died than confess this to Vera, whether he would be able to hold out till he got home.

But when she saw the water-splash at Upton, which had not been there on her outward journey, and through the windows of the bus caught sight of the river in places where it had never been visible before, her courage failed her. She did not mind disappointing Timothy, for experience had shown her that her relationships with men, or with some men, throve on the disappointments she handed out to them. They came back for more; and Timothy was essentially one of those who did. But for a moment, before his need for her renewed itself, he could be sulky and annoyed; and he might refuse to go unless she went with him. It would be a mistake in tactics for this to happen. Together they had worked the village up to a high pitch of expectation and excitement which, in all probability, could not be repeated at a later date, especially if the postponement was due to the organisers showing the white feather. Moreover, without vanity she knew that she had made herself a mascot, if not exactly a Lady Godiva, to a great many people in the village, and the demonstration would lose a good deal of its publicity value if she failed to take part in it. She was news, she felt, and Timothy was not. Headquarters would be dissatisfied with her if she cried off. On the other hand they would be much more disgusted if the demonstration, with whose progress she had kept them in touch, fizzled out altogether. And weighing in her mind the alternatives of warning Timothy of her defection, and not warning him, she realised that the latter was the better bet. With his obstinate regard for the sanctity of engagements and even of arrangements, he would certainly keep the rendezvous at the bridge, if he could, even supposing she did not turn up. He would assume she had been kept.

For another reason the expedition had become, personally, distasteful to her. As far as in her lay, she had fallen in love with Edgell Purbright; and her continued relationship with Timothy, though it was good, even necessary for business, was becoming increasingly irksome to her. She might pay the forfeit she had promised him, or she might not; but whichever she did, she was through with him. Whereas with Edgell—

But curiosity was strong in her; she must know what was going to happen. It would not do for her to stand on the bridge with the other spectators, and wait to see if Timothy would come; that would be trying him too far, and besides, she would lose face with her public, who expected to see her in the boat. She must find some point of vantage where she could see and not be seen. It was then that she remembered Lovers' Lane. She and Edgell had been there several times and he had entrusted her with the key which, he told her, he had borrowed from his mother. She had the key in her bag. Bare-legged and sandalled, she quietly waded through the water-splash. It might be a little awkward if any of the villagers spotted her before she reached the door, but she could easily think up some excuse, urgent business of Frances's or a late change of plan. As a matter of fact fortune favoured her; the coast was clear, and so exultant was she at her success that she forgot to lock the door behind her. Once inside, the lane enveloped her in its secrecy.

It ran between hedges until the trees began. Vera lost herself in reflections and speculations. How well everything had turned out for her! Magda's death had been most opportune; her presence would have been a serious embarrassment. She was of some value to the Party because of her social connections: 'Mrs. Vivian, whose left wing opinions are well-known.' But she was a play-girl and not taken seriously even in Curzon Street, which in its turn was not taken seriously by those of greater weight. In outline, she knew about Vera's Upton assignment, but in spite of her conversion to Communism her outlook was still that of a bourgeoise and an amoureuse who put love before politics. Had she come, she would never have let Vera have her way with Timothy; she was too feminine not to have warned him, too much a woman of the beau monde not to have made him feel that she, Vera, was not. The whole operation would have developed into a dog-fight between them, and the demonstration would never have come off. Nor would she have been as blind as Timothy seemed to be to Vera's relationship with Edgell.

At the thought of Edgell her steps came slower, for the wood she was now entering – it was little more than a coppice – was redolent of him. He excited her more than any man had for years; far, far more than Timothy with his anxious expression and his spaniel's eyes. She must not let herself fall too deeply in love, for there was work still to be done in Upton, and Edgell, the Rector's son, would make a better stalking-horse than Timothy, even if he was more difficult to handle. The gentry might ignore Timothy; they could not ignore Edgell. Suppose she married him for a time. . . .

She heard a sound, a continuous low murmur which had the force of a roar though not its volume. She looked up and saw at the end of the glade where only the sky used to be, the river.

The novelty excited her and she hurried forward. Yes, there it was, almost level with the bank, instead of several feet below it, sliding by her at what seemed a tremendous pace. Ordinarily Vera was not interested in Nature; it said nothing to her. If she liked it at all, she liked it to be unnatural: and the Swirrel today wore a most unnatural, indeed a revolutionary air. Something within her responded to its ruthlessness, its threat to enter houses and sweep down bridges, to flatten and destroy the old order – the old disorder – on its banks. She liked its lack of hesitancy, its wholesale methods and its singleness of purpose, as though all the whims of the water had been collected into one irresistible will, in which there was no waste of effort, every drop, indistinguishable from the others, lending its impulse to the whole.

Heavy with foliage, the trees overhung the river. Timothy would have his back to her at first; it was when he had passed by that he might see her; and this spot against the tree-trunk, where she and Edgell had often sat, exactly fulfilled the strategic requirements. Edgell had discovered it. Edgell. . . .

It came on her so suddenly, it was over so quickly, that Vera wondered if it really had happened. She found herself gazing into the eyes of two children who were sitting in the stern seat of the boat, leaning away from each other, their fingers trailing in the water. Afterwards she remembered they were little boys. Of Timothy all she noticed was that one of his shirt-sleeves had come down. But in the bows of the boat there had been a kind of figure-head, a sight so strange that she could hardly take it in. Could it have been a dog? Yes, of course, it was Felix. The sculls left spreading puddles in the water, which endured for a moment and then were dissolved in the brown flood. Vera leaned back against the tree-trunk. So it was accomplished, the task she had set herself and worked at, on and off, for nearly eighteen months. What a lot of labour she had put into it, and how distasteful much of it had been. She knew she ought to feel no emotion whatever; it was only a routine employment, one of a series of assignments which should mean no more to her than numbers in an addition sum; yet she could not repress a sense of satisfaction. How far the demonstration had succeeded she could not tell; but it was a beginning – a step in the right direction. The River Revolution had been launched and nothing in Upton would be quite the same again. Even if there were no further outbreaks – and she had reason to think there would be – the labourers would be less willing to touch their caps and the bosses would not get out their fishing-tackle with the same confidence as before. The two nations would be conscious of their apartness, their irreconcilability; and the rift would widen in preparation for the final struggle.

Her musings took on a more prophetic cast, and her face a sternness that Timothy had never seen there. But presently it softened again and a puzzled frown appeared between her brows. How was she to fit Edgell into the picture, for do what she would, she could not keep him out? And as the sweetness of the thought of him stole over her, she remembered Timothy with a dislike that bordered upon hatred. The price she was pledged to pay – the penance she must do this very night – Timothy's reward! In any case it would have been as ridiculous and meaningless as a forfeit in a child's game; but now the thought of it revolted her in a way she had not believed possible. Of course she would get out of it; but what a rumpus he would make!

She heard a sound, but there were many sounds, scarcely distinguishable above the toneless roar of the river. She heard it again – it was regular now – and knew that it was footsteps. Peering round the tree she saw a figure coming towards her, tripping and prancing down the glade. Her eyes dazzled by the light on the river, she could not tell at once who the apparition was, that looked so tall in the twilight of the trees. The apparition was muttering to itself – herself – and Vera recognized Mrs. Purbright in all her finery.

But Mrs. Purbright did not see her. She went straight to the river's brink and looked anxiously up and down, still muttering.

Vera, rigid against the tree-trunk, made no sound. Mrs. Purbright turned away from the river and looked back down the glade, with half-closed, unseeing eyes. 'She's going now,' was Vera's whispered thought and in that moment of relief she realised how absurd Mrs. Purbright looked, and nearly laughed.

She suppressed the laugh, but at the cost of a movement somewhere, and Mrs. Purbright heard it. She recoiled as though she had seen a snake. A dozen expressions crossed her face before she exclaimed, her mind harking back to a long-ago occasion, 'Oh, Miss Angell, I am so glad to see you. I'm feeling so uneasy about Mr. Casson.'

Vera rose from the tree-trunk and flicked some wet leaves from her skirt. On her feet, and nearly as tall as Mrs. Purbright, she felt better able to cope with the situation.

'Can I help you?' she asked civilly.

'Oh, Miss Angell, I wish you could. I don't know why I should appeal to you, but who else is there?' Mrs. Purbright was thinking aloud. 'Probably you know, he's gone out in his boat. It was brave of him, I think, but such a pity. You may not agree with me.'

'It wasn't the day I should have chosen,' said Vera, truthfully.

'No, indeed, that's just it, *not* a good day for the river. I tried to stop him before he started, and again at the bridge. But I was too late. Things went against me. Edgell . . . Edgell. . . .'

Vera said nothing, but looked at Mrs. Purbright with a pensive, sad regard.

'He's not well, poor boy, and I was so torn . . . but decided to come here in case, you know, I should be in time to head him off and persuade him to go back. Mr. Casson, I mean. You haven't seen him, have you?' Vera said nothing, and Mrs. Purbright hurried on, partly because her feelings were running away with her, partly because, dimly remembering her interview with Nelson, she felt she must not let the conversation get into other hands. And the sense of gratitude that the sight of beauty never failed to kindle in her, warmed her thoughts towards this Miss Angell, who so eminently possessed it.

'It's the waterfall that's worrying me, it's only a little way below us, you know, and it might be dangerous when the river is so swollen. Please, Miss Angell, you are younger than I am and your eyes are better, I am sure. Would you go to that little jutting-out place there, if you think you can safely, and call out to him if he comes by?'

Partly in automatic reaction to the vehemence of Mrs. Purbright's words, but more in a spirit of mischief, Vera complied. She had a good head, and did not mind perching on the grassy peninsula. Turning her beautiful back to Mrs. Purbright, she shaded her eyes and gazed up the river.

'How good of you,' said Mrs. Purbright. 'I should feel so terribly guilty, if he had an accident. He has been rather unlucky here, Miss Angell. . . .'

'Cross is my name, as a matter of fact,' said Vera pleasantly, still scanning the river.

'Cross, of course, how stupid of me. I don't think he ever quite understood how to take us, you know, and this boat has been such a barrier. . . . There's no sign of him, I suppose?'

Vera looked again. 'Not yet,' she said.

'There's still a chance. The path we came by is a tremendously short cut. It's two miles further by the river. If we stop him he can go quietly back and . . . and take up his ordinary life, writing and so on. This expedition will have cleared the air, perhaps. People speak so sympathetically of him, and would like him if they knew him. He has been such a good friend to me. I can't bear to think that somehow. . . .' Mrs. Purbright paused, suddenly realising the weight and density of all the imponderables she had battled against in her championship of Timothy. She came closer to Vera and tried to look over her shoulder, then drew back.

'Better that he shouldn't see me,' she said, 'now that you're here. Much better. He might resent my interference, I might do more harm than good. I have given him reason to dislike me.' Mrs. Purbright hesitated, and with an impulse of generosity that she was only too glad to obey, bundled into the background of her mind all that she knew, or had been told, or had surmised about Miss Cross.

'In this moment of our common anxiety – for I am sure you must feel even more anxious about him than I do – I will tell you something that I could tell to no one else. I too have loved him – yes, as much as I have loved my own son, perhaps more, or why should I be here? Is that a link between us? Miss Angell, I think it must be. I cannot say we share him – that would be both presumptuous and untrue, but we share our feeling for him.' Addressing Vera's back, unable to see her eyes which were still bent on the river, she broke off and said, 'I'm a little tired, I shall sit down now. Tell me if you see him coming.'

Vera turned round and said, 'But Mrs. Purbright, I *have* seen him.'

'You *have* seen him?' gasped Mrs. Purbright.

'Yes, he passed by about ten minutes ago.'

'And you never told me?'

'But Mrs. Purbright,' said Vera, opening wide her innocent eyes, 'you never gave me the chance!'

Mrs. Purbright stared at her with an expression of amazement and incredulity. She did not sit down but shuffled to and fro on the edge of the isthmus that separated her from Vera.

'It was a cruel trick to play on me,' she said. 'I believe you are a wicked woman, Miss Angell.'

With a slight stiffening of manner Vera said, 'The name is still Cross.'

Mrs. Purbright made no comment, but as though speaking to herself she said, 'I wonder how you got in here.'

'The same way as you did, I imagine,' said Vera, bored but polite.

'I found the door open: it was careless of somebody.'

'Very careless.'

'I must warn Sir Watson.'

'I think you should.'

'The door is marked Private. You didn't realise it was private property?'

Vera shrugged her shoulders.

'Of course with the door open, anyone can get in,' said Mrs. Purbright.

'It wasn't open,' said Vera.

'You must excuse me,' said Mrs. Purbright, who was trembling with rage, 'if I fail to understand. You climbed over, I suppose.'

'Does it matter?'

'Not to a woman of your sort.'

'But I didn't climb over, Mrs. Purbright. I came through the *ordinary* way.'

'You must have forced the lock, then.'

'I didn't have to.'

'But you have no key.'

Vera smiled and the corners of her mouth dropped.

'You have a skeleton key perhaps?' pursued Mrs. Purbright.

Vera shook her head. She couldn't resist the temptation to tease Mrs. Purbright a little further.

'Oh no, I don't need one. You see I have a *real* key.'

'You have a key?'

'Yes, the one Edgell gave me.'

Mrs. Purbright stiffened. Her eyes narrowed and she took a step forward.

'Please give me the key, Miss Cross.'

Vera bared her blue eyes and said despairingly, 'But I can't, Mrs. Purbright. I promised Edgell I wouldn't give it to *anybody*.'

'Give it to me, I say.'

'I can't,' cried Vera, frightened now. 'Let me pass, Mrs. Purbright.'

'I won't let you pass. If you don't give me the key, I shall take it.'

For a moment the two women struggled in silence on the river's brink. Then Vera cried hoarsely, 'Be careful, you nearly had me over. Let go, you fool. *Oh, Mrs. Purbright!*'

CHAPTER XXX

ON the morning of 'the day,' for Timothy's mind had long invested it with inverted commas, he awoke almost as exultant as if he had created it. The fact that it had rained all yesterday, rained all night, and was raining still, did not in the least depress him; if it rained before seven it would be fine before eleven. When eleven o'clock came, and brought no break in the downpour, he remembered how in Venice the weather often cleared up about three; and an ounce of personal observation was worth a pound of proverbs. He had reached a state, unknown to him before, when every circumstance, favourable or the reverse, combined to prick the sides of his intent.

How oddly does Fate take us by surprise! Timothy had foreseen and guarded against everything that could possibly go wrong on the voyage between the Old Rectory and the Devil's Staircase. Many times, in imagination, he had rowed and finished the course. He had also, which was more remarkable for him, studied the river itself, the actual terrain, if that was the word, wherever it was visible.

He had discovered, for instance, that there was, embedded in the Old Steps, a convenient ring to which he could moor the boat when he was addressing the spectators on the bridge. This ring, being near the top of the steps, would be available however high the water was. For Timothy had not ignored the possibility of a flood. Indeed he hoped the river would be rather full, for according to all the information he could get, the likeliest risk he ran was that of going aground and being left high and dry.

But one thing he had completely overlooked: the difficulty, in a flood, of getting the boat out of the boat-house.

When he went there, soon after breakfast, he found the path to the boat-house already awash, and the water, he could see, was a foot deep at the door. He would have to enlist the aid of Simpson. Simpson had a pair of gumboots.

Of all the people whom Timothy had canvassed about his attempt on the river Simpson was almost the only one who refused to see its symbolic significance. 'So you're going for a row, are you, sir?' he said, and a row for him it remained, in spite of Timothy's playful efforts to persuade him that the row, spelt the same but spoken differently, might gloriously turn into a row.

'So you won't be able to go for a row, after all,' was his comment when Timothy told him of the inaccessibility of the boat-house. 'You can't go for a row without a boat.'

'Oh, but we must get it out,' said Timothy. 'And I'm afraid I can't do it alone.'

'There you are, you see.'

This was one of Simpson's pet remarks; whatever happened, it established the fact of his ominiscience and his interlocutor's lack of foresight. However, he came not too grudgingly to Timothy's help, and together – he in his gumboots and Timothy with his trousers turned up to the knee – they tackled the boat-house.

Inside at any rate they had a roof to keep the rain out. The boat was now floating clear of its narrow dock. The pull of gravity had taken it to the farther wall, against which it kept up a gentle but impatient tapping. Already it had an air of partial freedom; it reminded Timothy of a butterfly that has emerged from the chrysalis but is not yet ready to fly. With the recovery of its mobility it had lost that static, expectant, rather sinister look that used to trouble Timothy; it was waiting to serve, not to be served. Or so he thought.

The doors were made to open outwards but they were immovable from disuse and the extra weight and pressure of the water. Timothy pushed at one door, Simpson at the other, but being at the side, and close against the hinges, they could not get a purchase. It was then that Timothy had the idea, which Simpson for a time resisted, of using two stakes as battering rams. Standing at opposite sides, their stakes crossing in the middle, they pushed and strained with rapt, expressionless faces, and eyes slewed sideways, like workmen in a mediæval woodcut. When at last the doors gave way, the pressure of the water flung them outwards and laid them flat against the boat-house. How to shut them was a problem that could wait.

Meanwhile there was a magnificent aperture, larger than the size of the doors when closed would have suggested. Daylight poured in, and the fact that the rain poured in also did not destroy the dramatic effect. With this influx of light Timothy felt that the shadows which had haunted the boat-house were forever exorcised.

'You see my plan did work,' said Timothy, who, being no engineer, was inordinately uplifted by the success of his invention. 'We should never have done it the way we were trying to before.'

'That's what I said,' replied Simpson, with a slightly repressive air. It wasn't what he had said; this phrase like the other, was one he frequently used to snatch verbal victory, and the prestige that went with it, from the jaws of defeat. Timothy had never convicted Simpson of making a mistake.

A flood is Nature at its most untidy. The opening framed a dismal prospect of things misplaced and acting out of character. The narrow conduit between the river and the boat-house had disappeared, with all the low-growing vegetation on its banks; instead, a mass of muddy water, pitted by raindrops, drifted slowly by. Eddies and tiny whirlpools were busy with leaves and twigs; bushes looked misshapen, deprived of half their height. Beetles and other insects, which had never seen water in their lives before, now looked like being drowned. Beyond, in the open, ridged and sinewy, the current raced; and beyond it were the rocks, their pinky glow dulled and dirtied by the rain.

'You'll never go out in this?' said Simpson, surveying the prospect with lack-lustre eye. ' 'Tisn't the day for a picnic, Mr. Casson.'

'I wasn't going for a picnic,' said Timothy.

'That's what I said: you want to choose your day.'

'I'm afraid the day has chosen me,' said Timothy, thinking of the posters, the handbills and the concourse on the bridge.

'It'll be fine at three o'clock, you'll see,' he promised the departing Simpson.

'Après le déluge, moi.' The thought pleased Timothy: it was material for a joke, and when the rain stopped he would work on it. 'There will be too much of me in the coming by and by.' A light dissertation on egotism, in his best 'Lombard' manner. Meanwhile he decided to manœuvre the boat into the garden and beach it on the lawn. He would have to bale it out afterwards, but what matter? He could no longer resist the lure of that open door. The moment he touched the craft meaning business it seemed to come to life, as it never had in the old days when he fingered it like a museum piece. He followed the sculls into the boat and sat down on the sliding seat. A throne! Tentatively he worked it backwards and forwards. The motion was freedom's very stride. What immediately followed was something of an anti-climax – the nosing out of the boat-house, the sudden swing against the corner of the building, hampering his movements; the branches above scratching his face, the branches below clutching at the keel; the discomfort of wetness spoiling the grandeur of water. But at last he fought his way clear of the undergrowth, and three good strokes brought the bow on

393

to the lawn, high if not dry. The boat heeled over gently and Timothy got out.

He pulled it half way up the lawn, tied a stone to the painter as a safeguard against advancing floods, took out the sculls and the sliding seat and with many a backward glance walked slowly to the house.

He tried to savour what he felt, to be at once the subject and object of his consciousness. But you cannot fill a cup fuller than it will hold; the rest is lost. Timothy's being could not contain the rapture that was being poured down on it with the rain; he was more than mortal, but had no measure to tell him by how much. He knew the precious elixir was running to waste and longed for other dimensions of the spirit which like a reservoir would hold and store it. But something warned him that transience was the essential condition of his joy, that the price of having it was to lose it, that like the manna of the desert it would not keep to the next day. As well try to recapture the thrill of speed when the toboggan has come to rest. His mind told him this yet he did not believe it; he did not believe that the warm soft rain would not fall forever on his spirit as it was now falling on his body.

Feeling like an emperor he entered the kitchen, but his words seemed woefully inadequate as he uttered them, and met with a like reception from the maids.

'But you're all wet' – so Beatrice greeted Timothy's halting but momentous announcement. 'He looks like a drowned rat, doesn't he, Effie?' Since the notice had been given and taken both maids had adopted a more familiar as well as a more friendly manner with him.

Effie looked at him speculatively.

'I shall have to iron Mr. Casson's suit,' she said, 'and Simpson won't half carry on about his shoes.'

Looking down Timothy saw that he was standing in a puddle and for the first time realised that he was wet through. At another time the discovery would have horrified him, as something that should never be allowed to happen, a departure from all his rules of life. But to-day he only said, and only felt, 'I suppose I must go and change.'

As he was going out Beatrice called after him, 'There are two telegrams for you in the hall. One came just after you had gone out, and the other a few minutes ago. Effie took them down, but she doesn't know if she got them right.'

'I couldn't hear, the line was that bad,' complained Effie. 'But they said they'd send you confirmation copies.'

Confirmation! Timothy's mind went back to that far-off divine event, from which his whole creation should have moved. How did his beliefs and aspirations then square with his present attitude? Suddenly he remembered Mrs. Purbright. Of all his thoughts she was the only one which still challenged his new conception of his rights and duties, and resisted the exaltation that had taken possession of him. He dared not risk the slightest parley with her. If one of the telegrams was from her, as well it might be, it would be wiser to destroy them both unread. Without looking at them he went up to change.

'But, Mrs. Purbright, I'm afraid I don't agree with you. In my opinion what I am doing now, or just going to do, is a highly Christian act. I'm doing it entirely for the benefit of the poor and the oppressed. . . . No, it does *not* matter dividing the village into two camps, we've been over all that before. For one thing, it's misleading, in the highest degree misleading, to say two camps, when there are only a handful of people in one camp, and practically the whole population of the village, some five hundred people, in the other. Of course if you happen to be in the minority – the, in my opinion, negligible minority – it's just too bad. I'm afraid we shall have to liquidate you, sorry as I am to say it. You're making use of a class argument, to protect your own skin. . . . No, I simply don't understand you when you say that human beings should not be looked at that way, on two sides of a barricade. It's the way they are, and the way they always will be, until we get rid of the people on the other side. . . . A personal matter? Really, Mrs. Purbright, I wonder that you should have brought that up again . . . especially when you yourself told me you thought I had been badly treated, in the first place, about the boat. The house-agent's blurb and all that – the farrago of lies by which I was induced to take the house, from that excellent woman of business, Miss Chadwick – have you forgotten? You must have a very short memory. *I* have forgotten it, I need hardly say; it doesn't enter into my calculations in the least. I assure you that I had completely forgotten it until this moment. . . . *I* stand to gain anything by defying them? I don't know what you mean, Mrs. Purbright. If you call vindicating other people's rights, by incidentally vindicating my own, *gain* – then it's a kind of gain I'm not ashamed of. . . . It wasn't that kind of gain, you say. Then, what kind of gain was it, pray? . . . I know Miss Vera Cross, yes, of course I know her. A very beautiful and distinguished woman, who has not been appreciated in this village as she should have been, if I may say so. Yes, she is a friend of mine, a close friend: do you object to that? Isn't that my affair? . . . Promise, promise, some form of prize or reward that may have influenced me? I know of no such promise. Please be more explicit, Mrs. Purbright. . . . What? . . . What? . . . Oh really to think that you, a clergyman's wife, should have made such an infamous suggestion! The indelicacy of it! If only you had been a man, instead of an interfering, elderly woman, I should know how to answer you . . .!'

Timothy's dry clothes supplied the answer. The new flannel suit, bought off the peg for the occasion, fitted surprisingly well and made him look younger and fresher. By renewing his personality it renewed also his morale and jerked his thoughts back into their proper groove. By choosing, by preferring one course to another, he had annihilated all the arguments on the other side; they had ceased to exist, and could not be reborn in a telegram.

The two slips of paper were identical. He took one up at random:

Many thanks letter stop completely disagree with what you say but will fight to the death for your right to say it stop Up the rebels stop Have leave at last and will be with you for week-end. TYRO.

And then the other:

Worried by your letter dearest Timothy. I sympathise deeply with your difficulties and would like to discuss them with you. Will come on Friday unless you tell me not convenient. Have little hope of finding servants for you. Most earnestly implore you to give up river plan. Love, ESTHER.

'Luncheon is served, sir,' said Effie to Timothy's new, smart back.

'Oh yes,' said Timothy. He turned round. 'Effie! You took down the telegrams perfectly all right. You didn't make a single mistake. I almost wish you had.'

'Thank you, sir.'

He followed her into the dining-room. It was Wednesday. Beatrice and Effie were due to leave on Saturday. Apart from a vague notion of going to an hotel in Swirrelsford, he had made no plans, except by making his will, for the future beyond today. After today, it had seemed to him, nothing mattered.

But the telegrams reminded him that something did matter. Two guests had proposed themselves, and unless he had the means of entertaining them he must put them off. The telegrams were directed to a dead self, a non-existent Timothy, whose mind was sterile to any idea that did not bear on his present project. Still, these were his friends, the only friends he had, even if friendship now meant little more to him that a sense of obligation.

'Effie,' he said timidly, 'you know that two of my friends' – he tried to speak as if their name was legion – 'have asked if they could come for the week-end.'

'Indeed, sir?' said Effie, too well-trained to admit that she had taken in the purport of the telegrams.

'Yes, Mrs. Morwen and Mr. MacAdam. I wonder if you and Beatrice would do me the great kindness of staying over Sunday?'

Effie's body wilted but her face went stiff and expressionless. 'I will go and ask Beatrice, sir,' she said, and left the room.

Timothy ate and pondered. Tyro had given his blessing to the River Revolt while disapproving of its motives; Esther sympathised with the motives but did not like the plan. How impossible it was to please everybody! How futile to try! The only thing was to do what one knew to be right, and Timothy did know. The sense of being right was the one state of mind that absorbed a man entirely, leaving nothing over, no stragglers, no malcontents to sabotage his effort. Nevertheless he began to wonder – for the mind sometimes has its fancies even when it is made up – how long this conviction of being right would last, after he had translated it into action. How would he feel, for instance, this evening? Or in two or three days' time, when Esther and Tyro were here? What would they find to talk about? What did people talk about, who were not engaged to the full of their natures in expressing in action their conviction of what was right?

Timothy had talked about nothing else for many days and thought about nothing else, it seemed, for several weeks. He no longer needed his own propaganda, but others did. The one task of his tongue was to convert them. But afterwards?

Well, afterwards the war would be on. Today was only the declaration of war. All he had done so far was to marshal his mass of manœuvre, as the strategists used to say. Afterwards it would be war. Esther and Tyro would be coming into a war area.

War, a war within a war. Suddenly he remembered the war outside his own, the World War, which he had not remembered for a long time, and immediately felt jealous of it. Yes, they would want to talk about the War, their war not his, for they were both, in their different ways, absorbed by it. They would brush his war aside. They would shake their heads over the German advance into Russia. They would discuss the food position and the submarine menace. They would speculate as to whether the German air bombardments were really weakening. They would have no time for his war. How could he bring himself to listen to them, chattering about a struggle in which the issues were so confused that none of the parties, except Russia, was certainly in the right? In which millions of innocent people were suffering and would suffer? In which nothing, Timothy was sure of it, would be settled when the conflict ended? Whereas here in Upton—

If Effie and Beatrice decided to leave he would have no option but to put off Esther and Tyro; and it would be a relief, a real deliverance if they did not come.

He raised his eyes. Effie was standing at his elbow, her colour heightened and her breath coming fast.

'If you please, sir, Beatrice says we will stay.'

'Oh, Effie, how good of you both! I was afraid you might be due at your next place.'

'No, sir, we're not suited yet. We could have been many times over, of course. But Beatrice thought we ought to take a holiday, "on my account," she says.'

'Oh yes, quite right. But are you sure you wouldn't rather go on Saturday?'

'Quite sure, sir. Beatrice said she wouldn't hear of it. We shan't let you down, sir, come what may.'

'Well, that's very good of you,' said Timothy, this time in an ungracious voice. 'I could so easily put them off,' he added, hopefully.

'Oh no, sir, we couldn't let you do that. Besides we want to know how it's all going to end.'

'How what's going to end?' asked Timothy.

'Well, sir, some people call it the River Riot and some people call it something which I couldn't very well tell you. But everyone thinks there'll be bloodshed before the end, sir.'

'Do they really, Effie?'

'Oh yes, sir,' said Effie, beginning to show a tremulous animation. 'There's been a lot of tar-barrels outside Captain Sturrock's house, and nobody knows what they're there for.'

'I had noticed them,' said Timothy.

'And their maid has given notice – only she's not a real maid, she's a waif brought up on charity. But she won't stay, not with those tar-barrels so close.'

'I don't blame her,' said Timothy heartily.

'And Sir Watson Stafford has received several anomalous letters.'

'Really?'

'And Commander Bellew tripped over a piece of rope, only it wasn't there by accident.'

'I hope he didn't hurt himself,' said Timothy without thinking.

'Oh yes, he did, sir, he strained his knee-cap. And they say he's asking for police protection, only Mr. Nelson doesn't tell us anything.'

'Has anything else happened?' asked Timothy.

'Oh yes, sir. Someone posted one of your notices inside the church door, and Mr. Purbright tore it down and burnt it. They say his face was something terrible when he lit the match.'

'Oh, I say,' said Timothy.

'Yes, and ever so many people have quarrelled, husbands and wives, too, and aren't on speaking terms. They say that Mr. Wimbush struck Mrs. Wimbush, but I shouldn't know that.'

'Oh dear, I'm sorry,' said Timothy. 'I always liked him so much.'

'Well, sir, it was her that was hurt, not him, though she was sticking up for you.'

'Most of the women seem to be on our side,' said Timothy, to change the conversation.

'Oh yes, sir, a good many, on account of always being unfairly treated. But it isn't the women who are calling for what they call the blood-bath, it's the men.'

'I don't want things to go too far, Effie,' said Timothy uneasily.

'Oh no, sir, but they'll have to be worse before they're better, won't they? Beatrice says she wouldn't miss it for worlds. Of course it was different before, but now she says she doesn't mind how long she stays.'

When referring to their departure both Beatrice and Effie always gave the impression that they, not Timothy, had decided on it. Timothy did not object to this version of the event, indeed he rather welcomed it, as it shifted the responsibility for their dismissal on to them. He had for some time suspected that they did not really want to go, and Effie's last remark confirmed it. If Timothy implored, perhaps if he even asked, them to reconsider 'their' intention to depart, they would do so gladly. And if they did, it would simplify everything. Timothy ought to have been glad, yet somehow he was not. He was relieved, on the whole, that they would stay over the week-end; but the thought of their presence beyond that was a burden. Not only, or chiefly, because he didn't think it would answer; because, assured of their position, no longer under notice, they would slip back into their old despotic ways. No, his real reason for hoping they would go was that he could not make plans beyond today; what was to happen next had no reality for him, he could not imagine himself taking part in the future, and he viewed with misgiving the commitments piling up all round him, which, he obscurely felt, he would never be able to discharge; even the week-end, so near, was an oppression. He was giving to the future unredeemable pledges. It was as though he had undertaken to climb the Matterhorn or do some other impossible feat. And these considerations disturbed the perfect image of felicity which the morning's work had brought him – the absolute harmony, the identification, one might say, between his time-conditioned being and the timeless desire that animated it. 'Après le déluge, moi.' Yes, he would still be there, picking up the pieces, clearing up the mess. Self-fulfilment was not the same as self-annihilation. It began to seem a grim joke, now.

'You'll be at the bridge, Effie, this afternoon?' he asked.

'Oh yes, sir, we're not going back on our promise and we're looking forward to it ever so much, at least Beatrice is. She says if anyone starts anything funny she's got something that will make them think twice. She won't tell me what it is but I believe it's a dagger. But you won't go, sir, not unless it clears up, will you?' added Effie, almost hopefully.

'Oh, it'll clear up all right, you'll see.'

The maids had the right spirit; he could talk to them. But what about his prospective guests? Timothy's mind went back to them. Esther and Tyro were bourgeois to the bone, capitalist drones, however hard they might appear to work. But after all, why must he have them? For months he had implored them to come, and they had always refused. Now, just because it happened to suit them, they had decided to come, both of them, and almost without consulting him, or his convenience. They had proposed themselves. Why? (The obvious answer never occurred to Timothy.) They would not get on with each other, they hardly knew each other, and what they knew they did not like. And least of all would they like what they would find: a militant revolutionary, almost a Communist, absorbed in his activities and surrounded, quite literally, by the articles of his faith.

Those pamphlets! Those inflammatory sheets, printed in smudged ink that showed through the paper, pathetic, perhaps, but proud, for they bore the tidings of the new gospel! They lay about the drawing-room for everyone to see; and though no one, except Effie and possibly Beatrice, *had* seen them (and of course, Vera, who had given them to him) was he to disown them, put them away, hide them, just because some people out of his dead life had chosen that moment to resurrect themselves? Never! They should be on view everywhere, even in his visitors' bedrooms; and he would insist on them being read, and commented on.

His mind grew hot as he envisaged his guests' inevitable opposition to the pamphlets. Unlike as they were, they would sink their differences and combine against him. Esther would be reticent, Tyro vociferous in disagreement. All the arguments of reaction! He would have to convince them, and what weary word-slinging it would entail, that reaction, in the new vocabulary of ethics, was a synonym for sin. And why should he take the trouble? Converts over fifty were little use to the cause anyhow, fellow-travellers at best. It was no good arguing with the elderly; they would only pit their wits against his, and speak from unreal premises, unreal because since Marx the fundamentals of thought had changed. Anyhow, the subject did not admit of argument; it could only be profitably discussed by people who agreed in principle, but possibly differed as to ways and means. The others must be eliminated.

Eliminated! Timothy did not wish to eliminate Esther and Tyro in a general sense, but he could eliminate them from the Old Rectory, and he would. They must be kept away. He only wanted to meet his own kind; he could not be bothered to talk to reactionaries whose attitude would not, of course, shake his faith but would irritate the surface of his mind, rub him up the wrong way and dissipate his mental energy. Little, dark, bearded men unobtrusively carrying despatch cases were the sort he wanted to know, and Vera had promised that he should know them.

He would write to Esther and Tyro, explaining that he now felt out of tune with people of their sort, and that their meeting would serve no useful purpose. He would say he still kept them in his thoughts, and wished them well and would welcome news of them from time to time; but any closer relationship between them must cease. Each would understand that this communication cancelled everything, *everything*, that he had said in previous letters.

Meanwhile he must concoct two putting-off telegrams. . . .

As he mused on how to phrase them, a shaft of sunlight came into the room. He jumped up and went out into the steamy, splashy afternoon to reconnoitre. It was still raining, but much less hard, and there was a break in the clouds which betokened the cessation of hostilities. 'Après le déluge, moi. . . .'

The water must have risen nearly a foot, for the boat, which he had left beached on the lawn, was once again afloat. It was lucky that he had anchored it; lucky, too, that he had taken the precaution of getting it out of the boat-house when he did, for by now it would have been immured beyond hope of release. But perhaps not lucky, perhaps he was merely fulfilling his own destiny. If only destiny would prompt him as effectually now!

He dragged the boat further up the slope, and the rainwater which had collected in it rushed tumultously into the stern, beyond the seat, lifting the rudder, which was lying there. He had not put the rudder in position yet. Vera would probably want to steer, but he hoped she wouldn't; on her own admission she knew little about water-craft and would almost certainly pull the wrong string; in this instance, her guidance would be a liability, not an asset. He would have to bale the boat out, but there would be time for that when the rain stopped.

As he returned to the house his thoughts went back to Vera. Where, among these intrusions from the future, did she come in? The future was irrelevant; and strangely enough, Vera had never made herself part of it. She had spoken of developments in the situation in Upton, but as to the further progress of *their* situation, what *they* would do, after the day's and the night's consummation, she had not said a word.

Timothy fell to thinking of that – for the past existed, however dubious the future. It seemed incredible now, but without that vulgar and trivial incentive, the carrot dangled before the donkey, he would never have embarked on this great enterprise. Indeed he remembered, as a matter of historic fact, that until she made the promise his whole being was opposed to the idea. And now, though the thought sweetened and revived his fancy, it seemed only an adjunct, an adjunct to the fulfilment of his dream, an adjunct that detracted from its disinterestedness. He almost wished she had not made it. . . .

But as the afternoon passed, and the sun came out in earnest, as he had known it would, and tea was announced, and the zero hour approached, his feelings underwent a revolution and he found himself longing for her and counting the minutes till she came. In telling him tea was ready Effie had adopted a manner she had never used to him before. He might have been a matador bound for the arena, and she an aficionada bidding him farewell. As the image entered his mind he seemed to see the tiers of seats, in which all humanity was congregated, gradually receding from him, leaving him alone but for a few skirmishers to await the onset of the bull.

As he sat looking at her empty place a sense of utter loneliness possessed him, of being cut off from humankind. Until then he had not realised how much he counted on her and to what a degree his grand idea, that had seemed so abstract, had its true lodging in her flesh and blood.

At half past five he went into the kitchen, carrying the cushions of the boat. The maids were moving about with an air of controlled excitement, dressed in their best clothes: they looked at him questioningly, without speaking. 'Miss Cross hasn't come yet,' he said, making the statement sound as flat and ordinary as he could; 'I shall go and get the boat ready, and if she doesn't come, I must start without her.' They stood still and made no comment; there was no sound in the room until suddenly Timothy heard the thud of Felix's tail and his chain grating on the flag-stones; and the next thing he knew was that the dog had launched itself on him, with the crafty and humorous smile which he kept for these assaults. Absently Timothy fondled his silky head and Felix lumbered up on to his hind-legs and tried to lick Timothy's face.

'Down, Felix, down, you'll ruin my new trousers.'

But Felix paid no attention. Only force could curb his appetite for love and as Timothy felt the weight and warmth of his body he became aware of the warmth and staunchness of his nature, too.

'Are you taking Felix with you?' he asked Beatrice.

'Oh no, sir, I shouldn't like to risk it. He might go mad and bite someone.'

'Well, could he come with me? After all, he's a water-dog.'

Beatrice demurred, but only formally; she saw that Timothy's heart was set on taking Felix; and Felix, the moment he divined from Timothy's voice that an adventure was afoot, went wild with excitement.

Disappointingly, he did not swim or take to the water in a large way; while Timothy baled out the boat he paddled in the shallows with a serious air, and so much absorbed was he by exploring this new element that he did not raise his head when Timothy, his task complete, went off to make a final telephone call to Vera.

'No, she's not come in yet,' said Frances, civil and non-committal. 'I can't think what's kept her.' Nor was she in sight when Timothy took a last look down the road.

She had promised to put on his favour with her own hands. Now Timothy had to pin on the paper boat himself. 'A Free River for a Free People!' The lonely drop of blood from Timothy's pricked finger did not warm as it should have done to this proud rallying-cry. Nor did he get the thrill he hoped for when he tied the Union Jack on to the stern, or the much greater afflatus of spirit when the Hammer and Sickle fluttered in the bow.

Simpson had gone home and Timothy must launch himself. Again it was the unexpected that gave trouble. The cushions must be kept clean for Vera who, Timothy still hoped, would join him at the bridge, but Felix had taken a fancy to them and would not be dislodged. Nor, which was much worse, would the boat. It had worn itself a groove in the soft turf and would not budge. Supposing he could not shift it? Supposing that the population of Upton, bridge-bound, awaited it in vain?

But in this crisis, Felix was a help. It needed only their joint weight in the stern to set the boat afloat. A single shove with the sculls and the

Argo was already under way. Argo! The name was emblazoned on the woodwork of the seat, in rather vulgar lettering, gold edged with black. As Argo the boat would lose its perilous associations; as Jason Timothy would shed his craven fears.

The blades of grass, pearl-grey with clinging air-bubbles, sank out of sight as they neared the river bank. How deep the water was Timothy could not tell, for churned-up mud made it almost opaque. Felix, who never really liked taking a back seat, squeezed his broad rump into the angle of the bows, and sat down back to back with Timothy, in an heraldic attitude, sniffing the air, and looking round him with insensate pride.

Once in the current all Timothy had to do was to keep straight and avoid the projecting branches, some of which had probably once over-hung, but now were in the water. Timothy was an experienced but not an expert oarsman; his style was nondescript but within limits he could make the boat obey him. So he was free to feast his eyes, as he flashed by, on the landscape that had been forbidden him so long. What he had hoped to see he hardly knew. Prairies? Jungles? Parakeets? Apes? It was all rather tame but he did not really mind, for he saw it with a conquer-or's enchanted eye. Only one thing disappointed him. His progress was too easy and too quick. He had stored up in himself enough nervous energy and resistance to tackle the Amazon, and nothing was calling it into play. He felt as an elephant might feel, picking up a pea.

After a bend or two the river straightened. On Timothy's right a path appeared, an asphalt urbanised path, down which he had often walked; and along it were running two small boys, their knees and elbows working like pistons. 'Give us a ride, Mister!' they chanted in a whining sing-song. 'Give us a ride!' So little did they look where they were going that Timothy was afraid they would fall into the river; and more for that than for any other reason he drew the boat into the bank and told them to get in.

Felix turned his head, moved forward and gave a growl, which said as plainly as possible, 'Keep out of my boat.'

The little boys, who were stepping in, scrambled back in a hurry.

'Will your dog hurt us, Mister?' asked the bigger of the two, in his plangent, lilting voice. Timothy assured them he would not. 'I've never known him growl before, except over a bone. Lie down, Felix!'

Still grumbling, his nose wrinkled in disgust, Felix resumed his heraldic posture at the prow. The Hammer and Sickle flapped against his chest. The little boys, so strangely reminiscent of Gerald and Billy Kimball, sat side by side, facing Timothy with tense, expectant eyes.

The bridge was in sight. Timothy swung the boat into midstream, braced himself and put on a spurt. He had already practised in his mind the manœuvre by which he must take the boat out of the current, turn it round and bring it to the steps; miraculously, he pulled it off, all in one movement, so it seemed; and it was this master-stroke which gave Nelson such a favourable impression of his oarsmanship. Evidently it impressed the rest of the on-lookers, too, for they gave him a ragged but rousing cheer. Landing on the steps, he tied the painter to the ring; it was taut in a moment. Retiring to his seat he looked up at the audience.

It was much smaller than he had expected and been promised, just enough people to line the parapet, with a handful looking over the others' shoulders. The faces were lively with curiosity and amusement, rather than stern with political resolve, yet they all kept their eyes on Timothy. One or two fathers lifted their children on to the parapet so that they could see him better, and silence fell when he began to speak.

He told them little that he had not told them personally, in his rounds from house to house. He reminded them of their rights and liberties which were being taken from them; landlords, he said, were becoming water-lords; soon they would claim the sky. 'We cannot boat or bathe without their permission; soon we shall not be allowed to breathe.' He had nothing against these gentlemen themselves, he said; he was as ready to touch his hat to them as any man in the village. He did not want to interfere with or curtail their pleasures, which were bringing them so much health and happiness in their declining years. But he did ask them, and begged his hearers to ask them, too, to share their privileges with those less fortunate than themselves. And it was no use asking politely; he had tried that. They must ask loudly and if necessary rudely; and if words brought no redress they must resort to deeds. Many of them were employed by these – he would not say tyrants, tyrants was an old-fashioned word. Nor would he say dictators. Dictators was too strong: the gentlemen in question were not dictators – yet. But they would be if nobody stood up to them and stopped them. 'They can't get on without you,' Timothy said. 'They rely on you to do their work – some of it is rather dirty work – for them, or how would they live? You must organize and tell them that unless they give you and your children your just rights (for I'm thinking about the children almost more than you, children like these in the boat – see how happy they look), you won't do any more to make their lives easy and comfortable for them; you will strike. Strike, that's the word to use. That will make them sit up and take notice. And if they answer, 'Strike if you like, we don't mind, we've got money in the bank and we can get on without you,' then you must use other methods. I won't say now what they are, because we don't want them to know, do we? If they knew, they might take steps to protect themselves. We want whatever comes, to come as a surprise.

'But if and when you do this I don't want you to feel any enmity for them in your hearts. I don't myself and I've suffered from them almost as much as you have. We must feel that we're doing it for them, not against them, to bring them to their senses. If they only knew it, they'd be much happier if they weren't so selfish.'

The little crowd continued to listen; but Timothy was too far away to see what effect his words were having. He only knew that he himself was moved by them; he even felt that they were being said for the first time. And encouraged by his eloquence he went on:

'You've been very patient. I don't want to talk about myself, because I've got no importance, I'm nothing but a mouthpiece. But you know all about me – I've lived with you for eighteen months, and I can honestly say – I can honestly say that I've become very fond of you all. You have treated me very kindly – all of you at Upton except a few I won't bother to name, and anyhow they aren't here with us to-day – very kindly, and much better than I had any right to expect, coming amongst you as a stranger. We've met together at the pub . . . and . . . and elsewhere, and had a lot of jolly talks. And I should like you to know how grateful I am for that, and to thank you, too, for coming here today, which didn't begin very promisingly, but has turned out, I can truly say, to be the happiest day of my life.'

Timothy stopped; he could no longer look at the spectators; his head drooped and he kept his eyes, where every oarsman should keep them, in the boat. It was the only speech he had made in his life, and it was over. There was no sound save the gurgling and rushing of the water. But suddenly the silence was broken by a note of music, which swelled into a song.

'For he's a jolly good fellow.' Timothy forgot that this had been arranged for. He was taken by surprise and deeply moved. Exposed in the boat, upright on the absurd sliding seat, with his feet against the stretcher, he had no way of concealing his embarrassment, except from himself, by closing his eyes. Pleased with this proof of modesty, enjoying his confusion, the crowd sang still more lustily, and at the end they gave him three cheers.

With tears in his voice Timothy thanked them. 'When I was a little chap,' he wound up, 'the thing I enjoyed most in the world was to be in a boat. I believe children are still the same, and I can't tell you how happy it makes me, on this, my first outing on the river, to have these little fellows with me. Turn round and wave to them, sonnies.' Cries of 'Ah! Aren't they sweet?' greeted the lads' salute.

'Is it over, Mister? Can we start now?' the talkative one asked. But it wasn't quite over. Most of the spectators waited on the bridge to see Timothy set off; some strolled towards the village, making comments to each other which Timothy longed to hear; and a few, chiefly mothers with children, came down from the bridge in his direction. At the steps they stopped.

'Could you give Frankie a ride?' a mother asked him. 'He's fond of boating, same as you are, only he hasn't never been in a boat.'

Frankie was pushed forward, and looked at Timothy appealingly.

'And Charlie would like to come, too,' said another mother. 'Ever since we told him what you meant to do, Mr. Casson, he's been on to us to let him go with you. He doesn't give us any peace, do you, Charlie? I expect it's in the blood, his father was a sailor.'

'My little girl would like to go, too,' said another woman, standing behind the others. 'She doesn't wish to push herself forward, of course, but she could help you to row, Mr. Casson, she's gone boating several times at Swirreslford.'

Several other children, unvouched for and unannounced, crowded on to the steps and fixed on Timothy glances eloquent with implied reproach.

'But we don't want any more, do we, Mister?' said the elder of Timothy's two passengers. 'We got here first, didn't we?' And Felix, evidently sharing this sentiment, underlined it with a growl.

'Shut up, Felix,' said Timothy, distressed by the exclusive and possessive attitude of his living freight.

'I wish I could take you all,' he said, addressing the embattled mothers, 'but I'm afraid I'm full up already. Soon, I hope, there'll be a whole fleet of boats stationed here, enough to take everybody.'

'I didn't think you'd descend to favouritism,' another, more educated woman said. 'What's the good of gassing about the freedom of the river, when you've packed the boat with your friends?'

Timothy had no answer to this, and felt his temper rising. Soon the heckling started in a new quarter.

'And you've got a dog. You said the boats were to be for human beings and children. Why can't you leave the dog and let Albert go instead?'

'Because he's *my* dog,' began Timothy angrily. Then, realising this was a bad gambit, suggesting delight in private property, he hastily explained that Felix, if landed, might get lost. 'Besides, he knows how to swim,' he added humorously.

'My Frankie knows how to swim,' said Frankie's mother. 'But I bet those two boys you've got there don't know how to. And they don't belong to Upton either. They're Birmingham bred, they are, they haven't any right on our river, Mr. Casson.'

The little boys, who had been following this closely, saw their trip threatened and looked at Timothy in alarm.

'But we're all right, aren't we, Mister?' said their spokesman, determined to have the word 'right,' whatever it meant, on his side. 'And we asked the gentleman first.'

'Those town boys are too blasted nippy, if you ask me,' said one of the women.

'Well, they did get there first,' admitted Timothy. 'And I don't think it would be safe to take any more.' Suddenly he had an idea. 'If you'll come here tomorrow at this time' – he stopped, assailed anew by the unreality of tomorrow. But he had to finish the sentence. 'I'll take any three of you,' he said.

Murmuring, only half satisfied, the rejected passengers edged away from the steps. The remaining spectators on the bridge, Nelson, Beatrice and Effie among them, craned their necks. This was the moment Timothy dreaded; the current was so strong that he might not get clear of the bank in time to avoid being swung against the masonry.

Stepping ashore he untied the painter and hauled the boat a few yards upstream, until a low-growing bush barred further progress. Clinging to the bush he lowered himself into the boat, holding it with his feet until he could sit down. Released, it swung outwards and backwards, but he was able to get two free strokes, putting the boat with its bow to the bridge, before the current caught him. Looking up, as he was swept under, he saw Nelson's admiring eyes and pride in the foreshortened faces of Beatrice and Effie.

The bridge disappeared from sight as though snatched away by a scene-shifter, and he was alone on the uncharted water. At least, he felt alone; for his three passengers made no demands on his thoughts, as the spectators had. He had discharged his human obligations; he had done what he could for mankind; now he could enjoy his reward, which was to be rid of them.

The rain-bright green of the trees was turning to gold. As the river bent outwards to his right, the westering sun shone down it into Timothy's eyes. But the current was not so strong as it had been: he could turn round and watch the glitter as it passed from tree to tree.

Once or twice he tried to fix a spot in his memory, thinking 'I'll come back there,' only to find his memory would not retain the image. Soon the trees grew thicker; their crests alone were lit up now; below, the gathering of a premature twilight enfolded him in a tingling secrecy of shade. On his right, the hills which bounded the re-entrant to the valley came down steeply to the water's edge; on his left the ground was flat, but more thickly wooded and no less mysterious – openings lengthened into glades, and glades into sunlit vistas, which were gone before his eye had time to explore them to the end.

Only one thing impaired the deep translucency which gave the scene its magic. Too turbid to hold a reflection, the surface of the river made a discordant streak in the melting symphony of trees and sky; they looked down on it in vain for shadows of themselves, and Timothy's thoughts, which in other directions were gently led on into infinity, rebounded from it like a stone from a wall.

The little boys, relaxed and happy, trailed grimy fingers in the grimy flood.

'Are you going to take us back, Mister?' one of them asked.

'Of course,' said Timothy. 'Did you think I should want you to walk?'

'We didn't know, Mister,' said the child. 'We *can* walk . . . oh ever such a long way, can't we, Reg?'

'Oh yes,' said Reg. 'We could walk to the moon.'

'We could walk to the sun.'

'We could walk right up to Heaven.'

They both thought this a tremendous joke, and laughed uproariously, pommelling each other with their watery fists.

'Can you swim, too?'

'Well, only when someone's holding us.'

They had reached the bend in the horseshoe; they were traversing its noble curve. Now the tree-tops in front of Timothy were beginning to light up, and little by little the golden radiance stole down their sides and the film of shadow lifted. Timothy could only see about fifty yards each way, so sharp was the curve. Soon it grew wider, then straightened out into an avenue which ended in the sun. Here the river gave the impression, which a river seldom gives, of going downhill, and Timothy felt the boat increase its pace.

From out of his reverie he saw the little boys looking fixedly at the left-hand bank.

'Who was that lady, Mister? She was pretty,' asked the smaller of the two.

'Lady? I didn't see any lady,' said Timothy.

'Pooh!' said the elder boy. 'I see her and she wasn't pretty, she was Miss Cross.'

'Miss Cross!' exclaimed Timothy. 'Are you sure?'

'Yes, she was sitting against a tree, watching us.' The boy spoke as if Vera's position established her identity beyond all possibility of mistake.

'I think you must be wrong.' But Timothy didn't think so. Spreading from his breast, the incredible news ran down his nerves to the tips of his fingers. One scull scraped the water; if he had been pulling hard he would have caught a crab. As it was, the boat swerved and heeled over.

'Ow, Mister! Do that again.' Anxious to repeat the sensation, the little boys tried to make the boat rock.

'Oh, do sit still.'

In vain Timothy tried to restore the rhythm of his rowing. The mechanism was no longer automatic; the thoughts that were jerking his mind jerked his body, too. Thinking of how to row made him nervous. He looked round anxiously. The children sensed his disquiet.

'Are you tired, Mister?'

Timothy shook his head. His lips were trembling and he did not trust himself to speak.

'Oh, what is that noise, Mister? Is it a wild animal got loose in the woods?' Timothy heard the noise but did not answer. The boat sped on.

'Oh, who's that man waving his arms, Mister?'

Uncertain of his balance, Timothy preferred not to look round.

' 'Tisn't a man,' said the elder scornfully. 'Don't you know who it is? It's Mr. Wimbush.'

'Wimbush!' exclaimed Timothy.

'Yes, Mister, he's waving his arms at us.'

Gingerly Timothy looked round and there sure enough was Wimbush, standing on the bank, gesticulating and shouting.

A wave of blind anger surged up in Timothy. 'So he's trying to turn us off the river, is he?' he muttered. 'Let him try.' He took his hand off the scull and, half-rising in his seat, tried to shake his fist at his ex-gardener. The boat lurched and shipped some water.

'Oh, Mister, be careful. The dog nearly fell out.'

Felix must have thought his position unsafe, for a moment later, at the end of his backward swing, Timothy touched the dog's body and felt his warm breath on his neck. Wimbush was running alongside, still

410

waving his arms, and calling out 'Go back, go back.' But Timothy couldn't go back, if he had wanted to.

The boat began to bump and toss as lateral waves – the flood water of the river thrown back by the bank – struck against it and passed under with a sucking sound. Streaks and patches of dirty foam appeared on the tormented surface. The boat writhed and wriggled beneath Timothy and would not answer to the sculls. The little boys clung to each other. Suddenly he saw terror staring in their eyes.

'Oh Mister, what's happening? The river's gone!'

Involuntarily Timothy looked round. It was true; the river had disappeared; a few yards ahead, beyond a fissured mound of spray-streaked water, there was no more river.

'Lie down in the bottom of the boat!' he called out, but the children were too frightened to understand and clung to each other, whimpering. A moment later they were flung forward on their faces as the boat plunged into the waterfall.

Timothy, too, was unseated, but Felix's body broke his fall and he managed to scramble back. He tried to ship the oars, for they were useless now and might get broken; but the crazy movement of the boat prevented him. All he could do was to cling, spread-eagled, to the struts of the rowlocks, while the boat crashed from boulder to boulder. Most of the boulders were invisible, sheathed in a curving muscle of water; but here and there one stuck out, jagged and threatening.

If only the boat did not turn broadside on, they might yet reach the bottom safely. Still clinging to the struts, Timothy strained his eyes. They were more than half way down the staircase but at the foot, guarding the pool, a big flat rock, only half covered by water, barred their way. Nearer and nearer it came. Timothy could already see the water of the pool, heaving and churning but promising safety. He glanced into the boat. The boys were lying on the floor, clasped in each other's arms, like kittens; Felix, shivering, was trying hard to keep his feet. The rock was upon them now. Timothy closed his eyes.

He felt a heavy blow and heard a crack, and the next thing he knew he was in the water.

His first feeling was one of immeasurable relief and freedom, combined with surprise that the water was so warm. Now at any rate he was his own master, and could act instead of being acted on. Round his head were clots of yellow spume like miniature mountains. He clove his way through them and saw, first the boat with a gash in its side, slowly turning round in the middle of the pool; then Felix, with a smile on his face, swimming towards him. But he could not see the boys.

The boat was only a few yards away and fending Felix off Timothy swam towards it. But his legs were swept from under him and in a moment he found himself in another part of the pool. From here he could see two little heads, and arms that feebly reached out to each other. He called out to them and renewed his efforts; this time he was on them in a trice and had hardly time to grasp the collar of one before he was again whirled away, this time in the main current towards the mouth of the pool. Frantically he fought with the current which, while it was carrying him, seemed to offer no more resistance to his strokes than if it had been air. They were nearing the edge when all of a sudden the water seemed to solidify, the ground rushed forward to meet him, and all he had to do was to lift the child, who was speechless with fright, on to the bank.

As he did so he heard a splash and saw another head in the water, a big, familiar head. Wimbush had come to the rescue, and was swimming with the same stroke that Felix used, but less expertly, towards the other boy. Good old Wimbush! Now all would be well.

Knee deep in water, he paused to get his breath. Wimbush was not making much headway. His strength, so triumphant on land, did not seem to serve him in the water. Felix was at the far side, looking for a landing. His head jerked to the rhythm of his strokes; he kept changing his direction and trying a fresh place. When he saw Timothy he swam towards him, still wearing his smile, though his eyes looked anxious and his nose was closer to the water-line. The boy had drifted nearer to the middle, where the whirlpool was turning him slowly round. Only the top of his head was visible, and just before a freak of the current brought Wimbush to the spot it sank. Timothy saw Wimbush put his head under the water, grope with his arm, and fish something up. It was the boy's elbow. His head followed, looking tiny beside Wimbush's. Timothy drew a long breath. Now they must all be safe. But no. A languor suddenly appeared in Wimbush's movements; he turned unseeing eyes towards Timothy and a great sigh seemed to bubble from his lips. Timothy ran round the pool to the place where Wimbush had got in, trusting that the current would take him to where Wimbush was. It did, but he was only just in time: Wimbush was sinking; the weight of the child's body on his arm was helping to thrust him under. Timothy got his hands under the man's shoulders and turning on his back struck out for the shore. The load was heavy and the current contrary and a sense of oncoming disaster dulled his mind and clogged his movements. But he was doing better than he knew when the boat, which was drifting about half full of water, suddenly spun round and struck him on the head. It was not a heavy blow but it was enough. Timothy's legs went down, his forehead bowed to meet the water, and his arms, losing their hold, spread out and hung downwards as if beginning an embrace.

From the bank, a few yards away, the little boy watched the group with terrified eyes, crying 'Mister! Mister! Mister!'

CHAPTER XXXI

COLONEL HARBORD did not feel altogether happy about the upshot of his conversation with the Purbrights. His mind was still convinced that a policy of non-interference was the right one; it had the Rector's approval and the approval of everyone he knew. No good would come of meddling, and left to itself the agitation would blow over. Casson was a crank of a kind which often turned up in country villages; a misfit, and his own worst enemy. What he wanted now was what he had always wanted: to be taken notice of. Centuries of tradition had made village people shrewd; they might be attracted by the novelty of a campaign like Casson's, but they did not really like self-advertisement and soon saw through it. No one else, he was quite sure, wanted to row on the river; none of the inhabitants of Upton had thought it a hardship that they couldn't until Casson had unsettled them.

Casson had invented a grievance in order to air his half-baked notions, and in doing so he had managed to stir up a lot of mud. He was the type of fellow – they were not unknown in the Army – who would always be up against it. The life he had lived since he came to Upton was not such as to induce ordinary level-headed people to feel much confidence in him. Live and let live, by all means, but there were limits, and Casson, from what he heard, had decidedly over-stepped them. Say what you would, a fellow who didn't play games, and didn't want to fish in a place where every normal man wanted to fish, must have something queer about him. If only he had been some kind of sportsman!

These were comforting opinions and comforting, too, was the knowledge that everyone he knew endorsed them – everyone except Mrs. Purbright.

Mrs. Purbright's eccentricity was well-known, and as much respected as Timothy's was not. People might smile at her and her affection for lame dogs and lost causes, but they recognised her sincerity. She was a scapegoat for their unavowable virtues and they were proud of her.

Colonel Harbord shared their regard for Mrs. Purbright, and he did not want to disappoint her. At the time, it had seemed enough to join her husband in good-naturedly confuting her views of what ought to be done – her fantastic, impracticable views, which were contrary to sense and reason. Afterwards she would see the force of the argument and come round to their way of thinking. At least a man would, and a woman who argued put herself in the position of a man.

But Mrs. Purbright had not seen reason; woman-like she had been thoroughly upset, and the memory of her distress tugged at his heart-strings as he walked home, and modified the half humorous account of the conversation that he was preparing for his wife. Nor, to his surprise, did Mrs. Harbord see eye to eye with him in unequivocally turning down Mrs. Purbright's proposal. 'Do you want me to go to the bridge, then?' he said, 'wearing my white sheet and taking my stool of repentance?' His wife laughed. 'No, but I think you could still do something. Men are always the same. They think that if someone holds a certain kind of opinion, then he must be a certain kind of person.'

'But doesn't it follow?'

Placid and quiet-eyed, Mrs. Harbord looked up from her sewing.

'Not necessarily.'

Colonel Harbord gave a despairing sigh.

'You don't tell me what I ought to do, I notice.'

'There are other places, besides the bridge,' said Mrs. Harbord. 'As a soldier, do you only attack at one point?'

To have introduced the military metaphor was a mistake. Colonel Harbord, though in many ways a broad-minded man, did not like amateurs to have opinions about military matters. He said that only the soldier in the field could judge. So he did not ask his wife what she meant. All the same, her observation lingered in his mind, reinforcing Mrs. Purbright's plea.

Though he would not go to the ceremony, neither could he quite keep away from it, and soon after six, when he believed that the meeting would be over, he strolled down to the bridge with a vague idea of asking someone how it had gone off. But when he saw the rabble coming away, wearing their favours and chatting to each other, he could not bring himself to. Great was his relief, therefore, to see Nelson on the bridge, a level-headed fellow and the guardian of law and order.

Nelson saluted him.

'Well, Nelson, it's nothing to do with me, but what's been happening?'

Nelson, fresh from his conversation with Mrs. Purbright, who even now might have been seen speeding down the road, had the whole thing at his tongue's end.

'Oh, nothing very much, sir. Mr. Casson just made an exhibition of himself, as I might say.'

'I can believe you,' said Colonel Harbord, drily. 'Is it true that he's some kind of Bolshy?'

'I couldn't tell you that, sir, but he rows a beautiful oar.'

'Oh, does he?' said Colonel Harbord, pricking up his ears.

'Yes, he does, sir. I've been in the rowing business myself, sir, so I know what I'm talking about. Mr. Casson's far and away the best oar I've ever seen, and I've seen a few.'

'You don't say so, Nelson.'

'It say it, sir, and what's more, I state it. There isn't another oarsman in the West Country as can touch Mr. Casson. That drive of his from the stretcher, sir, well, it's like a song.'

'I had no idea he was that kind of oar,' said Colonel Harbord, in a different tone.

'No, sir, and not many had. He never gave himself airs at all. But all the time he had it in him.'

'Evidently.'

'He used to be some kind of champion at college, I've been told. Head of the River, I think it's called. You couldn't count the number of cups he's won. But he's never had a chance to show what he's made of until now. The people were delighted with his display, especially his feathering.' Nelson demonstrated. 'They cheered and cheered.' Aware of the impression he was creating, Nelson made bold to add, 'You ought to have seen him, sir.'

'I almost wish I had,' said Colonel Harbord. He looked over the parapet at the swollen water.

He was not much of a judge of oarsmanship, and told himself that he would not have appreciated the fine points of Timothy's, but he was a judge of danger – an impartial, professional judge. A sixth sense that had come with training told him when this was present, just as surely as, or more surely than, it warns a stock-broker of the risk he runs.

Turning away from the angry, rushing river he said, 'Well, rather him than me. But he must be a sportsman to start out with the river in the state it is.'

The operative, the redeeming word slipped out without his noticing it; but Nelson noticed.

'Yes, sir, he is. A grand sportsman. And that ought to be known far and wide.'

Colonel Harbord pondered, and remembered his wife's remark, 'There are other places besides the bridge.'

'Is that your car down there, Nelson?' he asked.

'Yes, sir, it is, the same car that Mr. Casson kindly allows me to put in his subsidiary garage, and without charge. It's an Agamemnon eight, sir, with—'

'So I see,' said Colonel Harbord, 'and a very nice car, too. Could you run me down to some place where we could see Mr. Casson in . . . in action?'

'That would be above the Devil's Staircase, sir, but that's on Sir Watson Stafford's land.'

'Oh, he won't mind us going over it.'

Nelson complied with alacrity, and for a matter of a mile made the car show its best paces. Then gates had to be opened. At the last one they got out, to walk the rest of the way; and it was then that they heard, above the roar of the river, a shrill, repeated cry.

'Sounds like a child's voice,' said Colonel Harbord. They quickened their steps and the policeman had to remind the man in Nelson not to run.

Rivulets were trickling down the mound, which, artificially reinforced, held up the pool. The two men splashed through them and came panting to the top.

'Ah!' they both exclaimed, and the sound went to swell the sad gale of sighs that greets calamity in every land.

The three unfortunates, pathetically close to each other, were linked in a brotherhood of death. Humped bodies with dangling limbs, in attitudes from which the grace of life had fled, they were lying half in and half out of the water, where the current had carried them, a few feet from the shore. Between them and the shore, head down, tail drooping, stood Felix. He was whining and shivering, and from time to time he made short rushes at the bodies, and then backed away, as if afraid to touch them.

They had drifted over the river-bank on to the flood water; and Colonel Harbord and Nelson had only to wade in knee-deep to get them out. The policeman took Wimbush, the heaviest, whose hand still rested on the little boy; Colonel Harbord pulled out Timothy, then Nelson made a second journey for the child. To neither of them was the scene fraught with the horror it would have had for most people, but Colonel Harbord took his hat off, and Nelson, seeing this, removed his helmet.

'We'd better try artificial respiration,' Colonel Harbord said. 'You know your First Aid, Nelson. It's lucky I've rubbed up mine.' He took his coat off. The other boy, who had been silent since they came, partly from fright, partly from awe of Nelson, suddenly piped up, 'Are you going to take them to the lock-up, Mister?'

Neither of the men answered, but they exchanged glances, for the same thought had struck them both: which of the three victims was to be sacrificed for the sake of the others?

Colonel Harbord, however, was accustomed to making decisions.

'Let's leave the lad for the minute,' he said. 'He's . . . well, he's just unlucky. Perhaps we shall get one of the others round before long.'

They kneeled down in the approved fashion, and after a sidelong look to make sure they were both using the same method, they worked in silence, each throwing his weight against the lower ribs of the prone body under him. 'One, two, three, up! One, two, three, up!' They caught the rhythm from each other, and even breathed in unison; and the bodies breathed in unison, too, every few seconds exhaling bubbles, water and a gusty sigh.

Felix, meanwhile, could not bear to be left out. Nelson was his friend and therefore the first victim of his helpful attentions. He nuzzled against Nelson and tried to lick the back of Wimbush's neck. Nelson dug him in the ribs with his elbow and spoke to him in a way he had never been spoken to before; so Felix, after several such rebuffs, left him for Colonel Harbord.

'What are we to do about this damned dog, Nelson?'

'I'll get rid of him, sir.'

But it was difficult to convince Felix that he was not wanted. A kick was not enough; he merely backed away a yard or two, wagging his tail and waiting for the moment when his friendly advances should wear down human obtuseness. Nelson had to take a stick to him, of which there were several ready to his hand, before Felix, radiating backward glances loaded with love, vanished over the rushy rim, to be seen no more.

Nelson returned to his task. The little boy watched the two men avidly. Having assisted at Felix's expulsion he felt his self-importance rising; he was a man among men.

'Are you trying to squeeze them alive?' he asked.

'Yes,' said Nelson. Both he and Colonel Harbord were red in the face and breathing heavily.

'Aren't you going to do it to my brother?' the little boy went on. 'He's only small. You could do him easy.' He began to cry.

'All in good time,' said Colonel Harbord, gruffly. 'Elders first, you know. We haven't forgotten him.'

They worked on and were rewarded. At what precise moment the inertness left Wimbush's body, Nelson could not tell; nor did he confide his hopes to Colonel Harbord until he heard a catch in Wimbush's breath and, momentarily withdrawing his hands, saw a movement in the body which owed nothing to his agency.

Controlling his excitement he said:

'I believe he's coming round, sir.'

'Good man,' said Colonel Harbord, unemotionally. 'I wish I could say the same of this one.'

A few seconds later Wimbush was obviously breathing unaided. But he was still unconscious; when Nelson cautiously touched his eyeball, it did not move.

'Shall I take on the boy now, sir?'

Colonel Harbord heard the exultation which seemed to accuse him of failure and which Nelson could not keep out of his voice. But he was used to seeing others get the credit, and he only said, 'I should give him a few more rounds.'

And they were all that was necessary before the gurgling and snorting ceased to be the mechanical reactions of an inert object, and responding to the pressure of air and hand, turned into Wimbush. Nelson did not wait to see him re-animated but rose stiffly and dropped down beside the boy, whose slip of a body seemed to have no substance, so little resistance did it offer. Nelson's large thumbs nearly met in the middle of his back. Instinctively he reduced the force he had been using, and an expression that was almost tender spread across his face.

The other little boy was so excited that he did not know which to look at – the slowly reviving Wimbush, or the brother, on whom, he now felt sure, the same miracle was about to be performed. His eyes flickered to and fro between them. Wimbush was making curious twitching movements; his hands, extended horizontally above his head, clawed feebly at the rushes; his feet stirred, and water oozed out of his boots; he tried to turn his head which, in fulfilment of the regulations, had been laid sideways, into an easier position.

'Lie still, lie still, Wimbush,' said Colonel Harbord in a tired, jerky voice. 'You'll be all right if you lie still.'

Wimbush heard him, and ceasing to struggle began to breathe more naturally. At last he mumbled in a voice hardly above a whisper:

'Where's Mr. Casson?'

'He's all right. We're looking after him.'

'I . . . tried . . . to warn him,' Wimbush said. Having got that out, he spoke no more, and there was silence broken only by the sounds of respiration. It was as though all the manifold processes of life had been reduced to its bare essential: breathing.

Suddenly the little boy cried, 'Reg is waking up! I seed him move when the policeman wasn't shoving him! Look, Reg, look, it's me, it's Harold! Hurry up and get better, Reg! You won't half cop it when you get home!'

Both Nelson's patients had recovered; both had tasted the discomforts, the relapses, the tremulous joys of returning consciousness, both had been allowed to sit up, then to stand up. Both valued the blessings of the warm air and the bright sunlight as perhaps they never would again. To both had been re-granted the lease of life which seems eternal. Only Timothy lingered in the land of darkness.

Nelson was working at him now. Worn out, Colonel Harbord sat among the rushes feeling, in one part of his spirit, the resurgence of life around him, and in another a black spot of frustration which renewed itself each time he looked at Timothy. He looked as little as possible. He did not believe there was any chance for Timothy now. As a soldier he had seen too much of that kind of thing to be deeply affected by it but as a man he grieved – grieved not so much for Timothy, who was a stranger to him, as for a lost hope, a hope of restoring to harmony something which, on account of Timothy, had become discordant. And the fact that the others were on their legs again only made his sense of failure the more bitter.

He looked at the pool. The boat had sunk up to its gunwales, even the hole in its side was hidden. The blow that scuttled it had ripped off the Soviet standard; all that stuck up was the stern seat and behind, the Union Jack, which flapped idly in response to the aimless drifting of the boat. Colonel Harbord did not fail to notice his country's flag, and being ignorant of its previous association with the Hammer and Sickle, his heart warmed to Timothy.

From here, the Devil's Staircase looked a meagre torrent, hardly a cascade, just a slope down which the river came in gentle leaps, spreading fronds of water with no lethal suggestion in them. Indeed his eyes had grown so used to the waterfall as a shape that its texture hardly seemed to move. Some picked men could have scaled it, and given the enemy at the top a nasty shock. But to Timothy in his boat, bumping and slithering from ledge to ledge, it must have seemed a different proposition, and he could enter into the feelings of the oarsman, who had started out so gaily, when he found his skill did not avail him.

A champion, Nelson had said. Very likely Nelson exaggerated but the thought had taken root in Colonel Harbord's mind, and in all the long minutes through which he had tried to coax Timothy back to life it was a champion whose body he was manipulating, a champion who had come to Upton to enjoy his pastime, and who for one reason and another, had not been able to. A champion, a sportsman, one of us.

Still keeping his eyes on the landscape – it might have been a Naiad's loosened locks golden against the trees, he mused on what might have happened if Timothy had lived. Perhaps Mrs. Purbright was right and he could have been absorbed into the local life of Upton, once the question of the boat had been disposed of. His blunder at the smoking concert, his quarrel with Sturrock, even his infatuation with Miss Cross, all these were signs of spirit, and could have been forgiven to a baffled sportsman.

Had Timothy lived; but now the only thing was to forget the episode, as soon as the inevitable unpleasantness had died down.

How much longer should they give him? Colonel Harbord looked at his wrist-watch, its face heavily barred against flying shrapnel. Half past seven it said; they had been here nearly an hour. Wimbush and the boys ought to be taken home. Mild as the evening was, it would do the two survivors no good to hang about in their wet clothes, to exchange death by drowning for one by delayed shock or pneumonia.

Nelson's voice broke in on his meditation.

'Sir!'

'Yes, Nelson?'

'I believe Mr. Casson's coming round.'

Timothy took longer to recover than the others. More than once he seemed to be slipping back, not unwillingly, into unconsciousness; but Nelson was not to be cheated of his third success. The time came when Timothy could stagger to his feet and half walking, half carried, stumble down the slope to Nelson's car. The others followed in a ragged cluster, Reg prattling to Wimbush who returned monosyllabic answers. Timothy was laid on the back seat; Wimbush went in front and Colonel Harbord said he preferred to walk. The boys were told to sit on the floor. Reg, who seemed to have forgotten his ducking, jumped in gleefully, but his brother, on whom the episode had had a sobering effect, paused and said, 'Who was the lady in the water?'

Nelson, who had started up the car and was at last feeling the effects of strain, said rather shortly, 'Lady in the water? You're dreaming. There wasn't any lady in the water.'

'Yes, there was,' persisted the child. 'I seed her, mister. She looked as if she was looking at us.'

'I think he means someone he saw on the bank as we came by,' said Timothy.

But Nelson was in no mood for argument. 'Jump in,' he ordered in his best policeman's manner. 'You're too young to be thinking about ladies.'

Silenced by his tone, Harold obediently climbed into the car.

CHAPTER XXXII

AFTER his resuscitation Timothy was quite a different man from the Timothy who had organised the River Revolt. Lying in bed the next day, in accordance with doctor's orders, he was confronted with a consciousness which was strange to him. At first it was a blank; only gradually, and piecemeal, did recollections of what had happened before his accident come back. And still more partial was his reconstruction of his state of mind before the shipwreck. Indeed, he could hardly remember it at all, and would not have believed that his predecessor in his skin had any connection with him, had it not been for the testimony of events. Yes, he had done these things, so he must have been the kind of person who would have done them. There was no getting away from it; and hard as he tried to seal the doorways of his mind, the active historian who was collecting the evidence against him nearly always gained an entry.

This process of enforced enlightenment was most painful. Every recollection was a barb that wounded the pre-Upton Timothy to the quick. The dead self he had inherited from Upton hung round his neck like the albatross, and stank. Yet it must be recognised; it must be acknowledged; it must be worn for all, and especially for Timothy, to see, an emblem of penitence, and a pledge of reformation.

So he resolved; but a part of himself did not approve of this moral post-mortem and tried to sabotage it by concealing from his recollection certain facts and casting doubt on others. Had he, or had he not, sent telegrams to Esther and Tyro, putting them off? Had he, or had he not, advocated a campaign of violence in his oration at the bridge? Had he, or had he not . . .?

In his abasement Timothy took it for granted that he was socially as well as morally ruined. No one would ever speak to him again. Why should they? He had – pretentious as it might sound – tried to overthrow the established order. He was a Robespierre and would be a target for everybody's vengeance. He would have to start again on the bottom rung; even his health, which had served him so well, he had wantonly flung away. The doctor, who was to visit him again this morning, had told him that he might feel the effects of yesterday's exploit for months and even years. 'You're not a chicken, you know,' the doctor said kindly. 'And your nerves are none too good. After fifty, you've got to go slow.'

He heard the door-bell ring. Ah, that would be the doctor. Timothy pulled the sheet straight and arranged his expression in expectant and more cheerful lines.

Effie knocked and came in. Since his return her behaviour had been a miracle of tact; she had asked no questions and shown him every sympathy, as had Beatrice. But if he had been on his death-bed her expression could not have been graver.

'Colonel Harbord presents his compliments, sir,' she recited, 'and asks how you are feeling this morning.'

Timothy, who had been lying down, sat up.

'Please thank him very much and tell him I am feeling a great deal better.'

And he did feel better – for a time. Then conscience whispered to him that this had been but a routine inquiry, prompted by the automatic good manners of the kind of people from whom he had deliberately estranged himself. It did not mean anything else; how could it?

Yet there was one person, he felt almost sure, who would lament his misadventure, ridiculous and self-inflicted as it was. In spite of everything he had done to wound and anger her, he was surprised that he had not heard from Mrs. Purbright. She had been his tried, his constant friend. The doctor had forbidden him to write letters, or even to leave his bed. He had told Timothy, as he had told the maids, that he must do nothing to excite himself. If he disobeyed orders and telephoned to her, how could he expect her to answer, after all the rebuffs he had given her?

Mrs. Purbright had not asked about him, nor had someone else who might have been expected to.

Timothy had tried to keep his mind away from the thought of Vera; it was too tender, too painful; it was the core of his discomfort, the thorn from which the swelling came. But he had thought about Mrs. Purbright, and he must think about her. From the moment when the little boy told him he had seen her sitting on the bank his love for her had died. He did not hate her, but every tender association had been cut, not a fibre of feeling remained. She, not he, had been the promoter of the River Revolt; she had insisted on it, offering herself as the prize, and when the time of trial came she had deserted him; worse, she had secretly spied on him, unwilling to share the risk but callously curious

424

about his fate, the fate that she herself had caused. She, more than anything, or anyone, was the past from which he had to flee.

But presently his mind, though not (he believed) his heart, began to find excuses for her. She might have been delayed; she might have been unable to get into touch with him; she might have been frightened (was there anything unnatural or disgraceful in that?) and thought the best course was to go to the river-bank and, who knows? head him off, as Wimbush had tried to do. Behaviour as mad as his inevitably produced corresponding curiosities of behaviour in other people.

Or the child might have made a mistake; it might not have been Vera at all, but somebody else, her double. Miss Double-Cross! Here was indeed material for a joke, had he felt up to it. But what a fool, what a hasty fool, he had been to take a child's word as unquestioningly as if it had been a grown-up's! And to put on Vera's presence the worst possible construction – a construction that would never have occurred to him if his nature had not been warped by his besetting boat-lust. A construction that was as unfair to himself – his better self – as it was to her. One must be fair, even if one no longer loves.

But perhaps she had telephoned; perhaps they had both telephoned, she and Mrs. Purbright, and Effie had forgotten to give the messages. He rang the bell.

'Oh Effie,' he said as casually as he could, 'I just wanted to ask you – Has Mrs. Purbright telephoned today?'

Effie's face became expressionless – that is to say, it became tense with her desire to keep expression at bay.

'No, sir.'

'How odd – I mean she used to telephone every day, didn't she? This is almost the first day she hasn't. If she does ring up, would you thank her very much and explain why I can't answer?'

'Very good, sir.'

'And Effie—' still more carelessly, 'I suppose Miss Cross hasn't telephoned?'

Effie's whole body stiffened.

'No, sir.' And before he could say anything more she was gone.

It occurred to him that Effie might be keeping something from him, and in his anxiety to know the worst he rang again.

'I'm sorry to keep bothering you, Effie, but is Nelson anywhere about?'

'No, sir, Mr. Nelson came this morning to look at his car but he hasn't been in since. He asked how you were, sir, and we said as well as could be expected.'

425

'That was kind of him. Is Simpson in the garden?'

Reluctantly Effie admitted that he was. 'But he's very busy, sir,' she added.

'Ask him to come up and see me a minute.'

After a long wait, heavy shufflings were heard in the passage, and Simpson, preceded by Effie, with a good deal of lateral sway lumbered into the room. Effie retired but, though Timothy did not notice it, her footsteps ceased outside the door.

'Well, Simpson, you see what a crock I am. It didn't go very well, did it?'

Lugubriously, Simpson agreed that it had not.

'I suppose all the village are saying what a fool I made of myself.'

'Some do, sir, but quite a few say it was bad luck.'

'Oh, do they?' Timothy brightened. 'I had a nice message from Colonel Harbord.'

'There you are, you see.'

'I suppose I oughtn't to have chosen a day like yesterday.'

'That's what I said.'

Timothy couldn't remember his saying it, but he didn't argue the point.

'I wonder what became of the boat.'

Simpson began to show more animation.

'The boat, sir, that's quite finished. They've got it out of the water and there's a hole in her as would sink an ocean liner. 'Twon't be no good they say, except for firewood.'

Timothy sighed.

'Perhaps it's just as well.'

But Simpson did not agree with him.

'Indeed it isn't, it's a cruel pity, and you didn't ought to talk that way about a good boat that was a pleasure to look at, besides costing money. There's some say it should be kept like a relict, stuffed like and put in a glass case.'

'A relic!' exclaimed Timothy. 'Why, I should have thought it was better forgotten.'

'That's what you say, sir, but there's many as says the opposite, and thinks we ought to have something to remember you by, though damaged. It wasn't the boat's fault, when all's said and done.'

'I suppose not,' said Timothy, doubtfully. He had never felt sure of the bona fides of the boat.

'No, it wasn't, and it wasn't your fault either,' said Simpson, as heatedly as if he had been saying it was. 'It's the fault of that there old river. Ah, that river has a lot to answer for.'

'We were very lucky to get off with a soaking,' said Timothy.

'That's what I said. And that's what I meant when I said it wasn't your fault. *They* weren't in the boat.'

'They weren't? Who wasn't?'

Simpson didn't answer for a moment. His eyes narrowed and his wispy moustaches took on the impenetrability of a disguise.

'There's you saved, and Wimbush saved, as might not have been, carrying so much weight, and the child saved, though he was his mother's seventh. Providence will be served and you can't ask no more than that.'

'No, indeed,' said Timothy.

'And if there's sorrowing there'll be rejoicing, too.'

'Sorrowing?' said Timothy. 'Will some people be sorry we weren't drowned?' He couldn't get rid of the impression of himself as the village scapegoat.

'Well, the boy didn't count for much and Wimbush isn't easy to get on with, and it may not be as bad as we think, but if anyone's sorry it will be you, sir.'

'Me?' said Timothy. 'But you just said it wasn't my fault.'

'Nor it was, and they don't rightly know whose fault it was and it looks like they never would know. And when they ask you, sir, because ask you they will, you just keep mum, like I do, and say you have an ally by.'

'An alibi?' said Timothy, who thought Simpson must be referring to an impending judicial inquiry about the accident. 'But I couldn't have. I was in the boat.'

'That's what I said.'

Timothy realised they were talking at cross-purposes, but before he had time to question Simpson further, a knock at the door announced the doctor.

The doctor's report was favourable. Timothy could get up next day. 'But I'd rather you didn't go out,' he said, 'and if you want to celebrate, celebrate quietly at home.'

'I don't suppose anyone would want to celebrate with me,' said Timothy, still wallowing in a trough of guilt.

'Don't you be too sure,' said the doctor. 'People don't need much urging when there are a few drinks about – I wish they did.'

'I shouldn't have to compel them to come in?' asked Timothy, wistfully angling for evidence that his name was not mud in Upton.

'Well, publicans aren't a specially scrupulous race,' remarked the doctor, 'but I never yet heard of one who was so unpopular that he emptied the bar.'

Timothy thought of the Fisherman's Arms and wondered what sort of welcome he would have there. He thought, too, of Vera, but he could not ask the doctor about her. 'I expect you're right, that I'm better where I am,' he said.

'Yes,' said the doctor. 'You're still a bit dicky, you know. You've got a nice billet here,' he added, looking round appreciatively at the shabby amenities of the Old Rectory. 'Possess your soul in patience – Upton won't run away.'

Reading between the lines of his conversation with the doctor, Timothy couldn't help concluding that the doctor was giving him a friendly warning not to go where he wasn't wanted; and in his dejected mood this impression carried more weight than did Simpson's assertion that certain elements in the village wished to preserve the relics of the boat as a public monument. Even if that was true, it would be the rowdies who desired it – the riff-raff whom Timothy's political activities had inflamed. The better sort would fight shy of him. If his venture had been a success (and thank heaven it hadn't been) he would at least have been a foe to reckon with, Upton's Public Enemy Number One; as it was, the best he could hope for was to be a laughing-stock.

These reflections removed any temptation he might have felt to go out into the highways and byways and seek the countenances of his fellow-men. But he looked about for causes for thankfulness, and not in vain. He had been preserved, miraculously preserved, and preserved twice over; first from death, and secondly from having plunged Upton into civil war. For though he could not be sure (and the uncertainty gnawed at him) that some of the dragon's teeth he had sown might not take root, he did not think they would; for nothing is more fatal to subversive or, indeed, less dubious activities than a spectacular failure at the outset; no one was likely to rally to the sodden standard of a half-drowned rat.

Meanwhile he could once more trust in the innate benevolence of man and in the greater benevolence of the Power that watched over them. He had had proofs of both in plenty. The thought of the people who had come to his rescue – all of them, really, members of the other camp – filled him with thankfulness and wonder. He had been saved by the very people he had set out to destroy. If he could not now look them in the face, that was very salutary for him; he had sinned through pride, and his pride must be dragged in the dust. Let everyone despise him! Let everyone execrate his name! In humility of heart he would embrace

428

their reproof, finding, in his conviction of their goodness, some hope for his own.

Along these and similar lines of thought did Timothy try to reconcile his position with the order of the universe, and found, perhaps too readily, that the effect of not criticising others was to make him less critical of himself. By not seeing them, by being cut off from them by doctor's orders, he could the more easily regard them as abstractions; and just as the beholder of a beautiful picture partakes for a brief moment of the artist's unifying vision, so Timothy, looking out of his window could descry, above the pointed roof of the empty, exorcised boat-house, a vision of the human race as glorious as his humility painted it, with himself as its lowly and entranced spectator. Blessings had been poured on him without stint and of these the greatest was his sense of reunion with his fellows – his fellows beyond the window, above the boat-house, somewhere in the middle region of the sky.

Oh to stay indoors forever, and not only indoors but in bed! To receive the gift of humility from oneself, from one's comfortable sense of one's own unworthiness, not from the sneers of idle men, tittering on the village green! Not from individuals whose lives had been endangered by one's fault, whose constitutions had been impaired, whose clothes spoilt, whose wives had berated them, and whose mothers had smacked them! To repent at leisure in a bower of roses sealed against intrusion, not in a pillory in a public place, assailed by rotten eggs and brick-bats! To acknowledge and confess one's faults in a swooning assurance of forgiveness, and not to have to answer awkward questions about them, in a stuffy law court, perhaps, where blindfold justice held the scales, caring not a rap for one's fine feelings! In a word, to have the crown without the cross.

> And so through all eternity
> I forgive you, you forgive me.

Once a favourite couplet, he remembered it now for the first time since the War, and the time-proof litany of reciprocal forgiveness floated through the windows of the Old Rectory to the furthest shores of the world.

In this divided mood of loving his fellows in the spirit and dreading them in the flesh he spent most of the next day. But what, if that was to be his permanent condition, would his future be? A life of service in Upton, among the people whom he had insulted and injured, seemed the most suitable penance, and Timothy's imagination embraced it eagerly. But even in his exalted mood of selflessness he was aware of the practical difficulties. How would he begin? Whose doorstep should he ask to sweep? Whose brasses polish? The conditions of modern life did not lend themselves to acts of exemplary piety. Action demanded a retention of the self that contemplation, Timothy thought, could do without; to climb a ladder selflessly would probably mean falling off. In the distance, through the windows, he could see people walking along the road beside the Green, all intent on themselves. Timothy immediately stifled an impulse to think the worse of them. He must not think badly of anyone . . . or . . . . or. . . .

What was the inevitable consequence?

They would have the right to think badly of him, and that he was determined they should never do. No one must think badly of Timothy. He had committed a sin, a grievous sin, a sin more heinous than any of his acquaintance could lay claim to, but he had repented and been forgiven. Not a single ill result had happened from his act. He had abased himself and in doing so had qualified for happiness – in the near future, if not at once. Nobody must think badly of him, for if they did he might have to think badly of himself. And Timothy could not do that. It could not be expected of him. All his mental manœuvres of the past few hours, he realised as he walked up and down, watching the erring creatures in the world outside, had had one object: to put Timothy beyond criticism.

Whatever happened, Timothy was not to blame. Anyone who blamed him, or said a word against him, was grossly ignorant and unfair.

He was relieved when the telephone bell interrupted these meditations, but he did not go to answer it himself: he did not want to listen to the world's voice.

'A telegram for you, sir,' said Effie. Timothy had to read it. The message ran:

Arriving Swirrelsford 6.15. Shall take car unless you meet me.
Love.

ESTHER.

Timothy looked up, and just as his eyes took in the hour – it was past seven – he heard the crunch of wheels outside the door, and voices raised in dispute as to who should pay: a woman's and a man's. A moment later Esther and Tyro, surrounded by a mist of doubt and unreality, unbelievably came into the room.

'Timothy, my dear!'

'My dear Timothy!'

Unaccustomed to be shaken hands with, undear'd though not undarling'd for eighteen months, Timothy was completely overwhelmed. He clasped their friendly hands as if he could not let them go.

'We met on the platform,' Tyro explained, throwing his hat on to one chair and his haversack on to another. 'It was all so simple, Timothy, you might have thought of it yourself. I didn't remember Mrs. Morwen but she remembered me at once, wasn't it odd? When you didn't turn up we decided to come on together. Why weren't you there to meet us?'

Timothy, who had been helping Esther to take off her coat, said, 'Ah, that's a long story.'

'Tell us,' said Tyro. His glance strayed upwards to the cornice. 'About 1785, I should say. Yes, July, 1785. Not a day later.' His head was balder, his remaining hair wirier, his features were more alert and challenging than ever.

Timothy hesitated. He longed to tell them his story but at the mere thought of it his being shrivelled.

Esther who had been tidying herself before a looking-glass turned her much-lined, weather-beaten face to Timothy and said, 'You must choose your own time for telling us.'

Timothy made more than one false start, but before dinner was over the story was well under way. He had to edit it, of course. Vera had to be partially eliminated; a hush fell whenever Effie appeared, and she timed her entrances for the least appropriate moments. But as he got into the swing of it, he gained confidence. He meant it to be a confession; he could not, in the mood he was in, have told it any other way. But they listened more sympathetically than he had dared to hope, and as he went on he began to tell the story more objectively, not so much as a confession but as an adventure in which he had nearly lost his life. All the exaltation and excitement of the afternoon came back to him; his voice, which had been dull and flat, grew animated, his eyes glowed and he forgot to feel ashamed. By the time he had told them of the scene at the bridge and was launched on the final phase, with the Devil's Staircase almost in sight, he had put off the villain and put on the hero. What was his disappointment, therefore, to see that he was not holding his guests' attention. Their fingers fidgeted, their eyes signalled messages to each other or roamed the room as if in search of something. Timothy slowed down, he had not been able to on the river, and Tyro seized the opportunity to break in, his voice brittle with impatience:

'Excuse me, Timothy, but *could* we hear the news?'

'The news?'

'Yes, the news. It's nine o'clock now, and we may be missing something.'

Timothy was brought up with a jerk.

'I'm so sorry,' he said. 'The wireless set is in the drawing-room.'

Tyro made a bolt for the door, and by the time the others joined him he was on his knees beside the instrument, in a blare of shrieks and piercing whistles.

'Do help me, Timothy,' said Tyro, his voice plaintive with grievance. 'I can't get the beastly thing to go.'

As it turned out, nine o'clock had not yet struck, and they disposed themselves with reverent and expectant faces to listen to the chimes.

'Here is the news, and this is Alvar Liddell reading it.'

'Good,' remarked Tyro, setting himself more comfortably in his chair. 'I'm glad it's him. I can't stand some of the others.'

The news went on.

'Well, that's that,' said Tyro, energetically. 'It's always the same, I wonder why anyone bothers to listen. All the same we had to jog your memory, didn't we, Timothy? Shall I shut it off now, or do you want to listen to this?'

An orchestra was playing.

They looked at each other.

'Perhaps Timothy would finish his story for us,' said Esther. 'I'm afraid we interrupted you, Timothy.'

Tyro looked at his watch.

'There's just time before Lord Haw-Haw,' he said, 'but you must make it snappy, Timothy. I can't bear to miss him.'

Esther said gently, 'Do you know, I feel I can't bear to listen to him.'

'What, not to Timothy?'

'No, Lord Haw-Haw. He makes me feel quite ill.'

'Oh come, now, tell me why.'

For a minute or two they argued about Lord Haw-Haw, but Esther was not to be moved, and Tyro said, 'Very well then, I don't in the least agree with you, you seem to be confusing two things, his effect on you and his effect on the public. I enjoy him for his entertainment value. But let's have Timothy instead. At any rate he won't make our blood run cold. Come on, Timothy; you had just incited the Uptonians to riot and were about to shoot the rapids.'

Very haltingly, and feeling that he would rather not, Timothy took up his cold tale. But the zest had gone out of it, only the bare facts remained, and very bare they seemed. It might have been the epic of someone else. Moreover suspense was lacking; here he was, alive and well. He tried to concentrate on the fate of Wimbush and the boy; but he knew that already, by his manner, he had betrayed the happy ending: there were no casualties, even Felix had survived.

'And I've stayed indoors ever since,' he ended flatly. He looked at his audience, his eyebrows inviting comments.

'Well,' said Tyro, with a briskness of manner that showed he had his answer ready. 'I expect you were wise to do that. If you'd shown your face, they might have torn you to pieces, don't you think so, Mrs. Morwen?'

Esther was leaning back in her chair, looking at the ceiling. Her face, which had known much sorrow, perhaps a sorrow for every line, wrinkled itself anew for Timothy's problem. She did not answer at once, but at last she said, 'I think those things die down, you know.'

'Oh, I hope not,' exclaimed Tyro. 'In a way – excuse me, Timothy – it would have been better if you'd all been drowned, as a warning to the others.'

'But what good would that have done?' asked Mrs. Morwen.

'A great deal – it would have kept them on their toes, which is what these sleepy villages are so desperately in need of. Mind you, I don't agree with Timothy's political notions, any more than I approve of his present rather revolting state of penitence, they both seem to me deplorably half-baked. But having gone so far to stir up trouble – and there is no progress without it – where should we be, for instance, without this war? – it seems a thousand pities to let it fizzle out. If I were you, Timothy, I should buy another boat, and, as soon as you feel up to it, repeat the experiment, with knobs on.'

Timothy laughed, but Mrs. Morwen said, 'It's Timothy I'm thinking of, more than the village. A village can take care of itself. Everyone knows everyone else, everyone has a groove, which they'll slip back into. But Timothy hasn't.'

'But surely he doesn't want one!' Tyro cried. 'It's the last thing he ought to want.'

'I rather think he does want one,' said Mrs. Morwen. 'And this won't make it any easier. By the way, Timothy, what happened to the girl who you said helped you in the beginning?'

'I haven't heard from her since.'

'Wretched woman,' said Tyro, 'they're all alike— Excuse me, Mrs. Morwen— no moral fibre. Lady Macbeth is pure fiction. Now I know Timothy is waiting for us to tell him exactly what we think about the whole affair. You've both heard what I think, but I'll repeat it. It was a splendid effort in a perhaps unworthy cause, but we must be glad, I suppose, that it failed, because it could only have succeeded if Timothy had been drowned. Now, Mrs. Morwen?'

Mrs. Morwen sighed.

'Well, I'm only too thankful that Timothy wasn't drowned, or anyone else. We haven't said that yet, Timothy, have we? There seemed so much to say.' She gave him a fond look, which warmed his heart. 'We got switched on to other things; you must forgive us, Timothy.'

'Naturally we're glad that Timothy is safe,' said Tyro. 'It goes without saying. He wouldn't expect us to labour the obvious.'

'No, but all the same I'm sure we do want to say it. Politics are so intrusive. I almost wish you hadn't let them get hold of you, Timothy: they aren't for you. I agree with Mr. MacAdam that you've been awfully brave, in every way, to do something so . . . so unlike you. But, do you know, I almost wish you hadn't? I should so hate it if people misunderstood you and got the wrong idea of you – people like ourselves I mean – there must be some in the village, indeed, you've told me that there are. It would be such a pity if they got the idea that you were odd and eccentric, because you're not a bit, really. Is he, Mr. MacAdam?' For once Tyro couldn't find an answer, and Mrs. Morwen said, 'Of course artistic people often do *seem* different from others, in the way they dress and so forth, it's a sort of tradition and doesn't mean much, though I think it's a pity. But you were never like that, Timothy, it was one of the things that made us fond of you.' There was a hint of reproach in the look of approval which she bestowed on his dinner-jacket; Timothy had put it on to do honour to the occasion, after apologising to Tyro, who had not brought one. 'And I should be so sorry if, after this, your neighbours were – well, not suspicious, but puzzled and surprised, as I think they may be. After all, we must stick together, and be – forgive me – an example to those who look up to us. Otherwise, what are we for? I'm saying all the things one shouldn't say, I know, but sometimes they are in danger of being forgotten, and Mr. MacAdam asked me my opinion. I'm sure people will understand, in time, that it was just . . . just an aberration, your doing what you did, a sort of high spirits that anyone can overlook, but in a *way* I can't help being sorry that you did it.' Esther stopped, a little breathless, and did not look at Timothy.

Tyro's loud, rasping voice broke the silence. 'Bravo, Mrs. Morwen! I congratulate you. Your oratory has had ten times the effect of mine. When I told Timothy he ought to have been drowned he looked almost cheerful; now that you've told him you are glad he wasn't, he looks quite suicidal! I wish I knew how to be so persuasive! Do tell me, as a matter of interest' – he leaned towards her – 'where you learned your speech-making?'

His question, like many of his utterances, jarred on Esther, but she answered with a smile, 'I expect it was talking at Women's Institutes. I do a lot of that, I'm afraid.'

'Afraid? You ought to be proud. I wish I was eligible to be your audience. I must look into the work of these Women's Institutes. Hitherto they've only been a name to me. I suppose they exist in Liverpool—'

The buzz of the telephone bell interrupted him. Another shadow crossed Timothy's face. He stirred in his chair but did not get up.

'Shall I answer it?' Tyro was already on his feet.

'It would be kind, but why should you bother?'

'I enjoy answering the telephone.'

He was gone. Esther and Timothy exchanged glances, but both refrained from saying what was in their minds. A moment later the door was flung open.

'A Colonel Hardboiled, or words to that effect, wants to speak to you,' announced Tyro. 'I said you were off-colour and would he leave a message, but he said he would rather speak to you himself.'

Full of misgiving Timothy left the room.

'He's not looking well, is he?' remarked Tyro. 'It's lucky we are here to cheer him up.'

'He needs someone to look after him,' said Mrs. Morwen. 'I've felt that for a long time.'

'Funny we should both have chosen the same day,' said Tyro. 'But I'd just had a letter from him, as a matter of fact.'

'So had I,' said Esther. 'A nice letter.'

'So was mine,' said Tyro. 'It occurred to me he might be lonely,' he went on.

'Do you know, I had the same idea.' They looked at each other self-consciously, and then looked away.

Each underwent a self-examination, and each gave the same answer: it was Timothy's loneliness, not his legacy, that had brought them down to Upton. Meanwhile Timothy was nervously lifting the receiver.

'Is that you, Casson? Harbord here. Very sorry to disturb you, but how are you?'

'Oh much better, thank you.'

'I'm delighted to hear it, genuinely delighted. I rang up to ask, and also to say that we're having a few people in tomorrow between tea and dinner, and my wife wondered if you'd join us. If you feel like it, of course.'

Timothy said he would be very pleased, but explained that he had friends staying with him. Might he bring them?

'By all means,' said Colonel Harbord. 'The more the merrier. You'll find most of us here, except for Mrs. Purbright.'

'Is she away?' asked Timothy, enormously relieved, for the bare thought of her was still too sore to touch.

'Away?' Colonel Harbord's voice went up in surprise. 'No, she's ill. You didn't know?'

Timothy explained that he had been completely isolated for three days. 'Are you there?' he added, when Colonel Harbord didn't answer.

'Yes – well, I'm sure she'd rather we enjoyed ourselves.'

'How is she now?' asked Timothy.

'She was a bit better the last time I heard,' said Colonel Harbord. 'And Edgell's on the mend, too.'

'That's good.'

'Yes, isn't it?'

Of course it was sad Mrs. Purbright wasn't well, but one has to have a predominant feeling, and Timothy's predominant feeling, when he announced the invitation to his guests, was one of elation and expectancy. Lawnflete at last!

'So you're wrong, you see,' said Tyro to Mrs. Morwen. 'All his neighbours are getting ready to lick his boots.'

Esther smiled. 'I'm very glad,' she said.

CHAPTER XXXIII

'But what I chiefly want to show you, my dear chap,' Colonel Harbord was saying, 'is my lawn. We're very proud of our lawn, at Lawnflete. Perhaps your friends would like to see it, too?'

Taking Timothy's arm he led him from the drawing-room. Esther and Tyro followed. The other guests, who had seen the lawn before, stayed behind with their glasses and their conversation. The moment the newcomers had gone the buzz of talk died down. 'He doesn't *know*?' murmured Mrs. Sturrock to Mrs. Harbord. 'But is it possible?'

'Apparently it is,' Mrs. Harbord said. 'He didn't know about Volumnia either. We must try to keep it from him. But he's bound to find out some time. I wonder if he'll mind. I shouldn't, but then I'm not a man.'

Meanwhile Timothy, ignorant of these speculations, was treading Colonel Harbord's lawn. Enchanted ground! Ever since he had come to Upton, the lawn at Lawnflete had been, not quite the Mecca of his desire, but a serious rival to the boat. Had he been admitted to it earlier – who knows? – it might have dethroned the boat as his measure of achievement. He had caught a glimpse of it as he flashed by the other day; but that was in the other life, and as an enemy. Now he almost loved it, it was his; and though listening with only half an ear – for other voices less articulate were demanding his attention, he endorsed all the claims that Colonel Harbord was making for his lawn.

He learned that it had been made out of two pieces of sward, the junction of which was now almost invisible; challenged to find it, Timothy could not, to the Colonel's great content. For some years past Colonel Harbord had made a habit of uprooting from the serried greenness twelve weeds every day. Could his guest spot one now? Timothy, his eyes bent on the ground, fetched a wide circle and came back without seeing a single daisy. Esther and Tyro were similarly defeated, though it must be admitted that Tyro walked about with his head in the air and whispered to Timothy, nodding at the house, 'that hideous top storey is a nineteenth century addition.' The lawn, he learned, had not yet ceased to expand; it was forever making further conquests; this and that flower-bed, 'though my wife was against it,' had been incorporated; shrubs had been uprooted and waste ground reclaimed. 'It's lucky you didn't come yesterday,' Colonel Harbord said, 'or you wouldn't have seen it all – the water's only just gone down. Now I'd like to show you my landing stage and my old punt – not your sort of boat, my boy, just a tub for us fishermen to paddle about in.'

They strolled down to the wooden platform, now well above the water-line, and Timothy peered into the sturdy, shabby, roundabout craft.

'No fear of upsetting this one,' smiled Colonel Harbord, 'you could sit on the edge of it.'

Timothy was startled to find that there *had* been a boat on the river all the time he had believed it to be boatless; but the discovery, instead of annoying him, now seemed a happy bond between himself and Colonel Harbord. Yet he could not help thinking with a pang of his own boat, once so spick and span and riverworthy, which would never float again; and Colonel Harbord must have read what was in his mind, for he said, 'I hope that when you get your new boat you'll often tie up here. There are only a few preliminaries to be gone through, you know.' He gave Timothy a wink, and turning to Esther and Tyro, said, 'You must excuse me chattering so much to Casson. We seem to have a lot to talk about. I suppose he's told you how he tried to drown himself?'

'Yes,' said Tyro, 'we heard all about it and I understand that you, sir, are the villain of the piece.'

Colonel Harbord raised his eyebrows, Timothy looked horrified, and Esther blank; then Tyro, having thoroughly enjoyed their embarrassment, added, 'I mean, sir, that you rescued him. You shouldn't have done that, he was so set on being a martyr. You snatched the crown away from him.'

They all laughed and Colonel Harbord said, 'Well, to tell you the truth I'd just heard what a wonderful oarsman he was. The best in our part of the world, the local bobby told me. Couldn't let a man like that drown!'

All the way to the house he rallied Timothy on his prowess, and when they joined the party he continued for a while in the same strain. 'Only he must give an exhibition for *us*, this time! No parleying with Bolshies on the bridge!' This was the only reference that he or anyone else made to Timothy's political activities; and it drew a general smile, and a sigh of relief, as when a thorn, long probed for, finally comes out. 'Bellew shall start you with a pistol at your place,' said Colonel Harbord, 'and I shall hear it and time you with a stop-watch. We'll all be drawn up on the lawn to welcome you.'

Timothy smiled awkwardly and protested, as was indeed the fact, that he was no oarsman; but this they took, or chose to take, for modesty; and for two or three minutes all his ex-opponents, Sir Watson Stafford, Commander Bellew, and the rest, crowded round him, and questioned him flatteringly about his oarsmanship and where he had learnt it. At last Captain Sturrock joined the group. 'Remember me, Casson?' he said with a twisted smile, and when Timothy assured him that he did, they drew aside and talked together like old friends.

Soon Captain Sturrock surrendered him to the ladies, whose interest, being less professional, and more personal, Timothy found easier to cope with. They asked him about his health, and about his domestic difficulties, as to which their questions, though implying ignorance, betrayed the most intimate knowledge. 'I'm so sorry about it,' said Miss Chadwick, whom Timothy had not seen, or heard from, for some time; 'they kept everything in such good order, but I never thought Effie was strong. Perhaps that is why they are leaving?'

'Well,' said Timothy, 'I'm not sure that they are leaving, after all.'

'Not leaving?' Miss Chadwick opened her eyes wide.

'Why, Volumnia Purbright told me—' Seeing Timothy's face change she broke off and said, 'Anyhow, she would be the last to blame you.'

'But what has Mrs. Purbright to do with it?' asked Timothy.

'Nothing, directly. She was not in your . . . galère. We wondered why.'

'Please tell me what you mean,' Timothy urged her, but Mrs. Harbord, who was standing at his elbow, said, 'Mr. Casson, I want to introduce you to Lady Watson Stafford,' and a big purple bosom, with a grey head set cottage-loaf-wise on it, barred his way.

A bosom! A bosom was what he needed and what the ladies of Upton, under many veils of sophistication and good manners, were offering to him. In the faint, decorous perfume they exuded, in their smiles which chimed so musically with his, in the impression they conveyed that he mattered to them as a man, and not only as an oarsman – in this delicious solvent, the 'either . . . or,' the plus or minus sign, under which, as under a sign of the zodiac, he had lived, presenting a stark alternative to their husbands and to himself, melted away. If he mistook their affability for friendliness, and their curiosity for concern, it was no great matter; the effect on his spirits was the same.

But, he recollected, coming round from his intoxication, Esther and Tyro could not be feeling the same exhilaration at being absorbed into Upton society; to be one of them is less alluring than to be one of us. Excusing himself, he steered to where Tyro's impatient features towered above a puzzled matron. 'I couldn't tell you,' he was saying; 'Timothy's rowing record is a closed book to me.' Unobtrusively he collected Tyro and made towards Esther. She was seated between Commander Bellew and Captain Sturrock, who were both talking to her at once. It was clear that she satisfied all their preconceptions of what a woman ought to be; and from their anxiety to please her it looked as though she spoke their own language even better than they did. Timothy was loth to break up this conversation which, he felt, was doing him as much credit as Tyro's had done the reverse; but he, too, was a host, and Tyro must not be tried too far. They made farewells to little bursts of protest, which seemed to show they had not outstayed their welcome. 'Now you've found your way here,' said Mrs. Harbord, 'come again.'

'Yes, come again,' said Colonel Harbord escorting them to the door, 'whenever you feel you need resuscitation.'

Giving, as much for his own as for the Colonel's sake, a last look at the lawn, golden in the evening light, and carrying the glow of the occasion with him, Timothy walked away between his two companions. They were going through the gate in this formation, and Timothy, backed up by Esther, was defending the Uptonians from Tyro's taunts, when suddenly his foot caught against something, and the next thing he knew he was in a shower-bath. For a moment he thought that he was drowning; but it was not water, it was paint, red paint; and the vessel that contained it and the mechanism that discharged it were both plain to see – a big glass jar stuck in the empty lantern above the gateway, and a piece of string drawn across the ground and running up the iron-work. A simple but effectual device. He thought he heard a snigger in the bushes, but nothing moved.

'What the—' began Tyro. Both he and Esther were spattered by the paint.

'Quick, we can't leave it like this,' cried Timothy. He cut the string and the glass jar came tumbling through the opening in the lantern, and broke into several pieces. Stooping down he hurled them one after another in the direction that the laugh had come from, and was rewarded by a sharp squeal from the bushes. 'That's got 'em!' he muttered. 'That'll teach 'em!' With face as scarlet as his hair and shoulders he mumbled apologies and hurried his companions down the road. He had cut his hand on the glass and blood was mingling with the paint.

'We demand an explanation, please,' said Tyro.

'Oh, just some merrymakers, I suppose,' said Timothy.

But Tyro was not taken in. 'You mean your own supporters? What a joke!' His laughter rattled across the Green, and roosting birds tumbled out of the sentinel poplars. Neither Esther not Timothy joined in, but Tyro was used to laughing alone.

'It's being red that makes it so funny!' he gasped between the seizures. 'Your own colour! Blood-boltered Timothy! I wish you could see yourself!'

Timothy said it didn't seem funny to him. 'I've ruined two suits in the last few days,' he grumbled, 'and how am I to replace them? And you're in a mess, too,' he reminded Tyro.

'Am I? So I am, but it'll soon come off,' said Tyro, negligently dabbling his fingers in the squashy, blood-red spots. 'Never mind, it'll be a souvenir of Upton, and the most enjoyable episode of my visit! But Mrs. Morwen,' and his face took on an expression of the deepest concern, 'it's horrible for you! Your lovely dress all spoilt! Timothy might really have arranged things better! No, please don't do that,' he went on, for Esther was furtively trying to get the spots out with a deli-cate, exiguous handkerchief. 'Take mine,' and he handed her a magnifi-cent white silk one, which Timothy recognised as a gift he had made to Tyro several Christmases ago. 'You won't hurt this.'

Touched by his generosity, Esther nevertheless refused the loan. 'I don't mind a bit,' she declared, 'and in a way I'm glad it was us, not them. They are such nice, kind people.'

'Do you mean we aren't?' demanded Tyro.

'No, but it would have been so unlucky after they had made such an effort to be nice to us.'

'Effort, does it need an effort? Timothy, I protest. Still, I see what you mean. If the Colonel had received Timothy's libation it mightn't have gone down so well. But I wouldn't have missed the incident for worlds; it's been the highlight of our visit, don't you think so, Mrs. Morwen? Did you see Timothy's face as he bombarded the culprits skulking in the bushes? They were his own followers, remember, the very people he had been urging to take up arms against the Colonel and his ilk; but did he care? Not he! He was transformed. I never saw such magnificent determination on any human countenance. Gone was the old Timothy, Mr. Facing-Both-Ways; he really looked as if he would have liked to kill them! And perhaps you did, Timothy; whoever it was you hit squealed like a stuck pig.'

Timothy was about to make an angry answer, when his attention was diverted by some passers by, who stared at him with so much curi-osity and unfeigned amusement that he needed all his moral stamina to

441

outface them. Happily the gateway of the Old Rectory was at hand; into that they turned, Timothy leading, almost at a run; and as soon as they were in the house they dispersed to change for dinner.

Only when the meal was fairly started did Timothy realise, with dismay, from her silences and short answers, that Esther had taken a dislike to Tyro. He knew that they had very little in common; he would never have invited them to be fellow-guests; what bad luck that they had both hit on this weekend! And there was another whole day still to go; how would they get through it?

It was not that Tyro utterly effaced her, as he effaced so many people, reducing them to the mortifying status of unwilling controversialists who have no answer ready; but he forced her to assert herself in a way she did not like and was not used to. At home her word had so much authority that she did not need to be explicit. Here, in another context, and such a loud one, she felt like a violinist compelled to compete with a brass band, and she was too old and too sure of herself to find much fun in it. She was even tempted to stand a little on her dignity; for though she was intellectually diffident, and her mind was as vague and undisciplined as her memory, the self she turned to the world was more complete and confident than Timothy's or even Tyro's.

Oddly enough, the discovery that Esther had found Tyro tiresome allayed Timothy's own irritation against his too outspoken friend; his social conscience was aroused and he determined to make the party a success whatever the auspices. In this he was helped by Tyro's total unawareness of Esther's feeling for him; he appealed to her for her opinion just as freely as ever, disregarded it as freely, and as freely applauded it, both when it coincided with his own and when it scored a point against him. In spite of herself, Esther was somewhat mollified by this. Tyro still insisted that the booby-trap had been a huge joke, far more fun than the party; and every now and then when he looked up and saw the scarlet smears on Timothy's face and head he could not contain his laughter. But by degrees Timothy was able to wean the conversation away from the particular instance to a discussion of humour in the abstract. What constitutes a joke? Tyro declared that there must be an element of cruelty in it; Esther and Timothy demurred, and being on the same side they were the better able to keep their tempers.

So though the evening was not devoid of strain it passed off without an open breach, and ended with Tyro inviting Timothy to make him an apple-pie bed whenever he wanted to – now, if he liked.

Esther retired early, pleading the fatigue of an exciting day, and Tyro soon followed, leaving Timothy to do the rounds of the house, the doors, the windows, and the fire which had been a concession to cosiness rather than to cold. While thus occupied, a sense of his identity returned to him. All day long he had been dissipated by the tug of other minds and the need to adapt himself: now the scattered elements flocked to their matrix, like particles of quicksilver reunited to their parent ball. He was tempted to sit down a moment and enjoy his new-found wholeness of spirit. The presence of dear friends under his roof gave him a feeling of security, the wish to entertain them and compose their differences, a purpose. And he was convinced, perhaps mistakenly, that they only wanted him to be himself.

Now he could think of the Colonel's party and what it meant to him, in peace, unvexed by Tyro's gibes. A whole new area, hitherto forbidden, had been added to the territory of his spirit. It was the territory he had coveted ever since he came to Upton, and it seemed more than ever precious because of the sacrifices he had made to get it. But how else can one get anything worth while? With a great sum obtained I this freedom. The sacrifices had not all been on his side: there was Wimbush, there was Reg, he had not seen them yet to congratulate, to apologise to: he had seen no one to whom the account might seem a debit account. And there was the boat.

But the boat had been the only casualty; all the passengers had survived, none the worse for their exploit: indeed the better, for they would now know how dear life was, and those who loved them would know how dear they were; and such knowledge, which is granted to few, could only come by an escape from death. Providence had been on Timothy's side, had snatched him from the depths of abasement to set him on a pinnacle of success. Nor was the boat, though wrecked, a total loss. Its soul went marching on. A loftier Argo would appear, fraught with a later prize. Had not they all told him so? Had not Colonel Harbord assured him that, after a few preliminaries, the whole question of his status on the river, already accepted in principle, would be regularised? Was he not to give them a demonstration of his skill?

Timothy would never leave Upton now. It was his own place, consecrated to his use – not by his blood, not by anybody's blood, thank Heaven – but by the memory of a crisis in his life miraculously surmounted. The odds had seemed hopelessly against him, but somehow he had won through. Not only had he been preserved intact, but several cubits had been added to his stature. He had reached a position where all men, including himself, spoke well of him. They understood him, they knew what he was after, they loved and respected him. Of nothing, now, need he feel doubtful or ashamed. Tomorrow must be solemnised as a day of rejoicing, a Victory Celebration; on Monday he would begin the work of consolidating his gains. Beloved by rich and poor alike, he would be the acknowledged leader of Upton . . . its ruler, its King. . . .

Crossing the hall to go upstairs he met a stranger. It gave him quite a turn, this extraordinary face, this streaked and spotted face, coming to meet him from the opposite wall. Who on earth? – then he remembered – it was himself. He had not been able to get the paint off, and rather than wash his head in paraffin before dinner (a course which Tyro had advised, but which would have made him a noisome neighbour) he had put off cleansing himself until he went to bed. By the morning the smell would surely have worn off. Now the task remained to be done, just when he felt least like it.

In the bathroom he found the rusty paraffin container, placed there at his request by Effie. Slowly he began to take his clothes off, relishing less and less his coming baptism with the evil-smelling liquid. He would have given almost anything to postpone the ordeal. Suddenly he heard a sound as if the house were laughing to itself. Ha-ha! Ha-ha! Ha-ha! droned the mirthless, rhythmical guffaw.

Who could be ringing him up so late? What did they want with him? How could the voice of the outside world, which he had at last subdued, dare to intrude on his privacy? Let the thing ring itself hoarse, he would not answer.

Before he had got his head over the basin and begun to feel that he had only one sense, smell, and one object of that sense, paraffin, the ringing ceased. But it went on in his head, not indeed as a sound, but as an intensification of the smell, long after the shampoo was over.

At breakfast they assured Timothy that he had been completely purified, but he was not convinced, for paraffin, the most penetrating of all odours, had seeped into his thoughts. Partly with the idea that wind and sun would dispel it, he suggested going for a walk. He had also noticed that Esther was again getting restive under Tyro's pronouncements, made still more challenging by a sound night's sleep. In the open air they would have less explosive force. Esther confirmed his suspicions by saying she would like to go to church. At the word church Tyro shook his head – 'Do you think you are doing God a good turn by going to church?' he asked. Timothy excused himself from accompanying her on the plea that he would be a nuisance to his fellow-worshippers. The fact was he still shrank from meeting them. So Esther went off alone, leaving Timothy and Tyro to smoke a last cigarette before taking the road. Tyro was, for him, a little quiet.

'I hope Mrs. Morwen approves of me,' he said. 'I like her so much.'

Timothy assured him that she did, and even pretended she had said so.

'She is such a perfect example of her type,' said Tyro, warming at the thought. 'She runs absolutely true to form: she says exactly what one knows she will say. I'm sure I've shown my appreciation,' he added anxiously. 'I applaud her when she says the silliest things.'

'I hope she doesn't notice that,' said Timothy.

'How could she? She doesn't know they're silly. Of course she's one of the most valuable assets we have in England now, she doesn't think, she just does her job. Whereas you, Timothy—'

'What about me?'

'Oh, you think in terms of your feelings, as you always did. That's why you get in such a muddle. I wouldn't be surprised if, just because those old fogeys made a fuss of you yesterday, you now think they are delightful people.'

'Well, as a matter of fact, I do.'

'But they're dead, Timothy, dead from the waist up and for aught I know, from the waist down. They're utterly negligible. They're like the figure nought without its O.'

'I like them because they conform to type.'

'Type my foot! They've conformed to type for the last eighteen months, and all that time they've been your bitterest foes. Are they any different, just because they bill and coo?'

'Yes, just for that reason. They didn't, before.'

'Timothy, I can't believe you would use such a contemptible argument. Is your opinion of people *really* determined by the way they behave to you?'

'Yes, it is,' said Timothy, with more petulance than conviction, for he saw himself taking up a position which it would be hard to hold. 'I shouldn't be human if it wasn't.'

'Human!' cried Tyro. 'Did I hear you say "human," without using the word in a pejorative sense? What are we fighting this war for? Isn't it to establish other, non-human values, the values Christianity teaches? I'm not a Christian, Heaven forbid – you heard what I said when Mrs. Morwen mentioned church – but surely you realise that Christian values are essential for the preservation of the species?'

'Without the Christian faith?'

445

'I should hope so! All that mumbo-jumbo! You astonish me, Timothy! Do you really mean that you like a man because he agrees with you, not because he represents a point of view you can respect?'

'I respect my own point of view,' said Timothy, defiantly. 'And if they agree with that—'

'But what *is* your point of view? Yesterday, or at the most two days ago, it excluded from salvation all the people we met last night; you were ready to exterminate them, you know you were! Who put up the booby-trap, and for whom? You did, for them. And today, just because they butter you up they are your dearest friends, and, what is much more shameful, you appear to approve of them on moral grounds.'

'But I have converted them,' Timothy objected.

'Converted them! I like that! It is they who have converted you!'

'But I *have* converted them,' said Timothy angrily. 'They have recognised my right to row on the river.'

'What nonsense! They haven't recognised any right. They've got it into their heads, Heaven knows how, that you're some kind of champion oarsman – which I own was news to me, although I didn't say so – and out of pure sports-snobbery, of the sort that every Englishman of their class is riddled with, they've made an exception in your case. They're afraid that someone should come along and say, "I hear you had Timothy Casson living in your village, the chap who won the Diamonds in 1902, or whenever it was, and you wouldn't let him dip a blade in the river. What could you have been thinking of?" Then they'd feel small, because they had betrayed the cause of athletics – let down the side, so to speak. The mental age of those people is about nine or ten.'

'You talk like a schoolboy yourself,' retorted Timothy.

'Then I must have caught the language from them. And all the better, for out of the mouths of babes and sucklings— But don't hoodwink yourself into thinking you've converted them. It's the other way round. Have you given another thought to all those simple souls whom you wantonly misled with your Communist propaganda? No, you've deserted them. All you do now is to pelt them with broken bottles. You ought to make a public recantation, Timothy, you really ought.'

'But I haven't deserted them,' said Timothy. 'They'll be allowed to row, the same as I shall.'

'Don't you believe it,' chuckled Tyro. '*They're* not Olympic oarsmen. And let me tell you, Timothy, I'm not so sure they're going to let *you* row. You heard what your Colonel friend said about preliminaries. They'll still be talking about preliminaries this time next year.'

'Oh, don't be such a wet-blanket. Tyro.'

'Wet-blanket! I only want to bring you to a sense of reality.'

'Well, don't let's quarrel,' said Timothy, wearily.

'Quarrel, who talks of quarrelling? Well, I must go and put on my shoes. I see that true to country-house tradition, you've put on yours already. Or did you go to bed in them?'

They were crossing the Green, and Tyro was comparing the poplars to a group he remembered near Verona, when Timothy spied someone in the distance. She was by herself, but she was not alone; in front of and behind her a ragged group straggled down the road. They were all walking very slowly.

'Is it just your platform manner,' Tyro asked, 'or are you waving to someone?'

'It's Esther,' said Timothy. 'But I can't think why she's back so early.'

Esther had seen him signalling and was now coming towards them across the Green. She looked rather grave.

'Oh, Esther,' said Timothy anxiously. 'I hope you're not feeling ill?'

'Did you have a good church?' asked Tyro, before Esther had had time to answer. 'Or did you come out as a protest against ritualistic practices? We didn't expect you, pleased as we are to see you.'

'Well, as a matter of fact,' said Esther, 'there wasn't any church.' Her prayer book slipped from her hand, and she stooped to pick it up. 'There was a notice in the porch, saying that the Rector was unable to take the service because his wife had died.'

'Mrs. Purbright?' cried Timothy, incredulously.

'That was the name, I think.'

'Oh, but she *can't* be dead!'

'What stirring times you have in Upton,' observed Tyro. 'Every moment packed with drama. Do you always live like this?'

'Oh *please*, Tyro,' said Timothy. He looked imploringly in Esther's face. 'Was that all? Did you hear anything?'

'I heard someone say she'd had a sudden relapse. Everyone seemed very sorry. Several people were crying. Was she a nice woman, Timothy?'

Timothy couldn't speak for a moment.

'Very nice.'

A silence fell on them, then Tyro said, 'I suppose there's no reason why a clergyman's wife *shouldn't* be nice. What do you want us to do now, Timothy?'

Timothy couldn't think of anything to do, but felt he would like to keep on the move.

'If Esther cares to come for a walk—' he said.

'Certainly, if you don't mind me changing a little first.'

They strolled back to the house, and Esther went to her room.

'Isn't it extraordinary,' remarked Tyro, 'the way that women never can do something at the time you ask them? They always have to go away for half an hour to alter their appearances.'

Absently Timothy agreed, though he remembered that Tyro had had to go away to put his shoes on. Feeling too miserable to talk, but anxious in spite of himself for more news of Mrs. Purbright, he begged Tyro to excuse him and went into the kitchen.

Felix's tail thumped a welcome, but the maids' eyes gave him the guarded look they always wore now when he was with them.

'Oh, Beatrice,' he said, for of the two it always seemed natural to address Beatrice, so much did she command the pair, 'I've heard some bad news.'

At once their looks grew still more wary. Effie's eyes consulted Beatrice's. Beatrice, who had risen at Timothy's entry, sat down again and said, 'Well, you had to hear sometime, sir. But Effie and me were both determined that you should never hear it from our lips, and so were a good many more.'

'How kind of you,' said Timothy. Touched by their thought for him he, too, sat down, feeling almost for the first time completely at his ease with them. 'It is a great blow to me,' he said. 'I think she was the best friend I ever had.'

He thought they raised their eyebrows slightly. Beatrice said: 'We can well understand your saying that, sir. We both knew how you felt, though it's not for us to say so.'

'And not only to me,' said Timothy. Recollection unmanned him and he wiped his eyes. 'She was a good friend to all the village. She will be terribly missed.' He felt he would like to hear someone else's tribute, some other testimony to Mrs. Purbright's value as a human being. 'You liked her, didn't you, Beatrice?'

Again that faint look of surprise. How conventional they are, thought Timothy, they don't like one to display emotion, or even speak of it.

'We both liked her very much,' said Beatrice, rather primly. 'Though, of course, it wasn't in our place to have an opinion.'

'She was a most remarkable woman,' said Timothy, shaking his head in reminiscent sadness. He felt that the epithet was too literary; they wouldn't understand what it meant; they might even think it meant that Mrs. Purbright was eccentric and peculiar. Yet it was a relief

448

to talk to somebody who knew her. 'She was remarkable and . . . and generous,' he amended. 'She gave her mind to one so completely. I mean, she put everything she was, and had, at one's disposal. She kept nothing back.'

Again the formal, literary phrasing. It had not had the effect he aimed at; they looked uncomfortable and rather shocked. Yet he felt that he must go on; he would be eternally shamed, something in him would die and never come to life again, unless he testified to his feeling about Mrs. Purbright.

'She wasn't just unselfish, she was self-*giving*,' he pursued. That was better; they would understand that distinction. 'She didn't merely put *herself* in your place, she had the imagination to feel as you would; she really understood you. And at the same time she never lost sight of her own values. She kept them . . . not priggishly of course . . . as some people keep their choicest things . . . well, cakes and so on, for a visitor . . . Whatever one did, they were always there . . . to tempt any appetite for good that one might have. I'm afraid I don't explain myself very well.'

The maids listened in silence. Then Effie said suddenly, as though taking a plunge, 'And she was so pretty.'

'Yes, wasn't she?' exclaimed Timothy, delighted to have this welcome and unexpected addition to Mrs. Purbright's portrait. 'I'm so glad you noticed that. Not everyone would have. You might almost say beautiful. And she had so much distinction, of which she was quite unconscious, just as she was unconscious, and I believe half ashamed, of her own goodness. Well!' he shrugged his shoulders.

'Will you be going to the funeral, sir?' asked Beatrice. 'It's to be on Monday, so I understand. Effie and I will go of course, that is, if we're still here. We wouldn't like to miss it. There won't be many people, being as she was not well-known, and not a church-goer.'

Several things in what Beatrice had said struck Timothy as extremely odd.

'Not a churchgoer!' he exclaimed. 'Not many people! Why, the whole countryside will be there!' He thought again. 'Monday, did you say Monday? But she only died this morning or late last night.'

Both the women stared at him, and Effie gave a funny little cry, a sort of neigh, which might have been a warning. But Beatrice disregarded it. Sitting bolt upright, and with a solemn face, she said, 'Excuse me, sir, Miss Cross was drowned on Wednesday.'

Timothy gaped.

'Miss Cross?' he murmured in a wondering, uncertain voice.

'Drowned?' His head gave a jerk. 'I see now. I thought we were talking about Mrs. Purbright.'

It was their turn to look astonished.

'Is she dead, too?'

Timothy nodded.

Effie turned pale and began to cry. Beatrice rose, put an arm round her, and rocked her to and fro, like a child, caressing her and murmuring endearments.

'There, there,' she said, 'it's not half so bad now there are two of them, is it, sir?' Timothy could not see the logic of this, yet neither could he deny that in some mysterious way two deaths seemed less terrible than one. 'They'll be sort of company for each other, won't they, sir? We're not taught to believe otherwise.'

CHAPTER XXXIV

TIMOTHY's interview with Beatrice and Effie did not end there, but he only stayed long enough to blunt the edge of their appetite to enlighten him about Vera. The restraints they had put upon themselves the last few days to keep him in ignorance, had all broken down; a flood of mortuary information poured out, and Timothy, with bent head, had to extricate himself in the middle of a sentence. 'Of course they knew her by her hair' – he listened no more after that. In the few minutes' respite that he gave himself before rejoining the others he tried desperately to depersonalise the events, to strip them of the tegument of himself which clung to them; to feel them, not as his sorrows, but as other people's, which a merciful provision of Nature enables, indeed compels us, to forget.

In the course of their walk Tyro asked Timothy a good many questions about Vera, and Esther drew him on to speak of Mrs. Purbright. Tyro's interest was spontaneous; he wanted to know more of Vera, whereas Esther felt it would be good for Timothy to talk and insensitive to keep away from the subject of his double loss, simply because it was not hers. He was grateful to them for their interest in two people who could mean nothing to them, and for not leaving him alone with his thoughts; but each interrogatory embarrassed him in a different way. 'What a charming woman, how I wish I had known her.' Yes, but Timothy had known her, and for weeks (was it?) he had not thought fit to speak to her. But he could not tell them that.

'She sounds a lovely creature, Timothy, from your account. I often wonder which is rarer, to be really beautiful or really nice. I expect the incidence is about the same – one in a thousand. It would be interesting to take a census. We might do it together. Which would you choose for your province – the beautiful, or the nice?'

'Aren't they sometimes found together?' Timothy asked.

Tyro shook his head. 'Very rarely, wouldn't you agree, Mrs. Morwen?' He stared hard at her, as though wondering if she had a claim to either quality, and Esther and Timothy both smiled.

'I hope one grows nicer as one grows older,' Esther said.

'Possibly,' said Tyro. But the question didn't interest him and he turned to Timothy. 'How nice was your Miss Cross, Timothy?' Timothy took some time to answer.

'I don't think one thought of niceness in connection with her.'

'Bravo, well answered,' Tyro said. 'Of the two, you know, Timothy, I incline towards Miss Cross. Beauty is a fact, or nearly; niceness, whatever it means, is only an opinion. What did they think of each other?'

They scarcely knew each other, Timothy told him; they were poles apart, they didn't fit into the same thought, but Mrs. Purbright had always been grateful to Vera for her beauty. He couldn't remember what Vera had thought of Mrs. Purbright. 'She wasn't interested in individuals, you see, so much as in ... in social questions,' he explained.

'Yes, you told us; she belonged to your unmentionable past.' Timothy reddened; he wished they could get away from this criss-cross of comparisons between the two women, who were only alike in having died. They would not have wished to be thought of in relation to each other, nor would Timothy ever think of them like that.

Neither Esther, nor even Tyro, cross-examined him, of course, yet many random shafts went home. He watched the portraits taking shape, with most of what was vital and interesting in the originals left out. The beautiful girl, a stranger to Upton, who had cared for the poor and shared his indignation that they should be denied the freedom of the river, and had so inexplicably, yet so excusably (nil de mortuis!) failed to keep her tryst – how pallid did she seem! And the parson's wife with the amusing Christian name, who had interested herself in Timothy's career in Upton, and on one occasion had even tried to persuade him to give up the boat – what a poor travesty of Mrs. Purbright, with her passionate plea, her burning wish for justice, her face – he could see it now – damp and stained with her effort to convince him that in self-surrender lay the finest fulfilment of the spirit!

Nothing against the dead, and (still more essential) nothing against the living: Timothy must spare himself. So edited, so expurgated, the self-portrait that emerged between those of his two Egerias was indeed something to yawn over. His past was something to blush for; yet even more did he blush for himself as the narrator of such an insipid tale; made more insipid, more halting, by the fact that he could not remember how much more than he was now admitting to, he had told Tyro, and Esther, in letters written in the heat of his experiences.

So it was a relief, when Tyro, standing like stout Cortes on a bluff, suddenly burst through the half-hearted barrage of his talk with, 'Don't you adore the striations of the rock-formations here? There's nothing like it in Europe until you come to the Dordogne.'

For the rest of the walk they did not refer to what, in any case, Timothy had scarcely the right to call his bereavements. The see-saw in which now Vera, now Mrs. Purbright had been uppermost, had been put to rest, though he was still haunted by its ghostly rise and fall.

Of the nature of Mrs. Purbright's illness he knew nothing; of Vera's death only the details, the grisly details, of the finding of her body. Here, on the sunny hilltop with living friends beside him, his friends of thirty years, he did not speculate overmuch on how she died. It must have been before the watery curtain descended on his consciousness, distorting, obscuring, obliterating the details he had not deliberately entrusted to his waking mind. They belonged to another life, a past remoter than the real past. Into this almost limbo, both Vera and Mrs. Purbright were rapidly receding. They partook of its unreality. He had not seen them or communicated with them since his rebirth in a happier world. Mrs. Purbright remained to him, a beautiful and enriching memory, a blessing for which he could be forever thankful. (He did not know that she had saved his life.) Should Vera at any time obsess him – the black and silver phantom of the boat-house laying snares for his peace of mind – he could always invoke the shade of Mrs. Purbright, and the white magic would overcome the black. In her radiance the dark thing that was Vera would at once take flight. The two thoughts could not live together and Mrs. Purbright was by far the stronger. And even his recollections of Vera were softened now that he understood why, after his accident, she had never tried to get in touch with him.

One thing he was sure of: he had no responsibility for their deaths. At night he sometimes woke up sweating to think how nearly Wimbush and the boy had died. In spite of the hearty welcome at Lawnflete, all his surviving memories of the River Revolt were red-edged with guilt. But with regard to these two he was blameless; in a detective story he would have had an alibi that would have satisfied the sternest jury. He was as little implicated as if they had perished in an earthquake.

Only sadness remained to him, sadness that ennobles, not guilt that destroys. The living were nearer to him than the dead, whose bodies would lie in Upton churchyard, but whose souls, in spite of Beatrice, would never meet again.

*   *   *

Both Tyro and Esther thought that Timothy's future should be associated with some form of War Effort, though they did not agree as to what. At luncheon they discussed it. Tyro advised a daily job in Swirrelsford – 'You'd enjoy the bus rides so much' – while Esther was in favour of his confining his activities to Upton, where he was known and liked. 'I do deplore this continual drift away from the villages to the towns,' she said. 'It's so undesirable. One must keep a nucleus for people to gather round. It's as necessary as a fireplace in a room. Town life is disintegrating even for town-dwellers; it's poison to village people, who only make use of it for amusement in their idle hours. It makes them restless and discontented.'

Tyro made her trail her coat, and a rather fierce argument arose between them on the respective virtues of town and country life, in which Timothy's problem was lost sight of. Esther tried to define the intangibles and imponderables which, she said, went to make up village culture, and was vexed with herself for not being able to; while Tyro was maddeningly articulate about the benefits of urban existence and its value in sharpening the wits. 'I shouldn't mind so much,' he complained, 'if your villagers did anything with their ruminations; but they have no more to show for them than a cow has for chewing the cud.'

'The cow has its milk,' suggested Timothy, anxious to relieve Esther of the burden of argument.

'Yes, but what is milk but a mere product of digestion? What I look for is results in terms of art and culture. Excuse me, Timothy, but did the party yesterday do anything except stimulate our gastric juices?'

'It showed us a nice lawn,' said Timothy, 'and it brought us together.'

'I grant you the lawn,' said Tyro, 'though it reminded me of all the implications of the phrase "go out to grass." But as for bringing us together! Nothing brings people together except a common aim, and I didn't notice one.'

'The grass doesn't have a common aim,' said Timothy, 'but three million blades look better than three.'

'Oh, if you're talking of appearances!'

'Of course I am, though I'm nothing like so dependent on them as you are. If things weren't worth looking at, what would you do?' Tyro hesitated, but only for a moment.

'When I look, I use my mind. I compare, I discriminate, I classify, I condemn. And when I condemn I act, and when I act, I destroy. That's why at least three letters have gone into the waste-paper baskets of Liverpool instead of reaching their destinations.'

'The mountain labours' – began Timothy.

'Yes, but don't you see the difference? Don't you see that my mouse is worth a million of your cows, just because it is the offspring of a purpose? I don't deny that your cows may help to beat the Germans, but is that their intention? Do they remember with every cud they chew, why they are doing it? You say that I am over-conscious of purpose—'

'Excuse me, we never said anything of the sort,' snapped Timothy. Tyro seemed put out by having this opportunity for disagreement taken from him. 'Well, but you think it.'

'How do you know?'

'Then you ought to think it, it's not logical not to think it, holding the views you do. It follows directly from what you've been saying.'

'But we haven't said anything for quite a long time.'

'I'm not to blame for your running short of argument, but if you said that I set too much store on purpose, I should reply—'

So Tyro rambled on, inventing an enemy where none was, and investing this hypothetical foe with the likeness of Timothy or Esther, for an opponent he had to have; until at last the meal ended, and Timothy dismissed his guests to their siestas.

Timothy also tried to sleep, but could not. Treading softly so as not to disturb the slumbers of his friends, he went downstairs and out into the sunshine and shadow of the stable-yard. And what luck (for he felt in need of company) here was Nelson, most terre-a-terre of men, bending over the open bonnet of his car. If Timothy had been told he would find Nelson, he might have shrunk from the encounter. Now that it was forced on him he must pay his co-preserver his belated thanks.

'Hullo, Nelson.'

'Good afternoon, sir.' Nelson straightened himself.

'Rather different from when we last met.'

'Yes, indeed, sir.'

'I owe you more thanks than I can say, Nelson, and I should have come to tell you so only I wasn't feeling up to the mark.'

Nelson said he quite understood. 'You aren't looking yourself yet, sir, if I may say so.'

'Aren't I?' Timothy looked round anxiously as though a mirror might materialise from the air. 'Well, I suppose it takes time to wear off. Wimbush and the boy all right?'

'Fit as fiddles, sir. Wimbush says it has taken years off his life.'

'I shall look them up tomorrow. Perhaps a little present. . . . And I hope you'll accept one, Nelson, if it's not corrupting the police?'

'That's very good of you, sir, but why should you bother? Colonel Harbord, he have put in for a commendation for me.'

'My congratulations. You deserve it if any man ever did.' Timothy paused, and said with a rush, 'Isn't there a funeral tomorrow?'

'Yes, sir, Miss Cross.' Nelson's voice dropped.

'How did it happen, Nelson?'

The policeman drew a long breath.

'Well, sir, I don't know as I rightly ought to tell you.'

'Why, is it a secret?'

'No, sir, it came out at the inquest. But Mrs. Purbright, she said she didn't want you to know.'

'Mrs. Purbright! What had she to do with it?'

'She had a good deal to do with it, but all's well that ends well.'

In the context Timothy did not get much encouragement from this familiar phrase.

'Please tell me, Nelson.'

'Well, sir, being as you were a friend of the late lady. . . .'

'I was a friend of both of them, as a matter of fact.'

'I know, sir, but I meant Miss Cross. Mrs. Purbright was still alive then.'

'When?'

'When I went to see her, sir. She asked to make a deposition to the police, in this case myself.'

'But why, Nelson?'

'Because she thought she had been the cause – the occasion – of Miss Cross's death. She alleged it, sir.'

'But Nelson,' began Timothy, only half aware of the effect this announcement was having on his mind, 'was she in her senses?'

'Unfortunately yes, sir. An independent witness testified to having seen her enter the lane known as Lovers' Lane at about 6.20, the time stated.'

'And Miss Cross was there, I remember now,' said Timothy.

Nelson nodded. 'Asked why she entered the lane in the first place, the accused, Mrs. Purbright, only of course she accused herself, stated that her intention had been to call your attention, sir, to the danger of the Devil's Staircase, the river being above the normal level.'

Timothy stared at Nelson without speaking.

'She found Miss Cross, sir, and asked her to signal to you to stop, being younger than herself and more likely to catch your eye.'

'But I must already have gone by,' said Timothy. 'The boy, Reg, told me he had seen Miss Cross, but he didn't say anything about seeing Mrs. Purbright.'

'Your surmise is correct in every detail,' Nelson said. 'You *had* gone by. But Miss Cross didn't let on, if you take my meaning, that she had seen you; she held her on tenterhooks, which made the accused fly into a passion when she ascertained what were actually the facts. The other one had been having her on, you see. It was a provocative act.'

'Why do you keep saying the accused?' asked Timothy.

'Well, sir, she accused herself. She accused herself of having occasioned Miss Cross's death; in a way, she accused herself of—'

'Yes, I see. And what happened then?'

'Then, sir, she asked by what right Miss Cross came to be in Lovers' Lane, having regard to the fact that it was private property and she had no key; to which Miss Cross replied, in a nasty way, that she was in full possession of a key, the same having been given to her by her son, that is to say Mr. Edgell Purbright.'

'I see,' said Timothy again.

'Then, sir, the accused, Mrs. Purbright, said she saw red, if you understand me, on account of the other one's deceitful and provocative behaviour, and I suppose, though she did not say so, not regarding Miss Cross as a suitable companion for Mr. Edgell. So she tried to wrest the key from her, which the other one resisted. So they came to blows, though it sounded more like a kind of scrimmage, such as women have, and then they overbalanced and both fell in the river.'

'Yes, Nelson, and after that?'

'Well, sir, they floated together for a time, being as I might say still locked in conflict, they were that mad with each other, and Mrs. Purbright did not recollect very clearly, but she stated that the other released her hold and was carried down, while the current took Mrs. Purbright to the bank close to an overhanging bough which she clung to, and so managed to scramble out.'

'That was on the village side of the river, I suppose,' said Timothy.

'Yes, sir, and she walked home in a daze like, meaning to give the alarm, but when she reached the Rectory she collapsed.'

'I see,' said Timothy. He couldn't think of anything else to say.

'The boy was right, sir,' said Nelson suddenly, 'that was Miss Cross he saw in the water, but who would have believed it? It didn't seem natural, with three people nearly drowned, that there should be another, and quite unconnected.'

Timothy was silent. He was beginning to see all too many connections between the two occurrences.

'If she'd been in the boat,' Nelson went on, 'it would have been different. It was her friend, Mrs. Frances Bingham, who gave warning that she had disappeared and I remembered what the boy said and went down to the pool again. It was dark except for her hair and I identified the body at 11.5 p.m. It was lying just where yours was, sir, within easy reach.'

Nelson obviously expected some comment, but Timothy's mind was too much involved with the information he had already received to ask for more. But making an effort he said, 'Was that all Mrs. Purbright told you?'

Nelson reflected.

'Barring asking me not to tell you, sir, it was practically all. Of course she didn't know she wasn't going to get better. She thought she might be put on trial—'

'For what?'

Nelson read his thought.

'Oh not for murder, sir, for manslaughter at the most. And I don't think the jury would have convicted her, taking into account the insulting language and provocative behaviour of the other deceased. Mrs. Purbright was very much respected in the district, sir, you could almost say she was beloved, and Miss Cross had clawed her something terrible.'

'Clawed her?'

'Yes, sir, Miss Cross she kept her nails on the long side, and pointed, too. I never saw such scratches, deep they were and inches long, and I've had some experience in such matters, having often had to intervene in women's quarrels. Oh, they're a sight worse than men, sir, they don't abide by any rules. And she was marked, too, sir, Miss Cross was. The Coroner expressed astonishment at her condition. She didn't have everything her own way. Perhaps it was the brooch-pins that did *her* the damage, Mrs. Purbright wouldn't have scratched her, being a lady. Oh yes, sir, both women were very badly marked, but Mrs. Purbright, she was real mauled.' They were silent for a time, then Timothy said, 'Perhaps it's as well she didn't live, all things considered.'

'Oh, I don't know, sir,' said Nelson, 'these things blow over, and then, think of the loss to the district! The Rector's all right in his way, a bit hot-tempered, but she was the one. . . . And I forgot – her pearl necklace, that's gone, ripped off in the scrimmage, I shouldn't wonder.

And two brooches missing. The rings were all intact. But Mrs. Purbright said not to bother about the jewellery.'

'You can't think of anything else she said, Nelson?'

'Just let me look at my note-book, sir.'

He brought it out and turned the thin pages with his thick, clumsy fingers.

'I don't see anything else. She was that weak I had to bend over the pillow to hear what she said. But I remember she did say you were not to worry, it would all come right, but that not being applicable to the case in hand, and outside my sphere of duty, I didn't put it down.'

'Thank you very much, Nelson,' said Timothy. Rather to the surprise of both of them, he shook hands with the policeman. 'See you tomorrow,' he added, and walked towards the house. Nelson watched him go, and then with a sigh of pleasure, though still with a grave face, returned to the bonnet of the car.

Somewhere in the small hours Timothy dreamed that Mrs. Purbright had rung him up on the telephone. He was overjoyed to hear her voice; it brought him a most vivid feeling of her presence, and the transforming, almost tangible happiness that only comes in dreams. He did not know that she had died; he thought that she was ringing up to tell him that their long estrangement was over, and it seemed to him that nothing in the world mattered so much. 'Do come round,' he begged; 'I have some friends here but they're both asleep.' 'I can't come,' she said, 'because I have somebody with me.' Timothy was terribly disappointed. 'But couldn't you leave him for a little while?' When Mrs. Purbright couldn't come it usually meant she was engaged with Colonel Harbord or some of Timothy's one-time enemies.

'It's not a man, it's a woman.' 'Oh, I see, but couldn't you come when she's gone?' 'She won't go,' said Mrs. Purbright. 'Well, send her away.' Timothy had been intimate enough with Mrs. Purbright to say this. 'She won't go away,' repeated the voice in a tone of despairing sadness; 'you see, she's got mixed up with my thoughts.' To Timothy, in his dream, this didn't sound an irremediable catastrophe. 'Then I'll come round to you.' 'It wouldn't do any good,' said Mrs. Purbright, 'because we're both together in your mind,' and as she said this her voice changed and the new voice said, 'Hullo, darling, is it true you don't want to come and see us? It isn't very kind of you, darling, we look so nice twined together, you couldn't tell where I end or she begins.' 'But shan't I ever see her alone again?' 'No, darling, I'm afraid you'll always have to have me as a chaperone. Your girl-friends are

459

inseparable. I know you'll hate it, darling, but you can't have her without me.'

'Well, how do you feel this morning?' asked Tyro, when, rather late, Timothy joined them at the breakfast table. 'It's not for a guest to ask, but did you have a good night?'

'Not very,' Timothy admitted.

'You look rather wan, doesn't he, Mrs. Morwen?'

Esther, who had heard more than Tyro had of Nelson's narrative, said, 'Well, he's been under rather a strain.'

'Oh, but it was nothing,' said Timothy, repudiating almost violently his guests' concern. 'When I think what you have to go through, Esther, with so many of your relations at the war, and you, too, Tyro, in all the bombing at Liverpool, I can't see that I have *anything* to complain of.'

'He rejects our well-meant sympathy,' Tyro said, 'but wait, my lad, until you've seen the morning paper.'

Esther's look flashed a warning, but it missed Tyro, who rose from his chair and picked up the paper from the floor.

'It's the local rag,' he said, unfolding it. 'The *Western Daily Argus*. There's nearly a column. Upton *is* in the news. Would you like me to read it?'

'Let him wait till he's had his breakfast,' suggested Esther.

'No, no, I'd rather have it now,' said Timothy.

'Very well.' Tyro cleared his throat. 'First, there's the inquest on your friend, Miss Cross, you were telling us about. That doesn't concern you. You hardly come into it, except as explaining how the quarrel arose.'

'I can read that afterwards,' said Timothy.

'It's much the longest part. This is where you come in, after the asterisks.'

'By a curious coincidence, on the very day that saw Vera Cross being swept to her doom in the Bottomless Pool, the day that nearly brought tragedy to the family of Upton's Rector ('they don't know that she's dead, poor old girl,' interpolated Tyro) another accident, not unconnected with the above, was enacted on the flood-maddened waters of the River Swirrel. Protagonist was Upton bachelor, sixty-one-year-old Timothy Casson' ('I didn't know you were as old as that, Timothy') 'known in former years for his charming Nature Notes in *The Broadside*, who decided to throw a boating-party. The sexagenarian naturalist had taken as passengers six-year-old Reg Cartwright, and his brother, five-year-old Harold. Youngest joy-rider was the boys' retriever, Felix.' ('Apparently they couldn't find out *his* age.') 'Stopping at Upton's picturesque bridge with an impressive display of watersmanship that drew a cheer from the spectators, the literary oarsman gave a brief address, of a somewhat political character, in which he urged his hearers to take the river into their own hands and unleash it from the stranglehold of capitalist exploitation. This diatribe received a mixed reception of boos and cheers. Led by forty-one-year-old Mrs. Pendexter, one of Upton's foremost mothers, several of the village matrons asked that their young hopefuls might share the outing, but the *Broadside's* scholar-sculler (wisely, as it transpired) refused. Unmooring the boat, yclept the *Argo*, flying aft the Union Jack, and forward the Hammer and Sickle of our great ally, Mr. Casson shot the bridge in easy style, and was at once whirled out of view by the wild waste of waters. What happened afterwards must remain a mystery. Calling at Mr. Casson's residence, Upton's Rectory of an earlier day, our representative learned that the literary Leander was too ill to give an interview; but Colonel Harbord, of Lawnflete, Upton, and P.C. Nelson, of the same village, happening by chance to visit Upton's Bottomless Pool, found, in shallow water, the bodies of the three Argonauts to whom they at once applied the prescribed remedies, a task in which they received the able assistance of Mr. Wimbush, fifty-five-year-old water-bailiff to Mrs. Julia Lampard and ex-gardener to Mr. Casson.'

'I'll skip the next part,' Tyro said. 'It's all about bringing you round, Timothy – "unexampled efforts," and so on. The sting is in the tail.' CORONER ACCUSES CASSON – 'that's the headline.' Tyro put an official stiffening into his voice.

'Commenting on "Casson's harebrained act" the Coroner said, "He nearly drowned himself and two others, and it must be remembered that but for his insensate folly this poor woman would be alive today. Mrs. Purbright's sole object in going to the river was to warn him, and possibly, though we cannot be certain, a like intention may have inspired Miss Cross. The whole mad enterprise was, it seems, political in origin and should be a warning, if warning is needed, of the danger of Communism in our midst. I should like to make the strongest representations to the riparian lessees to prohibit any form of boating on their waters, and the municipality of Swirrelsford will, I understand, consider the advisability of withdrawing the licence for keeping pleasure-craft hitherto enjoyed by Mr. Gayflete."

'So that's that,' said Tyro. 'You seem to have queered everyone's pitch for rowing, Timothy; next year I expect the Boat Race will be cancelled – unless the war's already cancelled it. I think the Coroner's remarks are a bit strong, but I suppose he can say what he likes in his own court.' The words were scarcely out of his mouth when they heard the scrunch of wheels outside the window, followed by the ring of the front-door bell.

'The taxi,' said Tyro. He took out his watch. 'These country cabbies certainly have time to burn. He's come twenty minutes too soon.'

'Oh, must you really go?' cried Timothy. 'I feel I haven't seen you at all.' The conventional phrases came pat from his lips, but his heart was in a tumult of terror and despair. 'Oh, do stay,' he pleaded. 'Just for an hour or two— Isn't there a later train you could go by?'

'Afraid not,' said Tyro. 'Duty calls. You, lucky dog, are your own master.'

He pushed his chair back and to Timothy's dismay Esther, who was wearing a hat and showing other signs of impending travel, did the same.

'Oh but you can't *both* go,' he protested. 'I hoped that you, at least, Esther, would stay on until tomorrow. I know it isn't very cheerful here, but—' They had both risen and he looked up imploringly at their faces, on which the preoccupation of departure sat like an uneasy sunrise.

'You never told me you were going so early,' he reproached them. 'It is a blow, I own it is.'

Esther apologised.

'You seemed so distressed last night, that we didn't like to bother you to telephone for a taxi, and asked your nice Effie to do it, which she did, most efficiently.'

'Too efficiently,' said Timothy. The sense of horror which had oppressed him since his talk with Nelson, accentuated by his dream and by Tyro's reading of the newspaper, became almost unbearable.

'You mustn't leave me alone, you really mustn't!' he besought them.

They looked at each other in perplexity, and Tyro said, 'I've got to obey orders, I'm afraid. They didn't want to give me leave in any case. I had to spin the most terrific yarn, say that you were dying, and all that.'

'And I've left behind three grand-children with measles,' said Esther, giving Timothy a guilty smile. 'I didn't tell you, because I remember how you used to worry about infection.'

'Infection?' repeated Timothy. 'Infection?' In the mood he was in, the thought of infection was a blessed thought, recalling a comfortable white bed in the school sick-room, with starched and kindly nurses hovering near. He turned away.

'Well, I suppose I mustn't try to keep you,' he said.

Unwilling to leave him in his unhappiness, unable to relieve it, they gazed at Timothy with pitying eyes. Then the same thought simultaneously struck them both, though it was Tyro who voiced it.

'Why not come with us?'

'Yes, why not?' said Esther.

Timothy looked as startled as if they had suggested a journey to the North Pole.

'But how can I? I haven't made any arrangements, I haven't packed, I haven't— And there are the funerals,' he finished, in a lower voice.

'Oh, leave your old funerals,' Tyro said impatiently. 'Let the dead bury their dead. And you've plenty of time to pack, and say a fond farewell to Beatrice and Effie – nearly a quarter of an hour. Now be quick.'

Timothy stood, forgetful of their presence, his face working with his mind's effort to visualize the new prospect. All at once the obstacles seemed to roll away, leaving a sunlit vista shining straight into the future.

'I will!' he said. 'I will!'

'Good man,' said Tyro.

'But *where* shall I go?' said Timothy.

At that they both looked very much taken aback.

'We can discuss that in the taxi,' Tyro said.

They discussed it among themselves while Timothy was packing. Though by word of mouth they had often agreed, it was the first time during their visit that they had really seen eye to eye. It was decided that Timothy should go to Esther for a time, then, if Tyro could persuade him to, to Liverpool, to seek employment in the Censor's Office. 'It's just the thing for him,' Tyro declared. 'It'll do him a world of good. He was too static here, he was getting quite mossy.'

Tremendous thumps and scurryings to and fro came from the room above. 'It sounds as if there were a whole army of them,' Tyro remarked. 'Timothy never could do anything quietly. It's a sort of latent exhibitionism. He can't help wanting to draw attention to himself. I expect it adds to his sense of his own reality.'

'He's certainly made himself conspicuous here,' said Esther.

'Yes, hasn't he? They won't forget him in a hurry. Of course, he'll have done the place a power of good by shaking them all up. I wish we could make him realise that.'

'He has such excellent intentions,' Esther said.

'Yes, hasn't he? All stultified by that fatal desire to be a general favourite. He doesn't recognise the otherness of other people, though I've always tried to din it into him.'

'The ordinary doesn't appeal to him,' said Esther.

'No, for all his conventionality, it doesn't. He likes things to be raised to a higher power – some instinct of worship, I imagine – just as he likes people to be types of themselves. Miss Cross and Mrs. Purbright were; and no doubt we are, too, in his eyes.'

Esther didn't ask Tyro to tell her to what type she belonged, but he volunteered the information.

'You, of course, are the matriarchal type, the perfect grandmother; I – well . . .' he shrugged his shoulders, 'what would you say I am? The eternal spirit of the chainless mind?' He laughed. 'But if he could welcome imperfection, in himself and others, he'd be much happier and so would they. We can't all be masterpieces. You should like people for their faults, I told him. He didn't think it possible.'

'With their faults, perhaps,' amended Esther, and Tyro rather unwillingly assented.

'Now he's fretting about that accident to those two buddies of his, God rest their souls, and he either has to think (a) that he had nothing to do with it, or (b) that it was all his fault. When we said that neither was true, he didn't like it. When I told him to regard himself as an ordinary sinner, he looked quite cross. But it would be the salvation of his inner life if he could. "Practise embracing your faults," I said, "they're as much part of you as your virtues." But he wouldn't hear of it.'

'I'm not so sure,' said Esther. 'I think that with regard to the war—' One of the low-flying planes that haunted the sky over Upton drowned her voice. Tyro did not hear her remark, nor did he ask her to repeat it, so anxious was he to put forward his own view.

'There is something in what you say,' he told her shamelessly, 'though I can't altogether agree with it. But I do think that his more realistic attitude to the war may be a sign that he is taking himself more realistically. Last night he seemed quite pleased to listen to the news, boring as it was, and he even made some fairly intelligent comments. He didn't say that the battle of Marathon was more interesting, because more like a battle, than the battles of today. And you may have noticed that after we heard of the disaster to the destroyers he never again mentioned his boat.'

Esther nodded vigorously. She had at last begun to feel almost intimate with Tyro. 'I've always wondered,' she said, 'why he was so set on using his boat. It seemed a rather . . . well, a rather childish whim in a man of his age.'

'It's something a woman wouldn't understand,' said Tyro, glibly. 'It's perfectly plain to me, of course. It was a death-wish. He couldn't face modern life – he never has faced the self-evident truth that civilisation progresses only by disagreement – and the boat was his way out, a symbol of absolute peace, where no one could get at him – or let's face it' (Tyro was always facing things) 'contradict him. And, by Jove, he nearly found what he was after.'

Unnoticed by them, the racket overhead had now transferred itself to the stairs. Tyro looked mischievously at Esther. 'What a joke if, having weathered the Devil's Staircase, he broke his neck on his own!'

Esther had no time to answer, for Timothy with pale, perspiring face stood in the doorway.

'It's all settled,' said Tyro. 'You're to go to Mrs. Morwen.'

'If you don't mind the measles,' smiled Esther.

'Oh!' cried Timothy, remembering his eighteen months of unblemished health. 'But I *adore* measles!'

His tired face, which already looked as if he had spent a night in the train, grew radiant.

'The rest of the plan we shall tell you afterwards.'

'It's bound to be heaven.' Timothy could see no flaw in a future away from Upton.

'Have you remembered your ration-book?' said Esther anxiously.

'Good heavens, no! And I haven't said good-bye to Beatrice and Effie. Is there time?'

'Yes, if you hurry.'

Timothy dashed into the kitchen. 'My ration-book!' he cried. 'I'm going away! I'm leaving! I can't explain, but I'll write! Stay here as long as you like! Cheerio, Effie! Ta-ta, Beatrice!'

In a Grand Chain of outstretched arms and interposing tables he skirmished round the kitchen. A familiar thudding began; a crafty smile wrinkled a golden face; Felix, rampant, had barred the way. 'Down! Felix, down! Good dog, good-bye, good-bye, good dog!' There seemed no end to it. His thoughts as tangled as his tongue, he left the kitchen. Simpson, his quarry, was outside. His knees, his nose, his forehead, his moustaches, were pointing to the ground. Though standing up, his whole effect was of recumbency. 'Oh, Simpson, I'm off! I'm going! I shan't see you any more! Yes, perhaps I shall. I hope I shall, I'm coming back of course, but not for long! I'll send you your wages!' He paused, breathless, his hand held out.

With scarcely a change in his expression, Simpson took it. 'There you are, you see,' he said.

Beatrice and Effie were at the door, handkerchiefs poised for waving. The travelling companions bundled in, Tyro, beside the driver, Timothy and Esther at the back. The driver, admonished to make haste, started with a jerk and they proceeded at an anti-social pace through the long, familiar village street. People were opening their windows, kneeling at their doors; Timothy had never seen Upton in curl-papers before. Some passers-by, mostly women, looked incuriously at the big, dusty car which seemed to be in such a hurry, and looked away again.

They had passed the bridge, the southern boundary of the village, and the sense of its enveloping personality began to dwindle. Timothy screwed his head round to get a last glimpse of the poplars, but a twinge of superstition jerked it back – whether because he hoped to see them again, or because he hoped not to, he could hardly tell. Time, which had counted for little in Upton, suddenly became of great importance now, but for once Timothy was less anxious than his friends. For him each milestone was also a time-signal, and he knew that they would catch the train. Though the surface of his mind was soothed by speed, fatigue was bringing its reaction; he felt that Fate, like a police-car, was hard upon their heels. Under cover of something Tyro was saying to the driver he murmured to Esther, 'I wish I didn't have to think of them together.'

'Who, Timothy dear?'

'Mrs. Purbright and Vera Cross.'

'Which do you want to think of?' interrupted Tyro, turning round with a loud guffaw. 'One, you say, was an angel; the other – well! But remember *you* are just an ordinary sinner.'

Timothy frowned and again appealed to Esther.

'But, Timothy, we went over all that, and Mr. MacAdam said you must practise—' She stopped and Tyro supplied the missing words.

'Mental astigmatism.'

'And you were only a little to blame for what happened to them, not more than—' She waited for Tyro to prompt her.

'A negro might be for the people who get themselves crushed to death watching him lynched.'

'Thank you. What we mean is, *they* weren't in the boat.'

466

'I know,' said Timothy. 'And yet—' He left the sentence unfinished. Whether it was weariness, or the comfort of feeling that Esther and Tyro were beside him, neither of whom could be joined in thought to the other, or whether to be out of Upton was to be in safety – who can say? But he did not notice the next milestone. He was asleep.

From Byron, Austen and Darwin

to some of the most acclaimed and original contemporary writing, John Murray takes pride in bringing you powerful, prizewinning, absorbing and provocative books that will entertain you today and become the classics of tomorrow.

We put a lot of time and passion into what we publish and how we publish it, and we'd like to hear what you think.

Be part of John Murray – share your views with us at:

www.johnmurray.co.uk

▶️ johnmurraybooks

🐦 @johnmurrays

📘 johnmurraybooks